THE UNCONSOLED

KAZUO ISHIGURO

The Unconsoled

THIS BOOK WAS
SLIGHTLY DAMAGED IN
TRANSIT AND IS NOW
BEING SOLD AT A
SPECIAL BARGAIN PRICE

4

ff

faber and faber

LONDON · BOSTON

First published in Great Britain in 1995
by Faber and Faber Limited
3 Queen Square London WC1N 3AU

Phototypeset by Intype, London
Printed in England by Clays Ltd, St Ives plc

© Kazuo Ishiguro, 1995

Kazuo Ishiguro is hereby identified as author of this
work in accordance with Section 77 of the Copyright,
Designs and Patents Act 1988

A CIP record for this book
is available from the British Library

ISBN 0–571–17387–X

2 4 6 8 10 9 7 5 3 1

For Lorna and Naomi

I

1

The taxi driver seemed embarrassed to find there was no one – not even a clerk behind the reception desk – waiting to welcome me. He wandered across the deserted lobby, perhaps hoping to discover a staff member concealed behind one of the plants or armchairs. Eventually he put my suitcases down beside the elevator doors and, mumbling some excuse, took his leave of me.

The lobby was reasonably spacious, allowing several coffee tables to be spread around it with no sense of crowding. But the ceiling was low and had a definite sag, creating a slightly claustrophobic mood, and despite the sunshine outside the light was gloomy. Only near the reception desk was there a bright streak of sun on the wall, illuminating an area of dark wood panelling and a rack of magazines in German, French and English. I could see also a small silver bell on the reception desk and was about to go over to shake it when a door opened somewhere behind me and a young man in uniform appeared.

'Good afternoon, sir,' he said tiredly and, going behind the reception desk, began the registration procedures. Although he did mumble an apology for his absence, his manner remained for a time distinctly off-hand. As soon as I mentioned my name, however, he gave a start and straightened himself.

'Mr Ryder, I'm so sorry I didn't recognise you. Mr Hoffman, the manager, he was very much wanting to welcome you personally. But just now, unfortunately, he's had to go to an important meeting.'

'That's perfectly all right. I'll look forward to meeting him later on.'

The desk clerk hurried on through the registration forms, all the while muttering about how annoyed the manager would be to have missed my arrival. He twice mentioned how the preparations for 'Thursday night' were putting the latter under unusual pressure, keeping him away from the hotel far more than

3

was usual. I simply nodded, unable to summon the energy to enquire into the precise nature of 'Thursday night'.

'Oh, and Mr Brodsky's been doing splendidly today,' the desk clerk said, brightening. 'Really splendidly. This morning he rehearsed that orchestra for four hours non-stop. And listen to him now! Still hard at it, working things out by himself.'

He indicated the rear of the lobby. Only then did I become aware that a piano was being played somewhere in the building, just audible above the muffled noise of the traffic outside. I raised my head and listened more closely. Someone was playing a single short phrase – it was from the second movement of Mullery's *Verticality* – over and over in a slow, preoccupied manner.

'Of course, if the manager were here,' the desk clerk was saying, 'he might well have brought Mr Brodsky out to meet you. But I'm not sure . . .' He gave a laugh. 'I'm not sure if I should disturb him. You see, if he's deep in concentration . . .'

'Of course, of course. Another time.'

'If the manager were here . . .' He trailed off and laughed again. Then leaning forward, he said in a low voice: 'Do you know, sir, some guests have had the nerve to complain? About our closing off the drawing room like this each time Mr Brodsky requires the piano? It's amazing how some people think! Two different guests actually complained to Mr Hoffman yesterday. You can be sure, they were very quickly put in their place.'

'I'm sure they were. Brodsky, you say.' I thought about the name, but it meant nothing to me. Then I caught the desk clerk watching me with a puzzled look and said quickly: 'Yes, yes. I'll look forward to meeting Mr Brodsky in good time.'

'If only the manager were here, sir.'

'Please don't worry. Now if that's all, I'd very much appreciate . . .'

'Of course, sir. You must be very tired after such a long journey. Here's your key. Gustav over there will show you to your room.'

I looked behind me and saw that an elderly porter was waiting across the lobby. He was standing in front of the open elevator, staring into its interior with a preoccupied air. He gave a start as I came walking up to him. He then picked up my suitcases and hurried into the elevator after me.

*

As we began our ascent, the elderly porter continued to hold onto both suitcases and I could see him growing red with the effort. The cases were both very heavy and a serious concern that he might pass out before me led me to say:

'You know, you really ought to put those down.'

'I'm glad you mention it, sir,' he said, and his voice betrayed surprisingly little of the physical effort he was expending. 'When I first started in this profession, very many years ago now, I used to place the bags on the floor. Pick them up only when I absolutely needed to. When in motion, so to speak. In fact, for the first fifteen years of working here, I have to say I used that method. It's one that many of the younger porters in this town still employ. But you won't find me doing anything of that sort now. Besides, sir, we're not going up far.'

We continued our ascent in silence. Then I said:

'So you've worked in this hotel for some time.'

'Twenty-seven years now, sir. I've seen plenty here in that time. But of course, this hotel was standing long before I ever got here. Frederick the Great is believed to have stayed a night here in the eighteenth century, and by all accounts it was a long-established inn even then. Oh yes, there have been events here of great historic interest over the years. Some time when you're not so tired, sir, I'd be happy to relate a few of these things to you.'

'But you were telling me,' I said, 'why you consider it a mistake to place luggage on the floor.'

'Ah yes,' the porter said. 'Now that's an interesting point. You see, sir, as you can imagine, in a town of this sort, there are many hotels. This means that many people in this town have at some point or other tried their hand at portering. Many people here seem to think they can simply put on a uniform and then that will be it, they'll be able to do the job. It's a delusion that's been particularly nurtured in this town. Call it a local myth, if you will. And I'll readily confess, there was a time when I unthinkingly subscribed to it myself. Then once – oh, it was many years ago now – my wife and I took a short holiday. We went to Switzerland, to Lucerne. My wife has passed away now, sir, but whenever I think of her I remember our short holiday. It's very beautiful there by the lake. No doubt you know it. We took some lovely boat rides after breakfast. Well, to return to my point, during that holiday I observed that people in that town didn't make the same sorts of assumptions about their porters as people here do. How can I put it, sir? There was much greater *respect* paid to porters there. The best ones were figures of some renown and had the leading hotels fighting for their services. I must say it opened my eyes. But in this town, well, there's been this idea for many many years. In fact there are days when I wonder if it can ever be eradicated. Now I'm not saying people here are in any way rude to us. Far from it, I've always been treated with politeness and consideration here. But, you see, sir, there's always this idea that anyone could do this job if they took it into their heads, if the fancy just took them. I suppose it's because everyone in this town at some point has had the experience of carrying luggage from place to place. Because they've done that, they assume being a hotel porter is just an extension of it. I've had people over the years, sir, in this very elevator, who've said to me: "I might give up what I'm doing one of these days and take up portering." Oh yes. Well, sir, one day – it wasn't long after our short holiday in Lucerne – I had one of our leading city councillors say more or less those exact words to me. "I'd like to do that one of these days," he said to me, indicating the bags. "That's the life for me. Not a care in the world." I suppose he was trying to be kind, sir. Implying I was to be envied. That was when I was younger, sir, I didn't then hold the bags, I had them on the floor, here in this very elevator, and I suppose in those days I might have looked a bit that way. You know, carefree, as the gentleman implied. Well, I tell you, sir, that was the last straw. I don't mean the gentleman's words made me so angry in themselves. But when he said that to me, well, things sort of fell into place. Things I'd been thinking about for some time. And as I explained to you, sir, I was fresh from our short holiday in Lucerne where I'd got some perspective. And I thought to myself, well, it's high time porters in this town set about changing the attitude prevalent here. You see, sir, I'd seen something different in Lucerne, and I felt, well, it really wasn't good enough, what went on here. So I thought hard about it and decided on a number of measures I would personally take. Of course, even then, I probably knew how difficult it would be. I think I may have realised all those years ago that it was perhaps already too late for my own generation. That things had gone too far. But I thought, well, even if I could do my part and change things just a little, it would at least make it easier for those who came after me. So I adopted my measures, sir, and I've stuck to them, ever since that day the city councillor said what he did. And I'm proud to say a number of other porters in this town followed my lead. That's not to say they adopted precisely the same measures I did. But let's say their measures were, well, compatible.'

'I see. And one of your measures was not to put down the suitcases but to continue to hold them.'

'Exactly, sir, you've followed my gist very well. Of course, I have to say, when I took on these rules for myself, I was much younger and stronger, and I suppose I didn't really calculate for my growing weaker with age. It's funny, sir, but you don't. The other porters have said similar things. All the same, we all try to keep to our old resolutions. We've become a pretty close-knit group over the years, twelve of us, we're what's left of the ones who tried to change things all those years ago. If I were to go back on anything now, sir, I'd feel I was letting down the others. And if any of them were to go back on any of their old rules, I'd feel the same way. Because there's no doubt about it, some progress has been made in this town. There's a very long way to go yet, that's true, but we've often talked it over – we meet every Sunday afternoon at the Hungarian Café in the Old Town, you could come and join us, you'd be a most welcome guest, sir – well, we've often discussed these things and each of us agrees, without a doubt, there have been significant improvements in the attitude towards us in this town. The younger ones who came after us, of course, they take it all for granted. But our group at the Hungarian Café, we know we've made a difference, even if it's a small one. You'd be very welcome to join us, sir. I would happily introduce you to the group. We're not nearly as formal as we once were and it's been understood for some time that in special circumstances, guests can be introduced to our table. And it's very pleasant at this time of the year with this gentle sunshine in the afternoons. We have our table in the shade of the awning, looking across the Old Square. It's very pleasant, sir, I'm sure you'll like it. But to return to what I was saying, we've been discussing this topic a lot at the Hungarian Café. I mean about

7

these old resolutions we each made all those years ago. You see, none of us thought about what would happen when we got older. I suppose we were so involved in our work, we thought of things only on a day to day basis. Or perhaps we underestimated how long it would take to change these deeply ingrained attitudes. But there you are, sir. I'm now the age I am and every year it gets harder.'

The porter paused for a moment and, despite the physical strain he was under, seemed to get lost in his thoughts. Then he said:

'I should be honest with you, sir. It's only fair. When I was younger, when I first made these rules for myself, I would always carry up to three suitcases, however large or heavy. If a guest had a fourth, I'd put that one on the floor. But three, I could always manage. Well, the truth is, sir, four years ago I had a period of ill-health, and I was finding things difficult, and so we discussed it at the Hungarian Café. Well, in the end, my colleagues all agreed there was no need for me to be so strict on myself. After all, they said to me, all that's required is to impress on the guests something of the true nature of our work. Two bags or three, the effect would be much the same. I should reduce my minimum to two suitcases and no harm would be done. I accepted what they said, sir, but I know it's not quite the truth. I can see it doesn't have nearly the same effect when people look at me. The difference between seeing a porter laden with two bags and seeing one laden with three, you must admit, sir, even to the least practised eye, the effect is considerably different. I know that, sir, and I don't mind telling you it's painful for me to accept. But just to return to my point. I hope you see now why I don't wish to put down your bags. You have only two. At least for a few more years, two will be within my powers.'

'Well, it's all very commendable,' I said. 'You've certainly created the desired impact on me.'

'I'd like you to know, sir, I'm not the only one who's had to make changes. We discuss these things all the time at the Hungarian Café and the truth is, each one of us has had to make some changes. But I wouldn't have you think we're allowing each other's standards to slip. If we did that, all our efforts over these years would be for nothing. We would rapidly become a laughing stock. Passers-by would mock us when they saw us gathered at our table on Sunday afternoons. Oh no, sir, we remain very strict with each other and, as I'm sure Miss Hilde will vouch, the community has come to respect our Sunday gatherings. As I say, sir, you'd be most welcome to join us. Both the café and the square are exceptionally pleasant on these sunny afternoons. And sometimes the café proprietor will arrange for gypsy violinists to play in the square. The proprietor himself, sir, has the greatest respect for us. The café isn't large, but he'll always ensure there's plenty of room for us to sit around our table in comfort. Even when the rest of the café is extremely busy, the proprietor will see to it we don't get crowded out or disturbed. Even on the busiest afternoons, if all of us around our table at one and the same time were to rotate our arms at full stretch, not one of us would make contact. That's how much the proprietor respects us, sir. I'm sure Miss Hilde will vouch for what I'm saying.'

'Pardon me,' I said, 'but who is this Miss Hilde you keep referring to?'

No sooner had I said this, I noticed that the porter was gazing past my shoulder at some spot behind me. Turning, I saw with a start that we were not alone in the elevator. A small young woman in a neat business suit was standing pressed into the corner behind me. Perceiving that I had at last noticed her, she smiled and took a step forward.

'I'm sorry,' she said to me, 'I hope you don't think I was eavesdropping, but I couldn't help overhearing. I was listening to what Gustav was telling you, and I have to say he's being rather unfair on those of us in this town. I mean when he says we don't appreciate our hotel porters. Of course we do and we appreciate Gustav here most of all. Everyone loves him. You can see there's a contradiction even in what he's just told you. If we're so unappreciative, then how does he account for the great respect they're treated with at the Hungarian Café? Really, Gustav, it's very unkind of you to misrepresent us all to Mr Ryder.'

This was said in an unmistakably affectionate tone, but the porter seemed to feel real shame. He adjusted his posture away from us, the heavy cases thumping against his legs as he did so, and turned his gaze away sheepishly.

'There, that's shown him,' the young woman said smiling. 'But he's one of the very best. We all love him. He's exceedingly modest and so he'd never tell you himself, but the other hotel porters in this town all look up to him. In fact, it wouldn't be an exaggeration to say they're in awe of him. Sometimes you'll see them sitting around their table on Sunday afternoons, and if Gustav hasn't yet arrived, they won't start talking. They feel it would be disrespectful, you see, to start proceedings without him. You'll often see them, ten or eleven of them, sitting there silently with their coffees, waiting. At most, they might exchange the odd whisper, like they were in church. But not until Gustav arrives do they relax and start conversing. It's worth going along to the Hungarian Café just to witness Gustav's arrival. The contrast between before and after is very marked, I have to tell you. One moment there are these glum old faces sitting silently around the table. Then Gustav turns up and they start yelling and laughing. They punch each other in fun, slap each other on the back. They sometimes even dance, yes, up on the tables! They have a special "Porters' Dance", isn't that so, Gustav? Oh yes, they really enjoy themselves. But not a bit of it until Gustav's arrived. Of course he'd never tell you any of this himself, he's so modest. We do all love him here in this town.'

While the young woman was speaking, Gustav must have continued to turn himself away, for when I next looked at him he was facing the opposite corner of the elevator with his back to us. The weight of the suitcases was making his knees sag and his shoulders quiver. His head was bent right down so as to be practically hidden from us behind him, but whether this was due to bashfulness or sheer physical exertion was hard to say.

'I'm so sorry, Mr Ryder,' the young woman said. 'I haven't yet introduced myself. I'm Hilde Stratmann. I've been given the task of ensuring everything goes smoothly while you're here with us. I'm so glad you've managed to get here at last. We were all starting to get a little concerned. Everyone waited this morning for as long as they could, but many had important appointments and had to go off one by one. So it falls to me, a humble employee of the Civic Arts Institute, to tell you how greatly honoured we all feel by your visit.'

'I'm very pleased to be here. But concerning this morning. Did you just say . . .'

'Oh, please don't worry at all about this morning, Mr Ryder. No one was put out in the least. The important thing is that you're here. You know, Mr Ryder, something on which I can certainly agree with Gustav is the Old Town. It really is most attractive and I always advise visitors to go there. It has a marvellous atmosphere, full of pavement cafés, craft shops, restaurants. It's only a short walk from here, so you should take the opportunity as soon as your schedule allows.'

'I'll certainly try and do that. Incidentally, Miss Stratmann, speaking of my schedule . . .' I paused rather deliberately, expecting the young woman to exclaim at her forgetfulness, perhaps reach into her attaché case and produce a sheet or a folder. But although she did break in quickly, it was to say:

'It *is* a tight schedule, yes. But I do hope it's not unreasonable. We've tried to keep it strictly to the essential things. Inevitably we were inundated, by so many of our societies, the local media, everybody. You have such a following in this town, Mr Ryder. Many people here believe you to be not only the world's finest living pianist, but perhaps the very greatest of the century. But we think in the end we've managed to bring it down to the essentials. I trust there's nothing there you're too unhappy with.'

Just at this moment the elevator doors slid open and the elderly porter set off down the corridor. The suitcases made him drag his step along the carpet and Miss Stratmann and I, following on behind, had to measure our pace so as not to overtake him.

'I do hope no one was offended,' I said to her as we walked. 'I mean, about my not having time for them on my schedule.'

'Oh no, please don't worry. We all know why you're here and nobody wants it said that they distracted you. In fact, Mr Ryder, aside from two rather important social functions, everything else on your programme relates more or less directly to Thursday night. Of course, you've had a chance by now to familiarise yourself with your schedule.'

There was something about the way she uttered this last remark that made it difficult for me to respond entirely frankly. I thus muttered: 'Yes, of course.'

'It *is* a heavy schedule. But we were very much guided by your request to be allowed to see as much as possible at first hand. A very commendable approach, if I may say so.'

Ahead of us, the elderly porter stopped in front of a door. At last he lowered my suitcases and began fiddling with the lock. As we came up to him, Gustav picked up the suitcases again and staggered into the room, saying: 'Please follow me, sir.' I was about to do so, when Miss Stratmann placed a hand on my arm.

'I won't keep you,' she said. 'But I did just want to check at this stage if there was anything at all on your schedule you weren't happy with.'

The door swung shut, leaving us standing out in the corridor.

'Well, Miss Stratmann,' I said, 'on the whole, it struck me as . . . as a very well-balanced programme.'

'It was precisely with your request in mind that we arranged the meeting with the Citizens' Mutual Support Group. The Support Group is made up of ordinary people from every walk of life brought together by their sense of having suffered from the present crisis. You'll be able to hear first-hand accounts of what some people have had to go through.'

'Ah yes. That's sure to be most useful.'

'And as you'll have noticed, we've also respected your wish to meet with Mr Christoff himself. Given the circumstances, we perfectly appreciate your reasons for requesting such a meeting. Mr Christoff, for his part, is delighted, as you can well imagine. Naturally he has his own reasons for wanting to meet you. What I mean, of course, is that he and his friends will do their utmost to get you to see things their way. Naturally, it'll all be nonsense, but I'm sure you'll find it all very useful in drawing up a general picture of what's been going on here. Mr Ryder, you're looking very tired. I won't keep you any longer. Here's my card. Please don't hesitate to call if you have any problems or queries.'

I thanked her and watched her go off back down the corridor. When I entered my room I was still turning over the various implications of this exchange and took a moment to register Gustav standing next to the bed.

'Ah, here you are, sir.'

After the preponderance of dark wood panelling elsewhere in the building, I was surprised by the light modern look of the room. The wall facing me was glass almost from floor to ceiling and the sun was coming in pleasantly between the vertical blinds hung against it. My suitcases had been placed side by side next to the wardrobe.

'Now, sir, if you'll just bear with me a moment,' Gustav said, 'I'll show you the features of the room. That way, your stay here will be as comfortable as possible.'

I followed Gustav around the room while he pointed out switches and other facilities. At one point he led me into the bathroom and continued his explanations there. I had been about to cut him short in the way I am accustomed to doing when being shown a hotel room by a porter, but something about the diligence with which he went about his task, something about his efforts to personalise something he went through many times each day, rather touched me and prevented me from interrupting. And then, as he continued with his explanations, waving a hand towards various parts of the room, it occurred to me that for all his professionalism, for all his genuine desire to see me comfortable, a certain matter that had been preoccupying him throughout the day had again pushed its way to the front of his mind. He was, in other words, worrying once more about his daughter and her little boy.

When the arrangement had been proposed to him several months earlier, Gustav had little supposed it would bring him anything other than uncomplicated delight. For an afternoon each week, he was to spend a couple of hours wandering around the Old Town with his grandson, thereby allowing Sophie to go off and enjoy a little time to herself. Moreover, the arrangement had immediately proved a success and within weeks grandfather and grandson had evolved a routine highly agreeable to them both. On afternoons when it was not raining, they would start at the swing park, where Boris could demonstrate his latest feats of daring. If it was wet, they would start at the boat museum. They would then stroll about the little streets of the Old Town, looking in various gift shops, perhaps stopping at the Old Square to watch a mime artist or acrobat. The elderly porter being well known in the area, they would never get far without someone greeting them, and Gustav would receive numerous compliments regarding his grandson. They would next go over to the old bridge to watch the boats pass underneath. The expedition would then conclude at a favourite café, where they would order cake or ice cream and await Sophie's return.

Initially these little outings had brought Gustav immense satisfaction. But the increased contact with his daughter and grandson had obliged him to notice things he once might have pushed away, until he had no longer been able to pretend all was well. For one thing, there was the question of Sophie's general mood. In the early weeks, she had taken her leave of them cheerfully, hurrying away to the city centre to shop or to meet a friend. But lately she had taken to slouching off as though she had nothing to do with herself. There were, furthermore, clear signs that the trouble, whatever it was, had started to make its mark on Boris. True, his grandson was still for the most part his high-spirited self. But the porter had noticed how every now and then, particularly at any mention of his home life, a cloud would pass over the little boy's expression. Then two weeks ago something had happened which the elderly porter had not been able to expel from his mind.

He had been walking with Boris past one of the numerous cafés of the Old Town when he had suddenly noticed his daughter sitting inside. The awning had shaded the glass allowing a clear view through to the back, and Sophie had been visible sitting alone, a cup of coffee before her, wearing a look of utter despondency. The revelation that she had not found the energy to leave the Old Town at all, to say nothing of the expression on her face, had given the porter quite a shock – so much so that it had taken a moment before he had thought to try and distract Boris. It had been too late: Boris, following the porter's gaze, had got a clear glimpse of his mother. The little boy had immediately looked away and the two of them had continued with their walk without once mentioning the matter. Boris had regained his good humour within minutes, but the episode had none the less greatly perturbed the porter and he had since turned it over many times in his mind. In fact, it was the recollection of this incident that had lent him such a preoccupied air down in the lobby, and which was now troubling him once more as he showed me around my room.

I had taken a liking to the old man and felt a wave of sympathy for him. Clearly he had been brooding on things for a long time

14

and was now in danger of allowing his worries to attain unwarranted proportions. I thought about broaching the whole topic with him, but then, as Gustav came to the end of his routine, the weariness I had been experiencing intermittently ever since I had stepped off the plane came over me again. Resolving to take up the matter with him at a later point, I dismissed him with a generous tip.

Once the door had closed behind him, I collapsed fully clothed onto the bed and for a while gazed emptily up at the ceiling. At first my head remained filled with thoughts of Gustav and his various worries. But then as I went on lying there, I found myself turning over again the conversation I had had with Miss Stratmann. Clearly, this city was expecting of me something more than a simple recital. But when I tried to recall some basic details about the present visit, I had little success. I realised how foolish I had been not to have spoken more frankly to Miss Stratmann. If I had not received a copy of my schedule, the fault was hers, not mine, and my defensiveness had been quite without reason.

I thought again about the name Brodsky and this time I had the distinct impression I had either heard or read about him in the not so distant past. And then suddenly a moment came back to me from the long plane journey I had just completed. I had been sitting in the darkened cabin, the other passengers asleep around me, studying the schedule for this visit under the dim beam of the reading light. At one point the man next to me had awoken and after a few minutes had made some light-hearted remark. In fact, as I recalled, he had leaned over and put to me some little quiz question, something about World Cup footballers. Not wishing to be distracted from the careful study I was making of my schedule, I had brushed him off somewhat coldly. All this now returned to me clearly enough. Indeed, I could recall the very texture of the thick grey paper on which the schedule had been typed, the dull yellow patch cast on it by the reading light, the drone of the plane's engines – but try as I might, I could remember nothing of what had been written on that sheet.

Then after a few more minutes I felt my weariness engulfing me and decided there was little point in worrying myself further until I had had a little sleep. Indeed, I knew well from experience how much clearer things became after a rest. I could then go and find Miss Stratmann, explain to her about the misunderstanding, obtain a copy of my schedule and have her clarify whatever points needed clarifying.

I was just starting to doze off when something suddenly made me open my eyes again and stare up at the ceiling. I went on scrutinising the ceiling for some time, then sat up on the bed and looked around, the sense of recognition growing stronger by the second. The room I was now in, I realised, was the very room that had served as my bedroom during the two years my parents and I had lived at my aunt's house on the borders of England and Wales. I looked again around the room, then, lowering myself back down, stared once more at the ceiling. It had been recently re-plastered and re-painted, its dimensions had been enlarged, the cornices had been removed, the decorations around the light fitting had been entirely altered. But it was unmistakably the same ceiling I had so often stared up at from my narrow creaking bed of those days.

I rolled over onto my side and looked down at the floor beside the bed. The hotel had provided a dark rug just where my feet would land. I could remember how once that same area of floor had been covered by a worn green mat, where several times a week I would set out in careful formations my plastic soldiers – over a hundred in all – which I had kept in two biscuit tins. I reached down a hand and let my fingers brush against the hotel rug, and as I did so a memory came back to me of one afternoon when I had been lost within my world of plastic soldiers and a furious row had broken out downstairs. The ferocity of the voices had been such that, even as a child of six or seven, I had realised this to be no ordinary row. But I had told myself it was nothing and, resting my cheek back down on the green mat, had continued with my battle plans. Near the centre of that green mat had been a torn patch that had always been a source of much irritation to me. But that afternoon, as the voices raged on downstairs, it had occurred to me for the first time that this tear could be used as a sort of bush terrain for my soldiers to cross. This discovery – that the blemish that had always threatened to undermine my imaginary world could in fact be incorporated into it – had been one of some excitement for me, and that 'bush' was to become a key factor in many of the battles I subsequently orchestrated.

All this came back to me as I continued to stare up at the ceiling. Of course, I remained highly conscious of how all around the room features had been altered or removed. Nevertheless, the realisation that after all this time I was once more back in my old childhood sanctuary caused a profound feeling of peace to come over me. I closed my eyes and for a moment it was as though I were once more surrounded by all those old items of furniture. In the far corner to my right, the tall white wardrobe with the broken door knob. My aunt's painting of Salisbury Cathedral on the wall above my head. The bedside cabinet with its two small drawers filled with my little treasures and secrets. All the tensions of the day – the long flight, the confusions over my schedule, Gustav's problems – seemed to fall away and I felt myself sliding into a deep and exhausted sleep.

2

When I was roused by the bedside telephone, I had the impression it had been ringing for some time. I picked up the receiver and a voice said:

'Hello? Mr Ryder?'

'Yes, hello.'

'Ah, Mr Ryder. This is Mr Hoffman speaking. The hotel manager.'

'Ah yes. How do you do.'

'Mr Ryder, we're so extremely pleased to have you with us at last. You're very welcome here.'

'Thank you.'

'Very welcome indeed, sir. Please don't worry at all about your delayed arrival. As I believe Miss Stratmann told you, everyone present understood perfectly. After all, when one has the distances you have to cover, and with so many engagements around the world – ha ha! – such things are sometimes inevitable.'

'But . . .'

'No, really, sir, there's no need to utter another word on the matter. All the ladies and gentlemen, as I say, were very understanding. So let us put the matter behind us. The important thing is that you are here. And for that alone, Mr Ryder, our gratitude to you is unmeasurable.'

'Well, thank you, Mr Hoffman.'

'Now, sir, if you aren't too busy just now, I would very much like at last to greet you face to face. Extend to you my personal welcome to our town and to this hotel.'

'That's very kind of you,' I said. 'But just now I'm taking a short nap . . .'

'A short nap?' There was a flash of irritation in the voice. The next moment the geniality had returned completely. 'Why, of course, of course. You must be very tired. You've come such a long way. So then, let us say, whenever you are ready.'

'I'll look forward to meeting.you, Mr Hoffman. No doubt, I'll be down before long.'

'Please come absolutely in your own time. For my part, I shall continue to wait here – that is, down here in the lobby – however long you care to take. So please don't hurry at all.'

I thought about this for a moment. Then I said: 'But Mr Hoffman, you must have so many other things to do.'

'True, this is a very busy part of the day. But for you, Mr Ryder, I will happily wait here for as long as necessary.'

'Please, Mr Hoffman, don't waste your valuable time on my account. I'll be down presently and then I'll come and find you.'

'Mr Ryder, it's no bother at all. In fact, I'll be honoured to wait here for you. So as I say, come entirely in your own time. I assure you, I will remain standing here until you arrive.'

I thanked him again and put down the receiver. Sitting up, I looked around me and guessed from the light that it was now the late afternoon. I felt more tired than ever, but there seemed little option other than to go down to the lobby. I got to my feet, went to one of my suitcases and found a less crumpled jacket than the one I was still wearing. As I was changing into it, a strong craving came over me for some coffee and I left my room a few moments later with something approaching urgency.

I emerged from the elevator to find the lobby far livelier than before. All around me, guests were lounging in armchairs, leafing through newspapers or chatting together over cups of coffee. Near the reception desk several Japanese people were greeting one another with much jollity. I was slightly bemused by this transformation and did not notice the hotel manager until he had come right up to me.

He was in his fifties, and was larger and heavier than I had imagined from the voice on the phone. He offered me his hand, beaming broadly. As he did so, I noticed he was short of breath and that his forehead was lightly coated with sweat.

As we shook hands, he repeated several times what an honour my presence represented for the town and for his hotel in particular. Then he leaned forward and said with a confiding air: 'And let me assure you, sir, all the arrangements for Thursday night are in hand. There really is nothing you need worry about.'

I waited for him to say more, but when he merely went on smiling, I said: 'Well, that's good to hear.'

'No, sir, there really is nothing to worry about.'

There was an awkward pause. After a moment, Hoffman seemed about to say something else, but then stopped himself, gave a laugh and hit me lightly on the shoulder – a gesture I thought unduly familiar. Finally he said: 'Mr Ryder, if there is anything I can do to make your stay here more comfortable, please let me know without delay.'

'You're very kind.'

There was another pause. Then he laughed again, shook his head a little and once more hit me on the shoulder.

'Mr Hoffman,' I said, 'was there perhaps something in particular you wished to speak to me about?'

'Oh, nothing in particular, Mr Ryder. I just wished to greet you and make sure everything was to your satisfaction.' Then suddenly he gave an exclamation. 'Of course. Now you mention it, yes, there was something. But it was merely a small matter.' Yet again, he shook his head and laughed. Then he said: 'It's to do with my wife's albums.'

'Your wife's albums?'

'My wife, Mr Ryder, is a very cultured woman. Naturally she's a great admirer of yours. In fact she has followed your career with close interest and for some years has been collecting press cuttings about you.'

'Really? How very good of her.'

'In fact, she has compiled two albums of cuttings entirely devoted to you. The entries have been arranged chronologically and date back many years. Let me come to the point. It has always been my wife's great hope that you would one day peruse these albums for yourself. The news that you were to visit our town naturally gave new life to this hope. Nevertheless she knew how busy you would be here and was insistent you should not be bothered on her account. But I could see what she secretly hoped, and so I promised her I would at least raise the matter with you. If you could find even a minute just to cast an eye over them, you have no idea what it would mean to her.'

'You must convey my gratitude to your wife, Mr Hoffman. I shall be very happy to look at her albums.'

'Mr Ryder, that's very good of you! Very good of you indeed! As a matter of fact, I did bring the albums here to the hotel in readiness. But I can guess how busy you must be.'

'I do have quite a busy schedule. However, I'm sure I'll be able to find some time for your wife's albums.'

'How very good of you, Mr Ryder! But let me stress, the last thing I wish to do is put extra pressure on you. So let me make a suggestion. I will wait for you to indicate when you are ready to inspect the albums. Until you do so, I won't bother you. Any time, night or day, when you feel the moment is right, please come and find me. I am usually to be found quite easily and I don't leave the premises until late. I shall stop whatever it is I'm doing and go and fetch the albums. I'd feel much happier leaving it on such a basis. Really, I couldn't bear to think I was adding further pressure to your schedule.'

'That's very considerate of you, Mr Hoffman.'

'Actually it occurs to me, Mr Ryder. Over the coming days I may give the appearance of being frantically busy. But I would like you to understand, I shall never be too busy to attend to this matter. So even if I look very preoccupied, please don't be put off.'

'Very well. I'll remember that.'

'Perhaps we should agree on a signal of some sort. I say this because you may come searching for me and see me on the other side of a crowded room. It would be very onerous on you to have to push your way through such a seething mass. And in any case, by the time you reach the point in the room where you first saw me, I may myself have moved off. This is why a signal would be advisable. Something easily distinguishable which you can give above the heads of the crowd.'

'Indeed, that seems a very sound idea.'

'Excellent. I am heartened to discover you such an agreeable and kind person, Mr Ryder. If only one could say as much for certain other celebrities we have hosted here. So. It just remains for us to agree a signal. Perhaps I could suggest . . . well, let us say something like this.'

He raised a hand, palm outwards, the fingers fanned out, and described a motion as though he were wiping a window.

'Just an example,' he said, putting his hand quickly behind his back. 'Of course, another signal may be more to your liking.'

'No, that signal is fine. I'll give it to you as soon as I'm ready to look at your wife's albums. It really is very kind of her to have gone to such trouble.'

'I know it has given her profound satisfaction. Of course, if later on you think of some other signal you prefer, please phone me from your room, or else leave a message with one of the staff.'

'You're most kind, but the signal you suggest seems to me very elegant. Now, Mr Hoffman, I wonder if you would advise me where I might get some good coffee. I feel just now I could drink several cups.'

The manager laughed rather theatrically. 'I know the feeling very well. I shall take you to the atrium. Please, follow me.'

He led the way to the corner of the lobby and through a pair of heavy swing doors. We entered a long gloomy corridor with dark wood panelling along both walls. There was so little natural light in the corridor that even at this point in the day a row of dim wall lamps had been left on. Hoffman continued to walk briskly ahead of me, turning every few steps to smile over his shoulder. About half-way down, we passed a rather grand-looking doorway and Hoffman, who must have noticed me looking at it, said:

'Ah yes. Coffee would normally be served there in the drawing room. A splendid room, Mr Ryder, very comfortable. And now further adorned by some hand-made tables I found myself during a recent trip to Florence. I'm sure you'd approve of them. However, just now, as you know, we have closed off the room for Mr Brodsky.'

'Oh yes. He was in there earlier when I arrived.'

'He's still in there, sir. I would take you in to introduce you to each other except, well, I feel this is perhaps not quite the moment. Mr Brodsky may ... well, let us say, it may not yet be the moment. Ha ha! But not to worry, there will be many opportunities for you two gentlemen to get to know one another.'

'Mr Brodsky is in that room now?'

I glanced back towards the doorway and possibly slowed my pace a little. In any case, the manager grasped my arm and began firmly to lead me away.

'He is indeed, sir. Very well, he's sitting there silently just now, but I assure you, he will begin again at any moment. And this morning, you know, he rehearsed the orchestra for a full four hours. By all accounts, everything is going extremely well. So please, there's nothing to worry about.'

The corridor eventually turned a corner after which it grew much brighter. In fact this section of it had windows all along one side causing pools of sunlight to form on the floor. Only when we had gone some way along this section did Hoffman let go of me. As we slowed to a leisurely pace, the manager gave a laugh to cover his embarrassment.

'The atrium is just here, sir. Essentially it's a bar, but it's comfortable and you will be served coffee and whatever else you desire. Please, this way.'

We turned off the corridor and went under an arch.

'This annexe,' Hoffman said, leading me in, 'was completed three years ago. We call it the atrium and we're rather proud of it. It was designed for us by Antonio Zanotto.'

We came into a bright spacious hall. Owing to the glass ceiling high above us there was something of the feeling of stepping out into a courtyard. The floor was a vast expanse of white tiles, at the centre of which, dominating everything, was a fountain – a tangle of nymph-like figures in marble gushing water with some force. In fact it struck me the water pressure was quite excessive; one could hardly look across to any part of the atrium without having to peer through the fine mist hovering in the air. Even so, I managed quickly to ascertain that each corner of the atrium had its own bar, with its separate collection of high-stools, easy chairs and tables. Waiters in white uniforms were criss-crossing the floor and there appeared to be a fair number of guests spread about the place – though such was the feeling of space one hardly noticed them.

I could see the manager watching me with a smug expression, waiting for me to express approval of our surroundings. At that moment, however, the need for coffee came over me so strongly that I simply turned away and made for the nearest of the bars.

I had already seated myself on a high-stool, my elbows up on the bar counter, when the manager caught up with me. He snapped his fingers at the barman, who was in any case coming to serve me, saying: 'Mr Ryder would like a pot of coffee. Kenyan!'

Then, turning back to me, he said: 'I would enjoy nothing better just now than to join you, Mr Ryder. Converse in a leisurely way about music and the arts. Unfortunately there are a number of things I must do which I cannot possibly delay further. I wonder, sir, if you'd be so good as to excuse me?'

Although I insisted he had been more than kind, he spent several more minutes taking his leave of me. Then at last he glanced at his watch, let out an exclamation and hurried off.

Left alone, I must quickly have drifted off into my own thoughts, for I did not notice the barman return. He must have done so, however, for I was soon drinking coffee, staring at the mirrored wall behind the bar – in which I could see not only my own reflection but much of the room behind me. After a while, for some reason, I found myself replaying in my head key moments from a football match I had attended many years earlier – an encounter between Germany and Holland. I adjusted my posture on the high-stool – I could see I was hunching excessively – and tried recalling the names of the players in the Dutch team that year. Rep, Krol, Haan, Neeskens. After several minutes I had succeeded in remembering all but two of the players, but these last two names remained just beyond the rim of my recall. As I tried to remember, the sound of the fountain behind me, which at first I had found quite soothing, began to annoy me. It seemed that if only it would stop, my memory would unlock and I would finally remember the names.

I was still trying to remember when a voice said behind me:

'Excuse me, it's Mr Ryder, isn't it?'

I turned to find a fresh-faced young man in his early twenties. When I greeted him, he came up eagerly to the bar.

'I do hope I'm not intruding,' he said. 'But when I saw you just now I simply had to come over and say how excited I am you're here. You see, I'm a pianist myself. On a strictly amateur basis, I mean. And, well, I've always admired you terribly. When Father finally got word that you were coming, I was so thrilled.'

'Father?'

'I'm so sorry. I'm Stephan Hoffman. The manager's son.'

'Ah yes, I see. How do you do.'

'You wouldn't mind if I sat here for a minute, would you?' The young man climbed up onto the stool next to mine. 'You know, sir, Father's just as thrilled, if not more so. Knowing Father he may not have told you just how *much* he's thrilled. But believe me it means everything to him.'

'Is that so?'

'Yes, really, I'm hardly exaggerating. I remember the period when Father was still waiting for your reply. This peculiar silence would come over him whenever your name was mentioned. And then, when the pressure really built up, he'd start muttering under his breath about it all. "How much longer? How much longer until he replies? He's going to turn us down. I can sense it." I had to really work then, to keep his spirits up. Anyway, sir, you can imagine just what your being here now means to him. He's such a perfectionist! When he organises an event like Thursday night, everything, *everything*, has to be just right. He goes over every detail in his head, over and over. Sometimes it does get a bit much, all this single-mindedness. But then I suppose if he didn't have that side to him, he wouldn't be Father and he wouldn't achieve half of what he does.'

'Indeed. He seems an admirable person.'

'Actually, Mr Ryder,' the young man said, 'I did have something I wanted to ask you. It's a request really. If it's impossible, then please just say so. I won't take it amiss.'

Stephan Hoffman paused as though to gather up his courage. I drank a little more coffee and gazed at the reflection of the two of us sitting side by side.

'Well, this is also to do with Thursday night,' he went on. 'You see, Father's asked me to play the piano at the event. I've practised and I'm ready and it's not that I'm worried about it or anything . . .' As he said this, just for a second his assured manner faltered and I caught a glimpse of an anxious adolescent. But almost immediately he had recovered with a nonchalant shrug. 'It's just that with Thursday night being so important, I don't want to let him down. To come to the point, I was just wondering if you would have a few minutes to spare to listen to me run through my piece. I've decided to play Jean-Louis La Roche's *Dahlia*. I'm just an amateur and you'd have to be very tolerant. But I thought I could just run through it and you could give me a few tips about how I might polish things up.'

25

I thought about this for a moment. 'So,' I said after a while, 'you're set to perform on Thursday night.'

'Of course, it's a very small contribution to the evening alongside, well' – he gave a laugh – 'the other things taking place. All the same I want my bit to be as good as possible.'

'Yes, I can quite understand. Well, I'd be pleased to do what I can for you.'

The young man's face lit up. 'Mr Ryder, I'm speechless! It's the very thing I need . . .'

'But there *is* a problem. As you can guess, my time here is very restricted. I'll have to find a moment when I have a few minutes free.'

'Of course. Whenever it's convenient for you, Mr Ryder. My goodness, I'm so flattered. To be frank, I thought you'd turn me down flat.'

A bleeper began to sound somewhere within the young man's clothing. Stephan started, then reached inside his jacket.

'Awfully sorry,' he said, 'but that's the urgent one. I should have been somewhere else long ago. But when I saw you sitting here, Mr Ryder, I couldn't resist coming over. I hope we can continue this discussion very shortly. But for now, please excuse me.'

He got down off the stool, but then for a second seemed tempted to start another exchange. Then the bleeper went off again and he hurried away with an embarrassed smile.

I turned back to my reflection behind the bar counter and began to sip my coffee again. I could not, however, re-capture the mood of relaxed contemplation I had been enjoying before the young man's arrival. Instead, I found myself troubled once more by a sense that much was expected of me here, and yet that things were at present on a far from satisfactory footing. In fact, there seemed nothing for it but to seek out Miss Stratmann and clear up certain points once and for all. I resolved to go and find her as soon as I came to the end of my current cup of coffee. There was no reason for this to be an awkward encounter, and it would be simple enough to explain what had happened at our last meeting. 'Miss Stratmann,' I might say, 'I was very tired earlier and so when you asked about my schedule I misunderstood you. I thought you were asking me if I would have time to look at it straight away if you were to produce a copy then and there.' Or else I could go on the offensive, even adopting a tone of reproach. 'Miss Stratmann, I have to say I'm a little concerned and, yes, somewhat disappointed. Given the level of responsibility you and your fellow citizens seem content to place on my shoulders, I think I have a right to expect a certain standard of administrative back-up.'

I heard a movement near me and looking up saw that Gustav, the elderly porter, was standing by my stool. As I turned towards him, he smiled and said:

'Hello, sir. I just happened to see you here. I do hope you're enjoying your stay.'

'Oh, I am indeed. Though unfortunately I haven't yet had the opportunity to visit the Old Town as you recommended.'

'That's a pity, sir. Because that really is a very nice part of our city and it's so near. And the weather just now, I'd say it's ideal. A slight chill in the air, but sunny. Just warm enough still to sit outside, though I dare say you'll have to wear a jacket or a light coat. It's the best sort of day to see the Old Town.'

'You know,' I said, 'a little fresh air may be just what I need.'

'I really would recommend it, sir. It would be such a shame if it came to your leaving our town without having enjoyed even a brief walk around the Old Town.'

'You know, I think I'll do just that. I'll go off right now.'

'If you find time to sit down at the Hungarian Café in the Old Square, I feel certain you wouldn't regret it. I would suggest you order a pot of coffee and a piece of the apple strudel. Incidentally, sir, I did just wonder . . .' The porter paused a moment. Then he went on: 'I did wonder if I might ask a small favour of you. I wouldn't normally ask favours of guests, but in your case, I feel we've got to know one another pretty well.'

'I'd be pleased to do something for you if it were at all possible,' I said.

For a moment, the porter remained standing there silently.

'It's just a small thing,' he said eventually. 'You see, I know just now my daughter will be at the Hungarian Café. She'll have little Boris with her. She's a very pleasant young woman, sir, I'm sure you'd feel very sympathetic towards her. Most people do. She's not what you'd call beautiful, but she has an attractive sort of appearance. She's a very good-natured person at heart. But I suppose she's always had this small weakness about her. Perhaps it was the way she was brought up, who can say? But it's always been there. That's to say, she has this tendency to let things overwhelm her sometimes, even when they're well within her capacity to sort. Some little problem will come up, and instead of taking the few simple measures required, she just broods on it. That way, as you know, sir, small problems grow into larger ones. Before long, things look very deep to her and she gets herself into a mood of despair. It's all so unnecessary. I don't know what exactly is troubling her now, but I'm sure it's not anything so insurmountable. I've seen it so often before. But now, you see, Boris has started to notice. In fact, sir, if Sophie doesn't get a grip on things soon, I'm afraid the boy will become seriously worried. And he's such a delight at the moment. So full of openness and trust. I know it's impossible for him to go through the whole of his life like that, perhaps it's not even desirable. But still, at his age just now, I think he should have just a few more years of believing the world to be a place of sunshine and laughter.' He fell silent again and for a few moments seemed deep in thought. Then looking up he went on: 'If only Sophie could see clearly what was happening, I know she'd get a grip on things. She is at heart very conscientious, very keen to do the best for the people she most cares about. But the thing about Sophie, well, once she gets into this state, she does need a little help to recover her sense of perspective. A good talk, that's really all she needs. Just someone to sit down with her for a few minutes and make her look at things clearly. Help establish what the real problems are, which measures she should take to overcome them. That's all she needs, sir, a good talk, something to give her back her perspective. She'll do the rest herself. She can be very sensible when she means to be. Which brings me to my point, sir. If you happen to be going to the Old Town just now, I wondered if you wouldn't mind having a little word with Sophie. Of course, I realise this might be something of an inconvenience to you, but since you're going that way anyway, I thought I'd ask you. You wouldn't have to talk to her for long. Just a short talk, just to find out what's troubling her and to give her back a sense of proportion.'

28

The porter stopped and looked at me appealingly. After a moment, I said with a sigh:

'I'd like to be of some help, I really would. But listening to what you say, it seems to me quite likely that Sophie's worries, whatever they are, may well relate to family issues. And as you know, such problems tend to be very deeply enmeshed. An outsider such as myself may after some frank discussion get to the bottom of one thing, only to find it connected to another problem. And so on and so on. Frankly, in my opinion, to talk through the whole tangled net of family issues, I would have thought you were yourself best suited to do that. As Sophie's father and the boy's grandfather, after all, you'd have a natural authority I simply lack.'

The porter seemed immediately to feel the burden of these words and I almost regretted having spoken them. Clearly I had hit upon a sensitive point. He turned away slightly and for several moments gazed emptily across the atrium in the direction of the fountain. Finally he said:

'I appreciate what you're telling me, sir. By rights, yes, I should be the one to talk to her, I can see that. Well, let me be honest – I don't quite know how to put this – but let me be quite honest with you. The truth of the matter is, Sophie and I haven't spoken to each other for many years. Not really since she was a child. So you can appreciate, it's somewhat difficult for me to accomplish what's required.'

The porter looked down at his feet and seemed to be waiting for my next utterance as though for a judgement.

'I'm sorry,' I said after a while, 'but I'm not quite clear what you're saying. You mean you haven't seen your daughter all this time?'

'No, no. As you know, I *see* her regularly, each time I take Boris off her. What I mean is, we don't speak. Perhaps you'd understand better if I were to give an illustration. Take those times Boris and I are waiting for her after one of our little walks around the Old Town. We might be sitting in Mr Krankl's coffee house, say. Boris might be in high spirits, talking loudly, laughing about everything. But as soon as he sees his mother coming through the door, he'll go silent. Not in any upset sort of way. He'll just restrain himself. He respects the ritual, you see? Then

Sophie will come up to our table and address *him*. Did we have a nice time? Where did we go? Has Grandfather not been too cold? Oh yes, she always asks after me. She worries that I'll get ill wandering about the district like that. But as I say, we don't speak directly, Sophie and me. "Say goodbye to Grandfather," she'll say to Boris by way of farewell and off they go together. That's the way things have been with us for many years and there seems no real call to alter them at this stage. But then, you see, in a situation like this one, I find myself at something of a loss. I do feel a good talk is what's required. And someone like yourself would in my opinion be ideal. Just a few words, sir. Just to help her identify what the problems actually are. If you can just do that, she'll do the rest, you can be assured of that.'

'Very well,' I said after thinking this over. 'Very well, I'll see what I can do. But I must stress what I said earlier. These things are often too complicated for an outsider. But I'll see what I can do.'

'I'll be indebted to you, sir. She'll be at the Hungarian Café at this moment. You should have no difficulty recognising her. She has long dark hair and a number of my features. And if you're in any doubt, you could always ask the proprietor or one of his staff to point her out.'

'Very well. I'll set off straight away.'

'I'll be so indebted, sir. And even if for some reason a talk with her proves impossible, I know you'll enjoy walking around the area.'

I lowered myself off the high-stool. 'Well then,' I said to him, 'I'll let you know how I get on.'

'Thank you so much, sir.'

3

The route from the hotel to the Old Town – a walk of some fifteen minutes – was distinctly unpromising. For much of the way glassy office buildings loomed above me along streets noisy with the late-afternoon traffic. But when I came out to the river and started across the hump-backed bridge leading to the Old Town, I could sense I was about to enter a quite different atmosphere. Visible on the opposite bank were colourful awnings and café parasols. I caught the movement of waiters and of children running in circles. A tiny dog was barking excitedly at the quayside, perhaps having noticed my approach.

A few minutes later I had entered the Old Town. The narrow cobbled streets were full of people walking at an easy pace. I wandered around aimlessly for some minutes, past numerous little souvenir shops, confectioners and bakeries. I also passed several cafés and for a moment I wondered if I would have difficulty locating the particular one referred to by the porter. But then I came out to a large square at the heart of the district and the Hungarian Café was immediately obvious. The sprawl of tables occupying the entire far corner of the square was, I could see, emanating from one small doorway beneath a striped awning.

I paused a moment to recover my breath and take in the surroundings. The sun was starting to set over the square. There was, as Gustav had warned, a chilly breeze which every now and then caused a flutter to pass through the parasols surrounding the café. Regardless, the majority of the tables were occupied. Many of the customers seemed to be tourists, but I could see also a fair number who looked like locals who had left their work early and were unwinding over a coffee and newspaper. Indeed, as I crossed the square I passed many office workers standing in groups with their briefcases, talking cheerfully together.

On reaching the tables, I spent a few moments strolling around them, looking for someone likely to be the porter's daughter.

Two students were arguing about a movie. A tourist was reading *Newsweek*. An old woman was throwing pieces of bread to some pigeons gathered around her feet. But I could not see any young women with long dark hair and a small boy. I stepped inside the café and discovered a small, rather gloomy room with just five or six tables. I could see how the overcrowding problem mentioned by the porter might become a very real one during the colder months, but on this occasion the only occupant was an old man in a beret, seated near the back. Deciding I should give up on the matter, I returned outside and was looking about for a waiter from whom to order some coffee, when I became aware of a voice calling my name.

Turning, I saw a woman sitting with a young boy waving to me from a nearby table. The pair clearly matched the porter's description and I could not understand how I had failed to notice them earlier. I was a little taken aback, moreover, that they should be expecting me, and it was a moment or two before I waved back and began making my way towards them.

Although the porter had referred to her as a 'young woman', Sophie was in early middle age, perhaps around forty or so. For all that, she was somewhat more attractive than I had expected. She was quite tall, slimly built and her long dark hair gave her a gypsy-like quality. The boy beside her was a little on the tubby side, and at this moment was regarding his mother with a cross expression.

'Well?' Sophie was looking up at me with a smile. 'Aren't you going to sit down?'

'Yes, yes,' I said, realising I had been standing there hesitantly. 'That is, if you don't mind.' I gave the boy a grin, but he just looked back at me with disapproval.

'Of course we don't mind. Do we, Boris? Boris, say hello to Mr Ryder.'

'Hello, Boris,' I said seating myself.

The boy continued to look at me with disapproval. Then he said to his mother: 'Why did you tell him he could sit down? I was just explaining something to you.'

'This is Mr Ryder, Boris,' Sophie said. 'He's a special friend. Of course he can sit with us if he wants.'

'But I was explaining to you how the Voyager flew. I knew you weren't listening. You should learn to pay attention.'

'I'm sorry, Boris,' Sophie said, exchanging a quick smile with me. 'I was trying awfully hard, but all this science is way above my head. Now why don't you say hello to Mr Ryder?'

Boris looked at me for a moment, then said grumpily: 'Hello.' With that he turned his gaze away from me.

'Please don't let me be the source of any friction,' I said. 'Please, Boris, continue with what you were just explaining. In fact, I'd be very interested to hear about this aircraft myself.'

'It's not an aircraft,' Boris said wearily. 'It's a vehicle for going through star systems. But you wouldn't understand any better than Mother.'

'Oh? How do you know I wouldn't understand? I might have a very scientific mind. You shouldn't judge people so quickly, Boris.'

He sighed heavily and kept his gaze averted from me. 'You'll be just like Mother,' he said. 'You'd lack concentration.'

'Now come on, Boris,' Sophie said. 'You should be a little more accommodating. Mr Ryder's a very special friend.'

'Not only that,' I said, 'I'm a friend of your grandfather.'

For the first time, Boris regarded me with interest.

'Oh yes,' I said. 'We've become good friends, your grandfather and I. I'm staying at his hotel.'

Boris went on studying me carefully.

'Boris,' Sophie said, 'why don't you say hello nicely to Mr Ryder? You still haven't shown him any manners at all. You don't want him going away thinking you're an ill-mannered young man, do you?'

Boris went on looking at me a while longer. Then quite suddenly he flopped forward onto the table, burying his head in his arms. At the same time he began to swing his feet about underneath, for I could hear the clanging of his shoes against the metal table leg.

'I'm sorry,' Sophie said. 'He's been rather moody today.'

'As a matter of fact,' I said to her quietly, 'there was something I wished to talk to you about. But, er . . .' I signalled with my eyes towards Boris. Sophie looked at me, then turned to the little boy, saying:

33

'Boris, I've got to talk with Mr Ryder a moment. Why don't you go and look at the swans? Just for a minute.'

Boris kept his head in his arms as though asleep, though his feet continued to clang rhythmically. Sophie shook his shoulder gently.

'Come on now,' she said. 'There's a black swan out there too. Go and stand over by those railings, where those nuns are. You'll be able to see it for sure. You can come back in a few minutes and tell us what you've seen.'

For a few more seconds Boris gave no response. Then he sat up, let out another weary sigh and slid off his chair. For some reason best known to himself, he affected the mannerisms of someone utterly drunk and went staggering away from the table.

Once the boy was a sufficient distance away, I turned back to Sophie. Then an uncertainty came over me as to how I should begin and I sat hesitating for a moment. In any case, Sophie smiled and spoke first:

'I've got good news. That Mr Mayer phoned earlier about a house. It's just come on the market today. It sounds really promising. I've been thinking about it all day. Something tells me this might be it, the one we've been looking for all this time. I told him I'd go out there first thing tomorrow morning and have a good look. Really, it sounds perfect. About half an hour's walk from the village, all by itself on a ridge, three storeys. Mr Mayer says the views over the forest are the best he's seen in years. I know you're very busy just now, but if it turns out to be anything like as good as it sounds, I'll call you and perhaps you could come out. Boris too. It might be exactly what we've been looking for. I know it's taken a long time, but I might have found it at last.'

'Ah yes. Good.'

'I'll take the first bus out there in the morning. We'll have to act fast. It won't stay on the market long.'

She began to give me more details about the house. I remained silent, but only partly because of my uncertainty as to how I should respond. For the fact was, as we had been sitting together, Sophie's face had come to seem steadily more familiar to me, until now I thought I could even remember vaguely some earlier discussions about buying just such a house in the woods. Mean-

34

while my expression had perhaps grown preoccupied, for eventually she broke off, then said in a different, more tentative voice:

'I'm sorry about that last phone call. I hope you're not still sulking about it.'

'Sulking? Oh no.'

'I keep thinking about it. I shouldn't have said any of it. I hope you didn't take it to heart. After all, how can you be expected to stay at home just now? What home? And with that kitchen the way it is! And I've been taking so long, finding somewhere for us. But I'm so hopeful now, about this house tomorrow.'

She began to talk again about the house. As she did so, I tried to recall something of the phone conversation to which she had just referred. After a while, I found a faint recollection returning to me of listening to this same voice – or rather a harder, angrier version of it – on the end of a telephone in the not-so-distant past. Eventually I thought I could recall also a certain phrase I had been shouting at her down the mouthpiece: 'You live in such a small world!' She had continued to argue and I had gone on repeating contemptuously: 'Such a small world! You live in such a small world!' To my frustration, however, I found nothing more of this exchange would come back to me.

Possibly I had begun to stare at her in my endeavour to jog my memory, for she now asked rather self-consciously:

'Do you think I've put on weight?'

'No, no.' I turned away with a laugh. 'You're looking quite marvellous.'

It occurred to me I had not yet mentioned anything of the matter concerning her father and I tried again to think of a suitable way to broach the topic. But just then something jolted my chair from behind and I realised Boris had returned.

In fact the little boy was running around in circles near our table, kicking a discarded paper carton as though it were a football. Noticing that I was now watching him, he juggled the carton from one foot to the other, then kicked it hard through the legs of my chair.

'Number Nine!' he shouted, holding his arms aloft. 'A superb goal from Number Nine!'

'Boris,' I said, 'hadn't you better put that carton in the waste bin?'

'When are we going to go?' he asked, turning to me. 'We're going to be late. It'll be dark soon.'

Looking past him I saw that indeed the sun was beginning to set over the square and that many of the tables had become vacant.

'I'm sorry, Boris. What was it you were wanting to do?'

'Hurry up!' The little boy gave my arm a tug. 'We'll never get there!'

'Where is it Boris wants to go?' I asked his mother quietly.

'To the swing park, of course.' Sophie sighed and rose to her feet. 'He wants to show you the progress he's made.'

There seemed no choice but for me to rise also, and the next moment the three of us were setting off across the square.

'So,' I said to Boris as he fell in step beside me, 'you're going to show me a few things.'

'When we were there earlier on,' he said, taking my arm, 'there was this boy, he was bigger than me, and he couldn't even do a torpedo! Mother thought he was at least two years older than me. I showed him how to do it five times, but he was too scared. He just kept going to the top, then he couldn't do it!'

'Really. And of course, you're not scared to do this thing. This torpedo.'

'Of course I'm not scared! It's easy! It's completely easy!'

'That's good.'

'He was too scared! It was so funny!'

We left the square and began to make our way through the small cobbled streets of the district. Boris seemed to know the way well, often running a few paces ahead in his impatience. Then at one point, he fell in step beside me again and asked:

'Do you know Grandfather?'

'Yes, I told you. We're good friends.'

'Grandfather's very strong. He's one of the strongest men in the town.'

'Is that so?'

'He's a good fighter. He was a soldier once. He's old, but he's still a better fighter than most people. Street thugs don't realise that sometimes, then they get a nasty surprise.' Boris made a sudden lunging movement as he walked. 'Before they know it, Grandfather's got them on the ground.'

'Really? That's interesting, Boris.'

Just at that moment, as we continued through the little cobbled streets, I found myself remembering more of the argument I had had with Sophie. It had taken place perhaps a week or so ago, and I had been in a hotel room somewhere, listening to her voice at the other end of the line shouting:

'How much longer can they expect you to carry on like this? Neither of us are so young any more! You've done your share now! Let somebody else do it all now!'

'Look,' I had been saying to her, my voice still calm, 'the fact is, people need me. I arrive in a place and more often than not find terrible problems. Deep-seated, seemingly intractable problems, and people are so grateful I've come.'

'But how much longer can you go on doing this for people? And for us, I mean for me and you and Boris, time's slipping away. Before you know it, Boris will be grown up. No one can expect you to keep on like this. And all these people, why can't they sort out their own problems? It might do them some good!'

'You've no idea!' I had broken in, now angry. 'You don't know what you're saying! Some of these places I visit, the people don't know a thing. They don't understand the first thing about modern music and if you leave them to themselves, it's obvious, they'll just get deeper and deeper into trouble. I'm needed, why can't you see that? I'm needed out here! You don't know what you're talking about!' And it was then I had shouted at her: 'Such a small world! You live in such a small world!'

We had come to a small playground encircled by railings. It was empty of people and I thought it had a rather melancholy atmosphere about it. Boris though led us enthusiastically through the little gate.

'Look, this is easy!' he said, and went running off towards the climbing frame.

For a while, Sophie and I stood in the fading light watching his figure climb higher and higher. Then she said quietly:

'You know, it's funny. When I was listening to that Mr Mayer, the way he was describing the living room of the house, I kept getting these pictures in my mind, of the apartment we lived in when I was small. All the time he was talking, I kept getting these pictures. Our old living room. And Mother and Papa, the way they were then. It's probably nothing like that. I'm not really expecting it to be. I'll get there tomorrow and I'll find it's completely different. But it made me hopeful. You know, a sort of omen.' She gave a small laugh, then touched my shoulder. 'You're looking so glum.'

'Am I? I'm sorry. It's all this travelling. I suppose I'm rather tired.'

Boris had reached the top of the climbing frame, but the light had grown so dim he was barely more than a silhouette against the sky. He gave us a shout, then, gripping the top rung, somersaulted his body around it.

'He's so proud of being able to do that,' Sophie said. Then she called out: 'Boris, it's too dark now. Come on down.'

'It's easy. It's easier in the dark.'

'Come on down now.'

'It's all this travelling,' I said. 'Hotel room after hotel room. Never seeing anyone you know. It's been very tiring. And even now, here in this city, there's so much pressure on me. The people here. Obviously they're expecting a lot of me. I mean, it's obvious . . .'

'Look,' Sophie broke in gently, placing a hand on my arm, 'why don't we forget about it all for now? There'll be plenty of time for us to talk it over later. We're all tired. Come back with us to the apartment. It's only a few minutes' walk from here, just past the medieval chapel. I'm sure we could all do with a nice supper and a chance to put our feet up.'

She had spoken softly, her mouth close to my ear so that I could feel her breath. My earlier weariness came over me again and the idea of relaxing in the warmth of her apartment – perhaps lazing about with Boris on the carpet while Sophie prepared our meal – seemed suddenly highly enticing. So much so that for a brief moment I might even have closed my eyes and stood there smiling dreamily. In any case I was brought out of my reverie by Boris's return.

'It's easy to do it in the dark,' he said.

I saw then that Boris looked cold and somewhat shaken. All his earlier energy had evaporated and it occurred to me the performance he had just put on had required large resources on his part.

'We're all going back to the apartment now,' I said. 'We'll have something nice to eat there.'

'Come on,' Sophie said, setting off. 'Time's getting on.'

A fine drizzle had started to fall and now that the sun had set, the air was much chillier. Boris took my hand again and we followed Sophie out of the swing park into a deserted back street.

4

It was clear we had now left behind the Old Town. The dingy brick walls that towered up on either side were windowless and appeared to be the backs of warehouses. As we made our way along the street, Sophie kept up a purposeful pace and before long I could sense Boris having difficulty keeping up. But when I asked him: 'Are we going too fast?' he looked at me with a furious expression.

'I can go much faster!' he shouted and broke into a trot, tugging at my hand. But almost straight away he slowed down again with a hurt look on his face. After a while, despite my maintaining an easy pace, I could hear his breath coming with a struggle. He then started to whisper to himself. I did not pay much attention at first, assuming he was simply trying to keep up his spirits. But then I heard him whisper:

'Number Nine . . . It's Number Nine . . .'

I glanced at him with curiosity. He looked wet and cold, and it occurred to me I should keep him conversing.

'This Number Nine,' I said. 'Is he a footballer?'

'The top footballer in the world.'

'Number Nine. Yes, of course.'

Up ahead of us, Sophie's figure vanished around a corner and Boris's grip on my hand tightened. I had not until this moment appreciated how far in front we had allowed his mother to get, and though we increased our pace, it seemed to take an inordinate time for us to reach the corner ourselves. Once we finally turned it, I saw to my annoyance that Sophie had gained even further on us.

We went past more dirty brick walls, some with extensive damp patches. The paving was uneven and I could see before us puddles glinting under the street lighting.

'Don't worry,' I said to Boris. 'We're nearly there now.'

Boris was continuing to whisper to himself, repeating in time with his short breaths: 'Number Nine . . . Number Nine . . .'

From the first, Boris's mentions of 'Number Nine' had rung some distant bell for me. Now as I listened to his whispering, I recalled that 'Number Nine' was not in fact a real footballer, but one of Boris's miniature players from his table-football game. The footballers, moulded in alabaster and each one weighted at the base, could be made with flicks of the finger to dribble, pass and shoot a tiny plastic ball. The game was intended for two people each controlling a team, but Boris only ever played on his own, spending hours lying on his front orchestrating matches full of dramatic reversals and nail-biting comebacks. He possessed six full teams, as well as miniature goals with authentic netting and a green felt cloth that opened out to form the pitch. Boris despised the manufacturers' assumption that he would enjoy pretending the teams were 'real' ones, such as Ajax Amsterdam or AC Milan, and had given the teams his own names. The individual players, however – though Boris had come to know each one's strengths and weaknesses intimately – he had never named, preferring to call them simply by their shirt numbers. Perhaps because he was not aware of the significance of shirt numbers in football – or perhaps it was just another wilful quirk of his imagination – a player's number bore no relation to where Boris placed him in the team formation. Thus, the Number Ten of one team might be a legendary central defender, the Number Two a promising young winger.

'Number Nine' belonged to Boris's very favourite team, and was by far the most gifted of the players. However, for all his immense skill, Number Nine was a highly moody personality. His position in the team was somewhere in midfield, but often, for long stretches of a match, he would sulk in some obscure part of the pitch, apparently oblivious of the fact that his team was losing badly. Sometimes, Number Nine would continue in this lethargic manner for over an hour, so that his team would go four, five, six goals down, and the commentator – for indeed there was a commentator – would say in a mystified voice: 'Number Nine so far just hasn't found his form. I don't quite know what's wrong.' Then, perhaps with twenty minutes remaining, Number Nine would finally give a glimpse of his true ability, pulling back a goal for his side with some fine piece of skill. 'That's more like it!' the commentator would exclaim. 'At last, Number Nine shows what he can do!' From that moment on, Number Nine's form would grow steadily stronger, until before long he would be scoring one goal after another, and the opposing team would be concentrating entirely on preventing at virtually any cost Number Nine receiving the ball. But sooner or later he would, and then, no matter how many opponents stood between him and the goalmouth, he would manage to find a way through to score. Soon the inevitability of the outcome once he had received the ball was such that the commentator would say: 'It's a goal,' in tones of resigned admiration, not when the ball actually went into the net, but at the moment Number Nine first gained possession – even if this occurred deep within his own half. The spectators too – there were spectators – would commence their roar of triumph as soon as they saw Number Nine get the ball, the roar continuing intensely and evenly as Number Nine wove his way gracefully through his opponents, struck the ball past the goalkeeper, and turned to receive the adulation of his grateful team-mates.

As I was remembering all this, a vague recollection came into my head that some problem had recently arisen concerning Number Nine, and I interrupted Boris's whispering by asking:

'How is Number Nine these days? On good form?'

Boris walked a few steps in silence, then said: 'We left the box behind.'

'The box?'

'Number Nine came off his base. Quite a few of them do that, it's easy to fix. I put Number Nine in a special box and I was going to fix him once Mother got the right kind of glue. I put him in the box, it was a special one, so I wouldn't forget where he was. But we left him behind.'

'I see. You mean, you left him where you used to live.'

'Mother forgot to pack him. But she said we could go back soon. To the old apartment and he'd be there. I can fix him, we've got the right sort of glue now. I've got a bit saved up.'

'I see.'

'Mother says it'll be all right, she's going to see about everything. Make sure the new people don't throw him away by mistake. She said we'd go back soon.'

I had the distinct impression Boris was hinting at something, and when he fell silent again, I said to him:

'Boris, if you wanted, I could take you back. Yes, we could go back together, the two of us. Back to the old apartment and fetch Number Nine. We can do it soon. Perhaps even tomorrow if I find a spare moment. Then as you say, you've got the glue. He'll be back to his best in no time. So don't worry. We'll do that very soon.'

Sophie's figure once again disappeared from our view, this time so abruptly I thought she must have gone into a doorway. Boris tugged at my hand and we both hurried on towards the spot where she had vanished.

We soon discovered that Sophie had in fact turned down a side-alley, whose entrance was little more than a crack in the wall. It descended steeply and appeared so narrow it did not seem possible to go down it without scraping an elbow along one or the other of the rough walls to either side. The darkness was broken only by two street lamps, one half-way down, the other at the very bottom.

Boris gripped my hand as we began our descent, and soon his breath was coming with difficulty again. After a while I noticed that Sophie had already reached the bottom of the alley, but she seemed at last to have become aware of our plight, and was standing beneath the lower lamp, gazing back up at us with a vaguely concerned expression. When we finally joined her, I said angrily:

'Look, can't you see we've been having trouble keeping up with you? It's been a tiring day, both for me and for Boris.'

Sophie smiled dreamily. Then, putting an arm around Boris's shoulder, she drew the little boy close to her. 'Don't worry,' she said to him softly. 'I know it's a little unpleasant here and that it's got cold and rainy. But never mind, very soon now we'll be at the apartment. It'll be very warm, we'll see to that. Warm enough so that we can all just go around in T-shirts if we want. And there are those big new armchairs you can curl up in. A little boy like you could get lost in chairs like that. And you could look at your books, or watch one of the videos. Or if you like, we could bring down some board games from the cupboard. I could bring them all down for you, and you and Mr Ryder could play whichever one you wanted. You could put the big red cushions on the carpet and spread the game out on the floor. And all the time, I'll be cooking our evening meal and preparing the table in the corner. In fact, instead of one large dish, I think I might make a selection of small things. Little meatballs, tiny cheese flans, a few little cakes. Don't worry, I'll remember all your favourites and I'll lay it all out on the table. Then we can sit down and eat, and then afterwards all three of us can go on with the board game. Of course, if you didn't feel like playing any more, we wouldn't have to go on. Perhaps you'll want to talk with Mr Ryder about football. Then, only when you're really tired, you can go off to bed. I know your new room's very small, but it's very snug, you said so yourself. You're sure to sleep very soundly tonight. You'll have forgotten all about this cold unpleasant walk by then. In fact you'll forget all about it the moment you go in through the door and you feel the nice warm heating. So don't get discouraged. It's only a little way to go now.'

She had had Boris in a hug while saying this, but now she suddenly released him, turned and began to walk again. The abruptness with which she did so caught me by surprise – for I had myself become steadily lulled by her words and had for a moment closed my eyes. Boris too looked bewildered, and by the time I had taken his hand his mother was once more several paces in front.

I was keen not to let her get too far ahead again, but just at that moment I became conscious of footsteps coming down behind us and I could not help lingering a second to look back up the alley. Just as I did so, the person entered the pool of light cast by the lower lamp and I saw that it was someone I knew. His name was Geoffrey Saunders and he had been in my year at school in England. I had not seen him since schooldays, so was naturally struck by how much he had aged. Even allowing for the unflattering effects of the lamplight and the cold drizzle, he looked overwhelmingly down-at-heel. He was wearing a rain-coat that seemed to have lost its ability to fasten and which he was now clutching together at the front as he walked. I was not at all sure I wished to acknowledge him, but then, as Boris and I set off once more, Geoffrey Saunders fell in step alongside us.

'Hello, old chap,' he said. 'Thought it was you. Rotten evening it's turned out to be.'

'Yes, miserable,' I said. 'And earlier it was so pleasant.'

The alley had brought us out onto a dark deserted road. There was a strong breeze and the city seemed far away.

'Your boy?' Geoffrey Saunders asked, nodding towards Boris. Then, before I could reply, he continued: 'Nice boy. Well done. Looks very bright. Myself I never married. Always thought I would, but time's just slipped away and now I suppose I never shall. To be honest, I suppose there's more to it than that. But I don't want to bore you with all the rotten luck I've had over the years. I've had some good things happen too. Still. Well done. Nice boy.'

Geoffrey Saunders leaned forward and gave Boris a salute. Boris, either too upset or too preoccupied, gave no response.

The road was now leading us downhill. As we walked through the darkness, I recalled how at school Geoffrey Saunders had been the golden boy of our year, always distinguishing himself both academically and on the sports field. His was the example forever being used to rebuke the rest of us for lack of effort, and it was widely reckoned that he would in time become school captain. He never did so, I recalled, owing to some crisis that had obliged him to leave the school suddenly during our fifth year.

'I read in the papers you were coming,' he was saying to me. 'I've been expecting to hear from you. You know, to tell me when you'll be popping round. I went and bought some cakes from the bakery so that I had something to offer you along with a cup of tea. After all, my digs may be rather dreary, what with my being single and all, but I still expect people to come and visit sometimes and I feel quite capable of looking after them well. So when I heard you were coming, I immediately popped out and bought a selection of tea cakes. That was the day before yesterday. Yesterday, I thought they were still presentable, though the icing had got a bit on the tough side. But today, when you still hadn't called, I threw them away. Pride, I suppose. I mean, you've been so successful, and I don't want you going away thinking I'm leading this miserable existence in small rented rooms with only stale cakes to offer a visitor. So I went to the bakery and got some fresh cakes. And I tidied my room up a bit. But you didn't call.

Well, I suppose I can't blame you. I say' – he leaned forward again and looked at Boris – 'are you all right there? You sound completely puffed out.'

Boris, who indeed was struggling again, gave no sign of having heard.

'Better slow down for the little slowcoach,' Geoffrey Saunders said. 'It's just that I was a little unlucky in love at one stage. A lot of people in this town assume I'm homosexual. Just because I live alone in a rented room. I minded that at first, but I don't any more. All right, they mistake me for a homosexual. So what? As it happens, my needs are met by women. You know, the sort you pay. Perfectly adequate for me, and I'd say some of them are quite decent people. All the same, after a while, you start to despise them and they start to despise you. Can't help it. I know most of the whores in this town. I don't mean I've slept with them all. Not by any means! But they know me and I know them. I'm on nodding terms with a lot of them. You probably think I lead a miserable existence. I don't. It's just a matter of how you look at things. Occasionally friends come to visit me. I'm quite capable of entertaining them over a cup of tea. I do it quite well and they often say afterwards how much they enjoyed popping round.'

The road had been descending steeply for a while, but it now levelled, and we found ourselves in what appeared to be an abandoned farmyard. All about us in the moonlight there loomed the dark shapes of barns and outhouses. Sophie was continuing to lead the way, but she was now some distance in front and often I would glimpse her figure only as it disappeared around the edge of some broken building.

Fortunately Geoffrey Saunders seemed to know his way well, navigating a route through the dark with barely a thought. As I followed close behind him, a certain memory came back to me from our schooldays, of a crisp winter's morning in England, with an overcast sky and frost on the ground. I had been fourteen or fifteen and had been standing outside a pub with Geoffrey Saunders somewhere deep in the Worcestershire countryside. We had been paired together to mark a cross-country run, our task being simply to point the runners, as they emerged out of the mist, in the correct direction across a nearby field. I had been unusually upset that morning, and after fifteen minutes or so of our standing there together staring quietly into the fog, in spite of my best efforts, I had burst into tears. I had not known Geoffrey Saunders well at that point, though like everyone else I had always been keen to make a good impression on him. I had thus been quite mortified and my initial impression, once I had finally brought my emotions under control, had been that he was ignoring me with the utmost contempt. But then Geoffrey Saunders had begun to speak, at first without looking in my direction, then eventually turning to me. I could not now bring to mind just what it was he had said on that foggy morning, but I could recall well enough the impact his words had had. For one thing, even in my state of self-pity, I had been able to recognise the remarkable generosity he was displaying, and had felt a profound gratitude. It was also at that moment I had first realised, with a distinct chill, that there was another side to the school golden boy – some deeply vulnerable dimension that would ensure he would never live up to the expectations that had been placed on him. As we continued to walk together through the dark, I tried once more to remember just what he had said that morning, but to no avail.

With the ground levelling, Boris seemed to recover a little breath and he had once more begun to whisper. Now, perhaps encouraged by a sense that we were about to reach our destination, he found the energy to kick a stone in his path, exclaiming out loud as he did so: 'Number Nine!' The stone skipped across the rough ground and landed in water somewhere in the darkness.

'That's a bit more like it,' Geoffrey Saunders said to Boris. 'Is that your position? Number Nine?'

When Boris failed to answer, I said quickly: 'Oh no, it's just his favourite footballer.'

'Oh yes? I watch a lot of football. On the television, that is.' He leaned forward to Boris again. 'Which number nine is that?'

'Oh, it's just his favourite player,' I said again.

'As far as centre forwards go,' Geoffrey Saunders went on, 'I rather like that Dutchman, plays for Milan. He's quite something.'

I was about to say something further to explain about Number Nine, but at that moment we came to a halt. I saw then that we were standing at the edge of a vast grassy field. Just how large it was, I could not ascertain, but I guessed it extended far beyond what could be seen by the moon. As we stood there, a harsh wind swept across the grass and on into the darkness.

'We appear to be lost,' I said to Geoffrey Saunders. 'Do you know your way around here?'

'Oh yes. I live not so far from here. Unfortunately I can't ask you in just now because I'm very tired and have to go to sleep. But I'll be ready to welcome you tomorrow. Let's say any time after nine o'clock.'

I looked across the field into the blackness.

'To be frank, we're in a little trouble just now,' I said. 'You see, we were on our way to the apartment of that woman we were following earlier. Now we've got ourselves rather lost and I've no idea what her address is. She said something about living near a medieval chapel.'

'The medieval chapel? That's in the city centre.'

'Ah. Can we get to it by going across there?' I pointed over the field.

'Oh no, there's nothing that way. Nothing but emptiness. Only person living out there is that Brodsky fellow.'

'Brodsky,' I said. 'Hmm. I heard him practising in the hotel today. You all seem to know about this Brodsky here in this town.'

Geoffrey Saunders gave me a glance that made me suspect I had said something foolish.

'Well, he's been living here for years and years. Why shouldn't we know about him?'

'Yes, yes, of course.'

'A bit hard to believe the crazy old fellow's got it in him to conduct an orchestra. But I'm prepared to wait and see. Things can't very well get much worse. And if *you* start saying Brodsky's the thing, well, who am I to argue?'

I could not think what I might say to this. In any case, Geoffrey Saunders suddenly turned away from the field, saying:

'No, no, the city's over that way. I can direct you if you like.'

'We'd be very grateful,' I said as a chilly gust blew against us.

'Well now.' Geoffrey Saunders fell into thought for a moment. Then he said: 'To be honest, you'd be best off getting a bus. To walk from here would take a good half-hour or so. Perhaps the woman persuaded you her apartment was close by. Well, they always do that. It's one of their tricks. You should never believe them. But it's no problem if you take a bus. I'll show you where you can pick one up.'

'We'd be very grateful,' I said again. 'Boris is getting cold. I hope this bus stop isn't far.'

'Oh, very near. Just follow me, old man.'

Geoffrey Saunders turned and led us back towards the abandoned farmyard. I sensed, however, that we were not retracing our footsteps and, sure enough, before long we found ourselves walking down a narrow street in what seemed a less than affluent suburb. Small terraced houses stood in rows on either side. Here and there I could see lights in windows, but for the most part the occupants appeared to have turned in for the night.

'It's all right,' I said quietly to Boris, who I sensed was close to exhaustion. 'We'll be at the apartment now very soon. Your mother will have everything ready for us by the time we turn up.'

We walked on for a while past more rows of houses. Then Boris began to mutter again:

'Number Nine . . . It's Number Nine . . .'

'Look, which number nine *is* this?' Geoffrey Saunders said, turning to him. 'You mean that Dutchman, don't you?'

'Number Nine's the best player so far in history,' Boris said.

'Yes, but which number nine do you mean?' Geoffrey Saunders's voice had now gained an edge of impatience. 'What's his name? Which is his team?'

'Boris just likes to call him . . .'

'Once he scored seventeen goals in the last ten minutes!' Boris said.

'Oh nonsense.' Geoffrey Saunders seemed genuinely annoyed. 'I thought you were being serious. You're talking nonsense.'

'He did!' Boris shouted. 'It was a world record!'

'Quite!' I joined in. 'A world record!' Then, recovering my composure somewhat, I gave a laugh. 'That's to say, well, it's bound to be, isn't it.' I smiled appealingly at Geoffrey Saunders, but he ignored me.

'But who are you talking about? Do you mean that Dutchman? Anyway, young man, you've got to realise, scoring goals isn't

49

everything. The defenders are just as important. The *really* great players are often defenders.'

'Number Nine's the best player so far in history!' Boris said again. 'When he's on form, no defence can stop him!'

'That's right,' I said. 'Number Nine's without doubt the world's finest. Midfield, up front, everything. He does everything. Really.'

'You're talking nonsense, old man. Neither of you know what you're talking about.'

'We know perfectly well.' By this time I was getting quite angry with Geoffrey Saunders. 'In fact, what we're saying is universally acknowledged. When Number Nine's on form, really on form, the commentator shouts "goal" the moment he gets the ball, no matter where on the pitch . . .'

'Oh my goodness.' Geoffrey Saunders turned away in disgust. 'If that's the sort of rubbish you fill your boy's brain with, God help him.'

'Now look here . . .' I put my face right up to his ear and spoke in an angry whisper. 'Look here, can't you understand . . .'

'It's rubbish, old man. You're filling the boy's head with rubbish . . .'

'But he's young, just a small boy. Can't you understand . . .'

'No reason to fill his head with rubbish. Besides, he doesn't look as young as all that. In my view, a boy his age, he should be making a proper contribution to things by now. Starting to pull his weight a bit. He should be learning about wallpapering, say, or tiling. Not all this nonsense about fantastical footballers . . .'

'Look, you idiot, just be quiet! Be quiet!'

'A boy his age, it's high time he was pulling his weight . . .'

'He's my boy, I'll say when it's time for him to . . .'

'Wallpapering, tiling, something like that. To my mind, that's the sort of thing . . .'

'Look, what do you know about it? What do you know, a miserable, lonely bachelor? What do you know about it?'

I pushed his shoulder roughly. Geoffrey Saunders became suddenly crestfallen. He shuffled a few paces on ahead of us, where he continued walking with his head slightly bowed, still clutching the front of his raincoat.

'It's all right,' I said to Boris quietly. 'We'll be there soon.'

Boris did not respond and I saw that he was staring at Geoffrey Saunders's lurching figure before us.

As we continued to walk, my anger at my old schoolmate began to subside. Besides, I had not forgotten that we were entirely reliant on him to show us the way to our bus stop. After a few moments I drew up closer to him, wondering if we were still on talking terms. To my surprise I heard Geoffrey Saunders muttering away to himself softly:

'Yes, yes, we'll talk over all these things when you come round for your cup of tea. We'll talk over everything, spend a nostalgic hour or two discussing schooldays and old schoolfriends. I'll have my room tidied, and we can sit on the armchairs, on either side of the fireplace. Yes, it does look rather like the sort of room one might rent in England. Or at least might have done a few years ago. That's why I took it. Reminded me of home. Anyway, we could sit on either side of the fireplace and talk about the lot. The masters, the boys, exchange news of mutual friends we're still in touch with. Ah, here we are.'

We had emerged into what looked like a small village square. There were a few small shops – where presumably the inhabitants of this district bought their groceries – all of them closed and gridded up for the night. In the middle of the square was a patch of green not much bigger than a traffic island. Geoffrey Saunders pointed to a solitary street lamp in front of the shops.

'You and your boy should wait over there. I know there's no sign, but don't worry, it's a recognised bus stop. Now, I'm afraid I'll have to leave you.'

Boris and I stared across to where he had pointed. The rain had stopped, but a mist was hovering around the base of the lamppost. There was nothing stirring around us.

'Are you sure a bus will come?' I asked.

'Oh yes. Naturally, at this time of night it might take a little while. But certainly it'll come in the end. You have to be patient, that's all. You might get a little chilly standing here, but believe me the bus is well worth the wait. It will come out of the darkness, all brightly lit up. And once you step on board, you'll find it's very warm and comfortable. And it always has the most cheerful crowd of passengers. They'll be laughing and joking, handing out hot drinks and snacks. They'll make you and your boy very welcome. Just ask the driver to let you off at the medieval chapel. It's just a short journey by bus.'

Geoffrey Saunders bade us good night, then turned and walked off. Boris and I watched him disappear down an alleyway between two houses, then began to make our way over to the bus stop.

5

We stood beneath the street lamp for several minutes, surrounded by silence. Eventually I put my arm around Boris saying: 'You must be getting cold.'

He pressed himself against my body, but said nothing, and when I glanced down at him I saw he was gazing thoughtfully along the darkened street. Somewhere far away a dog began to bark, then stopped. When we had been standing like that for a time, I said:

'Boris, I'm sorry. I should have arranged things better. I'm sorry.'

The little boy remained silent for a moment. Then he said: 'Don't worry. The bus will come soon.'

I could see across the little square the mist drifting in front of the short row of shops.

'I'm not sure a bus is coming, Boris,' I said eventually.

'It's all right. You've got to be patient.'

We went on waiting for several more moments. Then I said again:

'Boris, I'm not at all sure a bus is going to come.'

The little boy turned to me and sighed wearily. 'Stop worrying,' he said. 'Didn't you hear what the man said? We just have to wait.'

'Boris. Sometimes things don't happen as you expect. Even when someone tells you it will.'

Boris gave another sigh. 'Look, the man said, didn't he? Anyway, Mother will be waiting for us.'

I was trying to think of what to say next when the sound of a cough made us both start. Turning, I saw, just beyond the light cast by the street lamp, someone leaning out of a stationary car.

'Good evening, Mr Ryder. Excuse me, but I was just going by and happened to see you. Is everything all right?'

I took a few steps towards the car and recognised Stephan, the hotel manager's son.

'Oh yes,' I said. 'Everything's fine, thank you. We were . . . well, we were waiting for a bus.'

'Perhaps I could give you a lift. I was just on my way some-where, a rather delicate mission Father's entrusted me with. I say, it's rather chilly out there. Why don't you jump in?'

The young man got out and opened the passenger doors front and back. Thanking him, I helped Boris into the rear seat and got into the front. The next moment, the car had begun to move.

'So this is your little boy,' Stephan said as we sped through deserted streets. 'How very nice to meet him, though he looks a bit exhausted just now. Oh well, let him rest. I'll shake his hand another time.'

Glancing behind me, I saw that Boris was in the process of falling asleep, his head against the cushioned armrest.

'So, Mr Ryder,' Stephan went on. 'I assume you're wanting to return to the hotel.'

'Actually, Boris and I were on our way to someone's apartment. In the centre, near the medieval chapel.'

'The medieval chapel? Hmm.'

'Is that going to be a problem?'

'Oh, not really. No problem at all.' Stephan steered round a tight corner into another narrow dark street. 'It's just that, well, as I mentioned, I was just on my way somewhere myself. To an appointment. Now let me see . . .'

'Your appointment is an urgent one?'

'Well actually, Mr Ryder, it *is* rather. It's to do with Mr Brodsky, you see. In fact, it's quite crucial. Hmm. I wonder, if you and Boris were generous enough to wait just a few minutes while I saw to it, then I could drive you wherever you want afterwards.'

'Naturally you must attend to your business first. But I'd be grateful if there's not too much delay. You see, Boris hasn't had supper yet.'

'I'll be as quick as I can, Mr Ryder. I only wish I could take you immediately, but you see, I daren't be late. As I say, it's rather a tricky little mission . . .'

'Of course, you must see to that first. We'll be very happy to wait.'

'I'll try and make it as quick as possible. Though to be honest, I don't see how I can take too many short cuts. In fact, it's the sort of thing Father would usually handle himself, or else one of the gentlemen, but well, it's just that Miss Collins has always had a soft spot for me . . .' The young man broke off, suddenly embarrassed. Then he said: 'I'll try not to be long.'

We were now moving through a more salubrious district – closer, I guessed, to the city centre. The street lighting was much better and I noticed tram lines running alongside us. There was the occasional café or restaurant closed for the night, but for the most part the area was full of stately apartment buildings. The windows were all dark and our vehicle seemed the only thing for miles disturbing the hush. Stephan Hoffman drove in silence for a few minutes. Then he said suddenly, as though he had for some time been working himself up to it:

'Look, it's awfully impertinent of me. But are you *sure* you don't want to go back to the hotel? It's just that, I mean, with those journalists waiting for you there and everything.'

'Journalists?' I looked out into the night. 'Ah yes. The journalists.'

'Golly, I hope you don't think I'm being cheeky. It's just that I happened to see them as I was leaving. Sitting in the lobby with their folders and briefcases on their laps, looking very keyed up at the thought of meeting you. As I say, it's none of my business and naturally you've got the whole thing worked out, I'm sure.'

'Quite, quite,' I said softly, and continued to look out of the window.

Stephan fell silent, no doubt deciding he should not press the matter further. But I found myself thinking about the journalists, and after a moment I thought I could perhaps remember some such appointment. Certainly, the image the young man had evoked of people sitting with folders and briefcases rang a bell. In the end, though, I could not recall with any definiteness such an item having been on my schedule and decided to forget the matter.

'Ah, here we are,' Stephan said beside me. 'Now if you'd excuse me for a little while. Please make yourselves as comfortable as you can. I'll be back as quickly as possible.'

We had come to a halt in front of a large white apartment building. Several storeys high, the dark wrought-iron balconies at each level gave it a Spanish flavour.

Stephan got out of the car and I watched him go up to the entrance. He stooped over the row of apartment buttons, pressed one, then stood waiting, a nervousness discernible in his posture. A moment later a light came on in the entrance hall.

The door was opened by an elderly, silver-haired woman. She looked slender and frail, but there was a certain gracefulness in her movement as she smiled and showed Stephan in. The door closed behind him, but by leaning right back in my seat I found I could still see the two of them clearly illuminated in the narrow pane to the side of the front door. Stephan was wiping his feet on the doormat, saying:

'I'm sorry to come like this at such short notice.'

'I've told you many times, Stephan,' the elderly woman said, 'I'm always here whenever you need to talk things over.'

'Well actually, Miss Collins, it wasn't . . . Well, it's not about the usual stuff. I wanted to talk to you about something else, a quite important matter. Father would have come himself, but, well, he was so busy . . .'

'Ah,' the woman interrupted with a smile, 'something else your father's put you up to. He's still giving you all the dirty work.'

There was a playful note in her voice, but Stephan seemed to miss it.

'Not at all,' he retorted earnestly. 'On the contrary, this is a mission of a particularly delicate and difficult nature. Father entrusted me with it and I was very happy to accept . . .'

'So I've now become a mission! And one of a delicate and difficult nature at that!'

'Well no. That's to say . . .' Stephan paused in confusion.

The elderly woman seemed to decide she had teased Stephan enough. 'All right,' she said, 'we'd better go inside and discuss this properly over some sherry.'

'How kind of you, Miss Collins. But actually, I mustn't stay long. I've got some people waiting out in the car.' He indicated in our direction, but the elderly woman was already opening the door into her apartment.

I watched her lead Stephan through a small and tidy front parlour, through a second doorway and down a shadowy corridor decorated on either side with little framed water-colours. The corridor ended at Miss Collins's drawing room – a large L-shaped affair at the back of the building. The light here was low and cosy, and at first glance the room looked expensively elegant in an old-fashioned way. On closer inspection, however, I could see much of the furniture was extremely worn, and that what at first I had taken for antiques were in fact little better than junk. Once luxurious couches and armchairs sat about the place in states of disrepair and the full-length velvet drapes were mottled and frayed. Stephan seated himself with an ease that betrayed his familiarity with the surroundings, but continued to look tense as Miss Collins busied herself at the drinks cabinet. When she eventually handed him a glass and sat down near him, the young man burst out abruptly: 'It's to do with Mr Brodsky.'

'Ah,' Miss Collins said. 'I rather suspected as much.'

'Miss Collins, the fact is, we wondered if you might consider helping us. Or rather, helping *him* . . .' Stephan broke off with a laugh and looked away.

Miss Collins tilted her head thoughtfully. Then she asked: 'You're asking me to help Leo?'

'Oh, we're not asking you to do anything you'd find distasteful or . . . well, painful. Father understands perfectly how you must feel.' He gave another short laugh. 'It's just that your help could prove crucial just at this stage in Mr Brodsky's . . . recovery.'

'Ah.' Miss Collins nodded and appeared to give this some thought. Then she said: 'May I take it from all this, Stephan, that your father's having only limited success with Leo?'

The teasing in her voice seemed to me more pronounced than ever, but again Stephan failed to notice it.

'Not at all!' he said crossly. 'On the contrary, Father's worked wonders, made enormous strides! It hasn't been easy, but Father's perseverance has been remarkable, even to those of us used to the way Father goes about things.'

'Perhaps he hasn't persevered enough.'

'But you've no idea, Miss Collins! No idea! Sometimes he's come home exhausted after a gruelling day at the hotel, so exhausted he's had to go straight upstairs to bed. I've had Mother come down complaining and I've gone up there, up to their room, and found Father snoring away on his back, collapsed right across their bed. As you know, it's been an important understanding for years that he goes to sleep on his side, never on his back, he always snores so badly otherwise, so you can imagine Mother's disgust at discovering him like that. It's usually God's own job for me to rouse him but I have to because otherwise, I told you before, otherwise Mother refuses to go back into the bedroom. She'll just hover out in the corridor with her angry look, she won't go back in until I've woken him up, undressed him, got him in his bathrobe and guided him into the bathroom. But what I'm meaning to tell you is that, well, even when he's that tired, sometimes the phone's gone and it's been one of the staff to say Mr Brodsky's right on the edge, that he's been demanding a drink, and, do you know, Father somehow finds more energy from somewhere. He pulls himself together, that look comes into his eyes, he gets dressed and goes off into the night, not to return for hours. He said he'd get Mr Brodsky fit and he's giving everything he's got, every last bit to accomplish what he said he would.'

'That's very commendable. But exactly how far is he getting?'

'I assure you, Miss Collins, the progress has been astonishing. Everyone who's seen Mr Brodsky recently has remarked on it. There's so much more going on behind those eyes. His comments too, they have more and more meaning by the day. But most crucially, his ability, Mr Brodsky's great ability, *that*'s returning without a doubt. By all accounts, the rehearsals have been going extremely promisingly. The orchestra, they've been completely won over by him. And when he's not been rehearsing at the concert hall, he's been busy working things out by himself. You can often catch little snatches of him at the piano now as you wander about the hotel. When Father hears that piano, he's so encouraged you can see he's ready to sacrifice any amount of sleep.'

The young man paused and looked at Miss Collins. For a moment she seemed far away, leaning her head to one side as though she too might catch a few notes from a distant piano. Then a gentle smile returned to her face and she looked again at Stephan.

'What I've heard,' she said, 'is that your father sits him up in that hotel drawing room, sits him up in front of the piano like he's some manikin, and Leo stays there for hours gently swaying on the stool without touching a note.'

'Miss Collins, that's quite unfair! Perhaps there were occasions like that in the early days, but it's a very different story now. In any case, even if he does sit there silently sometimes, surely you must remember this, it hardly means nothing's going on. Silence is just as likely to indicate the most profound ideas forming, the deepest energies being summoned. In fact, the other day, after a particularly long silence, Father actually went into the drawing room and there was Mr Brodsky staring down at the piano keys. After a while he looked up at Father and said: "The violins need to be harsh. They must sound harsh." That's what he said. There may have been silence, but inside his head, there'd been a whole universe of music. What he'll show us all on Thursday night, it's thrilling to think about. Just so long as he doesn't falter now.'

'But you said, Stephan, you wanted me to help in some way.'

The young man, who had become increasingly animated, now collected himself.

'Well yes,' he said. 'That's what I've come here tonight to speak to you about. As I say, Mr Brodsky's been rapidly regaining all his old powers. And, well, naturally, along with his great talents, various other things are now re-emerging. To those of us who never knew him very well before, it's been something of a revelation. These days he's often so articulate, so urbane. Anyway, the point is, along with everything else, he's started to remember. Well, to put it bluntly, he talks about you. Thinks and talks about you all the time. Last night, just to give you an example – this is embarrassing but I'll tell you – last night he started to weep and couldn't stop. He just kept weeping, pouring out all his feelings for you. It's the third or fourth time it's happened, though last night's was the most extreme instance. It was almost midnight, Mr Brodsky hadn't emerged from the drawing room, so Father went to listen at the door and heard him sobbing. So he went in and found the place in complete darkness, and Mr Brodsky bowed over the piano, weeping. Well, there was a suite vacant upstairs, so Father took him up there and had the kitchen bring up all Mr Brodsky's favourite soups – he tends only to eat soups – and plied him with orange juice and soft drinks, but frankly, last night, it was touch and go. Apparently he was attacking the

59

cartons of juice feverishly. If Father hadn't been there, it's very possible he would have cracked, even at this late stage. And all the time he continued to talk about you. Well, the point I'm getting at – oh dear, I shouldn't stay too long, I've got people waiting in the car – my point is, with so much of the future of our city depending on him, we have to do everything to ensure he'll pull through this last bit. Dr Kaufmann agrees with Father, we're close to the last hurdle now. So you see how much hangs in the balance.'

Miss Collins continued to look at Stephan with the same distant half-smile, but still said nothing. After a moment, the young man went on:

'Miss Collins, I realise what I'm saying might well be opening up old wounds. And I appreciate you and Mr Brodsky haven't spoken to each other now for many years . . .'

'Oh, that's not quite accurate. Only earlier this year, he shouted obscenities at me as I was strolling across the Volksgarten.'

Stephan laughed awkwardly, unsure how to handle Miss Collins's tone. Then he went on with some earnestness: 'Miss Collins, no one's suggesting you have any sort of extended contact with him. Good lord, no. You wish to put the past behind you. Father, everyone, they appreciate that. All we're asking, just one small thing, it might make such a difference, it would so encourage him and mean so much to him. We hoped you wouldn't mind us at least putting it to you.'

'I've already agreed to attend the banquet.'

'Yes, yes, of course. Father told me, we're so grateful . . .'

'On the strict understanding there'll be no direct contact . . .'

'That's completely understood, absolutely. The banquet, yes. But actually, Miss Collins, it was something further we wanted to ask of you, if you could just bear to think about it. You see, a group of gentlemen – Mr von Winterstein among them – will be taking Mr Brodsky to the zoo tomorrow. Apparently in all the years, he's never visited it. His dog can't be admitted, naturally, but Mr Brodsky has finally consented to leave it in good hands for just a couple of hours. It was felt that an outing of this sort would help calm him. The giraffes in particular we thought might be relaxing. Well, I'll come to the point. The gentlemen wondered if you might possibly care to join the group at the zoo.

Even say just a word or two to him. You wouldn't need to travel out with the party, you could just join them there, just for a few minutes, exchange a pleasant remark with him, perhaps say a few uplifting things, it could make all the difference. A few minutes, then you could be on your way. Please, Miss Collins, if you'd give this some consideration. So much might hang on it.'

While Stephan had been speaking, Miss Collins had risen from her seat and moved slowly over to her fireplace. She now remained standing quite still for several seconds, one hand resting on the mantelpiece as though to steady herself. When eventually she turned to Stephan again, I saw that her eyes had become moist.

'You see my problem, Stephan,' she said. 'I may have been married to him once. But for many years now, the only times I've encountered him, he's been shouting abuse at me. So you see, it's hard for me to guess what sort of conversation he'd best enjoy.'

'Miss Collins, I swear to you he's a different man now. These days he's so polite and urbane and . . . but surely, you'd remember. If you could even just think about it. There's so much at stake.'

Miss Collins sipped her sherry thoughtfully. She seemed about to reply, but just at this point I heard Boris shift behind me in the back of the car. Turning, I saw that the little boy must have been awake for some time. He was gazing through his window out across the still and empty street, and I sensed a sadness about him. I was about to say something, but he must have realised my attention was on him, for he asked quietly without moving:

'Can you do bathrooms?'

'Can I do bathrooms?'

Boris sighed heavily and went on gazing out into the darkness. Then he said: 'I'd never done tiles before. That's why I made all those mistakes. If someone had shown me, I could have done them.'

'Yes, I'm sure you could have done. This is the bathroom in your new apartment?'

'If someone had shown me, I could have done them all right. Then Mother would have been happy with the bathroom. She'd have liked the bathroom then.'

'Ah. So she's not happy with it at the moment?'

Boris looked at me as though I had said something immensely stupid. Then, with heavy irony, he said: 'Why would she cry about the bathroom if she liked it?'

'Why indeed? So she cries about the bathroom. I wonder why she does that.'

Boris turned back to his window and I could now see by the mixed light coming into the car that he was struggling not to burst into tears. At the last moment he managed to disguise his upset as a yawn and rubbed his face with his fists.

'We'll sort all these things out eventually,' I said. 'You'll see.'

'I could have done it all right if someone had shown me. Then Mother wouldn't have cried.'

'Yes, I'm sure you'd have made a very good job of it. But we'll sort everything out soon.'

I straightened in my seat and gazed through the windscreen. There was hardly a lit window anywhere down the street. After a while I said: 'Boris, we have to have a good think now. Are you listening?'

There was silence from the back of the car.

'Boris,' I went on, 'we've got to make a decision. I know earlier we were on our way to join Mother. But now it's got very late. Boris, are you listening?'

I threw a glance over my shoulder and saw he was still staring vacantly out into the darkness. We went on sitting silently for several more moments. Then I said:

'The fact is, it's very late now. If we went back to the hotel we could see your grandfather. He'd be delighted to see you. You could have a room of your own or, if you preferred, we could have them set up another bed for you in my room. We could have them bring up something good to eat, then you could get off to sleep. Then tomorrow morning we'll get up for breakfast and decide what we'll do.'

There was silence behind me.

'I should have organised things better,' I said. 'I'm sorry. I . . . I just wasn't thinking clearly tonight. It was so busy earlier on. But look, I promise we'll make it up tomorrow. We can do all kinds of things tomorrow. If you like, we could go back to the old apartment and get Number Nine. What do you say?'

Boris still said nothing.

'We've both had tiring days. Boris, what do you say?'

'We'd better go to the hotel.'

'I think that's the best idea. So that's settled then. When the gentleman comes back, we'll tell him our new plan.'

6

Just at this point a movement caught my eye and, glancing back to the apartment building, I saw that the front door was open. Miss Collins was in the process of showing Stephan out, and though they were parting amicably, something in both their manners suggested their meeting had concluded on an uneasy note. Soon the door closed and Stephan came hurrying back to the car.

'I'm sorry to have been so long,' he said, climbing into his seat. 'I hope Boris has been all right.' Placing his hands on the wheel, he let out a troubled sigh. Then he forced a smile and said: 'Well, let's get going.'

'Actually,' I said, 'Boris and I had a good talk while you were gone. We think we'll return to the hotel after all.'

'If I may say so, Mr Ryder, that's probably a good decision. So it's back to the hotel. Jolly good.' He glanced at his watch. 'We'll be there in no time. The journalists will have no real cause for complaint. No cause at all.'

Stephan started the engine and we set off again. As we drove through the deserted streets, the rain started once more and Stephan turned on the windscreen wipers. After a while, he said:

'Mr Ryder, I wonder if I could be cheeky enough to remind you of the conversation we were having earlier. You know, when I met you in the atrium this afternoon.'

'Ah yes,' I said. 'Yes, we were discussing your recital on Thursday night.'

'You were very kind and said you might be able to find a few minutes for me. To listen to me run through the La Roche. Of course, this is probably completely impossible, but, well, I thought you wouldn't mind my asking. It's just that I was going to get in a little more practice tonight, once we got back to the hotel. I was wondering if, when you'd finished with these journalists, I know it's a great nuisance, but if you could come and listen for even a few minutes and tell me what you thought . . .' He trailed off with a laugh.

I could see this was a matter of considerable importance for the young man and felt tempted to comply with his request. Nevertheless, after some consideration, I said:

'I'm sorry, tonight I'm so tired, it's imperative I get off to sleep as soon as possible. But don't worry, there's bound to be an opportunity in the near future. Look, why don't we leave it like this? I'm not sure precisely when I'll next have a few minutes to spare, but as soon as I do I'll phone the desk and get them to go and find you. If you're not in the hotel, I'll simply try again the next time I'm free and so on. That way we're bound to find a mutually convenient time before long. But tonight, really, if you don't mind, I really must get a good night's sleep.'

'Of course, Mr Ryder, I quite understand. By all means, let's do as you suggest. It's extremely kind of you. I'll wait to hear from you then.'

Stephan had spoken politely, but he seemed unduly disappointed, perhaps even mistaking my reply for some subtle refusal. Evidently he was in a state of such anxiety over his forthcoming performance that any setback, however minor, was apt to send him off into a cold panic. I felt some sympathy for him and said again reassuringly:

'Don't worry, we're bound to find an opportunity very soon.'

The rain continued to fall steadily as we travelled through the night-time streets. The young man remained silent for a long time and I wondered if he had become angry with me. But then I caught sight of his profile in the changing light and realised he was turning over in his mind a particular incident from several years ago. It was an episode he had pondered many times before – often when lying awake at night or when driving alone – and now his fear that I would prove unable to help him had caused him once more to bring it to the front of his mind.

It had been the occasion of his mother's birthday. As he had parked his car in the familiar driveway that night – those were his college days when he had been living in Germany – he had braced himself for a painful few hours. But his father had opened the door to him, whispering excitedly: 'She's in a good mood. A very good mood.' His father had then turned and shouted into the house: 'Stephan is here, my dear. A little late, but he's here nevertheless.' Then in a whisper again: 'A very good mood. The best for a long time.'

The young man had gone through into the lounge to discover his mother reclining on a sofa, a cocktail glass in her hand. She was wearing a new dress and Stephan had been struck afresh at just how elegant a woman his mother was. She had not risen to greet him, obliging him to stoop down to kiss her cheek, but nevertheless the warmth of her manner as she invited him to take the armchair opposite had quite taken him aback. Behind him, his father, greatly pleased by this start to the evening, had emitted a small chuckle, then, indicating the apron he was wearing, had gone hurrying back towards the kitchen.

Left alone with his mother, Stephan's first feeling had been one of sheer terror – that something he said or did would shatter her good mood, thus undoing hours, perhaps days, of painstaking effort on his father's part. He had thus begun by giving brief, stilted replies to her queries about his college life, but when her attitude had remained consistently appreciative, found himself answering at greater and greater length. At one point he had referred to a college professor as resembling 'a mentally balanced version of our foreign minister' – a phrase he had been particularly proud of and had used numerous times to his fellow students with considerable success. Had the early exchanges with his mother not gone so well, he would not have risked repeating it to her. But he had done so and with a leap of his heart had seen amusement momentarily light up her face. For all that, it had still come as a relief when his father had returned to announce dinner.

They had gone through to the dining room where the hotel manager had laid out the first course. The meal had started quietly. Then his father – a little abruptly, Stephan had thought – had commenced to tell an amusing anecdote concerning a group of Italian guests at the hotel. When he had finished, the hotel manager had urged Stephan to recount a story of his own, and when Stephan had started somewhat uncertainly his father had proceeded to support him with exaggerated laughter. So they had gone on, Stephan and his father taking turns to tell amusing stories and supporting each other with hearty responses. The tactic seemed to work, for eventually – Stephan could hardly believe it – his mother too had started to laugh for prolonged

66

spells. The meal itself, moreover, had been prepared with the fanatical attention to detail characteristic of the hotel manager and was an astounding piece of cuisine. The wine was clearly something very special and by the time they were midway through the main course – an exquisite concoction of goose and wild berries – the mood of the evening had become one of genuine gaiety. Then the hotel manager, his face pink with the wine and laughter, had leaned over and said:

'Stephan, tell us again about that youth hostel you stayed in. You know, that one in the woods in Burgundy.'

For a second Stephan had been horrified. How could his father, who had conducted everything thus far so faultlessly, make such an obvious misjudgement? The story he was referring to involved extensive references to the hostel's lavatory arrangements and was clearly unsuitable to put before his mother. Yet as he had hesitated, his father had given him a wink as though to say: 'Yes, yes, trust me, this will work. She'll love the story, it'll be a success.' Gravely doubtful though he was, Stephan's faith in his father had been such as to make him embark on the anecdote. He had not got far, however, before the thought ran through his mind that what had so far been a miraculously successful evening was about to come down in tatters around them. Nevertheless, egged on by his father's guffaws, he had continued, and then heard to his amazement his mother's open laughter. Looking up across the table, he had seen her shaking her head helplessly. Then, somewhere towards the end of his story, amidst all the laughter, Stephan had caught his mother giving his father a look of fondness. It was just a brief look, but there had been no mistaking it. The hotel manager, despite the tears of laughter in his eyes, had not missed it either, and turning to his son had given another wink, this time with an air of triumph. At that moment the young man had felt something very powerful rising in his breast. But before he had had the time clearly to identify it, his father had said to him:

'Now Stephan, before the sweet course we must rest. Why don't you play something for your mother on her birthday?' With this the hotel manager had waved towards the upright piano by the wall.

That gesture – that casual wave towards the dining-room

upright – was one Stephan was to recall again and again over the years. And each time he did so something of the sickening chill he had felt at that moment would come back to him. At first he had looked at his father in disbelief, but the latter had simply gone on smiling contentedly, holding his hand out towards the piano.

'Come on, Stephan. Something your mother would like. A little Bach, perhaps. Or something contemporary. Kazan maybe. Or Mullery.'

The young man, forcing his gaze round to include his mother, had seen her face, softened by laughter along unfamiliar lines, smiling at him. She had then turned to the hotel manager rather than to Stephan and said: 'Yes, dear, I think Mullery would be just the thing. That would be splendid.'

'Come on, Stephan,' the hotel manager had said jovially. 'This is your mother's birthday, after all. Don't disappoint her.'

An idea had flashed through Stephan's mind – an idea rejected the very next instant – that his parents were conspiring together against him. Certainly from the way they were gazing at him – so full of proud anticipation – it was as though they had no memory at all of the anguished history surrounding his piano playing. In any case, the protest he had started to formulate had faded in his mouth, and he had risen to his feet as though it were someone else doing so.

The piano's position against the wall was such that, when Stephan had sat down at it, he had been able to see at the edge of his vision the figures of his parents, their elbows upon the table, each leaning slightly towards the other. After a moment he had actually turned and glanced directly towards them, aware as he did so that he had wanted to see them like that one last time – sitting together as though bound by an uncomplicated happiness. He had then turned back to the piano, overwhelmed by the certainty that the evening was about to fall. Curiously he had realised he was no longer at all surprised by the latest turn of events, that in fact he had been waiting for it all along and that it had brought with it a sense of relief.

For a few seconds, Stephan had gone on sitting without playing, trying desperately to shake off the effects of the wine and to run through in his mind the piece he was about to attempt. For one giddying moment he saw the possibility – it had after all been an evening of remarkable things – that he would somehow perform at a level never before attained, and that he would finish to find his parents smiling, applauding and exchanging with each other looks of deep affection. But no sooner had he commenced the opening bar of Mullery's *Epicycloid*, he had realised the utter impossibility of any such scenario.

He had played on nevertheless. For a long time – throughout most of the first movement – the figures at the edge of his vision had remained very still. Then he had seen his mother lean back slightly in her chair and bring a hand up to her chin. Several bars later, his father had turned his gaze away from Stephan, placed both hands on his lap and had bowed his head forward so that he appeared to be studying a spot on the table before him.

Meanwhile the piece had gone on and on, and though the young man had felt tempted several times to abandon it, to stop altogether had somehow seemed the most dreadful option of all. So he had continued, and when at last the piece had finished, Stephan had sat staring at the keyboard for several moments before working up the courage to look round at the scene awaiting him.

Neither of his parents was looking at him. His father's head had now become so bowed the forehead was almost touching the table surface. His mother was looking in the other direction across the room, wearing the frosty expression Stephan was so familiar with and which, astonishingly, had been absent until that point in the evening.

Stephan had needed only a second to appraise this scene. Then he had got up and returned quickly to the dining table, as though by doing so the minutes since his leaving it could be expunged. For a little while, the three of them had continued to sit silently. Finally his mother had risen saying:

'It's been a very nice evening. Thank you, both of you. But I'm feeling tired now and I think I ought to go up to bed.'

At first the hotel manager had seemed not to have heard. But as Stephan's mother had moved towards the door, he had raised his head and said very quietly: 'The cake, my dear. The cake. It's . . . it's something rather special.'

'You're very kind, but really, I've had so much already to eat. I must get some sleep now.'

'Of course, of course.' The hotel manager had stared down at the table again with an air of resignation. But then, as Stephan's mother was about to pass through the door, the hotel manager had suddenly straightened and said loudly: 'At least, my dear, come and look at it. Just look at it. As I say, it's something special.'

His mother had hesitated, then said: 'Very well. Show it to me quickly. Then I really must sleep. It's the wine perhaps, but I feel extremely tired now.'

On hearing this, the hotel manager had started to his feet and the next instant had ushered his wife out of the dining room.

The young man had listened to his parents' footsteps going towards the kitchen, then, after no more than a minute, returning along the corridor and climbing the staircase. For some time after that Stephan had remained seated at the table. Various small noises had come from above but he had been unable to hear any voices. In the end it had occurred to him that his best course would simply be to drive back through the night to his digs. Certainly his presence at breakfast would hardly help his father on the slow, huge task of rebuilding his mother's good humour.

He had left the dining room intending to slip out of the house unnoticed, but out in the hallway he had encountered his father descending the staircase. The hotel manager had put his finger to his lips, saying:

'We must speak quietly. Your mother's just gone to bed.'

Stephan had informed his father of his intention to return to Heidelberg, to which the hotel manager had said: 'What a pity. Your mother and I thought you'd be able to stay longer. But as you say, you have lectures in the morning. I'll explain to your mother, she's sure to understand.'

'And Mother,' Stephan had said. 'I hope she enjoyed the evening.'

His father had smiled, but for a brief moment before he did so Stephan had seen a look of profound desolation cross his face.

'Oh yes. I know she did. Oh yes. She was so glad you could take a break from your studies and come all this way. I know she was hoping you would stay a few days, but don't worry. I'll explain it to her.'

70

As he had driven along the deserted highways that night, Stephan had turned over every aspect of the evening's events – just as he was to do again and again over the following years. The anguish he felt each time he recalled that occasion had gradually diminished with time, but now the steady approach of Thursday night had brought back many of the old terrors, causing him yet again, as we drove on through the rainy night, to be transported back to that painful evening of several years ago.

I felt sorry for the young man and broke the silence by saying to him:

'I realise it's none of my business, and I hope this doesn't sound rude, but I do think you've been treated rather unfairly by your parents over the matter of your piano playing. My advice to you would be to try and enjoy your playing as much as you can, drawing satisfaction and meaning from it regardless of them.'

The young man considered this for several moments. Then he said:

'I'm grateful to you, Mr Ryder, for giving my position thought and all that. But actually – well, to be quite blunt about it – I don't think you really understand. I can see how to an outsider my mother's behaviour that night might look a little, well, a little inconsiderate. But that would be doing her an injustice and I'd really hate for you to go away with such an impression. You see, you've got to understand the whole background to this matter. For one thing, you see, from when I was four I had Mrs Tilkowski as my piano teacher. I suppose there's no reason why that would mean much to you, Mr Ryder, but you have to understand, Mrs Tilkowski is a very revered figure in this city, certainly not just *any* piano teacher. Her services aren't for sale in the usual way – though of course she takes fees like anyone else. That's to say, she's very serious about what she does and will only take children of the city's artistic and intellectual elite. For instance, Paulo Rozario, the surrealist painter, lived here for a time and Mrs Tilkowski taught both his daughters. And Professor Diegelmann's children. The Countess's nieces too. She chooses her pupils very carefully, and so you see I was very fortunate to get her, particularly since in those days Father didn't have the sort of standing in the community he has today. But I suppose my parents were as dedicated to the arts then as they are now. All through my childhood I remember them talking about artists and musicians and how important it was that such people were supported. Mother stays at home most of the time now, but in those days she was much more outgoing. If a musician, say, or an orchestra came through the town, she'd always make a point of going along to lend her support. She'd not only attend the performance, she'd always try and go to the dressing room afterwards to give her praise personally. Even if a performer had done badly, she'd still go to his dressing room afterwards to give a little encouragement and a few gentle hints. In fact she'd often invite musicians to visit our house, or else offer to take them on a tour around the city. Usually their schedules were much too full to take up her offers, but, as no doubt you can vouch yourself, such invitations are always very uplifting to any performer. As for my father, he was extremely busy, but I remember he too used to do his best. Certainly, if there was a reception held in honour of some visiting celebrity, he'd always make a point of accompanying Mother to it, no matter how busy he was, so that he could play his part in welcoming the visitor. So you see, Mr Ryder, as far back as I can remember, my parents have been very cultured people who appreciated the importance of the arts in our society, and I'm sure that's why Mrs Tilkowski finally agreed to take me on as a pupil. I can see now it must have been a real triumph for my parents at the time, particularly for Mother, who'd gone about all the arrangements. There I was, having lessons from Mrs Tilkowski alongside Mr Rozario's and Professor Diegelmann's children! They must have been so proud. And for the first few years I did very well, I really did, so much so that Mrs Tilkowski once called me one of the most promising pupils she'd ever had. Things really went well until . . . well, until when I was ten years old.'

The young man suddenly went silent, perhaps regretting having talked so freely. But I could see another part of him was eager to carry on with his revelations, and so I asked:

'What happened when you were ten?'

'Well, I'm ashamed to admit this, and to you of all people, Mr Ryder. But when I was ten, well, I just stopped practising. I'd turn up at Mrs Tilkowski's not having practised my passages at all. And when she asked why I hadn't, I'd just not speak. This is awfully embarrassing, it's like someone else I'm talking about, and I just wish by some magic it could be. But that's the truth, there you are, that's how I behaved. And after a few weeks of this, there was nothing for it but for Mrs Tilkowski to inform my parents that if things didn't change, she could no longer carry on with me. I later found out Mother lost her temper a little and shouted at Mrs Tilkowski. Anyway it all ended rather badly.'

'And after that you went to another teacher?'

'Yes, a Miss Henze, who wasn't at all bad. But she was hardly Mrs Tilkowski. I still didn't practise, but Miss Henze wasn't so strict. Then when I was twelve, it all changed. It's hard to explain just what happened, it may sound a little odd. I was just sitting in the lounge of our house one afternoon. It was very sunny, I remember I was reading this football magazine, and my father came wandering into the room. I remember he was wearing his grey waistcoat and his shirt-sleeves were rolled up and he stood in the middle of the floor and stared out through the window out into the garden. I knew Mother was out there, sitting out on the bench we used to have in those days under the fruit trees, and I was waiting for Father to go out and sit with her. But he just kept standing there. He had his back to me, so I couldn't see his face, but whenever I looked up I could see he was staring out into the garden to where Mother was. Well, the third or fourth time I looked up and Father still hadn't gone out, something suddenly dawned on me. I mean, that's when I realised. That my mother and father had barely spoken to each other for months. It was very odd, this realisation just came over me, that they'd hardly spoken at all. It's odd I hadn't noticed it earlier but I hadn't, not until that moment. But then I saw it very clearly. All in a rush, a number of different instances came back to me – times when previously Father and Mother would have said something to each other, but in fact they hadn't. I don't mean they'd been totally silent. But, you know, this coolness had come between them and I hadn't seen it until that moment. I can tell you, Mr Ryder, it was a very strange feeling, that realisation coming over me. And almost at the same time this terrible other thing occurred to me – that this change must have dated back to when I'd lost Mrs Tilkowski. I couldn't be certain, because so much time had gone by, but once I'd thought about it I was sure that's when this thing had first started. I can't remember now if Father

73

ever went out into the garden or not. I didn't say anything, just pretended to keep reading my football magazine, then after a while I went up to my room, lay down on the bed and thought it all over. It was after that I started to work hard again. I started practising really very diligently and I must have made a lot of progress, because after a few months Mother went to see Mrs Tilkowski to ask if she'd consider taking me back. I can see now it must have been quite a humiliation for Mother, having shouted that last time, and she must have had to do a lot of work on Mrs Tilkowski. Anyway, the result was, Mrs Tilkowski agreed to take me back, and this time I worked hard all the time, practising and practising. But you see, I'd lost those crucial two years. The years between ten and twelve, you know better than anyone how crucial they are. Believe me, Mr Ryder, I tried to make up for those lost years, I did everything I could, but really it was just too late. Even now I often stop and ask myself: "What on earth could I have been thinking of?" Oh, what I'd give now to have those years again! But you see, I don't think my parents really appreciated how damaging those missing two years would be. I think they thought once I'd got Mrs Tilkowski back, so long as I worked hard, they wouldn't make much difference. I know Mrs Tilkowski tried to explain it to them on more than one occasion, but I think they were so full of love and pride for me they just didn't take on board the reality of the situation. For quite a few years, they went on assuming I was making fine progress, that I was really gifted. It was only when I was seventeen it really hit them. There used to be a piano competition in those days, the Jürgen Flemming Prize, it was organised by the Civic Arts Institute for promising young people in the city. It used to have a reputation of sorts, though it's stopped now due to lack of funds. When I was seventeen, my parents had this idea I should enter it, and my mother actually went about seeing to all the preliminaries for getting me entered. That was when they first realised how short of the mark I was. They listened very carefully to my playing – it was probably the first time they *really* listened – and they realised I'd only humiliate myself and the family by entering. I was quite keen to have a go anyway, but my parents decided it would damage my confidence too much. As I say, that was the first time they noticed how weak my playing was. Until then, their high hopes, and I suppose their love for me, just prevented them from listening at all objectively. That was the first time they took on board just how much damage those missing two years had done. Well, after that, naturally enough, my parents became very disappointed. Mother in particular seemed to resign herself to the idea that it had all been for nothing, all the effort she'd gone to, all the years with Mrs Tilkowski, that time she'd gone to beg her to take me back, all of it, she seemed to think of it all as a big waste. And she got rather despondent and stopped going out very much, stopped going to the concerts and functions. Father, though, he's always kept up some hope for me. That's typical of him really. He'll always keep hopeful right to the end. Every now and again, every year or so, he asks to hear me play, and whenever he does, I can see he's full of hope for me, I can see him thinking: "This time, this time it'll be different." But so far, each time I finish playing and look up I can see he's crestfallen again. Of course he does his best to hide it, but I can see it clearly enough. But he's never given up hope, and that's meant a lot to me.'

We were now speeding down a wide avenue flanked by tall office buildings. Although we sometimes passed rows of neatly parked cars, ours still seemed to be the only vehicle moving for miles.

'And it was your father's idea,' I asked, 'that you should perform on Thursday night?'

'Yes. There's faith for you! He first suggested it six months ago. He hasn't heard me play for almost two years, but he's showing real faith in me. Of course he gave me every chance to say no, but I was so moved that he should show such faith in me after all those disappointments. So I said yes, I'd do it.'

'That was very brave of you. I do hope it turns out to be the correct decision.'

'Actually, Mr Ryder, I said yes because, well, even though I say so myself, I think I've made something of a breakthrough recently. Perhaps you'll know what I'm talking about, it's rather hard to explain. It's as though something in my head, something that was always blocking my progress, like a dam or something, it's like it's suddenly burst and a whole new spirit's been allowed to flow. I can't quite explain it, but the fact is I think I'm a significantly better pianist now than when Father last heard me. So you see, when he asked if I wanted to perform on Thursday night, nervous though I was, I said yes. If I hadn't, it wouldn't have been fair on him, after all the faith he's invested in me. That's not to say I'm not worried about Thursday night. I've been working on my piece very hard and I'll admit, I *am* a bit worried. But I know I've got a very good chance of surprising my parents. In any case, you see, I've always had this fantasy. Even when my playing was at its most wretched. I had this fantasy of spending months somewhere locked away, practising and practising. My parents wouldn't see me for months and months. Then one day I'd suddenly come home. A Sunday afternoon probably. In any case some time when Father would be home too. I'd come in, hardly say a word, just go to the piano, lift the lid, start playing. I'd not even have taken my coat off. I'd just play and play. Bach, Chopin, Beethoven. Then on to the modern stuff. Grebel. Kazan. Mullery. I'd just play and play. And my parents would have followed me into the dining room and they'd just be looking on in astonishment. It would be beyond their wildest dreams. But then, to their amazement, they'd realise that even as I played I was reaching greater and greater heights. Sublime, sensitive adagios. Astounding fiery bravura passages. I'd climb higher and higher. And they'd be standing there in the middle of the room, Father still absently holding the newspaper he'd been reading, both of them completely astounded. In the end I'd finish with some stunning finale, then at last I'd turn to them and . . . well, I've never been sure what happens after that. But it's a fantasy I've had ever since I was thirteen or fourteen. Thursday night may not turn out quite like it, but it's possible it could be pretty close. As I say, something's changed and I'm sure I'm almost there now. Ah, Mr Ryder, here we are. Well in time, I'm sure, for your journalists.'

The city centre had been so silent and devoid of traffic I had not recognised it. But, sure enough, we were now approaching the entrance of the hotel.

'If you don't mind,' Stephan went on, 'I'll drop you and Boris off here. I have to take the car round to the back.'

In the rear, Boris was looking tired, but was still awake. We got out, and I made sure the little boy had thanked Stephan before leading him towards the hotel.

7

The lights had been dimmed in the lobby and the hotel in general seemed to have fallen into quiet. The young desk clerk I had met on first arriving was on duty again, though he appeared to be fast asleep in his seat behind the reception desk. As we approached, he looked up and, recognising me, made an effort to wake himself up.

'Good evening, sir,' he said very cheerfully, but the next moment his weariness seemed to overtake him again.

'Good evening. I'll need another room. For Boris.' I put my hand on the little boy's shoulder. 'As close to mine as possible please.'

'Let me see what I can do, Mr Ryder.'

'Actually, your porter here, Gustav, he happens to be Boris's grandfather. I wonder if by any chance he's still in the hotel.'

'Oh yes, Gustav lives here. He has a little room up in the attic. But just now, I think he'd be asleep.'

'Perhaps he wouldn't mind being woken up. I know he'll want to see Boris straight away.'

The desk clerk glanced worriedly at his watch. 'Well, anything you say, sir,' he said uncertainly and picked up the phone. After a short pause, I heard him get through.

'Gustav? Gustav, I'm very sorry. This is Walter. Yes, yes, I'm sorry to wake you. Yes, I know, I'm very sorry. But please listen. Mr Ryder has just come in. He has your grandson with him.'

For the next few moments, the desk clerk listened, nodding several times. Then he put the receiver down and smiled at me.

'He's coming immediately. He says he'll see to everything.'

'Jolly good.'

'Mr Ryder, you must be very tired now.'

'Yes, I am. It's been an exhausting day. But I believe I have one more appointment. There should be some journalists waiting here for me.'

'Ah. They finally left an hour or so ago. They said they'd

arrange another appointment. I suggested they deal directly with Miss Stratmann so that you're not bothered by them. Really, sir, you look very tired. You should stop worrying about such things and go off to bed.'

'Yes, I suppose so. Hmm. So they left. First they turn up early, then they leave.'

'Yes, sir, very annoying. But I would say, Mr Ryder, you should just go to bed now and sleep. You really ought to stop worrying. I'm very sure everything will be taken care of.'

I was grateful to the young clerk for these comforting words and indeed for the first time in hours began to feel a sense of relaxation coming over me. I put my elbows up on the reception desk and for a moment or so began to doze off there on my feet. I did not go quite to sleep, however, for I remained aware all the while of Boris leaning his head heavily against my side, and of the desk clerk's voice, continuing in the same reassuring tones, just in front of my face.

'Gustav won't be long now,' the latter was saying, 'and he'll see to it your boy's comfortable. Really, sir, there's nothing more to worry about. And Miss Stratmann, we've known her at this hotel for a long time. A most efficient lady. She's looked after the affairs of many important visitors in the past and they've all been a hundred per cent impressed by her. She just doesn't make mistakes. So you can leave her to worry about those journalists, there won't be any problems. And as for Boris, we're going to give him a room just across the hall from you. It has a very fine view in the morning he's bound to enjoy. So Mr Ryder, I really think you should just go off to sleep now. There's nothing more you could conceivably achieve today. In fact, if I may be so bold, I'd recommend you leave Boris to his grandfather once you've all got upstairs. Gustav will be here any minute, he's just putting on his uniform, that's what's holding him up just a little. He'll be down soon in all his finery, that's Gustav for you, uniform immaculate, not a thing out of place. Once he appears, you should just get him to take charge of everything. He's going as fast as he can. He'll just be tying his shoe-laces at this very moment, sitting on the edge of his little bed. Any moment now he'll be ready, he'll jump to his feet, though he'll have to take care not to hit his head on the rafters. A quick comb of his hair and then he'll be out into

79

the corridor. Yes, he'll be here any second, and you can just go off to your room, unwind a little then get a good night's sleep. I'd recommend you take a night cap, one of the special cocktails you'll find ready-mixed in your mini-bar. They're quite excellent. Or perhaps you'd prefer some hot beverage to be brought up to you. And you could listen to some soothing music on the radio. There's a channel that broadcasts from Stockholm at this time of the night, just quiet late-night jazz, very soothing indeed, I often use it myself to wind down. Or else if you need to *really* unwind, may I suggest you go along and see the movie? Many of our guests are doing just that at this very moment.'

This last remark – this talk of a movie – brought me out of my drowsiness. Straightening, I said:

'I'm sorry, what's that you just said? Many of your guests have gone off to a movie?'

'Yes, there's a cinema just round the corner. They have a late-night performance. Many guests find popping round there and watching a film helps them to unwind at the end of a hard day. You could always do that as an alternative to taking a cocktail or a hot beverage.'

The telephone rang beside the desk clerk's hand, and excusing himself he picked up the receiver. As he listened, I noticed he looked towards me awkwardly a few times. Then he said: 'He's just here, madam,' and handed me the receiver.

'Hello,' I said.

For a few seconds there was silence. Then a voice said: 'It's me.'

It took me a moment to realise it was Sophie. But as soon as I did so, I became consumed by an intense rage towards her, and it was only Boris's presence that stopped me shouting furiously down the line. In the end I said very coldly: 'So. It's you.'

There was another short silence before she said: 'I'm calling from outside. In the street. I saw you and Boris go in. It's probably better he doesn't see me just now. It's way past his bedtime. Try not to let him know you're talking to me.'

I glanced down at Boris, who had dozed off on his feet leaning against me.

'So what exactly do you think you're doing?' I asked.

I heard her sigh heavily. Then she said:

'You've got every right to be angry. I . . . I don't know what happened. I can see how silly I've been now . . .'

'Look,' I interrupted, anxious that I would not be able to keep my anger under control much longer, 'where exactly are you?'

'On the other side of the street. Under the arches, in front of the antique shops.'

'I'll be out in a minute. Just stay where you are.'

I handed the receiver back to the desk clerk and was relieved to see that Boris had remained asleep throughout the call. In any case, at that moment, the elevator doors opened and Gustav stepped out onto the carpet.

His uniform did indeed look immaculate. His thin white hair had been wetted and combed. A puffiness around the eyes and a slight stiffness in his gait were the only signs of his having been fast asleep just a few minutes earlier.

'Ah, good evening, sir,' he said as he approached.

'Good evening.'

'You've brought Boris with you. How very kind of you to have gone to such trouble.' Gustav came towards us a few more steps, observing his grandson with a gentle smile. 'My goodness, sir, look at him. Fallen fast asleep.'

'Yes, he got very tired,' I said.

'He still looks so young when he's asleep like that.' The porter went on gazing tenderly at Boris for another moment. Then he looked up at me and said: 'I was wondering, sir, if you managed to talk to Sophie. I've been thinking all afternoon about how you might have got on.'

'Well, I did speak to her, yes.'

'Ah. And did you get any inkling?'

'Inkling?'

'Of what's preoccupying her?'

'Ah. Well, although she said several quite revealing things . . . to be frank, as I said to you earlier, it's very difficult for an outsider like myself to make much sense of these things. Naturally I did form one or two vague ideas about what might be troubling her, but really I feel more than ever it would be best if you yourself spoke to her.'

'But you see, sir, as I believe I explained to you before . . .'

'Yes, yes, you and Sophie don't talk directly, I remember,' I said with a sudden rush of impatience. 'Nevertheless, surely, if this is a matter of importance to you . . .'

'It's a matter of the utmost importance to me. Oh yes, sir, the *utmost* importance. It's for Boris's sake, you see. If we don't get to the bottom of this matter soon, he's going to become seriously worried, I know he is. There are clear signs already. And you only have to look at him, the way he is now, sir, you look at him like this, and you see he really is still so young. We owe it to him to keep his world free of such worries for a little while longer, don't you think so, sir? In fact, to call this matter one of importance to me is something of an understatement. Latterly I've hardly stopped worrying about it day and night. But you see . . .' He paused, gazing blankly at the floor in front of him. Then he shook his head a little and sighed. 'You say I should speak to Sophie myself. It's not quite that simple, sir. You have to understand the history of the situation. You see, we've had this . . . this *understanding* now for many years. Ever since she was young. When she was *very* small, of course, things were different then. Up until she was eight or nine, oh, Sophie and I, we'd talk all the time. I'd tell her stories, we'd go for long walks around the Old Town, hand in hand, just the two of us, talking and talking. You mustn't misunderstand, sir, I loved Sophie dearly then and I do so to this day. Oh yes, sir. We were *very* close when she was small. This understanding only started when she was eight years old. Yes, that's how old she was then. Incidentally, sir, this understanding of ours, it wasn't something I originally imagined going on for very long. I suppose I saw it as something that might last just a few days. That was all, sir, that was all I intended. The first day, I remember I was off work and I was trying to put up a shelf in the kitchen for my wife. Sophie kept following me about, asking this, offering to fetch that, trying to help me. I maintained my silence, sir, I maintained it completely. She soon became bewildered and upset, of course, I could see that. But it was what I had decided and I had to be firm. It wasn't easy for me, sir. Oh goodness me, it wasn't easy at all, I loved my little girl more than anything in the world, but I told myself I had to be strong. Three days, I said to myself, three days would be sufficient, three days and that would be the end of it. Just three days, then I'd be able to come in from work, pick her up again, hold her close to me, we'd tell each other everything. Catch up, so to speak. In those days, I was working at the Alba Hotel and towards the end of that third day, as you can imagine, I was longing for my shift to end so that I could get home and see my little Sophie again. You can understand my disappointment, then, when on returning to the apartment, Sophie refused to come and greet me when I called to her. What's more, sir, when I went and found her she looked away from me very deliberately and left the room without speaking. As you can imagine, I was very hurt. And I suppose I got a little angry – as I say, I'd had a very hard day and had been so looking forward to seeing her. I said to myself, if *that*'s how she wants to behave, let her see where it leads. So I ate my supper with my wife, then went to bed not having said a single word to Sophie. I suppose things just went on from there. One day followed another, and before you knew it, it just became the norm between us. I don't want you to misunderstand me, sir, we weren't quarrelling as such, there ceased to be any animosity between us fairly quickly. In fact, it was in those days just as it is now. Sophie and I remained very considerate towards one another. It's simply that we refrained from speaking. I admit, sir, I didn't at that stage imagine the thing going on for as long as it has. My intention, I suppose, was always that at some opportune point – on a special day such as her birthday – we'd put it all behind us and go back to the way we'd been. But then her birthday came and went, Christmas also, it came and went, sir, and we somehow never resumed. Then when she was eleven, a certain sad little event occurred. In those days Sophie had this little white hamster. She called it Ulrich, she became greatly fond of it. She'd spend hours on end talking to it, taking it around the apartment in her hands. Then one day the creature disappeared. Sophie searched everywhere. Her mother and I also searched the apartment, we asked the neighbours about it, but to no avail. My wife did her best to reassure Sophie that Ulrich was safe – that he'd just gone on a little holiday and would be back before long. Then one evening, my wife had gone out and Sophie and I were alone in the apartment. I was in the bedroom with the radio up quite loud – there was a concert being broadcast – when I became aware that in the living room Sophie was sobbing uncontrollably. Almost immediately I guessed she'd at last found Ulrich. Or what remained of him – he'd been missing a few weeks by then. Well, the door between the bedroom and the living room was closed, and as I say, the radio was up loud, so it would have been perfectly conceivable I might not have heard her. So I remained in the bedroom, my ear close to the door, the concert playing behind me. I did of course think several times I'd go through to her, but then the longer I stood there at the door, the more odd it seemed that I should suddenly burst in. You see, sir, it wasn't as though she was sobbing so loudly. For a little while, I even sat down again, tried to pretend to myself I'd never heard her. But of course it just tore me up inside to hear her sob like that and I soon found myself standing at the door again, stooped over, trying to listen to Sophie over the sound of the concert. If she calls for me, I told myself, if she knocks or calls for me, then I'll go in. That's what I decided. If she shouts: "Papa!" then I'll go in, I'll explain I hadn't heard her before because of the music. I waited, but she neither called me nor knocked. The only thing she did, after some time of very distraught sobbing – it went straight to the heart, I can tell you, sir – she called out as though to herself – I emphasise this, sir, as though saying it to herself – she called out: "I left Ulrich in the box! It was my fault! I forgot! It was my fault!" What had happened, I ascertained later, was that Sophie had put Ulrich inside this little gift box. She'd wanted to take him out somewhere, she was often taking him out to "show" him things. She'd put him inside this little gift box she had, all ready to go out, but then something had happened, she'd been distracted and she hadn't gone out at all, and meanwhile she'd forgotten she'd put Ulrich inside the box. On this night I'm telling you about, sir, weeks later, she'd been doing something around the apartment and suddenly remembered. Can you imagine what an awful moment that would have been for my little girl! Suddenly remembering like that, perhaps hoping against hope she'd remembered incorrectly and rushing to the box. Of course, there was Ulrich, still inside. Listening through the door I couldn't of course determine at the time everything that had happened, but I more or less guessed the moment she shouted that out. "I left Ulrich in the box! It was my fault!" But I want you to understand, sir, she said this as though to herself. If she'd said: "Papa! Please come out . . ." But no. Even so, I did actually think to myself: "If she calls out like that again, I'll go in." But she didn't. She just went on sobbing. I could picture her holding Ulrich in her fingers, perhaps hoping he could still be saved . . . Oh, it wasn't easy for me, sir. But the concert was continuing behind me, and you see, I remained in the bedroom. I heard my wife come in much later and the two of them talking and Sophie crying again. And then my wife came into the bedroom and told me what had happened. "Didn't you hear anything?" she asked, and I said: "Oh dear, no, I was listening to the concert." The next morning, at breakfast, Sophie said nothing to me, and I said nothing to her. We just continued with our understanding, in other words. But I realised, there was no doubting it, I realised Sophie *knew* I'd been listening. And what was more, she wasn't resenting me for it. She passed me the milk jug, just as usual, the butter, she even took away my plate for me – an extra little service. What I'm saying, sir, is that Sophie understood our arrangement and respected it. After that, as you might imagine, things rather settled on that basis. You see, since we'd not brought an end to our understanding over the matter of Ulrich, it wouldn't have seemed right to bring it to an end until something at least as significant came along. Indeed, sir, to end it suddenly one day for no special reason would not only have been odd, really, it would have belittled the tragedy the whole Ulrich episode represented for my daughter. I do hope you can see this, sir. In any case, as I say, after that our understanding became, well, cemented, and even in these present circumstances it doesn't seem to me appropriate I should suddenly break such a long-standing arrangement. I dare say Sophie would feel much the same way. That's why, sir, I asked you, as a special favour, particularly since you happened to be walking that way this afternoon . . .'

'Yes, yes, yes,' I broke in, feeling another wave of impatience. Then I said more gently: 'I appreciate how things stand between you and your daughter. But I wonder, isn't it possible, this very matter – this matter of your understanding. Isn't it possible that this might itself be at the heart of what's bothering her? That it was this understanding of yours she was thinking about that time you saw her sitting so despondently in the café?'

This seemed to stun Gustav and for some time he remained silent. Finally he said: 'That's never occurred to me before, sir, what you've just suggested. I'll have to give it some thought. I must say, it's never occurred to me before.' He was silent again for a few moments, a troubled expression on his face. Then he looked up and said: 'But why would she be so concerned about our understanding *now*? After all this time?' He shook his head slowly. 'May I ask you, sir? Is this an idea you formed from speaking to her?'

Suddenly I felt very weary and wished the whole affair to be taken off my hands. 'I don't know, I don't know,' I said. 'As I keep saying, these family matters . . . I'm merely an outsider. How can I judge? I was simply saying it's a possibility.'

'Certainly it's something I'll have to give some thought to. For Boris's sake, I'm prepared to examine every possibility. Yes, I'll have to give it some thought.' Again he fell silent, the troubled expression growing on his face. 'I wonder, sir,' he said eventually, 'if I might request another favour. When you next see Sophie, perhaps you wouldn't mind investigating this particular possibility. I know you'd go about it in a very tactful way. I wouldn't normally ask such a thing, but, you see, I'm thinking of little Boris here. I'd be so grateful.'

He looked at me appealingly. In the end I gave a sigh and said: 'Very well. I'll do what I can for Boris's sake. But I can only say again, for an outsider like me . . .'

Perhaps it was the mention of his name, but at that moment Boris started awake.

'Grandfather!' he exclaimed and, releasing me, made excitedly for Gustav with the obvious intention of embracing him. But at the last moment, the little boy seemed to remember himself and held out his hand instead.

'Good evening, Grandfather,' he said with calm dignity.

'Good evening, Boris.' Gustav patted him gently on the head. 'It's good to see you again. What sort of a day have you had?'

Boris gave a casual shrug. 'Somewhat tiring. Just the usual sort of day.'

'Just one minute,' Gustav said, 'and I'll see to everything.'

His arm around his grandson's shoulders, the porter went up to the reception desk. For the next few moments, he and the desk clerk exchanged hotel jargon in lowered tones. Then they both nodded in agreement about something and the desk clerk handed over a key.

'If you'd follow me, sir,' Gustav said. 'I'll show you where Boris will be staying.'

'Actually, I have another appointment.'

'At this hour? You have such a busy life, sir. Well, in that case, may I suggest I take Boris up myself and install him?'

'That's an excellent idea. I'd be very grateful.'

I walked with them to the elevator and gave a final wave as the doors closed on them. Then all at once the frustration and anger I had thus far managed to keep in check came flooding back, and without uttering another word to the desk clerk, I crossed the lobby and went out again into the night.

8

The street was deserted and silent. It took me a while to spot – a little way down on the opposite side – the stone arches Sophie had mentioned on the phone. For a moment, as I made my way towards them, I wondered if she had lost her nerve and fled. But then I saw her figure emerge from the shadows and could feel my fury rising once more.

Her expression was not as meek as I would have expected. She was watching me carefully, and as I came up to her she said, almost calmly:

'You've got every right to be angry. I don't know what happened. I suppose I was confused. You've got every right to be angry, I know.'

I looked at her nonchalantly. 'Angry? Oh, I see. You're talking about your behaviour earlier this evening. Well, yes, I must say, I felt very disappointed on behalf of Boris. Obviously, he was very upset. But as far as I'm concerned, quite frankly, it's not something I've spent a lot of time thinking about. I've so much else on just now.'

'I don't know why it happened. I know how much you were depending on me . . .'

'I've never depended on you. I think you ought to calm down a little.' I gave a quick laugh and began to walk slowly. 'As far as I'm concerned, this simply isn't a major issue. I've always been quite ready to go about my tasks with or without your support. I'm just disappointed on Boris's behalf, that's all.'

'I've been very stupid, I see that now.' Sophie had fallen in step alongside me. 'I don't know, I suppose I thought you and Boris – you have to see it from my side – you and Boris were lagging behind and I thought perhaps you weren't so keen on what I'd planned for the evening and I supposed maybe you'd drift off anyway . . . Look, if you like, I'll tell you everything. Everything you want to know. Every detail . . .'

I stopped walking and turned to her. 'Obviously I haven't

made myself clear. I'm not interested in any of this. I only came out here because I wanted to get some fresh air and unwind a little. It's been a hard day. As a matter of fact, I came out here because I wanted to take in a movie before bed.'

'A movie? Which movie's that?'

'How do I know which movie? Some late-night film. There's a cinema just down here. I thought I'd go and see it whatever it is. It's been a very hard day.'

I began to walk again, this time more purposefully. After a moment, to my satisfaction, I heard her footsteps pursuing me.

'Are you really not angry?' she asked, catching up.

'Of course I'm not angry. Why should I be?'

'Can I come too? To this movie?'

I gave a shrug and continued to walk at a steady pace. 'Please yourself. You're perfectly welcome.'

Sophie grasped my arm. 'If you want, I'll make a completely clean breast of it. I'll tell you everything. Everything you want to know about . . .'

'Look, how many more times do I have to say this? I'm not in the least interested. All I want just now is to unwind. There's going to be a lot of pressure on me over these next few days.'

She continued to hold my arm and for a while we walked together in silence. Then she said quietly: 'It's so good of you. To be so understanding.'

I said nothing to this. In time we drifted off the pavement and continued down the centre of the deserted street.

'Once I find a proper home for us,' she said eventually, 'then everything will go better. It's bound to. This place I'm seeing in the morning, I'm really hopeful about it. It sounds exactly what we've always wanted.'

'Yes. Let's hope so.'

'You could sound a little more excited. This could be a turning point for us.'

I shrugged and continued to walk. The cinema was still some distance away, but being virtually the only thing illuminated in the darkened street, our eyes had for some time been fixed on it. Then as we came nearer, Sophie gave a sigh and brought us to a halt.

'Maybe I won't come in,' she said, disengaging her arm. 'I need plenty of time to look at this house tomorrow. I have to make an early start. I'd better be getting back.'

For some reason her words took me quite by surprise, and for a second I remained uncertain how I should respond. I glanced over towards the cinema, then back at Sophie.

'But I thought you said you wanted to . . .' I began, then, pausing, said in a calmer tone: 'Listen, this is a very good film. I'm sure you'll enjoy it.'

'But you don't even know which film it is.'

The idea flashed through my head that she was playing some sort of game. Even so, a strange panic had begun to seize me and I could not keep a pleading note out of my voice.

'You know what I meant. The desk clerk. He suggested it to me. He's someone I know to be very reliable. And the hotel has its reputation to think of. It's hardly likely to recommend . . .' I trailed off, the panic now mounting further as Sophie began to move away from me. 'Look' – I raised my voice, no longer caring who heard me – 'I know this will be a good movie. And we haven't been to one together for so long. That's true, isn't it? When did we last do something like this together?'

Sophie appeared to give this consideration, then finally smiled and came back towards me.

'All right,' she said, taking my arm gently. 'All right. It's late, but I'll come in with you. As you say, it's ages since we did anything like this together. Let's have a really good time.'

I experienced a considerable feeling of relief, and as we entered the cinema it was all I could do not to grasp her tightly to me. Sophie seemed to sense something and nestled her head on my shoulder.

'It's so good of you,' she said softly. 'Not to be angry with me.'

'What is there to be angry about?' I muttered, looking about the foyer.

A little way in front of us, the last of a queue was filing into the theatre. I looked around for somewhere to buy tickets, but the kiosk was closed, and it occurred to me there might exist some special arrangement between the hotel and the cinema. In any case, when Sophie and I brought up the rear of the queue, a man in a green suit standing at the threshold smiled and ushered us in along with everyone else.

It was virtually a full house. The lights had not yet gone down and many people were moving around finding their seats. I was looking to see where we might sit when Sophie squeezed my arm excitedly.

'Oh, let's get something,' she said. 'Ice creams or popcorn or something.'

She was pointing down to the front of the theatre where a short queue had formed in front of a uniformed woman holding a tray of confectioneries.

'Of course,' I said. 'But we'd better hurry or there'll be no seats left. It's very crowded in here.'

We made our way down to the front and joined the queue. After a while, as I was standing there, I could feel my anger rising again, until eventually I was obliged to turn away from Sophie altogether. Then I heard her say behind me:

'I have to be honest. I didn't actually come to the hotel tonight to find you. I didn't even know you two would turn up there.'

'Oh?' I leaned forward, looking towards the confectioneries.

'After what happened,' Sophie went on, 'I mean, once I'd realised how silly I'd been, well, I didn't know what to do. Then I suddenly remembered. About Papa's winter coat. I remembered I still hadn't given it to him.'

There was a rustling noise. Turning, I noticed for the first time that Sophie was carrying on one arm a large shapeless package in brown paper. She raised it in the air, but it was obviously quite heavy and she soon lowered it again.

'It was silly,' she said. 'There was no need to panic. But you see, I suddenly thought I could feel the winter in the air. And I remembered about the coat and I wanted to get it to him without any more delay. So I wrapped it up and came out. But then I got to the hotel and the evening was so mild. I could see I'd been panicking about nothing and I didn't know if I should go in and give it to him tonight or not. So I was standing there and it got later and later and eventually I realised Papa would have gone to bed. I thought about leaving it at the desk for him, but then I wanted to give it to him myself. And I was thinking, well, I could just as well give it to him in a few weeks' time, it's still so mild. That's when the car drove up and you and Boris got out. That's the truth of it.'

'I see.'

'I don't know if I'd have had the courage to face you otherwise. But there I was, right across the street from you, so I took a deep breath and phoned.'

'Well, I'm glad you did.' I gestured at our surroundings. 'After all, it's a long time since we've come to a movie together like this.'

She gave no response and when I looked at her she was gazing down fondly at the package on her arm. She patted it with her free hand.

'The season won't be turning for a little while yet,' she murmured, as much to the coat as to me. 'So there's no desperate hurry. We can give it to him in a few weeks.'

We had now reached the head of the queue and Sophie stepped in front of me to peer eagerly into the tray the uniformed woman was proffering.

'What are you going to have?' she asked. 'I think I want an ice-cream tub. No, a choc-ice. One of these.'

Looking over her shoulder, I saw the tray contained the usual ice creams and chocolate bars. But curiously these had all been pushed untidily to the edges of the tray to give pride of place to a large battered book. I leaned forward to examine it.

'That's a very useful manual, sir,' the uniformed woman said eagerly. 'I can heartily recommend it. I suppose I shouldn't be selling it here like this. But then the manager doesn't mind us selling the odd personal item, just so long as we don't do it too often.'

On the jacket was a photograph of a smiling man in overalls half-way up a step-ladder, a paint brush in his hand, a roll of wallpaper under his arm. When I picked it up I could feel the binding starting to come apart.

'Actually it belonged to my eldest son,' the uniformed woman continued. 'But he's grown up now and gone to Sweden. I was finally sorting through his things last week. I kept anything I thought had sentimental value and the rest of it I threw out. But then there were one or two things that didn't seem to fit into either category. This old manual, sir, I can't say it has much sentimental value, but it's such a useful volume, it shows you how to do so many things around the house, decorating, tiling, it teaches you everything step by step with very clear diagrams. I remember my son found it very useful when he was growing up. I realise it's a little ragged now, but it really is the most useful book. I'm not asking much for it, sir.'

'Perhaps Boris would like it,' I said to Sophie, flicking through the pages.

'Oh, if you've got a growing boy, sir, it really would be perfect. I can vouch from our own experience. Our son got so much from it when he was that age. Painting, tiling, it shows you everything.'

The lights were starting to dim and I remembered we had yet to find seats.

'Very well, thank you,' I said.

The woman thanked me profusely as I paid her and we came away with the book and the ice creams.

'It's good of you to think of Boris like that,' Sophie said as we moved up the aisle. Then she raised her package again with a rustle and hugged it to herself.

'It's odd to think Papa went the whole of last winter without a proper coat,' she said. 'But he was just too proud to wear that old one. It was mild last year, so it didn't matter so much. But he can't go another winter like that.'

'No, he certainly shouldn't.'

'I'm quite unsentimental about it. I know Papa's getting older now. I've been thinking things through. About his retirement, for instance. He's getting older and it has to be faced.' Then she added quietly: 'I'll give it to him in a couple of weeks. That should be fine.'

The lights had continued to dim and the audience had quietened in anticipation. I realised the theatre was even more crowded than before and I wondered if we had left it too late to find seats. But then as the darkness settled over us, an usher came down the aisle with a torch and pointed out two seats near the front. Sophie and I edged down the row, mumbling apologies, and sat down just as the advertisements were starting.

Most of the advertisements were for local businesses and seemed to go on interminably. When the main feature finally started we had been seated for at least half an hour, and I saw with some relief it was to be the science fiction classic, *2001: A Space Odyssey* – a favourite of mine which I never tired of seeing.

As soon as those impressive opening shots of a prehistoric world appeared on the screen, I could feel myself relaxing, and I was soon comfortably absorbed in the film. We were well into the central section of the narrative – with Clint Eastwood and Yul Brynner on board the spaceship bound for Jupiter – when I heard Sophie say beside me:

'But the weather could change. Just like that.'

I assumed she was referring to the film and murmured back something in assent. But a few minutes later, she said:

'Last year, it was a nice sunny autumn, just like this. It went on and on. People were sitting out on the pavements drinking coffee right into November. Then suddenly, virtually overnight, it got so cold. It could easily be like that again this year. You never know, do you?'

'No, I suppose not.' By this time, of course, I had realised she was again talking about the coat.

'But it's not so urgent yet,' she murmured.

When I next glanced at her, she appeared to be watching the film again. I too turned back to the screen, but then after a few seconds certain fragments of memory began to come back to me there in the darkness of the cinema and my attention once more drifted from the film.

I found myself recalling quite vividly a certain occasion when I had been sitting in an uncomfortable, perhaps dirty armchair. It was probably the morning, a dull grey one, and I had been holding a newspaper in front of me. Boris had been lying on his front on the carpet nearby, drawing on a sketch pad with a wax crayon. From the little boy's age – he was still very small – I supposed this to be a memory deriving from six or seven years ago, though what room we had been in, in which house, I could not remember. A door to a neighbouring room had been left ajar through which several female voices could be heard chattering away.

For some time I had gone on reading my newspaper on the uncomfortable armchair, until something about Boris – some subtle change in his demeanour or his posture – had made me glance down at him. Then in an instant I had seen the situation before me. Boris had managed to draw on his sheet a perfectly recognisable 'Superman'. He had been attempting to do just such a thing for weeks, but for all our encouragement had been unable to produce even a vague likeness. But now, perhaps owing to that mixture of fluke and genuine breakthrough so often experienced in childhood, he had suddenly succeeded. The sketch was not quite finished – the mouth and eyes needed completing – but for all that I had been able to see at once the huge triumph it represented for him. In fact I would have said something to him had I not noticed at that moment the way he was leaning forward in a state of great tension, his crayon held over the paper. He was, I had realised, hesitating whether to go on to refine his drawing at the risk of ruining it. I had been able to sense acutely his dilemma and had felt a temptation to say out loud: 'Boris, stop. That's enough. Stop there and show everyone what you've achieved. Show me, then show your mother, and then all those people talking now in the next room. What does it matter if it's not completely finished? Everyone will be astonished and so proud of you. Stop now before you lose it all.' But I had not said anything, continuing instead to watch him from around the edge of my newspaper. Finally Boris had made up his mind and begun to apply a few more touches with great care. Then, growing more confident, he had bent right forward and started to use the crayon with some recklessness. A moment later he had stopped abruptly, staring silently at his sheet. Then – and I could even now recall the anguish mounting within me – I had watched him attempting to salvage his picture, applying more and more crayon. Finally his face had fallen and, dropping the crayon onto the paper, he had risen and left the room without a word.

This whole episode had affected me to a surprising degree, and I had still been in the process of composing my emotions when Sophie's voice had said somewhere close by:

'You've no idea, have you?'

I had lowered my paper, startled by the bitterness of her tone, to find her standing in the room staring at me. Then she had said:

'You've no idea, what that was like for me, watching what happened then. It'll never be like that for you. Look at you, just reading the newspaper.' Then she had lowered her voice, making it gather even more intensity. 'That's the difference! He's not your own. Whatever you say, it makes a difference. You'll never feel towards him like a real father. Look at you! You've no idea what I went through just then.'

With that she had turned and disappeared out of the room.

It had occurred to me to follow her through into the next room, visitors or no visitors, and bring her back for a talk. But in the end I had decided in favour of waiting where I was for her return. Sure enough, a few minutes later, Sophie had come back into the room, but something in her manner had prevented me from speaking and she had gone out again. In fact, although during the following half-hour Sophie had entered and left the room several more times, for all my resolve to make my feelings known to her, I had remained silent. Eventually, after a certain point, I had realised any chance to broach the topic without looking ridiculous had passed, and I had returned to my newspaper with a strong sense of hurt and frustration.

'Excuse me,' I heard a voice say behind me and a hand touched my shoulder. Turning, I saw a man in the row behind leaning forward and studying me carefully.

'It *is* Mr Ryder, isn't it? My goodness, it is. Please forgive me, I've been sitting here all this time, I didn't recognise you in this poor light. I'm Karl Pedersen. I'd been so looking forward to meeting you at the reception this morning. But of course unforeseeable circumstances prevented you from attending. How opportune I should now meet you like this.'

The man had white hair, glasses and a kindly face. I adjusted my posture slightly.

'Ah yes, Mr Pedersen. I'm very pleased to make your acquaintance. It was, as you say, all very unfortunate this morning. I too had been greatly looking forward to, er, to meeting you all.'

'As it happens, Mr Ryder, there are several other councillors here now in this cinema, all of whom were most sorry to miss you this morning.' He looked about in the darkness. 'If I can just ascertain where they're sitting, I'd like to take you over to meet at least one or two of them.' Twisting round, he craned his neck to search the rows behind him. 'Unfortunately, just now I can't see anyone . . .'

'Of course I'd be very pleased to meet your colleagues. But it's rather late now, and if they're enjoying the film, perhaps we should leave it to another time. There are bound to be many more opportunities.'

'I can't see anyone just now,' the man said, turning back to me.

'What a pity. I know they're in this cinema somewhere. In any case, sir, as a member of the civic council, may I say how pleased and honoured we all are by your visit?'

'You're very kind.'

'Mr Brodsky has by all accounts made very good progress at the concert hall this afternoon. Three or four hours solid rehearsing.'

'Yes, I heard. It's splendid.'

'I wonder, sir, if you managed today to visit our concert hall.'

'The concert hall? Well, no. Unfortunately I've not yet had the chance . . .'

'Of course. You had a long journey coming here. Well, there's still plenty of time. I'm sure you'll be impressed by our concert hall, Mr Ryder. It really is a beautiful old building, and whatever else we've let deteriorate in this city, no one can accuse us of neglecting our concert hall. A very beautiful old building, and set in the most splendid surroundings too. That's to say, in Liebmann Park. You'll see what I mean, Mr Ryder. A pleasant walk through the trees, and then you come to the clearing – and there! The concert hall! You'll see for yourself, sir. An ideal place for the community to gather, away from the bustle of the streets. I remember when I was a boy, there was a city orchestra in those days, and the first Sunday of each month everyone would gather in that clearing before the concert. I can remember all the various families arriving, everyone smartly dressed, more and more people arriving through the trees and greeting one another. And we children, we'd be running everywhere. In the autumn we had a game, a special game. We'd rush around gathering up all the fallen leaves we could see, bring them up to the gardener's shed and pile them up against the side. There was a particular plank, about this high on the wall of the shed, it had a stain on it. What we told each other was that we had to collect enough leaves so that the pile reached up to that stain before the adults started to file into the building. If we didn't, the whole city was going to explode into a million pieces, some such thing. So there we all were, rushing back and forth, our arms full of wet leaves! It's easy for someone of my age to become nostalgic, Mr Ryder, but there's no doubt about it, this was a very happy community once. There were large happy families here. And real lasting friendships.

People treated one another with warmth and affection. We had a splendid community here once. For many many years. I'll be seventy-six next birthday, so I can vouch personally for that.'

Pedersen fell silent for a moment. He continued to lean forward, his arm on the back of my seat, and when I glanced at him I noticed his eyes were not on the screen but somewhere far away. Meanwhile, we were approaching that section of the film in which the astronauts first suspect the motives of the computer, HAL, central to every aspect of life aboard the spaceship. Clint Eastwood was stalking the claustrophobic corridors with a terse expression and a long-barrelled gun. I was just starting to become engrossed when Pedersen began to talk again.

'I have to be honest. I can't help feeling a little sorry for *him*. Mr Christoff, I mean. Yes, odd as this may sound to you, I feel *sorry* for him. I've said as much to a few colleagues and they've just thought, oh, the old fellow's going soft, who can feel an ounce of pity for that charlatan? But, you see, I have a better memory of it than most. I remember what happened at the time Mr Christoff first arrived in this city. Of course I feel as angry as any of my colleagues about him. But, you see, I know well enough that at the start, right at the start of it, it wasn't Mr Christoff that pushed himself forward. No, no, it was . . . well, it was *us*. That's to say, people like myself, I don't deny it, I was in a position of influence. We encouraged him. We celebrated him, flattered him, made it clear we looked to him for enlightenment and initiative. At least some of the responsibility for what happened lies with us. My younger colleagues, they perhaps weren't around so much in those early years. They only know Mr Christoff as this dominant figure around which so much revolved. They forget that he never asked to be put in such a position. Oh yes, I remember very well Mr Christoff first arriving in this city. He was a fairly young man then, on his own, very unassuming, modest even. If no one had encouraged him, I'm sure he'd have been happy to melt into the background, give the odd recital at a private function, nothing more. But it was the timing, Mr Ryder. The timing was unfortunate. Just when Mr Christoff turned up in our city, we were going through, well, a sort of hiatus. Mr Bernd, the painter, and Mr Vollmöller, a very fine composer, both of whom had for so long been at the helm of our cultural life here, they'd both died within months of each other and there was a certain feeling . . . well, a kind of *unsettled* feeling. We were all very sad at the passing of two such fine men, but I suppose everyone felt too that now there was a chance for a change. A chance for something new and fresh. Inevitably, happy as we'd all been, after so many years of those two gentlemen being at the centre of everything, certain frustrations had built up. So you can imagine, when word got around that the stranger lodging at Mrs Roth's was a professional cellist and one who'd performed with the Gothenburg Symphony Orchestra, and on several occasions under Kazimierz Studzinski, well, there was not a little excitement. I remember personally having much to do with the welcoming of Mr Christoff. I remember, you see, how it was, and also how unassuming he was at first. Now, with hindsight, I'd even say he was lacking in confidence. Most likely he'd had a few setbacks prior to coming here. But we fussed over him, pressed him for his views on everything, yes, that's how it all started. I remember personally helping to persuade him about that first recital. He was genuinely reluctant. And in any case, that first recital was originally to be just a small affair, to take place at the Countess's house. It was only two days before the date, when it became clear how many people were determined to attend, that the Countess was forced to move the venue to the Holtmann Gallery. From then on, Mr Christoff's recitals – we demanded at least one every six months – they were held at the concert hall, and they became our great talking points, year in, year out. But he was reluctant at the beginning. Not just that first time. For the first few years, we had to keep persuading him. Then naturally the acclaim, the applause, the flattery, they did their work, and soon enough Mr Christoff was putting himself and his ideas about. "I've flowered here," he was heard to say a lot around that time. "I've flowered since coming here." My point, you see, sir, was that it was *we* who pushed *him*. I do feel sorry for him now – though I dare say I'm probably the only person in this city who does. As you've noticed, there's a lot of anger directed at him. I'm realistic enough about the situation, Mr Ryder. One has to be ruthless. Our city is close to crisis. There's widespread misery. We have to start putting things right somewhere and we might as well start at the centre. We have to be ruthless, and as sorry as I feel for him, I can see there's nothing else for it. He and everything he has come to represent must now be put away in some dark corner of our history.'

Although I had continued to sit slightly turned towards him, thus making it clear I had not stopped listening, my attention had been drawn back to the movie. Clint Eastwood was talking into a microphone to his wife back on earth and tears were flowing down his face. I realised we were coming close to the famous scene in which Yul Brynner comes into the room and tests Eastwood's speed on the draw by clapping his hands in front of him.

'Excuse me,' I said, 'but how long ago was it Mr Christoff came to this town?'

I had asked this without a great deal of thought, at least half my attention on the screen. In fact I went on watching the movie for another two or three minutes before realising that behind me Pedersen was hanging his head in an attitude of profound shame. Sensing that my gaze had returned to him, he looked up and said:

'You're very right, Mr Ryder. Very right to reprimand us. Seventeen years and seven months. That's a long time. A mistake such as ours might have been made anywhere, but then not to rectify it for so long? I can see how we must look to an outsider, to someone like yourself, sir, and I feel thoroughly ashamed, let me say so. I make no excuses. It took us an eternity to admit our error. Not, I dare say, to *see* it. But to admit it, even to ourselves, that was difficult and took a long time. We had, you see, plunged deep with Mr Christoff. Virtually every council member had at some time invited him to his house. He had been regularly seated next to Mr von Winterstein at the annual civic banquets. His photograph had adorned the cover of our city almanac. He had written the introduction to the programme for the Roggenkamp Exhibition. There were yet other implications. Things had gone further. There was for instance the unfortunate case of Mr Liebrich. Ah, but excuse me, I think I've just spotted Mr Kollmann over there' – he craned his neck again, looking towards the back of the cinema – 'yes, that's Mr Kollmann, and with him, if I'm not mistaken, it's so difficult to see in this light, with him is Mr Schaefer. Both these gentlemen attended this morning's welcoming reception and I know they'd both be utterly delighted to meet you. Furthermore, on this matter we're discussing, I'm sure both these gentlemen will have much to say. I wonder if you'd care to go over and meet them.'

'I'd be honoured. But just now you were about to tell me . . .'

'Ah yes, of course. The unfortunate case of Mr Liebrich. You see, sir, for many years before Mr Christoff's arrival, Mr Liebrich had been one of our most respected violin teachers. He taught the children of the best families. He was highly admired. Now Mr Christoff, not long after his first recital, was asked his opinion on Mr Liebrich and he let it be known that he didn't care much for Mr Liebrich at all. Not for his playing nor his teaching methods. By the time of Mr Liebrich's death a few years ago, he had lost virtually everything. His pupils, his friends, his place in society. That was just one case that sprang to mind. To admit that we'd been wrong about Mr Christoff all along – can you imagine the enormity of it, sir? Yes, we were weak, I admit it. Then again we had no idea things would reach the present level of crisis. People seemed by and large happy still. Year after year slipped by and if some of us had doubts we kept them to ourselves. But I don't defend our negligence, sir, not for a second. And I, in my position on the council at that time, I know I'm as culpable as anyone. In the end, and I feel thoroughly ashamed to admit this, in the end it was the people of this city, the ordinary people who forced us to face up to our responsibilities. The ordinary people, their lives by this point growing ever more miserable, were at least a clear step ahead of us. I remember the exact moment this fact first dawned on me. It was three years ago, I was walking home after the latest of Mr Christoff's recitals – it was, I remember, Kazan's *Grotesqueries for Cello and Three Flutes*. I was hurrying home through the darkness of Liebmann Park, it was quite chilly, and I could see Mr Kohler the chemist walking a little way in front of me. I knew he'd also been at the concert and so I caught up with him and we started talking. At first I was careful to keep my thoughts to myself, but eventually I asked him if he'd enjoyed Mr Christoff's recital. Yes, he had, Mr Kohler said. There must have been something about the way he'd said it, because I recall asking him again a few moments later if he'd enjoyed the concert. This time Mr Kohler said yes, he'd enjoyed himself, but perhaps Mr Christoff's performance had been a little functional. Yes, "functional" was the word he used. As you can imagine, sir, I thought carefully before I next spoke. In the end I decided to throw caution to the wind, and I said: "Mr Kohler, I tend to agree with you. There was a certain dryness to it all." To which Mr Kohler remarked that "cold" was the word that had sprung to his mind. By then we'd reached the park gates. We wished each other good night and parted. But I remember I hardly slept that night, Mr Ryder. Ordinary people, decent citizens like Mr Kohler were now expressing such views. It was clear the pretence could no longer continue. It was time for us – all of us in positions of influence – to own up to our error, however far-reaching the implication. Ah, but excuse me, that is most definitely Mr Schaefer seated beside Mr Kollmann. Both of those gentlemen will, I know, have interesting viewpoints about what occurred. Being a generation younger than myself, they'll have seen things from a slightly different angle. Besides, I know how much they were longing to meet you this morning. Please, let's go over.'

Pedersen got to his feet and I watched his crouched figure edging down the row muttering apologies. On reaching the aisle, he straightened and gestured to me. Weary though I was, there seemed nothing for it but to join him, and I too rose and began to make my way towards the aisle. As I did so, I noticed that an almost festive mood was pervading the cinema. Everywhere people were exchanging jokes and little remarks as they watched the film, and no one seemed to mind at all my pushing past. On the contrary, people seemed to tuck their legs to one side or jump to a standing position with eagerness. A few people even rolled right back in their seats, feet stuck up in the air, squealing with delight as they did so.

Once I reached the aisle, Pedersen began to lead the way up the carpeted slope. Somewhere among the rear stalls, he halted and with an ushering motion said:

'After you, Mr Ryder.'

9

I once more found myself pushing past people, this time with Pedersen directly behind me, whispering apologies on our behalf. Before long we came upon a group of several men huddled together. It took me a moment to ascertain that a game of cards was in progress, some participants leaning forward from the row behind, while others leaned back from the row in front. They looked up as we approached, and when Pedersen announced me they all rose to a half-standing position. They seated themselves again only when I was comfortably installed in their midst, and I found myself shaking numerous hands proffered out of the darkness.

The man nearest me was dressed in a business suit, with his collar unbuttoned and his tie loosened. He smelt of whisky and I noticed he was having difficulty focusing on me. His companion, looking over his shoulder, was thin, with an oddly freckled face, and seemed more sober, though he too had his tie loosened. I did not have time to take in the rest of the company before the drunken man shook my hand a second time, saying:

'I hope you're enjoying the film, sir.'

'I am indeed. In fact, it happens to be one of my all-time favourites.'

'Ah. Well then, it's fortunate that's what's showing tonight. Yes, I too like this film. A classic. Mr Ryder, would you care to take over this hand?' He held his cards up to my face.

'No thank you. Please don't interrupt your game on my account.'

'I was just telling Mr Ryder,' Pedersen said behind me, 'that life here wasn't always the way it is today. Even you gentlemen who are younger than me, I'm sure you'll be able to vouch . . .'

'Ah yes, the good old days,' the drunken man said dreamily. 'Ah yes. Things were good here in the good old days.'

'Theo's thinking about Rosa Klenner,' said the freckled man behind him, causing laughter all around.

'Nonsense,' the drunken man protested. 'And stop trying to embarrass me in front of our distinguished guest.'

'Oh yes, oh yes,' his friend went on. 'In those days Theo here was completely in love with Rosa Klenner. That's to say, the present Mrs Christoff.'

'I was never in love with her. Anyway, I was already married by then.'

'All the more pitiful then, Theo. All the more pitiful.'

'It's complete nonsense.'

'I can remember, Theo,' a new voice said from the row behind, 'you used to bore us for hours talking about Rosa Klenner.'

'I didn't know her true nature in those days.'

'It was precisely her true nature that appealed to you,' the voice went on. 'You've always hankered after women who wouldn't look at you for three seconds.'

'There's some truth in that,' the freckled man said.

'There's no truth at all . . .'

'No, let me explain to Mr Ryder.' The freckled man put his hand on his drunken friend's shoulder and leaned towards me. 'The present Mrs Christoff – we still tend to call her Rosa Klenner – she's a local girl, one of us, grew up with us. She's still a beautiful woman, and in those days, well, she had us all captivated. She was very beautiful and very distant. She used to work at the Schlegel Gallery, which has closed now. She used to be there behind a desk, no more than an attendant really. She used to be there on Tuesdays and Thursdays . . .'

'Tuesdays and *Fridays*,' the drunken man interrupted.

'Tuesdays and Fridays. Sorry. Naturally, Theo would remember. After all, he used to go to the gallery – it was just this little white room – he used to go there all the time and pretend to be looking at the exhibits.'

'Nonsense . . .'

'You weren't the only one, were you, Theo? You had a lot of rivals. Jürgen Haase. Erich Brull. Even Heinz Wodak. They were all regulars.'

'And Otto Röscher,' Theo said nostalgically. 'He was often there.'

'Was that so? Yes, Rosa had a lot of admirers.'

'I never spoke to her,' Theo said. 'Except once, when I asked her for a catalogue.'

'The thing that became apparent about Rosa,' the freckled man continued, 'ever since we were all teenagers, was that as far as she was concerned all the local males were beneath her. She developed a reputation for turning down advances in the cruellest possible ways. That's why poor souls like Theo here, very wisely, never said a word to her. But then whenever someone of note, an artist, a musician, a writer, someone like that passed through the town, she'd pursue them with no shame whatsoever. She was always on this or that committee, which meant she had access to virtually every celebrity visiting the town. She'd get to go to all the receptions and half an hour into an event she'd have the guest in a corner, talking and talking, staring into his eyes. Of course, there was a lot of speculation – about her sexual behaviour, I mean – but no one could ever prove anything. She was always very clever. But if you saw the way she flung herself at visiting celebrities, you couldn't doubt she'd have relations with at least some of them. She certainly charmed a whole lot of them, she was extremely attractive. But as for the local men, she wouldn't look at them.'

'Hans Jongboed always claimed to have had a fling with her,' the man called Theo put in. This caused much laughter, several voices nearby repeating derisively: 'Hans Jongboed!' Pedersen, however, was stirring uneasily.

'Gentlemen,' he began, 'Mr Ryder and I were just discussing . . .'

'I never spoke to her. Except that once. To ask for a catalogue.'

'Ah, Theo, never mind.' The freckled man slapped his friend on the back, causing the latter to slump forward a little. 'Never mind. Look at her plight now.'

Theo seemed lost in thought. 'She was like that about everything,' he said. 'Not just about love. She'd only really have any time for members of the artistic circle, and then only for the real elite. You couldn't get any respect from her otherwise. She was disliked here. Long before she ever married Christoff, she was disliked.'

'If she wasn't so beautiful,' the freckled man said to me, 'she'd have been universally hated. As it was, there were always men like Theo here willing to fall under her spell. Anyway, Christoff arrived in this town. A professional cellist, and one with a distinguished track record! Rosa made a completely unashamed go for him. Didn't seem to care what any of us thought. She knew what she wanted and went about it quite ruthlessly. It was admirable in an appalling sort of way. Christoff was charmed and they got married during his first year here. Christoff was what she'd been waiting for all that time. Well, I hope she's got her money's worth. Sixteen years of being his wife. It hasn't been so bad. But what now? He's finished here. What's she going to do now?'

'She won't even get a job in a gallery now,' Theo said. 'She's hurt us too much over the years. Hurt our pride. She's through in this city, every bit as much as Christoff himself.'

'One school of thought has it,' the freckled man said, 'that Rosa will leave town with Christoff and not ditch him until they're well settled elsewhere. But Mr Dremmler here' – he indicated someone in the row in front – 'is convinced she'll stay on here.'

The man in the row in front turned at the mention of his name. Evidently he had been listening to the discussion, for he now said with some authority: 'What you've got to remember about Rosa Klenner is that she's got a really timid side to her. I was at school with her, we were in the same year. She's always had it, that side to her, and it's her curse. This city isn't good enough for her, but she's too timid to leave. You notice, for all her ambitions, she's never attempted to leave us. This timid side to her, a lot of people don't notice it, but it's there. That's why my bet's on her staying. She'll stay and try her luck again here. She'll be hoping to hook some other celebrity passing through. After all, she's still a beautiful woman for her age.'

A high reedy voice somewhere nearby said: 'Maybe she'll go for Brodsky.'

This provoked the largest burst of laughter yet.

'It's perfectly possible,' the voice went on in a mock-hurt tone. 'All right, he's old, but she's no longer so young. And who else is there here in her league?' Again there was much laughter, spurring the speaker on. 'In fact, Brodsky's the best course for her. I'd recommend it to her. Anything else and all the resentment the town now feels towards Christoff will stay with her. But if she becomes Brodsky's mistress, or even Brodsky's *wife*, ah, by far the best way to obliterate her connection with Christoff. And it means she can just carry on in her . . . her present *position*.'

By this point there was laughter all around us, with people even three rows in front turning and displaying their mirth. Next to me, Pedersen cleared his throat.

'Gentlemen, please,' he said. 'I'm disappointed. What will Mr Ryder make of all this? You're still thinking of Mr Brodsky – *Mr* Brodsky, please – you're still thinking of him in the old way. You're making yourselves look foolish. Mr Brodsky is no longer a figure of fun. Whatever one thinks of Mr Schmidt's proposition about Mrs Christoff, Mr Brodsky is *not* in any case an amusing option . . .'

'It's good of you to have come here, Mr Ryder,' Theo cut in. 'But it's too late. Things have just reached a point here, it's just too late . . .'

'That's rubbish, Theo,' Pedersen said. 'We're at a turning point, an important turning point. Mr Ryder has come here to tell us that. Haven't you, sir?'

'Yes . . .'

'It's too late. We've lost it. Why don't we resign ourselves to being just another cold, lonely city? Other cities have. At least we'll be moving with the tide. The soul of this town, it's not sick, Mr Ryder, it's dead. It's too late now. Ten years ago, perhaps. There was still a chance then. But not now. Mr Pedersen' – the drunken man pointed limply at my companion – 'you, sir. It was you and Mr Thomas. And Mr Stika. All you good gentlemen. You all *prevaricated* . . .'

'Let's not have this again, Theo,' the freckled man broke in. 'Mr Pedersen's right. It's not quite yet time for such resignation. We've found Brodsky – *Mr* Brodsky – and for all we know he may be . . .'

'Brodsky, Brodsky. It's too late. We're done for now. Let's just be a cold modern city and be done with it.'

I felt Pedersen's hand on my arm. 'Mr Ryder, I'm very sorry . . .'

'You *prevaricated*, sir! Seventeen years. Seventeen years, Christoff's been left to get on with things unchallenged. And what do you offer us now? Brodsky! Mr Ryder, it's too late.'

'I'm truly sorry,' Pedersen said to me, 'you've had to listen to such talk.'

Someone behind us said: 'Theo, you're just drunk and depressed. Tomorrow morning you'll have to search out Mr Ryder and apologise to him.'

'Well,' I said, 'I'm interested to hear all sides of the discussion . . .'

'But this is no side at all!' Pedersen protested. 'I assure you, Mr Ryder, Theo's sentiments are not in the least typical of what people here are now feeling. Everywhere, in the streets, in the trams, I sense a tremendous feeling, a feeling of optimism.'

This brought a general murmur of agreement.

'Don't believe it, Mr Ryder,' Theo said, grasping my sleeve. 'You're here on a fool's errand. Let's take a quick poll here in this cinema. Let's ask a few of the people here . . .'

'Mr Ryder,' Pedersen said quickly, 'I'm going to go home, turn in for the night. It's a wonderful film, but I've seen it a number of times already. And you yourself, sir, you must be getting tired.'

'Actually, I'm very tired indeed. I might leave with you, if I may.' Then, turning, I said to the others: 'Excuse me, gentlemen, but I think I'll now return to my hotel.'

'But Mr Ryder,' the freckled man said, concern in his voice, 'please don't go just yet. You must stay at least until the astronaut dismantles HAL.'

'Mr Ryder,' a voice said from further down the row, 'perhaps you'd care to take over my hand here. I've had enough of this game for tonight. And it's always so hard to see the cards in this sort of light. My eyesight isn't what it used to be.'

'You're very kind, but really I must go.'

I was about to exchange good nights, but Pedersen was already on his feet and starting to edge his way out. I followed on behind him, giving a few waves back to the company as I went.

Pedersen was clearly upset by what had taken place, for when we reached the aisle he continued walking silently with his head down. As we left the auditorium, I threw a last glance towards the screen and saw Clint Eastwood preparing for the dismantling of HAL, carefully checking over his giant screwdriver.

The night outside – its deathly hush, the chill, the thickening mist

– was such a contrast to the warm hubbub in the cinema that we both paused on the pavement as though to regain our bearings.

'Mr Ryder, I don't know what to say,' Pedersen said. 'Theo's an excellent fellow, but sometimes after a big dinner . . .' He shook his head despondently.

'Let's not worry. Hard-working people need to unwind. I very much enjoyed the evening.'

'I feel thoroughly ashamed . . .'

'Please. Let's forget it. Really, I enjoyed myself.'

We began to walk, our footsteps echoing in the empty street. For a time, Pedersen maintained a preoccupied silence. Then he said:

'You must believe me, sir. We've never underestimated the difficulties of introducing such an idea to our community. I mean, this idea of Mr Brodsky. I can assure you we've gone about everything with considerable caution.'

'Yes, I'm sure that's so.'

'At the start we took great care to whom we even mentioned the idea. It was vital that only those most likely to be sympathetic should hear of it during the earlier stages. Then, via these persons, we allowed the thing to seep out slowly to the public at large. That way we ensured that the whole notion was presented in the most positive light. At the same time, we took other measures. For instance, we gave a series of dinners in Mr Brodsky's honour to which we invited carefully chosen guests from our higher ranks. At first these dinners were small and virtually secret, but gradually we have been able to spread our net wider and wider, gaining more and more support for our position. At any important public event, too, we've made sure Mr Brodsky has been seen amidst the dignitaries. When the Peking Ballet came here, for instance, we had him seated in the same box as Mr and Mrs Weiss. Then of course, at the personal level, we've all made a point when referring to him of employing only the most respectful tones. We've been working hard at it now for two years, and by and large we've been very satisfied. The general picture of him has definitely been changing. So much so that we judged it time to take this vital step. That's why it was so discouraging just now. Those gentlemen in there, they're the very ones who should be setting an example. If *they* revert to such an attitude each time they unwind a little, how can we ever expect the people at large . . .' He trailed off and shook his head again. 'I feel let down. On my behalf and on yours, Mr Ryder.'

He became silent again. After we had not spoken for a while, I said with a sigh:

'Public opinion is never easy to shift.'

Pedersen remained silent for a few more steps, then said: 'You have to consider our starting point. When you look at it that way, when you consider our starting point, then I think you'll see we *have* made considerable progress. You must understand, sir, Mr Brodsky's been living here with us now for a long time, and in all those years no one had heard him talk about, let alone play, any music. Yes, we'd all vaguely known he'd once been a conductor in his old country. But you see, because we never saw anything of that side of him, we never thought of him like that. In fact, to be frank, until recently, Mr Brodsky was really only ever noticed when he got very drunk and went staggering about the town shouting. The rest of the time he was just this recluse who lived with his dog up by the north highway. Well, that's not quite true, he was also seen regularly at the library. Two or three mornings a week he'd come into the library, take his usual seat beneath the windows and tie his dog to the table leg. It's against the rules, to bring the dog in, but the librarians long ago decided it was the simplest thing, just to let him bring it in. Far simpler than starting a fight with Mr Brodsky. So you sometimes saw him there, his dog at his feet, thumbing through his pile of books – always these same turgid-looking volumes of history. And if anyone in the room started even the briefest of whispered exchanges, even merely greeted someone, he'd stand up and bellow at the culprit. Theoretically, of course, he was in the right. But then we've never been so strict about silence in our library. People like to talk a little when they meet, after all, as in any other public place. And when you think that Mr Brodsky was himself breaking the rules bringing his dog in, it's not surprising there was this notion that his behaviour was unreasonable. But then just every once in a while, on certain mornings, a particular mood would descend on him. He'd be there reading at the table and then this forlorn look would come over him. You'd notice him sitting there, staring off into space, sometimes with tears welling in his eyes. Once that happened, people would know it was all right to talk. Usually someone would test the water first. And if Mr Brodsky made no response, then very quickly the whole room would start talking. Sometimes – people are so perverse! – the library becomes much noisier on such occasions than at any time when Mr Brodsky is absent. I remember one morning going in to return a book and the place sounded like a railway station. I had virtually to shout to make myself heard at the issue desk. And there was Mr Brodsky, very still in the middle of it all, in a world of his own. I must say he was a sad sight. The morning light made him look rather feeble. There was a droplet on the end of his nose, his eyes seemed so far away and he'd quite forgotten the page he was holding. And it occurred to me it was a little cruel, the way the atmosphere had turned. It was as though they were taking advantage of him, though I'm not quite sure in what sense. But you see, another morning, he'd have been quite capable of silencing the lot of them in an instant. Well anyway, Mr Ryder, what I'm trying to say is that for many years that's who Mr Brodsky was to us. I suppose it's too much to expect people to change *completely* their view of him in such a relatively short time. Considerable progress has been made, but as you saw just now ...' Again, exasperation seemed to overtake him. 'But *they* should know better,' he muttered to himself.

We came to a halt at a crossroad. The fog had got much thicker and I had lost my bearings. Pedersen glanced around, then began to walk again, leading me down a narrow street with rows of cars parked on the pavements.

'I'll see you to your hotel, Mr Ryder. I might as well go home this way as any other. The hotel is to your satisfaction, I trust?'

'Oh yes, it's fine.'

'Mr Hoffman runs a fine establishment. He's an excellent manager and an excellent fellow all round. Of course, as you know, it's Mr Hoffman we have to thank for Mr Brodsky's, er, recovery.'

'Ah yes, of course.'

For a little while the cars on the pavement obliged us to walk in single file. Then we drifted out into the middle of the street, and when I drew up alongside him I saw that Pedersen's mood had lightened. He smiled and said:

'I understand you're going to the Countess's house tomorrow

to listen to those records. Our mayor, Mr von Winterstein, I know he intends to join you there. He's very keen to take you aside and talk matters over with you. But the main thing, of course, is those records. Extraordinary!'

'Yes. I'm very much looking forward to it all.'

'The Countess is a remarkable lady. Time and again she's demonstrated a dimension to her thinking that puts the rest of us to shame. I've asked her more than once what on earth gave her the idea in the first place. "A hunch," she always says. "I woke up one morning with this hunch." What a lady! It could have been no easy task, obtaining those gramophone records. But she managed, using a specialist dealer in Berlin. Of course the rest of us knew nothing of it at the time, and I dare say if we had we'd have just laughed at the whole idea. And then she summoned us one evening to her residence. Just two years ago last month, a very pleasant, sunny evening. So there we all were, eleven of us, gathered in her drawing room, none of us knowing quite what to expect. She served us refreshments, then almost immediately began to address us. We had fretted long enough, she said. It was time we acted. Time we admitted how misguided we had been and took some positive steps to repair the damage as best we could. Otherwise our grandchildren, their children after them, would never forgive us. Well, none of this was new, we'd been repeating such sentiments to each other for months by that point and we all just nodded, made the usual noises. But then the Countess continued. As far as Mr Christoff was concerned, she said, little further action was necessary. He was now thoroughly discredited in every walk of life throughout the city. But that in itself was hardly sufficient to put into reverse the spiral of misery gaining ever greater momentum at the heart of our community. We had somehow to build a new mood, a new era. We all nodded to this, but again, Mr Ryder, these were sentiments we had exchanged many times before. I believe Mr von Winterstein even said as much, though in the most courteous sort of way. This was when the Countess started to reveal just what was in her mind. The solution, she declared, had quite possibly been in our midst the whole time. She proceeded to explain herself further and, well, at first, naturally, we could hardly believe our ears. Mr Brodsky? Of the library and the drunken walks? Was she

112

seriously talking about Mr *Brodsky*? Had it been anyone other than the Countess, I'm sure we'd have fallen about laughing. But the Countess, I remember, remained very sure of herself. She suggested we all make ourselves comfortable, she had some music for us to listen to. To listen to very carefully. Then she began to play those records to us, one after the other. We sat there and listened, the sun going down outside. The recording quality was poor. The Countess's stereogram, you'll see tomorrow, it's a somewhat dated affair. But none of this mattered. Within minutes the music had cast a spell over us all, had lulled us into a deeply tranquil mood. Some of us had tears in our eyes. We realised we were listening to something we had so sorely missed over the years. Suddenly it seemed more incomprehensible than ever that we should have come to celebrate someone like Mr Christoff. Here we were, listening to true music again. The work of a conductor not only immensely gifted, but who *shared our values*. Then the music stopped, we stood up and stretched our legs – we'd been listening for well over three hours – and then, well, the idea of Mr Brodsky – Mr Brodsky! – seemed as absurd as ever. The recordings were very old, we pointed out. And Mr Brodsky for reasons best known to himself had abandoned music a long time ago. And besides, he had his . . . his problems. One could hardly call him the same person. We were soon all shaking our heads. But then the Countess spoke up again. We were approaching crisis point. We had to keep an open mind. We had to seek out Mr Brodsky, talk with him, ascertain the present state of his powers. None of us needed reminding, surely, of the urgency of the situation. Each of us could recount dozens of sad cases. Of lives blighted by loneliness. Of families despairing of ever rediscovering the happiness they'd once taken for granted. It was at this point that Mr Hoffman, the manager of your hotel, suddenly cleared his throat and declared that he would see to Mr Brodsky. He would take it upon himself – he said this all very solemnly, he actually stood up to do so – he would take it upon himself to assess the situation, and if there was any hope at all of rehabilitating Mr Brodsky, then he, Mr Hoffman, would take personal charge. If we would entrust him with this task, he would vow to us not to let the community down. That was, as I say, just over two years ago. Since then we've watched with astonishment the dedication with which Mr Hoffman has gone about fulfilling his promise. The progress, if not always smooth, has been remarkable overall. And now Mr Brodsky is, well, he has been brought to his present condition. So much so that we felt we should wait no longer to take the crucial step. After all, we can only go so far simply *presenting* Mr Brodsky in a better light. At some point, the people of this town have to judge with their own eyes and ears. Well, so far, every indication is that we have not been over-ambitious. Mr Brodsky has been rehearsing regularly, and by all accounts has won fully the respect of the orchestra. It may be a great many years since he last gave a public performance, but it seems little has been lost. That passion, that fine vision we encountered in the Countess's drawing room that evening, it's all been waiting somewhere deep inside and is now steadily re-awakening. Yes, we have every confidence he will do us all proud come Thursday night. Meanwhile, for our part, we have done everything in our power to ensure the success of the evening. The Stuttgart Nagel Foundation Orchestra, as you know, if not of the very highest rank, is very well respected. Its services do not come cheaply. Nevertheless, there was hardly a dissenting voice over our hiring them for this most important of occasions, nor about the period involved. At first, two weeks' rehearsal time had been envisaged, but in the end, with full support from the Finance Committee, we stretched it to three weeks. Three weeks board and hospitality for a visiting orchestra, on top of fees, you can see, sir, it is no small undertaking. But there was hardly a whisper of opposition. Each council member has now come to understand the importance of Thursday night. Everyone sees that Mr Brodsky must be given every chance. For all that' – Pedersen suddenly heaved a sigh – 'for all that, as you saw yourself this very evening, old ingrained ideas are hard to erase. This is precisely why your help, Mr Ryder, your agreeing to come to our humble city may prove absolutely crucial to us. The people will listen to you in a way they would never listen to one of us. In fact, sir, I can tell you, the mood in this town has altered simply at the news of your arrival. There's the greatest anticipation building up around what you'll tell us on Thursday night. In the trams, in the cafés, people are talking of virtually nothing else. Of course, I don't know precisely what you've prepared for us. Perhaps you've taken care not to paint too rosy a picture. Perhaps you'll warn us of the hard work that lies ahead for each one of us if we're ever to re-discover the happiness we once had. You'll be very right to give us such warnings. But I know too how skilfully you'll appeal to the positive, public-spirited part of your listener. One thing in any case is certain. When you finish speaking, no one in this city will ever again look at Mr Brodsky and see the shabby old drunk they once did. Ah, I can see you looking concerned, Mr Ryder. Please don't worry. We may look like a backwater town, but there are certain sorts of occasions at which we excel. Mr Hoffman in particular has been working hard to structure a truly magnificent evening. Rest assured, sir, every citizen of any standing will attend. And as for Mr Brodsky himself, as I say, I'm sure he won't let us down. He'll surpass everyone's expectations, I'm certain of it.'

In fact the look on my face noted by Pedersen had not to do with 'concern', so much as the growing annoyance I was feeling towards myself. For the truth was that my forthcoming address to this city was not only far from ready, I had yet to complete even the background research. I could not understand how with all my experience I had arrived at such a state of affairs. I remembered how that very afternoon in the hotel's elegant atrium, I had sat sipping the strong bitter coffee, reiterating to myself the importance of planning the rest of the day with care so as to make the best use of the very limited time. As I had sat watching the misty fountain in the mirror behind the bar, I had even pictured myself in a situation not unlike the one I had just encountered at the cinema, making a striking impression on the company with my easy authority over the range of local issues, producing at least one spontaneous witticism at Christoff's expense memorable enough to be quoted throughout the town the next day. Instead I had allowed myself to be deflected by other matters, with the result that, during my entire time at the cinema, I had been unable to manage a single noteworthy comment. It was even possible I had created the impression of being less than urbane. Suddenly I felt again an intense irritation with Sophie for the chaos she had caused and for the way she had obliged me to compromise so thoroughly my usual standards.

We came to a halt again and I realised we were standing in front of the hotel.

'Well, it's been a great pleasure,' Pedersen said, holding out his hand to me. 'I look forward to enjoying more of your company over the coming days. But now you must get some rest.'

I thanked him, wished him a good night and entered the lobby as his footsteps faded away into the darkness.

The young desk clerk was still on duty. 'I hope you enjoyed the movie, sir,' he said, handing me my key.

'I did, very much. Thank you for suggesting it. It was very relaxing.'

'Yes, many guests find it a good way to round off the day. Oh, Gustav reports that Boris was very happy with his room and went off to sleep immediately.'

'Ah, good.'

I wished him a good night and hurried across to the elevator.

I arrived in my room feeling very grimy after the long day and, changing into my dressing gown, began to prepare for a shower. But then, as I was investigating the bathroom, an intense surge of weariness came over me, so that it was virtually all I could do to stagger back to my bed and collapse on top of it, sinking at once into a deep sleep.

10

I had not been asleep long when the telephone rang beside my ear. I let it ring for a while, then finally sat up on the bed and picked up the receiver.

'Ah, Mr Ryder. It's me. Hoffman.'

I waited for him to explain why he was disturbing me, but the hotel manager did not continue. There was an awkward silence and then he said again:

'It's me, sir. Hoffman.' There was another pause, then he said: 'I'm down here in the lobby.'

'Oh yes.'

'I'm sorry, Mr Ryder, perhaps you were in the middle of something.'

'Actually I was just getting a little sleep.'

This remark seemed to stun Hoffman, for there followed another silence. I laughed quickly and said:

'What I meant was, I was lying down, as it were. Naturally I won't be having a full sleep until . . . until all the day's business is concluded.'

'Quite, quite.' Hoffman sounded relieved. 'Just catching your breath, so to speak. Very understandable. Well, in any case, I shall be here in the lobby waiting for you, sir.'

I put down the receiver and sat on the bed wondering what to do. I felt as exhausted as ever – I could not have slept more than a few minutes – and it was tempting to forget the whole matter and simply go back to sleep. But I eventually saw the impossibility of doing so and got to my feet.

 I discovered I had fallen asleep in my dressing gown, and I was about to remove it and get dressed when it occurred to me I might go down and deal with Hoffman still wearing it. At this time of night, after all, I was unlikely to encounter anyone except Hoffman and the desk clerk, and my going down in such attire would emphasise subtly but pointedly the lateness of the hour and the fact that he was keeping me from my sleep. I stepped out into the corridor and made my way to the elevator feeling not a little annoyed.

Initially at least, the dressing gown seemed to have the desired impact, for Hoffman's opening words as I entered the lobby were: 'I'm sorry to have disturbed your rest, Mr Ryder. It must be so tiring for you, all this travelling.'

I made no attempt to hide my weariness. Passing a hand through my hair, I said: 'It's perfectly all right, Mr Hoffman. But I trust this won't take too long. I am, in fact, feeling pretty tired now.'

'Oh, this won't take long, not long at all.'

'Fine.'

I noticed that Hoffman was wearing a raincoat and, underneath it, full evening dress with cummerbund and bow tie.

'You'll have heard, of course, the bad news,' he said.

'The bad news?'

'It's bad news, but let me say, sir, I am confident, very confident, it will not lead to anything serious. And before the evening is out, I trust you will be equally convinced of it, Mr Ryder.'

'I'm sure I will,' I said, nodding reassuringly. Then after a moment I decided the situation was hopeless and asked point blank: 'I'm sorry, Mr Hoffman, but what bad news are you referring to? There's been so much bad news lately.'

He looked at me in alarm. 'So much bad news?'

I gave a laugh. 'I mean the fighting in Africa and so on. Everywhere, bad news.' I gave another laugh.

'Oh, I see. I was of course referring to the bad news about Mr Brodsky's dog.'

'Ah yes. Mr Brodsky's dog.'

'You'll agree, sir, this is most unfortunate. The timing of it. One can proceed with the utmost care, and then something like this happens!' He gave an exasperated sigh.

'Yes, it's awful. Awful.'

'But as I say, I am confident. Yes, confident it will not lead to any major setback. Well now, may I suggest we go off at once? Actually, now I think of it, you were quite right, Mr Ryder. This is a much better time to set off. It means we shall arrive neither too early nor too late. Quite right, one must take these things calmly. Never get panicked. Well, sir, let's be off.'

'Er . . . Mr Hoffman. I seem to have made a little misjudgement about my attire for this occasion. Perhaps you'll allow me a few minutes to go back upstairs and change into something else.'

'Oh' – Hoffman glanced fleetingly at me – 'you look splendid, Mr Ryder. Please don't worry. Now' – he looked anxiously at his watch – 'I suggest we be on our way. Yes, this is just the right sort of time. Please.'

Outside the night was dark and the rain was coming down steadily. I followed Hoffman around the hotel building, down a path and into a small outdoor car park containing five or six vehicles. There was a solitary lamp fastened to a fence post by which I could make out the large puddles on the ground before me.

Hoffman ran across to a large black car and held open its passenger door. As I made my way towards it I could feel wetness seeping through my carpet slippers. Just as I was stepping into the car, one foot sank deep into a puddle, completely soaking it. I let out an exclamation but Hoffman was already hurrying around to the driver's side.

Hoffman drove us out of the car park as I did my best to dry my feet on the soft flooring. When I looked up we were already out in the main street and I was surprised to see how heavy the traffic had become. Moreover, many shops and restaurants had now come awake, and crowds of customers were milling about inside the illuminated windows. As we continued, the traffic grew steadily until somewhere near the heart of the city, amidst three lanes of vehicles, we came to a complete standstill. Hoffman looked at his watch then banged his hand against the wheel in frustration.

'How unfortunate,' I said sympathetically. 'And when I was out only a little while ago, the whole town seemed to be asleep.'

He appeared very preoccupied and said absent-mindedly: 'The traffic in this town, it just gets worse and worse. I don't know what the solution is.' He banged the steering wheel again.

For the next few minutes, we sat in the car in silence as we edged slowly forwards. Then Hoffman said quietly:

'Mr Ryder has been travelling.'

I thought I had misheard him, but then he said it again – this time with a suave little wave of his hand – and I realised he was rehearsing what he would say upon arrival to explain our lateness.

'Mr Ryder has been travelling. Mr Ryder – has been *travelling*.'

As we proceeded through the dense night-time traffic, Hoffman continued occasionally to mutter things under his breath, most of which I failed to catch. He had gone into a world of his own and appeared to be growing increasingly tense. Once, after we had failed to reach a green light in time, I heard him mutter: 'No, no, Mr Brodsky! He was magnificent, a magnificent creature!'

Then at last we took a turning and found ourselves driving out of the city. Before long the buildings disappeared and we were travelling on a long road with dark open spaces – perhaps farmland – to either side. The traffic grew sparse enabling the powerful car to pick up speed. I could see Hoffman relaxing visibly, and when he next addressed me he had regained much of his usual urbane manner.

'Tell me, Mr Ryder. Is everything at the hotel to your satisfaction?'

'Oh yes. Everything's fine, thank you.'

'You're happy with your room?'

'Oh yes, yes.'

'Your bed. It's comfortable?'

'Very comfortable.'

'I ask because we do pride ourselves on our beds. We renew our mattresses at very frequent intervals. No other hotel in this town renews as many mattresses as we do. This I know for a fact. The mattresses we throw out would be considered serviceable for several further years by many of our so-called rivals. Did you know, Mr Ryder, that if one were to stand up, lengthways, end to end, all the used mattresses we throw out during five financial years, one would be able to make a line along our main street starting at the civic chambers, going right along to the fountain, round the corner of Sterngasse and as far down as Mr Winkler's pharmacy?'

'Really. That's most impressive.'

'Mr Ryder, let me speak frankly. I've been giving much thought to the matter of your room. Naturally in the days leading to your arrival, I spent a long time considering which room to give you.

Most hotels would have a simple answer to the question: "Which is the best room in the house?" But this is not the case in my hotel, Mr Ryder. Over the years, I've given so much individual attention to so many different rooms. There have even been times when I've become – ha ha! – some would say *obsessed*, yes, obsessed, with one room or another. Once I see the potential of a particular room, I spend many days thinking about it, and then I take the greatest care in having it renovated to match my vision as closely as possible. I am not always successful, but on a number of occasions the results, after much work, have come close to what I pictured in my head, and of course, that is very satisfying. But then – perhaps it's some sort of defect in my nature – no sooner have I completed the renovation of one room to my satisfaction, I am seized by the potential of another. And before I know it, I find myself devoting great time and thought to the new project. Yes, some would call this obsessional, but I see nothing so wrong with it. Few things are as dull as a hotel with room after room completed along the same tired concepts. As far as I am concerned, each room must be thought about according to its own unique characteristics. In any case, what I'm getting at, Mr Ryder, is that I have no one favourite room in the hotel. So after a lot of thought, I concluded you'd be most happy in the room you are presently occupying. But having met you, I am now no longer certain.'

'Oh no, Mr Hoffman,' I said, interrupting. 'The present room is fine.'

'But I've been thinking about it on and off all day since meeting you, sir. It seems to me you'd be more temperamentally suited to another room I have in mind. Perhaps in the morning I'll show it to you. I'm quite sure you'll like it better.'

'No, Mr Hoffman, really. The present room . . .'

'Let me be frank, Mr Ryder. Your coming has put the room you're now occupying under its first true test. You see, this is the first time I've had a truly distinguished guest in that room since its reconceptualisation four years ago. Of course, there was no way I could predict that you yourself would one day honour us. But the fact is, I worked on that room with someone very much like yourself in mind. What I'm trying to say, you see, is that it's only now, with your arrival, that it's been properly put to the use for which it was intended. And, well, I can see quite clearly that I made several crucial misjudgements four years ago. It's so difficult, even with my experience. No, without doubt I'm dissatisfied. It is not a happy match. My proposal to you, sir, is that we move you to 343, which I feel is much closer to your spirit. You'll feel much calmer there and sleep better. And as for your present room, well, I've been thinking about it on and off all day. I have a good mind to have it demolished in its present form.'

'Mr Hoffman, really, no!'

I had shouted this and Hoffman took his eyes off the road to stare at me in surprise. I laughed and, quickly recovering, said:

'What I meant was, please don't go to such trouble and expense on my account.'

'It would be for my own peace of mind, I assure you, Mr Ryder. My hotel is my life's work. I made a bad mistake concerning that room. I see nothing for it but demolition.'

'Mr Hoffman, that room . . . The fact is, I feel a lot of affection for it. I really am very happy there.'

'I don't understand, sir.' He seemed genuinely puzzled. 'The room is clearly not correct for you. Now that I've met you, I can state that with some certainty. You don't have to be so polite. I am surprised to find you so peculiarly attached to it.'

I gave a sudden laugh, perhaps an unnecessarily loud one. 'Not at all. Peculiarly attached?' – I gave another laugh – 'It's just a room, nothing more. If it needs to be demolished, then demolished it must be! I'll gladly move to another room.'

'Ah. I'm very pleased you see it that way. It would have been a source of great frustration to me, Mr Ryder, not simply during the rest of your stay, but throughout the years to come, to think that you once stayed at my hotel and were forced to endure such an unsuitable room. I really can't think what could have been going on in my mind four years ago. A complete miscalculation!'

We had been speeding through the darkness for some time without encountering other headlights. Off in the distance I could see what may have been a few farmhouses, but otherwise there was little to break the empty blackness to either side. We travelled on in silence for a little while. Then Hoffman said:

'This is a cruel stroke of luck, Mr Ryder. That dog, well, it wasn't young, but it might easily have lasted another two or three years. And the preparations had been going so well.' He shook his head. 'It's such bad timing.' Then, turning to me with a smile, he went on: 'But I'm confident. Yes, I'm confident. He won't be deflected now, not even by something like this.'

'Perhaps Mr Brodsky should be offered another dog as a sort of present. Perhaps a young puppy.'

I had said this without much thought, but Hoffman made a show of considering it respectfully.

'I'm not sure, Mr Ryder. You must realise, he was extremely attached to Bruno. He kept little other company. He'll be in a state of mourning. But you may be right, we must alleviate his loneliness now that Bruno has gone. Perhaps some other animal. Something soothing. A bird in a cage, say. Then in time, when he is ready, another dog could be introduced. I'm not sure.'

He fell silent for the next several minutes and I thought his mind had gone on to something else. But then suddenly, as he stared at the dark road unwinding before us, he muttered intensely under his breath:

'An ox! Yes, an ox, an ox, an ox!'

But by this stage I was tired of the whole business of Brodsky's dog and I leaned back in my seat without speaking, determined to relax for the remainder of the journey. At one point, in an attempt to find out something about the event to which we were travelling, I said to him: 'I hope we shan't be very late.'

'No, no. Just right,' Hoffman replied, but his mind seemed to be elsewhere. Then a few minutes later, I heard him mutter sharply once more: 'An ox! An ox!'

After a while we turned off the open road and found ourselves in a salubrious residential district. I could see in the darkness large houses in their own grounds, often surrounded by high walls or hedges. Hoffman drove carefully around the leafy avenues, and I could hear him once more rehearsing his lines under his breath.

We passed through some tall iron gates into the courtyard of a substantial residence. There were already many vehicles parked around the grounds and it took the hotel manager a little while to find a space. He then got out and hurriedly went off towards the front entrance.

I remained in my seat a moment longer, studying the large

house for clues concerning the occasion we were about to attend. The front comprised a long row of huge windows coming almost to the ground. Most of these were lit behind their curtains, but I could see nothing of what was going on within.

Hoffman rang the doorbell and gestured for me to join him. When I got out of the car, the rain had eased to a drizzle. I pulled my dressing gown close around me and walked towards the house, taking care to avoid the puddles.

The door was opened by a maid who showed us into an expansive hallway decorated with grand portraits. The maid appeared to know Hoffman and there was a quick exchange as she took his raincoat. Hoffman paused a moment to straighten his tie in the mirror, before leading the way deeper into the building.

We arrived at a vast room flooded with lights in which a reception was in full swing. There were at least a hundred people present, standing about in smart evening dress, holding glasses and exchanging conversation. As we stood at the threshold, Hoffman raised an arm in front of me as though to protect me and searched the room with his gaze.

'He's not here yet,' he muttered eventually. Then, turning to me with a smile, he said: 'Mr Brodsky isn't here yet. But I'm confident, *confident* he'll be here before long.'

Hoffman turned back to the room and for a second seemed at a loss. Then he said: 'If you'd just wait here a moment, Mr Ryder, I'll go and fetch the Countess. Oh, and if you wouldn't mind standing a little way back over here – ha ha! – just out of sight. As you'll remember, you're supposed to be our big surprise. Please, I won't be long.'

He went into the room and for a few moments I watched his figure moving about the guests, his worried demeanour in marked contrast to the merriment all around him. I saw a number of people try to speak to him, but each time Hoffman hurried on with a distracted smile. Eventually I lost sight of him and possibly drifted forward a little in my effort to locate him again. I must in any case have made myself conspicuous for I heard a voice next to me say: 'Ah, Mr Ryder, you've arrived. How delightful you're with us at last.'

A large woman of around sixty had placed her hand on my arm. I smiled and muttered some pleasantry, to which she said:

'Everyone here is so eager to meet you.' With that she began to lead me firmly into the heart of the gathering.

As I followed her, squeezing my way past the guests, the large woman began to ask me questions. At first these were the usual enquiries about my health and my journey. But then, as we continued to make our way around the room, she proceeded to quiz me with great thoroughness about the hotel. Indeed she went into such detail – did I approve of the soap? what did I make of the carpet in the lobby? – that I began to suspect she was some professional rival of Hoffman much peeved that I was staying at his establishment. However, her general attitude and the manner in which she regularly nodded and smiled at people as we passed left little doubt that she was the hostess of these proceedings, and I concluded that this was indeed the Countess herself.

I had assumed she was leading me either to a particular spot in the room or to a particular person, but after a while I got the distinct impression we were walking around in slow circles. In fact several times I felt certain we had already been in a part of the room at least twice before. The other thing I noticed with curiosity was that although heads would turn and greet my hostess she made no effort to introduce me to anyone. Moreover, although some people smiled politely at me from time to time, no one seemed especially interested in me. Certainly no one broke off a conversation on account of my passing by. I was somewhat puzzled by this, having steeled myself for the usual smotherings of questions and compliments.

Then after a while I noticed there was an odd quality to the whole atmosphere in the room – something forced, even theatrical about its conviviality – though I was unable immediately to put my finger on it. But then we finally came to a halt – the Countess falling into conversation with two women covered in jewellery – and I at last had the chance to look about me and gather some impressions. Only then did I realise that the occasion was not a cocktail party at all, but that in fact all these people were waiting to be called into dinner; that dinner should have been served at least two hours earlier, but that the Countess and her colleagues had been obliged to hold off its commencement due to the absences of both Brodsky – the official guest of honour – and myself – the evening's great surprise. Then, as I continued to cast my gaze about me, I began steadily to realise just what had taken place before our arrival.

The present occasion was the largest to date of the dinners given in Brodsky's honour. Being also the last before the crucial event on Thursday evening, it was never likely to have been a relaxed affair, and Brodsky's lateness had turned the tension up further. At first, though, the guests – all of them highly conscious of being the city's elite – had remained calm, everyone scrupulously avoiding any comment likely to be construed as casting doubt on Brodsky's dependability. Most, in fact, had managed not to mention Brodsky at all, relieving their anxiety simply by endless speculation over when dinner would be served.

Then had come the news concerning Brodsky's dog. How such news had come to be given out in so haphazard a manner was not clear. Possibly a phone call had come to the house and one of the civic leaders, in a misguided attempt to settle the atmosphere, had blurted it out to some guests. In any case, the consequences of allowing such a thing to spread mouth to mouth through a gathering already tense with worry and hunger was entirely predictable. Very soon, every sort of wild rumour had begun to circulate around the room. Brodsky had been discovered, utterly drunk, cradling his dog's corpse. Brodsky had been found lying in a puddle in the street outside, talking gibberish. Brodsky, overcome with grief, had tried to kill himself by drinking paraffin. This last story had had its origins in an incident several years earlier when indeed, during a drunken binge, Brodsky had been rushed to hospital by a neighbouring farmer after imbibing a quantity of paraffin – though whether he had done so in a bid to kill himself or simply out of drunken confusion had never been established. Before long, in the wake of these rumours, despairing talk had started up everywhere.

'That dog meant everything to him. The man will never get up from this. We have to face it, we're right back at square one.'

'We have to call off Thursday night. Call it off straight away. It can't be anything but a disaster now. If we let it go ahead, the people of this city will never give us a second chance.'

'That fellow was always too risky. We should never have let it get this far. But what do we do now? We're lost, hopelessly lost.'

Then, even as the Countess and her colleagues had sought to

regain control of the evening, a burst of shouting had erupted from near the centre of the room.

Many people were rushing towards the incident, a few retreating in panic. What had occurred was that one of the younger councillors had pinned to the floor a tubby, bald-headed figure who after a moment everyone had recognised to be Keller the vet. The young councillor had been pulled off but had held onto Keller's lapel so tenaciously the vet had been pulled up with him.

'I did my best!' Keller was shouting, red in the face. 'I did my best! What more could I have done? Two days ago the animal was fine!'

'Fraud!' the young councillor had bellowed and attempted another assault. Again he had been pulled off, but by now a number of others, recognising a good scapegoat, had begun also to shout at Keller. For a moment accusations had rained down on the vet from all sides, charging him with negligence, and with jeopardising the future of the whole community. At this point a voice had shouted: 'What about the Breuers' kittens? You spend all your time playing bridge, you let those kittens die one by one . . .'

'I only play bridge once a week and even then . . .' the vet had started to protest hoarsely, but immediately more voices had shouted over him. Suddenly everyone in the room had seemed to have a long-borne grievance against the vet concerning some beloved animal or other. Then someone had shouted that Keller owed him money, another that Keller had never returned a gardening fork borrowed six years earlier. Soon the feelings against the vet had risen to such a pitch it had seemed quite natural that those restraining the young councillor should slacken their grip. And when the latter had made yet another lunge, he had seemed this time to do so on behalf of the great majority of those present. The situation had looked on the verge of turning quite unpleasant, when a voice booming across the room had at last brought everyone to their senses.

That the room had fallen silent as quickly as it had perhaps owed more to the astonishment caused by the speaker's identity than to any natural authority he commanded. For the figure everyone had turned to see glaring down at them from the platform had been that of Jakob Kanitz, a man noted in the town principally for his timidity. Now in his late forties, Jakob Kanitz had for as long as anyone could remember held the same dull clerical post at the town hall. He was rarely known to venture an opinion, still less contradict or argue. He had no close friends and several years earlier had moved out of the small house he had shared with his wife and three children to rent a tiny attic room further down the same street. Whenever anyone had broached the matter, he had intimated he would very soon rejoin his family, but the years had gone by and his arrangements had not changed. Meanwhile, largely on account of his willingness to volunteer for the many mundane tasks around the organising of a cultural event, he had become an accepted, if somewhat patronised member of the town's artistic circles.

The room had had little time to get over its surprise before Jakob Kanitz – perhaps aware that his nerve would hold out for only so long – had begun to speak.

'Other cities! And I don't just mean Paris! Or Stuttgart! I mean smaller cities, no more than us, other cities. Gather together their best citizens, put a crisis like this before them, how would they be? They'd be calm, assured. Such people would know what to do, how to behave. What I'm saying to you, all of us here, we're the best of this town. It isn't beyond us. Together we can come through this crisis. Would they be fighting in Stuttgart?! There's no need for panic yet. No need to give up, to start quarrelling among ourselves. All right, the dog, it's a problem, but it's not the end, it doesn't mean anything yet. Whatever condition Mr Brodsky may be in at this moment, we can put him back on course again. We can do it, provided we all play our part tonight. I'm sure we can, we have to. Have to put him back on course. Because if we don't, if we don't pull together and get this right tonight, I tell you this, there's nothing left for us except misery! Yes, deep, lonely misery! There's no one else for us to turn to, it has to be Mr Brodsky, there's no one else now. He's probably on his way at this moment. We've got to stay calm. What are we doing, fighting? Would they fight in Stuttgart? We've got to think clearly. In his shoes, how would we feel? We must show we're all grieving with him, that the whole town shares his sorrow. Then again, friends, think about it, we must cheer him up. Oh yes! We can't spend the whole evening in gloom, send him away believing there's nothing left, he might as well go back to . . . No, no! The right balance! We've got to be cheerful too, make him see there's so much more to life, that we're all looking to him, depending on him. Yes, we have to get it right, these next few hours. He's probably on his way now, God knows in what condition. These next few hours, they're crucial, crucial. We've got to do it right. Otherwise there's only misery. We must . . . we must . . .'

At this point Jakob Kanitz had become covered in confusion. He had remained standing there on the platform for several more seconds, not speaking, a huge embarrassment steadily engulfing him. Some residue of his earlier emotion had caused him to give one last glare to those assembled, then he had turned sheepishly and stepped down.

But this clumsy appeal had had an immediate impact. Even before Jakob Kanitz had finished speaking, a low assenting murmur had started up and more than one person had pushed reproachfully the shoulder of the young councillor – by this point shamefacedly shuffling his feet. Jakob Kanitz's departure from the stage had been followed by a few seconds of awkward silence. Then, steadily, conversation had broken out around the room, with everywhere people discussing in serious but calm tones what should be done once Brodsky arrived. Before long a consensus had emerged to the effect that Jakob Kanitz had got it more or less right. The task was to strike the correct balance between the sorrowful and the jovial. The atmosphere would have to be carefully monitored at all times by each and every person present. A feeling of resolution had gone around the room, and then, in time, people had begun gradually to relax, until eventually they were smiling, chatting, greeting one another in gracious, urbane tones, all as though the unseemly episodes of the last half-hour had not taken place. It had been somewhere around this point – no more than twenty minutes after Jakob Kanitz had finished speaking – that Hoffman and I had arrived. No wonder then that I should have detected something odd beneath the layer of refined merriment.

I was still turning over all that had happened prior to our arrival when I caught sight of Stephan on the other side of the room, talking to an elderly lady. Next to me, the Countess seemed still to be engrossed in her conversation with the two bejewelled women, and so, muttering an excuse under my breath, I drifted away from them. As I came towards him, Stephan saw me and smiled.

'Ah, Mr Ryder. So you've arrived. I wonder if I might introduce you to Miss Collins.'

I then recognised the thin old lady to whose apartment we had driven earlier in the night. She was dressed simply but elegantly in a long black dress. She smiled and held out her hand as we exchanged greetings. I was about to make further polite conversation with her when Stephan leaned forward and said quietly:

'I've been such a fool, Mr Ryder. Frankly I don't know what's for the best. Miss Collins has been very kind as usual, but I'd like also your opinion on it all.'

'You mean . . . about Mr Brodsky's dog?'

'Oh. No, no, that's all awful, I realise that. But we were just discussing something else altogether. I really would appreciate your advice. In fact, Miss Collins was just now suggesting I seek you out, wasn't that so, Miss Collins? You see, I hate to be a bore about this, but there's been a complication. I mean, about my performance on Thursday night. God, I've been such a fool! As I told you, Mr Ryder, I've been preparing Jean-Louis La Roche's *Dahlia*, but I never told Father about it. Not until tonight, that is. I'd been thinking I'd keep it a surprise for him, he so loves La Roche. What's more, Father would never dream I was capable of mastering such a difficult piece, and so I thought it would be a tremendous surprise for him on both counts. But then just recently, with the big night so near now, I'd been thinking it wasn't practical to keep it a secret any more. For one thing, it's all got to be printed on the official programme, there's going to be a copy next to each napkin, Father's been agonising over the design, trying to decide about the embossments, the illustration on the back, everything. I realised a few days ago I'd have to tell him, but I still wanted it to be something of a surprise, so I was waiting for the right sort of moment to come along. Well, earlier on, just after I dropped you and Boris off, I went into his office to put back the car keys, and there he was on the floor, going through a pile of papers. On his hands and knees, all the papers round him on the carpet, nothing unusual about it, Father often works like that. It's quite a small office, and his desk takes up a lot of the space anyway, so I had to tiptoe around everything to put the keys back. He asked me how everything was, then before I'd said anything seemed to become engrossed in his papers again. Well, for some reason, just as I was leaving, I caught sight of him on the carpet like that and I suddenly felt it would be the right moment to tell him. It was just an impulse. So I said to him, quite casually: "By the way, Father, I'm going to play La Roche's *Dahlia* on Thursday night. I thought you'd like to know." I didn't say it in any special way, I just told him and waited to see his reaction. Well, he put aside the document he was reading, but he kept gazing at the carpet in front of him. Then a smile came over his face and he said something like: "Ah yes, *Dahlia*," and for a few seconds he looked very happy. He didn't look up, he was still on his hands and knees, but he looked very happy. Then he closed his eyes and started to hum the opening of the adagio, he started to hum it there on the floor, moving his head in time. He seemed so happy and tranquil, Mr Ryder, at that point I was congratulating myself. Then he opened his eyes and smiled dreamily up at me and said: "Yes, it's beautiful. I've never understood why your mother despises it so." As I was just telling Miss Collins, I thought at first I'd misheard him. But then he said it again. "Your mother despises it so much. Yes, as you know, she's come to despise La Roche's later work so intensely these days. She won't let me play his recordings anywhere in the house, not even with the headphones on." Then he must have noticed how flabbergasted and upset I was. Because – typical Father! – he started straight away trying to make me feel better. "I should have asked you a long time ago," he kept saying. "It's all my fault." Then he suddenly slapped his forehead like he'd just remembered something else and said: "Really, Stephan, I've let you *both* down. I thought at the time I was doing the right thing, not interfering, but I see now I've let you both down." And when I asked what he meant, he explained how Mother's been looking forward all this time to hearing me play Kazan's *Glass Passions*. Apparently she'd let Father know some time ago this was what she wanted, and well, Mother would assume Father would arrange it all. But you see, Father saw my side to it. He's very sensitive about such things. He realised that a musician – even an

131

amateur like me – would want to make his own decision about such an important performance. So he'd not said anything to me, fully intending to explain it all to Mother when a chance came along. But then of course – well, I suppose I'd better explain it a bit more, Mr Ryder. You see, when I say Mother let Father know about the Kazan, I don't mean she actually *told* him. It's a little hard to explain to an outsider. The way it works is that Mother would somehow, you know, somehow just *let it be known* to Father without ever directly mentioning it. She'll do it through signals, which to him would be very clear. I'm not sure precisely what she did this time. Perhaps he'd come home and found her listening to *Glass Passions* on the stereo. Well, since she very rarely puts anything on the stereo, that would be a pretty obvious sign. Or perhaps Father had come to bed after his bath and found her reading a book in bed on Kazan, I don't know, it's just the way things have always been done between them. Well, as you can see, it's not as though Father could have suddenly said: "No, Stephan's got to make his own choice." Father was waiting, trying to find a suitable way of conveying his reply. And of course he wasn't to know that, of all pieces, I was preparing La Roche's *Dahlia*. God, I've been so stupid! I had no idea Mother hated it so! Well, he told me how things stood, and when I asked him what he considered the best course, he thought about it and said I ought to carry on with what I'd prepared, it was too late to change it now. "Mother wouldn't blame you," he kept saying. "She wouldn't blame you for a moment. She'll blame me and quite rightly." Poor Father, he was trying so hard to comfort me, but I could see how distressed he was getting about it all. After a while he was looking at a spot on the carpet – he was still on the floor but by this time all crouched up, like he was doing a press-up – he was looking at the carpet and I could hear him muttering things to himself. "I'll be able to take it. I'll be able to take it. I've lived through worse. I'll be able to take it." He seemed to have forgotten I was there, so in the end I just left, just quietly closed the door behind me. And since then – well, Mr Ryder, I've not been thinking about much else all evening. To be frank, I'm at a bit of a loss. So little time left. And *Glass Passions* is such a difficult piece, how can I possibly have it ready? In fact, if I had to be honest, I'd say that piece is still a little beyond my ability, even if I had the whole year to prepare it.'

The young man came to a halt with a troubled sigh. When after a few moments neither he nor Miss Collins had spoken, I concluded he was waiting for my opinion. So I said:

'Of course, this is none of my business, you must decide for yourself. But my own feeling is that at this late stage you should just stick with what you've prepared . . .'

'Yes, I suppose you would say that, Mr Ryder.'

It was Miss Collins who had broken in. There was an unexpected cynicism in her tone which made me stop and turn to her. The old lady was looking at me in a knowing, slightly superior manner. 'No doubt,' she went on, 'you'd call it – what? – ah yes, "artistic integrity".'

'It's not so much that, Miss Collins,' I said. 'It's just that from a practical viewpoint, I'd think it rather too late at this stage . . .'

'But how do you know it's too late, Mr Ryder?' she interrupted again. 'You know very little about Stephan's abilities. To say nothing of the deeper implications of his current predicament. Why do you take it upon yourself to pronounce like this, as though you're blessed with some extra sense the rest of us lack?'

I had been feeling increasingly uncomfortable since Miss Collins's initial intervention, and while she was saying this I had found myself turning away in an effort to avoid her gaze. I could not think of any obvious retort to her questions and after a moment, deciding it best to cut short the encounter, I gave a small laugh and drifted off into the crowd.

For the next several minutes I found myself wandering aimlessly around the room. As earlier, people sometimes turned as I went by, but no one seemed to recognise me. At one point I saw Pedersen, the man I had met in the cinema, laughing with a few other guests and thought I would go over to him. But before I could do so I felt something touch my elbow and turned to find Hoffman beside me.

'I'm sorry I had to leave you for a moment. I hope you're being well looked after. What a situation!'

The hotel manager was breathing heavily, his face covered in perspiration.

'Oh yes, I've been enjoying myself.'

'I'm sorry, I had to leave the room to take a phone call. But now they're on their way, definitely, they're on their way. Mr Brodsky will be here any minute. My goodness!' He glanced around, then leaned closer and lowered his voice. 'This guest list was ill-judged. I warned them. Some of these people here!' He shook his head. 'What a situation!'

'But at least Mr Brodsky is on his way . . .'

'Oh yes, yes. I must say, Mr Ryder, I'm so relieved you're with us tonight. Just when we need you. By and large, I see no reason to change your speech too much on account of the, er, the circumstances. Perhaps a mention or two of the tragedy wouldn't go amiss, but we'll organise someone else to say a few words about the dog, so really, there's no need for you to deviate from what you've prepared. The only thing – ha ha! – your address shouldn't be too long. But of course, you're the last person to . . .' He trailed off with a small laugh. Then he was looking around the room again. 'Some of these people,' he said again. 'Very ill-judged. I warned them.'

Hoffman went on casting his gaze around the room, and I was thus able for a moment to turn my mind to the matter of the speech the hotel manager had mentioned. After a while, I said:

'Mr Hoffman, in view of the circumstances we now find our-selves in, I feel a little uncertain about when precisely I should get up and . . .'

'Ah, quite, quite. How sensitive of you. As you say, if you just stood up at the usual point, one never knows what might be . . . yes, yes, how far-sighted of you. I shall be sitting next to Mr Brodsky, and so perhaps you might leave it to me to assess when the best moment would be. Perhaps you'd be good enough to wait for me to signal to you. My goodness, Mr Ryder, it's so reassuring to have someone like you with us at a time like this.'

'I'm only too pleased to be of help.'

A noise on the other side of the room caused Hoffman to turn away abruptly. He craned his neck to see across the room, though it seemed obvious nothing of significance had occurred. I gave a cough to regain his attention.

'Mr Hoffman, there's just one other small matter. I was just wondering' – I indicated my dressing gown – 'I thought I might change into something a little more formal. I wondered if it was possible to borrow some clothes. Nothing special.'

Hoffman glanced distractedly at my attire, then almost immediately looked away again, saying absent-mindedly: 'Oh, don't worry, Mr Ryder. We're not at all stuffy here.'

He was craning his neck once more to see across the room. It seemed to me clear he had not taken on board at all my problem and I was about to raise the matter again when there was a flurry of activity near the entrance. Hoffman started, then turned to me with a ghastly smile. 'He's here!' he whispered, touched me on the shoulder and hurried off.

A hush fell across the room, and for a few seconds everyone was looking towards the door. I too tried to see what was going on, but found my view hopelessly obstructed. Then suddenly, as though remembering their resolve, people all around me were resuming their conversations in tones of controlled gaiety.

I made my way through the crowd until eventually I managed to see Brodsky being led across the room. The Countess was supporting one arm, Hoffman the other, and four or five others were fluttering anxiously nearby. Brodsky, evidently oblivious of his attendants, was gazing darkly up at the room's ornate ceiling. He was taller, more upright than I had expected, though at this moment he was carrying himself with such stiffness – and at an oddly sloping angle – that from a distance it seemed his entourage were rolling him along on castors. He was unshaven, but not outrageously so, and his dinner jacket was slightly askew as though it had been put on him by someone else. His features, though coarsened and aged, had a trace left about them of the debonair.

For an instant I thought they were leading him to me, but then realised they were heading for the adjoining dining room. A waiter standing at the threshold ushered through Brodsky and his attendants and as they disappeared another hush fell on the room. Before long, the guests resumed their talking again, but I could sense a new tension in the air.

I noticed at this point a solitary upright chair left against a wall and it occurred to me that a fresh vantage point might better enable me to assess the prevailing mood and decide on the most appropriate sort of talk to give at dinner. I thus walked over, seated myself and for several minutes sat watching the room.

The guests were still laughing and talking, but there was no doubt the underlying tension was increasing. In view of this, and in view of the fact that someone else would be speaking specifically about the dog, it seemed wise that I make my talk as light-hearted as was reasonable. In the end I decided the best thing might be to recount some amusing behind-the-scenes anecdotes concerning a series of mishaps that had beset my last Italian tour. I had told these stories in public often enough to be quite confident of their ability to defuse tensions and felt sure they would be much appreciated in the present circumstances.

I was testing out to myself a few possible opening lines when I noticed the crowd had thinned considerably. Only then did I realise people were steadily going through into the dining room and rose to my feet.

A few people smiled vaguely at me as I joined the procession into dinner, but no one spoke to me. I did not really mind this, since I was still trying to shape in my mind a really captivating opening statement. As I moved closer to the dining-room doors, I found myself undecided between two possibilities. The first was: 'My name over the years has tended to be associated with certain qualities. A meticulous attention to detail. Precision in perform- ance. The tight control of dynamics.' This mock-pompous start could then be rapidly undercut by the hilarious revelations of what had actually occurred in Rome. The alternative was to strike a more obviously farcical note from the start: 'Collapsing curtain rails. Poisoned rodents. Misprinted score sheets. Few of you, I trust, would readily associate my name with such phenomena.' Both openings had their pros and cons and in the end I decided against making a final choice until I had gained a better sense of the mood over dinner.

I entered the dining room, people talking excitedly all around me. Immediately I was struck by its vastness. Even with the present company – well over a hundred – I could see why it had been necessary to illuminate only one part of the room. A gen- erous number of round tables had been laid with white table- cloths and silver, but there seemed to be just as many others, bare and without seating, disappearing in rows into the darkness on the far side. Many guests were already seated and the overall picture – the gleam of the ladies' jewellery, the crisp whiteness of the waiters' jackets, the backdrop of black dinner suits and the darkness beyond – was not unimpressive. I was surveying the scene from just inside the doorway, taking the opportunity to straighten my dressing gown, when the Countess appeared at my side. She began to lead me by the arm, much as she had done earlier, saying:

'Mr Ryder, we've placed you at this table over here where you won't be quite so conspicuous. We don't want people spotting you and spoiling the surprise! But don't worry, once we announce your presence and you stand up, you'll be perfectly visible and audible to everyone.'

Although the table she led me to was in a corner, I could not see why it was particularly more discreet than any of the others. She seated me, then, saying something with a laugh – I could not hear her in the hubbub – hurried away.

I found I was sitting with four others – one middle-aged couple, another slightly younger – who all smiled routinely towards me before resuming their conversation. The husband of the older couple was explaining why their son wished to continue living in the United States, and then the conversation moved on to the couple's various other children. Occasionally one or the other of them remembered to include me in a nominal sort of way – by looking in my direction or, if a joke was made, by smiling at me. But none of them addressed me directly and I soon gave up trying to follow.

But then, as the waiters began to serve the soup, I noticed that their conversation had become sparse and distracted. Finally, somewhere during the main course, my companions seemed to drop all pretences and began to discuss the real matter preoccupying them. Casting barely disguised glances towards where Brodsky was seated, they exchanged speculations in lowered tones concerning the old man's present condition. At one point the younger of the women said:

'Surely, *some*body should go up there and tell him how sorry we feel. We should all be going up there. No one seems to have said a word to him yet. Look, the people with him, they're hardly talking to him. Perhaps *we* should go up, we should start it off.

Then everyone else might follow. Perhaps everyone's waiting, just like us.'

The others hastened to reassure her that our hosts had everything under control, that in any case Brodsky looked to be very well, but then the next minute they also were looking uneasily across the room.

Naturally I too had been taking the opportunity to observe Brodsky quite carefully. He had been placed at a table a little larger than the rest. Hoffman was to one side of him, the Countess on the other. The rest of his company comprised a ring of solemn grey-haired men. The way these latter seemed continuously to be conferring under their breaths gave the table a conspiratorial air hardly helpful to the general atmosphere. As for Brodsky himself, he was showing no obvious sign of drunkenness and was eating steadily, if without enthusiasm. He nevertheless seemed to have retreated into a world of his own. For much of the main course, Hoffman had an arm behind Brodsky's back and appeared constantly to be murmuring into his ear, but the old man went on staring gloomily into space without responding. Once when the Countess touched his arm and said something, he again failed to reply.

Then towards the end of dessert – the food, if not spectacular, had been satisfying – I saw Hoffman making his way across the floor past the hurrying waiters and realised he was coming towards me. Arriving, he bent down and said in my ear:

'Mr Brodsky seems to wish to say a few words, but quite frankly – ha ha! – we've been trying to persuade him against doing so. We believe he shouldn't be put under any extra strain tonight. So, Mr Ryder, perhaps you would be good enough to watch carefully for my signal and rise promptly as soon as I give it. Then immediately you finish speaking, the Countess will bring the formal part of the proceedings to an end. Yes, really, we think it best Mr Brodsky isn't put under any extra strain. Poor man, ha ha! This guest list, really' – he shook his head and sighed – 'thank goodness you're here, Mr Ryder.'

Before I could say anything, he was dodging through the waiters again, hurrying back to his table.

I spent the next several minutes surveying the room and weighing up the two possible openings I had prepared for my speech. I was still prevaricating when the noise in the room suddenly subsided. I then became aware that a severe-faced man who had been sitting next to the Countess had risen to his feet.

The man was quite elderly and silver-haired. He exuded authority and almost immediately there was complete silence in the room. For a few more seconds the severe-faced man simply looked at the assembled guests with an air of reprimand. Then he said in a voice at once restrained and resonant:

'Sir. When such a fine, noble companion passes away, there is little, so little others can say that does not seem empty and shallow. Nevertheless, we could not possibly let this evening go by without a few formal words on behalf of everyone in this room, to convey to you, Mr Brodsky, the deep sympathy we feel for you.' He paused while a murmur of assent went around the room. Then he continued: 'Your Bruno, sir, was not only much loved by those of us who saw him going about his business around our town. He came to achieve a status rare among human beings, let alone among our quadrupeds. That is to say, he became an emblem. Yes, sir, he came to exemplify for us certain key virtues. A fierce loyalty. A fearless passion for life. A refusal to be looked down upon. An urge to do things in one's own special way, however seemingly outlandish to the eyes of grander observers. That is to say, the very virtues that have gone to build this unique and proud community of ours over the years. Virtues, sir, which if I may venture' – his voice slowed with significance – 'we hope very soon to see flower here again in every walk of life.'

He paused and looked around once more. He continued to hold the audience in his frosty gaze for another moment, then said finally:

'Let us now, together, observe a minute's silence in memory of our departed friend.'

As he lowered his eyes, people everywhere bowed their heads and complete silence reigned once more. At one point I looked up and noticed that some of the civic leaders on Brodsky's table – perhaps in their anxiety to set a good example – had adopted ludicrously exaggerated postures of grief. One of them, for instance, was clutching his forehead in both hands. For his part, Brodsky – who had remained immobile throughout the speech, not looking up once either at the speaker or the room in general – continued to sit quite still, and there was again something odd-angled about his whole posture. It was even possible he had fallen asleep in his chair and that the function of Hoffman's arm behind his back was primarily physical.

At the end of the minute, the severe-faced man sat down without speaking further, creating an awkward hiatus in the proceedings. A few people began cautiously to converse again, but then there came a movement from another table and I saw that a large balding man with blotchy skin had stood up.

'Ladies and gentlemen,' he said in a powerful voice. Then, turning to Brodsky, he bowed slightly and muttered: 'Sir.' He looked down at his hands for a few seconds, then gazed around the room. 'As many of you will already know, it was I who found the body of our beloved friend earlier this evening. I hope then that you will indulge me for a few moments while I say a few words concerning . . . concerning what took place. For you see, sir' – he looked again at Brodsky – 'the fact is, I must beg your forgiveness. Let me explain myself.' The large man paused and swallowed. 'This evening, as usual, I was making my deliveries. I had almost finished by then, I had just two or three calls left to make, and I took a short cut down the alley running between the railway line and Schildstrasse. I would not normally take such a short cut, particularly after dark, but today I was earlier than usual, and as you know, there was a pleasant sunset. So I took the short cut. And there, at just about the half-way point along the alley, I saw him. Our dear friend. He had placed himself in a discreet position, virtually hidden between the lamp-post and the wooden fence. I knelt beside him to make sure that he had indeed passed on. As I did so, many thoughts went through my mind. I thought, naturally, of you, sir. Of what a great friend he had always been to you, and what a tragic loss this would be. I thought too of how much the city at large would miss Bruno, how it would join you in your hour of grieving. And let me say it, sir, I felt, for all the sorrow of the moment, that fate had handed me a privilege. Yes, sir, a privilege. It had fallen to me to transport the body of our friend to the veterinary clinic. Then, sir, for what happened next, I . . . I have no excuse. Just now, as Mr von Winterstein was speaking, I was sitting here tormented by indecision. Should I too stand up now and speak? In the end, as you see, I decided that yes, I would. Much better that Mr Brodsky hears it from my own lips than as gossip in the morning. Sir, I am bitterly ashamed of what took place next. I can only say that I had no intention, not in a hundred years . . . I can now only beg your forgiveness. I have gone over it in my head many times in the last few hours and I see now what I should have done. I should have put down my packages. You see, I was still carrying two of them, the last of my deliveries. I should have put them down. They would have been safe enough in the alley, tucked in next to the fence. And even if someone had made off with them, what of it? But for some foolish reason, some idiotic professional instinct perhaps, I did not. I did not think. That is to say, as I lifted up Bruno's body, I was still clinging to the packages. I don't know what I expected. But the fact is – you will learn of this tomorrow, so I will tell you now myself – the fact is your Bruno must have been there for some time, for his body, magnificent though it was in death, had become cold and, well, it had stiffened. Yes, sir, stiffened. Forgive me, what I have to say now may bring you distress, but . . . but let me continue. In order to carry my packages – how I regret it, a thousand times I've regretted it already – in order to continue carrying my packages, I hoisted Bruno high up onto my shoulder, not taking into account his stiffened condition. Only when I had gone most of the way down the alley in this manner did I hear a child's shout from somewhere and stop. Then of course the enormity of my error dawned on me. Ladies and gentlemen, Mr Brodsky, need I spell it out to you? I see I must. The fact was this. On account of our friend's stiffness, on account of the foolish way I had chosen to transport him up on my shoulder, that is to say, in a virtually upright position . . . Well, the point is, sir, from any of the houses in Schildstrasse the whole upper part of his body would have been visible over the top of the fence. In fact, cruelty upon cruelty, it was just that time of the evening when most households were gathered in their back rooms for their evening meals. They would have been gazing at their gardens as they ate and would have seen our noble friend gliding past, his paws thrust in front of him – ah, the indignity of it! Household after household! I have become haunted by it, sir, I can see it before me, how it must have looked.

Forgive me, sir, forgive me, I could not remain sitting here a moment longer without unburdening myself of this . . . this testimony to my bungling nature. What a misfortune that this sorrowful privilege should have fallen to a clod such as myself! Mr Brodsky, please, I beg you to accept these hopelessly inadequate apologies for the humiliation to which I subjected your noble companion so soon after his moment of departure. And the good people of Schildstrasse, perhaps some of them are here now, they like everyone else would have been deeply fond of Bruno. To have glimpsed him for the last time in such a manner . . . I beg you, sir, everyone, I beg you, I beg your forgiveness.'

The large man sat down, shaking his head mournfully. Then a woman at a table near him rose, touching her eyes with a handkerchief.

'Surely there's no doubt about it,' she said. 'He was the greatest dog of his generation. Surely there's no doubt about it.'

A murmur of agreement went around the room. The civic leaders around Brodsky were nodding earnestly, but Brodsky himself still had not looked up.

We waited for the woman to say something more, but although she remained on her feet, she said nothing, merely continuing to sob and dab at her eyes. After a while a man in a velvet dinner jacket beside her rose and gently helped her back into her chair. He himself remained on his feet, however, and glared accusingly around the room. Then he said:

'A statue. A bronze statue. I propose we build a bronze statue to Bruno so that we can remember him for ever. Something big and dignified. Perhaps in Walserstrasse. Mr von Winterstein' – he addressed the severe-faced man – 'let us resolve here, this evening, to build a statue to Bruno!'

Someone called out 'hear, hear' and a clamour of voices rose up expressing approval. Not only the severe-faced man, but all the civic leaders at Brodsky's table looked suddenly confused. Several panicky glances were exchanged before the severe-faced man said without rising:

'Of course, Mr Haller, it's something we would consider very carefully. Along of course with other ideas as to how we might best commemorate . . .'

'This is going too far,' a man's voice suddenly interrupted from the other end of the room. 'What an absurd idea. A statue for that dog? If that animal deserves a bronze statue, then our tortoise, Petra, she deserves one five times as big. And she met such a cruel end. It's absurd. And that dog attacked Mrs Rahn only earlier this year . . .'

The rest of this statement was drowned out by uproar all around the room. For a moment everyone seemed to be shouting at once. The man who had spoken, still on his feet, now turned to someone at his own table and began a furious argument. In the growing chaos, I became aware that Hoffman was waving across at me. Or rather, he was describing with his hand an odd circular motion – as though he were wiping an invisible window – and I recalled vaguely that this was some form of signal favoured by him. I rose to my feet and cleared my throat emphatically.

The room almost immediately fell silent and all eyes turned to me. The man who had objected to the statue broke off his argument and hurriedly took his seat. I cleared my throat a second time and was about to embark on my talk when I suddenly became aware that my dressing gown was hanging open, displaying the entire naked front of my body. Thrown into confusion, I hesitated for a second then sat back down again. Almost immediately, a woman stood up across the room and said stridently:

'If a statue isn't practical, then why not name a street after him? We've often changed street names to commemorate the dead. Surely, Mr von Winterstein, this isn't too much to ask. Perhaps Meinhardstrasse. Or even Jahnstrasse.'

A chorus of approval went up for this idea and soon people were calling out all at once the names of other possible streets. The civic leaders were again looking profoundly uncomfortable.

A tall bearded man at a table near mine stood up and said in a booming voice: 'I agree with Mr Holländer. This is going too far. Of course, we all feel sorry for Mr Brodsky. But let's be honest, that dog was a menace, to other dogs and to humans alike. And if Mr Brodsky had thought to comb the creature's fur from time to time, and treat him for the skin infection it obviously had for years . . .'

The man was engulfed by a storm of angry protests. There were shouts of 'Disgraceful!' and 'Shame!' everywhere, and several people left their tables in order to lecture the offender. Hoffman was again signalling to me, wiping the air furiously, a horrible grin on his face. I could hear the bearded man's voice booming over the mayhem: 'It's true. The creature was a disgusting mess!'

I checked that my gown was fastened tightly and was about to stand up again, when I saw Brodsky suddenly stir and rise to his feet.

The table made a noise as he rose and all heads turned towards him. In an instant, those who had left their seats had returned and silence reigned in the room once more.

For a second I thought Brodsky would crash across the table. But he maintained his balance, surveying the room for a moment. When he spoke his voice had a gentle huskiness about it.

'Look, what is this?' he said. 'You think that dog was so important to me? He's dead and that's it. I want a woman. It gets lonely sometimes. I want a woman.' He paused and for a while seemed to become lost in his thoughts. Then he said dreamily: 'Our sailors. Our drunken sailors. What would have become of them now? She was young then. Young and so beautiful.' He drifted back into his thoughts, gazing up at the lights suspended from the high ceiling, and for a second time I thought he might crash forward across the table. Hoffman must have feared something similar for he stood up and, placing a gentle hand behind Brodsky's back, whispered something in his ear. Brodsky did not immediately respond. Then he muttered: 'She loved me once. Loved me more than anything. Our drunken sailors. Where are they now?'

Hoffman gave a hearty laugh as though Brodsky had made a witticism. He smiled broadly at the room then whispered again in Brodsky's ear. Brodsky finally seemed to recall where he was and, turning vaguely to the hotel manager, allowed himself to be coaxed back down into his chair.

There followed a silence during which no one stirred. Then the Countess stood up with a vivacious smile.

'Ladies and gentlemen, at this point in the evening, we have a lovely surprise! He arrived only this afternoon, he must be very tired indeed, but he has consented nevertheless to be our surprise guest. Yes, everyone! Mr Ryder is here among us!'

The Countess made a flourishing gesture in my direction as excited exclamations broke out across the room. Before I could do anything, the people at my table had quickly engulfed me and were trying to shake my hand. The next instant I was aware of people all round me, gasping with pleasure, greeting me and holding out their hands. I responded to these advances as courteously as I could, but when I glanced over my shoulder – I had not had a chance to get up off my chair – I could see a crowd gathering at my back with many people pushing and standing on tip-toes. I saw I would have to take control of the situation before it disintegrated into chaos. With so many already on their feet, I decided the best course would be to elevate myself above them on some pedestal. Quickly ensuring my dressing gown was fastened, I clambered up onto my chair.

The clamour ceased instantly, people freezing where they stood to stare up at me. From my new vantage point I saw that over half the guests had left their tables and I decided to begin without delay.

'Collapsing curtain rails! Poisoned rodents! Misprinted score sheets!'

I became aware of a single figure walking towards me through the stationary clusters of people. On arrival, Miss Collins pulled towards her a chair from the neighbouring table, sat down and proceeded to gaze up at me. Something about the way she did so distracted me sufficiently that for a moment I could not think of my next line. Seeing me hesitate, she crossed one leg over the other and said in a concerned voice:

'Mr Ryder, are you feeling unwell?'

'I'm fine, thank you, Miss Collins.'

'I do hope,' she went on, 'you didn't take too much to heart what I said to you earlier. I wanted to come and find you to apologise, but I couldn't see you anywhere. I may have spoken much more abrasively than was called for. I do hope you'll forgive me. It's just that even now, when I come upon someone of your calling, things suddenly come back to me and I find myself adopting that sort of tone.'

'It's quite all right, Miss Collins,' I said quietly, smiling down at her. 'Please don't worry. I wasn't really upset at all. If I walked

145

away rather abruptly, it was just that I thought you might want the opportunity to talk unhindered with Stephan.'

'It's good of you to be so understanding,' Miss Collins said. 'I *am* sorry I got a little angry. But you must believe me, Mr Ryder, it wasn't just anger on my part. I do quite honestly wish to be of some help to you. It would greatly sadden me to see you making the same mistakes over and over. I wanted to say to you, now that we've met, you'd be very welcome to visit me for tea some afternoon. I'd be more than happy to talk over whatever happens to be on your mind. You'd have a sympathetic ear, I can assure you.'

'That's good of you, Miss Collins. I'm sure it's well meant. But if I may say so, it would seem your past experiences have left you less than well-disposed towards, as you yourself put it, those of my calling. I'm not at all sure you would enjoy having me visit you.'

Miss Collins appeared to give this some thought. Then she said: 'I can appreciate your misgivings. But I feel it would be perfectly possible for us to get on in a civil way. If you like it need only be a short visit. If you found you enjoyed it then you could always come back. Perhaps we could even go for a short walk. The Sternberg Garden is very close to my apartment. Mr Ryder, I've had many years to reflect on the past and I really am ready to put it behind me. I would very much like once more to lend a hand to someone such as yourself. Of course, I can't promise I'll have answers to every question. But I'll listen to you with sympathy. And you can be sure, I won't idealise or sentimentalise you in the way a less experienced person might.'

'I'll think carefully about your invitation, Miss Collins,' I said to her. 'But I can't help thinking you've mistaken me for someone I clearly am not. I say this because the world seems full of people claiming to be geniuses of one sort or another, who are in fact remarkable only for a colossal inability to organise their lives. But for some reason there's always a queue of people like yourself, Miss Collins – very well-meaning people – eager to rush to the rescue of these types. Perhaps I flatter myself, but I can tell you, I am not one of their number. In fact, I can say with confidence that at this point in time, I'm not in any need of rescuing.'

Miss Collins had been shaking her head for some time. Now

she said: 'Mr Ryder, it really would be a great sadness to me if you were to continue making your mistakes over and over. And to think that all the time, I was here, simply watching you and doing nothing. I really do think I might be of some help to you in your present plight. Of course, when I was with Leo' – she waved a hand vaguely towards Brodsky – 'I was too young, I didn't know nearly enough, I couldn't really see it, what was going on. But now I've had many years to think about everything. And when I heard you were coming to our town, I told myself it really was time I learnt to contain the bitterness. I've grown old, but I'm far from done yet. There are certain things in life I've come to understand well, very well, and it's not too late, I should try and put it to some use. It's in this spirit I'm inviting you to visit me, Mr Ryder. I apologise again for being a little short with you earlier when we met. It won't happen again, I promise. Please, do say you'll come.'

As she was speaking, the image of her drawing room – the low cosy light, the worn velvet drapes, the crumbling furniture – had drifted before me, and for a brief moment the thought of reclining on one of her couches, far from the pressures of life, seemed peculiarly enticing. I took a deep breath and sighed.

'I'll bear your kind invitation in mind, Miss Collins,' I said. 'But for now, I'll have to go to bed and get some rest. You must appreciate, I've been travelling for months, and since arriving here I've hardly had a moment's pause. I'm extremely tired.'

As I said this, all my tiredness came back to me. The skin under my eyes felt itchy and I rubbed my face with the palm of my hand. I was still rubbing at my face when I felt a touch on my elbow and a voice said gently:

'I'll walk back with you, Mr Ryder.'

Stephan was reaching up to help me off the chair. I leant a hand on his shoulder and climbed down.

'I'm very tired now too,' Stephan said. 'I'll walk back with you.'

'Walk back?'

'Yes, I'm going to sleep in one of the rooms tonight. I often do that if I'm on duty early in the morning.'

For a moment his words continued to puzzle me. Then, as I looked past the clusters of standing and seated dinner guests, past the waiters and the tables, to where the vast room disappeared into darkness, it suddenly dawned on me that we were in the atrium of the hotel. I had not recognised it because earlier in the day I had entered it – and had viewed it – from the opposite end. Somewhere in the darkness on the far side would be the bar where I had drunk my coffee and planned the day ahead.

I had no chance to dwell on this realisation, however, for Stephan was leading me away with surprising insistence.

'Let's be getting back, Mr Ryder. Besides, there's something I wanted to speak to you about.'

'Good night, Mr Ryder,' Miss Collins called as we strode past.

I glanced back to wish her good night, and would have done so in a less cursory manner had Stephan not continued to lead me away. Indeed, as we made our way across the floor, I could hear people wishing me good night on all sides, and although I smiled and waved as best I could, I was conscious I was not making as gracious an exit as I might. But Stephan was clearly preoccupied and, even while I was still returning good nights over my shoulder, he tugged at my arm and said:

'Mr Ryder, I've been thinking. Perhaps I'm just getting above myself now, but I really think I ought to try the Kazan. I've remembered your advice earlier, just to stick to what I've prepared. But really, I've been thinking and I feel I might be able to conquer *Glass Passions*. It's within my capabilities now, I really believe that. The real problem is time. But if I really go at it, really work at it, at night and everything, I think I might be able to do it.'

We had entered the darkened section of the atrium. Stephan's heels echoed in the emptiness, the flip-flopping of my slippers marking a counterpoint. I could make out in the gloom, somewhere to our right, the pale marble of the large fountain, now silent and still.

'This is none of my business, I know,' I said. 'But in your position I would just carry on with what you were originally going to play. It's what you've chosen and that should be good enough. Anyway, in my opinion, it's always a mistake to change a programme at the eleventh hour . . .'

'But Mr Ryder, you don't quite understand. It's Mother. She . . .'

'I'm aware of everything you told me earlier. And as I say, I don't wish to interfere. But with respect, I think there comes a point in one's life when one must stand by one's decisions. A time to say: "This is me, this is what I've chosen to do." '

'Mr Ryder, I appreciate what you're saying. But I think perhaps you're only saying it – I know you're advising me with the best of intentions – but I think you're only saying what you're saying because you don't believe an amateur like me could possibly give a decent rendering of the Kazan, particularly with the limited time I have left. But you see, I was thinking hard about it all through dinner, and I really believe . . .'

'Really, you miss my point,' I said, feeling a touch of impatience with him. 'You really miss my point. What I'm saying is you have to make a stand.'

But the young man seemed not to be listening. 'Mr Ryder,' he went on, 'I realise it's awfully late and you're getting tired. But I wondered. If you could just give me a few minutes, even fifteen minutes, say. We could go now to the drawing room and I could play you a snatch of the Kazan, not all of it, just a snatch. Then you could advise me whether I have any chance at all of coming up with the goods by Thursday night. Oh, excuse me.'

We had reached the far end of the atrium and we paused in the dark while Stephan unlocked the doors leading out to the corridor. I glanced back and the area where we had been dining looked hardly more than a small illuminated pool in the darkness. The guests seemed to be seated again, and I could see the figures of the waiters milling around with their trays.

The corridor was very dimly lit. Stephan locked behind us the doors to the atrium and we made our way side by side, not talking. After a while, when the young man had glanced towards me a few times, it occurred to me he was waiting for my decision. I gave a sigh, saying:

'I'd certainly like to help you. I have much sympathy for you in your present situation. It's just that it's got so late now and . . .'

'Mr Ryder, I realise you're getting tired. May I make a suggestion? What if I were to go into the drawing room by myself and you could stand outside the door and listen. Then as soon as you'd heard enough to form your opinion, you could go quietly off to bed. Of course, I won't know if you're still standing out there or not, so I'll have every incentive to perform to my utmost right to the end – which is just what I need. You could tell me in the morning whether I have any chance at all for Thursday night.'

I thought about this. 'Very well,' I said eventually. 'Your proposal strikes me as very reasonable. It serves both our needs very conveniently. Very well, we'll do as you say.'

'Mr Ryder, that's jolly good of you. You've no idea what a help this is to me. I've been in such a quandary.'

In his excitement, the young man increased his pace. The corridor turned the corner and became very dark, so much so that as we hurried down it I had more than once to put my hand out for fear of veering into one or the other wall. Apart from at its very end, where some light was coming in from the glazed doors leading to the hotel lobby, there appeared to be no lighting whatsoever. I was making a mental note to raise the matter with Hoffman the next time I saw him when Stephan said: 'Ah, here we are,' and came to a halt. I then became aware we were standing by the drawing-room doors.

Stephan jingled about with more keys, and when the doors eventually opened I could see nothing beyond them except blackness. But the young man stepped eagerly into the room, then peeked his head back out into the corridor.

'If you could give me just a few seconds to find the score,' he said. 'It's somewhere in the piano stool, but everything's such a mess in there.'

'Don't worry, I won't go until I've formed a clear opinion.'

'Mr Ryder, this is so good of you. Well, I won't be a second.'

The doors closed with a rattle and for a few minutes there was silence. I remained standing in the darkness, glancing now and then to the end of the corridor and the light from the lobby.

Then at last Stephan commenced the opening movement of *Glass Passions*. After the first few bars, I found myself listening more and more intently. It was clear at once the young man was far from familiar with the piece, and yet, beneath the uncertainty and stiffness, I could discern an imagination of an originality and emotional subtlety that quite surprised me. Even in its present rough form, the young man's reading of Kazan seemed to present certain dimensions never glimpsed in the great majority of interpretations.

I leaned forward closer to the doors, straining to catch his every hesitant nuance. But then, towards the end of the movement, fatigue suddenly engulfed me and I remembered how late it was. It occurred to me there was no real need to hear any more – given adequate time, the Kazan was very obviously within his capabilities – and I began to walk slowly away in the direction of the lobby.

II

11

I was woken by the ringing of the telephone on the bedside cabinet. My first thought was that I had again been disturbed after only a few minutes, but then I saw from the light that it was now well into the morning. I picked up the receiver, seized by a sudden concern that I had overslept.

'Ah, Mr Ryder,' Hoffman's voice said. 'You slept well, I hope.'

'Thank you, Mr Hoffman, I slept very well. But of course I was just now in the process of getting up. With such a busy day in front of me' – I gave a laugh – 'it's high time I was making a start.'

'Indeed, sir, and what a day you have before you! I can well understand your wish to conserve your energy as much as possible at this point of the morning. Very wise, if I may say so. And particularly after giving us so much of yourself last night. Ah, that was such a marvellously witty address! The whole town is talking of nothing else this morning! In any case, Mr Ryder, since I knew you would be rising about this time I thought I might call you and let you know the situation. I am happy to inform you that 343 is now fully prepared. May I suggest you commence your occupancy of it immediately? Your belongings, if you have no objection, will be transferred while you are having your breakfast. 343, I know, will be so much more satisfactory than your present room. I do apologise once again for this mistake. It grieves me that it was made. But as I think I explained last night, it can sometimes be very hard to gauge these things.'

'Yes, yes, I quite understand.' I looked around the room and felt a desperate sadness starting to engulf me. 'But Mr Hoffman' – with an effort I brought my voice under control – 'there's a slight complication. My boy, Boris, he's now here with me at this hotel and . . .'

'Ah yes, and very welcome the young man is too. I've looked into the matter and he has been transferred to 342 adjoining you. In fact, Gustav saw to the young man's move earlier this morning. So you've nothing at all to worry about. Please, then, return to 343 after breakfast. You'll find all your belongings there. It's just one floor up from where you are now, I'm confident you'll find it much more to your taste. But of course if you're unhappy with it, please let me know immediately.'

I thanked him and replaced the receiver. I then climbed out of bed, looked around me again and took a deep breath. In the morning light my room did not look anything so special – just a typical hotel room – and it occurred to me that I was indeed displaying an unseemly attachment to it. Nevertheless, as I showered and dressed, I found myself growing increasingly emotional again. Then suddenly the thought came to me that before going down to breakfast, before anything, I should go and check that all was well with Boris. For all I knew, he was at this moment sitting alone in his new room in a state of some disorientation. I quickly finished dressing and, taking one last look behind me, went out of the room.

I was going along the corridor of the third floor searching for 342 when I heard a noise and saw Boris running towards me from the far end. He was running in a curious manner and I stopped in my tracks at the sight of him. Then I saw he was making steering motions with his hands and guessed he was impersonating someone in a speeding car. He was muttering furiously under his breath to an invisible passenger on his right and showed no sign of noticing me as he went hurtling past. A door was ajar further down the corridor, and as Boris approached it he yelled: 'Look out!' and swerved sharply into the room. From within came the sound of Boris's vocal impression of things crashing. I walked up to the door and, checking that it was indeed 342, stepped inside.

I found Boris lying on his back on the bed, both feet high in the air.

'Boris,' I said, 'you shouldn't run around shouting like that. This is a hotel. For all you know, people might be asleep.'

'Asleep! At this time of day!'

I shut the door behind me. 'You shouldn't make all this noise. There'll be complaints.'

'Tough luck if they complain. I'll just get Grandfather to deal with them.'

His feet were still in the air and now he began languidly clap-

156

ping his shoes together. I took a chair and watched him for a moment.

'Boris, I have to talk to you. What I mean is, *we* have to talk, both of us. It's good for us. You must have so many questions. About all this. Why we're here in the hotel.'

I paused to see if he would say anything. Boris went on clapping his feet together in the air.

'Boris, you've been very patient until now,' I went on. 'But I know there's all kinds of things you're wanting to ask. I'm sorry if I've always been too busy to sit and talk to you about them properly. And I'm sorry about last night. That was disappointing, for both of us. Boris, you must have so many questions. Some of them won't have easy answers, but I'll try and answer them the best I can.'

For some reason as I said this – perhaps it was to do with my old room and the thought that I might now have left it behind for ever – a powerful sense of loss welled up inside me and I was obliged to pause a moment. Boris went on clapping his feet for a little longer. Then his legs appeared to grow tired and he allowed them to flop onto the bed. I cleared my throat, then said:

'So Boris. Where shall we begin?'

'Solar Man!' Boris shrieked suddenly and chanted loudly the opening bars of some theme tune. With this he crashed over, disappearing into the gap between the bed and the wall.

'Boris, I'm being serious. For goodness sake. We've got to talk these things over. Boris, please, come out from there.'

There was no reply. I sighed and got to my feet.

'Boris, I want you to know that whenever you want to ask me anything, you can just ask. I'll stop whatever I'm doing and come to talk things over with you. Even if I'm with people who seem very important, I want you to understand, they're not as important to me as you. Boris, can you hear me? Boris, come out from there.'

'I can't. I can't move.'

'Boris. Please.'

'I can't move. I've broken three vertebrae.'

'Very well, Boris. Perhaps we'll talk when you're feeling better. I'm going downstairs now to get some breakfast. Boris, listen. If you like, after breakfast, we could go back to the old apartment.

If you want, we can do that. We could go and get that box then. The one with Number Nine in it.'

There was still no response. I waited a moment longer, then said: 'Well, think about it, Boris. I'm going down to have breakfast now.'

With that, I left the room, closing the door quietly behind me.

I was shown into a long sun-filled room adjoining the front of the lobby. The large windows appeared to face the street at pavement level, but opaque glass had been used on the lower panes to give some privacy, and the sound of the traffic passing outside could be heard only in muffled tones. Tall palms and ceiling fans gave the place a vaguely exotic air. The tables had been arranged in two long rows and, as the waiter led me down the gangway between them, I noticed most of the tables had already been cleared.

The waiter seated me near the back and poured me some coffee. As he went away, I saw the only other guests present were a couple talking in Spanish near the doorway and an old man reading a paper a few tables from me. I supposed I was perhaps the last guest down to breakfast, but then again, I had had an exceptionally demanding night and saw no reason to feel any guilt about it.

On the contrary, as I sat watching the palms waving gently under the rotating fans, a feeling of contentment began to come over me. I had, after all, reason enough to be well satisfied with what I had achieved in the short time since my arrival. Naturally there were still many aspects to this local crisis that remained unclear, even mysterious. But then, I had not yet been here twenty-four hours and answers to questions were bound to present themselves before long. Later in the day, for instance, I would be visiting the Countess, when I would have the opportunity not just to refresh my memory of Brodsky's work from his old gramophone records, but to talk over the whole crisis in detail with both the Countess and the mayor. Then there was the meeting with the citizens most directly affected by the current problems – the importance of which I had stressed to Miss Stratmann the previous day – and the encounter with Christoff himself. In other words, several of my most significant appointments still lay in front of me, and it was pointless to attempt to draw any real conclusions or even to begin thinking about finalising my speech at this stage. For the time being, I was entitled to feel pleased with the amount of information I had already absorbed, and could certainly afford a few minutes of indulgent relaxation as I ate my breakfast.

The waiter returned bearing cold meats, cheeses and a basket of fresh rolls, and I began to eat unhurriedly, pouring the strong coffee into my cup a little at a time. When eventually Stephan Hoffman appeared in the room, I was in something approaching a tranquil mood.

'Good morning, Mr Ryder,' the young man said, coming towards me with a smile. 'I heard you'd just come down. I don't want to disturb your breakfast, so I won't stay long.'

He remained hovering beside my table, the smile still on his face, clearly waiting for me to speak. Only then did I remember our arrangement of the previous night.

'Ah yes,' I said. 'The Kazan. Ah yes.' I put down my butter knife and looked at him. 'It is of course one of the most difficult pieces ever composed for piano. Given that you've only just started to practise it, it hardly surprised me to hear certain rough edges. Nothing much more than that, simply rough edges. With that piece there's little one can do but devote time. A *lot* of time.'

I paused again. The smile had faded from Stephan's face.

'But on the whole,' I went on, 'and I don't say such things lightly, I thought your rendering last night showed exceptional promise. Provided you have enough time, I'm certain you'll give a very fair account of even that difficult piece. Of course the question is . . .'

But the young man was no longer listening. Coming a step closer to me, he said:

'Mr Ryder, let me get this clear. You're saying practice is all it will take? That it's within my grasp?' Suddenly Stephan's face contorted, his body doubled over and he hammered his fist into his raised knee. Then he straightened, took a deep breath and beamed with delight. 'Mr Ryder, you've no idea, no idea what this means to me. What marvellous encouragement, you've no idea! I know this sounds immodest, but I'll tell you, I always felt it, deep within myself, I always felt I had it. But to hear you say

159

so, you of all people, my God, it's priceless! Last night, Mr Ryder, I played on and on. Each time I felt tiredness coming over me, whenever I was tempted to stop, a little voice inside would say: "Wait. Mr Ryder may still be outside. He may need just a little more to make his assessment." And I'd put even more into it, everything, I went on and on. When I finished, about two hours ago, I must confess I did go up to the door and peek out. And of course, I found you'd gone to bed – very sensibly. But it was so good of you to have stayed as long as you did. I just hope you didn't sacrifice too much sleep on my account.'

'Oh no, no. I stayed at the door for . . . a certain period. Enough to make my assessment.'

'It was so kind of you, Mr Ryder. I feel like someone else this morning. The clouds have lifted from my life!'

'Now look, you mustn't get the wrong idea. What I'm saying is that the piece is within your capabilities. But whether you have enough time left before . . .'

'I'll make sure I have enough time. I'll take every single opportunity to get to the piano and practise. I'll forget about sleep. Don't you worry, Mr Ryder. I'll do my parents proud tomorrow night.'

'Tomorrow night? Oh yes . . .'

'Oh, but here I am talking on selfishly about myself, I haven't even mentioned how sensationally you went down last night. At the dinner, I mean. Everyone's been talking about it, all over the city. It really was such a charming speech.'

'Thank you. I'm glad it was appreciated.'

'And I'm sure it helped enormously to create the atmosphere for what came afterwards. Yes, apparently – this is the *really* good news I should have reported to you immediately – as you saw, Miss Collins turned up last night. Well, at one point, as she was leaving, she and Mr Brodsky, apparently they exchanged smiles. Yes, really! Many people witnessed it. Father saw it himself. He'd been making no effort at all to bring them into direct contact, he'd been very careful things weren't pushed too fast, especially with Miss Collins thinking it over about the zoo and everything. But it was just as she was leaving. Apparently Mr Brodsky noticed she was leaving and stood up. He'd been sitting at his table the whole evening, even though by this time people were milling about freely in the way they always do. But now Mr Brodsky, he got to his feet and looked across the room to the doorway where Miss Collins was saying good night to a few people. One of the gentlemen, I think it was Mr Weber, was escorting her out, but some instinct must have told her. Anyway, she glanced back at the room and of course saw Mr Brodsky on his feet gazing at her. Father noticed this, and so did quite a few others and the room got quite a bit quieter, and Father says he thought for a terrible moment she was going to give him a cold bitter look, her face had shaped up as though she was going to. But then at the last moment, she smiled. Yes, she gave Mr Brodsky a smile! Then she went out. Mr Brodsky, well, you can imagine what that would have meant to him. Just imagine, after all these years! According to Father, I saw him just now, Mr Brodsky's been working with a new energy this morning. Already he's been at the piano for an hour! It's just as well I vacated it when I did! Father says there's something entirely different about him this morning, and of course no suggestion whatsoever of needing a drink. It's all been a triumph for Father as much as anyone, but I'm sure your speech contributed enormously to everything. We're still waiting to hear from Miss Collins, about her coming to the zoo, I mean, but after what happened last night, we can't help but be optimistic. What a morning it's turning into! Well, Mr Ryder, I won't keep you any longer, I'm sure you're longing to finish your breakfast. I'll just say thank you again for everything. I'm sure we'll run into each other during the day and I'll report to you how things are going with the Kazan.'

I wished him luck and watched him stride purposefully out of the room.

The encounter with the young man left me feeling more contented than ever. For the next several minutes I went on with my breakfast at the same leisurely pace, enjoying in particular the fresh taste of the local butter. At one point the waiter appeared with another pot of coffee then left again. After a while, for some reason, I found myself trying to remember the answer to a question once put to me by a man sitting beside me on a plane. Three pairs of brothers had played together in World Cup finals, he had said. Could I remember them? I had made some excuse and returned to my book, not wishing to be drawn into conversation. But then ever since, on occasions such as this when I found myself with a rare few minutes to myself, I would find the man's question coming back to me. The annoying thing was that I had at times over the years managed to remember all three sets of brothers, but then at other times would discover I had forgotten one pair or another. And so it was this morning. I remembered that the Charlton brothers had played for England in the 1966 final, the van der Kerkhof brothers for Holland in 1978. But try as I might I could not remember the third pair. After a while I began to grow quite annoyed at myself, and at one stage became quite determined I would not leave the breakfast table nor embark on my day's commitments until I had succeeded in remembering the third pair of brothers.

I was brought out of my reverie by the realisation that Boris had come into the room and was making his way towards me. He was doing so gradually, drifting nonchalantly from table to empty table, as though it were merely by chance he was getting closer to me. He avoided looking at me and even when he had arrived at the next table he loitered there fingering the tablecloth, his back turned to me.

'Boris, have you had breakfast?' I asked.

He continued fiddling with the tablecloth. Then he asked in a tone that suggested he did not care much one way or the other: 'Are we going to the old apartment?'

'If you want to. I promised we'd go if you wanted to. Do you want to go, Boris?'

'Haven't you got work to do?'

'Yes, but I can manage to do that later. We could go to the old apartment if you want. But if we're going, we'll have to set off straight away. As you say, I have quite a busy day in front of me.'

Boris seemed to be thinking things over. He kept his back to me and went on fiddling with the tablecloth.

'Well, Boris? Shall we go?'

'Will Number Nine be there?'

'I should think so.' Deciding I should take the initiative, I stood up and tossed my napkin next to my plate. 'Boris, let's set off straight away. It looks like a sunny day outside. We don't even need to go up for jackets. Let's just go straight away.'

Boris continued to look hesitant, but I put my arm around his shoulders and led him out of the breakfast room.

As Boris and I were crossing the lobby, I noticed the desk clerk waving to me.

'Oh Mr Ryder,' he said. 'Those journalists came back earlier. I thought it best to send them away for now and suggested they try again in an hour's time. Don't worry, they were perfectly agreeable.'

I thought for a moment, then said: 'Unfortunately, I'm in the middle of something important just now. Perhaps you might ask these gentlemen to arrange a time properly through Miss Stratmann. Now if you'll excuse us, we have to be getting along.'

It was only when we had made our way out of the hotel and were standing on the sunny pavement that it occurred to me I could not remember how to get to the old apartment. For a few seconds I looked at the traffic moving slowly in front of us. Then Boris, perhaps sensing my difficulty, said: 'We can get a tram. From outside the fire station.'

'That's good. Okay then, Boris, you lead the way.'

The noise of the traffic was such that for the next few minutes we hardly talked. We dodged along narrow crowded pavements, crossed two busy little streets, then came out onto a broad avenue with tram lines and several lanes of slow traffic. The pavement was much wider here and we walked more freely through the pedestrians, past banks, offices and restaurants. Then I heard footsteps running up behind me and felt a hand touch my shoulder.

'Mr Ryder! Ah, here you are at last!'

The man I turned to find resembled an ageing rock singer. He had a weather-beaten face and long messy hair parted down the middle. His shirt and trousers were loose and cream-coloured.

'How do you do,' I said cautiously, aware that Boris was eyeing the man with suspicion.

'What a most unfortunate series of misunderstandings!' the man said laughing. 'We've been given so many different appointments. And last night we waited a long time, over two hours, but never mind! These things happen. I dare say none of it is your fault, sir. In fact, I'm sure it isn't.'

'Ah yes. And you were waiting again this morning. Yes, yes, the desk clerk mentioned it.'

'This morning, again, there was some misunderstanding.' The long-haired man shrugged. 'They said to come back in another hour. So we were just killing time over there, in that café, the photographer and I. But now that you're passing, I wonder if we shouldn't just do the interview and the photographs right now. Then we won't need to bother you ever again. Of course, we realise that for someone such as yourself, talking to a small local paper like ours won't be high among your priorities . . .'

'On the contrary,' I said quickly, 'I always place the highest importance on periodicals such as yours. You hold the key to the local feelings. People like yourself I regard as being among my most valued contacts in a town.'

'How very kind of you to say so, Mr Ryder. And if I may say so, rather insightful.'

'But I was going on to say that, unfortunately, just at this moment, I'm in the middle of something.'

'Of course, of course. For that very reason, I was suggesting we just get the whole thing over and done with now, rather than that we continue to bother you throughout the day. Our photographer, Pedro, he's over there now in that café. He can take a few quick pictures while I ask you two or three questions. Then you and this young gentleman, you can hurry along to wherever it is you're going. The whole thing would take only about four or five minutes. It seems by far the simplest solution.'

'Hmm. Just a few minutes, you say.'

'Oh, we'd be more than delighted with a few minutes. We fully appreciate how many other important demands there must be on your time. As I say, we're just over there. That café there.'

He was pointing to a spot a little distance away where some tables and chairs were spilling onto the pavement. It did not look the sort of place I would ideally conduct an interview, but it occurred to me this might be the simplest way to bring the matter of the journalists to an end.

'Very well,' I said. 'But I have to emphasise, I have a particularly tight schedule this morning.'

'Mr Ryder, it's so gracious of you. And for a humble little paper like ours! Well, let's get it done as quickly as possible. Please, this way.'

The long-haired journalist began to lead us back along the pavement, almost colliding with another pedestrian in his eagerness to return to his café. He was soon a few paces ahead and I took the opportunity to say to Boris:

'Don't worry, this won't take any time at all. I'll make sure of that.'

Boris continued to wear a disgruntled expression and so I added:

'Look, you can sit and have something nice while you're waiting. Some ice cream or cheesecake. Then we'll set off immediately.'

We came to a halt by a narrow courtyard busy with parasols.

'Here we are,' the journalist said, gesturing towards one of the tables. 'We're just over here.'

'If you don't mind,' I said to him, 'I'll first of all install Boris inside. I'll come back out and join you in just one minute.'

'An excellent idea.'

Although many of the tables out in the courtyard were occupied, there were no customers at all inside. The décor was light and modern, and the room was full of sunshine. A plump young waitress of Nordic appearance was standing behind a glass counter inside which was displayed a range of cakes and pastries. As Boris seated himself at a table in the corner, the young woman came towards us with a smile.

'So what would you like?' she asked Boris. 'We have this morning the freshest cakes in the whole town. They just arrived ten minutes ago. Everything's very fresh.'

Boris proceeded to quiz the waitress very thoroughly about her cakes before settling on the almond and chocolate cheesecake.

'Okay, I won't be long,' I said to him. 'I'll just go and see these people, then come right back. If you want anything, I'll be just outside.'

Boris shrugged, his attention fixed on the waitress, now in the process of extricating an elaborate confection from out of the display cabinet.

12

When I came back out into the courtyard, I could not see the long-haired journalist anywhere. I strolled among the parasols for a while, peering at the faces of the people sitting at the tables. When I had gone once round the courtyard, I stopped to consider the possibility that the journalist had changed his mind and gone away. But this seemed extraordinary, and I looked around me once more. There were various people reading newspapers over their coffees. An old man was talking to the pigeons around his feet. Then I heard someone mention my name and, turning, saw the journalist sitting at a table directly behind me. He was in deep conversation with a squat, swarthy man whom I took to be the photographer. Letting out an exclamation I went up to them, but curiously the two men continued their discussion without looking up at me. Even when I drew up the remaining chair and sat down, the journalist – who was in mid-sentence – gave me no more than a cursory glance. Then, turning back to the swarthy photographer, he continued:

'So don't give him any hints about the significance of the building. You'll just have to make up some arty justification, some reason why he has to be constantly in front of it.'

'No problem,' the photographer said nodding. 'No problem.'

'But don't push him too much. That seems to be where Schulz went wrong in Vienna last month. And remember, like all these types, he's very vain. So pretend to be a big fan of his. Tell him the paper had no idea when they sent you, but you happen to be a really huge fan. That'll get him. But don't mention the Sattler building until we've developed a rapport.'

'Okay, okay.' The photographer was still nodding. 'But I kind of thought this would have been fixed up by now. I thought you'd have got him to agree already.'

'I was going to try and fix it on the phone, but then Schulz warned me what a difficult shit the guy is.' As he said this, the journalist turned to me and gave me a polite smile. The photographer, following his companion's gaze, gave me a distracted nod, then the two of them returned to their discussion.

'The trouble with Schulz,' the journalist said, 'is he never flatters them enough. And he's got that manner, like he's really impatient, even when he's not. With these types, you just have to keep up the flattery. So all the time you snap, keep shouting "great". Keep exclaiming. Don't stop feeding his ego.'

'Okay, okay. No problem.'

'So I'll start in with . . .' The journalist gave a weary sigh. 'I'll start talking about his performance in Vienna or something like that. I've got some notes on it here, I'll bluff my way. But let's not waste too much time. After a few minutes, you make out you've had this inspiration about going out to the Sattler building. I'll make out I'm a bit annoyed at first, but then end up admitting it's a brilliant idea.'

'Okay, okay.'

'You're sure now. Let's have no mistakes. Remember he's a touchy bastard.'

'I understand.'

'Anything starts to go wrong, just say something flattering.'

'Fine, fine.'

The two men nodded to each other. Then the journalist took a deep breath, clapped his hands together and turned to face me, brightening suddenly as he did so.

'Ah, Mr Ryder, here you are! It's so good of you to give us some of your precious time. And the young man, he's enjoying himself in there, I trust?'

'Yes, yes. He's ordered a very large piece of cheesecake.'

Both men laughed pleasantly. The swarthy photographer grinned and said:

'Cheesecake. Yeah, that's my favourite. From when I was a little kid.'

'Oh, Mr Ryder, this is Pedro.'

The photographer smiled and held out his hand eagerly. 'Very pleased to meet you, sir. This is a real break for me, I tell you. I was put on this assignment only this morning. When I got up, all I had to look forward to was another shoot in the council chambers. Then I get this call while I'm having my shower. Do you want to do it? they ask. Do I want to do it? The man's been my

, hero since I was a kid, I tell them. Do I want to do it? Jesus, I'll do it for nothing. I'll pay *you* to do it, I tell them. Just tell me where to go. I swear I've never been this excited over an assignment.'

'To be frank, Mr Ryder,' the journalist said, 'the photographer who was with me last night at the hotel, well, after we'd been waiting a few hours he started to get a little impatient. Naturally I was quite angry with him. "You don't seem to realise," I said to him. "If Mr Ryder has been delayed, it's bound to be by the most important sorts of engagements. If he's good enough to consent to give us some of his time and we need to wait a little, then wait we shall." I tell you, sir, I got quite angry with him. And when I got back I told the editor it just wasn't good enough. "Find me another photographer for the morning," I demanded. "I want someone who fully appreciates Mr Ryder's position and shows him the appropriate gratitude." Yes, I suppose I got quite worked up about it. Anyway, we've got Pedro now, who turns out to be almost as big a fan of yours as I am.'

'Bigger, bigger,' Pedro protested. 'When I got the call this morning, I just couldn't believe it. My hero's in town and I'm going to get to shoot him. Jesus, I'm going to do the best job I've ever done, that's what I said to myself while I was taking my shower. A guy like that, you have to do the best job ever. I'll take him up against the Sattler building. That's how I saw it. I could see the whole composition in my head while I was taking my shower.'

'Now, Pedro,' the journalist said, looking at him sternly, 'I doubt very much if Mr Ryder cares to go over to the Sattler building just for the sake of our photographs. All right, it's only a few minutes drive at the most, but a few minutes is still no inconsiderable thing to a man on a tight schedule. No, Pedro, you'll just have to do the best you can here, take a few shots of Mr Ryder as we talk at this table. Okay, a pavement café, it's very clichéd, it will hardly show to good effect the unique charisma Mr Ryder carries around him. But it will just have to do. I admit, your idea of Mr Ryder against the Sattler building, it's inspired. But he simply doesn't have the time. We'll have to be satisfied with a much more ordinary picture of him.'

Pedro punched his fist into his palm and shook his head. 'I guess that's right. But Jesus, it's tough. A chance to take the great

Mr Ryder, a once-in-a-lifetime chance, and I have to make do with another café scene. That's the way life deals you a hand.' He shook his head again sadly. Then for a moment the two of them sat there looking at me.

'Well,' I said eventually, 'this building of yours. Is it literally a few minutes drive away?'

Pedro sat up abruptly, his face lit with enthusiasm.

'You mean it? You'll pose in front of the Sattler building? Jesus, what a break! I just knew you'd be a great guy!'

'Now wait . . .'

'Are you sure, Mr Ryder?' the journalist said grasping my arm. 'Are you really sure? I know you've got a heavy schedule. Why, that's really magnificent of you! And truly, it will take no more than three minutes by taxi. In fact, if you'll just wait here, sir, I'll go and hail one now. Pedro, why don't you get a few shots of Mr Ryder here anyhow while he's waiting.'

The journalist hurried off. The next moment I saw him at the edge of the pavement, leaning towards the oncoming traffic, an arm held poised in the air.

'Mr Ryder, sir. Please.'

Pedro was crouched down on one knee, squinting up at me through a camera. I arranged myself in my chair – adopting a relaxed but not overly languid posture – and put on a genial smile.

Pedro snapped the shutter a few times. Then he retreated some distance and crouched down again, this time beside an empty table, disturbing as he did so a flock of pigeons pecking away at some crumbs. I was about to re-adjust my posture, when the journalist came rushing back.

'Mr Ryder, I can't find a taxi just now, but here's a tram just arrived. Please hurry, we can jump on. Pedro, quickly, the tram.'

'But will it be as quick as a taxi?' I asked.

'Yes, yes. In fact with the traffic like this the tram will be quicker. Really, Mr Ryder, you've no need to worry. The Sattler building is very near. In fact' – he raised his hand to shade his eyes and looked into the far distance – 'in fact, you can almost see it from here. If it weren't for that grey tower over there, we'd be able to see the Sattler building right at this moment. That's how close we are, really. In fact, if someone of normal height – no taller than you or me – if such a person were to climb onto the roof of the Sattler building, stand up straight and hold up some pole-like object – a household mop, say – on a morning like this, we'd be able to see it quite easily above that grey tower. So you see, we'll be there in no time at all. But please, the tram, we must hurry.'

Pedro was already down at the kerb. I could see him, his heavy bag of equipment on his shoulder, trying to persuade the tram driver to wait for us. I followed the journalist out of the courtyard and clambered aboard.

The tram started up again as the three of us made our way down the central aisle. The carriage was crowded, making it impossible for us to sit near one another. I squeezed myself into a seat towards the back of the carriage, between a small elderly man and a matronly mother with a toddler on her lap. The seat was surprisingly comfortable and after a few moments I began rather to enjoy the journey. Opposite me were three old men reading one newspaper, held open by the man in the middle. The jogging of the tram seemed to give them difficulties and at times they tussled for command of a particular page.

We had been travelling for a while when I became aware of activity around me and saw that a ticket inspector was making her way down the aisle. It occurred to me then that my companions must have purchased my ticket for me – I certainly had not acquired one on boarding. When I next glanced over my shoulder I saw that the ticket inspector, a petite woman whose ugly black uniform could not entirely disguise her attractive figure, had all but reached our part of the carriage. All around me, people were producing their tickets and passes. Suppressing a sense of panic, I set about formulating something to say that would sound at once dignified and convincing.

Then the ticket inspector was looming above us and my neighbours all proffered their tickets. While she was still in the process of clipping them, I announced firmly:

'I'm without a ticket, but in my case there are special circumstances which, if you'll allow me, I'll explain to you.'

The ticket inspector looked at me. Then she said: 'Not having a ticket is one thing. But you know, you really let me down last night.'

As soon as she said this, I recognised Fiona Roberts, a girl from my village primary school in Worcestershire with whom I had developed a special friendship around the time I was nine years old. She had lived near us, a short way along the lane in a cottage not unlike ours, and I had often wandered down to spend an afternoon playing with her, particularly during the difficult period before our departure to Manchester. I had not seen her at all since those days, and so was quite taken aback by her accusing manner.

'Ah yes,' I said. 'Last night. Yes.'

Fiona Roberts went on looking at me. Perhaps it was to do with the reproachful expression she was now wearing, but I suddenly found myself recalling an afternoon from our childhood, when the two of us had been sitting together under her parents' dining table. We had, as usual, created our 'hide-out' by hanging an assortment of blankets and curtains down over the sides of the table. That particular afternoon had been warm and sunny, but we had persisted in sitting inside our hide-out, in the stuffy heat and near-darkness. I had been saying something to Fiona, no doubt at some length and in an upset manner. More than once she had tried to interrupt, but I had continued. Then finally, when I had finished, she had said:

'That's silly. That means you'll be all on your own. You'll get lonely.'

'I don't mind that,' I had said. 'I like being lonely.'

'You're just being silly again. No one likes being lonely. I'm going to have a big family. Five children at least. And I'm going to cook them a lovely supper every evening.' Then, when I did not respond, she had said again: 'You're just being silly. No one likes being on their own.'

'I do. I like it.'

'How can you *like* being lonely?'

'I do. I just do.'

In fact, I had felt some conviction in making this assertion. For by that afternoon it had already been several months since I had commenced my 'training sessions'; indeed, that particular obsession had probably reached its peak just around that time.

My 'training sessions' had come about quite unplanned. I had been playing by myself out in the lane one grey afternoon –

171

absorbed in some fantasy, climbing in and out of a dried-out ditch running between a row of poplars and a field – when I had suddenly felt a sense of panic and a need for the company of my parents. Our cottage had not been far away – I had been able to see the back of it across the field – and yet the feeling of panic had grown rapidly until I had been all but overcome by the urge to run home at full speed across the rough grass. But for some reason – perhaps I had quickly associated the sensation with immaturity – I had forced myself to delay my departure. There had not been any question in my mind that I would, very soon, start to run across the field. It was simply a matter of holding back that moment with an effort of will for several more seconds. The strange mixture of fear and exhilaration I had experienced as I had stood there transfixed in the dried-out ditch was one that I was to come to know well in the weeks that followed. For within days, my 'training sessions' had become a regular and important feature of my life. In time, they had acquired a certain ritual, so that as soon as I felt the earliest signs of my need to return home I would make myself go to a special spot along the lane, under a large oak tree, where I would remain standing for several minutes, fighting off my emotions. Often I would decide I had done enough, that I could now set off, only to pull myself back again, forcing myself to remain under the tree for just a few seconds more. There was no doubting the strange thrill that had accompanied the growing fear and panic of these occasions, a sensation which perhaps accounted for the somewhat compulsive hold my 'training sessions' came to have over me.

'But you know, don't you,' Fiona had said to me that afternoon, her face close to mine in the darkness, 'when *you* get married, it needn't be like it is with your mum and dad. It won't be like that at all. Husbands and wives don't always argue all the time. They only argue like that when . . . when special things happen.'

'What special things?'

Fiona had remained silent for a moment. I had been about to repeat my question, this time more aggressively, when she had said with some deliberation:

'Your parents. They don't argue like that just because they don't get on. Don't you know? Don't you know why they argue all the time?'

Then suddenly an angry voice had called from outside our hide-out and Fiona had vanished. And as I had continued sitting alone in the darkness under the table, I had caught the sounds from the kitchen of Fiona and her mother arguing in lowered voices. At one point I had heard Fiona repeating in an injured tone: 'But why not? Why can't I tell him? Everybody else knows.' And her mother saying, her voice still lowered: 'He's younger than you. He's too young. You're not to tell him.'

These memories were brought to a halt as Fiona Roberts came a few steps closer, saying to me:

'I waited till ten-thirty. Then I told everyone to eat. People were starving by then.'

'Of course. Naturally.' I laughed weakly and looked around the carriage. 'Ten-thirty. By that time, yes, people are bound to get hungry . . .'

'And by that time, it was obvious you weren't coming. No one believed any of it any more.'

'No. I suppose by that time, inevitably . . .'

'At first it was going fine,' Fiona Roberts said. 'I'd never held anything like that before, but it was going fine. They were all there, Inge, Trude, all of them in my apartment. I was a little nervous, but it was going fine and I was really excited too. Some of the women, they'd prepared so much for the evening, they'd come with folders full of information and photos. It wasn't until around nine o'clock the restlessness started up, and that's when it first occurred to me you might not come. I kept going in and out of the room bringing in more coffee, refilling the bowls of snacks, trying to keep things going. I could see they were all starting to whisper, but I still thought, well, you might come along yet, you were probably just caught up in the traffic somewhere. Then it got later and later, and in the end they were talking and whispering quite openly. You know, even when I was still in the room. In my own apartment! That's when I told them just to eat. I just wanted the whole thing over with then. So they all sat around eating, I'd prepared all these little omelettes, and even as they were eating, some of them like that Ulrike, they kept whispering and sniggering. But you know, in some ways I actually preferred the ones who sniggered. I preferred them to the likes of Trude, pretending to feel so sorry for me, taking care to be nice right to

173

the end, oh, how I loathe that woman! I could see her as she was leaving, thinking to herself: "Poor thing. She lives in a fantasy world. We really should have guessed." Oh, I hate the lot of them, I really despise myself for having got involved with them at all. But, you see, I was living on the estate for four years, I hadn't made a single proper friend, I was very isolated. For ages, those women, the people who were in my apartment last night, they wouldn't have anything to do with me. They consider themselves the elite on the estate, you see. They call themselves the Women's Arts and Cultural Foundation. It's silly, it's not a foundation in any real sense, but they think it sounds grand. They like to busy themselves whenever something's being organised in the city. When the Peking Ballet came, for instance, they made all the bunting for the welcoming reception. Anyway, they consider themselves very exclusive and until recently they wouldn't consider having anything to do with someone like me. That Inge, she wouldn't even say hello if I saw her around the estate. But that all changed, of course, once it got around. That I knew you, I mean. I'm not sure how it got out, I wasn't going around boasting about it. I suppose I must have just mentioned it to someone. Well anyway, as you can imagine, that changed everything. Inge herself stopped me one day earlier this year, when we were passing on the stairs, and invited me to one of their meetings. I didn't really want to get involved with them, but I went along, I suppose I thought I might make some friends at last, I don't know. Well right from the start, some of them, Inge and Trude too, they weren't at all sure whether to believe it or not, you know, about my being an old friend of yours. But they went along with it in the end, it made them feel pretty good, I suppose. This whole idea about looking after your parents, it wasn't mine, but obviously the fact that I knew you had a lot to do with it. When the news first came about your visit, Inge went along and put it to Mr von Braun, saying the Foundation was ready now, after the Peking Ballet, ready to take on something really important, and anyway, one of the group was an old friend of yours. That sort of thing. And so the Foundation got the job, of looking after your parents during their stay here, and everybody was thrilled of course, though some of those women, they got pretty nervous about such a responsibility. But Inge kept them all confident,

174

saying it was no more than we deserved now. We kept having these meetings when we'd come up with ideas about how to entertain your parents. Inge told us – I was sorry to hear this – neither of your parents is very well now, and so quite a lot of the obvious things, tours around the city, that sort of thing, weren't very suitable. But there were a lot of ideas, and everyone was beginning to get pretty excited. Then at the last meeting someone said, well, why shouldn't we ask *you* to come and personally meet us all? Talk over what your parents might like. There was dead silence for a moment. Then Inge said: "Why shouldn't we? After all, we're uniquely qualified to invite him." Then they were all staring at me. So in the end I said: "Well, I expect he's going to be busy, but if you like I could ask him." And I could see how thrilled they all were when I said that. Then once your reply came in, well, I became a princess, they treated me with such appreciation, smiling and caressing me whenever they ran into me, bringing presents for the children, offering to do this or that for me. So you can just imagine the effect it had last night when you didn't turn up.'

She gave a deep sigh and was silent for a moment, staring blankly through the window at the buildings going by outside. Eventually, she went on:

'I suppose I shouldn't blame you really. After all, we haven't seen each other for so long now. But I thought you'd want to come for your parents' sake. Everyone had so many ideas about what we could do for them here. This morning, they'll all be talking about me. Hardly any of them go out to work, they have husbands who bring in good money, they'll all be phoning each other or paying each other visits, they'll all be saying: "Poor woman, she lives in a world of her own. We should have seen it earlier. I'd like to do something to help her, except that, well, she's so *wearying*." I can just hear them now, they'll be really enjoying themselves. And Inge, a part of her will be very angry. "The little bitch tricked us," she'll be thinking. But she'll be pleased, she'll be relieved. Inge, you see, as much as she liked the idea of my knowing you, she always found it threatening. I could tell that. And the way the others were all treating me these last few weeks, ever since your reply, that might have given her something to think about. She's been really torn, they all have. Anyway, they'll be enjoying themselves this morning, I know they will be.'

Naturally, as I listened to Fiona, I sensed I should be feeling considerable remorse over what had happened the previous night. However, despite her vivid account of the scenes at her apartment, as much as I felt deeply sorry for her, I found I had only the vaguest recollection of such an event having been on my schedule. Besides, her words had made me realise with something of a shock how little consideration I had so far given to the whole question of my parents' imminent arrival in the city. As Fiona had mentioned, they were neither of them in good health and could hardly be left to fend for themselves. Indeed, as I looked at the harsh traffic and the glassy buildings going by outside, I felt a strong sense of protectiveness towards my elderly parents. It was in fact the ideal solution that a group of local women be entrusted with their welfare, and it had been immensely foolish of me not to have taken the opportunity to meet and talk to them. I felt a panic beginning to seize me about what to do with my parents – I could not imagine how I could have given so little thought to this whole dimension to my visit – and for a moment my mind was racing. I suddenly saw my mother and my father, both small, white-haired and bowed with age, standing outside the railway station, surrounded by luggage they could not hope to transport by themselves. I could see them looking at the strange city around them, and then eventually my father, his pride getting the better of his good sense, picking up two, then three cases, while my mother tried in vain to restrain him, holding his arm with her thin hand, saying: 'No, no, you can't carry that. It's much too much.' And my father, his face hard with determination, shaking off my mother saying: 'But who else is going to carry them? How else will we ever reach our hotel? Who else is going to help us in this place if we don't help ourselves?' All this while cars and lorries roared past them and commuters rushed by. My mother, sadly resigning herself, watching my father as he tottered with his heavy burden, four paces, five, then finally overcome, lowering the suitcases, shoulders stooped, his breath coming heavily. Then my mother, after a while, going to him, placing a gentle hand on his arm. 'Never mind. We'll find someone to help us.' And my father, now resigned, perhaps satisfied because he had demonstrated at least his spirit, looking quietly into the rush before him, searching for someone who might have come to meet them, who would see to their luggage, make welcoming conversation and take them off to a hotel in a comfortable car.

All these images filled my head as Fiona was speaking so that I was for some moments hardly able to consider her own unfortunate situation. But then I became aware of her saying:

'They'll be talking about how they'll have to be more careful from now on. I can just hear them. "We've become so much more prestigious now, we're bound to get all sorts trying to trick their way in. We have to be careful, especially now we've got so much responsibility. That little bitch should be a lesson to us." That sort of thing. God knows what kind of life I'm going to lead now on that estate. And my children, they've got to grow up there . . .'

'Look,' I said interrupting, 'I can't tell you how badly I feel about this. But the fact is, something quite unforeseeable happened last night, I won't bore you with it here. I was of course extremely annoyed at having to let you down, but it was quite impossible even to get to a phone. I hope you hadn't gone to too much trouble.'

'I'd gone to a *lot* of trouble. It's not easy for me, you know, a single mother with two growing children . . .'

'Listen, I really feel very badly about this. Let me make a suggestion. Just now I've got something I have to do with these journalists over there, but that won't take long. I'll get away from them as quickly as possible, I'll jump into a taxi and come to your apartment. I'll be there in, say, half an hour – forty-five minutes at the most. Then what we can do is this. We'll walk together all around your estate, so all these people, your neighbours, this Inge, this Trude, they can all see with their own eyes that we really are old friends. Then we'll call in on the more influential ones, like this Inge person. You could introduce me, I'll apologise about last night, explain how at the last moment I'd been unavoidably delayed. One by one, we'll win them over and repair the harm I did you last night. In fact, if we do this well, you might be even better established with your friends than you ever would have been. What do you say to that?'

For a few moments Fiona went on staring at the passing view.

Then finally she said: 'My first instinct would be to say: "Forget the whole thing." It's got me nowhere, my claiming to be an old friend of yours. And anyway, maybe I don't need to be part of Inge's circle. It's just that I was so lonely before on the estate, but having had a taste of how they behave, I'm not sure I won't be happier just having my children for company. I could read a good book or watch the television in the evenings. But then I have to think not just about myself, but about my children. They have to grow up on the estate, they have to be accepted. For their sake, I ought to take up this suggestion of yours. As you say, if we do what you suggest, I might be better off than I would have been even if the party had been a roaring success. But you have to promise, swear on everything you hold dear, you won't let me down a second time. Because, you see, if we're to carry out your plan, it means as soon as I get in from this shift, I'll have to start phoning round to fix up our visits. There's no way we can just go knocking on doors unexpectedly, it's just not that sort of neighbourhood. So you see how it would be if I made all these appointments and you didn't show up. There'd be nothing for it but for me to go the rounds on my own, explaining your absence all over again. So you must promise me you won't let me down once more.'

'You have my promise,' I said. 'As I say, I'll just finish off this small chore here then I'll jump into a taxi and be with you. Don't worry, Fiona, everything will sort itself out.'

Just as I said this I felt someone touch my arm. Turning, I saw Pedro on his feet, his large bag once more hoisted on his shoulder.

'Mr Ryder, please,' he said and pointed down the aisle to the exit.

The journalist was standing near the front ready to disembark.

'This is our stop here, Mr Ryder,' he called down, waving to me. 'If you don't mind, sir.'

I could feel the tram slowing to a halt. Rising to my feet, I squeezed out and made my way down the carriage.

13

The tram rattled away leaving the three of us standing in open countryside surrounded by windswept fields. I found the breeze refreshing and for a few moments stood watching the tram disappear across the fields into the horizon.

'Mr Ryder, this way if you please.'

The journalist and Pedro were waiting a few paces away. I went up to them and we began to make our way across the grassy field. Now and then powerful gusts of wind tugged at our clothes and sent ripples across the grass. Eventually we reached the foot of a hill where we paused to recover our breath.

'It's just a short way up here,' the journalist said, pointing up the hill.

After the struggle we had had walking through the long grass I was glad to see there was a dirt path leading us up the hill.

'Well,' I said, 'I don't have much time, so perhaps we'd better be on our way.'

'Of course, Mr Ryder.'

The journalist led the way up the path which climbed steeply in zig-zags. I managed to keep up with him, following just a step or two behind. Pedro, perhaps slowed down by his bags, quickly fell behind altogether. As we climbed, I found myself thinking about Fiona, about how I had let her down the previous night, and it struck me that for all the assurance with which I had so far conducted myself on this present visit, for all I had so far achieved, my handling of certain matters – at least by my own standards – left something to be desired. Quite aside from the embarrassment I had caused Fiona, with my parents' arrival in the town now so imminent, it was vexing in the extreme that I had let slip such an opportunity to discuss their many complicated needs with the people in whose care they were to be entrusted. As my breath came harder, I could feel returning to me an intense sense of irritation with Sophie for the confusion she had brought into my affairs. Surely it was not too much to ask that, at such crucially important points in my life as this, she somehow contained her chaos to herself. All sorts of words I suddenly wished to say to her began filling my head and, had I not been short of breath, I might well have started to mutter them out loud.

After the path had turned three or four corners, we stopped to rest. Raising my gaze, I saw we now commanded a sweeping view over the surrounding countryside. There was field after field stretching into the distance. Only far on the horizon was there something that looked like a huddle of farm buildings.

'A splendid view,' the journalist said, panting and clawing his hair back off his face. 'It's so exhilarating to come up here. The fresh air will set us up well for the rest of the day. Well, better not waste time, pleasant as this all is.' He laughed cheerfully, then began to walk again.

As before I kept up closely with him, while Pedro lagged behind. Then at one point, as we were struggling up a particularly steep section, Pedro called out something from below. I thought he was appealing to us to slow down, but the journalist did not break his step, simply shouting over his shoulder against a blast of wind: 'What did you say?'

I could hear Pedro struggling to gain a few paces. Then I heard him shout:

'I said, we seem to have got the shit convinced. I think he's going to go along with it.'

'Well,' the journalist shouted back, 'he's co-operated so far, but you can never take these types for granted. So keep up the flattery. He's come this far up and he seems quite happy about it. But then I don't think the fool even knows the significance of the building.'

'What do we tell him if he asks?' Pedro shouted. 'He's bound to ask.'

'Just change the subject. Ask him to alter his pose. Any talk about his appearance is bound to deflect him. If he keeps asking, well, we'll have to tell him in the end, but by then we'll have a whole lot of pictures and there'll be nothing the shit can do.'

'I'll be glad when this is all over,' Pedro said, his breath coming even harder now. 'God, the way he keeps stroking his hands together makes my flesh creep.'

'We're almost there now. We've been doing fine, now let's not blow it at the last moment.'

'Excuse me,' I said interrupting, 'but I need to stop for a second.'

'Of course, Mr Ryder, how inconsiderate of me,' the journalist said and we came to a halt. 'I myself am a marathon runner,' he went on, 'and so have an unnatural advantage. But I must say, sir, you seem extremely fit indeed. And for a man of your age – I only know your age from my notes here, I'd never have guessed it otherwise – really, you've completely outpaced poor Pedro.' Then he shouted to Pedro as the latter caught up with us: 'Come on, slowcoach. Mr Ryder's laughing at you.'

'It's not fair,' Pedro said smiling. 'Mr Ryder's so gifted, and then on top of it all, to be blessed with such athleticism. Some of us aren't so lucky.'

We stood looking out over the view, recovering our breath. Then the journalist said:

'We're very nearly there now. Let's keep going. After all, Mr Ryder has a busy day ahead.'

The last part of the journey was the most arduous. The path grew ever steeper and frequently disintegrated into muddy puddles. Ahead of me the journalist continued on steadily, though I could see he was now bent forward with the effort. As I staggered on after him, my head began to fill again with things I wished to say to Sophie. 'Do you realise?' I caught myself muttering through clenched teeth in time to my steps. 'Do you realise?' Somehow the sentence never got any further, but with each step, either in my head or under my breath, I repeated this line over and over until the words themselves began to fuel my irritation.

The path at last levelled off and I could see a white building at the peak of the hill. The journalist and I stumbled towards it and the next moment we were leaning against its wall, panting away. After a while Pedro joined us, wheezing frantically. He collapsed against the wall, sagging down onto his knees, and I feared for a second he was about to have a seizure. But even as he continued to wheeze and pant, he began to unzip his bag. He pulled out a camera, then a lens. At this point the effort seemed to overwhelm him and, putting an arm to the wall, he buried his head in its crook and went on gasping for air.

When at last I felt reasonably recovered, I moved a few steps away from the building in order to get a view of it. A gust of wind almost flattened me back against the wall, but eventually I reached a spot from which I found myself looking at a tall cylinder of white brickwork, windowless apart from a single vertical slit near the top. It was as though a single turret had been removed from a medieval castle and transplanted here on top of the hill.

'Mr Ryder, whenever you're ready, sir.'

The journalist and Pedro had taken up a position some ten metres from the building. Pedro, now evidently recovered, had set up his tripod and was peering through his viewfinder.

'Right up against the wall, if you will, Mr Ryder,' the journalist called.

I made my way back up to the building. 'Gentlemen,' I said, raising my voice above the wind, 'before we begin, I'd like you just to explain to me the precise nature of this setting we've chosen.'

'Mr Ryder, please,' Pedro called, waving his hand in the air. 'Stand right back against the wall. Perhaps an arm against it. Like this.' He held his elbow out to the wind.

I stepped closer to the wall and did as requested. Pedro proceeded to take a number of photographs, occasionally shifting his tripod or changing his lens. All the while, the journalist remained close by, peering over Pedro's shoulder and conferring with him.

'Gentlemen,' I said after a time, 'surely it's not unreasonable of me to ask . . .'

'Mr Ryder, please,' Pedro said, jumping up from behind the camera. 'Your tie!'

My tie had blown over my shoulder. I corrected it, taking the opportunity also to rearrange my hair.

'Mr Ryder,' Pedro called, 'if we could please have some with your hand raised like this. Yes, yes! As though you're ushering someone towards the building. Yes, that's perfect, perfect. But please, smile proudly. Very proud, as though the building is your baby. Yes, that's perfect. Yes, you look magnificent.'

I obeyed the instructions as best I could, though the powerful gusts made it difficult to maintain a suitably genial expression on my face.

Then after a time I became aware of a figure standing over to my left. I gained an impression of a man in a dark coat huddling close to the wall, but at that moment I was having to hold a pose and could only see him at the edge of my vision. Pedro continued to shout instructions through the wind – to move my chin a fraction to one side, to smile more broadly – and some time seemed to pass before I was free to turn and look at the figure. When I finally did so, the man – he was tall and stick-like, with a bald head and bony features – started immediately to come towards me. He was holding his raincoat tightly to himself, but as he approached he held out his hand.

'Mr Ryder, how do you do? It's an honour to meet you.'

'Ah yes,' I said, studying him. 'I'm very pleased to meet you, Mr . . . er . . .?'

The stick-like man looked taken aback. Then he said: 'Christoff. I am Christoff.'

'Ah, Mr Christoff.' A particularly strong blast obliged us to brace ourselves for a few seconds, allowing me to recover somewhat. 'Ah yes, Mr Christoff. Of course. I've heard a great deal about you.'

'Mr Ryder,' Christoff said, leaning towards me, 'may I say straight away how grateful I am to you for agreeing to attend this lunch. I knew what a civilised person you were and so wasn't in the least surprised when you responded positively. I knew, you see, you were the sort at least to give us a fair hearing. The sort that would be actually keen to hear our side of things. No, I wasn't surprised at all, but I remain immensely grateful. Well now' – he looked at his watch – 'we're a little late, but no matter. The traffic shouldn't be so bad. Please, this way.'

I followed Christoff around to the back of the white building. Here the wind was less strong and a mass of piping spilling out of the brickwork was emitting a low humming noise. Christoff continued to lead the way towards a spot on the rim of the hill marked by two wooden posts. I pictured a steep drop beyond the posts, but on reaching them I looked down to see a long flight of rickety stone steps leading dizzyingly down the hillside. Far below, the staircase met a paved road where I could make out the shape of a black car waiting, presumably, for us.

'After you, Mr Ryder,' Christoff said. 'Please, descend at your own pace. There's no hurry.'

However, I noticed he glanced anxiously again at his watch.

'I'm very sorry we're late,' I said. 'Those photographs took a little longer than I expected.'

'Please don't worry, Mr Ryder. I'm sure we'll get there in good time. Please, after you.'

I felt a little giddy negotiating the first steps. There was no banister on either side and I was obliged to concentrate hard through fear that I would miss a step and fall right the way down the hillside. But thankfully the wind was less troublesome and after a while I found myself growing more confident – it was not so different from descending any other staircase – to the extent that I occasionally took my eyes off my feet altogether to survey the panoramic view before us.

The sky was still overcast, but the sun was beginning to break through the clouds. The road on which the car was waiting, I could now see, was built into a plateau. Beyond it the hill continued its descent down through a mass of tree-tops. Further below yet I could see fields stretching off in all directions into the distance. Faintly visible on the horizon was the skyline of the city.

Christoff remained directly behind me. For the first few minutes, perhaps noticing my nervousness about the descent, he refrained from conversing. But once I had built up my rhythm, he sighed and said:

'Those woods, Mr Ryder. Down there to your right. Those are the Werdenberger Woods. Many of the wealthier people in this town, they like to have a chalet down there. The Werdenberger Woods are very pleasant. Only a short drive to the city, and yet one feels so far from everything. Once we're in the car and we drive down the mountainside, you'll see the chalets. Some are perched right on the edge of sheer drops. The views must be stunning. Rosa would have loved one of those chalets. In fact we had a particular one in mind, I'll point it out to you as we drive down. One of the more modest ones, but very attractive just the same. The present owner hardly uses it, no more than two or three weeks in the year. If I'd made a good offer, he'd certainly have given it serious consideration. But there's no point thinking about all that now. That's all finished with.'

He fell silent for a few moments. Then his voice started again behind me.

'It's nothing grand. Rosa and I have never even seen inside it. But we've driven past it so many times, we can imagine what it would be like. It sits out on this little promontory, there's a sheer drop, oh, you'd get the feeling of being suspended high in the sky. You'd see clouds from every window as you walked from room to room. Rosa would have loved it. We used to drive past, slow the car right down, sometimes even stop and sit there imagining it, how it would be inside, picturing it room by room. Well, as I say, that's all in the past now. Useless to dwell on it. In any case, Mr Ryder, you didn't agree to give us your precious time just to hear all this. Forgive me. Let us return to more important matters. You know, sir, we are all *immensely* gratified by your agreeing to come and talk with us. And what a telling contrast to these people, these men who claim to lead this community! On three separate occasions we invited them to attend one of our luncheons, to come and talk over the issues just as you're about to do. But they wouldn't entertain it. Not for a second! Far too proud, all of them. Von Winterstein, the Countess, von Braun, all of them. It's because they're uncertain, you see. In their hearts they know they don't understand anything, so they refuse to come and have a proper discussion with us. Three times we've invited them, and each time the bluntest of refusals. But it would have been futile anyway. They wouldn't have understood the half of what we are saying.'

I became silent again. I felt I should make some comment, but it struck me I could only make myself audible by shouting back over my shoulder and I was not prepared to risk taking my eyes off the steps. For the next few minutes, then, we continued our descent in silence, Christoff's breathing becoming increasingly laboured behind me. Then I heard him say:

'To be perfectly fair, it's not their fault. The modern forms, they're so complex now. Kazan, Mullery, Yoshimoto. Even for a trained musician such as myself, it's hard now, very hard. The likes of von Winterstein, the Countess, what chance do they have? They're completely out of their depth. To them it's just crashing noise, a whirl of strange rhythms. Perhaps they've convinced themselves over the years they can hear something there, certain emotions, meanings. But the truth is, they've found nothing at all. They're out of their depth, they'll never understand how modern music works. Once it was simply Mozart, Bach, Tchaikovsky. Even the man in the street could make a reasoned guess about that sort of music. But the modern forms! How can people like this, untrained, provincial people, how can they ever understand such things, however great a sense of duty they feel towards the community? It's hopeless, Mr Ryder. They can't distinguish a crushed cadence from a struck motif. Or a fractured time signature from a sequence of vented rests. And now they misread the whole situation! They want things to go the opposite way! Mr Ryder, if you're getting tired, why don't we take a short rest?'

In fact I had paused a second because a bird, flying alarmingly close to my face, had caused me almost to lose my footing.

'No, no, I'm fine,' I called back, recommencing the descent.

'These steps are rather too grimy to sit on. But if you liked, we could always just pause and stand.'

'No, really, thank you. I'm fine.'

We proceeded down in silence for the next few minutes. Then Christoff said:

'In my most detached moments, I actually feel sorry for them. I don't blame them. After all they've done, after all they've said about me, I still at times see the situation objectively. And I say to myself, no, it's really not their fault. It's not their fault music has become so difficult and complicated. It's unreasonable to expect anyone in a place like this to comprehend it. And yet these people, these civic leaders, they must give the appearance of knowing what they're doing. So they repeat certain things to themselves, and after a while, they begin to believe themselves authorities. You see, in a place like this, there's no one to contradict them. Please be very careful of the next few steps, Mr Ryder. They're a little crumbled at the edges.'

I took the next several steps very slowly. Then when I glanced up I noticed we had not much further left to go.

'It would have been useless,' Christoff's voice said behind me. 'Even if they'd accepted our invitation, it would have been useless. They wouldn't have understood the half of it. You, Mr Ryder, you'll at least understand our arguments. Even if we fail to convince you, you will, I feel sure, go away with some respect for our position. But of course we hope to persuade you. Convince you that, regardless of my personal fate, the present direction must at all costs be maintained. Yes, you're a brilliant musician, one of the most gifted presently at work anywhere in the world. But nevertheless, even an expert of your calibre needs to apply his knowledge to a particular set of local conditions. Each community has its own history, its own special needs. The people I'll shortly introduce you to, Mr Ryder, are among the few, the very few in this town one might reasonably describe as intellectuals. They've taken the trouble to analyse the particular conditions that prevail here, and what's more, they – unlike von Winterstein and his sort – they do understand something of how the modern forms work. With their help, in the most civilised and respectful way, naturally, I'm hoping to persuade you, Mr Ryder, to modify your present stance. Of course, everyone you'll meet has the utmost respect for you and all you stand for. But we feel it's possible, even with your powerful insight, there may be certain aspects of the situation here you may not yet have fully appreciated. Here we are.'

In fact there were another twenty or so steps before we reached the road. Christoff remained silent for this last part of the descent. I was relieved, for his latter utterances had begun to annoy me. His implication that I was more or less ignorant of the local conditions, that I was the sort to draw conclusions without bothering with such factors, was quite insulting. I recalled how since my arrival in the city – in spite of my tight schedule, in spite of my fatigue – I had applied myself to this very task of acquainting myself with the local situation. I remembered, for instance, how the previous afternoon, when I could so easily have been taking a well-earned rest in the comfort of the hotel's atrium, I had instead set off into the town to gather my impressions. Indeed, the more I thought about Christoff's words, the more irked I felt, so that when we finally came down to the car and Christoff held open the passenger door for me, I climbed in with barely a word.

'We're not too behind time,' he said, getting into the driver's seat. 'If the traffic's good, we'll be there very quickly.'

As he said this, I remembered all at once my many other commitments for the day. There was, for instance, Fiona – no doubt expecting me at her apartment at any moment. The situation, I could see, would require a certain firmness on my part.

He started the car and we soon found ourselves descending a steeply curving road. Christoff, who appeared to know the road well, took each sharp bend with assurance. As we came lower the road became less vertiginous and the chalets he had mentioned, often precariously perched, began appearing to either side of us. Eventually I turned to him saying:

'Mr Christoff, I've been looking forward very much to this lunch with you and your friends. To hearing your side of things. However, several things have come up unexpectedly this morning, and as a result I find I have a very busy day ahead of me. As a matter of fact, even as we speak . . .'

'Mr Ryder, please, you don't have to explain. We knew from the outset how very busy you were likely to be and everyone present, I assure you, will be most understanding. If you leave after an hour and a half, even after an hour, no one, I can assure you, will be in the least offended. They're a fine bunch, the only ones in this town with the ability to think and feel to this level. Whatever the outcome of this lunch, Mr Ryder, I'm sure you'll be pleased to have met them. Many of them I remember when they were young and eager. A fine bunch, I can vouch for each of them. They'd once have thought themselves my protégés, I suppose. They still look up to me. But these days we're colleagues, *friends*, perhaps something even deeper. These last few years have only made us draw closer. Naturally a few have left me, that's inevitable. But the ones who've stayed, oh, they've been unwavering. I'm proud of them, I love them dearly. They're the best hope for this town, though I know they'll not be allowed any influence here for a good while yet. Ah, Mr Ryder, we'll soon be passing the chalet I was telling you about. It's around this next corner. It'll appear on your side.'

He fell silent, and when I looked at him I noticed he was close to tears. I felt a wave of sympathy for him and said gently:

'One never knows what the future might bring, Mr Christoff. Perhaps you and your wife will find a chalet very much like this some day. If not here, then in some other city.'

Christoff shook his head. 'I know you're trying to be kind, Mr Ryder. But really, there's no point. It's all finished between Rosa and me. She'll leave me. I've known that for some time. In fact the whole town knows it. No doubt you've heard them gossiping.'

'Well, I suppose I did hear one or two things . . .'

'I'm sure there's a lot of gossip going about. I don't much care now. The essential thing is that Rosa will soon leave me. She won't tolerate being married to me much longer, not after what's happened. You mustn't get the wrong idea. We've grown to love each other over the years, grown to love each other very much. But you see, with us, that was always the understanding, right from the start. Ah, there it is, Mr Ryder. On your right. Rosa often sat in that seat you're in now and we'd drive past it slowly. Once we were driving past so slowly, we were so absorbed, we nearly collided with a vehicle coming up the hill. But yes, we had an understanding. While I enjoyed the pre-eminence I did in this community, she was able to love me. Oh yes, she loved me, she genuinely loved me. I can say this with utter conviction, Mr Ryder. Because you see, for Rosa, nothing else in life would be more important than to be married to someone in the position I was in. Perhaps that makes her sound a little shallow. But you mustn't misunderstand her. In her own way, in the way she knew, she loved me deeply. In any case, it's nonsense to believe people go on loving each other regardless of what happens. It's just that in Rosa's case, well, the way she is, she's able to love me only under certain circumstances. That doesn't make her love for me any less real.'

For a little while, Christoff was silent again, evidently deep in thought. The road was turning a slow curve, offering a plunging view on my side. I gazed down at the valley below us and could make out what seemed to be an affluent suburb of large houses, each with an acre or so of its own ground.

'I was just remembering,' Christoff said, 'when I first came to this town. How excited they all were. And Rosa, how she came up to me that first time at the Arts Building.' He fell silent again for a moment. Then he said: 'You know, back then, I had no fanciful ideas about myself. By that point in my life I'd come to accept I was no genius. Or anything approaching one. I'd had a career of sorts, but a number of things had happened which had forced me to see my limitations. When I came to this town, my plan was to live quietly – I have a small private income – perhaps do a little teaching, something like that. But then people here, they were so appreciative of my small talents. So pleased I had come here! And after a while, I began thinking. I had, after all, worked hard, very hard, trying to come to terms with modern musical methods. I did understand something about them. I looked around me and thought, well, yes, I could make a contribution here. In a town like this, the way things were then, I saw how I might do it. I saw how I might do some real good. Well, Mr Ryder, after all these years, my belief is that I did do something worthwhile. I believe it sincerely. It's not simply that my protégés – my colleagues, I should say, my *friends* whom you'll meet shortly – it's not just that they've got me thinking it. No, I believe it, believe it very firmly. I did something worthwhile here. But you know how it is. A town like this. Sooner or later things start to go wrong with people's lives. Discontent grows. And the loneliness. And people like this, who understand almost nothing about music, they say to themselves, oh, we must have had everything entirely wrong. Let's do the complete opposite. These accusations they make against me! They say my approach celebrates the mechanical, that I stifle natural emotion. How little they understand! As we'll demonstrate to you very shortly, Mr Ryder, I merely introduced an approach, a system that would allow people like this some way into the likes of Kazan and Mullery. Some way of discovering meaning and value in the works. I tell you, sir, when I first came here, they were crying out for precisely this. For some ordering, for a system they could comprehend. The people here, they were out of their depth, things were breaking down. People were afraid, they felt things slipping out of control. I have documents with me, you'll see everything shortly. You'll see then, I'm sure, just how misguided the present consensus is. Very well, I'm a mediocrity, that much I don't deny. But you'll see I was always on the right track. That what little I did achieve was a start, a useful contribution. What's needed now – I hope you'll see it, Mr Ryder, if only you would see it, then all might not be lost for this city – what's needed is someone, someone more gifted than myself, very well, but someone to continue, to *build* on what I've done. I made a contribution, Mr Ryder. I have the proof, you'll see when we arrive.'

We had come out onto a major highway. The road was broad

and straight, revealing a large expanse of sky before us. Off in the distance, I could see two heavy lorries travelling in the inner lane, but otherwise the road ahead was virtually empty.

'I hope you don't imagine, Mr Ryder,' said Christoff after a while, 'that my bringing you to this lunch today is some desperate ploy on my part to regain my former pre-eminence here. I fully realise my personal position has become impossible. Besides, I've nothing left to give. I've given it all, everything I had, I've given it all to this city. I want to go away somewhere now, far away, somewhere quiet, by myself, and have nothing more to do with music. My protégés, naturally, they'll be devastated when I leave. They still haven't accepted it. They want me to fight back. One word from me, they'd set to work, they'd do their utmost, go door to door even. I've told them how things stand, I've explained very frankly, but they still can't accept it. It's so difficult for them. They've looked up to me for so long, always found their meanings through me. They'll be devastated. But it makes no difference, it has to finish now. I want it to end. Even Rosa. Every minute of our marriage has been precious to me, Mr Ryder. But knowing it will finish, yet not knowing quite when – it's been terrible. I want it all to end now. I wish Rosa well. I hope she finds someone else, someone of proper stature. I just hope she has the sense to look beyond this town. This town can't provide the sort of figure she needs for a husband. No one here understands music properly. Ah, but if only I had your talent, Mr Ryder! Then Rosa and I, we could grow old together.'

The sky had become overcast. The traffic remained sparse and we found ourselves regularly overtaking long-distance lorries before speeding on. Thick forests appeared to either side, then eventually gave way to flat expanses of farmland. The tiredness of the last several days began to catch up with me, and as I continued to watch the highway unwind before us, I found it difficult not to doze. Then I heard Christoff's voice say: 'Ah, here we are,' and I opened my eyes again.

14

We had slowed right down and were approaching a small café – a white bungalow – standing alone on the roadside. It was the sort of place one might imagine lorry drivers stopping for a sandwich, though as Christoff steered the car across the gravelled forecourt and brought it to a halt, there were no other vehicles to be seen.

'We're having lunch here?' I asked.

'Yes. Our little circle, we've gathered here for years now. Everything's very informal.'

We got out and walked towards the café. As we approached I could see bright pieces of cardboard hung from the awning, announcing various special offers.

'Everything's very informal,' Christoff said again, opening the door for me. 'Please make yourself at home.'

The décor inside was very basic. There were large picture windows going all the way round the room. Here and there posters advertising soft drinks or peanuts had been put up with sellotape. Some had become faded in the sunlight and one of them had turned simply into a rectangle of pale blue. Even now, with the sky overcast, there was a harshness to the daylight falling across the room.

There were eight or nine people already present, all seated at the tables near the back. They each had in front of them steaming bowls of what looked to be mashed potato. They had been eating hungrily with long wooden spoons, but now they all stopped and stared at me. One or two began to stand up, but Christoff greeted them cheerily, waving to them to remain seated. Then, turning to me, he said:

'As you can see, lunch has started without us. But given our lateness, I'm sure you'll excuse them. As for the others, well, I'm sure they won't be much longer. In any case, we shouldn't waste any more time. If you'd just step this way, Mr Ryder, I'll introduce you to my good friends here.'

I was about to follow him when we became aware of a heavy

bearded man in a striped apron signalling furtively to us from behind the service counter nearby.

'Very well, Gerhard,' Christoff said, turning to the man with a shrug. 'I'll start with you. This is Mr Ryder.'

The bearded man shook my hand saying: 'Your lunch will be ready in no time, sir. You must be very hungry.' Then he muttered something quickly to Christoff, glancing as he did so towards the rear of the café.

Both Christoff and I followed the bearded man's gaze. As though he had been waiting for our attention to turn to him, a man who had been sitting by himself in the far corner now rose to his feet. He was portly and grey-haired, perhaps in his mid-fifties, dressed in a brilliant white jacket and shirt. He started to come towards us, then, stopping near the middle of the room, smiled at Christoff.

'Henri,' he said, and held up his arms in greeting.

Christoff stared coldly at the man, then turned away. 'There's nothing for you here,' he said.

The white-jacketed man seemed not to hear. 'I was just watching you, Henri,' he continued genially, gesturing out of the window. 'Walking across from your car. You're still walking with that stoop. It used to be a sort of affectation, but now it seems to be there for real. There's no need for it, Henri. Things may not be going your way, but there's no need for a stoop.'

Christoff continued to keep his back turned to the man.

'Come on, Henri. This is childish.'

'I've told you,' Christoff said. 'We've nothing to say to each other.'

The white-jacketed man shrugged and took a few more steps towards us.

'Mr Ryder,' he said, 'since Henri is determined not to introduce us, I'll introduce myself. I'm Dr Lubanski. As you know, Henri and I were very close once. But now, you see, he doesn't even talk to me.'

'You're not welcome here.' Christoff was still not looking at the man. 'Nobody wants you here.'

'You see, Mr Ryder? Henri's always had this childish side to him. So silly. Myself, I long ago came to terms with the fact that our paths have diverged. Once we used to sit and talk for hours.

Didn't we, Henri? Dissecting some work or other, arguing it through from every angle over our beers at the Schoppenhaus. I still think back fondly to those days at the Schoppenhaus. Sometimes I even wish I'd never had the good sense to disagree. That we could sit down again tonight, spend more hours arguing and discussing music, about how you'd prepare this or that piece. I live alone, Mr Ryder. As you can imagine' – he laughed lightly – 'things can get a little lonely at times. And then I start remembering how it was in those days. I think to myself, how good it would be, just to sit down with Henri again and talk over some score he's preparing. There was a time he wouldn't do anything without first consulting me about it. Wasn't that so, Henri? Come on, let's not be childish. Let's at least be civil.'

'Why today of all days?' Christoff shouted suddenly. 'No one wants you here! They're all still very angry at you! Look! Look for yourself!'

Dr Lubanski, ignoring this outburst, embarked on some other reminiscence concerning himself and Christoff. The point of the story quickly eluded me and I found my gaze wandering past him to those watching nervously from the tables at the back.

None of them appeared to be over forty years of age. Three were women and one of them in particular, I noticed, was looking at me with a peculiar intensity. She was in her early thirties, dressed in long black clothes and wearing spectacles with small, thick lenses. I would have studied the others more closely, but just at this point I remembered again what a busy day still lay before me, and how imperative it was that I remained firm with my present hosts if I were not to be detained here beyond the allotted time.

As Dr Lubanski came to a pause, I touched Christoff's arm, saying quietly: 'I wonder if the others will be much longer.'

'Well . . .' Christoff glanced around the room. Then he said: 'It seems this might be all for today.'

I had the impression he was hoping to be contradicted. When no one said anything he turned back to me with a short laugh.

'A small gathering,' he said, 'but nevertheless we have . . . we have the best minds of the town here, I assure you. Now Mr Ryder, please.'

He began to introduce his friends to me. Each smiled nervously

194

and uttered a greeting as his or her name was called. All the while, I was aware of Dr Lubanski walking away slowly towards the back of the room, never taking his gaze off the proceedings. Then, as Christoff was coming to the end of his introductions, Dr Lubanski let out a loud laugh, causing the former to break off and throw a look of cold fury towards him. Dr Lubanski, who by this time had seated himself again at his table in the corner, gave another laugh and said:

'Well, Henri, whatever else you've lost over the years, you've not lost your nerve. You're going to repeat the whole Offenbach saga to Mr Ryder? To Mr *Ryder*?' He shook his head.

Christoff went on staring at his former friend. Some devastating retort seemed about to leave his lips, but then at the last moment he turned away without speaking.

'Throw me out if you like,' Dr Lubanski said, starting on his mashed potato again. 'But it's beginning to look as though' – he waved his spoon around the room – 'as though not everyone here is finding my presence so irksome. We could put it to a vote perhaps. I'd gladly leave if I'm genuinely not wanted. What about a show of hands?'

'If you insist on staying, I don't care in the least,' Christoff said. 'It makes no difference. I have my facts. I have them here.' He raised a blue folder he had produced from somewhere and tapped it. 'I'm quite sure of my ground. You can do what you want.'

Dr Lubanski turned to the others with a shrug that seemed to say: 'What can you possibly do with someone like this?' The young woman with the thick spectacles immediately looked away, but her companions seemed mostly confused, one or two of them even smiling back shyly.

'Mr Ryder,' Christoff said, 'please sit down and make yourself comfortable. As soon as Gerhard returns, he will serve you lunch. Now' – he clapped his hands together and his voice assumed the tones of someone addressing a large hall – 'ladies and gentlemen. I must first of all thank Mr Ryder, on behalf of each of us present today, for agreeing to come and debate with us in the midst of what must surely be a very busy few days . . .'

'You've certainly got nerve,' Dr Lubanski called from the back.

195

'Not intimidated by me, not even by Mr Ryder. Quite a nerve, Henri.'

'I'm not intimidated,' Christoff retorted, 'because I have the facts! Facts are facts! I have it here! The evidence! Yes, even Mr Ryder. Yes, sir' – he turned to me – 'even a man of your reputation. Even you are obliged to defer to *facts*!'

'Well, this will be worth witnessing,' Dr Lubanski said to the others. 'A provincial cellist lecturing Mr Ryder. Fine, let's hear it, let's hear it.'

For a second or two, Christoff hesitated. Then with some resolve he opened his folder saying: 'If I may start with a single case, which I think leads us to the heart of the controversy concerning ringed harmonies.'

For the next few minutes, Christoff outlined the background to the case of a certain local business family, leafing through his folder, reading out the occasional quotation or statistic. He seemed to present his case competently enough, but there was something about his tone – his unnecessarily slow delivery, the way he explained things twice and three times – that quickly got on my nerves. Indeed, it occurred to me Dr Lubanski had a point. There *was* something preposterous about this failed local musician presuming to lecture me.

'Now *that* you call a fact?' Dr Lubanski suddenly broke in as Christoff was reading from the minutes of a civic committee meeting. 'Ha! Henri's "facts" are always interesting, aren't they?'

'Let him have his say! Let Henri present his case to Mr Ryder!'

The young man who had spoken up had a pudgy face and a short leather jacket. Christoff smiled at him approvingly. Dr Lubanski raised his hands, saying: 'All right, all right.'

'Let him have his say!' the pudgy-faced young man said again. 'Then we'll see. We'll see what Mr Ryder makes of it all. Then we'll find out once and for all.'

It seemed to take Christoff a good few seconds to absorb the implication of these last words. At first he remained frozen, the folder held aloft in his arms. Then he looked around at the faces surrounding him as though for the first time. All about the room there were searching gazes directed at him. For a moment Christoff appeared badly shaken. Looking away he muttered, almost to himself:

'These are indeed facts. I've gathered evidence here. Any one of you can see it, peruse it.' He peered into his folder. 'I'm just summarising the evidence for brevity. That's all.' Then with an effort he seemed to regain his poise. 'Mr Ryder,' he said, 'if you will bear with me a moment. I believe things will be much clearer very shortly.'

Christoff carried on with his argument, a slight tension in his voice, but otherwise in much the same manner as before. As he talked on, I remembered how the previous night I had given up precious hours of sleep in order to carry out further my investigations of the local conditions. How, despite my great tiredness, I had sat in the cinema, talking through the issues with the town's leading citizens. Christoff's repeated assumptions about my ignorance – even now, he was embarking on a long digression to explain a point completely obvious to me – were steadily bringing me to the point of exasperation.

I was not, it seemed, alone in my impatience. A number of others in the room were shifting uncomfortably. I noticed the young woman with the thick spectacles glaring from Christoff's face to mine, and several times she looked to be on the verge of interrupting. But in the end it was a man with closely cropped hair sitting somewhere behind me who broke in.

'Just one moment, one moment. Before we go further, let's just get one thing settled. Once and for all.'

Dr Lubanski's laugh again came from the back of the café. 'Claude and his pigmented triad! You still haven't resolved that?'

'Claude,' Christoff said, 'this is hardly the time . . .'

'No! Now that Mr Ryder's here, I want it settled.'

'Claude, this isn't the time to raise that again. I'm presenting an argument to show . . .'

'Perhaps it's trivial. But let's get it settled. Mr Ryder, Mr Ryder, is it truly the case that pigmented triads have intrinsic emotional values regardless of context? Do you believe that?'

I sensed the focus of the room fixing upon me. Christoff gave me a swift look, something like a plea mingled with fear. But in view of the earnestness of the enquiry – to say nothing of Christoff's presumptuous behaviour up to this point – I saw no reason not to reply in the frankest terms. I thus said:

'A pigmented triad has no intrinsic emotional properties. In fact, its emotional colour can change significantly not only according to context, but according to volume. This is my personal opinion.'

No one spoke, but the impact of my statement was discernible. One by one, hard gazes turned towards Christoff – who meanwhile was pretending to be engrossed in his folder. Then the man called Claude said quietly:

'I knew it. I always knew it.'

'But he convinced you you were wrong,' Dr Lubanski said. 'He bullied you into believing you were wrong.'

'What has this to do with anything?' Christoff cried. 'Claude, look, you've taken us on a complete tangent. And Mr Ryder has so little time. We must return to the Offenbach case.'

But Claude seemed to be lost in thought. Eventually he turned and looked towards Dr Lubanski, who nodded and smiled back gravely.

'Mr Ryder has very little time,' Christoff said again. 'So if you'd all allow me, I'll try and summarise my argument.'

Christoff began to go through what he considered the key points concerning the tragedy of the Offenbach family. He was affecting an air of nonchalance, though by now it was clear to everyone he was badly upset. In any case, around this point, I ceased to attend to him, his remark concerning my lack of time having caused me suddenly to remember Boris sitting waiting for me in that little café.

A considerable period, I realised, had elapsed since I had left him there. A picture came into my mind of the little boy, shortly after my departure, sitting in his corner with his drink and cheesecake, still full of anticipation about the trip before him. I could see him gazing cheerfully towards the other customers out in the sunny courtyard, now and then looking beyond them to the traffic in the street, thinking how before long he too would be out there travelling. He would recall once more the old apartment, the cupboard in the corner of the living room where, he had become increasingly certain, he had left the box containing Number Nine. Then as the minutes went by, the doubts that had always been lurking somewhere, doubts he had so far kept well buried, would begin creeping to the surface. But for a while yet, Boris would succeed in keeping up his spirits. I had simply been detained unexpectedly. Or perhaps I had gone somewhere to buy a picnic to take on the trip. In any case, there was still plenty remaining of the day. Then the waitress, the plump Scandinavian girl, would ask if he wanted anything further, betraying as she did so a note of concern which Boris would not fail to detect. And he would make a renewed show of being unworried, perhaps ordering with bravado another glass of milk shake. But the minutes would tick on. Boris would notice, outside in the court-yard, customers who had sat down long after his arrival closing their newspapers, getting up and leaving. He would see the sky clouding over, the day moving into the afternoon. He would think again of the old apartment he had so loved, the cupboard in the living room, Number Nine, and slowly, as he picked away at the remains of his cheesecake, he would begin to resign himself to the idea that yet again he would be let down, that we would not set off on the journey after all.

Several voices were shouting around me. A young man in a green suit had risen to his feet and was trying to make a point to Christoff, while at least three others were waving their fingers to emphasise something.

'But that's an irrelevance,' Christoff was shouting over them. 'And in any case, it's just Mr Ryder's personal opinion . . .'

This brought an onslaught down on him, almost everyone in the room attempting to respond at the same time. But in the end Christoff again managed to shout them down.

'Yes! Yes! I'm aware of *exactly* who Mr Ryder is! But local con-ditions, local conditions, that's another matter! He doesn't yet know about our particular conditions! While I . . . I have here . . .'

The rest of this statement was drowned out, but Christoff raised the blue folder high above his head and waved it.

'The nerve! The nerve!' Dr Lubanski was calling from the back with a laugh.

'With all respect, sir' – Christoff was now addressing me directly – 'with all respect, I am surprised you aren't more interested in hearing about the conditions here. In fact, I'm *sur-prised*, your expertise notwithstanding, I'm *surprised* you should simply leap to your conclusions . . .'

The chorus of protest came again, now more furious than ever.

'For instance . . .' Christoff yelled over the top. 'For instance, I was very surprised that you should allow the press to photograph you in front of the Sattler monument!'

To my consternation, this brought sudden silence.

'Yes!' Christoff was clearly delighted at the effect he had created. 'Yes! I saw him! When I picked him up earlier on. Standing right in front of the Sattler monument. Smiling, gesturing towards it!'

The shocked silence continued. Some of those present seemed to grow embarrassed, while others – including the young woman with the thick spectacles – stared at me questioningly. I smiled and was about to make some comment when Dr Lubanski's voice, now controlled and authoritative, said from the back:

'If Mr Ryder chooses to make such a gesture, it can only indicate one thing. That the extent of our misguidedness is even deeper than we suspected.'

All eyes turned to him as he rose and came a few steps closer to the gathering. Dr Lubanski stopped and leant his head to one side as though listening to the distant sounds of the highway. Then he continued:

'His message is one we must each of us examine carefully and take to our hearts. The Sattler monument! Of course, he's right! It's not overstating the case, not for one moment! Look at you, still trying to cling onto Henri's foolish notions! Even those of us who've seen them for what they are, even us, the truth is we've remained complacent. The Sattler monument! Yes, that's it. This city is at crisis point. Crisis point!'

It was gratifying that Dr Lubanski had immediately highlighted the preposterousness of Christoff's statement, at the same time underlining the strong message I had wished to send out to the city. Nevertheless, my indignation towards Christoff was now considerable and I decided it was high time I cut him down to size. But the whole room was again shouting all at once. The man named Claude was repeatedly banging his fist on a table surface to emphasise a point to a grizzled man with braces and muddy boots. At least four people, from different parts of the room, were shouting at Christoff. The situation seemed on the verge of chaos and it occurred to me this was as good a point as any to take my leave. But as I stood up, the young woman with thick spectacles materialised in front of me.

'Mr Ryder, please tell us,' she said. 'Let's get to the bottom of it. Is Henri right in believing we can't at any cost abandon the circular dynamic in Kazan?'

She had not spoken loudly, but her voice had a penetrating quality. The whole room heard her question and immediately became quiet. A few of her companions gave her searching looks, but she glared back defiantly.

'No, I'll ask it,' she said. 'This is a unique opportunity. We can't waste it. I'll ask it. Mr Ryder, please. Tell us.'

'But I have the facts,' Christoff muttered miserably. 'Here. I have it all.'

No one paid him any attention, every gaze having focused once more on me. Realising I would have to choose my next words carefully, I paused a moment. Then I said:

'My own view is that Kazan never benefits from formalised restraints. Neither from the circular dynamic, nor even a double-bar structure. There are simply too many layers, too many emotions, especially in the later works.'

I could feel, almost physically, the tide of respect sweeping towards me. The pudgy-faced man was looking at me with something close to awe. A woman in a scarlet anorak was muttering: 'That's it, that's it,' as though I had just articulated something she had been struggling to formulate for years. The man named Claude had risen to his feet and now took a few steps towards me, nodding vigorously. Dr Lubanski was also nodding, but slowly and with his eyes closed as if to say: 'Yes, yes, here at last is someone who really knows.' The young woman with the thick spectacles though had remained quite still, continuing to watch me carefully.

'I can understand,' I went on, 'the temptation to resort to such devices. There's a natural fear of the music flooding the musician's resources. But the answer surely is to rise to such a challenge, not to resort to restraints. Of course, the challenge might be too great, in which case the answer is to leave Kazan well alone. One should not, in any case, attempt to make a virtue out of one's limitations.'

At this last remark, many in the room seemed no longer able to hold back their feelings. The grizzled man with the muddy boots broke into vigorous applause, throwing snarling looks towards

Christoff as he did so. Several others started to shout again at Christoff, and the woman in the scarlet anorak was again repeating, this time more loudly: 'That's it, that's it, that's it.' I felt strangely exhilarated and, raising my voice above the mounting excitement, continued:

'These failures of nerve are, in my experience, very often associated with certain other unattractive traits. A hostility towards the introspective tone, most often characterised by an over-use of the crushed cadence. A fondness for pointlessly matching fragmented passages with each other. And at the more personal level, a megalomania masquerading behind a modest and kindly manner . . .'

I was obliged to break off because everyone in the room was now shouting at Christoff. He in turn was holding up his blue folder, thumbing its pages in the air, crying: 'The facts are here! Here!'

'Of course,' I shouted above the noise, 'this is another common failing. The belief that putting something in a folder will turn it into a fact!'

This was met by a roar of laughter that had at its heart an uncoiling fury. Then the young woman with the thick spectacles rose to her feet and went up to Christoff. She did so very calmly, transgressing the small area of space that had hitherto been maintained around the cellist.

'You old fool,' she said, and again her voice penetrated clearly through the clamour. 'You've dragged us all down with you.' Then, with some deliberation, she struck Christoff's cheek with the outside of her hand.

There was a stunned pause. Then suddenly people were rising from their chairs, pushing one another aside in an attempt to reach Christoff, the desire to follow the young woman's example evidently seizing them with some urgency. I was aware of a hand shaking my shoulder but for the moment was too preoccupied with what was unfolding before me to attend.

'No, no, that's enough!' Dr Lubanski had somehow reached Christoff first and was holding up his hands. 'No, let Henri be! What do you think you're doing? That's enough!'

Possibly it was only Dr Lubanski's intervention that saved Christoff from a full-scale assault. I caught a glimpse of Christoff's bewildered, frightened face, and then an angry circle settled around him and he ceased to be visible to me. The hand was shaking my shoulder again and I turned to find the bearded man with the apron – I recalled that his name was Gerhard – holding a steaming bowl of mashed potato.

'Would you care for some lunch, Mr Ryder?' he asked. 'I'm sorry it's a little late. But you see, we had to start a new vat.'

'That's very kind of you,' I said, 'but actually I really have to be going. I've left my little boy waiting for me.' Then, leading him away from the noise, I said to him: 'I wonder if you would show me through to the front.' For indeed, I had at that moment remembered that this café and the one in which I had left Boris were in fact parts of the same building, this being one of those establishments offering contrasting rooms – opening onto separate streets – catering to different kinds of clientele.

The bearded man was clearly disappointed by my refusal of lunch, but he recovered quickly, saying: 'Of course, Mr Ryder. It's this way.'

I followed him to the front of the room and round the service counter. There he unlatched a small door and indicated for me to go through. As I was doing so I took a last glance back and saw the pudgy-faced man up on a table top, waving Christoff's blue folder in the air. There were now hoots of laughter amidst the angry shouts, while Dr Lubanski's voice could be heard appealing with some emotion: 'No, Henri's had enough! Please, please! That's enough!'

I came through into a spacious kitchen tiled entirely in white. There was a strong smell of vinegar and I caught a glimpse of a large woman bent over a sizzling stove, but the bearded man had already crossed the floor and was opening another door in the far corner of the kitchen.

'It's this way, sir,' he said, ushering me.

The door was peculiarly tall and narrow. Indeed, it was so narrow I saw I would only pass through it by turning myself sideways. Moreover, when I peered in, I could see only darkness; there was nothing to suggest I was looking into anything other than a broom cupboard. But the bearded man made his ushering motion again and said:

'Please be careful of the steps, Mr Ryder.'

I then saw there were three steps – they appeared to be made from wooden boxes nailed one on top of the other – rising immediately from the threshold. I eased myself through the doorway and took each one with caution. As I reached the top step, I saw in front of me a small rectangle of light. Two paces forward brought me right up to it and I found myself looking through a glass panel into a room filled with sunlight. I saw tables and chairs, and then I recognised the room where I had earlier left Boris. There was the plump young waitress – I was viewing the room from behind her counter – and, over in the corner, Boris gazing into space with a disgruntled expression. He had finished his cheesecake and was absent-mindedly running his fork up and down the tablecloth. Apart from a young couple sitting near the windows, the interior of the café was otherwise empty.

I felt something pushing against my side and realised the bearded man had squeezed up behind me and was now crouched down in the dark, jangling a set of keys. The next moment the whole of the partition before me opened and I found myself stepping into the café.

The waitress turned to me and smiled. Then she called across to Boris: 'Look who's here!'

Boris turned to me and pulled a long face. 'Where've you been?' he said wearily. 'You've been ages.'

'I'm very sorry, Boris,' I said. Then I asked the waitress: 'Has he been behaving himself?'

'Oh, he's a complete charmer. He's been telling me all about where you used to live. On that estate by the artificial lake.'

'Ah yes,' I said. 'The artificial lake. Yes, we were just about to go there now.'

'But you've been absolutely ages!' Boris said. 'Now we'll be late!'

'I'm very sorry, Boris. But don't worry, we still have plenty of time. And the old apartment isn't about to go away, is it? Still, you're quite right, we ought to be setting off straight away. Now let me see.' I turned back to the waitress who had started to say something to the bearded man. 'Excuse me, but I wonder if you could tell us how we can most easily get to this artificial lake.'

'The artificial lake?' The waitress pointed out of the window. 'That bus waiting outside. That will take you right there.'

I looked where she was pointing and saw beyond the parasols in the courtyard a bus parked in the busy street more or less directly in front of us.

'It's been waiting there a long time already,' the waitress went on. 'So you'd better jump on. I think it's due to leave any moment.'

I thanked her and, motioning to Boris, led the way out of the building into the sunshine.

15

We boarded the bus just as the driver was starting his engine. As I bought the tickets from him, I saw the bus was very full and remarked worriedly:

'I hope my boy and I will be able to sit together.'

'Oh, don't worry,' the driver said. 'They're a good crowd. Just leave it to me.'

With that he turned and bellowed something over his shoulder. There had been an unusually merry hubbub in progress, but the whole bus went quiet. Then the next moment, all over the bus, passengers were getting up from their seats, pointing, waving and generally conferring about how we might be best accommodated. A large woman leaned into the central aisle and called: 'Over here! You can sit here!' But another voice from another part of the bus shouted: 'If you've got a little boy, it's better over here, he won't get sick. I'll move over next to Mr Hartmann.' Then another conference seemed to commence concerning our options.

'You see, they're a good crowd,' the driver said cheerfully. 'Newcomers always get a special welcome. Well, if you'd make yourselves comfortable, I'll start us on our way.'

Boris and I hurried down the bus to where two passengers were standing in the aisle pointing to our seat. I let Boris in nearest the window and sat down just as the bus began to pull away.

Almost immediately I felt a tap on my shoulder and someone in the seat behind was reaching over to offer a packet of sweets.

'The little boy might like this,' a man's voice said.

'Thank you,' I said. Then more loudly to the whole bus, I said: 'Thank you. Thank you, all of you. You've all been most civil.'

'Look!' Boris clutched excitedly at my arm. 'We're going out onto the north highway.'

Before I could respond, a middle-aged woman appeared beside me in the aisle. Grasping the head-rest of my seat to maintain her balance, she held out a piece of cake on a paper napkin.

'A gentleman at the back had this left over,' she said. 'He wondered if the young man would like it.'

I accepted it gratefully, once more thanking the bus in general. Then, as the woman disappeared, I heard a voice a few seats away saying: 'It's good to see a father and son getting on so well. Here they are, going on a little day trip together. We don't see this sort of thing nearly enough these days.'

I felt a powerful surge of pride at these words and glanced towards Boris. Perhaps he too had heard, for he gave me a smile that had more than a hint of the conspiratorial about it.

'Boris,' I said, handing him the cake, 'isn't this a marvellous bus? It was worth the wait, don't you think?'

Boris smiled again, but he was now examining the cake and said nothing.

'Boris,' I went on, 'I've been meaning to say to you. Because you might wonder sometimes. You see, Boris, I could never have wished for anything better . . .' I laughed suddenly. 'I'm sounding silly. What I mean is, I'm very happy. About you. Very happy we're together.' I gave another laugh. 'Aren't you enjoying this bus ride?'

Boris nodded, his mouth full of cake. 'It's good,' he said.

'I'm certainly enjoying it. And what kind people.'

At the back of the bus a few of the passengers began to sing. I felt very relaxed and sank deeper into my seat. Outside the day had grown overcast again. We were still in a built-up part of the town, but as I watched I saw two road signs go by, one after the other, marked: 'North Highway'.

'Excuse me,' a man's voice said somewhere behind us. 'But I heard you saying to the driver you were going to the artificial lake. I hope it won't be too chilly out there for you both. If you were just wanting somewhere nice to spend the afternoon, I'd recommend you get off a few stops earlier at the Maria Christina Gardens. There's a boating pond there the young man might like.'

The speaker was sitting directly behind us. The backs of our seats were tall and I could not see the man clearly even though I craned round to do so. In any case I thanked him for his sugges-tion – it was clearly well meant – and started to explain the special nature of our visit to the artificial lake. I had not intended to go into detail, but once I had started I found there was something about the convivial atmosphere around us that compelled me to go on talking. In fact, I was rather pleased by the tone I happened to strike, perfectly poised between seriousness and jocularity. Moreover, I could tell from the sensitive murmurs coming from behind me that the man was listening carefully and sympathetically. In any case, before long, I found myself explaining about Number Nine and just why he was so special. I was just recounting how Boris had come to leave him behind in the box when the passenger interrupted with a polite cough.

'Excuse me,' he said, 'but a trip of this kind is almost bound to cause a little worry. It's perfectly natural. But really, if I may say so, I think you have every reason to be optimistic.' He was presumably leaning right forward in his seat, for his voice, calm and soothing, was coming from a spot just behind where Boris's shoulder was touching mine. 'I feel sure you'll find this Number Nine. Of course, you're worried just now. So many things could have gone wrong, you're thinking. That's only natural. But from what you've just told me, I feel sure it'll turn out well. Of course, when you first knock on the door, the new people might not know who you are and be a little suspicious. But then once you've explained they're bound to welcome you in. If it's the wife who's answered the door, she'll say: "Oh, at last! We've been wondering when you'd be coming round." Yes, I'm sure she will. And she'll turn and shout to her husband: "It's the little boy who used to live here!" And then the husband will come out, he'll be some kindly man, perhaps he'll be in the middle of re-decorating the apartment. And he'll say: "Well, at last. Come on in and have some tea." And he'll show you into the main room, while his wife slips into the kitchen to prepare the refreshments. And you'll notice straight away how much the place has changed since you were there, and the husband will see this and at first he'll be a little apologetic. But then, once you've made it quite clear you're not at all resentful about their changing things, he's sure to start showing you around the place, around the whole apartment, pointing out this change, that change, most of which he's seen to with his own hands and about which he's very proud. And then the wife will come into the living room with the tea and some little cakes she's made, and you'll all sit down and enjoy yourselves, eating and drinking, listening to this couple talking about how much they like the apartment and the estate. Of course, through all this, you'll both be concerned about Number Nine and be waiting for the right moment to bring up the purpose of your visit. But I expect they'll raise it first. I expect the wife will say, after you've been talking and drinking tea for a good while, she'll say: "And was there something you came back for? Something you left behind?" And that's when you could mention this Number Nine and the box. And then she's bound to say: "Oh yes, we kept that box in a special place. We could see it was something important." And even as she's saying this, she'll give her husband a little signal. Perhaps not even a signal, husbands and wives become almost telepathic when they've lived happily together for as many years as this couple have done. Of course, that's not to say they don't quarrel. Oh no, they may even have quarrelled quite often, perhaps even gone through patches over the years when they seriously fell out. But you'll see when you meet them, a couple like this, you'll see these things sort themselves out in the end and that they're essentially very happy together. Well, the husband, he'll go and fetch the box from some place where they keep important things, he'll bring it in, perhaps it'll be wrapped up in tissue paper. And of course, you'll open it straight away and this Number Nine, he'll be there inside, just the way you left him, still waiting to be glued to his base. So then you can close the box and the nice people will offer you some more tea. Then after a while you'll say you'll have to be going, you don't wish to impose on them too much. But the wife will insist you have more of her cake. And the husband will want to show you both around the apartment one last time to admire all his re-decorating. Then finally they'll wave you off from the doorstep, saying to be sure to call whenever you're passing by again. Of course, it may not happen precisely like this, but from what you've told me, I feel sure, by and large, that's how things will turn out. So there's no need to worry, no need at all . . .'

The man's voice in my ear, together with the gentle swaying of the bus as it proceeded along the highway, was producing an enormously relaxing effect. I had already closed my eyes soon after the man had started to speak, and now around this point, sinking further into my seat, I dozed off contentedly.

*

I became aware that Boris was shaking my shoulder. 'We've got to get off now,' he was saying.

Becoming fully awake, I realised the bus had come to a halt and that we were the only remaining passengers. At the front the driver had risen to his feet and was patiently waiting for us to disembark. As we made our way down the aisle, the driver said:

'Do take care. It's very chilly out there. That lake, in my opinion, should be filled. It's nothing but a nuisance and every year several people drown in it. Admittedly some of these are suicides, and I suppose if the lake weren't there, they might choose some other more unpleasant method. But in my view the lake should be filled.'

'Yes,' I said. 'Obviously the lake provokes controversy. I'm an outsider myself so I tend to keep out of these arguments.'

'Very wise, sir. Well, do enjoy your day.' Then, saluting Boris, he said: 'Enjoy yourself, young man.'

Boris and I stepped down off the bus and as it drove away looked around at our surroundings. We were standing on the outer rim of a vast concrete basin. Some distance away, at the centre of the basin, was the artificial lake, its kidney shape making it resemble some gigantic version of the kind of vulgar swimming pool Hollywood stars were once reputed to own. I could not help admiring the way the lake – indeed the whole estate – proudly announced its artificiality. There was no trace of grass anywhere. Even the thin trees dotted around the concrete slopes had all been encased in steel pots and cut precisely into the paving. Looking down on the whole scene, completely encircling us, were the countless identical windows of the high-rise housing blocks. I noticed there was a subtle curve to the front of each block, making possible the seamless circular effect reminiscent of a sports stadium. But for all the apartments now surrounding us – at least four hundred, I guessed – there were hardly any people to be seen. I could make out a few figures walking briskly on the other side of the lake – a man with a dog, a woman with a pram – but there was clearly something about the atmosphere that kept people indoors. Certainly, as the bus driver had warned, the climate was not conducive. Even as Boris and I stood there a bitter wind came blowing across the water.

'Well, Boris,' I said, 'we'd better get a move on.'

The little boy seemed to have lost all his enthusiasm. He was staring emptily at the lake and did not move. I turned towards the block behind us, making an effort to put a spring into my step, but then remembered I did not know where in all this vastness our particular apartment was situated.

'Boris, why don't you lead the way? Come on, what's the matter?'

Boris sighed then began to walk. I followed him up several flights of concrete stairs. Once, as we were turning the corner to climb the next flight, he let out a shriek and stiffened into a martial arts posture. I was startled, but saw immediately there was no assailant other than in the boy's imagination. I said simply:

'Very good, Boris.'

Thereafter, he repeated the shriek and the pose before turning up each new flight of stairs. Then to my relief – I was growing short of breath – Boris led us off the stairs and along a walkway. From this higher vantage point, the kidney shape of the lake was all the more evident. The sky was a dull white and although the walkway was covered – there must have been two or three more running directly above – there was scant shelter and gusts of wind blew at us with savage force. On our left-hand side were the apartments, a series of short concrete stairways linking the walkway to the main building like little bridges across a moat. Some of the stairways led up to apartment doors while others led down. As we walked on, I found myself studying each of these doors, but when after a few minutes none of them had stirred even the faintest memory I gave up and glanced out at the view over the lake.

Boris, all the while, had been walking purposefully a few paces ahead, his excitement for our venture having apparently returned. He was whispering to himself, and the longer we walked the more his whispering seemed to grow in intensity. Then he began to jump as he walked, throwing karate blows at the air, the clatter of his feet echoing about us each time he landed. But he refrained from shrieking as he had on the stairs, and since we had not yet encountered a single person on the walkway, I decided there was no cause to restrain him.

After a while I happened to glance down at the lake and was

211

surprised to find I was now looking at it from a considerably different angle. Only then did it occur to me that the walkway described a gradual circle right the way round the estate. It was perfectly possible that we could walk in circles indefinitely. I watched Boris hurrying on in front of me, busily performing his antics, and wondered if he remembered the way to the apartment any better than I did. Indeed, it occurred to me I had not planned matters at all well. I should at the very least have taken the trouble to contact beforehand the new occupants of the apartment. After all, when one thought about it, there was no reason why they would particularly wish to entertain us. A pessimism about the whole expedition began to come over me.

'Boris,' I called to him, 'I hope you're paying attention. We don't want to walk right past it.'

He glanced back at me without ceasing his furious mutterings, then ran on further ahead and recommenced his karate movements.

Eventually it struck me we had been walking an inordinate time, and when I glanced down again at the lake, I could see we had come at least a full circle around it. Ahead of me Boris was still muttering busily to himself.

'Look, wait a moment,' I called to him. 'Boris, wait.'

He stopped walking and gave me a sulky look as I came up to him.

'Boris,' I said gently, 'are you sure you remember the way to the old apartment?'

He shrugged and looked away. Then he said lamely: 'Of course I do.'

'But we seem to have gone right the way round.'

Boris shrugged again. He had become engrossed by his shoe, which he was angling one way and then the other. Eventually he said: 'They would have kept Number Nine safe, wouldn't they?'

'I should think so, Boris. He was in a box, an important-looking box. They would keep something like that aside. High up on a shelf, somewhere like that.'

For a moment Boris continued to regard his shoe. Then he said: 'We went past it. We've gone past it twice.'

'What? You mean we've been walking round and round up

here in this chilly wind for nothing? Why didn't you say so, Boris? I don't understand you.'

He remained silent, moving his foot one way, then the other.

'Well, do you suppose we should go back?' I asked. 'Or do we have to circle the lake yet again?'

Boris sighed and for a moment seemed deep in thought. Then he looked up and said: 'All right. It's back there. Just back there.'

We retraced our steps a short distance along the walkway. Before long Boris stopped at one of the stairways and glanced quickly up at the apartment door. Then almost immediately he turned his back to it and began once more to study his shoe.

'Ah yes,' I said, looking carefully up at the door. In fact the door – painted blue and with virtually nothing to distinguish it from any of the others – aroused no memories for me at all.

Boris glanced over his shoulder up at the apartment, then looked away again, poking his toe at the ground. For a while I remained at the bottom of the stairway, a little uncertain what to do next. Eventually, I said:

'Boris, why don't you just wait here a minute? I'll go up and see if anyone's in.'

The little boy went on prodding with his foot. I went up the steps and knocked on the door. There was no response. When I had knocked a second time with no result, I put my face up to the small glass panel. The glass was frosted and I could see nothing.

'The window,' Boris called from behind me. 'Have a look through the window.'

I saw to my left a sort of balcony – really no more than a ledge running along the front of the building, too narrow even to put out an upright chair. I reached out a hand to its iron balustrade, and by leaning my body right over the wall of the stairway I was just able to peer in through the nearest window. I found myself looking into an open-plan lounge with a dining table at one end against a wall and rather dated modern furnishings.

'Can you see it?' Boris was calling. 'Can you see the box?'

'Just a minute.'

I tried to lean my body even further over the wall, conscious though I was of the gaping drop below me.

'Can you see it?'

'Just a minute, Boris.'

The room was by now growing steadily more familiar to me. The triangular clock on the wall, the cream foam sofa, the three-tiered hi-fi cabinet; I found object after object, as my gaze fell on it, bringing with it a poignant nudge of recognition. However, as I continued to peer into the room, I gained the strong impression that the whole of the rear section – which adjoined the main portion to form an 'L' – had not previously been there at all, that it was a very recent addition. Nevertheless, as I continued to look at it, this same rear section seemed in itself strongly reminiscent, and after a moment I realised this was because it resembled exactly the back part of the parlour in the house my parents and I had lived in for several months in Manchester. The house, a narrow city terrace, had been damp and badly in need of redecorating, but we had put up with it since we were staying only until my father's work enabled us to move away to something much better. To me, a nine-year-old, the house quickly came to represent not only an exciting change, but the hope that a fresh, happier chapter was unfolding for us all.

'You won't find anyone in there,' a man's voice said behind me. Straightening, I saw that the speaker had emerged from the neighbouring apartment. He was standing in front of his door at the top of a stairway parallel to the one I was standing on. The man was around fifty, with heavy, bulldog-like features. He was unkempt and his T-shirt had a damp patch around the chest.

'Ah,' I said, 'so this apartment is empty?'

The man shrugged. 'Maybe they're coming back. My wife and I, we don't like an empty apartment next to us, but after all that trouble, we're relieved, I can tell you. We're not unfriendly people. But after all of that, well, we'd much sooner have it the way it is now. Empty.'

'Ah. So it's been empty for some time. Weeks? Months?'

'Oh, a month at least. They might be coming back, but we wouldn't care if they didn't. Mind you, I felt sorry for them at times. We're not unfriendly people. And we've been through difficult times ourselves. But when it goes on like that, well, you just want them to go. We'd rather have it empty.'

'I see. A lot of trouble.'

'Oh yes. To be fair, I don't think there was physical violence.

But still, when you had to listen to them shouting late at night, it was very upsetting.'

'Excuse me, but look here . . .' I came a step closer to him, signalling with my eyes that Boris was within earshot.

'No, my wife didn't like it one bit,' the man went on, ignoring me. 'Whenever it started, she used to bury her head in the pillow. Even in the kitchen once. I came in and there she was cooking with a pillow around her head. It wasn't pleasant. Whenever we saw him he was sober, very respectable. He'd give us a quick salute, be on his way. But my wife was convinced that's what was behind it. You know, drink . . .'

'Look,' I whispered angrily, leaning over the concrete wall separating us, 'can't you see I have my boy with me? Is this the sort of talk to come out with in front of him?'

The man looked down towards Boris with a surprised expression. Then he said: 'But he's not so young, is he? You can't protect him from everything. Still, if you don't like talk of this kind, fine, let's talk about something else. You think of a better topic if you can. I was just telling you how it was. But if you don't want to talk about it . . .'

'No, I certainly don't! I certainly don't wish to hear . . .'

'Well, it wasn't important. It's just that, quite naturally, I tended to side with him rather than with her. If he'd actually got violent, well, that would have been something else, but there was never any evidence of that. So I tended to blame *her*. Okay, he went away a lot, but from what we understood he had to, that was all part of his work. It wasn't a reason, that's what I'm saying, it wasn't a reason for her to behave in the way she did . . .'

'Look, will you stop it? Don't you have any sense? The boy! He can hear . . .'

'All right, he may be listening. So what? Children always hear these things sooner or later. I was just explaining why I tended to take his side, and that's why my wife brought up the drinking. The going away was one thing, my wife would say, but the drinking was another . . .'

'Look, if you carry on like this, I'll be forced to terminate this conversation here and now. I'm warning you. I'll do it.'

'You can't hope to protect your boy for ever, you know. How

215

old is he? He doesn't look so young. It's not good to over-shelter them. He's got to come to terms with the world, warts and all . . .'

'He doesn't have to yet! Not just yet! Besides, I don't care what you think. What is it to you anyway? He's my boy, he's in my charge, I won't have this sort of talk . . .'

'I don't know why you're getting so angry. I'm only making conversation. I was just telling you what we made of it. They weren't bad people, it's not that we disliked them, but it sometimes got too much. Mind you, I suppose it always sounds much worse when it's coming through a wall. Look, it's useless trying to hide it from a boy his age. You're fighting a losing battle. And what's the point . . .'

'I don't care what you think! Not for a few years yet! He won't, he won't hear about such things . . .'

'You're foolish. These things I'm talking about, it's just what happens in life. Even my wife and me, we've had our ups and downs. That's why I sympathised with him. I know what it feels like, that first moment you suddenly realise . . .'

'I warn you! I'll terminate this conversation! I'm warning you!'

'But then I never drank. That does change things. Going away a lot is one thing, but to drink like that . . .'

'This is your last warning! Any more and I'll leave!'

'He was cruel when he was drunk. Not physical, all right, but we could hear a lot of it, he was cruel all right. We couldn't make out all the words, but we used to sit up in the dark and listen . . .'

'That's it! That's it! I warned you! Now I'm going! I'm going!'

Turning my back on the man, I ran down the steps to where Boris was standing. I took his arm and began to hurry away, but as I did so the man started to yell after us:

'You're fighting a losing battle! He has to find out what it's like! It's just life! There's nothing wrong with it! It's just real life!'

Boris was looking back with some curiosity and I was obliged to tug hard at his arm. For several moments we kept up a steady pace. More than once I sensed Boris trying to slow down, but I kept going, anxious to put beyond possibility any threat of the man pursuing us. By the time we slowed to a halt, I found I was badly out of breath. Staggering over to the wall – it was disconcertingly low, finishing only just above my waist – I put my elbows up and leaned over. I looked out at the lake, at the high-rise blocks beyond, at the pale wide sky, and waited for my chest to stop heaving.

After a while I became aware of Boris standing alongside me. He had his back to me and was fiddling with a loose fragment of masonry near the top of the wall. I began to feel a certain embarrassment about what had just occurred, and realised I would have to offer him some sort of explanation. I was still trying to think of something to say, when Boris, keeping his back to me, muttered:

'That man was mad, wasn't he?'

'Yes, Boris, completely mad. Possibly deranged.'

Boris went on fiddling with the wall. Then he said: 'It doesn't matter any more. We don't have to get Number Nine.'

'If it wasn't for that man, Boris . . .'

'It doesn't matter. It doesn't matter any more.' Then Boris turned to me and smiled. 'It's been a great day so far,' he said brightly.

'You're enjoying it?'

'It's been great. The bus trip, everything. It's been great.'

I was seized by an impulse to reach out and embrace him, but it struck me he would be puzzled, possibly alarmed by such a gesture. In the end I lightly tousled his hair then turned back to the view.

The wind was no longer troublesome, and for a moment we stood there quietly side by side, looking out over the estate. Then I said:

'Boris, I know you must be wondering. I mean, why it is we can't just settle down and live quietly, the three of us. You must, I know you do, you must wonder why I have to go away all the time, even though your mother gets upset about it. Well, you have to understand, the reason I keep going on these trips, it's not because I don't love you and dearly want to be with you. In some ways, I'd like nothing better than to stay at home with you and Mother, live in an apartment like that one over there, anywhere. But you see, it's not so simple. I have to keep going on these trips because, you see, you can never tell when it's going to come along. I mean the very special one, the very important trip, the one that's very very important, not just for me but for everyone, everyone in the whole world. How can I explain it to you, Boris, you're so young. You see, it would be so easy just to miss it. To say one time, no, I won't go, I'll just rest. Then only later I'll discover that was the one, the very very important one. And you see, once you miss it, there's no going back, it would be too late. It won't matter how hard I travel afterwards, it won't matter, it would be too late, and all these years I've spent would have been for nothing. I've seen it happen to other people, Boris. They spend year after year travelling and they start to get tired, perhaps a little lazy. But that's often just when it comes along. And they miss it. And, you know, they regret it for the rest of their lives. They get bitter and sad. By the time they die, they've become broken people. So you see, Boris, that's why. That's why I've got to carry on for the moment, keep travelling all the time. It makes things very difficult for us, I realise. But we have to be strong and patient, all three of us. It won't be much longer, I'm sure. It'll come soon, the very important one, then it will all be done, I'll be able to relax and rest then. I could stay at home all I wanted, it wouldn't matter, we could enjoy ourselves, just the three of us. We could do all the things we haven't been able to do. It won't be long now, I'm sure of it, but we'll just have to be patient. Boris, I hope you can understand what I'm saying.'

Boris remained silent for a long time. Then suddenly he straightened and said sternly: 'Move off quietly. All of you.' With that he ran a few steps away and began his karate movements again.

For the next few minutes I went on leaning against the wall, looking out at the view, listening to the sounds of Boris whispering furiously to himself. Then when I glanced at him again, I realised he was enacting in his imagination the latest version of a fantasy he had been playing through over and over during the past weeks. No doubt the fact of our being so close to its actual setting had made irresistible the prospect of going through it all again. For indeed, the scenario involved Boris and his grandfather fighting off a large gang of street thugs, in this very walkway, directly outside the old apartment.

I continued to watch him moving busily, now several yards away from me, and supposed he was coming to that part where he and his grandfather, standing shoulder to shoulder, ready themselves for another onslaught. There would already be a sea of unconscious bodies over the ground, but a number of the most persistent thugs would now be re-grouping for another assault. Boris and his grandfather would wait calmly side by side, while the thugs whispered strategies in the darkness of the walkway. In this, as in all such scenarios, Boris was in some vague way older. Not an adult exactly – which would make things too remote, as well as raising complications as to his grandfather's age – but somehow old enough to make credible the necessary physical feats.

Boris and Gustav would allow the thugs all the time they required to take up their formation. Then once the wave came, grandfather and grandson, a smoothly co-ordinated team, would deal efficiently, almost sadly, with the assailants flying at them from all sides. Eventually the attack would be over – but no, one last thug might leap out of the dark wielding some hideous blade. Gustav, being the nearest, would deliver a quick blow to the neck and then the battle would at last be over.

For a few silent moments, Boris and his grandfather would gravely survey the bodies littered about them. Then Gustav, casting his experienced gaze one last time over the scene, would give a nod, at which the two of them would turn away with the expressions of men who had undertaken work they had had to do, but had not enjoyed. They would ascend the short stairway to the door of the old apartment, take a last look at the defeated street thugs – some of them by now beginning to moan or crawl away – before going inside.

'It's all right now,' Gustav would announce at the door. 'They're gone.'

Sophie and I would then emerge nervously into the entrance hall. Boris, coming in behind his grandfather, would add: 'But it's not quite over yet. They'll attack once more, perhaps before morning.'

This assessment of the situation, which had been so obvious to grandfather and grandson they had not even bothered to confer, would be greeted with anguish by myself and Sophie.

'No, I can't stand it!' Sophie would wail, then break down sobbing. I would hold her in my arms in an attempt to comfort her, but my own features would be crumpling. Faced with this pathetic spectacle, Boris and Gustav would not show a flicker of disparagement. Gustav would place a reassuring hand on my shoulder, saying: 'Don't worry. Boris and I will be here. And after this last attack, that will be the end of it.'

'That's right,' Boris would confirm. 'One more battle is the most they'll take.' Then turning to Gustav he would say: 'Grandfather, perhaps this next time, I'll try reasoning with them again. Give them a last chance to back away.'

'They won't listen,' Gustav would say, shaking his head gravely. 'But you're right. We should give them a last chance.'

Sophie and I, overwhelmed with fear, would disappear deeper into the apartment weeping in each other's arms. Boris and Gustav would look at each other, sigh wearily, then, unbolting the front door, go back outside.

They would find the walkway dark, silent and empty.

'We might as well get some rest,' Gustav would say. 'You sleep first, Boris. I'll wake you if I hear them coming.'

Boris, nodding, would sit down on the top step of the stairway and, with his back against the front door, go promptly to sleep.

Some time later, a touch on his arm, and he would spring to his feet instantly awake. His grandfather would already be staring down at the street thugs gathering before them in the walkway. They would be more numerous than ever, the last confrontation having compelled them to recruit every one of their number from every dark recess of the city. Now they would all be there, dressed in torn leathers, army jackets, cruel belts, holding metal bars or bicycle chains – but their own sense of honour forbidding them to bring guns. Boris and Gustav would come slowly down the stairway towards them, pausing perhaps on the second or third step up. Then Boris, at a signal from his grandfather, would begin to speak, raising his voice so that it rang around the concrete pillars:

'We've fought you many times. There are even more of you this time, I can see. But you must each of you know in your hearts you cannot win. And this time my grandfather and I can't guarantee some of you won't get seriously hurt. There's no sense in this fighting. You must all have had homes once. Mothers and fathers. Perhaps brothers and sisters. I want you to understand what's happening. These attacks of yours, your continual terrorising of our apartment, has meant that my mother is crying all the time.

She's always tense and irritable, and this means she often tells me off for no reason. It also means Papa has to go away for long periods, sometimes abroad, which Mother doesn't like. This is all the result of your terrorising the apartment. Perhaps you're simply doing it because you're high-spirited, because you come from broken homes and you know no better. This is why I'm trying to get you to understand what's really happening, the real effects of your inconsiderate behaviour. What it could come to sooner or later is that Papa won't come back home at all. We might even have to move out of the apartment altogether. This is why I've had to bring Grandfather here, away from his important work in charge of a big hotel. We can't allow you to continue with what you've been doing. And this is why we've been fighting you. Now that I've explained things to you, you have a chance to think it all over and go back. If you don't, then Grandfather and I will have no choice but to fight you again. We'll do our best to knock you unconscious without doing any long-lasting damage, but in a large fight, even with our level of skill, we can't guarantee some of you won't end up with bad bruises, even broken bones. So take your chance and go back.'

Gustav would give a small smile of approval at this speech, then the two of them would survey again the brutish faces before them. A significant proportion would be looking uncertainly at each other, fear rather than reason causing them to re-consider. But then their leaders – horrific, scowling characters – would start up a war-like growl, which would steadily spread through their ranks. Then they would surge forward. Quickly, Boris and his grandfather would take up positions, back to back, moving neatly in formation, employing their own carefully developed blend of karate and other combat techniques. The street thugs would come at them from every direction, only to be sent spinning, stumbling, flying away emitting grunts of surprised horror, until once again the ground would be covered with unconscious bodies. For the next several moments Boris and Gustav would stand together waiting, watching carefully, until the thugs began to stir, some groaning, others shaking their heads trying to determine where they were. At this point, Gustav would take a step forward, saying:

'Now go, let that be the finish. Leave this apartment alone. This was a very happy home before you started to terrorise it. If you return again, my grandson and I will have no choice but to start breaking bones.'

This speech would hardly be necessary. The street thugs would know that this time they had been thoroughly defeated, that they were fortunate not to be more badly hurt. Slowly they would begin to clamber to their feet and hobble away, supporting each other in twos and threes, many moaning in pain.

Once the last thug had limped away, Boris and Gustav would exchange a look of quiet satisfaction, turn and go back up to the apartment. As they came in, Sophie and I – we would have witnessed the entire scene from the window – would welcome them back jubilantly. 'Thank God it's over,' I would say excitedly. 'Thank God.'

'I've already started to cook a celebratory meal,' Sophie would announce, beaming happily, all the tension now fallen from her face. 'We're so grateful to you and Grandfather, Boris. Why don't we all play a board game tonight?'

'I'll have to be going,' Gustav would say. 'I've got a lot to do back at the hotel. If there's any further trouble, let me know. But I'm certain that's the end of it.'

We would wave Gustav off as he went down the stairway. Then, closing the door, Boris, Sophie and I would settle in for the evening. Sophie would move in and out of the kitchen, preparing the meal, singing lightly to herself, while Boris and I lounged about on the floor of the living room, engrossed in the board game. Then, after we had been playing for an hour or so, at a point when Sophie was out of the room, I would suddenly look up at Boris with a serious expression and say quietly:

'Thank you for what you did, Boris. Now things can be as they were. The way they were before.'

'Look!' Boris shouted, and I saw he was standing beside me again, pointing over the wall. 'Look! It's Aunt Kim!'

Sure enough, down on the ground below us, a woman was waving frantically to attract our attention. She was wearing a green cardigan which she was holding tightly to herself, and her hair was blowing about messily. Noticing we had at last spotted her, she shouted something, but it was lost in the wind.

'Aunt Kim!' Boris called down.

The woman gesticulated and shouted something again.

'Let's go down,' Boris said, and began to lead the way, suddenly full of excitement once more.

I followed Boris as he ran down several flights of concrete stairs. As we came out at ground level, the wind immediately hit at us with great force, but Boris still managed to perform for the woman's benefit a staggering motion as though landing from a parachute jump.

'Aunt Kim' was a stocky woman of around forty, whose somewhat stern face was definitely familiar to me.

'You must be deaf, both of you,' she said as we came up to her. 'We saw you get off that bus and we were calling and calling, but were you listening? And then I come down here to get you and you're nowhere to be found.'

'Oh dear,' I said. 'We didn't hear anything, did we, Boris? It must be this wind. So' – I cast my gaze around me – 'you were watching us from your apartment.'

The stocky woman pointed vaguely to one of the countless windows overlooking us. 'We were calling and calling.' Then, turning to Boris, she said: 'Your mother's up there, young feller. She's just *longing* to see you.'

'Mother?'

'You'd better come on up straight away, she's just longing to see you. And you know what? She's been cooking all afternoon, getting the most fantastic feast ready for when you get home tonight. You're just not going to believe it, she says she's prepared everything, all your favourites, everything you can think of. She was just telling me all about it, and then we looked out of the window and there you were, getting off the bus. Listen, I've just spent half an hour looking for you guys, I'm frozen. Do we have to keep standing out here?'

She had been holding out her hand. Boris took it and we all started towards the section of the building she had indicated. As we got closer, Boris ran on ahead, pushed open a fire door and disappeared inside. The door was swinging shut as the stocky woman and I approached. She held it open for me, saying as she did so: 'Ryder, aren't you supposed to be somewhere else? Sophie was just telling me how her phone's been ringing all afternoon. People trying to track you down.'

'Really? Ah. Well, as you see, I'm here.' I gave a laugh. 'I brought Boris here.'

The woman shrugged. 'I suppose you know your business.'

We were standing in a dimly lit space at the bottom of a stairwell. On the wall next to me was a bank of mail boxes and some fire equipment. As we started up the first flight – there were at least five more flights above us – the clatter of Boris's running feet came from somewhere over our heads, and then I heard him shout: 'Mother!' There were exclamations of delight, more clatter of feet, and Sophie's voice saying: 'Oh my darling, my darling!' A muffled quality to her voice suggested they were embracing, and by the time the stocky woman and I arrived on the landing they had disappeared inside the apartment.

'Excuse the mess,' the woman said, ushering me in.

I went through a tiny entrance hall into an open-plan room furnished with simple modern items. A large picture window dominated the room, and as I came in I saw Sophie and Boris standing together in front of it, their figures almost silhouettes against the grey sky. Sophie smiled briefly at me, then resumed her conversation with Boris. They seemed excited about something and Sophie kept hugging Boris's shoulders. From the way they were pointing out of the window, I thought that perhaps Sophie was recounting how she and the stocky woman had spotted us earlier. But as I moved closer I heard Sophie saying:

'Yes, really. Everything's virtually ready. We just have to heat a few things up, like the meat pies.'

Boris said something I did not catch, to which Sophie replied:

'Of course we can. We'll play whichever one you like. You can see which one you want once we've finished eating.'

Boris looked at his mother questioningly, and I noticed a guardedness had entered his manner, preventing him from becoming as excited as perhaps Sophie would have liked. Then, as he wandered off to another part of the room, Sophie stepped closer to me and shook her head sadly.

'I'm sorry,' she said quietly. 'It wasn't any good. If anything, it was worse than the one last month. The views are stunning, it's built right on a cliff edge, but it's just not sturdy enough. Mr Mayer agreed in the end. He thinks the roof could fall down in a strong gale, perhaps even within the next few years. I came straight back, I was home by eleven. I'm sorry. You're disappointed, I can tell.' She glanced across towards Boris, who was examining a portable cassette player left on a shelf.

'There's no need to get discouraged,' I said with a sigh. 'I'm sure we'll find something soon.'

'But I was thinking,' Sophie said. 'On the coach coming back. I was thinking there's no reason we can't start doing all sorts of things together now, house or no house. So as soon as I got in, I started cooking. I thought tonight we could have a great feast, just the three of us. I remembered the way Mother used to do it when I was small, before her illness. She used to cook lots and lots of different little things and put them all out for us to pick and choose. They were such great evenings and I thought, well, tonight there's no reason we couldn't do something like that, just the three of us. I hadn't really considered it before, not with that kitchen the way it is, but I had a good look around it and realised I was being silly. Okay, it's far from ideal but a lot of it works. So I started cooking. I've been cooking right through the afternoon. And I've managed to make just about everything. All Boris's favourites. It's just sitting there waiting for us, it just needs warming up. We'll have a great feast tonight.'

'That's good. I'm very much looking forward to it.'

'There's no reason why we can't, even in that apartment. And you've been so understanding about . . . about everything. I was thinking about it all. On the coach coming back. We've got to put the past behind us now. We've got to start doing things together again. Good things.'

'Yes. You're quite right.'

Sophie stared out of the window for a few seconds. Then she said: 'Oh, I nearly forgot. That woman kept phoning. All the time I was cooking. Miss Stratmann. Asking if I knew where you were. Did she get hold of you?'

'Miss Stratmann? Well no. What was she wanting?'

'She seemed to think there'd been a mix up over some of your appointments today. She was very polite, kept apologising for disturbing me. She said she was sure you were well on top of everything, she was just phoning to check up, that was all, she wasn't worried in the least. But then fifteen minutes later the phone would ring and it would be her again.'

'Well, it's nothing to be concerned about. Er . . . she was under the impression I should have been somewhere else, you say?'

'I'm not sure what she was saying. She was very nice, but she kept on phoning. I over-cooked a tray of chicken tarts because of that. Then, the last time she phoned, she asked if I was looking forward to it. To this reception this evening at the Karwinsky Gallery. You hadn't told me about it, but she said it like they were expecting me. So I said, yes, I was very much looking forward to it. Then she asked if Boris was, and I said yes, he was too, and so were you, that you were really looking forward to it. That seemed to reassure her. She said she wasn't worried, she was just mentioning it, that was all. I put the phone down and I was a little disappointed at first. I thought this reception might interfere with our feast. But then I saw I had time to get everything ready first, that we could all go and come back, as long as we didn't have to stay too long we could still have our evening together. And then I thought, well, it's a good thing really. A good thing both for me and for Boris, to go to a reception like this.' She suddenly reached out to Boris, who had come wandering back towards us, and hugged him roughly. 'Boris, you'll be a big hit, won't you? You won't mind all these people. You just be yourself and you'll really enjoy it. You'll be a big hit. Then before you know it, it'll be time to go home and then we'll have a really great evening, just the three of us. I've got everything ready, all your favourites.'

Boris wearily fought off his mother's embrace and went off again. Sophie watched him with a smile, then turned to me, saying:

'Hadn't we better be setting off soon? The Karwinsky Gallery, it might take some time from here.'

'Yes,' I said and glanced at my watch. 'Yes, you have a point.' I turned to the stocky woman who had come back into the room. 'Perhaps you could advise us,' I said to her. 'I'm not entirely certain which bus will take us to this gallery. Do you know if it's coming in soon?'

'To the Karwinsky Gallery?' The stocky woman gave me a look of contempt and only Boris's presence seemed to stop her adding something sarcastic. Then she said: 'You won't get a bus out to the Karwinsky Gallery from here. You'd have to take a bus back into the city centre. Then you'd have to wait for a tram outside the library. There's no way you'll make it on time.'

'Ah. What a pity. I'd been relying on a bus being available.'

The stocky woman gave me another scornful look, then said: 'Take my car. I won't be needing it this evening.'

'That's awfully kind of you,' I said. 'But are you sure we won't be . . .'

'Oh, cut the crap, Ryder. You need the car. There's no other way you'd get out to the Karwinsky Gallery in time. Even with a car, you'd have to be starting out right now.'

'Yes,' I said, 'that's just what I was thinking. But look, we don't want to inconvenience you.'

'You can just take a few boxes of books with you. I won't be able to carry them if I have to go in by bus tomorrow.'

'Yes, of course. Whatever we can do.'

'Just drive them round to Hermann Roth's shop in the morning, any time before ten.'

'Don't worry, Kim,' Sophie said before I could say anything. 'I'll see to all that. You're so good.'

'Okay, you guys had better start moving. Hey, young feller' – the stocky woman gestured to Boris – 'why don't you help me load up these books?'

For the next few minutes I found myself alone at the window gazing out at the view. The others had disappeared into a bedroom and I could hear them talking and laughing behind me. It occurred to me I should go in and assist them, but then I saw the importance of my taking the opportunity to collect my thoughts on the evening ahead, and I went on staring down at the artificial lake. Some children had started to kick a ball against the fence on the far side of the water, but otherwise the perimeter areas were deserted.

Eventually I heard the stocky woman calling me and became aware that they were waiting to leave. I came into the hallway to find Sophie and Boris, each carrying a cardboard box, already going out into the corridor. They began to argue about something as they set off down the staircase.

The stocky woman was holding open the front door for me. 'Sophie's determined it goes well tonight,' she said, her voice lowered. 'So don't let her down again, Ryder.'

'Don't worry,' I said. 'I'll make sure everything goes well.'

She gave me a hard look, then turned and went down the staircase jingling her keys.

I followed after her. We were on the second flight down when I saw a woman coming up the stairs with a tired gait. The figure squeezed past the stocky woman with a muttered 'excuse me' and we had already passed each other before I realised that it was Fiona Roberts, still in her ticket inspector's uniform. She too did not seem to recognise me until the last moment – the light was poor on the stairs – but she turned wearily, a hand on the metal banister, and said:

'Oh, here you are. It's good of you to be so punctual. I'm sorry I was a little longer than I said. There was a re-routing, a tram on the eastern circuit, so my shift went on much longer. I hope you haven't been waiting here long.'

'No, no.' I drifted back up a step or two. 'Not long at all. But unfortunately, my schedule has got very tight . . .'

'It's all right, I won't take any more of your time than necessary. Actually, I have to tell you, I phoned round the girls, just as we said, I phoned from the depot canteen during my break. I told them to expect me with a friend, but I didn't actually tell them it was *you*. I was going to at first, just as we'd agreed, but I started by phoning Trude and as soon as I heard that voice, the way she said: "Oh yes, it's you, dear," I could hear so much in that voice, so much patronising bile. I could tell how all day she'd been talking about me, one phone call after another, with Inge and all the rest of them, discussing last night, all of them pretending to feel pity for me, saying how they'd have to treat me with sympathy, after all I was like an ill person, it was their duty to be kind. But of course they couldn't keep me, how could someone like me be part of the Foundation? Oh, they'll have enjoyed themselves today, I could hear it all, just in the way she said it as soon as I phoned. "Oh yes, it's *you*, dear." And I thought, all right then, let's not give you any warning. Let's see where you get by not believing me. That's what I thought to myself. I thought, let's hope you're completely thrown when you open the door and see who's standing there next to me. Let's hope you've got your worst clothes on, perhaps your *sportswear*, and all your make-up's off so that mound next to your nose is completely visible, and that your hair's pinned back the way you do sometimes that makes you look at least fifteen years older. And let's hope your apartment's looking a mess, with all those stupid magazines, those scandal sheets and romantic novelettes you read littering the furniture, and you'll be so thrown you won't know what to say, you'll be so embarrassed about everything, and you'll make it worse by saying one completely inane thing after another. And you'll offer refreshments then find you're short of everything, and you'll feel so foolish for never having believed me. Let's do that, I thought. So I never told her, I didn't tell any of them. I just said I'd be coming round with a friend.' She stopped and calmed herself a little. Then she said: 'I'm sorry. I hope I didn't sound vindictive. But I've been longing for this all day. It kept me going, doing all those tickets, it kept me going. The passengers must have wondered why I was going around like that, you know, with a gleam in my eye. Well, if you've got a tight schedule, I suppose we ought to start straight away. We can start at Trude's. Inge should be with her, she usually is at this time of the day, so we can deal with them both first off. I hardly care about the others. I just want to see the looks on the faces of those two. Well, let's go.'

She started up the stairs, all her former weariness gone. The stairs seemed to go on endlessly, one flight after another, until I was struggling for breath. Fiona, however, did not appear to be exerting herself at all. As we climbed she continued to talk, her voice lowered as though people might be listening all around us.

'You don't have to say too much to them,' I heard her saying at one point. 'Just let them fawn over you for a few minutes. But of course you might want to discuss your parents with them.'

When we finally came off the staircase I was so out of breath – my chest was actually wheezing – I was unable to attend much to the surroundings. I was aware of being led down a dim corridor past rows of doors and that Fiona, oblivious of my difficulties, was marching on ahead. Then suddenly she stopped and knocked at a door. Catching up with her, I was obliged to lean a hand on the door frame, my head bowed, in an effort to recover my breath. When the door opened, I must have presented a somewhat crumpled figure beside the triumphant Fiona.

'Trude,' Fiona said. 'I've brought a friend with me.'

With an effort I straightened myself and smiled pleasantly.

16

The woman who had opened the door was around fifty, plump with short white hair. She was wearing a loose pink jumper and baggy striped trousers. Trude glanced towards me briefly, then, noticing nothing out of the ordinary, turned to Fiona and said: 'Oh, yes. Well, I suppose you ought to come in.'

The condescension was obvious, but appeared only to heighten Fiona's anticipation, and she gave me a conspiratorial smile as we followed Trude inside.

'Is Inge here with you?' Fiona asked as we came into a tiny entrance hall.

'Yes, we've just come back,' Trude said. 'As it happens, we've got a lot to report. And since you just happened to call, you'll be the first to hear our news. That's lucky for you.'

This last remark seemed to be made entirely without irony. Trude then disappeared through a door, leaving us standing in the tiny hall, and we could hear her voice from within saying: 'Inge, it's Fiona. And some friend of hers. I suppose we ought to tell her what happened to us this afternoon.'

'Fiona?' Inge's voice sounded mildly outraged. Then with an effort, she said: 'Well, I suppose she ought to come in.'

Hearing this exchange, Fiona once again smiled excitedly at me. Then Trude's head peered round the door and we were shown into the lounge.

The room was not unlike the stocky woman's in size and shape, though the furniture was fussier and dominated by floral patterns. Perhaps it was simply that this apartment faced a different direction, or perhaps the sky outside had cleared a little. In any case, the afternoon sun was drifting in through the large window and as I stepped into the light I fully expected the two women to start with recognition. Fiona obviously did so too for I noticed how she carefully stood to one side in case her presence lessened the impact. Neither Trude nor Inge, however, appeared to register anything. They each cast a quick uninterested glance at me and then Trude invited us, rather coldly, to sit down. We did so side by side on a narrow couch. Fiona, though initially bewildered, seemed to conclude that this unexpected turn of events could serve only to intensify the moment of revelation once it came, and gave me another gleeful little grin.

'Shall I tell her or do you want to?' Inge was saying.

Trude, who clearly deferred to the younger woman, said: 'No, you tell it, Inge. You deserve to. But Fiona' – she turned to us – 'you're not to go around telling people yet. We want to keep it a surprise for the meeting tonight, that's only fair. Oh, didn't we tell you about tonight's meeting? Well, there, we've just told you. Do come if you've got time. Though since you've got your friend staying with you' – she nodded towards me – 'we'll understand perfectly if you're not able to come. But Inge, you tell it, you deserve to, really.'

'Well, Fiona, I'm sure you'll be interested in this, we've had a most exciting day. As you know, Mr von Braun had invited us to his office today to discuss with him personally our plans for looking after Mr Ryder's parents. Oh, you didn't know? I thought you *all* knew. Well, we'll be reporting in detail tonight just how the meeting went, I'll just tell you for now it went very nicely indeed, even if it had to be cut a little short. Oh, Mr von Braun was so apologetic about that, he couldn't have been more so, could he, Trude? He was so apologetic about having to get away early, but when we learnt the reason, well, then we understood perfectly. You see, there'd been this very important trip arranged to the zoo. Ah, you might laugh, Fiona dear, but this was no ordinary trip to the zoo. An official party, including naturally Mr von Braun himself, was going to take Mr Brodsky there. Do you know, Mr Brodsky had never been to the zoo? But the point was, Miss Collins had been persuaded to be there. Yes, at the zoo! Can you imagine that? After all these years! And no more than Mr Brodsky deserves, that's what we both said immediately. Yes, Miss Collins was going to be there when they arrived, she'd be waiting at an agreed place, and the official party would encounter her, and she would exchange conversation with Mr Brodsky. It had all been arranged. Can you imagine it? They were going to meet and actually talk after all this time! We said we could understand *perfectly* why our meeting had to be cut short, but Mr von Braun, he was so kind to us, he obviously felt badly about it, he said to us: "Why don't you ladies also come along to the zoo? I can't very well ask you to join the official party, but you could perhaps look on from a little distance." We said we'd be absolutely thrilled. And that's when he said to us: "Of course, if you do as I suggest, you'll not only get a glimpse of Mr Brodsky's first encounter with his wife after all this time, you'll" – and he paused, didn't he, Trude? he paused, then he said, cool as you like – "you'll also be able to see at close quarters Mr Ryder, who has most kindly agreed to be part of the official party. And if an opportune moment arises, though I can't guarantee this, I'll signal to you ladies and I could introduce you both to him." We were absolutely stunned! But of course, when we thought about it afterwards on the way home, we were just saying so to each other just now, when you think more carefully about it, it wasn't so surprising really. After all, we've come a long way in the last few years, what with the bunting for the Peking people, and all the effort we put into the sandwiches for the Henri Ledoux lunch . . .'

'The Peking Ballet, that was the real turning point,' Trude put in.

'Yes, that was the turning point. But I suppose we'd never really stopped to think about it, we'd just been getting on with things, going hard at it, we probably never realised how much we were going up all the time in everyone's esteem. The truth is, quite honestly, we've now become a very important part of life in this city. It's high time we realised that. Let's face it, that's why Mr von Braun invites us *personally* to his office, why he ends up suggesting the sorts of things he suggested today. "If an opportune moment arises, I'll introduce you to him." That's what he said, wasn't it, Trude? "I know Mr Ryder would be delighted to meet you both, especially since you'll be looking after his parents, a matter of the utmost concern for him." Of course, we'd always said, hadn't we, that once we'd been given this assignment, we had a good chance of being introduced to Mr Ryder. But we hadn't expected it to happen quite so soon and so we were very excited. Fiona, what's wrong, dear?'

Beside me, Fiona had been shifting impatiently, trying to interrupt the flow of Inge's words. Now that Inge had paused, Fiona nudged my arm and gave me a look as though to say: 'Now! This is the moment!' Unfortunately I was still a little out of breath from the climb up the stairs and this perhaps caused me to hesitate. In any case there was an awkward moment when all three women were staring at me. Then, when I said nothing, Inge went on:

'Well, if you don't mind, Fiona, I'll just finish what I was saying. I'm sure you have plenty of very interesting stories to tell us, dear, and we're very keen to hear them. No doubt you've had another very interesting day on your trams while we were in the city centre doing all this I'm now telling you about, but if you'd like to wait just a minute, you might hear something of passing interest to you. After all' – and here the sarcasm in her voice struck me as crossing the boundary of civilised behaviour – 'this does involve your *old friend*, your *old friend* Mr Ryder . . .'

'Inge, really!' Trude put in, but a smile was hovering around her lips and the two of them exchanged a quick smirk.

Fiona was nudging me again. Glancing at her, I could see her patience had run out and that she was wanting her tormentors to get their comeuppance without further delay. Leaning forward, I cleared my throat, but before I could actually say anything, Inge had started to talk again.

'Well, what I was saying was that when you think about it, it's no more than we deserve now, this level of treatment. Clearly Mr von Braun believes so anyway. He was very kind and courteous to us the whole time, wasn't he? He was so apologetic when he had to go off to the city hall to join the official party. "We'll be arriving at the zoo in about thirty minutes," he kept saying. "I do hope you ladies will be there." It would be perfectly all right, he told us, if we came as close as five or six metres from the official party. After all, it wasn't as though we were just members of the public! Oh, I'm sorry, Fiona, we hadn't forgotten, we were *going* to mention to Mr von Braun how one of our group, that's to say *you*, dear, how one of us was a very dear friend of Mr Ryder, a very dear friend of many years' standing. We had every intention of mentioning it, but somehow we just never got round to it, did we, Trude?'

Again the two women exchanged smirks. Fiona stared at them in cold fury. I saw at this point things had gone too far and decided to intervene. However, two possible ways of doing so immediately presented themselves to me. One option was to draw attention to my identity in a way that elegantly entered the flow of what Inge happened to be saying. For instance, I might have interjected calmly: 'Well, we didn't have the pleasure of meeting at the zoo, but what does that matter when we can meet in the comfort of your own home?' or some such thing. The alternative was simply to rise abruptly, perhaps throwing my arms out as I did so, and making the blunt declaration: 'I am Ryder!' I naturally wished to choose the course that would yield the maximum impact, but the resulting hesitation caused me once more to miss my opportunity, for Inge had begun to talk again.

'We got to the zoo and we waited, oh, it was about twenty minutes, wasn't it, Trude? We waited by the little stand-up place where you can drink a cup of coffee, and after about twenty minutes we saw these cars come driving right up to the gates, and this very distinguished party got out. About ten or eleven of them, all gentlemen, Mr von Winterstein was there, and Mr Fischer and Mr Hoffman. And Mr von Braun, of course. And in the middle of it there was Mr Brodsky, looking very distinguished indeed, wasn't he, Trude? Nothing like the way he used to be. Of course we looked immediately for Mr Ryder but he wasn't there. Trude and I were looking from face to face, but they were all the usual ones, the councillors, you know. For a second we thought Mr Reitmayer was Mr Ryder, just as he was getting out of the car. Anyway, he wasn't with them, and we were saying to each other, he's probably coming along just a little later, what with his busy schedule. And there they were, all these gentlemen coming up the path, all wearing dark overcoats, except for Mr Brodsky who was wearing a grey one, very distinguished looking, with a matching hat. They came up past the maple trees, all at a leisurely pace, up to the first of the cages. Mr von Winterstein seemed to be the host, pointing things out to Mr Brodsky, pointing out the animals in each cage. But you could see no one was paying much attention to the animals, they were so keyed up about Mr Brodsky's encounter with Miss Collins. And we couldn't resist, could we, Trude? We went on ahead, we went round the corner to the central concourse and sure enough, there was Miss Collins, all by herself, standing in front of the giraffes, looking at them. There were a few other people strolling about, but of course they had no idea, it was only when the official party came round the corner people realised something was happening and moved away respectfully, and there was Miss Collins still standing in front of the giraffes, looking more alone than ever, and you could see her glancing towards the official party as they came closer. She seemed so calm, you wouldn't know what was going on inside. And Mr Brodsky, we could see his expression, very stiff, stealing glances towards Miss Collins, even though they were still quite a long way apart, there were all the monkey and racoon cages still to go. Mr von Winterstein seemed to be introducing all the animals to Mr Brodsky, it was like the animals were all official guests at a banquet, wasn't it, Trude? We didn't know why the gentlemen couldn't just go straight to the giraffes and Miss Collins, but obviously this was the way it had been decided. And it was so exciting, so *moving*, for a moment we even forgot about the possibility of Mr Ryder turning up. You could see Mr Brodsky's breath in the air, all misty, and all the other gentlemen's too, and then, when there was only a few cages left, Mr Brodsky seemed to lose all interest in the animals and he took off his hat. It was a very old-fashioned, respectful sort of gesture, Fiona. We felt privileged to be there to see it.'

'You could see so much,' Trude broke in. 'So much in the way he did it, then just held his hat to his chest. It was like a declaration of love and apology all at the same time. It was very moving.'

'But I was telling the story, thank you, Trude. Miss Collins, she's so elegant, you'd never guess she was that age from a distance. Such a youthful figure. She turned to him very nonchalantly, just a cage or so separating them. Any members of the public there'd been had backed right away by this time, and Trude and I, we remembered what Mr von Braun had said, about the five metres, and we crept forward as much as we dared, but it seemed such a private moment, we didn't dare get up too close. First they nodded to each other and exchanged some very ordinary sort of greeting. Then Mr Brodsky, he suddenly took a few steps forward and reached out, quite swiftly, it was like he'd been planning it beforehand, Trude thought . . .'

'Yes, like he'd been rehearsing it in private for days . . .'

'Yes, it was like that. I agree with that. It was just like that. He reached out and took her hand and kissed it very lightly and politely, then let go. And Miss Collins, she just bowed gracefully, then immediately turned her attention to the other gentlemen, greeting them and smiling, we were too far away to catch what they were all saying. So there they all were and for a little while no one seemed to know what to do next. Then Mr von Winterstein took the initiative and started to explain something about the giraffes to both Mr Brodsky and Miss Collins, addressing them as though they were a couple – wasn't he, Trude? As though they were a nice old couple who'd arrived together from the start. So there they were, Mr Brodsky and Miss Collins, after all these years, standing side by side, not touching, just standing side by side, both of them staring at the giraffes, listening to Mr von Winterstein. This went on for some time, and you could see the other gentlemen whispering among themselves about what ought to happen next. Then gradually, before you knew it, the gentlemen had all melted back, it was all very well done, so *civilised*, they all pretended to be in conversation with each other and drifted away a little at a time so that in the end there was just Mr Brodsky and Miss Collins left in front of the giraffes. Of course, we were watching very closely now and everyone else must have been too, but of course everyone was pretending not to look. And we saw Mr Brodsky turn very gracefully to Miss Collins, raise a hand towards the giraffes' cage and he said something. It seemed to be something very heartfelt and Miss Collins bowed her head just a little, even she couldn't remain unmoved, and then Mr Brodsky went on talking, occasionally you'd see him raise his hand again, like this, very gently, towards the giraffes. We couldn't be sure if he was talking about the giraffes or about something else, but he kept raising his hand to the cage. Miss Collins did seem very overcome, but she's such an elegant lady, she straightened herself and smiled and then the two of them came strolling over to where the other gentlemen were talking. You could see her exchanging a few words with the gentlemen then, very pleasant and polite, she seemed to have quite a long talk with Mr Fischer, and then she was saying goodbye to them all, each of them in turn. She gave a little bow to Mr Brodsky, and you could see how pleased Mr Brodsky was with it all. He was standing there in a sort of dream, holding his hat to his chest. Then off she went up the path, all the way up to the refreshments hut, up past the fountain and out of sight by the polar bear enclosure. And once she'd gone, the gentlemen, they seemed to drop all their earlier pretence and gathered round Mr Brodsky, and you could see everyone was very pleased and excited and they seemed to be congratulating him. Oh, we'd have loved to have known what Mr Brodsky had said to Miss Collins! Perhaps we should have been bolder and gone a few steps nearer, we might have caught at least the odd word. But then, now we're who we are, we have to be more careful. In any case, it was all wonderful. And those trees at the zoo, they're so beautiful at this time of year. I do wonder what they said to each other. Trude thinks they really will get back together again now. Did you know, they never divorced? Isn't that interesting? All those years, and for all of Miss Collins's insisting on being called Miss Collins, they never divorced. Mr Brodsky deserves to win her back again. Oh, but I'm sorry, with all this excitement, we haven't even started telling you the main point! About Mr Ryder! You see, since Mr Ryder wasn't with the official party, we didn't really think we could come forward, even after Miss Collins had left. After all, Mr von Braun had suggested we come forward specifically to meet Mr Ryder. In any case, although we were watching Mr von Braun carefully, and we were quite near sometimes, he never looked towards us, he was probably very taken up with Mr Brodsky. So we didn't come forward. But then as they were leaving, we were watching them about to go through the gate, they all stopped and they were joined by someone, a man, but they were so far away by this time we couldn't see clearly. But Trude felt sure it was Mr Ryder who'd joined them – her long sight's better than mine and I wasn't wearing my lenses. She was sure, weren't you, Trude? She was certain it was him, that he'd very tactfully kept out of the way so as not to make things any more difficult than they were for Mr Brodsky and Miss Collins, and he was now re-joining the official party at the gates. I thought at first it was just Mr Braunthal, but I didn't have my lenses in, and Trude was very sure it was Mr Ryder. And afterwards, when I thought about it, I too felt perhaps it *was* Mr Ryder. So we missed the opportunity to be introduced to him! They were so far away by this point, you see, already at the gates, and the drivers were already holding open the car doors. Even if we'd rushed across, we wouldn't have got there in time. So we didn't, in the *strictest* sense, meet Mr Ryder. But Trude and I were just discussing it, and we were saying, in almost every other sense, I mean in any sense that really matters, it's fair to say we met him today. After all, if he'd been with the official party, then certainly, that time by the giraffe cage, just after Miss Collins had gone, Mr von Braun would definitely have introduced us. It was hardly our fault we didn't realise how tactful Mr Ryder was going to be, that he'd stay down by the gates. Anyway, the point is, it's beyond question it *would have been appropriate*, our being introduced to him. That's the point. Mr von Braun for one obviously thought so, now that we occupy the position we do, it would clearly have been appropriate. And you know, Trude' – she turned to her friend – 'now I think about it further, I agree with you. We might as well announce to the meeting tonight that we actually met him. As you say, that's closer to the truth than saying we didn't. And we've so much to get through tonight, we simply don't have time to explain everything all over again. After all, it's only a quirk of fate that kept us from being formally introduced, that's all. To all intents and purposes, we *have* met him. He'll certainly hear all about us, if he hasn't already, he's bound to enquire very closely about how his parents are to be looked after. So we've as good as met him, and as you say, it would be unfair if people thought otherwise. Oh, but please forgive me' – Inge suddenly turned to Fiona – 'I've forgotten, I'm talking to an *old friend* of Mr Ryder. This must all seem a fuss about nothing to such an *old friend* . . .'

'Inge,' Trude said, 'poor Fiona, she's very confused. Don't tease her.' Then, smiling at Fiona, she said: 'It's all right, dear, don't worry.'

As Trude was saying this, memories came back to me of the warm friendship Fiona and I had had as children. I recalled the small white cottage where she had lived, just a little walk away down that muddy lane in Worcestershire, and the two of us playing for hours under her parents' dining table. I remembered the times I had wandered down to the cottage, upset and confused, and how skilfully she had comforted me, allowing me quickly to forget whatever scene I had just left behind. The realisation that it was this same precious friendship that was being mocked before my eyes caused a fury to well up in me, and although Inge had again started to speak, I decided I could not let the situation go on unchecked another second. Determined not to repeat my earlier mistake of prevaricating, I leaned forward decisively, my intention to cut Inge off with a bold announcement of who I was, then to recline back again as the impact settled on the room. Unfortunately, although I put much force behind my intervention, all that came out was a slightly strangled grunt, which was nevertheless loud enough to cause Inge to stop and all three women to turn and stare at me. There was an awkward moment, before Fiona, no doubt wishing to cover up for my embarrassment – perhaps something of her old protectiveness towards me momentarily re-awakening – burst out:

'You two, you've no idea how foolish you look! Do you know why? No, you wouldn't guess, you two, you'd never guess just how stupid, how unspeakably ridiculous you both look at this moment. You really wouldn't, it's typical, just typical of you both! Oh, I've meant to tell you for so long, ever since we met, well, you'll see for yourselves now, you can judge for yourselves now if you're fools or what. Look!'

Fiona jerked her head in my direction. Inge and Trude, both bewildered, once again stared at me. I made another concerted effort to announce myself, but to my dismay all I could manage was another grunt, more vigorous than the last but no more coherent. I took a deep breath, a panic now beginning to seize me, and tried again, only to produce another, this time more prolonged, straining noise.

'What on earth is she saying to us, Trude?' Inge said. 'Why's this little bitch speaking to us like this? How dare she? What's come over her?'

'It's my fault,' Trude said. 'It was my mistake. It was my idea to invite her into our group. It's just as well she's revealing her true colours before Mr Ryder's parents arrive. She's jealous, that's all. She's jealous that we met Mr Ryder today. While all she has are these pathetic little stories . . .'

'What do you mean you met him today?' Fiona exploded. 'You said yourself just now you didn't . . .'

'You know perfectly well it was as good as meeting him! Wasn't it, Trude? We're perfectly entitled to say we've met him now. It's just something you'll have to come to terms with, Fiona . . .'

'Well in that case' – Fiona was now almost shrieking – 'let's see you come to terms with *this*!' She flung her arm towards me as though announcing the most dramatic of stage entrances. Once more I did my best to oblige. This time, fuelled by my mounting anger and frustration, the straining noise was more intense than ever and I could feel the sofa shake with my effort.

'What's wrong with this friend of yours?' Inge asked, suddenly noticing me. But Trude was paying no attention.

'I should never have listened to you,' she was saying to Fiona bitterly. 'It should have been obvious from the start what a little liar you were. And we let our children play with those brats of yours! They're probably little liars too and now they've probably taught all our children how to tell lies. How ridiculous your party was last night. And the way you've decorated your apartment! How absurd! We were all laughing about it this morning . . .'

'Why don't you help me!' Fiona suddenly addressed me directly for the first time. 'What's the matter, why don't you do something?'

In fact, all this time I had been continuing to strain. Now, just as Fiona turned to me, I caught a glimpse of myself in a mirror hung on the opposite wall. I saw that my face had become bright red and squashed into pig-like features, while my fists, clenched at chest level, were quivering along with the whole of my torso. Catching sight of myself in this condition took the wind right out of my sails and, losing heart, I collapsed back into the corner of the sofa, panting heavily.

'I think, Fiona dear,' Inge was saying, 'it's time you and this . . . this friend of yours went on your way. I don't think your attendance will be required this evening.'

'It's out of the question,' Trude shouted. 'We've got responsibilities now. We can't afford to indulge little birds with broken wings like her. We're no longer just a group of volunteers. We've got very important work to do and anyone not up to the mark will have to be let go.'

I could see tears appearing in Fiona's eyes. She looked at me again, now with growing bitterness, and I thought of trying just once more to declare my identity, but the thought of the figure I had glimpsed in the mirror made me decide against doing so. Instead, I staggered to my feet and went in search of the exit. I was still considerably out of breath from the straining, and when I reached the doorway I was obliged to stop a moment to lean against its frame. Behind me, I could hear the two women continuing to talk in heated tones. At one point, I heard Inge say: 'And what a disgusting person to bring to your apartment.' With an effort, I hurried out across the small hallway and, after some moments of fumbling frantically at the locks of the main door, succeeded in letting myself out into the corridor. Almost at once, I began to feel better and proceeded towards the staircase in a more composed manner.

17

Going down the successive flights of stairs, I looked at my watch and saw that it was high time we were setting off for the Karwinsky Gallery. Naturally I felt considerable regret about the situation I was having to leave behind, but clearly my priority had to be to ensure our punctual arrival at the evening's important event. I resolved nevertheless to attend to Fiona's problems in the reasonably near future.

When I finally reached the ground floor, I was greeted by a sign marked 'Car Park' on the wall and an arrow pointing the way. I went past several storage cupboards, then out through an exit.

I emerged at the rear of the apartment buildings, on the other side from the artificial lake. The evening sun was now low in the sky. There was an expanse of green land before me, sloping gradually away into the distance. The car park, immediately in front of me, was simply a rectangle of grass that had been fenced off, like a corral on an American ranch. The ground had not been concreted, though the to-ing and fro-ing of vehicles had worn it down virtually to bare earth. There was enough space for perhaps fifty cars, but at this moment there were only seven or eight, each parked some way away from the other, the sunset glancing off their bodywork. Near the back of the car park I could see the stocky woman and Boris loading the boot of an estate car. As I moved towards them, I noticed Sophie sitting in the front passenger seat, gazing emptily through the windscreen at the sunset.

The stocky woman was closing the boot as I came up to them.

'I'm sorry,' I said to her. 'I didn't realise you had so much to load up. I'd have given a hand except . . .'

'It's all right. This one here gave me all the help I needed.' The stocky woman ruffled Boris's hair, then said to him: 'So don't worry, okay? You're all going to have a great evening. Really. She's cooked all your favourites.'

She bent down and gave Boris a reassuring squeeze, but the

little boy seemed to be in a dream and stared off into the distance. The stocky woman held out the car keys to me.

'There should be plenty of petrol. Take care how you drive.'

I thanked her and watched her walk off towards the apartment buildings. When I turned to him, Boris was staring at the sunset. I touched his shoulder and led him round the car. He climbed into the back seat without speaking.

Evidently the sunset was having an hypnotic effect, for when I got in behind the wheel Sophie too was still staring into the distance. She seemed hardly to notice my arrival, but then, as I was familiarising myself with the controls, she said quietly:

'We can't let this house business drag us all down. We can't afford to. We don't know when it'll be, the next time you're back with us. House or no house, we've got to start doing things, *good* things together. That's what I realised this morning, coming back in the bus. Even with that apartment. And that kitchen.'

'Yes, yes,' I said and put the key into the ignition. 'Now. Do you know the way to the gallery?'

The question brought Sophie out of her trance-like condition. 'Oh,' she said, putting her hands up to her mouth as though she had just remembered something. Then she said: 'I could probably find the way from the city centre. But from here, I don't know.'

I sighed heavily. I could sense things were in danger of slipping out of control again, and I felt returning some of the intense annoyance I had experienced earlier in the day about the way Sophie had brought such chaos into my life. But then I heard her voice beside me say brightly:

'Why don't we ask the car park attendant? He might know.'

She was pointing to the entrance of the car park where, sure enough, there was a little wooden kiosk housing a uniformed figure, visible from the waist up.

'All right,' I said. 'I'll go and ask him.'

I got out and made my way towards the wooden kiosk. A car in the process of leaving the enclosure had paused beside the kiosk, and as I came closer I could see the attendant – a bald, fat man – leaning over his hatch, smiling jovially and gesturing to the driver. Their conversation went on for some time and I was on the verge of stepping in between them when the car at last started to pull away. Even then, the attendant continued to follow the vehicle with his eyes as it drove off along the long curving road that ran the perimeter of the housing estate. Indeed, he too seemed to have become transfixed by the sunset and, although I coughed directly under his hatch, he continued to gaze dreamily after the car. In the end I simply barked: 'Good evening.'

The plump man started, then, looking down at me, replied: 'Oh, good evening, sir.'

'I'm sorry to disturb you,' I said. 'But we happen to be in something of a hurry. We need to get to the Karwinsky Gallery, but you see, being a visitor to this town I'm not at all sure of the quickest route from here.'

'The Karwinsky Gallery.' The man thought for a moment, then said: 'Well, to be honest, it's not at all straightforward, sir. In my opinion, the simplest thing would be for you to follow that gentleman who just left. In that red car.' He pointed into the distance. 'That gentleman, as luck would have it, lives very near the Karwinsky Gallery. I could of course try and give you directions, but I'd have to sit and work it all out first, all those different turnings, particularly towards the end of your journey. I mean, when you come off the highway and you have to find your way through all those little roads around the farms. Simplest by far, sir, just to follow that gentleman in the red car. If I'm not mistaken, he lives just two or three turnings on from the Karwinsky Gallery. It's a very pleasant area and that gentleman, he and his wife very much like it there. It's the countryside out there, sir. He tells me he has a nice cottage with hens in the back yard and an apple tree. A nice sort of area for an art gallery, even if it's a bit out of the way. Well worth the drive, sir. The gentleman in that red car, he says he doesn't ever think of moving even though it's quite some way for him to come every day, here to this estate. Oh yes, he works here, he works in the administration block' – the man suddenly leaned right out of his hatch and pointed to some windows behind him – 'that block over there, sir. Oh no, these aren't all residential apartments by any means. To run an estate of this size, oh, it requires a lot of paperwork. That gentleman in the red car, he's been working here right from the first day the water company began building here. And now he oversees all the maintenance work on the estate. It's a big job, sir, and it's a long way for him to have to commute each day, but he says he never thinks

244

about moving nearer. And I don't blame him, it's very nice out there. But here I am chattering on, and you must be in a hurry. I do apologise, sir. As I say, if you just follow that red car, that's by far the simplest way to do it. I'm sure you'll enjoy the Karwinsky Gallery. It's a nice part of the country, and the gallery itself, I'm told it has some very beautiful objects.'

I thanked him tersely and walked back to the car. When I climbed back in behind the wheel, Sophie and Boris were again gazing at the sunset. I started the engine without speaking. Only after we had bumped past the wooden kiosk – I gave the car park attendant a quick wave – did Sophie ask: 'So you found out the way?'

'Yes, yes. We just follow the red car that left just now.'

As I said this, I realised how angry I still was at her. But I said nothing further and moved the car onto the road that circled the edge of the estate.

We passed block after block of apartments, the sunset reflected in the countless windows. Then the housing estate vanished and the road turned into a highway bound on either side by fir forests. The road was virtually empty, offering a clear view, and before long I spotted the red car up ahead, a small dot in the distance, travelling at an easy speed. Given the sparse traffic, I saw no necessity to follow hard up behind him and I too dropped to a leisurely speed with a respectful distance still between us. All the while, Sophie and Boris had both remained dreamily silent, and eventually I too began to get lulled into a tranquil mood watching the sun setting over the deserted highway.

After a little time, I found myself re-playing in my head the second goal scored by the Dutch football team in a World Cup semi-final against Italy some years ago. It had been a stupendous long-range shot and had always been one of my favourite sporting memories, but now, to my annoyance, I found I had forgotten the identity of the goal scorer. The name of Rensenbrink came drifting through my mind, and certainly he had been playing in that match, but in the end I felt certain he had not been the scorer. I saw again the ball floating through the sunshine, past the curiously transfixed Italian defenders, drifting on and on, beyond the outstretched hand of the goalkeeper. It was frustrating to have forgotten such a detail and I was systematically going through the names of all the Dutch footballers I could recall from that era, when Boris suddenly said behind me:

'We're too near the centre of the road. We're going to crash.'

'Nonsense,' I said. 'We're fine.'

'No, we're not!' I could feel him banging the back of my seat. 'We're too near the centre. If something comes the other way, we'll crash!'

I said nothing, but moved the car a little more towards the edge of the road. This seemed to reassure Boris and he became quiet again. Then Sophie said:

'You know, I have to admit, I wasn't at all happy when I first heard. About this reception, I mean. I thought it would spoil our evening together. But when I thought about it some more, and especially when I realised it wouldn't stop us having our meal tonight, I thought, well, it's a good thing. In some ways, it's exactly what we need. I know I can do well at it, and Boris too. We'll both do well, and then we'll have something to celebrate when we get back. The whole evening, it could really seal things for us.'

Before I could say something to this, Boris shouted again:

'We're much too near the centre!'

'I'm not moving any further over,' I said. 'We're perfectly fine now.'

'Perhaps he's frightened,' Sophie said to me quietly.

'Of course he's not frightened.'

'I'm frightened! We're going to have a major accident!'

'Boris, please be quiet. I'm driving perfectly safely.'

I had spoken quite sternly and Boris fell silent. But then, as I continued to drive, I became aware that Sophie was watching me uneasily. Occasionally she would glance back at Boris, then her gaze would return to me. Finally, she said quietly:

'Why don't we stop somewhere?'

'Stop somewhere? Why do we want to do that?'

'We'll get to the gallery in good time. A few minutes wouldn't make us late.'

'I think we should just find the place first.'

Sophie fell into silence for another few minutes. Then she turned to me again and said: 'I think we should stop. We could all have a drink and some refreshments. It'll help you cool down.'

'What do you mean, cool down?'

'I want to stop!' Boris called from the back.

'What do you mean, cool down?'

'It's so important you two don't have another quarrel tonight,' said Sophie. 'I can see it starting up again. But not this evening. I won't let it. We should all go and relax. Get ourselves into the right sort of mood.'

'What do you mean, right sort of mood? There's nothing the matter with any of us.'

'I want to stop! I'm frightened! I feel sick!'

'Look' – Sophie pointed at a passing sign – 'there's a service station coming up soon. Please, let's stop there.'

'This is completely unnecessary . . .'

'You're getting really angry. And tonight's so important. It's not to happen tonight.'

'I want to stop! I want the toilet!'

'There it is now. Please, let's stop. Let's put it right before it gets any worse.'

'Put what right?'

Sophie did not reply, but went on looking anxiously out through the windscreen. We were now moving through mountainous country. The fir forests had gone and in their place were craggy slopes towering up on either side of us. The service station was visible on the horizon, a structure resembling a spaceship built high into the cliffs. All my anger at Sophie had for the moment returned with a fresh intensity, but for all that – almost in spite of myself – I slowed down into the inside lane.

'It's all right, we're stopping,' Sophie said to Boris. 'Don't worry.'

'He wasn't worried in the first place,' I said coldly, but Sophie did not seem to hear.

'We'll have a quick snack,' she was telling the little boy. 'We'll all feel much better then.'

I followed a sign off the highway and up a steep narrow road. We climbed on through a number of hair-pin bends, then the road levelled off and we pulled into an open-air car park. Several lorries were parked side by side, as well as a dozen or so cars.

I climbed out and stretched my arms. When I glanced back, I saw Sophie helping Boris out of the car. I watched him take a few steps across the tarmac looking rather dozy. Then, as though to wake himself up, he turned his face up to the sky and let out a Tarzan yell, actually beating his chest as he did so.

'Boris, stop that!' I shouted.

'But he's not disturbing anyone,' Sophie said. 'No one can hear him.'

We were, it was true, high on a cliff-top and standing some distance away from the glassy structure that was the service station. The sunset had become a deep red and was reflecting off all the surfaces of the building. Without speaking, I strode past the pair of them and on towards the entrance.

'I'm not disturbing anyone!' Boris shouted after me. There came a second Tarzan yell, this time tailing off into a yodel. I carried on without turning. Only when I got to the entrance did I pause and wait, holding open the heavy glass door for them.

We crossed a lobby area with a bank of public telephones, and then through a second glass door into the café area. An aroma of grilled meat greeted us. The room was vast, with long rows of oval tables. On all sides were large glass panes through which we could see expanses of sky. From somewhere far off came the sounds of the highway beneath us.

Boris hurried over to the self-service counter and picked up a tray. Asking Sophie to buy me a bottle of mineral water, I went off to select a table. There were not many customers – only four or five tables were occupied – but I walked right to the end of one of the long rows and sat down with my back to the clouds.

After a few minutes Boris and Sophie came down the aisle holding their trays. They sat down in front of me and began to spread out their refreshments in an oddly muted manner. I then noticed Sophie giving Boris glances and supposed that while at the counter she had been urging the little boy to say something to me – something to make good the damage done by our recent altercation. It had not until this point occurred to me any sort of reconciliation was necessary between me and Boris, and I was annoyed to see Sophie so clumsily meddling in the situation. In an attempt to lighten the mood, I made some humorous remark concerning the futuristic décor surrounding us, but Sophie replied distractedly and darted another glance at Boris. The lack of subtlety was such that she might as well have nudged him with an elbow. Boris, understandably, seemed reluctant to comply and continued grumpily to twist around his fingers a packet of nuts he had purchased. Finally he mumbled without looking up:

'I've been reading a book in French.'

I shrugged and looked out at the sunset. I was aware of Sophie urging Boris to say something further. Eventually he said sulkily:

'I read a whole book in French.'

I turned to Sophie and said: 'Myself, I've never got on with the French language. I still have more trouble with French than I do with Japanese. Really. I get by in Tokyo better than in Paris.'

Sophie, presumably dissatisfied with this response, fixed me with a hard stare. Irritated by her coerciveness, I turned away and looked again over my shoulder at the sunset. After a while, I heard Sophie say:

'Boris is getting so much better at languages now.'

When neither Boris nor I responded, she leaned over towards the little boy, saying:

'Boris, you've got to make more effort now. We'll arrive at the gallery soon. There'll be a lot of people there. Some of them might look very important, but you won't be afraid, will you? Mother's not going to be afraid of them, and neither will you. We'll show everyone how well we can cope. We'll be a big success, won't we?'

For a moment Boris went on twisting his little packet round and round his fingers. Then he looked up and gave a sigh.

'Don't worry,' he said. 'I know what you have to do.' Then he sat up and went on: 'You have to put one hand in your pocket. Like this. And then you hold your drink, like this.'

He held the posture for a while, putting on as he did so an expression of great haughtiness. Sophie burst out laughing. I too could not help smiling a little.

'And when people come up to you,' Boris continued, 'you just say over and over: "Quite remarkable! Quite remarkable!" Or if you like, you can say: "Priceless! Priceless!" And when the waiter comes up with things on a tray, you do this to him.' Boris made a sour face and shook his finger from side to side.

Sophie was still laughing. 'Boris, you'll be a big hit tonight.'

Boris beamed, clearly pleased with himself. Then suddenly he got up, saying: 'I'm going to the toilet now. I forgot I wanted to go. I won't be a minute.'

He performed his disdainful finger shake for us one last time, then hurried off.

'He's very amusing sometimes,' I said.

Sophie was watching over her shoulder Boris going off up the aisle. 'He's growing so fast,' she said. Then she sighed and her expression grew more thoughtful. 'Soon he'll be grown. We don't have much time.'

I said nothing, waiting for her to continue. For a few seconds she went on gazing over her shoulder. Then turning to me she said quietly: 'This is his childhood, now, slipping away. Soon he'll be grown and he'll never have known anything better.'

'You talk as though he's having an awful time. He has a perfectly good life.'

'All right, I know, his life isn't so bad. But this is his childhood. I know what it should be like. Because I remember, you see, the way it was. When I was very small, before Mother got ill. Things were good then.' She turned back to face me, but her eyes seemed to focus on the clouds behind my back. 'I want something like that for him.'

'Well, don't worry. We'll sort things out very soon. In the meantime, Boris is doing just fine. There's no need to worry.'

'You're like everyone else.' There was now a hint of anger in her voice. 'You go on like there's all the time in the world. You just don't realise, do you? Papa may have a good few years left in him yet, but he's not getting any younger. One day he'll be gone and then there'll be only us. You and me and Boris. That's why we have to get a move on. Build something for ourselves soon.' She took a deep breath and shook her head, her eyes falling to the cup of coffee in front of her. 'You don't realise. You don't realise what a lonely place the world can become if you don't get on with things.'

I saw no point in taking issue. 'Well, that's what we'll do then,' I said. 'We'll find something soon.'

'You don't realise how little time there is. Look at us. We've hardly started.'

The accusing tone in her voice was growing. Meanwhile she

appeared to have forgotten entirely the not insignificant role her own behaviour had played in preventing us from 'getting on with things'. I felt a sudden temptation to point out all kinds of things to her, but in the end remained silent. Then, when neither of us had spoken for some time, I rose to my feet, saying:

'Excuse me. I think I'll get something to eat after all.'

Sophie was staring again at the sky and seemed hardly to notice my departure. I made my way to the self-service counter and took a tray. It was as I was studying the choice of pastries, I suddenly remembered I did not know the way to the Karwinsky Gallery and that we were for the time being entirely dependent on the red car. I thought about the red car, even now travelling out there on the highway, getting further and further from us, and I realised we could not afford to waste much more time lingering around the service station. In fact, it occurred to me we should set off again without delay, and I was on the verge of returning my tray and hurrying back to our table when I became aware that two people sitting nearby were talking about me.

Glancing round, I saw they were two middle-aged women, both smartly dressed. They were leaning across their table towards one another, speaking in lowered voices and, as far as I could make out, had no idea I was at that moment standing so close to them. They rarely referred to me by name and for this reason I could not at first be certain I was the subject of their discussion, but before long it became impossible to suppose they were talking of anyone else.

'Oh yes,' one of the women was saying. 'They've been in touch with that Stratmann woman any number of times. She keeps assuring them he'll turn up to inspect, but so far he hasn't. Dieter says they don't mind so much, it's not as though they don't have plenty of work to be getting on with, but they're all of them so keyed up now, thinking he's about to turn up any minute. And of course, Mr Schmidt keeps coming in every so often, shouting at them to tidy the place up, what if he came now and found the civic concert hall in such a condition? Dieter says they're all nervous, even that Edmundo. And you never know with these geniuses, what they'll pick out to criticise. They all still remember the time Igor Kobyliansky came to inspect and he tested every-thing so minutely. How he got down on all fours while they all stood in a big circle on the stage around him, how they all watched him while he crawled about, tapping all the floorboards, putting his ear right down to them. The last two days Dieter's not been the same, he's been so on edge when he's set off to work. It's been awful for all of them. Each time he doesn't show at an appointed time, they wait an hour or so then phone this Stratmann woman again. She's always very apologetic, she's always got excuses, and arranges another time with them.'

As I listened to this, a thought that had occurred to me several times during the past few hours came to the fore of my mind: namely that it would be wise for me to contact Miss Stratmann more frequently than I had been doing thus far. In fact I could even see some point in telephoning her from the public call boxes I had seen out in the lobby. But before I could give further consideration to this idea, the woman went on:

'And this is all after this Stratmann woman had been insisting for weeks how anxious he was to carry out the inspection, that he wasn't concerned just about the acoustics and all the usual things, but about his parents, how they were to be accommodated in the hall during the evening. Apparently they're neither of them very well, so they require special seating, special facilities, they require trained people nearby in case one or the other has a seizure or whatever. The arrangements needed are quite complicated and, according to this Stratmann woman, he was keen to go over each and every detail with all the staff. Well, that part of it was quite touching, to show so much concern about his aged parents. But then what do you know, he doesn't show up! Of course, it could be to do with this Stratmann woman rather than him. That's what Dieter thinks. By all accounts *he*'s got an excellent reputation, he doesn't sound at all the type to keep inconveniencing people like this.'

I had been getting quite annoyed at the women and was naturally relieved to hear these latter remarks. But it was what they had said concerning my parents – about the need to see to their various special requirements – that convinced me I could not afford to put off phoning Miss Stratmann a moment longer. Abandoning my tray on the counter, I hurried out into the lobby.

I stepped into a phone booth, searching through my pockets for

Miss Stratmann's card. After a moment I found it and dialled the number. The phone was answered immediately by Miss Stratmann herself.

'Mr Ryder, how good of you to call. I'm so glad everything has been going so well.'

'Ah. So you think everything is going well.'

'Oh splendidly! You've been such a success everywhere. People have been so thrilled. And your after-dinner speech last night, oh, *every*one's talking about how witty and entertaining it was. It's such a pleasure, if I may say so, having someone like you to work with.'

'Well, thank you, Miss Stratmann. It's kind of you to say so. It's a pleasure to be so well looked after. I was ringing just now because, er, because I wanted to check certain things relating to my schedule. Of course, there have been some unavoidable delays today, leading to one or two unfortunate consequences.'

I paused, expecting Miss Stratmann to say something, but there was silence at the other end. I gave a small laugh and continued: 'But of course, we're on our way at this moment to the Karwinsky Gallery. I mean, we're actually in the middle of our journey at this very moment. Naturally we wanted to get there in plenty of time, and I must say, we're all greatly looking forward to it. The countryside around the Karwinsky Gallery, I understand, is quite splendid. Yes, we're very happy to be on our way.'

'I'm so pleased, Mr Ryder.' Miss Stratmann sounded uncertain. 'I do hope you'll find the event enjoyable.' Then she said suddenly: 'Mr Ryder, I do hope we haven't offended you.'

'Offended me?'

'We really didn't mean to imply anything. I mean, by suggesting you go to the Countess's house this morning. We all knew you'd be thoroughly familiar with Mr Brodsky's work, no one ever dreamt otherwise. It's just that some of those recordings were quite rare and the Countess and Mr von Winterstein both thought . . . Oh dear, I do hope you're not offended, Mr Ryder! We really didn't mean to imply anything.'

'I'm not offended in the least, Miss Stratmann. On the contrary, I've been very concerned that the Countess and Mr von Winterstein aren't offended I was unable to turn up . . .'

'Oh, please don't worry on that score, Mr Ryder.'

'I was very keen to meet and talk with them, but when circumstances made it impossible for me to do everything we had originally hoped, I thought they would understand, particularly since, as you say, there was no actual necessity for me to listen to Mr Brodsky's recordings . . .'

'Mr Ryder, I'm sure the Countess and Mr von Winterstein both understand the situation perfectly. It was, in any case, I can see it now, a very presumptuous thing to have arranged, especially with your time so limited. I *do* hope you're not offended.'

'I assure you I'm not at all offended. But actually, Miss Stratmann, if I may. I was phoning you just now to discuss certain aspects, that is, certain *other* aspects of my schedule here.'

'Yes, Mr Ryder?'

'For instance, my visit to inspect the concert hall.'

'Ah yes.'

I waited to see if she would say anything more, but when she said nothing, I went on: 'Yes, I simply wanted to make sure everything was in order for my coming.'

Miss Stratmann at last responded to the troubled tone in my voice. 'Oh, I see,' she said. 'I take your point. I haven't scheduled very much time for you to carry out your inspection. But as you can see' – she paused and I could hear the rustle of a sheet of paper – 'as you can see, on either side of the concert hall visit, you have these two very important appointments. So I thought if you had to be a little squeezed for time anywhere, it should be at the concert hall. You could always return there at another point if you really needed to. Whereas, you see, we couldn't really afford to give less time to either of the other appointments. For instance, the meeting with the Citizens' Mutual Support Group, I know how much importance you place on meeting the ordinary people affected . . .'

'Yes, of course, you're quite right. I agree absolutely with what you say. As you point out, I can always squeeze in a second visit to the concert hall at some later point. Yes, yes. It's just that I was slightly concerned about the, er, the arrangements. That's to say, for my parents.'

There was again silence at the other end. I cleared my throat and continued:

'That's to say, as you know, my mother and father are both

advanced in years. It will be necessary to have special facilities for them at the concert hall.'

'Yes, yes, of course.' Miss Stratmann sounded slightly puzzled. 'And medical help nearby in the event of any unfortunate occurrences. Yes, it's all well in hand, as you'll see when you carry out your inspection.'

I thought about this for a moment. Then I said: 'My parents. That's who we're talking about. There's no confusion here, I trust.'

'Not at all, Mr Ryder. Please don't worry.'

I thanked her and came away from the telephone booths. As I stepped back into the café, I paused a moment inside the doorway. The sunset was causing long shadows to fall across the room. The two middle-aged women were still talking earnestly, though I could not guess if they were still discussing me. Over at the far end, I could see Boris explaining something to Sophie and the two of them laughing happily. I continued to stand there for a few moments, turning over in my mind the conversation I had just had with Miss Stratmann. Thinking further about it, I could see there *was* something presumptuous in the notion that I would benefit from having the Countess play me Brodsky's old records. No doubt she and von Winterstein had been looking forward to guiding me step by step through the music. The thought irritated me and I felt thankful I had been obliged to miss the appointment.

Then I glanced at my watch and saw that, for all my words of reassurance to Miss Stratmann, we were in danger of arriving late at the Karwinsky Gallery. I made my way over to our table and, without sitting down, said:

'We'll have to be getting on now. We've been here quite some time.'

I had spoken with a certain urgency, but Sophie simply looked up and said:

'Boris thinks these doughnuts are the best he's ever tasted. That's what you were saying, wasn't it, Boris?'

I glanced at Boris and saw he was ignoring me. I then recalled our recent little altercation – I had for the moment forgotten all about it – and it struck me it would be best to say something conciliatory.

'So the doughnuts are good, you say,' I said to him. 'Are you going to let me try a piece?'

Boris continued to look the other way. I waited for a few seconds, then gave a shrug.

'All right,' I said. 'If you don't want to talk, that's fine.'

Sophie touched Boris on the shoulder and was about to appeal to him, but I turned away saying: 'Come on, we have to be on our way.'

Sophie nudged Boris once more. Then she said to me, a touch of desperation in her voice: 'Let's stay just a little longer. You've hardly sat with us at all yet. And Boris is so enjoying it here. Aren't you, Boris?'

Again Boris showed no sign of having heard.

'Look, we've got to get a move on now,' I said. 'We're going to be late.'

Sophie looked again at Boris, then at me, anger gathering in her expression. Then finally she began to get up. I turned and made my way out of the café without looking back at them.

18

By the time I brought the car down the steep winding road and back onto the highway, the sun was very low in the sky. The traffic was as sparse as ever and I drove for a while at a good speed, scanning the horizon for signs of the red car. After several minutes we had left the mountains and were crossing vast expanses of farmland. On both sides of the highway the fields stretched on into the distance. It was while the road was taking a long slow curve across a piece of flat land that I spotted the red car again. It was still some way ahead, but I could see the driver proceeding as before at a leisurely speed. I reduced my own speed, and soon began to enjoy the scenery unfolding before me; the evening fields, the low sun flickering behind far-off trees, the occasional clusters of farm buildings – and all the while, the red car in front of us, drifting in and out of view with each turn of the road. Then I heard Sophie say beside me:

'How many people do you think there'll be?'

'At this reception?' I shrugged. 'How should I know? I have to say, you seem to be getting yourself very worked up about this thing. It's just another reception, that's all.'

Sophie went on staring out at the view. Then she said: 'A lot of the people tonight. They'll be the same ones who were at the Rusconi banquet. That's why I'm nervous. I thought you'd have realised that.'

I tried to recall the banquet she was referring to, but the name meant little to me.

'I was getting so much better at these things until then,' Sophie went on. 'Those people were so horrible to me. I haven't really recovered yet. There's bound to be a lot of the same people tonight.'

I was still trying without success to recall this event. 'You mean, people were actually rude to you?' I asked.

'Rude? Well, I suppose you could call it that. They certainly made me feel pretty small and pathetic. I do hope they're not all there again tonight.'

'If anyone's rude to you tonight, you just come and tell me. And as far as I'm concerned, you can be as rude as you like back to them.'

Sophie turned and looked at Boris in the back seat. After a moment I realised the little boy had fallen asleep. Sophie went on watching him for a little longer, then turned back to me.

'Why are you starting it again?' she asked in a quite different voice. 'You know how much it upsets him. You're starting it all again. How long do you plan to keep it up this time?'

'Keep what up?' I asked tiredly. 'What are you talking about now?'

Sophie stared at me for a moment, then turned away. 'You don't realise,' she said almost to herself. 'We've no time for things like this. You just don't realise, do you?'

I felt my patience coming to an end. All the chaos I had been subjected to throughout the day came back to me and I found myself saying loudly:

'Look, why do you think you've got the right to criticise me like this all the time? Perhaps you haven't noticed, but I happen to be under great pressure just now. But instead of supporting me, you decide to criticise, criticise, criticise. And now you seem to be getting all ready to let me down at this reception. At least, you appear to be preparing the ground well enough for doing just that . . .'

'All right! We won't come in then! Boris and I will wait in the car. You go to this thing by yourself!'

'There's no need for that. I was only saying . . .'

'I mean it! You go by yourself. That way we won't be able to let you down.'

After this we travelled on for several minutes without speaking. Eventually I said:

'Look, I'm sorry. You'll probably be fine at this reception. In fact, I'm sure you will be.'

She did not reply. We continued to travel in silence and each time I glanced at her, I found her staring blankly at the red car in the distance. An odd sense of panic began to grow within me until finally I said:

'Look, even if things don't go right this evening, well, it won't matter. What I mean is, it won't make any difference to anything important. There's no need for us to be silly like this.'

Sophie continued to stare at the red car. Then she said: 'Do I look like I've put on weight? Be honest.'

'No, not at all. You look marvellous.'

'But I have. I've put on a little.'

'It doesn't matter. Whatever happens tonight, it won't make any difference. Look, there's no need to worry. We'll have everything ready soon. A home, everything. So there's no need to worry.'

As I said this something began to come back to me of the banquet she had mentioned earlier. In particular, an image came into my mind of Sophie, in a dark crimson evening dress, standing awkwardly by herself in the centre of a crowded room, while all around her people stood laughing and talking in little groups. I found myself thinking about the humiliation she must have endured and eventually touched her gently on the arm. To my relief she responded by resting her head on my shoulder.

'You'll see,' she said, almost under her breath. 'I'll show you. And so will Boris. Whoever's there tonight, we'll show you.'

'Yes, yes. I'm sure you will. You'll both be fine.'

It was several minutes later that I noticed the red car indicating to turn off the highway. I reduced the distance between us and soon we were following our guide up a quiet road rising between meadows. The noise of the highway receded as we continued to climb, and then we were travelling on dirt tracks hardly fit for modern transportation. At one point a thick hedge scraped all along one side of our car, and soon afterwards we were bumping across a muddy yard full of broken-down farm vehicles. Then we came out onto some good country roads weaving smoothly through the fields and picked up speed again. Eventually I heard Sophie shout: 'Oh, there it is!' and saw a wooden board on a tree announcing the Karwinsky Gallery.

I slowed right down as we approached the gateway. Two rusted gateposts were still standing, but the gate itself had gone. As the red car continued down the road, finally vanishing from our view, I steered between the posts into a large overgrown field.

There was a dirt path running up the middle of the field and for a little while we moved slowly uphill. As we reached the crest, a fine view opened before us. The field swept down into a shallow valley, in the pit of which sat an imposing house built in the manner of a French chateau. The sun was setting in the woods behind it, and even from this distance, I could see the building was full of faded charm, evoking the slow decline of some dreamy land-owning family.

I engaged a low gear and took the car carefully down the hill. I could see in my mirror Boris, now fully awake, looking left and right, but the grass was so high it obscured entirely any view from the side windows.

As we came closer, I saw that a large area of the field near the house had become taken over with parked cars. I steered towards these as we completed our descent and saw there were almost a hundred vehicles in all, many of them polished to a gleam for the occasion. I drove around a little, trying to find a suitable spot to park, and came to a halt not far from the crumbling courtyard wall.

I got out of the car and stretched my limbs about. When I glanced back I saw that Sophie and Boris had also got out and that Sophie was fussing over Boris's appearance.

'Just remember,' I could hear her saying to him. 'No one in the room's more important than you. You just keep telling yourself that. Anyway, we won't be staying long.'

I was about to set off for the house when I became distracted by something at the corner of my eye. Turning, I saw that an old ruined car had been left abandoned in the grass close to where I was standing. The other guests had all left a space around it, as though its rust and general dilapidation might spread to their own vehicles.

I took a few steps towards the wreck. It had sunk some way into the earth and the grass had grown all around it, so that I might not have noticed it at all had the sunset not been striking its bonnet. There were no wheels and the driver's door had been torn off at the hinges. The paintwork had been gone over on numerous occasions, on the last of which the painter appeared to have used house paint before giving up mid-way. Both rear fenders had been replaced by mismatched substitutes from other vehicles. For all that, and even before I had examined it more closely, I knew I was looking at the remains of the old family car my father had driven for many years.

It was, of course, a long time since I had last laid eyes on it. Seeing it again in this sad state brought back to me its final days with us, when it had become so old I was acutely embarrassed my parents should continue to go about in it. Towards the end, I recalled, I had started to invent elaborate ploys to avoid taking journeys in it, so much did I dread being spotted by a school-friend or a teacher. But that had only been at the end. For many years I had clung to the belief that our car – despite its being quite inexpensive – was somehow superior to almost any other on the road and that this was the reason my father chose not to replace it. I could remember it parked in the drive of our little cottage in Worcestershire, its paint and metalwork gleaming, and my gazing at it for minutes at a time, feeling immensely proud. And on many afternoons – particularly on Sundays – I had spent hours playing in and around it. Occasionally I had brought out toys – perhaps even my collection of plastic soldiers – to lay out in the back seat. But more often I had simply built endless imaginary scenarios around the car, firing pistols through its windows, or conducting high-speed chases behind the wheel. Every so often, my mother would emerge from the house to tell me to stop slamming the car doors, the noise was driving her mad, and that if I did it once more she would 'skin me alive'. I could see her again quite vividly, standing at the back door of the cottage, shouting towards the car. The cottage had been a small one but, being deep in the countryside, had stood in a half-acre of grass. A lane went past our gate and on to the local farm, and twice a day a line of cows would go by, driven on by farmboys with muddy sticks. My father always left the car in the drive with its rear pointing to this lane, and I would often break off from what I was doing to watch the procession of cows through the back windscreen.

What we called our 'drive' was just an area of grass to the side of the house. It had never been concreted and in heavy rain the car would stand deep in water – a fact that could not have helped its rust problems and had possibly hastened it to its present condition. But as a child I had found wet days a particular treat. Not

261

only did the rain create an especially cosy atmosphere inside the car, it provided me with the challenge of having to leap over canals of mud each time I got in or out. At first my parents had disapproved of this practice, claiming I was making marks all over the car's upholstery, but once the vehicle was a few years old they had ceased to care about this point. The slamming doors, however, continued to annoy my mother throughout the time we owned the car. This was unfortunate since this slamming was central to the enacting of my scenarios, invariably punctuating key moments of dramatic tension. Matters were complicated by the fact that my mother sometimes went weeks, even months, without complaining about the doors, until I would have all but forgotten they could be a source of conflict. Then one day, when I was completely absorbed in some drama, she would suddenly appear, highly distressed, telling me just one more time and she would 'skin me alive'. On a few occasions this threat had been issued at a point when a door was actually ajar, leaving me in a quandary as to whether I should leave it open once I had finished playing – even though it might then remain open all night – or whether I should risk shutting it as quietly as possible. This dilemma would torment me throughout the remainder of my time playing with the car, thoroughly poisoning my enjoyment.

'What are you doing?' Sophie's voice said behind me. 'We ought to be going in.'

I realised she was talking to me, but I had become so taken up by the discovery of our old car that I murmured something back without really thinking. Then I heard her say:

'What's got into you? You seem to have fallen in love with that thing.'

Only then did I realise I was holding the car in a virtual embrace; I had been resting my cheek on its roof while my hands made smooth circular motions over its scabbed surface. I straightened with a quick laugh, and turned to see Sophie and Boris staring at me.

'In love with this? You have to be joking.' I gave another laugh. 'It's criminal the way people leave wrecks like this lying around.'

They continued to stare at me, so I shouted: 'What a disgusting heap!' and gave the car a few good kicks. This seemed to satisfy them and they both turned away. I then saw that Sophie, despite her show of hurrying me, was still preoccupied with Boris's appearance and had now resumed combing his hair.

I turned my attention back to the car, anxiety mounting that I might have inflicted some damage with my kicks. Closer examination showed that I had done no more than dislodge a few rusted flakes, but I was already full of remorse at having shown such callousness. I made my way through the grass around to the other side of the vehicle and peered in through the rear side window. Some flying object had struck the window but the glass had stayed intact, and I stared through the spiderweb cracks into the rear seat where I had once spent so many contented hours. Much of it, I could see, was covered with fungus. Rain water had pooled in one corner where the seat cushion met the arm-rest. When I tugged at the door, it came open with little trouble, but then became stuck half-way in the thick grass. There was just enough of a gap to enable me to squeeze in, and after a small struggle I managed to clamber onto the seat.

Once inside, it became clear that one end of the seat had fallen through the floor of the car, and I found myself unnaturally low. Through the window nearest my head I could see blades of grass and a pink evening sky. Re-adjusting myself I tugged at the door until it was almost shut again – something obstructed it from closing completely – and, after a few moments, found myself in a reasonably comfortable position.

Before long, a deep restfulness started to settle over me and I allowed my eyes to close for a moment. As I did so, I found a memory coming back of one of the happier family expeditions undertaken in the vehicle, a time we had driven all over the local countryside in search of a second-hand bicycle for me. It had been a sunny Sunday afternoon and we had gone from village to village, examining bicycle after bicycle, my parents conferring earnestly in the front while I sat behind them in this very seat, watching the Worcestershire scenery go by. Those were the days before telephones were routinely owned in England, and my mother had had on her lap a copy of the local newspaper in which people advertising items for sale printed their whole addresses. Appointments had been unnecessary; a family like us could simply materialise at a door and say: 'We've come about the boy's bike' and be shown around to the back shed for the inspection. The more friendly people would offer tea – which my father would decline each time with the identical humorous remark. But one old woman – who had turned out to be selling not a 'boy's bike' at all, but her husband's after the latter's death – had insisted on our coming in. 'It's always such a pleasure,' she had said to us, 'to receive people like yourselves.' Then, as we had sat in her little sunlit parlour with our teacups, she had referred to us once more as 'people like yourselves', and suddenly, in the midst of listening to my father talking about the sort of bicycle most suitable for a boy of my age, it had dawned on me that to this old woman my parents and I represented an ideal of family happiness. A huge tension had followed this realisation, one which had continued to mount within me throughout the half-hour or so we had stayed. It was not that I had feared my parents would fail to keep up their usual show – it was inconceivable they would have started even the most sanitised version of one of their rows. But I had become convinced that at any second some sign, perhaps even some smell, would cause the old woman to realise the enormity of her error, and I had watched with dread for the moment she would suddenly freeze in horror before us.

Sitting in the back of the old car, I tried to recall how that afternoon had ended, but I found my mind wandering instead to another afternoon altogether, one full of pouring rain, when I had come out to the car, to the sanctuary of this rear seat, while the troubles had raged on inside the house. On that afternoon, I had lain across the seat on my back, the top of my head squeezed under the arm-rest. From this vantage point, all I had been able to see from the windows had been the rain streaming down the glass. At that moment my profound wish had been that I would be allowed just to go on lying there undisturbed, hour after hour. But experience had taught me my father would at some stage emerge from the house, that he would walk past the car, go down to the gate and out into the lane, and so I had lain there for a long time, listening intently through the rain for the rattle of the back door latch. When at last the sound had come, I had sprung up and begun to play. I had mimicked an exciting tussle over a dropped pistol in such a way as to make clear I was far too absorbed to notice anything. Only when I had heard the wet tread of his feet go right to the end of the drive had I dared to stop. Then, quickly kneeling up on the seat, I had peered cautiously out of the back windscreen in time to see my father's raincoated figure, pausing by the gate, hunching slightly as he opened his umbrella. The next moment he had stepped purposefully into the lane and out of view.

I must have dozed off for I awoke with a jolt and saw that I was sitting in the back of the ruined car in complete darkness. In a slight panic I pushed at the door nearest me. At first it remained stuck, but then shifted a little at a time until I was able at last to squeeze myself out.

Brushing down my clothes, I looked about me. The house was brightly lit – I could see glittering chandeliers inside tall windows – and over beside our car Sophie was still fussing with Boris's hair. I was standing beyond the pool of light cast by the house, but Sophie and Boris were virtually floodlit. As I watched, Sophie leaned down to the wing mirror to add some finishing touches to her make-up.

Boris turned to me as I emerged into the light. 'You've been ages,' he said.

'Yes, I'm sorry. We ought to be going in now.'

'Just one second,' Sophie muttered distractedly, still bending over the mirror.

'I'm getting hungry,' Boris said to me. 'When do we go home?'

'Don't worry, we won't stay long. All these people, they're waiting to meet us, so we'd better just go in and say hello. But we'll leave pretty quickly. Then we'll go home and have a good evening. Just ourselves.'

'Can we play Warlord?'

'Of course,' I said, delighted the little boy seemed now to have forgotten our earlier altercation. 'Or any other game you fancy. Even if we start playing one and half-way through you want to stop and play a different one, because you're bored or because you're losing, that's fine, Boris. Tonight we'll just change to whichever one you want to play. And if you wanted to stop altogether and just talk for a while, about football, say, then that's what we'll do. It'll be a marvellous evening, just the three of us. But first let's go in and get this over with. It won't be so bad.'

'Okay, I'm ready now,' Sophie announced, but then she bent down to the mirror one last time.

We passed under a stone arch into the courtyard. As we made our way towards the front entrance, Sophie said: 'I'm actually looking forward to this now. I feel good about it.'

'Fine,' I said. 'Just relax and be yourself. Everything will be fine.'

19

The door was opened by a stout housemaid. As we wandered into the spacious entrance hall, she muttered:

'It's nice to see you again, sir.'

Only when I heard her say this did I realise I had been to the house before – that in fact it was the same one Hoffman had brought me to the previous evening.

'Ah yes,' I said, looking around at the oak-panelled walls, 'it's nice to be back again. This time, as you see, I've brought my family.'

The maid did not reply. Possibly this was due to deference, but when I glanced quickly at the woman standing sullenly by the door, I could not avoid sensing hostility. It was then that I noticed, on the round wooden table next to the umbrella stand, my face peering up from amid a spread of magazines and newspapers. Going up to the table, I pulled out what I saw to be the evening edition of the local newspaper, the entire front of which comprised a photograph of myself – taken apparently in a wind-swept field. Then I spotted the white building in the background and remembered the morning's photo-session on the hilltop. I took the newspaper over to a lamp and held the picture under the yellow light.

The force of the wind was causing my hair to be flung right back. My tie was fluttering stiffly out behind an ear. My jacket was also flying behind me so that I looked to be wearing a cape. More puzzlingly, my features bore an expression of unbridled ferocity. My fist was raised to the wind, and I appeared to be in the midst of producing some warrior-like roar. I could not for the life of me understand how such a pose had come about. The headline – there was no other text at all on the front page – proclaimed: 'RYDER'S RALLYING CALL'.

Somewhat nervously, I opened the newspaper and was confronted by a spread of six or seven smaller pictures, each a variation on the one on the front. My belligerent demeanour was evident in all but two of them. In these latter, I appeared to be presenting proudly the white building behind me, displaying as I did so a strange smile that revealed extensively my lower teeth but none of the upper. Scanning the columns beneath, my eye caught repeated references to someone named Max Sattler.

I would have examined the newspaper further but, suspecting as I did that the maid's hostility had to do with these very photographs, I began to feel distinctly uncomfortable. I put the paper down and came away from the table, resolving to study the report carefully at a later opportunity.

'It's time we went in,' I said to Sophie and Boris, who had been hovering in the middle of the hall. I had spoken loudly enough for the maid to hear and fully expected her to lead us through to the reception. But she made no movement and, after an awkward few seconds, I smiled at her saying: 'Of course, I can remember from last night.' With that I led the way into the house.

In fact the building was not at all as I remembered it, and we quickly found ourselves in a long panelled corridor quite unfamiliar to me. This proved not to matter, however, for a hubbub could be heard as soon as we had gone a little way down, and before long we were standing at the doorway of a narrow room packed with people in evening dress holding cocktail glasses.

At first glance the room appeared to be of a much smaller scale than the grand ballroom in which guests had gathered the night before. In fact on closer inspection I saw that originally it had probably not been a room at all, but a corridor, or at best a long curving vestibule. Its curve was such as to suggest it might eventually describe a semi-circle, though it was impossible to ascertain this glancing in from the doorway. I could see on its outer side the huge windows, now covered by curtains, going on round the curve, while the inner wall appeared to be lined by doors. The floor was marble, chandeliers hung from the ceiling, and here and there around the room were art objects displayed on pedestals or in elegant glass cabinets.

We paused at the threshold, taking in this scene. I looked about for someone to come and usher us in, perhaps even announce our arrival, but though we stood and watched for some time no one came to us. Occasionally some person would come striding hurriedly in our direction, but then at the last moment turn out to have been making for some other guest.

I glanced at Sophie. She had an arm around Boris and both were staring apprehensively at the crowd.

'Come on, let's go in,' I said nonchalantly. We all took a few steps into the room, but then came to a halt again a little way inside.

I looked around for Hoffman or Miss Stratmann or anyone else I recognised, but could see no one. Then, as I continued to stand there looking from face to face, the thought came to me that a great many of these same people might well have attended the event at which Sophie had been so appallingly treated. Suddenly I could see all the more vividly what Sophie had had to endure and felt a dangerous anger rising in me. Indeed, as I continued to look around the room, I could spot at least one group of guests – standing together almost where the room curved out of our view – who almost certainly had been among the major culprits. I studied them through the crowd: the men with their self-satisfied smiles, the pompous way they took their hands in and out of their trouser pockets as though to demonstrate to one and all how at ease they were in a gathering of this sort; and the women, with their ridiculous costumes, and their way of shaking their heads helplessly when they laughed. It was unbelievable – utterly pre-posterous – that such people should presume to sneer or look down on anyone, let alone on someone like Sophie. In fact I saw no reason not to go immediately up to this group to give them a firm dressing down under the full gaze of their peers. Murmur-ing a quick word of reassurance in Sophie's ear, I set off across the floor.

As I made my way through the crowd, I saw that the room did indeed turn a slow semi-circle. I could now see also the waiters standing like sentries all along the inner wall, holding their trays of drinks and canapés. Sometimes people would jog me and apologise pleasantly, or I would exchange smiles with someone trying to push through in the opposite direction, but curiously no one appeared actually to recognise me. At one stage I found myself squeezing past three middle-aged men who were shaking their heads despondently at something, and I noticed that one was holding under his arm a copy of the evening newspaper. I saw my windswept face peeking from behind his elbow and wondered vaguely if the appearance of the photographs could in some way account for the odd way our arrival had thus far been ignored. But I was now virtually next to the people I had been making for and gave this idea no further thought.

Noticing my approach, two of the group stepped aside as though to welcome me into their circle. They were, I realised, discussing the art objects surrounding us, and as I came into their midst they were all nodding over something the last speaker had said. Then one of the women said:

'Yes, it's so clear you could draw a line across this room, just after that Van Thillo.' She pointed to a white statuette on a stand not far from us. 'Young Oskar never had the eye. And to be fair, he knew it, but he felt a duty, a duty to his family.'

'I'm sorry, but I have to agree with Andreas,' one of the men said. 'Oskar was too proud. He should have delegated. To people who knew better.'

Then one of the other men said to me, smiling pleasantly: 'And what is your feeling on this, sir? About Oskar's contribution to the collection?'

I was momentarily taken aback by this enquiry, but I was not in a mood to be deflected.

'It's all very well you ladies and gentlemen standing here discussing Oskar's inadequacy,' I began. 'But more important and to the point . . .'

'It would be going too far,' a woman interrupted, 'to call young Oskar inadequate. His taste was very different to his brother's, and yes, he did make the odd mistake, but all in all I think he's brought a welcome dimension to the collection. It breaks up the austerity. Without it, well, this collection would be like a good dinner without the sweet course. That caterpillar vase over there' – she pointed through the crowd – 'it really is rather delightful.'

'It's all very well . . .' I began again heatedly, but before I could get further, a man said firmly:

'The caterpillar vase is the *only* one, the only one of his choices that earns its place here. His problem was that he had no sense of the collection as a whole, the balance of the thing.'

I could feel my patience running out.

'Look,' I shouted, 'just stop this! Just for one second stop this,

this inane chatter! Just stop it for one second and let someone else say something, someone else from outside, outside this closed little world you all seem so happy to inhabit!'

I paused and glared at them. My assertiveness had paid off for they were all of them – four men and three women – staring at me in astonishment. Having at last gained their attention, my anger now felt deliciously under control, like some weapon I could wield with deliberation. I lowered my voice – I had shouted a little more loudly than I had intended – and continued:

'Is it any wonder, is it any wonder at all that in this little town of yours, you have all these problems, this *crisis* as some of you choose to term it? That so many of you are so miserable and frustrated? Does it puzzle anyone, anyone from outside? Is it a surprise? Do we, we observers from a bigger, broader world, do we scratch our heads in bewilderment? Do we say to ourselves, how can it possibly be that a town such as this' – I could feel someone tugging at my arm, but I was now determined to have my say – 'that a town, a community like *this* should have such a crisis on its hands? Are we puzzled and amazed? No! Not for a moment! One arrives and immediately what does one see all around? Exemplified, ladies and gentlemen, by people like you, yes, you here! You *typify* – I'm sorry if I'm being unfair, if there are examples yet more gross and monstrous to be found under the rocks and paving stones of this city – but to my eyes, you, sir, and you, madam, yes, as much as I regret to break it to you, yes, you *exemplify* everything that's so wrong here!' The hand tugging at my sleeve, I realised, belonged to one of the women I was addressing, who for some reason was reaching behind the man standing next to me. I glanced a second in her direction, then went on: 'For one thing, you lack basic manners. Look at the way you treat each other. Look at the way you treat my family. Even myself, a distinguished figure, your guest, look at you, far too concerned about Oskar's art collecting. In other words, too obsessed, obsessed with the little internal disorders of this thing you call your community, too obsessed to display even the minimum level of good manners to us.'

The woman tugging my arm now moved round so that she was directly behind me and I was aware that she was saying

271

something to me in her effort to tear me away. I ignored her and continued:

'And it's here, of all places, what a cruel irony! Yes, it's here, to *this* place my parents have to come. Of all places, here, to receive your so-called hospitality. What an irony, what a cruelty, of all places, after all these years, that it should be somewhere like this, with people like you! And my poor parents, coming all this way, to hear me perform for the very first time! Do you suppose this makes my task any easier, that I'm obliged to leave them in the care of people like you, and you, and you?'

'Mr Ryder, Mr Ryder . . .' The woman at my elbow had been pulling insistently for some time and I now saw that this was none other than Miss Collins. This realisation made me lose my momentum and before I knew it she had succeeded in pulling me back from the group.

'Ah, Miss Collins,' I said to her, a little confused. 'Good evening.'

'You know, Mr Ryder,' Miss Collins said, continuing to lead me away. 'I'm genuinely surprised, I have to say it. I mean by the level of fascination there is. A friend told me just now that the whole town is gossiping about it. Gossiping, she assures me, in the kindest possible way! But I really can't see what all the fuss is about. Just because I went today to the zoo! I really can't understand it. I only agreed because they convinced me it was in everyone's interests, you know, for Leo to do well tomorrow night. So I merely agreed to be there, that was all. And I suppose, to be truthful, I wished to say a few encouraging words to Leo, now that he's gone this long without drinking. It seemed only fair I acknowledged it in some way. I assure you, Mr Ryder, if he'd gone this long without drinking at any other point in these last twenty years, I would have done exactly the same. It's just that it hadn't happened until now. There really wasn't anything so significant about my presence at the zoo today.'

She had ceased to pull at me, but had kept her arm in mine and we now settled to a slow walk through the crowd.

'I'm sure there wasn't, Miss Collins,' I said. 'And let me assure you, when I came over to you just now, I didn't have the slightest intention of raising the subject of yourself and Mr Brodsky.

Unlike the great majority of this town, I'm quite content not to pry into your private concerns.'

'That's very decent of you, Mr Ryder. But in any case, as I say, our meeting this afternoon didn't amount to anything so significant. People would be so disappointed if they knew. All that happened was that Leo came up to me and said: "You're looking very lovely today." Just the sort of thing you'd expect Leo to say after twenty years of being drunk. And that was just about all there was to it. Of course I thanked him, and said that he was looking better than I'd seen him for some time. He looked down at his shoes then, something I don't recall him ever doing when he was younger. He never did anything so timid in those days. Yes, his fire's burnt out, I could see that. But something's replaced it, something with some gravity. Well, there he was, looking down at his shoes, and Mr von Winterstein and the other gentlemen were all hovering about a little way behind, looking the other way, pretending they'd forgotten about us. I made some remark to Leo about the weather and he looked up and said, yes, the trees were looking splendid. Then he began to tell me which animals he'd liked of the ones he'd just seen. It was clear he hadn't been attending at all, because he said: "I love all these animals. The elephant, the crocodile, the chimpanzee." Well, the monkeys' cages were nearby and certainly they would have come that way, but they certainly wouldn't have passed the elephants or crocodiles and I said as much to Leo. But Leo brushed this aside as though I'd brought up something completely irrelevant. Then he seemed to get into a slight panic. Perhaps it had to do with Mr von Winterstein coming a little closer just then. You see, my original agreement had been that I'd say a few words to Leo, just literally a few words. Mr von Winterstein had assured me he'd intervene after a minute or so. Well, those had been my conditions but then, once we'd started to talk, it did feel hopelessly short. I myself began to dread the sight of Mr von Winterstein hovering nearby. Anyway, Leo knew we had very little time because then he plunged right in. He said: "Perhaps we might try again. To live together. It's not too late." You must accept, Mr Ryder, this was somewhat blunt after all these years, even allowing for this afternoon's time restrictions. I simply said: "But what would we do together? We've hardly a thing in common now."

And for a second or two, he looked about bewildered, as though I'd brought up a point he'd never before thought of. Then he pointed to the cage in front of us and said: "We could keep an animal. We could love and care for it together. Perhaps that was what we didn't have before." And I didn't know what to say so we were just standing there, and I could see Mr von Winterstein starting to come over, but then he must have sensed something, something in the way Leo and I were standing there, because he changed his mind and moved away again and started talking to Mr von Braun. Then Leo put up a finger in the air, that's a gesture of his from long ago, he put up his finger and said: "I had a dog, as you know, but he died yesterday. A dog's no good. We'll choose an animal that will live a long time. Twenty, twenty-five years. That way, so long as we look after it well, we'll die first, we won't have to mourn it. We never had children so let's do this." To which I said: "You simply haven't thought this through. Our beloved animal may well outlive us both, but it's unlikely the two of us will die at the same time. You may not have to mourn the animal, but if, say, I died before you, you'd have to mourn *me*." To which he said quickly: "That's better than having no one mourn you after you've gone." "But I have no fear of such a thing," I said to him. I pointed out that I'd helped many people in this town over the years and that when I died I wouldn't be at all short of mourners. To which he said: "You never know. Things might go well for me from here. I too might have many mourners when I die. Perhaps hundreds." Then he said: "But what would that matter, if none of them really cared for me? I'd swap them all. For someone whom I'd loved and who'd loved me." I must admit, Mr Ryder, this conversation was making me a little sad and I was unable to think of anything else to say to him. Then Leo said: "If we'd had children back then, how old would they be? They would be beautiful by now." As though they take years to become beautiful! Then he said again: "We never had children. So let's do this instead." When he said this again, well, I suppose I became confused and I glanced past his shoulder at Mr von Winterstein, and immediately Mr von Winterstein came towards us making some jokey remark, and that was it. That was the end of our conversation.'

We were continuing to walk slowly around the room, her arm

still in mine. I spent a moment digesting what she had told me. Then I said:

'I was just recalling, Miss Collins. The last time we met, you were kind enough to invite me to your apartment to discuss my problems. Ironically there seems now much more to discuss about the decisions *you* must make in life. I do wonder what you'll decide to do. If I may say so, you stand at something of a crossroad.'

Miss Collins laughed. 'Oh dear, Mr Ryder, I'm much too old to be standing at any crossroad. And it's really much too late for Leo to be talking like this. If this had all happened even just seven or eight years ago . . .' She gave a sigh and for a fleeting moment a profound sadness crossed her face. Then she was once more wearing her gentle smile. 'This is hardly the time to be starting out with a whole new set of hopes and fears and dreams. Yes, yes, you'll hasten to tell me I'm not so elderly, that my life is far from over, I do appreciate it. But the fact is, it *is* all very late in the day and it would be . . . well, let us say it would be *messy* to complicate things now. Ah, the Mazursky! It never fails to captivate me!' She gestured towards a red clay cat mounted on a stand we were just passing. 'No, Leo has created quite sufficient mess in my life already. I've long since built up a different life for myself and if you ask people in this town, most of them I hope will tell you I've acquitted myself rather well. That I've been of much service to many of them over a time of increasing hardship here. Of course, I've not been able to achieve anything on your sort of scale, Mr Ryder. But that doesn't mean I can't enjoy a certain sense of satisfaction when I look back and see what I've been able to do. Yes, by and large, I feel quite satisfied with the life I've made for myself since Leo, and I'm quite content to let it stand at that.'

'But surely, Miss Collins, you should at least consider very carefully the present situation. I can't understand why you wouldn't see it as a fine reward, after all your good work, to be able to share the evening of your life with the man who – excuse me – with the man whom at some level one assumes you still love. I say this because, well, why else have you continued to live here in this city all these years? Why else have you never considered another marriage?'

'Oh, I've *considered* other marriages, Mr Ryder. At least three men over the years I might easily have settled for. But they . . . they weren't right. Perhaps there *is* something in what you say. Leo was nearby and that made it impossible for me to feel sufficiently towards these others. Well, in any case, I'm talking of long ago. Your question, and perhaps an understandable one, is why shouldn't I now end my days with Leo? Well, let us consider for a moment. Leo is sober and calm now. Will he remain like that for long? Perhaps. There's a chance, I'll allow that. Particularly if he now wins recognition here, becomes a figure of renown again with large responsibilities. But if I agree to return to him, well, that'll be a different matter. He will decide after a little time to destroy everything he's built, just as he did before. And where would that leave everyone? Where would that leave this city? In fact, Mr Ryder, I rather think I have a public duty not to accept these proposals of his.'

'Forgive me, Miss Collins, but I can't help feeling you're really not as convinced by your own arguments as you would like to be. That somewhere deep down you've always been waiting and waiting for your old life, your life with Mr Brodsky, to resume. That all your good work, for which I don't doubt the people of this town will always be grateful, you nevertheless looked on it essentially as something to be getting on with while you waited.'

Miss Collins leant her head and considered my words with an amused smile.

'Perhaps there's something in what you say, Mr Ryder,' she said eventually. 'Perhaps I wasn't so aware of the speed at which time went by. It was only recently, last year in fact, that it really struck me how time was getting on. That we were both of us getting old and that it was perhaps too late to think about retrieving what we had. Yes, you may be right. When I first left him, I didn't see it as such a permanent thing. But was I *waiting*, as you claim? I really don't know. I thought about things on a day by day basis. And now I find the time's all gone. But when I look at it all now, my life, what I've done with it, it doesn't seem so bad. I'd like to finish things this way, the way I have it now. Why must I get involved with Leo and his animal? It really will be much too messy.'

I was about to express again, in the gentlest sort of way, my

276

scepticism as to whether she really believed all she was saying, when I became aware of Boris at my elbow.

'We've got to go home soon,' he said. 'Mother's getting upset.'

I looked across to where he was pointing. Sophie was standing a few steps from where I had originally left her, quite isolated, not talking to anyone. A feeble smile hovered on her face, though there was no one to display it to. Her shoulders were hunched and her gaze seemed to be fixed on the footwear of the group of guests nearest her.

The situation was clearly hopeless. Containing my fury at the whole room, I said to Boris: 'Yes, you're right. We'd better go. Bring your mother over. We'll try and slip out without people noticing. We attended, so no one can complain.'

I recalled from the previous evening that the house adjoined the hotel. As Boris disappeared into the crowd, I turned to look at the doors lining the wall, trying to recall which of them it had been that had led Stephan Hoffman and myself through to the hotel corridor. But just then Miss Collins, who was still holding my arm, started to talk again, saying:

'If I had to be honest, perfectly honest, then I'd have to admit it. Yes, in my less rational moments, it's been my dream.'

'Oh, what's that, Miss Collins?'

'Well, everything. Everything that's happening now. That Leo would pull himself together, that he'd find some position in this town worthy of him. That it would all be fine again, that the terrible years would be behind us for ever. Yes, I have to admit it, Mr Ryder. It's one thing, in the daylight hours, to be wise and reasoned. But during the nights, that's a different matter. Often enough over these years, I've woken up in the darkness, in the small hours, and I've lain awake thinking about it, thinking about just something like this happening. Now it's starting to happen for real, it's rather confusing. But then you see, it's not *really* starting. Oh, Leo might well be capable of achieving something here, he did once have a lot of talent, it can't all have faded away. And it's true, he never got a chance, a proper chance before, where we were. But for the two of us, it's too late. Whatever he says, it's surely too late.'

'Miss Collins, I'd very much like to discuss this whole matter

277

with you at greater length. But unfortunately, just now, I'm afraid I have to be going.'

Indeed, as I said this, I could see Sophie and Boris coming across the room towards me. Disentangling myself from Miss Collins, I considered again the choice of doors, stepping back a little to take in those hidden round the curve. When I studied them in turn, each door looked vaguely familiar, but I found I did not feel confident about any of them. It occurred to me to ask someone's advice, but I decided against this for fear of attracting attention to our early departure.

I led Sophie and Boris towards the doors, still in a quandary. For some reason, there had come into my head the numerous scenes from movies in which a character, wishing to make an impressive exit from a room, flings open the wrong door and walks into a cupboard. Although for exactly the opposite reason – I wished us to leave so inconspicuously that when it was discussed afterwards no one would be quite sure at which point we had done so – it was equally crucial I avoided such a calamity.

In the end I settled for the door most central in the row simply because it was the most imposing. There were pearl inlays within its deep panels and stone columns flanking each side. And at this moment, in front of each column, there stood a uniformed waiter as rigid as any sentry. A doorway of this status, I reasoned, while it might not necessarily take us directly through to the hotel, was certain to lead somewhere of significance from where we could work out our route, away from the public gaze.

Motioning Sophie and Boris to follow, I drifted towards the door and, giving one of the uniformed men a curt nod, as though to say: 'There's no need to stir, I know what I'm doing,' pulled it open. Whereupon, to my horror, the very thing I had most feared occurred: I had opened a broom cupboard and, at that, one which had been filled beyond its capacity. Several household mops came tumbling out and fell with a clatter onto the marble floor, scattering a dark fluffy substance in all directions. Glancing into the cupboard, I saw an untidy heap of buckets, oily rags and aerosol cans.

'Excuse me,' I muttered to the uniformed man nearest me as he hastened to gather up the mops and, with glances now turning accusingly our way, I hurried in the direction of the neighbouring door.

Determined not to make the same mistake twice, I set about opening this second door with caution. I proceeded very slowly, and even though I could sense many eyes on my back, even though I could hear a rise in the hubbub and a voice saying close by: 'My God, that's Mr Ryder, isn't it?' I resisted the temptation to panic, inching the door toward me a little at a time, all the while peering into the crack to ensure there was nothing about to fall out. When to my relief I saw the door led into a corridor, I stepped quickly through and gestured urgently to Sophie and Boris.

20

I closed the door behind them and we all three looked about us. With some triumph I saw that I had, at the second attempt, chosen exactly the right door and we were now standing in the long dark corridor that led past the hotel drawing room and into the lobby. At first we remained motionless, a little stunned by the hush after the noise of the gallery. Then Boris yawned and said: 'That was a really boring party.'

'Atrocious,' I said, feeling furious again at every one of the people at the reception. 'What a pathetic lot. No idea at all about civilised behaviour.' Then I added: 'Mother was by far the most beautiful woman there. Wasn't she, Boris?'

Sophie giggled in the darkness.

'She was,' I said. 'By far the most beautiful.'

Boris seemed about to say something, but just then we all became aware of a slithering noise coming from somewhere in the darkness around us. Then, as my eyes accustomed themselves, I managed to make out further down the corridor the outline of some large beast, coming towards us slowly, emitting the noise each time it moved. Sophie and Boris had become aware of its presence at the same time and for a moment we all seemed to become transfixed. Then Boris exclaimed in a whisper:

'It's Grandfather!'

I then saw that the beast was indeed Gustav, hunched right over, holding one suitcase under his arm, a second by its handle and dragging behind him a third – the source of the slithering noise. For a moment he appeared to be hardly moving forward at all, but simply rocking himself to a slow rhythm.

Boris made eagerly for him, while Sophie and I followed somewhat hesitantly. As we approached, Gustav, at last becoming aware of our presence, stopped and partially straightened. I could not see his expression in the darkness, but his voice sounded cheerful as he said:

'Boris. What a pleasant surprise.'

'It's Grandfather!' Boris exclaimed again. Then he said: 'Are you busy?'

'Yes, there's lots of work.'

'You must be very busy.' There was an odd tension in Boris's voice. 'Very, *very* busy.'

'Yes,' Gustav said, recovering his breath. 'It's very busy.'

I stepped up to Gustav and said: 'We're sorry to interrupt you in the middle of your duties. We've just been attending a reception, but we're now on our way home. To a big supper.'

'Ah,' the porter said looking at us. 'Ah yes. That's jolly good. I'm very pleased to see you all together like this.' Then he said to Boris: 'How are you, Boris? And how is your mother?'

'Mother's a bit tired,' Boris said. 'We're all looking forward to the supper. We're going to play Warlord afterwards.'

'Now that sounds splendid. I'm sure you'll enjoy yourselves. Well . . .' Gustav paused for a moment. Then he said: 'I'd better be getting on with my work. We're very busy at the moment.'

'Yes,' Boris said quietly.

Gustav ruffled Boris's hair. Then he hunched down again and recommenced his pulling. Reaching a hand out to Boris, I guided the little boy out of Gustav's way. Perhaps because we were watching, perhaps because the brief pause had restored some of his energy, the porter seemed this time to make much steadier progress as he moved past us into the darkness. I began to lead the way towards the lobby, but Boris was reluctant to follow, staring back down the corridor to where his grandfather's hunched shape could still be made out.

'Come on, let's hurry,' I said, putting an arm around his shoulder. 'We're all getting very hungry.'

I had started to walk again when I heard Sophie say behind me: 'No, it's this way.' I turned to find her stooping down by a small door I had not previously noticed. In fact, had I noticed it at all, I would not have assumed it to be anything more than a cupboard door, for it barely came up to my shoulder. Nevertheless, Sophie was now holding it open and Boris, with the air of someone who had done so numerous times before, stepped through it. Sophie continued to hold the door open and, after a little hesitation, I too stooped down and crept through after Boris.

I had half expected to find myself in a tunnel having to crawl

281

on hands and knees, but in fact I was standing in another corridor. If anything it was more spacious than the one we had just left, but clearly intended only for staff. The floor was uncarpeted and there were bare pipes running along the wall. We were again in near-darkness, though a little further down, a bar of electric light was falling across the floor. We walked a short way towards the light, then Sophie stopped again and pushed a fire door by its bar. The next moment we were outside, standing in a quiet side-street.

It was a fine night with many stars visible. Glancing down the street I saw it was deserted and that all the shops were closed. As we started to walk, Sophie said lightly:

'That was a surprise, meeting Grandfather like that. Wasn't it, Boris?'

Boris did not respond. He was striding on in front of us, muttering quietly to himself.

'You must be very hungry too,' Sophie said to me. 'I just hope there'll be enough. I got so carried away cooking all these things earlier, I forgot to prepare a really substantial course. This afternoon I thought there'd be plenty, but now I think about it . . .'

'Don't be silly, it'll be fine,' I said. 'That's exactly what I feel like anyway. A lot of small things, one after the other. I quite understand why Boris enjoys eating like that.'

'Mother used to do it this way, when I was small. For our special evenings. Not birthdays or Christmas, we did the same as everyone else then. But for evenings we wanted to make special, just the three of us, Mother used to do it this way. Lots of delicious little things, one after the next. But then we moved, and Mother wasn't well, and so we never did it much after that. I hope I've made enough for you. You must both be so hungry.' Then suddenly she added: 'I'm sorry. I wasn't very impressive tonight, was I?'

I saw her again, standing alone helplessly in the middle of the throng, and I reached out and placed my arm around her. She responded by drawing herself close against me, and for the next few minutes we walked like that, not talking, through a series of deserted side-streets. At one point Boris fell in step beside us to ask:

'Can I eat sitting on the sofa tonight?'

Sophie thought for a moment, then said: 'Yes, all right. For this meal, yes, all right.'

Boris walked alongside us for several more paces, then asked: 'Can I lie on the floor and eat?'

Sophie laughed. 'Just tonight, Boris. Tomorrow morning, at breakfast, you have to sit at the table again.'

This seemed to please Boris and he ran on ahead with some enthusiasm.

Eventually we came to a halt in front of a door squeezed between a barber's shop and a bakery. The street was a narrow one, made narrower by the many cars parked up on the pavement. As Sophie sorted through her keys, I glanced up and saw there were four more storeys above the shops. Some of the windows had lights on and I could hear faintly a television.

I followed the pair of them up two flights of stairs. As Sophie unlocked the front entrance the thought struck me that I was perhaps expected to behave as though familiar with the apartment. On the other hand, it was equally possible I was expected to behave like a guest. As we stepped inside, I decided to observe carefully Sophie's manner and take my cue from that. As it happened, no sooner had she closed the door behind us than Sophie announced she would have to turn on the oven and vanished further into the apartment. Boris, for his part, threw off his jacket and went running off making a noise like a police siren.

Left standing in the entrance hall, I took the opportunity to take a good look at my surroundings. There could be little doubt both Sophie and Boris expected me to know my way around, and certainly, the longer I stood gazing at the choice of half-open doors facing me, the dingy yellow wallpaper with its faint floral pattern, the exposed piping climbing from floor to ceiling behind the coat stand, I could feel some memory of this entrance hall gradually returning to me.

After a few minutes I went through into the living room. Although there were a number of features I did not recognise – the pair of old sunken armchairs to either side of the disused fireplace were undoubtedly recent acquisitions – my impression was that I could remember this room more clearly than I had the entrance hall. The large oval dining table pushed against the wall, the second door leading through to the kitchen, the dark shapeless sofa, the tired orange carpet were all distinctly familiar. The overhanging light – a single bulb covered by a chintz shade – was casting a shadowy pattern all around so that I could not be sure the wallpaper was not here and there developing damp patches. Boris was lying in the middle of the floor and rolled over onto his back as I came further into the room.

'I've decided to try an experiment,' he declared, as much to the ceiling as to me. 'I'm going to keep my neck like this.'

I looked down and saw that he had shortened his neck so that his chin was squeezed into his collar bone.

'I see. And for how long are you going to do that?'

'At least twenty-four hours.'

'Very good, Boris.'

I stepped over him and went through into the kitchen. This was a long narrow room and once again unmistakably familiar. The grimy walls, the traces of cobweb near the cornicing, the dilapidated laundry equipment all tugged naggingly at my memory. Sophie had put on an apron and was kneeling down arranging something inside the oven. She looked up as I came in, made some remark about the food, pointed inside the oven and laughed cheerfully. I too gave a laugh, then, casting one more look about the kitchen, turned and went back into the living room.

Boris was still lying on the floor and as I entered he immediately shortened his neck again. I paid him no attention and sat down on the sofa. There was a newspaper on the carpet nearby and I picked it up thinking it might be the one containing the pictures of me. It was in fact several days old, but I decided to peruse it anyway. As I read through the front story – the man von Winterstein was being interviewed about plans to conserve the Old Town – Boris continued to lie there on the carpet, not speaking, emitting occasionally some little robot-like noise. Whenever I stole a glance at him, I saw his neck was still shortened and decided to say nothing to him until he at least stopped this ridiculous game. Whether he was shortening his neck each time he guessed I was about to look at him, or whether he had it in a permanently contracted state, I could not tell and quickly ceased to care. 'Let him just lie there then,' I thought to myself and went on reading.

Eventually, after twenty minutes or so, Sophie came in with a platter laden with food. I could see vol-au-vents, savoury parcels, pies, all hand-sized and much of it intricate. Sophie laid the platter down on the dining table.

'You're very quiet,' she said looking about the room. 'Come on, let's enjoy ourselves now. Boris, look! And there's another plate like this to come. All your favourites! Now, why don't you choose a board game for us to play while I go and get the rest.'

As soon as Sophie disappeared back into the kitchen, Boris leapt to his feet, went to the table and stuffed a pie into his mouth. I was tempted to point out that his neck had returned to normal, but in the end went on reading the newspaper without speaking. Boris made his siren noise again and, moving rapidly across the room, stopped in front of a tall cupboard in the far corner. I remembered this was the cupboard inside which all the board games were kept, the broad flat boxes piled precariously on top of other toys and household items. Boris went on looking at the cupboard for a moment, then suddenly flung open the door.

'Which one are we going to play?' he asked.

I pretended not to hear and went on reading. I could see him at the edge of my vision, first turning towards me, then, as the realisation dawned on him that I would not reply, turning back to the cupboard. For some time, he stood there contemplating his pile of board games, now and then reaching out to finger the edge of one or another box.

Sophie returned with more food. As she set about arranging the table, Boris went over to her and I could hear the two of them arguing quietly.

'You said I could eat on the floor,' Boris was maintaining.

Then after a while, he slumped down in front of me on the carpet again, placing a heaped plate beside him.

I rose to my feet and went to the table. Sophie hovered about me anxiously as I took a plate and regarded the choice.

'It looks quite magnificent,' I said, as I served myself.

Returning to my sofa, I saw that, by putting my plate down on a cushion beside me, I would be able to eat and continue to read my newspaper at the same time. I had decided earlier to examine the newspaper very carefully, scrutinising even the adverts for

285

local businesses, and I now continued with this project, reaching over occasionally to my plate without taking my eyes off the newsprint.

Meanwhile Sophie had sat down on the floor near Boris, from time to time asking him a question – about how he liked a particular meat tart, or about some schoolfriend. But whenever she tried to start a conversation in this way, Boris had his mouth too full to reply with anything more than a grunt. Then Sophie said: 'Well, Boris, did you decide which game you wanted?'

I could sense Boris's gaze turning to me. Then he said quietly:

'I don't mind which one we play.'

'You don't mind?' Sophie sounded incredulous. There was a lengthy pause, then she said: 'All right then. If you really don't care, I'll choose one.' I heard her rising to her feet. 'I'm going to choose one now.'

This strategy appeared to win Boris over for a moment. Getting up with some excitement, he followed his mother to the cupboard and I could hear the two of them conferring in front of the stack of boxes, their voices lowered as though in deference to the fact that I was reading. Eventually they came back and sat down on the floor again.

'Come on, let's set this out now,' Sophie said. 'We could start playing while we're eating.'

When I next glanced down at them, the board had been opened out and Boris was positioning the cards and plastic counters with some enthusiasm. I was thus surprised when a few minutes later I became aware of Sophie saying:

'What's the matter? You said you wanted this one.'

'I did.'

'Then what's the matter, Boris?'

There was a pause before Boris said: 'I'm too tired. Like Papa.'

Sophie gave a sigh. Then suddenly she said in a brighter voice:

'Boris, there's something Papa's bought for you.'

I could not resist peering round the edge of the newspaper, and as I did so Sophie threw me a conspiratorial smile.

'Can I give it to him now?' she asked me.

I had no idea what she was talking about and returned a puzzled look, but she rose to her feet and left the room. She returned almost immediately, holding up the tattered handyman's manual

286

I had bought at the cinema the previous night. Boris, forgetting his supposed tiredness, leapt to his feet, but Sophie teasingly held the book away from him.

'Papa and I went out together last night,' she said. 'It was a wonderful evening and, in the middle of it all, he remembered you and he bought this for you. You've never had anything like this before, have you, Boris?'

'Don't tell him it's anything so marvellous,' I said from behind the newspaper. 'It's just an old manual.'

'It was very kind of Papa, wasn't it?'

I stole another peek. Sophie had now let Boris take the book and he had dropped to his knees to examine it.

'It's great,' he murmured, going through it. 'This is really great.' He paused at a page and stared at it. 'It shows you how to do everything.'

He turned over some more pages and as he did so the book gave a sharp crack and fell apart into two sections. Boris carried on turning the pages as though nothing had happened. Sophie, who had started to reach down, stopped on seeing Boris's reaction and straightened again.

'It shows you everything,' Boris said. 'It's really good.'

I had the distinct impression he was trying to address me. I went on reading, and a few seconds later I heard Sophie say softly: 'I'll get some sellotape. That's all it needs.'

I heard Sophie leave the room and carried on reading. I could see, at the corner of my eye, Boris still turning the pages. After a little while, he looked up at me and said:

'There's a special sort of brush you can get for putting up wallpaper.'

I continued to read. Eventually Sophie came wandering back in.

'It's odd, I can't find the sellotape anywhere,' she was mumbling.

'This book's great,' Boris said to her. 'It shows you how to do everything.'

'It's odd. Perhaps we finished it.' Sophie went back through into the kitchen.

I had a faint recollection of various rolls of adhesive tape being kept in the same cupboard as the board games, inside one of the small drawers near the bottom right-hand corner. I was thinking about putting down my newspaper and going over to conduct a search, but then Sophie came back into the room again.

'Never mind,' she said. 'I'll buy some tape in the morning and we'll mend the book then. Now come on, Boris, let's get started with the game or we'll never finish before bed.'

Boris did not reply. I could hear him down on the carpet, still turning pages.

'Well, if you're not going to play,' Sophie said, 'I'll just start on my own.'

There came the sound of a dice being rattled in its beaker. As I continued through my newspaper, I could not help feeling a little sorry for Sophie about the way the evening was turning out. But then, she could hardly have expected to introduce the level of chaos she had done without our having to pay some sort of price. Moreover, it was not even as though she had particularly excelled herself with the cooking. She had not thought to provide, for instance, any sardines on little triangles of toast, or any cheese and sausage kebabs. She had not made an omelette of any sort, or any cheese-stuffed potatoes, or fish cakes. Neither were there any stuffed peppers. Nor those little cubes of bread with anchovy paste on them, nor those pieces of cucumber sliced lengthways, not even wedges of hard-boiled egg with the zig-zag edges. And for afterwards, she had made no plum slices, no buttercream fingers, not even a strawberry Swiss roll.

I became gradually conscious that Sophie had been rattling the dice for an inordinate period. In fact, the rattling had changed in character since she had first started to play with the dice. She now seemed to be shaking it with a feeble slowness, as though in time to some melody running through her head. I lowered the newspaper with a sense of alarm.

On the floor, Sophie was leaning on one stiffened arm, a posture that made her long hair plunge down over her shoulder, concealing her face entirely. She appeared to have become completely absorbed with the game, and her weight had tipped forward oddly, so that she was hovering right over the board. The whole of her body was rocking gently. Boris was watching her sulkily, passing his hands over the crack in his book.

Sophie went on and on shaking the dice, for thirty, forty

seconds, before finally letting it roll out in front of her. She studied it dreamily, moved some pieces about the board, then began to shake the dice again. I could sense something dangerous in the atmosphere and decided it was time I took charge of the situation. Throwing the newspaper aside, I clapped my hands together and got to my feet.

'I have to be getting back to the hotel,' I announced. 'And I'd suggest, very strongly, you both go off to bed. We've all had a long day.'

I glimpsed Sophie's surprised expression as I strode out into the hall. The next moment she appeared behind me.

'You're going already? But have you had enough to eat?'

'I'm sorry, I know you've worked hard to prepare the meal. But it's got too late now. I have a very busy morning tomorrow.'

Sophie sighed and looked despondent. 'I'm sorry,' she said eventually. 'The evening wasn't very successful. I'm sorry.'

'Don't worry. It's not your fault. We were all rather tired. Now, I really have to be going.'

Sophie let me out sullenly, saying she would call me in the morning.

I spent the next several minutes wandering through the deserted streets trying to remember the way back to the hotel. I eventually came out onto a street I recognised, and began rather to enjoy the quiet of the night and the chance to be alone with just my thoughts and the sound of my footsteps. Before long, however, I felt again a certain regret about the way the evening had ended. But then the fact was, along with so much else, Sophie had succeeded in reducing my carefully planned time-table to chaos. And now here I was, reaching the end of my second day in the city having gained only the most superficial insights into the crisis I had come to assess. I recalled that I had even been prevented from keeping my morning's appointment with the Countess and the mayor, when I would have had the chance at last to hear for myself something of Brodsky's music. There was, of course, still plenty of time for me to make up lost ground; a number of substantial meetings still in front of me – such as that with the Citizens' Mutual Support Group – were certain to give me a much fuller picture of the situation here. Nevertheless, there could be no denying I had been placed under some pressure, and Sophie could hardly complain if I had not finished the day in the most relaxed of moods.

I had been strolling over a stone bridge thinking these thoughts. As I paused to gaze down into the water and at the row of lamps along the canalside, it occurred to me I still had the option of accepting Miss Collins's invitation to call on her. She had certainly intimated she was in a unique position to be of assistance, and now, with my time here growing ever more limited, I could see how a good talk with her might greatly expedite matters, providing me with virtually all the information I would by now have gathered myself had Sophie not had her way. I thought again of Miss Collins's drawing room, the velvet drapes and the weary furniture, and felt a sudden wish that I was there at this very moment. I began to walk again, over the bridge and into the dark street, resolving to call on her in the morning at the first opportunity.

III

21

I awoke to find bright sunlight pouring in through the vertical blinds and was seized by the panicky feeling I had let far too much of the morning slip by. But then I remembered my decision of the night before to pay a call on Miss Collins and got out of bed feeling much calmer.

The room was smaller and distinctly stuffier than my former one and I again felt annoyed at Hoffman for having obliged me to move. But the whole matter of the rooms no longer seemed as important as it had done the previous morning and as I washed and dressed I found no difficulty placing my mind firmly on the important meeting with Miss Collins upon which so much now depended. By the time I left my room, I had stopped worrying altogether about having slept in – the sleep, I knew, would prove invaluable in the long run – and was looking forward to a good breakfast over which I could organise my thoughts on the issues I would raise with Miss Collins.

I was surprised, then, on arriving down at the breakfast room to be greeted by the sound of a vacuum cleaner. The doors to the room were closed and when I pushed them open a little I saw two women in overalls cleaning the carpet, the tables and chairs pushed against the walls. The prospect of facing such a crucial meeting without breakfast was not a happy one and I returned to the lobby more than a little disgruntled. I walked past a group of American tourists up to the reception desk. The desk clerk was sitting reading a magazine, but on seeing me rose to his feet.

'Good morning, Mr Ryder.'

'Good morning. I'm somewhat disappointed to find breakfast is not being served.'

For a second, the desk clerk looked puzzled. Then he said: 'Normally, sir, even at this hour, someone would have been able to serve you breakfast. But of course, today being today, naturally enough, a great many of our staff are over at the concert hall to assist with the preparations. Mr Hoffman has himself been there since the early hours. I'm afraid we're very much running at half strength. Unfortunately the atrium also has had to be closed until lunch time. Of course, if it's a matter of coffee and a few rolls . . .'

'It's quite all right,' I said coldly. 'I simply don't have time to wait around while it's organised. I'll just have to do without breakfast this morning.'

The desk clerk began to apologise again, but I cut him off with a wave of my hand and walked away.

I stepped out of the hotel into the sunshine. It was not until I had walked some distance alongside the heavy traffic that I realised I was not at all sure of the location of Miss Collins's apartment. I had not attended carefully the night Stephan had driven us there, and besides, with the streets now so crowded with pedestrians and traffic, nothing was recognisable. I paused a moment on the pavement and considered asking a passer-by for directions. It was just conceivable Miss Collins was sufficiently well known in the city for me to do this. In fact I was about to stop a man in a business suit striding towards me, when I felt someone touch my shoulder from behind.

'Good morning, sir.'

I turned to find Gustav, holding a large cardboard box whose dimensions virtually obscured the upper half of his body. He was panting heavily, but whether this was due solely to his burden or because he had come hurrying after me, I could not tell. In any case, when I greeted him and enquired where he was going, it was a little while before he could reply.

'Oh, I was just taking this to the concert hall, sir,' he said eventually. 'The larger items were all transported by van last night, but then there are so many things still needed. I've been having to go back and forth between the hotel and the concert hall since early morning. Everyone's very excited over there already, I can tell you, sir. There's a real atmosphere there.'

'That's good to hear,' I said. 'I'm also very much looking forward to the event. But I wonder if you might be able to assist me. You see, I have an appointment at Miss Collins's apartment this morning, but I've just for the moment lost my way a little.'

'Miss Collins? Well then you're not far at all. It's this way, sir.

I'll walk with you, if I may. Oh no, don't worry, sir, it's directly on my route.'

His box was perhaps not as heavy as it looked, for once we started to walk, Gustav set a steady pace alongside me.

'I'm very glad we've coincided like this, sir,' he went on, 'because to be quite frank, there's a matter I'd been meaning to raise with you. In fact, I'd been meaning to raise it ever since we met, but somehow with one thing then another I never got around to it. And now tonight's almost upon us and I still haven't asked you. It's just something that came up a few weeks ago, at the Hungarian Café, at one of our Sunday gatherings. It wasn't long after we heard the news about you coming to our town, and of course, like everyone else, we were talking about it. And someone, I think it was Gianni, he was saying how he'd read you were a very decent sort, as different as you could get from these prima donna types, how you had a reputation for being very concerned about the ordinary citizen, he was saying all these things, sir. And there we were around the table, eight or nine of us, Josef wasn't there that night, we were watching the sun go down over the square and I think we each had the same thought all at once. At first we were all just sitting there in silence, none of us daring to say it aloud. In the end it was Karl, typical of him, Karl said what we were all thinking. "Why don't we ask him?" he said. "What have we got to lose? We should at least ask him. He sounds completely different to that other one. He might even agree, you never know. Why don't we ask him, it might be our last chance." And then we were all suddenly talking and talking about it, and ever since then, sir, to tell you the truth, we haven't sat together for any length of time without bringing up the topic. We'd be talking about something else, everyone laughing, and then this silence would come over us and we'd realise we were all thinking about it again. That's why I was starting to feel rather sorry for myself, sir. I thought, I'd seen you a few times, I'd had the honour of talking with you and yet I hadn't worked up the nerve to ask. Now here we are, the big event only hours away and I still haven't asked. How could I ever explain that to the boys on Sunday? As a matter of fact, when I got up this morning, sir, I said to myself, I must find him, I must at least put it to Mr Ryder, the boys are depending on it. But then everything was so busy, and you were bound to have so much to do, and I thought, well, I may well have lost my chance. So you see, I'm very glad we've coincided like this, I hope you won't mind my putting it to you, and of course, if you felt we were asking the impossible, then naturally that would be the last of it, the boys would accept that, oh yes.'

We had turned a corner into a busy boulevard. Gustav fell silent as we crossed at a set of lights and it was not until we were on the other side walking past a row of Italian cafés that he said:

'I'm sure you've guessed what I'm going to ask, sir. All we're requesting is a small mention. That's all, sir.'

'A small mention?'

'Just a small mention, sir. As you know, many of us, we've worked and worked over the years to try and change the attitude in this town towards our profession. We may have had a small effect, but by and large we've failed to make a general impact and, well, it's perfectly understandable, there's frustration setting in. We're none of us getting any younger, there's a feeling that things may never really change. But one word from you tonight, sir, that could alter the course of everything. It could be an historic turning point for our profession. That's how the boys see it. In fact, sir, some of the boys believe this is our last chance, at least for our generation. When will we get a chance like this again? That's what they keep asking. So here I am, I've put it to you, sir. Of course, if you feel it's not quite the thing, and I could well understand your feeling that way, after all you've come here to address some very important issues, and what I'm talking about is a small matter. Big for us, but seen overall, I appreciate, it's a small matter. If you felt it was impossible, sir, please say so and that'll be the last you'll hear of it.'

I thought for a moment, conscious that he was watching me intensely from around the edge of his box.

'What you're suggesting,' I said after a while, 'is that I make some small mention of you during . . . during my address to the people of this town.'

'No more than a few words at the most, sir.'

Certainly, the notion of coming to the help of the elderly porter and his colleagues in such a way had its appeal. I thought for a moment, then said: 'Very well. I'd be happy to say something on your behalf.'

I heard Gustav take a deep breath as the impact of my reply sank in. Then he said quite quietly:

'We'd be forever indebted to you, sir.'

He was about to say more, but I had somehow become taken by the idea of frustrating, for a while, his attempts to express his gratitude to me.

'Yes, let's think about it, how could we do it?' I said quickly, assuming a preoccupied air. 'Yes, I could say as I came up to the podium something like: "Before I begin, there's a small yet rather important point I'd like to make." Something like that. Yes, that would be easy enough.'

I suddenly saw quite vividly the gathering of sturdy old men around a café table, the looks on their faces – of disbelief, of unfathomed joy – as Gustav announced the news to them. I saw myself entering their midst, quietly and modestly, and their faces turning to me. All the while, I was conscious of Gustav walking by my side, no doubt virtually bursting to finish thanking me, but I nevertheless kept up my talk.

'Yes, yes. "A small but important point," I could say to them. "There is something which I, having seen many other cities around the world, find somewhat peculiar here . . ." Perhaps "peculiar" is too strong a word. Perhaps I might say "eccentric".'

'Ah yes, sir,' Gustav broke in. ' "Eccentric" would be a fine word. None of us wants any antagonism stirred up. But this is precisely why you're such a unique opportunity for us. You see, even if in a few years' time another celebrity agreed to come to our town, and even if we were to succeed in persuading him to speak for us, what are the chances of his having your sort of tact, sir? "Eccentric" would be a perfect way to put it, sir.'

'Yes, yes,' I went on, 'and I'd perhaps pause a second, looking at them with mild accusation, so that everyone, the whole hall, they'd be hushed and waiting. Then finally I might say some-thing like, well, let me see, I might say: "Ladies and gentlemen, to all of you, living here as you have for so many years, certain things may have come to appear normal, certain things which an outsider would immediately deem *conspicuous* . . ." '

Suddenly Gustav stopped walking. At first I thought he had

perhaps done so because his urge to express his thanks had become overwhelming. But then I looked at him and realised this was not the case. He had frozen on the pavement, his head pushed right over to one side by the box so that his cheek was squashed against its side. His eyes were closed tight, and his expression bore a slight frown as though he was trying to make a difficult calculation in his head. Then, as I watched, his Adam's apple moved slowly up and down his neck – once, twice, three times.

'Are you all right?' I asked, putting an arm behind him. 'Good gracious, you'd better sit down somewhere.'

I started to take the box from him, but Gustav's hands did not relinquish their grip.

'No, no, sir,' he said, his eyes still closed. 'I'm perfectly all right.'

'Are you sure?'

'Yes, yes. I'm perfectly all right.'

For a few more seconds he remained standing quite still. Then he opened his eyes and glanced about him, gave a faint laugh and began to walk again.

'You've no idea what this will mean to us, sir,' he said after we had gone several steps together. 'And after all these years.' He shook his head with a smile. 'I'll convey the news to the boys at the first opportunity. There's a lot of work this morning, but one phone call to Josef, that will do it. He'll let the others know. Can you imagine, sir, what it will mean to them? Ah, but there's your turning. I have to go on a little further. Oh, don't worry, sir, I'm perfectly all right. Miss Collins's apartment, as you know, is just down there on your right. Well, sir, I can't tell you how grateful I am. The boys will wait for tonight as they've waited for little else in their lives. I know it, sir.'

Wishing him a good day, I took the turning he had indicated. When, after a few steps, I glanced over my shoulder, Gustav was still standing on the corner watching me from around the edge of his box. Seeing me turn, he nodded his head emphatically – the box prevented him from waving – then went on his way.

The street I found myself in was a predominantly residential one. After a few blocks it grew quieter and there appeared above me the apartment houses with the Spanish-style balconies which I recognised from the night I had come down the street in Stephan's car. They stretched ahead block after block, and as I continued to walk I began to fear I might never recognise the one in front of which Boris and I had waited that night. But then I found myself stopping before a distinctly familiar entrance and after a moment I went up and peered through the glass panels on either side of the door.

The entrance hall was furnished in a tidy neutral way, and I was able to ascertain almost nothing from it. Then I remembered how that night I had watched Stephan and Miss Collins talk for a while in the front parlour before going further inside the building, and at the risk of being mistaken for an intruder I hooked a leg over the low wall and leaned across to look through the nearest window. The bright sun made it difficult for me to see inside, but I managed to make out a small stocky man in a white shirt and tie sitting alone in an armchair, more or less directly facing the window. His gaze appeared to be fixed on me, but his expression was empty and it was not at all clear whether he had registered me at all, or was simply staring out of the window lost in thought. None of this told me much, but when I pulled my leg back off the wall and looked again at the door, I felt convinced it was indeed the right one and pressed the bell for the ground-floor apartment.

After a short wait, I was gratified to see through the glazed panels Miss Collins's figure coming towards me.

'Ah, Mr Ryder,' she said opening the door. 'I was wondering if I would see you this morning.'

'How do you do, Miss Collins. After some consideration, I decided I'd take advantage of your kind suggestion that I come and call on you. But I see you have a guest already this morning.' I gestured towards her front parlour. 'Perhaps you'd prefer I came back another time.'

'I won't hear of you going away, Mr Ryder. Actually, although you suggest I'm busy, compared to an average morning it's rather quiet here today. As you see, I've only one person waiting. Just now I'm with a young couple. I've been talking to them for an hour already, but they have such deep-seated problems, they've so much to talk about and haven't been able to until today, I haven't the heart to rush them. But if you wouldn't mind waiting in the front room, it really shouldn't take much longer.' Then, suddenly lowering her voice, she said: 'The gentleman waiting now, poor man, he's just miserable and lonely and wants a few minutes of someone listening to him say so, that's all. He won't be long, I'll send him away quite quickly. He comes virtually every morning, he doesn't mind being hastened on now and again, he gets a lot of my time.' Her voice then resumed its normal tones as she continued: 'Well, please come in, Mr Ryder, don't just keep standing out there like that, even though I see it's a very pleasant day. If you liked, if no one's waiting by then, we could go and walk in the Sternberg Garden. It's very close and we've a lot to discuss, I'm sure. In fact, I've given your position quite a lot of thought already.'

'How kind of you, Miss Collins. Actually, I knew you might be busy this morning, and I wouldn't have intruded on you like this if there wasn't a certain amount of urgency involved. You see, the fact is' – I gave a heavy sigh and shook my head – 'the fact is, for one reason or another, I've not been able to go about things in quite the way I originally planned, and now, here we are, time is getting on and . . . Well, for one thing, as you know, I have to give my talk to the people here tonight, and to be absolutely frank with you, Miss Collins . . .' I almost came to a stop, but then saw her looking at me with a kindly expression and made an effort to continue. 'To be frank, there are a number of issues, local issues here, I'd like your advice on before . . . before I can finalise' – I paused in an attempt to stop my voice wobbling – 'before I can finalise my address. After all, all these people are depending so much on me . . .'

'Mr Ryder, Mr Ryder' – Miss Collins had placed her hand on my shoulder – 'please calm yourself. And do come in, please. That's better, come right in. Now please stop worrying yourself. It's very understandable you'd get a little agitated at this stage, that's perfectly natural. In fact, it's rather commendable you should be so concerned. We can discuss all these things, these local issues, don't worry, we'll do that very shortly. But let me say this much now, Mr Ryder. I do think you're worrying unduly. Yes, you'll have a lot of responsibility on your shoulders tonight, but then you've been in similar situations many many times before

and by all accounts you've acquitted yourself more than credit-
ably. Why would it be any different this time?'

'But what I'm saying to you, Miss Collins,' I said interrupting,
'is that this time it's been quite different. This time I've not been
able to go *about things* . . .' I sighed heavily again. 'The fact is I
haven't had a chance to prepare my ground in the usual way . . .'

'We'll talk about it all very soon. But Mr Ryder, I feel certain
you're getting things out of all proportion. What have you to so
concern yourself about? You have unrivalled expertise, you're a
man of internationally recognised genius, really, what have you
to fear? The truth is' – she lowered her voice again – 'the people
in a town like this, they'd be grateful for *anything* from you. Just
talk to them about your general impressions, they're not about to
complain. You've nothing at all to fear.'

I nodded, realising that she indeed had a point, and almost
immediately I felt a tension lifting from me.

'But we'll discuss it all very thoroughly in just a little while.'
Miss Collins, her hand still on my shoulder, was guiding me
through into her front parlour. 'I promise I shan't be long. Please
take a seat and make yourself comfortable.'

I went into a small square room filled with sunlight and fresh
flowers. The disparate assortment of armchairs suggested the
waiting room of a dentist or doctor, as did the magazines on
the coffee table. At the sight of Miss Collins, the stocky man rose
immediately to his feet, either out of courtesy or because he
hoped she would now invite him through into the drawing room.
I was expecting to be introduced, but the prevailing protocol
seemed indeed to be that of a waiting room, for Miss Collins
merely smiled at the man before disappearing through the inner
door, murmuring apologetically as she did so, apparently to us
both: 'I shan't be long.'

The stocky man sat down again and gazed at the floor. I
thought for a moment he would say something, but when he
remained silent I turned and seated myself on a wicker couch
occupying the sun-filled bay of the window I had earlier looked
through. The basket work creaked reassuringly as I settled myself
into it. A broad band of sunlight was falling across my lap, and
there was a large vase of tulips close to my face. I immediately felt
very comfortable and in a quite different frame of mind concern-

ing what lay before me than when I had rung the doorbell only minutes before. Of course, Miss Collins was absolutely right. A town of this sort would be grateful for virtually anything I cared to offer it. It was hardly conceivable that people would scrutinise my points closely or become critical. And as Miss Collins had again pointed out, I had been in such positions countless times before. Even with my ground less well prepared than I would like, I was still bound to be able to deliver an address of some authority. As I continued to sit there in the sunshine, I found myself growing ever more tranquil, and more and more amazed I could ever have worked myself into such a state of anxiety.

'I was just wondering,' the stocky man suddenly said to me. 'Are you still in touch with any of the old crowd? People like Tom Edwards? Or Chris Farleigh? Or those two girls who used to live at the Flooded Farmhouse?'

I realised then that the stocky man was Jonathan Parkhurst, whom I had known reasonably well during my student days in England.

'No,' I said to him, 'unfortunately I've rather lost touch with everyone from those days. Having to move around from country to country as I do, it's just impossible.'

He nodded without smiling. 'I suppose it must be difficult,' he said. 'Well, *they* all remember *you*. Oh yes. When I was back in England last year I met up with a few of them. They'd all apparently been meeting once a year or so. I envy them sometimes, but mostly I'm glad I haven't got myself stuck in a circle like that. That's why I like living out here, I can be anyone I want here, people don't expect me to be the clown all the time. But you know, when I went back, when I met them in this pub, they immediately started again. "Hey, it's old Parkers!" they all shouted. They still call me that, as though no time at all had gone by. "Parkers! It's old Parkers!" They actually made this big braying noise to welcome me when I first came in, oh God, I can't tell you how awful it was. And I could feel myself turning back into that pathetic clown I came here to get away from, yes, from the moment they started that braying noise. It was a nice enough pub, mind you, a typical old English country pub, a real fire, those little brass things all over the bricks, an old sword over the mantelpiece, a hearty landlord saying cheerful things, all of that was very nostalgic, I do miss it all living out here. But the rest of it, my God, it makes me shudder just to think of it. They made that braying noise, fully expecting me to come bounding up to the table clowning away. And all through the evening, they kept mentioning one name after another, it wasn't as though they even discussed them, they just made more noises, or else laughed immediately they mentioned another name. You know, they'd mention someone like Samantha, and they'd all laugh and cheer and whoop. Then they'd call out some other name, Roger Peacock, say, and they'd all break out into some sort of football chant. It was quite awful. But the worst of it was they all expected me to be the clown again and I just couldn't do anything about it. It was like it was completely unthinkable I could have become someone else, and so I started it all again, the funny voices, the faces, oh yes, I found I could still do it all very well. I suppose they'd no reason to suppose I didn't carry on like that out here. In fact, that's exactly what one of them said. I think it was Tom Edwards, at one point in the evening, they were all very drunk, he slapped me hard on the back and said: "Parkers! They must love you out there! Parkers!" I suppose this must have been just after I'd done another of my turns for them, perhaps I'd been telling them about some aspect of life out here and I'd been clowning it up a bit, who knows, anyway that's what he said and the others were laughing and laughing. Oh yes, I was a big hit. They all kept saying how much they missed me, I was always such a good laugh, oh it was so long since I'd heard anyone say such a thing, so long since I'd been received like that, it was so warm and friendly. And yet what was I doing that for again? I'd vowed never to be like that, that's why I came out here. Even as I was walking to the pub, I'd been saying to myself all the way down the lane, it was very chilly that night, foggy and very chilly, I was telling myself all the way down the lane, that was years ago, I'm not like that any more, I'm going to show them how I am now, and I said it over and over trying to make myself strong, but as soon as I walked in and saw that warm fire and they did that braying noise to welcome me, oh, it's been so lonely out here. Okay, here I don't have to do all those faces and funny voices, but at least that all worked. It may have been intolerable, but it worked, they all loved me, my old university friends, poor sods, they must believe I'm still like that. They'd never guess it, that my neighbours think I'm this very solemn, rather dull Englishman. Polite, they think, but very dull. Very lonely and very dull. Well, at least that's better than being Parkers again. That braying noise, oh, how pathetic, a group of middle-aged men making that sort of noise, and me, pulling my faces and doing those silly voices, oh God, it was truly nauseating. But I couldn't help it, it was so long since I'd been surrounded by friends like that. What about you, Ryder, don't you long for those days sometimes? Even you with all your success? Oh yes, that's what I was going to tell you. You may not remember any of them very well now, but they certainly remember *you* all right. Whenever they have one of these little reunions, it seems, there's a little part of the evening devoted specially to you. Oh yes, I've witnessed it. They go through a lot of the other names first, they don't like to get to you straight away, you know, they like a good run-up. They actually have little pauses when they all pretend they can't think of any more people from those days. Then finally one of them says: "What about Ryder? Anyone heard of him lately?" Then they all explode, making the most disgusting noise, something half-way between a jeer and a retch. They do it all together, repeatedly, really, that's all they do for about the first minute after your name's mentioned. Then they start to laugh and then they all start to mimic piano-playing, you know, like this' – Parkhurst put on a haughty expression and played an invisible keyboard in a highly precious manner – 'they all do this, then make more retching noises. Then they start in on the stories, little things they remember about you, and you can tell they've already told them to each other many times over because they all know, they all know at which points to make the noises again, at which point to say: "What? You're kidding!" and so on. Oh, they really enjoy themselves. The time I was there, someone was remembering the evening the finals finished, how they were all getting ready to go out on the piss for the night and saw you coming up the road looking very serious. And they'd said to you: "Come on, Ryder, come and get pissed out of your brain with us!" and apparently you'd replied, and here whoever's telling it puts on this face, apparently you'd said' – Parkhurst once more transformed into the haughty creature and his voice assumed a preposterously

pompous tone – ' "I'm much too busy. I can't afford not to practise tonight. I've missed two days' practice on account of these
horrid exams!" Then they all make the retching noise together,
and do their piano-playing in the air, and that's when they
start . . . Well, I won't tell you some of the other things they get up
to, they're quite appalling, they're a loathsome lot and so
unhappy, most of them, so frustrated and angry.'

As Parkhurst had been talking, a fragment of memory had
come back to me from my student days, one which for a moment
made me feel very tranquil, so much so that for a while I hardly
cared what Parkhurst was saying. I was recalling a fine morning
not unlike the present one, when I had also been relaxing in a
couch beside a sunny window. I was in my little room in the old
farmhouse I was sharing with four other students. On my lap
was the score of some concerto I had been studying in a lacka-
daisical way for the previous hour, which I had been considerer-
ing abandoning for one of the nineteenth-century novels piled on
the wooden floor near my feet. The window was open allowing a
breeze to drift through, and from outside came the voices of
several students sitting in the uncut grass arguing about philo-
sophy or poetry or some such thing. My small room had had little
else in it apart from that couch – just a mattress on the floor and,
in the corner, a small desk and upright chair – but I had been very
fond of it. Often the floor had become entirely covered with the
books and magazines I browsed through on those long afternoons, and I had got into the habit of leaving my door ajar so that
whoever happened to be passing could just wander in for a talk. I
closed my eyes and for a moment was seized by a powerful
longing to be back in that little farmhouse again surrounded by
open fields and companions lazing in the tall grass, and it was
some time before what Parkhurst was actually saying began to
sink in. Only then did it occur to me that it was some of these
same people, whose faces had now merged with one another in
the memory, whom I had once languidly welcomed when they
had peered around my door, and with whom I had spent a casual
hour or two discussing some novelist or Spanish guitarist, it was
some of these very people Parkhurst was now speaking of. But
even then, such was the almost sensuous pleasure I was experiencing as I reclined in Miss Collins's wicker couch in the sun-filled

bay that I still felt no more than a vague and distant discomfort concerning Parkhurst's words.

He went on talking and I had long since ceased to attend to him when I was startled by the sound of someone tapping the window pane behind me. Parkhurst seemed not to want to hear this and continued talking, and I too tried to ignore the noise as one might an alarm clock when disturbed in luxurious sleep. But the tapping persisted and Parkhurst finally broke off, saying: 'Oh goodness, it's that Brodsky fellow.'

Opening my eyes, I looked over my shoulder. Indeed Brodsky was peering in intently. The brightness outside, or perhaps something about his own vision, appeared to be giving him difficulty seeing in. His face was pressed against the glass and he was shading his eyes with both hands, but he seemed still not to see us and it occurred to me he was tapping the glass believing Miss Collins herself to be here in the room.

Eventually Parkhurst got to his feet, saying: 'I suppose I'd better see what he wants.'

22

I could hear Parkhurst opening the door and then voices arguing out in the hallway. Eventually Parkhurst came back into the room, rolled his eyes at me and gave a sigh.

Brodsky came in behind him. He looked taller than when I had last seen him across a crowded room, and I again noticed the odd way he held himself – at a slightly tilted angle as though about to topple over – but saw too that he was completely sober. He had on a scarlet bow tie and a rather dandy-ish black suit which looked brand-new. The collars of his white shirt were pointing outwards – whether by design or through excessive starching, I could not tell. He was holding a bouquet of flowers and his eyes were weary and sad. Brodsky paused at the threshold and peered tentatively around the door frame, perhaps expecting to discover Miss Collins in the room.

'She's busy, I told you,' Parkhurst said. 'Look, I happen to be a confidant of Miss Collins and I can say with certainty she will not wish to see you.' Parkhurst glanced at me, expecting me to confirm this, but I had decided not to get involved and simply gave Brodsky a weak smile. Only then did Brodsky recognise me.

'Mr Ryder,' he said, and bowed his head gravely. Then he turned again to Parkhurst. 'If she's in there, please, go and get her.' He indicated his bouquet as though it would in itself explain why his seeing her was so imperative. 'Please.'

'I told you, I can't help you. She won't see you. Besides, she's talking to some people.'

'Okay,' Brodsky murmured. 'Okay. You won't help me. Okay.'

With that he began to move towards the inner door through which Miss Collins had earlier disappeared. Parkhurst quickly blocked his route and for a moment Brodsky's tall gangly frame and Parkhurst's small stocky one came into conflict. Parkhurst's method of halting Brodsky consisted simply of pushing at the latter's chest with both hands. Brodsky, meanwhile, had placed a hand on Parkhurst's shoulder and was gazing over it towards the inner door, as though he were in a crowd and was politely peering over the person in front of him. All the while he continued to make a steady shuffling motion with his feet, intermittently mumbling the word 'please'.

'All right!' Parkhurst eventually shouted. 'All right, I'll go and talk to her. I know what she'll say, but all right, all right!'

They separated. Then Parkhurst said, raising his finger:

'But you wait here! You make jolly sure you wait here!'

Giving Brodsky a final glare, Parkhurst turned and went through the door, closing it firmly behind him.

At first Brodsky stood staring at the door and I thought he was about to follow Parkhurst. But in the end he turned around and sat down.

For some time Brodsky appeared to be rehearsing something in his head, his lips mouthing the odd word, and it did not feel appropriate to say anything to him. From time to time he would scrutinise the bouquet as though everything depended on it and the slightest blemish would be a major setback. Then, after we had been sitting without speaking for some time, he finally looked towards me and said:

'Mr Ryder. I'm very pleased to make your acquaintance at last.'

'How do you do, Mr Brodsky,' I said. 'I hope you're well.'

'Oh . . .' He waved his hand in a vague gesture. 'I can't say I feel well. I have, you see, a pain.'

'Oh? A pain?' Then, when he said nothing, I asked: 'You mean an emotional pain?'

'No, no. It's a wound. I got it many years ago and it's always given me trouble. Bad pain. Perhaps that's why I drank so much. If I drink, I don't feel it.'

I waited for him to say more, but he became silent. After a moment I said:

'You're referring to a wound of the heart, Mr Brodsky?'

'Heart? My heart's not so bad. No, no, it's to do with . . .' Suddenly he laughed loudly. 'I see, Mr Ryder. You think I am being poetic. No, no, I meant simply, I had a wound. I was injured, very badly, many years ago. In Russia. The doctors weren't so good, they did a bad job. And the pain's been bad. It's never healed properly. I've had it for so long now, it still hurts me.'

'I'm sorry to hear that. It must be a great nuisance.'

308

'Nuisance?' He thought about this then laughed again. 'You could say that, Mr Ryder, my friend. A nuisance. It's been a hell of a nuisance to me.' He suddenly seemed to remember he was holding his flowers. He sniffed them and breathed in deeply. 'But let's not talk of this. You asked how I felt and I told you, but I didn't mean to talk about it. I try to be brave about the wound. For years I never mentioned it, but now I'm old and I don't drink, it's got very painful. It hasn't really healed at all.'

'Surely there's something you can do about it. Have you seen a doctor? Perhaps a specialist of some sort?'

Brodsky looked at his flowers again and smiled. 'I want to make love to her again,' he said almost to himself. 'Before this wound gets worse. I want to make love to her again.'

There was an odd silence. Then I said:

'If your wound is so old, Mr Brodsky, I wouldn't have thought it's likely to get worse.'

'These old wounds.' He gave a shrug. 'They stay the same for years. You think you've got the measure of it. Then you get old and they start to grow again. But it's not so bad just now. Perhaps I can still make love. I'm old now, but sometimes . . .' He leaned forward confidentially. 'I tried it. You know, on my own. I can still do it. I can forget the pain. When I was drunk, my prick, you know, it was nothing, nothing. I never thought about it. Just for the toilet. That was all. But now I can do it, even with all the pain. I tried it, the night before last. I can't necessarily, you know, not all the way, not everything. My prick's so old and for so many years it was just, well, it was just the toilet. Ah.' He leaned back in his chair and gazed past my shoulder into the sunshine. A wistful look had come into his eyes. 'I so want to make love to her again. But we wouldn't live here. Not in this place. I've always hated this place. I used to come by here, yes, I admit it, I used to walk by here late at night when no one could see me. She never knew, but I often used to come and stand out there, looking at the building. I used to hate this street, this apartment. We wouldn't live here. You know, this is the first time, the first time I've come inside this terrible place. Why did she choose a place like this? It's not what she likes. We'll live outside the city. If she doesn't want to come back to the farmhouse, that's okay. We'll find something else, another cottage maybe. Something surrounded by grass and trees

309

where our animal can enjoy itself. Our animal, it won't like it here.' He looked around carefully at the walls and ceilings, perhaps for a moment re-considering the merits of the apartment. Then he concluded: 'No, how can our animal enjoy it here? We'll live somewhere, grass, trees, fields. You know, in a year's time, six months, if the pain gets too much, my prick can't do it, we can't make love any more, I don't care. As long as I can make love to her just once more. No, once wouldn't be enough, we'll have to get back, you know, like we used to be. Six times, that's it, six times and we'll have remembered everything, that's all I want. After that, all right, all right. If someone, a doctor, God, if he said you can make love to her just six more times, then that's it, you'll be too old, your wound will hurt too much, after that it's the finish, it's just the toilet, I won't care. I'll say, all right, fine by me. As long as I can take her in my arms again, six times is enough, so we're like we used to be, back where we were, then I don't care, I don't care after that. We'll have our animal anyway. We won't need to make love. That's for young lovers who don't know each other enough, who've never hated each other and loved each other again. You know, I can do it still. I tried it, on my own, the night before last. Not all the way, but I could make it stiff.'

He paused and nodded to me with a serious expression.

'Really,' I said smiling. 'That's marvellous.'

Brodsky leaned back in his chair and gazed out of the window again. Then he said: 'It was different, not like when you're young. When you're young you think of whores, you know, whores doing filthy things, stuff like that. I don't care about any of that now, there's only one thing left I want my prick to do, I want to make love to her again in the old way, just where we left off, that's all. Then if it wants to rest, that's okay, I don't ask any more. But I want to do it again, six times, that's enough, the way we used to do it. When we were young, we weren't great lovers. We didn't do it everywhere like young people maybe do now, I don't know. But we had, well, a good understanding. Yes, at times, it's true, when I was young I got tired of it, the same way every time. But she was like that, she was . . . she didn't want to do it any other way, I used to get angry with her, and she didn't know why. But now I want to repeat that old routine, step by step, exactly as we used to do it. The night before last, when I was, you know, when I was trying, I thought about whores, imaginary ones, fantastic ones doing fantastic things, and nothing, nothing, nothing. And then I thought, well, that's reasonable. My old prick, there's only one last mission, why taunt it with all these whores, what's that got to do with my old prick now? There's only one last mission, I should think about that. So I did. I lay there in the dark, remembering, remembering, remembering. I could remember how we used to do it, step by step. And that's how we're going to do it again. Of course our bodies are old now, but I've thought it through. We'll do it just the way we did. And she'll remember, she'll not have forgotten, step by step by step. Once we're in the darkness, under the sheet, we were never so bold, you see, it was her, she was modest, she wanted it that way. I minded it then, I always wanted to say to her: "Why can't you be like a whore? Display yourself in the light?" But now I don't mind, I want to do it just the way we used to, pretend we're going to sleep, keep quiet, ten minutes, fifteen minutes. Then I'll say something suddenly, something bold and dirty in the dark. "I want them to see you naked," I'll say. "Drunken sailors in a bar. A sea-port tavern, drunken filthy men, I want them to see you naked on the floor." Yes, Mr Ryder, I used to say such things, suddenly, after we'd been lying there pretending to go to sleep, yes, suddenly break the silence, that's important, suddenly. Of course, she was young then, she was beautiful, now it sounds strange, an old woman naked on the floor of a tavern, but I'll say it anyway because that's how we used to get it started. She'll say nothing and so I'll say more. "I want them all to stare at you. On all fours, on the floor." But can you imagine it? A frail old woman doing that? What would our drunken sailors say now? But then maybe they've grown old with us, our sailors in the seaport tavern, maybe in their mind's eye she'll be just as she was then and they wouldn't care. "Yes, they'll be staring at you! All of them!" And I'll touch her, just the side of her hip, I remember that, she liked me to touch her sides, I'll touch her just as I used to, then I'll get close to her and whisper: "I'll make you work in a brothel. Night after night." Can you imagine it? But I'll say it, because that's how it was. And I'll throw off the bedclothes and bend over her, I'll part her thighs, maybe they'll click, the joint between the thigh and the hip, it might make a little snapping noise, someone said she'd hurt her hip, maybe she can't part her thighs widely now. Well, we'll do it the best we can because that's what came next. Then I'll bend down to kiss her pussycat, I won't expect it to smell the way it did then, no, I've thought it through, it might smell bad, like stale fish, her whole body will smell bad maybe, I've thought hard about it. And me, my body, look at me now, it's not so good either. My skin, I have these scales, they keep flaking off, I don't know what it is. When it started, last year, it was just the scalp. When I combed my hair, these huge flakes, like fish scales, you could see through them, they came off. It was just the scalp, but now it's all over, my elbows, then my knees, now my chest. They smell like fish too, these flakes. Well, they'll keep falling, I won't be able to stop that, she'll have to put up with it, so I won't complain about her pussycat smelling the way it does, or the way her thighs won't part properly without clicking, I won't get angry, you won't see me trying to force them apart like something broken, no, no. We'll do it exactly like we used to. And my old prick, maybe only half stiff, when the time comes she'll reach down and she'll whisper: "Yes, I'll let them! I'll let the sailors all see me! I'll tease them till they can bear it no more!" Can you imagine it? The way she is now? But we won't care. And anyway, like I said, maybe the sailors will have aged with us. She'll reach down for it, my old prick, back then it would have been very hard, nothing in the world would have made it slack except for . . . well, but now maybe it'll be only half stiff, that was the best I could get it the other night, who knows, maybe it will be all the way, and we'll try and put it in, but she might be like a shell, but we'll try. And at just the right moment, we'll remember when, even if nothing's happening down there, we'll know how to finish the steps, because by then we'll have remembered so well, there'll be nothing to stop us, even if there's nothing happening down there, even if all we're doing is holding ourselves against each other, it won't matter, we'll still say it at just the right time. "They'll take you! They'll take you, you've teased them too long!" And she'll say: "Yes, they'll have me, all the sailors, they'll have me!" and even if nothing's happening down there, we can still hold each other, we'll hold each other and say it like we used to, it won't matter. Maybe the pain will be too much for my old prick, you know, because of my wound, but it won't matter, she'll remember how we did it. All these years, but she'll remember, every step. Mr Ryder, you don't have a wound?'

He was suddenly looking at me.

'A wound?'

'I have this old injury. Maybe that's why I drink. It gives me so much pain.'

'How unfortunate.' Then, after a short silence, I added: 'I did once injure a toe quite badly in a football match. I was nineteen. It wasn't anything too serious.'

'In Poland, Mr Ryder, when I was a conductor, even then, I never thought the wound would heal. When I conducted my orchestra, I always touched my wound, caressed it. Some days I picked at its edges, even pressed it hard between the fingers. You realise soon enough when a wound's not going to heal. The music, even when I was a conductor, I knew that's all it was, just a consolation. It helped for a while. I liked the feeling, pressing the wound, it fascinated me. A good wound, it can do that, it fascinates. It looks a little different every day. Has it changed? you wonder. Maybe it's healing at last. You look at it in a mirror, it looks different. But then you touch it and you know it's the same, your old friend. You do this year after year, and then you know it's not going to heal and in the end you get tired of it. You get so tired.' He fell silent and looked again at his bouquet. Then he said again: 'You get so tired. You're not tired yet, Mr Ryder? You get so tired.'

'Perhaps,' I said tentatively, 'Miss Collins has the power to heal your wound.'

'Her?' He laughed suddenly then went silent again. After a while he said quietly: 'She'll be like the music. A consolation. A wonderful consolation. That's all I ask now. A consolation. But heal the wound?' He shook his head. 'If I showed it to you now, my friend, I could show it to you, you'd see that was an impossibility. A medical impossibility. All I want, all I ask for now is a consolation. Even if it's like the way I said, just half-way stiff and we're doing no more than just dancing, six more times, that'll be enough. After that the wound can do what it likes. We'll have our animal by then, the grass, the fields. Why did she choose a place like this?'

He looked around again and shook his head. This time he

remained silent for a long time, perhaps for as long as two or three minutes. I was about to say something when he suddenly leaned forward in his chair.

'Mr Ryder, I had a dog, Bruno, he died. I've . . . I've still not buried him. He's in a box, a sort of coffin. He was a good friend. Just a dog, but a good friend. I planned a small ceremony, just to say goodbye. Nothing special. Bruno, he's the past now, but a small ceremony just to say goodbye, what's wrong with that? Mr Ryder, I wanted to ask you. A small favour, for me and Bruno.'

The door suddenly opened and Miss Collins came into the room. Then, as Brodsky and I rose to our feet, Parkhurst came in behind her and closed the door.

'I'm very sorry, Miss Collins,' he said, giving Brodsky an angry look. 'He just wouldn't hear of respecting your privacy.'

Brodsky was standing stiffly in the middle of the room. As Miss Collins came closer, he gave a bow and I could see the shadow of a considerable elegance he must once have possessed. He held the bouquet out to her saying: 'Just a small gift. I picked them myself.'

Miss Collins took the flowers from him, but otherwise completely disregarded them. 'I might have guessed you'd come here like this, Mr Brodsky,' she said. 'I came to the zoo yesterday and now you think you can take any liberties you wish.'

Brodsky lowered his eyes. 'But there's so little time,' he said. 'We can't afford to waste time now.'

'Waste time to do what, Mr Brodsky? It's quite ridiculous, your coming here like this. You must know I'm busy in the mornings.'

'Please.' He raised his palm. 'Please. We're old now. We don't have to argue like we used to. I just came by to give you the flowers. And to make a simple proposal. That was all.'

'A proposal? What sort of proposal was that, Mr Brodsky?'

'Simply that you meet me this afternoon at St Peter's Cemetery. Half an hour, that's all. To be on our own and talk a few things over.'

'But there's nothing to talk over. It was clearly a mistake for me to come to the zoo yesterday. And did you say the *cemetery*? Why on earth are you proposing such a place for a rendez-vous? Have you altogether taken leave of your senses? A restaurant, a café, perhaps some gardens or a lake. But you propose a cemetery!'

'I'm sorry.' Brodsky seemed genuinely crestfallen. 'I didn't think. I'd forgotten. That is, I'd forgotten St Peter's Cemetery was a cemetery.'

'Don't be so absurd.'

'I mean, I've been there so often, we used to feel so peaceful there, Bruno and I. Even when things were at their worst, I felt not so bad when I was there, it was peaceful, very beautiful, we liked it there. That's why I asked. Really, I'd forgotten. About the dead people being there.'

'And what did you intend for us to do there? Sit on a gravestone and reminisce about old times? Mr Brodsky, you really ought to think more carefully about your proposals.'

'But we used to like it there, Bruno and I. I thought you'd like it too.'

'Oh, I see. Now that your dog has died, you wish me to go in its place.'

'I didn't mean it like that.' Brodsky suddenly lost his demure look and a flash of impatience crossed his face. 'I didn't mean it that way at all, you know it. You always did this. I spend a long time thinking, trying to find something good for us, and then you, you scorn it, you laugh at it, you make out it's a ridiculous thing. Anyone else and you'd say what a charming idea. You always did this. Like the time I arranged for us to sit in the front at the Kobylainsky concert . . .'

'That was over thirty years ago. How can you still be talking about such things?'

'But it's the same, the same. I think of something, something good for us, because I know deep down you like things to be a little unusual. Then you just laugh at them. Maybe it's because my ideas, like the cemetery, they really appeal to you, deep down, and you can see I understand your heart. So you pretend . . .'

'This is a nonsense. There's no reason on earth why we should be discussing such matters. It's much too late, there's nothing for us to discuss, Mr Brodsky. I can't meet you in a cemetery whether it appeals to me or not, because I have nothing to discuss with you . . .'

'I just wanted to explain. Why it happened, everything, why I was the way I was . . .'

'It's much too late for that, Mr Brodsky. At least twenty years too late. Besides, I couldn't bear to listen to you trying to apologise all over again. Even now, I'm sure, I wouldn't be able to hear an apology on your lips without shuddering. For many, many years, an apology from you was not the end but the beginning. The beginning to another round of pain and humiliation. Oh, why don't you just leave me alone now? It's simply too late. Besides, you've taken to dressing absurdly since you became sober. What are these clothes you've started to wear?'

Brodsky hesitated, then said: 'It's what I've been advised to wear. By the people helping me. I'm to be a conductor again. I have to dress so people see me that way.'

'I almost said to you yesterday at the zoo. That ridiculous grey coat! Who told you to wear it? Mr Hoffman? Really, you should have a little more sense of your own appearance. These people are dressing you like some puppet, and you let them do it. And now look at you! This ridiculous suit. Do you imagine you look artistic like that?'

Brodsky glanced down at his attire, a hurt expression in his eyes. Then he looked up and said: 'You're an old woman. You don't know about the fashions now.'

'It's the prerogative of the old to deplore the clothes of the young. But how ridiculous that *you* should be the one dressed like that. Really, it's no use, it's simply not your style. Quite frankly, I think the town will prefer you in what you used to wear a few months ago. That's to say, rather elegant rags.'

'Don't laugh at me. I'm no longer like that. I might soon be a conductor again. These are my clothes now. When I looked at myself, I thought I looked right. You forget, in Warsaw, I had clothes like these. A bow tie like this one. You forget now.'

For a second, a sad look came into Miss Collins's eyes. Then she said:

'Of course I forget. Why would I remember such things? There have been so many more vivid things to remember in the years since.'

'Your dress,' he said suddenly. 'It's very good. Very elegant. But your shoes, they're as bad as ever, a disaster. You never accepted you have fat ankles. For a woman so thin, your ankles were always fat. And now look, even now.' He pointed at Miss Collins's feet.

'Don't be so childish. Do you think it's like those days in Warsaw when you could make me change my whole costume minutes before we left with just one remark like that? How much you live in the past, Mr Brodsky! Do you think it means the slightest thing to me, what you think of my footwear? And do you think I don't realise now that it was all merely a trick you played, deliberately leaving it to the last possible moment to make your criticism? Of course, I'd change everything then, go out in something thrown on in a terrible rush. Then once we were sitting in the car, or perhaps at the concert hall, only then would I remember my eye-shadow was the wrong colour for the dress, or the necklace looked awful with the shoes. And it was all so important for me in those days. The conductor's wife! It was so important for me and you knew that. Do you suppose I don't see now just what you were doing? How you would say: "Good, good, very nice," right until there were only a few minutes left. Then, yes, it would be something exactly like this. "Your shoes are a disaster!" As if you would know such a thing! What would *you* know about fashions today, you've been drunk for the last two decades.'

'Nevertheless,' Brodsky said, a hint of imperiousness now entering his expression, 'nevertheless, what I say is true. Those shoes make the lower half of your figure look absurd. It's true.'

'Look at this ridiculous suit! Some Italian creation, no doubt. The sort of thing a young ballet dancer might wear. And you believe this will help you gain credibility in the eyes of people here?'

'Absurd shoes. You look like one of those toy soldiers with a base so you don't fall over.'

'It's time for you to leave! How dare you come here like this, disturbing my morning! The young couple in there, they're very distressed, they need my counsel more than ever this morning, and here, you've disturbed us. This is our last conversation. It was a mistake to have met you yesterday at the zoo.'

'The cemetery.' There was suddenly a desperate note in his voice. 'You must meet me, this afternoon. Okay, I didn't think, the dead people, I didn't think. But I explained that. We have to talk before . . . before this evening. Or else how can I? How can I do it? Can't you see how important tonight is? We have to talk, you must meet me . . .'

'Look here.' Parkhurst stepped forward and glared at Brodsky. 'You heard what Miss Collins said. She's requested you leave her residence. Leave her sight, leave her life. She's too polite to say it, so I'll say it on her behalf. After everything you've done, you have no right, not the shred of a right to make the request you've just made. How can you stand there requesting a meeting, as though all those things never occurred? Perhaps you're pretending you were so drunk you don't remember. Well then I'll remind you. It's not so long ago you stood out there in that street, urinating on the wall of this building, shouting obscenities at this very window. The police took you away in the end, dragged you away while you shouted the vilest things about Miss Collins. This was no more than a year ago. No doubt, you're expecting Miss Collins to have forgotten by now. But I can assure you it was only one of many incidents like it. And as for your sartorial pronouncements, wasn't it less than three years ago you were found unconscious in the Volksgarten in clothes you'd repeatedly vomited over, taken to the Holy Trinity Church and there found to have body lice? Do you expect Miss Collins to care what such a man has to say about her dress sense? Let's face it, Mr Brodsky, once a man falls to the depths to which you fell, his position is irredeemable. You'll never, *never* win back a woman's love, I can tell you that with some authority. You'll never win back even her respect. Her pity perhaps, but nothing more. Conductor! Do you imagine this town will ever look at you and see anything other than a disgusting down-and-out? Let me remind you, Mr Brodsky, four years ago, perhaps five now, you physically attacked Miss Collins just off the Bahnhofplatz, and if not for two students who were passing you'd certainly have caused her serious injury. And all the time you were attempting to strike her, you were shouting the vilest . . .'

'No, no, no!' Brodsky suddenly cried, shaking his head and covering his ears.

'You were shouting the vilest obscenities. Of a sexual and deviant nature. There was talk you should have been imprisoned for it. Then of course there was the episode at the telephone kiosk in Tillgasse . . .'

'No, no!'

Brodsky grabbed Parkhurst by the lapel, causing the latter to recoil in alarm. But then Brodsky carried out no further aggression, simply clutching Parkhurst's lapel as though it were a lifeline. For the next few seconds, Parkhurst struggled to prise off Brodsky's fingers. When he finally succeeded, the whole of Brodsky's posture seemed to sag. The old man closed his eyes and sighed, then turned and walked silently out of the room.

At first the three of us remained standing in silence, unsure what to do or say next. Then the sound of Brodsky slamming the front door brought us to life and Parkhurst and I both moved to the window.

'There he goes,' Parkhurst said, his forehead against the glass. 'Don't worry, Miss Collins, he won't be back.'

Miss Collins appeared not to hear. She wandered towards the door, then turned back again.

'Please excuse me, I must . . . I must . . .' She walked dreamily up to the window and looked out. 'Please, I must . . . You see, I hope you understand . . .'

She was speaking to neither of us in particular. Then her confusion appeared to clear and she said: 'Mr Parkhurst, you had no right to speak in that way to Leo. He has shown enormous courage this past year.' She gave Parkhurst a piercing look, then hurried out of the room. The next moment we heard the door slam again.

I was still beside the window and could see Miss Collins's figure hurrying away down the street. She had caught sight of Brodsky already a good way ahead and after a few seconds broke into a trot, perhaps wishing to avoid the indignity of having to call to him to make him wait. But Brodsky, with his odd lop-sided gait, kept up a surprisingly brisk pace. He was obviously upset and it appeared genuinely not to have occurred to him she would come out after him.

Miss Collins, her breath coming harder, pursued him past the rows of apartment houses, then past the shops at the upper end of the street, without appreciably closing the distance. Brodsky

319

continued to walk steadily, now turning the corner where I had earlier parted with Gustav, and past the Italian cafés on the wide boulevard. The pavement was even more crowded than when I had come along it with Gustav, but Brodsky walked without looking up, so that he often came close to colliding with people in his path.

Then, as Brodsky approached the pedestrian crossing, Miss Collins appeared to realise she stood no chance of overtaking him. Coming to a halt, she cupped her hands around her mouth, but then seemed caught in some last dilemma, perhaps concerning whether to call out 'Leo' or else, as she had called him throughout their conversation, 'Mr Brodsky'. No doubt some instinct warned her of the urgency of the situation at which they had now arrived, for she called out: 'Leo! Leo! Leo! Please wait!'

Brodsky turned with a startled expression as Miss Collins came hurrying towards him. She was still holding the bouquet, and in his confusion Brodsky held out both hands as though offering to relieve her of it. But Miss Collins kept hold of the flowers and, though short of breath, sounded quite calm as she said: 'Mr Brodsky, please. Please wait.'

They stood together awkwardly for a moment, both suddenly conscious of the passers-by all around them, many of whom were starting to look their way, some barely hiding their curiosity. Then Miss Collins gestured back in the direction of her apartment, saying softly: 'The Sternberg Garden is very beautiful at this time of year. Why don't we go there and talk?'

They set off with more and more people looking their way, Miss Collins a step or two in front of Brodsky, both grateful for a clear reason to delay conversation until they had reached their destination. They turned the corner back into her street and before long were passing once again in front of the apartment houses. Then just a block or so away, Miss Collins stopped by a small iron gate tucked discreetly back from the pavement.

She reached for the latch, but paused a moment before opening the gate. It occurred to me then that the simple walk they had just completed together, the mere fact that they were now standing side by side at the entrance to the Sternberg Garden, would hold a significance for her far beyond anything Brodsky could at that moment have suspected. For the truth was, she had made that same short journey with him, from the bustle of the boulevard, finishing at the little iron gate, countless times in her imagination down the years – ever since the mid-summer's afternoon they had chanced upon one another on the boulevard in front of the jeweller's shop. And in all those years, she had not forgotten the look of studied indifference with which he had turned away from her that day, pretending to be engrossed by something in the shop's window.

At that point – a good year before the start of the drunkenness and the abuse – such shows of indifference had still been the principal feature of any contact between them. And although by that afternoon she had already resolved several times to set in motion some form of reconciliation, she too had looked away and gone on walking. Only when she had gone further along the boulevard, beyond the Italian cafés, had she given in to her curiosity and glanced back. It was then she had realised he had been following her. He had again been peering into a shop window, but there he had been none the less, only a short way away.

She had slowed her walk, assuming he would sooner or later catch up. When she had reached her corner and he had still not done so, she had taken another glance back. On that day, as on this, the broad sunny pavement had been crowded with pedestrians, but she had had the satisfaction of gaining a clear view of him as he checked himself in mid-stride and looked away towards the flower stall he was passing. A smile had come to her lips, and as she had turned her corner she had been pleasantly surprised by the lightness of her own mood. Her walk now reduced to a dawdle, she too had started to peer into shop windows. She had looked in turn at the pâtisserie, the toy shop, the drapers – in those days the bookshop had not been there – all the while trying to formulate in her head her opening remark to him when he finally came up to her. 'Leo, what children we must be,' she had considered saying. But that had seemed altogether too sensible and she had thought about something more ironic: 'I notice we seem to be going the same way' or some such thing. Then his figure had appeared around the corner and she had seen he was holding a bright bouquet. Turning away quickly, she had started to walk again, now at a reasonable pace. Then as she had approached her apartment, for the first time that day, she had been seized by a sense of annoyance at him. Her afternoon had been neatly planned. Why had he chosen this of all moments to seek a conversation with her? When she had arrived at her door, she had stolen another quick glance up the street, only to discover he was still at least twenty yards away.

She had closed her door behind her and, resisting the urge to look out of the window, had hurried to her bedroom at the rear of the building. There she had checked her appearance in her mirror and composed her emotions. Then, emerging from the bedroom, she had come to a startled halt in the corridor. The door at the far end had been standing ajar and she had been able to see right through, across her sun-filled front parlour and through the bay windows, to the pavement outside where he was now visible, his back to the house, loitering there as though he had arranged to meet someone at that very spot. For a moment she had not moved, suddenly afraid he would turn, look in through the glass and see her. Then his figure had drifted out of view and she had found herself gazing at the fronts of the houses on the opposite side, listening intently for the ring of the doorbell.

When after a minute he had still not rung, she had again felt a flash of anger towards him. He was, she had realised, waiting for her to come and invite him in. She had again calmed herself and, thinking over the situation carefully, had resolved to do nothing until he had rung the bell.

For the next several minutes she had proceeded to wait. Once she had returned to her bedroom for no particular reason, then drifted back out into the corridor. Then eventually, when it had finally occurred to her he had gone, she had made her way slowly out to the entrance hall.

Opening the door and looking left and right, Miss Collins had been surprised to find no trace of him whatsoever. She had expected to discover him lurking a few doors away – or at least the flowers to be on the doorstep. For all that, at that moment, she had felt no regret. A small sense of relief, certainly, and a not unpleasant feeling of excitement that the reconciliation process had at last begun, but she had felt no regret at all. In fact, as she had sat down in her front parlour she had experienced a triumphant glow at having stood her ground. Such small victories, she had told herself, were very important and would help them to avoid repeating the errors of the past.

Only several months later had it occurred to her she had made a mistake that day. Even then, at first, the idea had remained a very vague one she did not examine carefully. But then as the months had continued, that summer's afternoon had come to occupy an increasingly dominant place in her thoughts. Her great error, she had concluded, had been to enter her apartment. By doing so, she had asked just a little too much of him. Having led him all that way, around the corner and down past the shops, what she should have done was to have paused at the little iron gate, then, making quite sure he had a clear view of her, gone into the Sternberg Garden. Then, without a doubt, he would have followed. And even if for a while they had wandered about the shrubs in silence, sooner or later they would have started to talk. And sooner or later he would have given her the flowers. Throughout the twenty odd years that had passed since then, Miss Collins had rarely glanced towards that iron gate without experiencing a small tug somewhere within her. And so it was that on this morning, as she finally led Brodsky into the garden, she did so with a certain sense of ceremony.

For all the prominence the Sternberg Garden had come to assume in Miss Collins's imagination, it was not an especially appealing place. Essentially a concreted square no larger than a supermarket car park, it seemed to exist primarily for horticultural interest, rather than to provide beauty or comfort to the neighbourhood. There was no grass or trees, simply rows of flower beds, and at this point in the day the square was a suntrap with no obvious sign of shade anywhere. But Miss Collins, looking around at the flowers and ferns, clapped her hands in delight. Brodsky, closing the iron gate carefully after him, looked at the garden without enthusiasm, but seemed to take satisfaction from the fact that, aside from the apartment windows overlooking them, they had complete privacy.

'I sometimes bring them here, the people who come to see me,' Miss Collins said. 'It's so fascinating here. You'll see specimens you won't find anywhere else in Europe.'

She continued to stroll slowly, glancing admiringly about her, while Brodsky walked respectfully a few paces behind. The awkwardness they had displayed in each other's presence only a few minutes before had now evaporated entirely, so that someone glimpsing them from the gate might easily have mistaken them for an elderly couple of many years standing taking an habitual walk together in the sunshine.

'But of course,' Miss Collins said, pausing by a shrub, 'you've never liked gardens like these, have you, Mr Brodsky? You despise all this harnessing of nature.'

'Won't you call me Leo?'

'Very well. Leo. No, you'd prefer something wilder. But you see, it's only with careful control and planning some of these species can survive at all.'

Brodsky regarded solemnly the leaf Miss Collins was touching. Then he said: 'Do you remember? Every Sunday morning, after we'd had our coffee together at the Praga, we used to go to that bookstore. So many old books, so cramped and dusty whichever way you turned. You remember? You used to get so impatient. But we used to go anyway, every Sunday, after our coffee at the Praga.'

Miss Collins remained silent for a few seconds. Then she laughed lightly and began to walk slowly again. 'The tadpole man,' she said.

Brodsky smiled. 'The tadpole man,' he repeated, nodding. 'That was it. If we went back now, maybe he'll still be there, behind his table. The tadpole man. Did we ever ask him his name? He was always so polite to us. Even though we never bought his books.'

'Except for that morning he shouted at us.'

'He shouted at us? I don't remember that. The tadpole man was always so polite. And we never bought his books.'

'Oh yes. Once we went in, it was raining, and we took great care not to drip water over his books, we shook our coats at the doorway, and yet he was very ill-tempered that morning and shouted at us. Don't you remember? He shouted about my being English. Oh yes, he was very rude, but only that morning. The next Sunday, he seemed to have no memory of it.'

'That's funny,' Brodsky said. 'I don't remember. The tadpole man. I always remember him as so shy and polite. I don't remember this time you're talking about.'

324

'Perhaps I've remembered incorrectly,' said Miss Collins. 'Perhaps I've muddled him with someone else.'

'I think so. The tadpole man, he was always respectful. He wouldn't have done such a thing. About you being English?' Brodsky shook his head. 'No, he was always respectful.'

Miss Collins stopped again, for a moment absorbed by a fern.

'So many people in those days,' she said eventually. 'They were like that. They would be so polite, so long-suffering. They'd go out of their way to be kind to you, sacrifice all sorts of things, and then one day, for no reason, the weather, anything, they'd just explode. Then back to normal again. There were so many like that. Like Andrzej. He was like that.'

'Andrzej was crazy. You know, I read somewhere, he was killed in a car accident. Yes, I read it, in a Polish journal, five, six years ago. Killed in a car accident.'

'How sad. I suppose many of those people from those days might be gone now.'

'I liked Andrzej,' Brodsky said. 'I read it in a Polish journal, just a mention in passing, saying he'd been killed. A road accident. It was sad. I thought about those evenings, sitting in the old apartment. How we'd wrap up in blankets, share the coffee between us, all those books and journals everywhere and talk. About music, about literature, hours and hours, looking at the ceiling, talking, talking.'

'I used to want to go to bed, but Andrzej would never go home. Sometimes he stayed till dawn.'

'That's right. If he was losing an argument, then he wouldn't go. He'd never go until he thought he was winning. That's why sometimes he stayed till dawn.'

Miss Collins smiled, then sighed. 'How sad to hear he was killed,' she said.

'It wasn't the tadpole man,' Brodsky said. 'It was the man in the picture gallery. He was the one who shouted. A strange one, always pretended not to know who we were. You remember? Even in the days after that performance of *Lafcadio*. Waiters, taxi drivers wanting to shake my hand, but when we went to the gallery, nothing. He looked at us, face like a stone, same as always. Then at the end, when things were going badly, we went in, it was raining that day, and he shouted at us. We were making his floor wet, he said. And we'd always done it, whenever it rained, for years we'd done it, got his floor wet, all these years and he was sick of it. He was the one who shouted, said about you being English, it was him, not the tadpole. The tadpole was always respectful, right to the end. The tadpole shook my hand, I can remember, just before we left. You remember? We went to the bookshop, he knew it was the last time, he came out from behind his table and shook my hand. Most people didn't want to shake my hand by then, but he did. He was respectful, the tadpole, always.'

Miss Collins shielded her eyes with a hand and looked across to the far corner of the garden. Then she began to walk slowly again, saying: 'It's nice to remember some of these things. But we can't live in the past.'

'But you remember it,' Brodsky said. 'You remember it, the tadpole, the bookshop. Remember too that wardrobe? The door that fell off? You remember it all, just as I do.'

'Some things I remember. Other things, inevitably, I've forgotten.' Her voice had now become guarded. 'Some things, even from those times, are best forgotten.'

Brodsky appeared to give this consideration. Finally he said: 'Maybe you're right. The past, it's full of too many things. I'm ashamed, you know I'm ashamed, so let's finish. Let's finish with the past. Let's choose an animal.'

Miss Collins went on walking, now several steps in front of Brodsky. Then she stopped again and turned to him. 'I'll meet you this afternoon in the cemetery if that's what you wish. But you mustn't take that to mean anything. It doesn't mean I'm agreeing about your animal or about anything else. But I can see you're worried about tonight, that you'd wish to talk over your anxieties with someone else.'

'These last months. I saw the caterpillars, but I went on, I went on, I made myself ready. It will be for nothing if you don't come back.'

'I'm only agreeing to meet you for a short time this afternoon. Half an hour perhaps.'

'But you'll think about it. You'll think about it before we meet. You'll think about it. The animal, everything.'

Miss Collins turned away and for a long time stood examining another shrub. Finally she said: 'Very well, I'll think about it.'

'You can see how it's been for me. How hard. Sometimes it was so terrible I wanted to die, just to stop it, but I went on because this time I could see a way. Conductor again. You'd come back. It will be like it was, even better maybe. Sometimes it got terrible, the caterpillars, there's nothing more I can do to prove it. We never had children. So let's get an animal.'

Miss Collins began to walk again, and this time Brodsky kept up alongside her, gazing gravely into her face. Miss Collins seemed about to speak again, but just at that moment Parkhurst said suddenly from behind me:

'I never join in with them, you know. I mean when they start in on you the way they do. I don't even laugh, not even smile, I don't join in at all. You probably think I'm just saying that, but it's true. They disgust me, the way they go on. And that braying noise! As soon as I walk through the door, that braying noise again! Not even a minute, they won't even give me that, they won't give me sixty seconds to show them I've changed. "Parkers! Parkers!" Oh, they disgust me . . .'

'Look,' I said, feeling suddenly very impatient with him, 'if they annoy you so much, why don't you just speak your mind? Next time, why don't you confront them? Tell them to stop the braying noise. And ask them why, just why they hate me so much. Why my success offends them so. Yes, ask them that! In fact, for maximum impact, why don't you do it right in the middle of your clowning? Yes, right in the middle of one of your anecdotes, when you're doing all those funny voices and faces. When they're all laughing and slapping you on the back, so delighted you haven't changed a bit, do it right then. Ask them suddenly: "Why? Why does Ryder's success challenge you so much?" That's what to do. That would not only do me a service, it would demonstrate to these fools in one elegant move that there is, and always was, a much deeper person behind your clowning exterior. Someone not easily manipulated or compromised. That would be my advice.'

'That's all very well!' Parkhurst shouted angrily. 'It's very easy for you to say that! You've nothing to lose, they hate you anyway! But these are my oldest friends. When I'm out here, surrounded by all these continentals, most of the time I'm fine. But now and again something happens, something unpleasant, and then I say to myself: "So what? What do I care? These are just foreigners. In my own country, I've got good friends, I've only to go back, they'll all be waiting there." It's all very well, you coming out with smart advice like that. Actually, come to think of it, it probably isn't all very well for you at all. I don't see why you're so complacent. You can't afford to forget your old friends any more than I can. It's right, you know, some of these things they say. You're downright complacent and you'll pay for it one day. Just because you've become famous! They're right, you know. "Why don't you confront them?" What arrogance!'

Parkhurst continued in this vein for a while longer, but I had stopped listening. For his mention of my 'complacency' had triggered something, causing me suddenly to remember that my parents were due shortly to arrive in the city. And there came over me, there in Miss Collins's front parlour, seizing me with an icy panic that was almost tangible, the realisation that I had not prepared at all the piece I was to perform before them this evening. Indeed, it was several days, perhaps even weeks, since I had last touched a piano. Now here I was, only hours from this most important of performances, not even having made arrangements to rehearse. The more I thought over my situation, the more alarming it appeared. I saw I had allowed myself to become far too preoccupied with the talk I was to deliver, and somehow, unaccountably, had neglected the more fundamental matter of the performance. In fact, I could not for a moment even remember which piece I had decided to play. Was it Yamanaka's *Globe-structures: Option II*? Or was it Mullery's *Asbestos and Fibre*? Both pieces, when I came to think about them, were disturbingly hazy in my mind. Each, I remembered, contained sections of great complexity, but when I tried to think further about these passages, I found I could recall almost nothing. And meanwhile, for all I knew, my parents were already here in the city. I saw there was not a minute to be lost, that whatever the other calls on my time I had first to secure for myself at least two hours of quiet and privacy with a good piano.

Parkhurst was still talking earnestly.

'Look, I'm sorry,' I said, moving towards the door. 'I have to go immediately.'

Parkhurst jumped to his feet and his voice now took on a pleading tone.

'I don't join in, you know. Oh no, I don't join in at all.' He came after me as though to grasp my arm. 'I don't even smile. It's disgusting, the way they go on about you . . .'

'That's fine, I'm grateful,' I said, moving out of his reach. 'But I really have to go now.'

Letting myself out of Miss Collins's apartment I hurried up the street, now unable to think of anything other than the need to get back to the hotel and the piano in the drawing room. In fact I was so preoccupied I not only neglected to glance towards the little iron gate as I passed it, I failed to see Brodsky standing before me on the pavement until I was virtually on top of him. Brodsky bowed and greeted me calmly in a way that suggested he had been watching my approach for some time.

'Mr Ryder. We meet again.'

'Ah, Mr Brodsky,' I replied, not breaking my stride. 'Please excuse me, but I'm in a terrible hurry.'

Brodsky fell in step alongside me and for a while we walked together without speaking. Although it occurred to me there was something odd about this, I was too preoccupied to attempt any conversation.

We turned the corner together into the wide boulevard. Here the pavement was more crowded than ever – the office workers had come out for their lunch break – and we were obliged to slow down. It was then that Brodsky said beside me:

'All that talk the other night. A big ceremony. A statue. No, no, we won't have any of that. Bruno hated all these people. I'm going to bury him quietly, just me, what's wrong with that? I found a place this morning, a little spot to bury him, just me, he wouldn't want anyone else, he hated them all. Mr Ryder, I wanted music for him, the best music. A quiet little spot, I found it this morning, I know Bruno would like it there. I'll dig. No need to dig so deep. Then I'll sit beside the grave, think about him, all the things we did, say goodbye, that's all. I wanted music while I think about him, the best music. Will you do it for me, Mr

Ryder? Will you do it for me and Bruno? A favour, Mr Ryder. I'm asking you.'

'Mr Brodsky,' I said, walking briskly again, 'I'm not clear what exactly you're requesting. But I have to tell you, I'm in no position to consider any more calls on my time.'

'Mr Ryder . . .'

'Mr Brodsky, I'm very sorry about your dog. But the fact is, I've been obliged to attend to too many requests, and as a result I'm now very hard pressed to get done the most important things I came here to . . .' Suddenly I felt a flash of impatience seize me and came to an abrupt halt. 'Frankly, Mr Brodsky,' I said, almost shouting, 'I must ask you and everybody else to stop asking favours of me. The time has come for it to stop! It must stop!'

For a second Brodsky regarded me with a slightly puzzled expression. Then his gaze fell away and he looked utterly dejected. I immediately regretted my outburst, realising also the unreasonableness of blaming Brodsky for the numerous distractions I had had to deal with since arriving in the city. I sighed and said more gently:

'Look, let me make a suggestion. Just now I'm going back to the hotel to rehearse. I'll require at least two hours completely undisturbed. But after that, depending on how things have gone, I might be in a position to discuss further with you this matter concerning your dog. I must emphasise I can't promise anything, but . . .'

'He was just a dog,' Brodsky said suddenly. 'But I want to say goodbye. I wanted the best music.'

'Very well, Mr Brodsky, but I must now hurry on. I really am very short of time.'

I began to walk again. I had fully expected Brodsky to fall in step with me as before, but he did not move. I hesitated a second, somewhat reluctant simply to leave him on the pavement, but then remembered I could not now afford to be side-tracked at all. I hurried on past the Italian cafés, and did not glance back until I had reached the crossing and was waiting for the lights to change. For a moment, I could not see past the throngs of pedestrians, but then Brodsky's figure came into view standing exactly where I had left him, leaning forward a little to gaze at the approaching traffic. The thought occurred to me that the spot

where I had halted earlier was in fact a tram stop and that Brodsky had remained standing there for the simple reason he was
waiting for a tram. But then the lights changed and, as I crossed
the boulevard, I found my thoughts turning back again to the
much more pressing matter of my evening's performance.

23

When I came into the hotel I gained the impression the lobby was busy, but I had by this time become so preoccupied about my practice arrangements I did not look around at all. In fact I might even have pushed in front of some other guests as I leaned against the reception desk to address the clerk.

'Excuse me, but is there anyone in the drawing room at the moment?'

'The drawing room? Well, yes, Mr Ryder. Guests like to go there after lunch, so I should think . . .'

'I need to speak to Mr Hoffman immediately. It's a matter of the utmost urgency.'

'Yes, of course, Mr Ryder.'

The desk clerk picked up a phone and exchanged a few words. Then putting down the receiver he said: 'Mr Hoffman won't be a moment, Mr Ryder.'

'Very well. But this is a matter of some urgency.'

As I said this, I felt a touch on my shoulder and turned to find Sophie next to me.

'Oh hello,' I said to her. 'What are you doing here?'

'I was just trying to deliver something. You know, for Papa.' Sophie gave a self-conscious laugh. 'But he's busy, he's over at the concert hall.'

'Oh, the coat,' I said, noticing the package she was holding over her arm.

'It's getting chillier, so I brought it along, but he's over at the concert hall and hasn't come back. We've been waiting almost half an hour now. If he isn't back in the next few minutes, we'll have to leave it for today.'

I noticed Boris sitting on a sofa on the other side of the lobby. My view of him was largely obscured by a group of tourists standing in the middle of the floor, but I could see that he was engrossed in the tattered handyman's manual I had bought at the cinema. Sophie followed my gaze and laughed again.

'He's been so absorbed in that book,' she said. 'After you left last night, he was looking at it right up until bed. And then this morning, from the time he got up.' She gave another laugh and looked over towards him again. 'It was such a good idea, to buy it for him.'

'I'm glad he's enjoying it,' I said, turning back to the reception desk. I raised my hand to enquire of the desk clerk what had become of Hoffman, but just then Sophie came a step closer and said in a different voice:

'How much longer are you planning to keep it up? It's really upsetting him, you know.'

I gave her a puzzled look, but she continued to fix me with a severe stare.

'I know things are difficult for you just now,' she went on. 'And I haven't helped much, I realise. But the fact is he's upset and worried by it. How much longer is it going to go on?'

'I'm not sure what you're referring to.'

'Look, I said I realise it's my fault too. What's the point in pretending it's not happening?'

'Pretending what's not happening? I suppose this is that Kim's suggestion, is it? To come to me with all these accusations?'

'As a matter of fact, Kim always says it's best I be much more frank with you. But this time, it's nothing to do with her. I'm bringing this up because . . . because I can't bear to see Boris worrying like this.'

A little bewildered, I began to turn back to the desk clerk. But before I could attract his attention, Sophie said:

'Look, I'm not accusing you of anything. You've been very understanding about everything. I couldn't ask you to have been more reasonable. You haven't even shouted at me. But I always knew there'd have to be some anger and it's coming out like this.'

I gave a laugh. 'I suppose this is the sort of pop psychology you talk with that Kim, is it?'

'I always knew it,' Sophie continued, ignoring my remark. 'You've been very understanding about everything, more than anyone could ever expect, even Kim admits that. But it was never realistic. We couldn't just go on like this, as though nothing had happened. You're angry. Who can blame you? I always knew it

333

would have to come out somehow. I just never thought it would be like this. Poor Boris. He doesn't know what he's done.'

I looked again over to where Boris was sitting. He seemed still to be completely absorbed in his manual.

'Look,' I said, 'I'm still not at all sure what you're talking about. Perhaps you're just referring to the fact that Boris and I, we've been adjusting our behaviour towards one another a little. But surely that's only appropriate given the circumstances. If I've been a little distant towards him recently, it's simply because I don't want to mislead him about the true nature of our life together now. We have to all be more cautious. After what's happened, who knows what the future holds for the three of us? Boris has to learn to become more resilient, more independent. I'm sure in his own way, he understands this as much as I do.'

Sophie looked away and for a moment seemed to be thinking something over. I was about to attract the desk clerk's attention again when she said suddenly:

'Please. Come over now. Say something to him.'

'Come over? Well, the problem is, I've a matter of some urgency to attend to and just as soon as Hoffman turns up . . .'

'Please, just a few words. It would make such a difference to him. Please.'

She was looking at me intently. When I gave a shrug, she turned and began to lead the way across the lobby.

Boris glanced up briefly as we approached, then stared down at his book again with a serious expression. I had assumed Sophie was going to say something, but to my annoyance, she simply gave me a meaningful look then walked on past Boris's sofa towards a magazine rack next to the windows. I thus found myself standing alone next to Boris while the little boy went on with his reading. Eventually I pulled up an armchair and sat down opposite him.

Boris continued to read, showing no sign of having noticed my presence. Then, without looking up, he muttered to himself:

'This book's great. It shows you everything.'

I was wondering how to respond, but then caught sight of Sophie, her back to us, pretending to examine a magazine she had just taken off the rack. I suddenly felt a wave of anger and bitterly regretted having followed her across the lobby. She had, I realised, managed to manoeuvre things so that, whatever I now said to Boris, she could count it a triumph and a vindication. I cast another look at her back, the slight stoop she was affecting around the shoulders to suggest her fascination with the magazine, and felt steadily more angry.

Boris turned over a page and continued to read. After a while he muttered once more without looking up: 'Tiling the bathroom. I'll be able to do it easily now.'

There was a selection of newspapers on a coffee table nearby and I saw no reason why I too should not be reading. I picked a paper and held it open before me. A few moments passed in silence. Then, as I was glancing over an article about the German car industry, I heard Boris say suddenly:

'Sorry.'

He had uttered the word in a somewhat aggressive manner and at first I wondered if Sophie had managed to prod him or give him a signal while I had been reading. But when I stole a glance towards Sophie, her back was still turned and she appeared not to have moved at all. Then Boris said:

'I'm sorry I was selfish. I won't be any more. I won't talk about Number Nine ever again. I'm much too old for that now. It'll be easy with this book. It's great. I'll be able to do everything soon. I'm going to do the bathroom again. I didn't realise before. But it shows you in here, it shows you everything. I won't talk about Number Nine ever again.'

It was as though he were uttering lines he had memorised and rehearsed. None the less, there was something emotional in his voice and I felt a strong urge to reach out and comfort him. But then I saw Sophie's shoulders rise and fall, and remembered my annoyance at her. I could see, moreover, that in the long run none of our interests would be served if I allowed Sophie to manipulate matters in the manner she was now attempting.

I closed the newspaper and rose to my feet, glancing behind me to see if Hoffman was anywhere to be seen. As I did so, Boris spoke again, a panic now evident in his voice.

'I promise. I promise I'll learn to do everything. It'll be easy now.'

His voice wobbled a little, but when I looked at him again, his eyes were still fixed firmly on his page. His face, I noticed, looked strangely flushed. I then caught a movement across the lobby and saw Hoffman waving to me from beside the reception desk.

'I have to go now,' I called to Sophie. 'I've got something very important. I'll see you both another time.'

Boris turned over a page, but did not look up.

'Very soon,' I said to Sophie, who had now turned. 'We'll talk more very soon. But I have to go now.'

Hoffman had made his way into the centre of the lobby and was waiting for me with an anxious demeanour.

'I'm sorry to have kept you waiting, Mr Ryder,' he said. 'I should have anticipated you'd turn up well before time for a meeting such as this. I've just this moment come from the board-room, and I can tell you, sir, these people, these ordinary ladies and gentlemen, they're so extremely grateful, so grateful you've agreed to meet with them in person. That you, Mr Ryder, appreci-ate the importance of hearing from their own lips what they've been through.'

I looked at him sternly. 'Mr Hoffman, there appears to be a misunderstanding. I require at this point in time two hours in which to practise. Two hours of complete privacy. I must ask you to clear the drawing room as quickly as possible.'

'Ah yes, the drawing room.' Then he gave a laugh. 'I'm sorry, Mr Ryder, I don't quite understand. As you know, the committee of the Citizens' Mutual Support Group is at this very moment waiting up in the boardroom . . .'

'Mr Hoffman, you don't seem to appreciate the urgency of the situation. Owing to one unforeseen event after another, I haven't had a chance to touch a piano now for many days. I must insist I be allowed access to one as quickly as possible.'

'Ah yes, Mr Ryder. Of course, that's perfectly understandable. I'll do everything I can to be of assistance. But as far as the drawing room is concerned, it would not be at all practical at this moment. You see, it's so full of guests . . .'

'You appear quite ready to clear it for Mr Brodsky.'

'Ah, yes, quite right. Well, sir, if you were absolutely insistent you wanted the piano in the drawing room above all other pianos in the hotel, then certainly, yes, I would gladly comply. I would go in there now, personally, and request that all the guests leave, never mind if they are in the middle of taking coffee or whatever. Yes, I would do that ultimately. But perhaps before I resort to such extreme measures, you'd be so good as to consider certain other options. You see, sir, it is by no means the case that the piano in the drawing room is the best in the hotel. In fact some of the bass notes are distinctly dubious.'

'Mr Hoffman, if it isn't to be the drawing room, then by all means, please, tell me what else you have available. I have no peculiar attachment to the drawing room itself. What I need is simply a good piano and privacy.'

'The practice room. That would serve your needs much better.'

'Very well, then. The practice room it is.'

'Excellent.'

He began to lead me away. Then after just a few steps he stopped again and leaned forward confidentially.

'I take it then, Mr Ryder, you'll be requiring the practice room immediately you come out of the meeting?'

'Mr Hoffman, I don't wish to have to stress to you yet again the urgency of the present situation . . .'

'Ah yes, yes, Mr Ryder. Of course, of course. I very much understand. So . . . you're requiring to practise *before* the meeting. Yes, yes, I understand perfectly. That will be no problem, these people will be more than happy to wait a little. Well, no matter, this way please.'

We left the lobby via a door I had not noticed before situated to the left of the elevator, and we were soon walking along what was clearly a service corridor. The walls were undecorated and the fluorescent tubes overhead lent everything a hard, stark aspect. We passed a series of large sliding doors from behind which came various kitchen noises. One door was open and I glimpsed a harshly lit room with metal canisters piled in columns on a wooden bench.

'We're having to do much of the catering for tonight here on hotel premises,' said Hoffman. 'The concert hall, as you can imagine, has very limited kitchen facilities.'

The corridor turned a corner and we passed what I supposed were the laundry rooms. At one point we passed a set of doors from behind which came the sound of two women screaming at each other with alarming venom. Hoffman, however, seemed to register nothing and walked on in silence. Then I heard him mutter:

'No, no, these citizens. They'll be grateful regardless. A little delay, they won't mind at all.'

He eventually stopped in front of an unmarked door. I expected him to hold it open for me, but instead he averted his eyes from it and turned his whole body away.

'In there, Mr Ryder,' he mumbled and made a quick furtive gesture over his shoulder.

'Thank you, Mr Hoffman.' I pushed open the door.

Hoffman continued to stand rigidly on his spot, his gaze still averted. 'I shall wait here for you,' he muttered.

'No need to do that, Mr Hoffman. I'll be able to find my way back out.'

'I shall be here, sir. Don't you worry.'

I could not be bothered to argue and hurried on through the doorway.

I entered a long narrow room with a grey stone floor. The walls were covered to the ceiling with white tiles. I had the impression there was a row of sinks to my left, but I was by this point so anxious to get to the piano I paid little attention to such details. My gaze, in any case, had been immediately drawn to the wooden cubicles on my right. There were three of these, painted an unpleasant frog-green colour, standing side by side. The doors to the two outer cubicles were closed, but the central cubicle – which looked to have slightly broader dimensions – had its door ajar and I could see inside it a piano, the lid left open to display the keys. Without further ado I attempted to make my way inside, only to find this a frustratingly difficult task. The door – which swung inwards into the cubicle – was prevented from opening fully by the piano itself, and in order to get inside and close the door again I was obliged to squeeze myself tightly into a corner and to tug the edge of the door slowly past my chest. Eventually I succeeded in closing and locking the door, then managed – again with some difficulty in the cramped conditions – to pull the stool out from under the piano. Once I had seated myself, however, I felt reasonably comfortable, and when I ran my fingers up and down the keys I discovered that for all its discoloured notes and scratched outer body, the piano possessed

338

a mellow sensitive tone and had been perfectly tuned. The acoustics within the cubicle, moreover, were not nearly as claustrophobic as one might have supposed.

A great sense of relief swept over me at this discovery and I suddenly realised how tense I had been over the past hour. I took several slow deep breaths and set about preparing myself for this most important of practice sessions. It was then I remembered I had still not resolved the question of which piece to perform this evening. My mother, I knew, would find particularly moving the central movement of Yamanaka's *Globestructures: Option II*. But my father would certainly prefer Mullery's *Asbestos and Fibre*. In fact it was even possible he would not approve much of the Yamanaka. I sat gazing at the keys for a few more moments before deciding firmly in favour of the Mullery.

The decision made me feel all the better and I was just preparing to embark on those explosive opening chords when I felt something hard tap against the back of my shoulder. Turning, I saw with dismay that the door of the cubicle had somehow come unlocked and was hanging open.

I clambered to a standing position and pushed the door closed. I then noticed the latch mechanism was dangling upside down on the door frame. After further examination, and with a little ingenuity, I managed to fix the latch back in place, but even as I locked the door once more I could see I had effected only the most temporary of solutions. The latch was liable to slip down again at any moment. I could be in the middle of *Asbestos and Fibre* – in the midst, say, of one of the highly intense passages in the third movement – and the door could easily swing open again exposing me to whoever happened by then to be wandering about outside my cubicle. And certainly, if some obtuse person, not realising I was inside, were to attempt to gain entry, the lock would not offer even nominal resistance.

All these thoughts ran through my mind as I seated myself back on the stool. But after a little while, I came to the conclusion that if I did not make full use of this opportunity to practise, I might never get another. And if the conditions were less than ideal, the piano itself was perfectly adequate. With some determination, I willed myself to stop worrying about the faulty door behind me and to prepare myself once more for the opening bars of the Mullery.

Then, just as my fingers were poised over the keys, I heard a noise – a small creaking sound such as might be made by a shoe or some piece of clothing – somewhere alarmingly close by. I spun round on my stool. Only then did I notice that although the door had stayed closed, the whole of its upper section was missing, so that it more or less resembled a stable door. I had been so preoccupied with the faulty latch I had somehow completely failed to register this glaring fact. I now saw how the door ended at a rough edge just above waist height. Whether the upper section had been torn off as a result of wanton vandalism or because some renovation was taking place I could not be sure. In any case, even from my seated position I could, by craning my neck slightly, gain a clear view of the white tiles and sinks outside.

I could not believe Hoffman had had the effrontery to offer me such conditions. To be sure, no one else had come into the room so far, but it was perfectly conceivable a group of six or seven hotel staff could come in at any moment and begin using the sinks. The situation seemed to me untenable and I was about to abandon the cubicle angrily when I caught sight of a rag hanging from a nail on the door post close to the upper hinge.

I stared at this for a second, and then spotted another nail on the other door post at exactly the same height. Immediately guessing the purpose of the rag and the nails, I rose to my feet again to examine them further. The rag turned out to be an old bath towel. When I opened it out and hung it across the two nails, I found it formed a perfectly good curtain over the missing section of the door.

I sat down again feeling much better and prepared myself once more for the opening bars. Then, just as I was about to start playing, I was yet again stopped by the creaking noise. Then I heard it once more, and I realised it was coming from the cubicle on my left. It now dawned on me not only that someone had been in the next cubicle the whole time, but that the sound insulation between the cubicles was virtually non-existent, and that I had remained unaware of the person until this point only because – for whatever reason – he had remained very still.

Furious, I rose again and pulled at the door, causing the latch to come loose again and the towel to fall to the ground. As I squeezed my way out, the man in the next cubicle, perhaps seeing no further reason to restrain himself, cleared his throat noisily. I hurried out of the room feeling thoroughly disgusted.

I was a little surprised to find Hoffman waiting for me in the corridor, but then remembered that he had indeed promised to do so. He was standing with his back to the wall, but as soon as I emerged straightened himself and stood to attention.

'Now, Mr Ryder,' he said smiling, 'if you'd follow me. The ladies and gentlemen are very eager to meet you.'

I looked at him coldly. 'What ladies and gentlemen, Mr Hoffman?'

'Why, the members of the committee, Mr Ryder. Of the Citizens' Mutual Support Group . . .'

'Look, Mr Hoffman . . .' I was very angry, but the delicacy of what I had to explain caused me to pause. Hoffman, at last noticing that something was troubling me, stopped in the middle of the corridor and gazed at me with concern.

'Look, Mr Hoffman. I'm very sorry about this meeting. But it is imperative I get to practise. I cannot do anything else until I've first been allowed to practise.'

Hoffman appeared genuinely puzzled. 'I'm sorry, sir,' he said, his voice lowered discreetly. 'But you didn't practise just now?'

'I did not. I was . . . I was unable to.'

'You were unable? Mr Ryder, is everything in order? I mean, you're not feeling unwell?'

'I'm pefectly well. Look' – I gave a sigh – 'if you must know, I was unable to practise in there because . . . well, frankly, sir, the conditions do not provide the necessary level of privacy. No, sir, let me speak. The level of privacy is inadequate. It might be fine for some people, but for me . . . Well, I'll tell you, Mr Hoffman, I'll tell you quite frankly. It's been the same since I was a child. I've never been able to practise unless I had complete, utter privacy.'

'Is that so, sir?' Hoffman was nodding gravely. 'I see, I see.'

'Well, I hope you do see. The conditions in there' – I shook my head – 'they are nowhere near adequate. Now the point is, I must, must, have satisfactory practice facilities . . .'

'Yes, yes, of course.' He nodded sympathetically. 'I think, sir, I have the solution. The practice room in the annexe will give you absolute privacy. The piano is excellent, and as for the privacy, I can guarantee it, sir. It is very, very private.'

'Very well. That sounds like the answer. The annexe, you say.'

'Yes, sir. I'll take you there myself as soon as you've finished your meeting with the Citizens' Mutual Support . . .'

'Look, Mr Hoffman!' I suddenly shouted, only just resisting the urge to grab his lapel. 'Listen to me! I do not care about this group of citizens! I do not care how long they are kept waiting! The fact is, if I am not able to practise, I will pack up and leave this city immediately, in the next hour! That's right, Mr Hoffman. There will be no lecture, no performance, nothing! You understand me, Mr Hoffman? You understand me?'

Hoffman stared at me, the colour draining from his face. 'Yes, yes,' he muttered. 'Yes, of course, Mr Ryder.'

'So I must ask you' – I managed to control my voice a little – 'please. Kindly lead me to this annexe without further delay.'

'Very well, Mr Ryder.' He laughed oddly. 'I understand perfectly. After all, these are just ordinary citizens. What need is there for someone such as yourself . . .' Then he collected himself and said firmly: 'This way, Mr Ryder, if you'd care to follow me.'

24

We walked a little way further along the corridor, then crossed a large laundry room containing several growling machines. Hoffman then ushered me through a narrow exit and I stepped out to find the double doors of the drawing room facing me.

'We'll take a short cut through here,' Hoffman said.

As soon as we entered the drawing room, I understood better his earlier reluctance to clear the room for me. It was packed to overflowing with people, laughing and talking, some of them dressed very flamboyantly, and my first thought was that we had stumbled into a private party. But as we slowly made our way through the crowd, I could make out several distinct groups. Some exuberant locals were occupying one section of the room. Another group appeared to be comprised of rich young Americans – many of whom were singing in unison some college anthem; while in yet another area a group of Japanese men had drawn several tables together and were also carrying on boisterously. Curiously, though these groups were clearly separate, there appeared to be much interaction between them. All around me, people were wandering from table to table, slapping one another on the back, taking photographs of each other and passing plates of sandwiches back and forth. A harassed-looking waiter in a white uniform was going among them with a coffee jug in each hand. I thought to look for the piano, but found myself too busy squeezing past people in an effort to keep up with Hoffman. Eventually I reached the other side of the drawing room where Hoffman was holding open another door for me.

I went through into a passageway, one end of which was open to the outdoors. The next moment I stepped out into a small sunny car park, which I quickly recognised as the one Hoffman had led me to the night we had driven to Brodsky's banquet. Hoffman ushered me towards a large black car, and a few minutes later we were moving slowly through the lunch-time congestion.

'The traffic in this town,' Hoffman sighed. 'Mr Ryder, would you like the air-conditioning? Are you sure? My goodness, look at this traffic. Thankfully we won't have to put up with it for long. We'll take the south road.'

Sure enough, at the next traffic lights Hoffman turned down a road on which the vehicles were moving much more smoothly, and in no time we were travelling at a good speed across open countryside.

'Ah yes, this is the wonderful thing about our town,' Hoffman said. 'No need to drive far before you find yourself in pleasant surroundings. You see, the air is improving already.'

I said something in agreement and fell silent, not wishing to be drawn into conversation at this point. For one thing I had begun to have misgivings about my earlier decision to perform *Asbestos and Fibre*. The more I thought about it, the more some recollection seemed to come back to me of my mother once expressing her irritation specifically with this composition. I considered for a moment the possibility of something altogether different, something like Kazan's *Wind Tunnels*, but then remembered the piece would take two and a quarter hours to perform. There was no doubting that the short, intense *Asbestos and Fibre* was the obvious choice. Nothing else of that length would provide quite the same opportunity to demonstrate such a wide range of moods. And certainly, on the surface at least, it was a piece one could expect my mother very much to appreciate. And yet there was still something – admittedly nothing more than the shadow of a recollection – that prevented me from feeling at ease with the choice.

Apart from a lorry far up ahead in the distance, we appeared now to be alone on the road. I watched the farmland going by on either side of us and tried again to recall this elusive fragment of memory.

'We won't be long now, Mr Ryder,' Hoffman said beside me. 'I'm sure you'll find the practice room in the annexe much more to your liking. It's very tranquil, an ideal place to practise for an hour or two. Very soon now, you'll be lost in your music. How I envy you, sir! You'll soon be browsing among your musical ideas. Just as if you were wandering through some magnificent gallery where by some miracle you'd been told you could pick up a shopping basket and take home whatever you fancied. Forgive me' – he gave a laugh – 'but I've always entertained just such a fantasy. My wife and I, walking together through some wonderful gallery full of the most beautiful objects. Apart from ourselves, the place is deserted. Not even an attendant. And yes, there is a shopping basket on my arm, we have been told we can take whatever we wish. There would be certain rules, naturally. We could not take more than could be held in the basket. And of course, we would not be permitted to sell anything later on – not that we would dream of abusing such a sublime opportunity in that way. So there we would be, my wife and I, walking together through this heavenly hall. This gallery, it would be part of some large country mansion somewhere, perhaps overlooking vast areas of land. The balcony would have a spectacular view. And great statues of lions at each corner. My wife and I, we would stand there gazing over the scenery, discussing which items we should take. In this fantasy, for some reason, there is always a storm about to break. The sky is a slate grey, and yet somehow the shadows are all as though the brightest summer sun were shining on us. Creepers, ivy, all over the terrace. And just my wife and I, our supermarket basket still empty, discussing our choice.' He laughed suddenly. 'Forgive me, Mr Ryder, I'm being indulgent. It's just that this is how I imagine it must be for someone like yourself, someone of your genius, left at a piano for an hour or so in tranquil surroundings. That this is how it must be for the inspired. You will wander amidst your sublime musical ideas. You will examine this one, shake your head, put it back. Beautiful as it is, it isn't quite what you were looking for. Ha! How beautiful it must be inside your head, Mr Ryder! How I would love to be able to accompany you on the journey you will embark on the moment your fingers touch the keys. But of course, you will go where I can't possibly follow. How I envy you, sir!'

I muttered something nondescript and we travelled on in silence for a while. Then Hoffman said:

'My wife, in the early days before we married. I think that's how she saw our life together. Something like that, Mr Ryder. That we would enter arm in arm some beautiful deserted museum with our shopping basket. Though of course she would never have seen it in quite such fanciful terms. You see, my wife comes from a long line of talented people. Her mother was a very fine painter. Her grandfather one of the greatest poets in the Flemish language of his generation. For some unaccountable reason, he was neglected, but that alters nothing. Oh, there are others in the family, very talented, all of them. Being brought up in a family like that, she always took beauty and talent for granted. How could it have been otherwise? I tell you, sir, it led to certain misunderstandings. In fact it led to a very large misunderstanding early in our relationship.'

He fell silent again and for a while stared at the road unwinding before us.

'It was music that first brought us together,' he said eventually. 'We would sit in the cafés in Herrengasse and talk about music. Or rather, I talked. I suppose I talked and talked. I remember once walking through the Volksgarten with her and describing in great detail, perhaps for a full hour, my feelings about Mullery's *Ventilations*. Of course, we were young, we had time to indulge ourselves in such things. Even in those days, she didn't talk so much, but she listened to what I had to say and I could see she was deeply moved. Oh yes. Incidentally, Mr Ryder, I say we were young, but then I suppose neither of us were as young as all that. We were both the sort of age when we might already have been married for some time. Perhaps she was feeling some sense of urgency, who knows? In any case we talked of getting married, I was so in love with her, Mr Ryder, from the first I was very much in love with her. And she was so beautiful then. Even now, if you saw her, you'd see how very beautiful she must have been then. But beautiful in a special sort of way. You could see immediately she had a sensitivity to the finer things. I don't mind admitting to you, I was very much in love with her. I can't tell you what it meant to me when she agreed to marry me. I thought my life would be a joy, a continuous unbroken joy. But then it was just a few days later, a few days after she agreed to marry me, she came to visit me in my room for the first time. I was at that time working at the Hotel Burgenhof, and I was renting a room nearby in Glockenstrasse, beside the canal. Not exactly desirable, but a perfectly fine room. There were good bookshelves on one wall and an oak desk at the window. And as I say, it looked over the canal. It was the winter, a splendid sunny winter's morning, there was a beautiful light coming into the room. Of course, I had tidied everything, made it just so. She came in and looked around, she looked all around. Then she asked quietly: "But where do you compose your music?" I remember that very well, that actual instant, Mr Ryder, I remember it very vividly. I see it as a sort of turning point in my life. I don't exaggerate, sir. In many ways, I see it now, my present life started from that moment. Christine, standing by the window, that January light, her hand on the desk, just a few fingers as though to steady herself. She looked very beautiful. And she asked me that question with genuine surprise. You see, sir, she was puzzled. "But where do you compose your music? There's no piano." I didn't know what to say. I saw in an instant there had been a misunderstanding, a misunderstanding of catastrophically cruel proportions. Can you blame me, sir, if I felt the temptation to save myself? I wouldn't have told an out and out lie. Oh no, not even to save myself. But it was a very difficult moment. I think of it now and I feel a shudder go through me, even now as I tell you this. "But where do you compose your music?" "No, there's no piano," I said cheerfully. "There's nothing. No manuscript paper, nothing. I've decided not to compose again for two years." That's what I said to her. I was very quick, I said it with no outward sign of distress or hesitation. I even gave a specific date on which I planned to return to my composing. But for the time being, no, I wasn't composing. What could I say, sir? Did you expect me to look at this woman, this woman I loved desperately, who had only a few days earlier agreed to marry me, did you expect me to take it lying down? To say to her: "Oh dear, it's all been a misunderstanding. Naturally I release you from any obligation. Please, let's part herewith . . ." Of course I could not, sir. You might think I was dishonest. That's too harsh. In any case, you see, at that point in my life what I said wasn't entirely a lie. As it happened, I had every intention of taking up an instrument one day, and yes, I wished to try my hand at composition. So it wasn't a complete lie. I was disingenuous, yes, I admit it. But what else could I do? I couldn't let her go. So I told her I had made a decision to stop composing for two calendar years. In order to clear my head and my emotions, some such thing, I remember talking about it for some time.

347

And she listened to me, taking it all in, nodding her beautiful, intelligent head in sympathy to this nonsense I was telling her. But what could I do, sir? And you know, after that morning, she never mentioned my composing again, never in all these years. Incidentally, Mr Ryder, I can see you're about to ask, I will tell you, I will assure you. I had never before that morning, never at any time during our courtship, during all our walks along the canal, the times we met for coffee in the cafés on Herrengasse, I never, *never*, intentionally led her to believe I composed music. That I was perpetually in love with music, that it fuelled my spirit every day, that I heard it in my heart each morning I awoke, yes, these things I implied and they were true. But I never deliberately misled her, sir. Oh no, never. It was simply a terrible misunderstanding. She, coming from the family that she comes from, inevitably she *assumed* . . . Who knows, sir? But until that morning in my room, I had never uttered a single word to imply such a thing. Well, as I say, Mr Ryder, she never mentioned the matter again, not once. We married in due course, bought a small apartment over Friedrich Square, I found a good position at the Ambassadors. We began our life together and for a time we were reasonably happy. Of course, I never forgot about . . . about the misunderstanding. But it didn't worry me as much as you might suppose. You see, as I said before, in those days, well, I had every intention, when the time came, when there was an opportunity, to take up my instrument. Perhaps the violin. I had certain plans then, such as you do when you are young, when you don't realise how limited time is, when you don't realise there's a shell built around you, a hard shell so you *can't – get – out!*' Suddenly he took both hands off the steering wheel and pushed upwards against an invisible dome around him. The gesture contained more weariness than anger, and the next second he let his hands fall back onto the wheel again. He went on with a sigh: 'No, I didn't know about such things then. I still hoped I would become in time the sort of person she believed me to be. Indeed, sir, I believed I would succeed in becoming such a person precisely because of her presence, because of her influence. And the first year of our marriage, Mr Ryder, as I say, we were reasonably happy. We bought that apartment, it was perfectly adequate. There were days when I thought she'd realised about the misunderstanding and that she didn't mind. I don't know, every sort of thought ran through my mind in those days. Then in time, naturally, the date I'd mentioned, the two-year point when I was to return to composing, it came and went. I watched her carefully, but she said nothing about it. She was quiet, that was true, but she was always quiet. She said nothing, did nothing unusual. But I suppose it was from around that time, around the time of the two-year mark, the tension came into our lives. It was a sort of low-lying tension, it seemed always to be there, however happily we might spend an evening, it would still be there. I would arrange little surprise outings to her favourite restaurant. Or bring home flowers or her favourite perfumes. Yes, I worked diligently to delight her. But there was always this tension. For a lot of the time I managed not to notice it. I told myself I was imagining it. I suppose I didn't wish to admit it was there and growing by the day. I only knew for sure it had been there the day it went away. Yes, it went away and then I realised what it had been. It was one afternoon, we'd been married three years by then, I came in from work, I'd brought her a little present, a book of poetry I happened to know she was wanting. She hadn't explicitly said so, but I had guessed it. I came into the apartment and found her looking down at the square. You could see all the people returning from work at that time of the afternoon. It was a noisy apartment, but not so bad when one is relatively young. I handed her the volume. "Just a small gift," I said to her. She continued to look out of the window. She was kneeling up on the sofa, her arms resting on the back of it so she could cradle her head as she gazed out. Then she took the book from me, very wearily, and without saying a word went on looking down at the square. I remained standing in the middle of the room waiting for her to say something, to acknowledge my gift. Perhaps she wasn't well. I stood waiting with some concern. Then finally she turned round and looked at me. Not unkindly, oh no, but she looked at me, it was a particular look. The look of someone *confirming* with her eyes what she had been thinking. Yes, that's what it was, and I knew then she had finally seen through me. And that was when I realised, realised what the tension had been. I had been waiting, all that time, I had been waiting for this moment. And you know, it may seem odd, but it was a huge

349

relief. At last, at last, she had seen through me. Oh, what a relief! I felt so liberated. I actually exclaimed: "Ha!" and smiled. She must have thought it odd and the next second I pulled myself together. I realised immediately – oh yes, my feeling of liberation was all too brief – I realised immediately what new dragons I had to wrestle and in a moment I was all caution. I saw I would have to work doubly, triply hard if I were to keep her. But you see, I still thought then that if I worked at it, even though she had *realised*, if I worked very hard at it, I could yet win her. What a fool I was! Do you know, for several years after that day, I continued to believe it, I actually believed I was succeeding? Oh, I attended very carefully. I did all in my power to please her. And I never grew complacent. I realised that her tastes, her preferences, were bound to change with time and so I watched every nuance, ready to anticipate any change. Oh yes, even though I say so myself, Mr Ryder, for those few years, I performed my role as her husband quite magnificently. If a composer she had liked for years was beginning to please her less, I would pick it up instantly, almost before she had articulated the change to herself. The next time the composer was mentioned, I would say quickly, even as she was hesitantly thinking of expressing her doubt, I would say quickly: "Of course, he's not what he was. Please, we won't bother to go to the concert tonight. You'll find it tiresome." And I would be rewarded by the unmistakable look of relief on her face. Oh yes, I was extremely attentive, and as I say, sir, I believed it. I fooled myself, I loved her so, I fooled myself into believing I was slowly winning her. For just a few years, I actually felt confident. And then it all changed, all changed in one evening. I saw how inevitable it all was, how all my great efforts could only add up to nothing. I saw it all in one evening, sir. We'd been invited to Mr Fischer's house, he'd organised a little reception for Jan Piotrowski following his concert here. We were just starting to get invited to such things then, I was beginning to earn a certain respect here for my keen appreciation of the arts. Well, in any case, there we were at Mr Fischer's house, in his fine drawing room. Not a large gathering, forty at the most, it was a very relaxed sort of evening. I don't know if you ever met Piotrowski, sir. He turned out to be a very pleasant man indeed, most skilled at putting everyone at their ease. The conversation flowed very easily, we were all enjoying ourselves. Then at one point I went over to the table where there was a buffet, and I was helping myself to a few things when I realised Mr Piotrowski was standing there right next to me. I was still quite young then, I hadn't so much experience of celebrities, and I admit, yes, I was a little nervous. But then Mr Piotrowski smiled pleasantly, asked me if I was enjoying the evening, very quickly put me at my ease. And then he said: "I was just speaking to your most charming wife. She was telling me about her great love of Baudelaire. I had to confess to her I didn't know Baudelaire's work in any depth. She very correctly reprimanded me for this deplorable state of affairs. Oh, she made me thoroughly ashamed. I mean to put it right without delay. Your wife's love for the poet is absolutely infectious!" To which I nodded and said: "Yes, of course. She's always loved Baudelaire." "And with such passion," Piotrowski said. "She made me thoroughly ashamed." And that was all that took place, all that was said between us. But you see, Mr Ryder, my point is this. *I had never known of her love of Baudelaire!* Never even suspected it! You see what I am saying. *She had never revealed this passion to me!* And when Piotrowski said this to me, something fell into place. All of a sudden I saw clearly something I'd been trying not to see over the years. I mean, that she had always hidden certain parts of herself from me. Preserving them, as though contact with my coarseness would damage them. As I say, sir, I had perhaps always suspected it. That there was a whole side to herself she was preserving from me. And who could blame her? A woman of great sensitivity, brought up in a household such as hers. She had not hesitated to tell Piotrowski, but at no point during our years together had she once hinted of this love of Baudelaire. For the next several minutes I wandered about the reception hardly knowing what I was saying to people, just mouthing pleasantries, in a turmoil inside. Then I looked across the room, it must have been half an hour after the conversation with Piotrowski, I looked across the room and I saw her, my wife, laughing happily on the sofa beside Piotrowski. There was nothing flirtatious, you understand. Oh no, my wife has always been meticulous where propriety is concerned. But she was laughing with an ease I realised I had not seen since our walks together along the canal in the days before we were married.

That's to say, before she *realised*. It was a long sofa and there were two others sitting on it, and some people were also sitting on the floor in order to be near Piotrowski. But Piotrowski had just spoken to my wife and she was laughing happily. But it was not just this laugh, Mr Ryder, that spoke volumes to me. As I watched, I was standing on the other side of the room, as I watched, what happened next was this. Piotrowski until that point had been sitting on the edge of the sofa, his hands clasped around his knee, like so! As he laughed and made some remark to my wife, he began to recline, yes, as though he wished simply to sit back in the sofa. And as he began to recline, very swiftly, very deftly, my wife took a cushion from behind her and placed it for Piotrowski, so that by the time his head touched the back of the sofa, the cushion was there. It was done so swiftly, almost without thinking, a very graceful movement, Mr Ryder. And when I saw it, I felt my heart breaking. It was a movement so full of natural respect, a desire to be solicitous, to please in a small way. That little action, it revealed a whole realm of her heart she kept tightly closed to me. And I realised at that moment how deluded I had been. I realised then what I have known and never doubted since. I mean, sir, I realised she would leave me. Sooner or later. It was just a matter of time. Ever since that evening, I've known it.'

He fell silent and seemed once more to become lost in his thoughts. There was now farmland to either side of the road and I could see tractors moving slowly in the distance across the fields. I said to him:

'Excuse me, but this particular evening you talk of. How long ago was it?'

'How long ago?' Hoffman seemed slightly affronted by the question. 'Oh ... I suppose it was, well, Piotrowski's concert here, that must have been twenty-two years ago.'

'Twenty-two years,' I said. 'I take it your wife has remained with you all that time?'

Hoffman turned to me angrily. 'What are you implying, sir? That I don't know the state of affairs in my own home? That I don't understand my own wife? Here I am confiding in you, sharing with you these intimate thoughts, and you care to lecture me about these matters as though you know far better than I ...'

'I apologise, Mr Hoffman, if I appeared to be intruding. I simply wished to point out . . .'

'Point out nothing, sir! You know nothing of all this! The fact is, my situation is desperate and has been now for some time. I saw it that evening at Mr Fischer's, as clear as daylight, as clear as I see this road before me now. Very well, it hasn't happened yet, but that's only because . . . only because I've made *efforts*. Yes, sir, and what efforts I've made! Perhaps you would laugh at me. If I know it's a lost cause, why do I torture myself? Why do I cling to her like this? It's very easy for you to ask such a thing. But I love her deeply, sir, more today than ever. It's unthinkable for me, I could never watch her leave, everything would become meaningless. Very well, I know it's pointless, that sooner or later she'll leave me for someone like Piotrowski, someone like that, someone like the man she thought I was before she realised. But you can't scoff at a man for clinging on. I've done my very best, sir, I've done my best in the only way open to someone like me. I've worked hard, I've organised events, sat on committees, and I've succeeded over the years in becoming a figure of some stature among the artistic and musical circles of this city. And then of course, there was always the one hope. There was the one hope, which perhaps explains how I've managed to keep her so long. That hope is now dead, has been dead for a good few years already, but you see, for a while, there was this one, single hope. I refer, of course, to our son, Stephan. If he'd been different, if he'd been blessed with at least some of the gifts her side of the family possess in such abundance! For a few years, we both hoped. In our separate ways, we both watched Stephan and hoped. We sent him to piano lessons, we watched him carefully, we hoped against hope. We strained to hear some spark that was never there, oh, we listened so hard, each for our different reasons, we wanted so much to hear something, but it was never there . . .'

'Excuse me, Mr Hoffman. You say this about Stephan, but I can assure you . . .'

'For years I fooled myself! I said, well, perhaps he will develop late. There's something there, some little seed. Oh, I fooled myself and I dare say my wife did too. We waited and waited, then in the last few years it became useless to pretend any more. Stephan is now twenty-three years of age. I can no longer tell myself he will suddenly blossom tomorrow or the next day. I've had to face it. He takes after me. And I know now, she realises it too. Of course, as a mother, she loves Stephan dearly. But far from being the means to my salvation, he has become the very opposite. Each time she looks at him, she sees the great mistake she made in marrying me . . .'

'Mr Hoffman, really, I've had the pleasure of listening to Stephan's playing, and I have to say to you . . .'

'An embodiment, Mr Ryder! He's become an embodiment of the great mistake she made in her life. Oh, if you'd met her family! When she was young she must always have *assumed*. She must have thought she'd one day have beautiful, talented children. Sensitive to beauty, like herself. And then she made her mistake! Of course, as a mother, she loves Stephan utterly. But that's not to say she doesn't look at him and see in him her mistake. He's so like me, sir. I can't deny it any longer. Not now he's virtually a grown man . . .'

'Mr Hoffman, Stephan is a very gifted young man . . .'

'You don't have to say such things, sir! Please don't insult the frank intimacy into which I've taken you with such banal expressions of courtesy! I'm not a fool, I can see what Stephan is. For a while, he was my one hope, yes, but since then, since I saw it was useless, and if I am honest, I suppose I saw it at least six or seven years ago, I've tried – who can blame me? – I've tried to cling to her virtually one day at a time. I've said to her, look, wait at least until this next event I'm organising. Wait at least until that's over, you might see me differently then. And when that event has come and gone, I'll say to her immediately, no, wait, here's something else, another magnificent event, I'm working at it. Please wait for that. That's how I've worked it, sir. For the last six or seven years. Tonight, I know, is my last chance. I've staked everything on it. When I told her last year, when I first told her of my plans for this evening, when I outlined to her all the details, how the tables would be, the programme for the evening, even – you'll forgive me – I had foreseen that you, or someone else of almost comparable stature, would accept the invitation and form the centrepiece of the evening, yes, when I first explained it all to her, explained how because of *me*, this mediocrity she has been chained to for so long, how because of me, Mr Brodsky would win the hearts and confidence of the citizens of this town, and on the crest of this great evening, turn the whole tide here – ha ha! – I tell you, sir, she looked at me as though to say: "Here we go again." But I could see in her eyes a flicker. Something that said: "Perhaps you really will bring it off. That would be something." Yes, just a flicker, but it's just such flickers that have kept me going for this long, sir. Ah, here we are, Mr Ryder.'

We had pulled into a lay-by beside a field of tall grass.

'Mr Ryder,' Hoffman said. 'The fact is, I'm running a little late. I wonder if I could be so discourteous as to ask you to make your own way up to the annexe.'

Following his gaze, I saw that the field rose steeply up a hill and that perched at the very top was a small wooden hut. Hoffman rummaged about in the glove compartment and produced a key.

'You'll find a padlock on the door of the hut. The facilities are not luxurious, but then you'll have privacy, just as you requested. And the piano is an excellent example of the sort of uprights Bechstein produced in the twenties.'

I looked up at the hill again, then said: 'That hut up there?'

'I shall return for you, Mr Ryder, in two hours' time. Unless you would require a car sooner?'

'Two hours would be fine.'

'Well then, sir, I hope you find everything to your satisfaction.' Hoffman waved his hand towards the hut as though politely ushering me, but there was a trace of impatience in the gesture. I thanked him and got out of the car.

355

25

I pulled open a barred gate and followed a footpath that climbed up to the little wooden hut. The field was at first disconcertingly muddy, but as I climbed higher the ground grew firmer. Half-way up, I glanced over my shoulder and found I could see the long road curving through the farm fields, and the roof of what might well have been Hoffman's car going off into the distance.

I was a little out of breath by the time I reached the hut and unlocked the rusted padlock on the door. From the outside, the hut looked no different to an ordinary garden shed, but I was nevertheless taken aback to find it entirely undecorated inside. The walls and the floor were just rough boards, some of which had warped. I could see insects moving along the cracks in between them, while above me the remains of old cobwebs dangled from the rafters. An upright piano of somewhat grubby appearance took up most of the space, and when I pulled out the stool and sat down, I found my back virtually touching the wall behind me.

This same wall contained the only window in the hut, and by twisting round on my stool and craning my neck I found I had a view of the field outside descending steeply down to the road. The floor of the hut did not seem entirely level, and once I turned to face the piano again I had the uneasy feeling I was about to slide backwards down the hill. However, when I opened the piano and played a few phrases, I found it had a perfectly fine tone, the bass notes in particular having a pleasing richness to them. The action was not too light and the instrument had been very adequately tuned. It occurred to me the rough timber around me might even have been carefully chosen to provide the optimum level of absorption and reflection. Aside from a slight creaking each time I pressed the sustaining pedal, the facilities left me with little to complain of.

After a short moment to collect my thoughts I went into the vertiginous opening of *Asbestos and Fibre*. Then as the first movement settled into its more reflective phase, I became increasingly relaxed, so much so that I found myself playing most of the first movement with my eyes closed.

As I began the second movement, I opened my eyes again and found the afternoon sunshine streaming through the window behind me, throwing my shadow sharply across the keyboard. Even the demands of the second movement, however, did nothing to alter my calm. Indeed, I realised I was in absolute control of every dimension of the composition. I recalled how worried I had allowed myself to become over the course of the day and now felt utterly foolish for having done so. Moreover, now I was in the midst of the piece, it seemed inconceivable that my mother would not be moved by it. The simple fact was, I had no reason whatsoever to feel anything other than utter confidence concerning the evening's performance.

It was as I was entering the sublime melancholy of the third movement that I became aware of a noise in the background. At first I thought it was connected with the soft pedal, and then that it was something to do with the floor. It was a faint, rhythmic noise that would stop and start, and for some time I tried not to pay any attention to it. But it continued to return, and then, during the pianissimo passages mid-way through the movement, I realised that someone was digging outside not far away.

The discovery that the sound had nothing to do with me enabled me to ignore it all the more easily and I continued with the third movement, enjoying the ease with which the tangled knots of emotion rose languidly to the surface and separated. I closed my eyes again, and before long began to picture the faces of my parents, sitting side by side, listening with looks of solemn concentration. Oddly I did not picture them sitting in a concert hall – as I knew I would see them later in the evening – but in the living room of a neighbour in Worcestershire, a certain Mrs Clarkson, a widow with whom my mother had for a time been friendly. Possibly it was the tall grass outside the hut that had reminded me of Mrs Clarkson's. Her cottage, like ours, had been in the middle of a small field and naturally enough, being on her own, she had been unable to keep the grass under any sort of control. The inside of her house, by contrast, had been impecc- ably tidy. There had been a piano in one corner of her living room, which I could not remember ever having seen with the lid raised. For all I knew, it might well have been out of tune or broken. But a particular memory came back to me, of sitting quietly in that room, my cup of tea on my knee, listening to my parents chatting to Mrs Clarkson about music. Perhaps my father had just asked if she ever played her piano, for certainly, music had not been a regular topic with Mrs Clarkson. In any case, for no real logical reason, as I continued with the third movement of *Asbestos and Fibre* there in the wooden hut, I allowed myself the satisfaction of pretending I was back in that room in Mrs Clarkson's cottage, my father, my mother, Mrs Clarkson listening with serious expressions while I played the piano in the corner, the lace curtain threatening to blow across my face in the summer breeze.

As I approached the latter stages of the third movement I became conscious again of the digging noise. I was not sure whether it had ceased for a while then started up again or if it had been going on all the time, but in any case it now seemed much more conspicuous than before. The thought then suddenly occurred to me that the noise was being made by none other than Brodsky in the process of burying his dog. Indeed, I recollected his having declared on more than one occasion this morning his intention to bury his dog later in the day, and I even had a vague memory of having agreed to some arrangement whereby I played the piano while he performed the burial ceremony.

I now began to picture something of what must have taken place prior to my arrival at the hut. Brodsky, presumably, had arrived some time earlier and had been waiting at a spot just over the peak of the hill, a stone's throw from the wooden hut, where there was a cluster of trees and a slight dip in the ground. He had stood at the spot quietly, having placed his spade against a tree trunk, and nearby on the ground, concealed almost entirely by the surrounding grass, the body of his dog wrapped in a bed sheet. As he had said to me this morning, he had planned a simple ceremony for which my piano accompaniment was to be the sole embellishment, and understandably he had not wished to commence proceedings until my arrival. He had thus waited, perhaps for as long as an hour, gazing at the sky and the view from the hill.

At first, naturally enough, Brodsky would have turned over memories of his late companion. But as the minutes had ticked by and there had continued to be no sign of me, his thoughts had turned to Miss Collins and their forthcoming rendez-vous at the cemetery. Before long, Brodsky had found himself remembering again a particular spring morning of many years ago, when he had carried two wicker chairs out into the field behind their cottage. That had been no more than a fortnight after their arrival in the city, and despite their depleted funds Miss Collins had been going about furnishing their new home with considerable energy. On that spring morning she had come down to breakfast and expressed a desire to take a short rest sitting in the fresh air and sunshine.

Thinking back to that morning, he had found he could recall vividly the wet yellow grass and the morning sun overhead as he had positioned the chairs side by side. She had emerged a little later and they had sat together for a time, exchanging the occasional relaxed remark. For a small moment that morning, there had been for the first time in months a feeling that the future might hold something for them after all. Brodsky had been on the verge of articulating such a thought but then, remembering that it touched on the delicate topic of his recent failures, had changed his mind.

Then she had made her statement about the kitchen. Since he would not remove the sheets of hardboard from it, despite his having promised to do so for days, her progress there was hopelessly impeded. He had remained silent for a while, then had responded by saying, quite calmly, that he had much work waiting for him in the workshed. As they were unable to sit together even for a few minutes without becoming unpleasant, he might as well be making a start. And he had got up and walked through the cottage to the small shed in the front yard. Neither of them had raised their voices at any point and the entire altercation had lasted no more a few seconds. He had not attached much significance to it at the time and had soon become absorbed in his carpentry projects. On a few occasions during the course of the morning, he had looked up and seen her through the dusty shed window, wandering aimlessly about the front yard. He had gone on working, half expecting her to appear in the doorway, but each time she had gone back inside. He had come in for lunch – admittedly rather late – to discover she had already finished hers and disappeared upstairs. He had waited for a while then, returning to his shed, had gone on working there all through the afternoon. In time he had found himself watching the darkness falling and the lights coming on in the cottage. Close to midnight he had finally gone inside.

The whole of the downstairs of the cottage had been in darkness. In the living room, he had sat down on a wooden chair and, gazing at the moonlight falling over their ramshackle furniture, had thought over the curious way the day had gone. He had not been able to remember when they had ever spent an entire day in the way they had just done and, resolving to end things on a better note, had got to his feet and made his way up the staircase.

On reaching the landing, he had seen the light was still on in their bedroom. As he had made his way towards it, the floorboards had creaked loudly under him, announcing his approach as clearly as if he had called out to her. Arriving in front of their door he had paused and, looking down at the bar of light beneath it, had tried to collect himself a little. Then, just as he was reaching for the handle, from the other side of the door had come her cough. It had only been a small cough, almost certainly involuntary, and yet something about it had made him stop, then slowly retract his hand. Somewhere in that small sound had been a reminder of a dimension of her personality he had managed of late to keep shut out of his mind; a trait he had in happier times much admired, but which – he had suddenly realised it – he had been trying to ignore with increasing determination ever since the débâcle from which they had recently fled. Somehow, the cough had contained in it all her perfectionism, her high-mindedness, that part of her that would always ask of herself if she was applying her energies in the most useful way possible. He had suddenly felt enormous irritation at her, for the cough, for the whole way the day had gone, and had turned and walked away, not caring how loudly the boards creaked under him. Then, back in the mottled darkness of the living room, he had lain down across the old sofa under an overcoat and fallen asleep.

The next morning he had woken early and prepared breakfast for them both. She had come down at her usual time and they had greeted each other not unpleasantly. He had started to express his regret about what had happened, but she had stopped him, saying they had both been astonishingly childish. They had then continued their breakfast, both clearly relieved the dispute was behind them. And yet for the rest of that day, for several of the days that had followed, something cold had remained in their lives. And when in the months to come, after the periods of silence between them had grown in both duration and frequency, and he had paused to puzzle over their origins, he had found himself returning to that spring day, to the morning that had started so promisingly for them sitting side by side in the wet grass.

It was while he had been lost in such memories that I had finally arrived at the hut and begun to play. For the first several bars, Brodsky had gone on staring emptily into the distance. Then, with a sigh, he had brought his mind back to the task in hand and had picked up his spade. He had tested the ground with its edge, but then had gone no further, perhaps deciding the mood of the music was not yet what he required. Only when I had started upon the slow melancholy of the third movement had Brodsky commenced his digging. The ground was soft and had given him little trouble. He had then dragged the body of the dog across the tall grass and into the grave with little fuss, not feeling the temptation even to turn back the bed sheet for a last look. He had actually started to shovel some earth back when something, perhaps the sadness of the music drifting through the air to him, had finally made him pause. Then, straightening, he had allowed himself a few quiet moments looking down at the half-filled grave. Only as I had approached the end of the third movement had Brodsky retrieved his spade and recommenced his shovelling.

As I concluded the third movement, I could hear Brodsky still hard at work and decided I would forget the final movement – it was hardly suitable for the proceedings – and simply recommence the third once more. This, I felt, was the least I could do for Brodsky after having kept him waiting. The shovelling went on for a little longer, then came to a stop with almost half of the movement left to play. This would suit Brodsky well enough, I supposed, giving him a little more time to stand over the grave with his thoughts, and I found myself lending a greater emphasis to the elegiac nuances than I had previously.

When I had come once more to the end of the movement, I remained sitting quietly at the piano for several minutes before rising to stretch my limbs in the confined space. The afternoon sunshine was now filling the hut, and I could hear crickets in the grass nearby. After a little while, it occurred to me I should go out and say at least a few words to Brodsky.

When I pushed open the door and looked out, I was surprised to see how low the sun had sunk over the road below. A few steps through the grass brought me to the footpath again and I climbed the remaining distance to the peak of the hill. I was then able to see how on the other side the ground descended more gradually down into a pleasant valley. Brodsky was standing over the grave under a cluster of thin trees a short way below me.

He did not turn as I came down to him, but he said quietly, not taking his eyes from the grave: 'Mr Ryder, thank you. That was very beautiful. I'm grateful, very grateful.'

I muttered something and stopped in the grass a respectful distance from the grave. Brodsky went on looking downwards for a while, then said:

'Just an old animal. But I wanted the best music. I'm very grateful.'

'Not at all, Mr Brodsky. It's my pleasure.'

He gave a sigh and glanced towards me for the first time. 'You know, I can't cry for Bruno. I tried, but I can't cry. My mind, it's full of the future. And sometimes, full of the past. I think, you know, of our old life. Let's go now, Mr Ryder. Let's leave Bruno here.' He turned and started to walk slowly down towards the valley. 'Let's leave now. Goodbye, Bruno, goodbye. You were a good friend, but just a dog. Let's leave him, Mr Ryder. Come, walk with me. Let's leave him. It was good you played for him. The very best music. But I can't cry now. She'll be coming soon. It won't be long now. Please, let's walk.'

I looked again down at the valley before us and now noticed it was entirely covered with gravestones. It occurred to me then that we were walking towards the very cemetery where Brodsky had arranged to meet Miss Collins. Indeed, as I fell in step alongside him, I heard Brodsky say:

'Per Gustavsson's tomb. We're meeting there. No special reason. She said she knew the grave, that's all. I'll wait there, I don't mind waiting a little.'

We had been walking through the rough grass, but now we came to a footpath, and as we made our way further down the hillslope I found I could make out the cemetery more and more clearly. It was a tranquil, secluded setting. The gravestones were set out in orderly rows across the bed of the valley, with some making their way up the grass slopes on either side. Even at this moment, I noticed, a burial was taking place; I could make out the dark figures of the bereaved party, perhaps thirty people in all, gathered in the sunshine over to our left.

'I do hope it goes well,' I said. 'I mean, of course, your meeting with Miss Collins.'

Brodsky shook his head. 'This morning, I felt good. I thought if we only talked, things could come right again. But now, I don't know. Maybe that man, your friend at her apartment this morning, maybe he's right. Maybe she can never forgive me now. Maybe I went too far and she'll never forgive me.'

'I'm sure there's no need to be so pessimistic,' I said. 'Whatever happened, it's all in the past now. If the two of you could just . . .'

'All these years, Mr Ryder,' he said. 'Deep down. I never really accepted it, what they said about me back then. I never believed I was just this . . . this nobody. Maybe with my head, yes, I accepted what they said. But in my heart, no, I never believed it. Not for a minute, in all these years. I could always hear it, I could hear the music. So I knew I was better, better than they said. And for a little while after we came here, she knew it too, I know she did. But then, well, she began to doubt it, who can blame her? I don't blame her for going away. No, I don't. But I *do* blame her, I *do* blame her for not having done better. Oh yes, she should have done better! I made her hate me, can you imagine what that cost me? I gave her her freedom and what does she do? Nothing. Not even leave this town, just waste her time. On these *people*, these weak, useless people she talks to all day. If I'd known that was all she would do! A painful thing, Mr Ryder, to push away someone you love. You think I'd have done it? You think I'd have turned myself into this creature if that was all she was going to do? These weak, unhappy people she talks to! Once she had the highest

363

goals. She was going to do great things. That's how it was. And look, she wasted it all. Didn't even leave this town. Do you wonder that I shouted at her from time to time? If that's all she was going to do, why didn't she say so back then? Does she think it's a joke, a big joke, being a drunken beggar? People think, okay, he's drunk, he doesn't care about anything. That's not true. Sometimes everything gets clear, very clear, and then . . . do you know how awful it is then, Mr Ryder? She never took it, the chance I gave her. Never even left the city. Just talk, talk, these weak people. I shouted at her, can you blame me? She deserved it, everything I said, every piece of filthy abuse, she deserved it . . .'

'Mr Brodsky, please, please. This is hardly the way to prepare yourself for this most important encounter . . .'

'Does she think I enjoyed it? That I did it for fun? I didn't have to do it. Look, you see, when I want to stop the drink, I can. Does she think I did it for a joke?'

'Mr Brodsky, I don't wish to intrude. But surely the time has come to put such thoughts away for ever. Surely all these differences, misunderstandings, it's time they were forgotten. You must try and make the best of what's left of your lives. Please, try and calm yourself. It won't do to meet with Miss Collins like this, you're sure to regret it later. In fact, Mr Brodsky, if I may say so, you've been quite correct so far in emphasising to her the future. Your idea of an animal is, in my view, a very good one. I really think you should continue to pursue that idea and others like it. There's really no reason to go over the past again. And of course there's every hope for the future now. For my part, I intend to do what I can tonight to see that you're accepted by the people of this city . . .'

'Ah yes, Mr Ryder!' His mood seemed suddenly to change. 'Yes, yes, yes. Tonight, yes, tonight I intend . . . I intend to be magnificent!'

'That's more the spirit, Mr Brodsky.'

'Tonight, I won't compromise, not at all. Yes, all right, they hounded me, I gave up, we ran away, came to this place. But in my heart I never gave up completely. I knew I'd never had a proper chance. And now, at last, tonight . . . I've waited a long time, I won't compromise. This orchestra, they won't believe it, the way I'll stretch them. Mr Ryder, I'm grateful to you. You've been an inspiration. Until this morning I was afraid. Afraid of tonight, afraid what will happen. I'd better be careful, that's what I thought. Hoffman, all of them, go carefully, slowly, that's what they said. Take it slowly at the beginning, they said. Win them over little by little. But this morning, I saw your photograph. In the paper, the Sattler monument. I said that's it, that's it! All the way, take it all the way! Hold back nothing! This orchestra, they won't believe it! And these people, this city, they won't believe it either. Yes, take it all the way! She'll see it then. She'll see me again, she'll see who I really am, who I was all along! The Sattler monument, that's it!'

By this time the ground had levelled and we were walking along the grassy central path of the cemetery. I became aware of some movement behind us and, glancing over my shoulder, saw one of the mourners from the funeral running towards us, signalling with some urgency. As he came nearer, I saw he was a dark, thick-set man of around fifty.

'Mr Ryder, this is a real honour,' he said breathlessly as I turned to him. 'I'm the brother of the widow. She'd be so delighted if you'd join us.'

Looking where he was indicating, I saw we were now quite close to the funeral. Indeed, I could even catch in the breeze the sounds of forlorn sobbing.

'This way, please,' the man said.

'But surely, at such a private moment . . .'

'No, no, please. My sister, everyone, they'd be so honoured. Please, this way.'

Somewhat reluctantly I began to follow. The ground became more marshy as we made our way through the gravestones. I was unable at first to see the widow amidst the rows of dark hunched-over backs, but as we came up to the gathering I spotted her at the front, bowed over the unfilled grave. Her distress seemed so immense, she looked perfectly capable of throwing herself onto the coffin. Perhaps because of this possibility, an old white-haired gentleman was holding her tightly by the arm and shoulder. Behind her, the great majority were sobbing in what appeared to be genuine grief, but even so, the widow's anguished moans remained clearly distinguishable – slow, exhausted, yet shockingly full-chested cries such as might emerge from a victim of prolonged torture. The sound made me want to turn away, but the thick-set man was now gesturing for me to make my way to the front. When I did not move, he whispered none too quietly:

'Mr Ryder, please.'

This caused a few mourners to turn and look at us.

'Mr Ryder, this way.'

The thick-set man took my arm and we began to make our way through the crowd. As we did so, a number of faces turned to me and I heard at least two voices murmur: 'It's Mr Ryder.' By the time we had emerged at the front, much of the sobbing had abated and I could feel many pairs of eyes focused on my back. I adopted a posture of quiet respect, painfully aware that I was dressed in a casual light green jacket with not even a tie. My shirt, moreover, had a breezy orange and yellow pattern. I quickly buttoned the jacket while the thick-set man tried to attract the widow's attention.

'Eva,' he was saying gently. 'Eva.'

Although the white-haired gentleman turned to look at us, the widow gave no sign of having heard. She remained lost in her anguish, her cries falling rhythmically over the grave. Her brother glanced back at me with obvious embarrassment.

'Please,' I whispered, beginning to retreat, 'I'll offer my condolences a little later.'

'No, no, Mr Ryder, please. Just one moment.' The thick-set man now placed a hand on his sister's shoulder and said again, this time with distinct impatience: 'Eva. Eva.'

The widow straightened and finally, controlling her sobs, turned to face us.

'Eva,' her brother said. 'Mr Ryder is here.'

'Mr Ryder?'

'My deepest sympathies, madam,' I said lowering my head solemnly.

The widow continued to stare at me.

'Eva!' her brother hissed.

The widow started, looked at her brother, then at me again.

'Mr Ryder,' she said in a surprisingly composed voice, 'this is truly an honour. Hermann' – she gestured towards the grave – 'is a great admirer of yours.' Then suddenly she was overcome by sobs once more.

'Eva!'

'Madam,' I said quickly, 'I came here merely to express my deepest sympathies. I really am very sorry. But please, madam, everyone, let me now leave you to your grief . . .'

'Mr Ryder,' the widow said, and I saw she had composed herself again. 'This is an honour indeed. I'm sure everyone here would join me in saying that we are greatly, profoundly flattered.'

A chorus of assenting murmurs rose up behind me.

'Mr Ryder,' the widow went on, 'how are you enjoying your stay in our town? I do hope you've found one or two things at least to fascinate you.'

'I'm enjoying myself very much. Everyone here has been so kind. A delightful community. I'm very sorry about . . . about the death.'

'Perhaps you'd care for some refreshments. Some tea or coffee perhaps?'

'No, no, really, please . . .'

'Do at least stay for something to drink. Oh dear, has no one brought any tea or coffee? Nothing?' The widow gazed searchingly into the crowd.

'Really, please, I had no intention of interrupting like this. Please, continue with . . . what you were doing.'

'But you must have something. Somebody, hasn't somebody even a flask of coffee?'

Behind me many voices were consulting one another, and when I glanced over my shoulder I could see people searching through their bags and pockets. The thick-set man was waving to the back of the crowd and then something was passed to him. As he stood examining it, I could see it was a slice of cake in a cellophane wrapper.

'Is this the best we can do?' the thick-set man shouted. 'What is this?'

There was by now quite a hubbub building behind me. One voice in particular was asking angrily: 'Otto, where's that cheese?' Eventually a packet of peppermints was handed to the thick-set man. The latter glared angrily back at the gathering, then turned to present the cake and the peppermints to his sister.

'Really, you're most kind,' I said, 'but I only came because . . .'

'Mr Ryder,' the widow said, her voice now tense with emotion, 'it seems this is all we can offer you. I don't know what Hermann would have said, to be disgraced like this on this of all days. But here we are, I can only apologise. Look, this is all, this is all we can offer, all the hospitality we can offer.'

The voices behind me, which had quietened as the widow had started to speak, now broke into numerous arguments. I could hear someone shouting: 'I didn't! I didn't say anything of the sort!'

Then the white-haired gentleman who earlier had been holding the widow at the graveside stepped forward and bowed to me.

'Mr Ryder,' he said, 'forgive us for the shabby way we are returning this great compliment. You find us, as you can see, woefully unprepared. I can assure you, nevertheless, that each of us here is profoundly grateful. Please, accept the refreshments, inadequate though they are.'

'Mr Ryder, here, please sit down.' The widow was brushing with a handkerchief the surface of a flat marble tomb adjacent to her husband's grave. 'Please.'

I could now see a retreat was out of the question. I moved apologetically towards the tomb the widow had cleaned for me, saying: 'Well, you're all very kind.'

As soon as I sat down on the pale marble, the mourners seemed all to step forward and gather around me.

'Please,' I heard the widow say again. She was standing above me tearing at the cellophane containing the cake. When she had finally got it open, she handed me the cake, wrapper and all. I thanked her and began to eat. It was some sort of fruit cake and I had to make an effort to prevent it crumbling in my hands. It was, moreover, a somewhat generous slice and not something I could devour in a few quick mouthfuls. As I went on eating I had the feeling the mourners were steadily edging closer around me, though when I looked up at them, I saw they were all standing quite still, their eyes lowered respectfully. There was silence for some time, and then the thick-set man coughed and said:

'It's been a very pleasant day.'

'Yes, very pleasant,' I replied, though my mouth was full. 'Very pleasant indeed.'

Then the elderly white-haired gentleman took a step forward and said: 'There are some wonderful walks around our city, Mr

Ryder. Just a little way out of the centre, some splendid rural walks. If you find yourself with a spare hour, I'd be very happy to take you on one of them.'

'Mr Ryder, won't you have a peppermint?'

The widow was holding the opened packet close to my face. I thanked her and put a peppermint in my mouth even though I knew it would go oddly with the cake.

'And as for the city itself,' the white-haired gentleman was saying. 'If you have any interest in medieval architecture, there are a number of houses that would be of immense fascination. Particularly in the Old Town. I'd be very happy to show you around.'

'Really,' I said, 'you're very kind.'

I carried on eating, wishing now to finish the cake as quickly as possible. There was another silence and then the widow sighed and said:

'It's turned out very nice.'

'Yes,' I said, 'the weather has been marvellous here ever since my arrival.'

This was met by a general murmur of approval all round, some people even laughing politely as though I had made a witticism. I forced what remained of the cake into my mouth and brushed the crumbs from my hands.

'Look,' I said, 'you've all been so kind. But now, please, go on with the ceremony.'

'Another peppermint, Mr Ryder. It's all we can offer.' The widow again thrust the packet towards my face.

It was then that the realisation suddenly dawned on me that at this precise moment the widow was feeling the most intense hatred towards me. Indeed, it occurred to me that, polite though they all were, virtually everyone else present – the thick-set man included – was bitterly resenting my presence. Curiously, just as this thought flashed through my head, a voice from the back said, not loudly but quite distinctly:

'Why's he so special anyway? This is Hermann's time.'

There was an uneasy rumble of voices and at least two shocked whispers of: 'Who said that?' The white-haired gentleman coughed, then said:

'The canals are also very beautiful to walk beside.'

369

'What's so special about him anyway? Interrupting everything.'

'Shut up, you fool!' someone retorted. 'A fine time to disgrace us all.'

A number of voices growled support for this last utterance, but now a second voice had started to shout something aggressively.

'Mr Ryder, please.' The widow was again thrusting the peppermints at me.

'No, really . . .'

'Please. Take another.'

A furious exchange involving four or five people started at the back of the crowd. A voice was shouting: 'He'll take us too far. The Sattler monument, that's going too far.'

Then more and more people were starting to shout at each other, and I could sense a full-scale row about to erupt.

'Mr Ryder' – the thick-set man was bending down to me – 'please ignore them. They've always disgraced the family. Always. We're ashamed of them. Oh yes, we're ashamed. Please don't double our shame by listening.'

'But surely . . .' I began to stand up, but felt something push me down again. I then saw the widow had a hand grasped around my shoulder.

'Please relax, Mr Ryder,' she said sharply. 'Please finish your refreshments.'

There were now arguments raging everywhere and towards the back some people seemed to be jostling one another. The widow was continuing to hold me down by the shoulder, looking at the crowd with an expression of proud defiance.

'I don't care, I don't care,' a voice was shouting. 'We're better off the way we are!'

There was more jostling, and then a fat young man pushed his way out to the front. His face was very round and at this moment he was clearly worked up. He glared at me, then shouted:

'It's all very well your coming here like this. Standing in front of the Sattler monument! Smiling like that! Then you'll move on. It's not that simple for those of us who have to live here. The Sattler monument!'

The round-faced young man did not look like someone accustomed to making bold utterances and there seemed no doubting the sincerity of his emotions. I felt a little taken aback and for a moment found myself unable to respond. Then, as the round-faced young man began another volley of accusations, I felt something inside me give way. It occurred to me that I had some-how, unaccountably, made a miscalculation the previous day in choosing to be photographed in front of the Sattler monument. At the time, certainly, it had seemed the most telling way of sending out an appropriate signal to the citizens of this city. I had, of course, been all too aware of the pros and cons involved – I could recall how at breakfast that morning I had sat carefully weighing these up – but I now saw the possibility that there was even more to the business of the Sattler monument than I had supposed.

Encouraged by the round-faced young man, a few more people had begun to shout in my direction. Others were trying to restrain them, though not with the urgency one might have expected. Then, amidst all the shouting, I became aware of a new voice, speaking gently just behind my shoulder. It was a male voice, cultured and calm, which struck me as vaguely familiar.

'Mr Ryder,' it was saying. 'Mr Ryder. The concert hall. You really ought to be on your way. They're waiting for you there. Really, you must allow yourself plenty of time to inspect the facilities and conditions . . .'

Then the voice was drowned out as another particularly noisy exchange erupted in front of me. The round-faced young man pointed at me and began to say something over and over.

Then quite suddenly a hush descended over the crowd. At first I thought the mourners had finally calmed down and were waiting for me to speak. But then I noticed that the round-faced young man – indeed, everyone – was staring at a spot somewhere above my head. It was a few seconds before it occurred to me to twist round, and then I saw that Brodsky had stepped up onto a tomb and was standing directly over me.

It was perhaps simply the angle at which I was looking up at him – he was leaning forward slightly so that I could see against a vast background of sky much of the underside of his jaw – but there was something strikingly commanding about him. He seemed to loom above us like a huge statue, his open hands poised in the air. In fact, he was surveying the gathering before him in much the way I imagined he would an orchestra in the

371

seconds before he began to conduct. Something about him suggested a strange authority over the very emotions which had just been running riot in front of him – that he could cause them to rise and fall as he pleased. For a little while longer, the silence continued. Then a solitary voice shouted:

'What do *you* want? You old drunk!'

Perhaps the person had intended this cry to set off another round of shouting. As it was, no one showed any sign of having heard it.

'You old drunk!' the person tried again, but already the conviction was evaporating from his voice.

Then there was silence as all eyes stared up at Brodsky. After what seemed an inordinate length of time, Brodsky said:

'If that's what you want to call me, fine. We'll see. We'll see who I am. In these days, weeks, months to come. We'll see if that's all I am.'

He had spoken unhurriedly, with a calm power that did nothing to undermine his initial impact. The mourners went on staring up at him, seemingly spellbound. Then Brodsky said tenderly:

'Someone you loved has died. This is a precious moment.'

I felt the ends of his raincoat brush the back of my head, and I realised he was extending a hand down towards the widow.

'This is a precious time. Come. Caress your wound now. It will be there for the rest of your life. But caress it now, while it's raw and bleeding. Come.'

Brodsky stepped off the tomb, his hand still extended to the widow. She took it with a dreamy look, and then Brodsky placed his other hand behind her and began gently to lead her back to the edge of the open grave.

'Come,' I could hear him saying quietly. 'Come now.'

They moved slowly through the fallen leaves until she was once again at the graveside looking down at the coffin. Then, as the widow began once more to sob, Brodsky withdrew carefully and took a step away from her. By this time there were many others weeping again, and I could see that in no time things would be as they had been prior to my arrival. For the moment, in any case, all attention had turned from me and I decided to take the opportunity to slip away.

I rose to my feet quietly and had managed to make my way past several graves when I heard someone walking close behind me. A voice said:

'Indeed, Mr Ryder, it's high time you got to the concert hall. One never can tell what adjustments might be called for.'

Turning, I recognised Pedersen, the elderly councillor I had met in the cinema on my first evening. I realised, furthermore, that it had been his voice I had heard speaking softly behind my shoulder earlier on.

'Ah, Mr Pedersen,' I said as he fell in step beside me. 'I'm rather glad you reminded me about the concert hall. With feelings running so high back there, I must confess, I'd started to lose track of the time.'

'Indeed and so had I,' Pedersen said with a small laugh. 'And I too have a meeting to get to. Hardly of comparable importance, but nevertheless, it has to do with this evening.'

We came to the grassy path running through the middle of the cemetery and both paused.

'Perhaps you might assist me, Mr Pedersen,' I said, looking about me. 'I've arranged for a car to take me to the concert hall, it should be waiting for me. It's just that I'm not certain how to get back down to the road.'

'I'll be pleased to show you, Mr Ryder. Please follow me.'

We began to walk again, away from the hill down which I had come with Brodsky. The sun was now setting over the valley and the shadows cast by the gravestones had noticeably lengthened. As we walked on, I sensed on at least two occasions that Pedersen was about to speak, but then he seemed to change his mind. In the end, I said to him matter-of-factly:

'Some of those people just now. They seemed extremely exercised. I mean, about those photographs of me in the newspaper.'

'Well you see, sir,' Pedersen said with a sigh, 'it's the Sattler monument. Max Sattler has today as strong a hold on people's emotions as he ever did.'

'I suppose you too have some views. I mean, about those photographs in front of the Sattler monument.'

Pedersen smiled awkwardly and avoided my gaze. 'How can I explain it?' he said eventually. 'It's so hard for an outsider to understand. Even an expert like yourself. It's not at all clear why

373

Max Sattler – why that whole episode in the city's history – has come to mean so much to people here. On paper, it hardly amounts to anything very significant. And yes, it all happened almost a century ago. But you see, Mr Ryder, as you've no doubt discovered, Sattler has gained a place in the *imaginations* of citizens here. His role, if you like, has become mythical. Sometimes he's feared, sometimes he's abhorred. And at other times, his memory is worshipped. How can I explain it? Let me put it to you like this. There's a certain man I know, a good friend. Getting on in years now, but he's not had a bad life. He's well respected here, still plays an active role in civic affairs. Not a bad life at all. But this man, every now and then, he looks back over this life he's led and wonders if he didn't perhaps let certain things slip by. He wonders how things might have been if he'd been, well, a little less *timid*. A little less timid and a little more passionate.'

Pedersen gave a small laugh. The path had now curved round and I could see up ahead the dark iron gateway of the cemetery.

'Then he might, you know, start to think back,' Pedersen went on. 'Back to some pivotal point somewhere in his youth, before he became so set in his ways. He might recall, let us say, a moment when some woman tried to seduce him. Of course, he didn't allow it, he was much too proper. Or perhaps it was cowardice. Perhaps he was too young, who knows? He wonders if he'd taken another path then, if he'd been just a little more confident about . . . about love and passion. You know how it is, Mr Ryder. You know the way old men dream sometimes, wondering how it would have been if some key moment had gone another way. Well it can also be like that for a town, for a community. Every now and then, it looks back, looks back at its history and asks itself: "What if? What might we have become by now if we'd only . . ." Ah, if we'd only what, Mr Ryder? Allowed Max Sattler to take us where he wished? Would we now be something else altogether? Would we be today a city like Antwerp? Like Stuttgart? I honestly don't think so, Mr Ryder. There are, you see, certain things about this town, certain things that are so embedded. They will never change, not in five, six, seven generations. Sattler, in practical terms, was an irrelevance. Just a man with wild dreams. He would never have changed anything fundamentally. It's just the same as with this friend of mine. He's the way he is. No experience, however crucial, would have changed that for him. Now, Mr Ryder, here we are. If you go down these steps, you'll find yourself back on the road.'

We had passed through the tall iron gates of the cemetery and were now standing in a large, carefully landscaped garden. Pedersen was pointing towards a hedge on my left behind which I could see some stone steps commencing a curving descent. I hesitated a moment, then said:

'Mr Pedersen, you've been exceedingly polite. But let me assure you, whenever the possibility arises that I've made an error of judgement, I'm not one to turn and hide from it. In any case, sir, this is something a person in my position has to come to terms with. That's to say, during the course of any one day I'll be called upon to make many important decisions, and the truth is, the most I can do is to weigh up the evidence available at the time as best I can and forge on. Sometimes, inevitably, yes, I'll be guilty of a miscalculation. How could it be otherwise? This is something I've long come to terms with. And as you can see, when such a thing occurs, my only concern is how I might make good the error at the first opportunity. So please, feel free to speak frankly. If it's your view that I've made a mistake in posing in front of the Sattler monument, then please say so.'

Pedersen looked uncomfortable. He gazed back towards a mausoleum in the distance, then said: 'Well, Mr Ryder, this is simply my opinion.'

'I'd be very keen to hear it, sir.'

'Well, since you ask. Yes, sir. To be frank, I was rather disappointed when I saw the newspaper this morning. In my opinion, sir, as I've just explained, it's simply not in this city's nature to embrace the extremes of Sattler. He holds an attraction for certain people *precisely because* he's so distant, a piece of local myth. Reintroduce him as a serious prospect . . . then frankly, sir, people here will panic. They will recoil. They will suddenly find themselves clinging to what they know, never mind what misery it has already brought them. You asked my view, sir. I feel that the introducing of Max Sattler into these discussions has seriously undermined the possibility of progress. But of course there is still tonight. In the end, it will all hinge on what happens tonight. On what you will say. And on what Mr Brodsky will show us. And as you point out, there's no one more adept than yourself at recovering lost ground.' For a moment he appeared to be pondering something quietly to himself. Then he shook his head gravely. 'Mr Ryder, the best thing you can do now, sir, is to get to the concert hall. Tonight, everything must go according to plan.'

'Yes, yes, you're quite right,' I said. 'I'm sure my car's at this moment waiting to take me there. Mr Pedersen, I'm grateful to you for your frankness.'

26

The steps descended steeply past tall hedges and shrubs. I then found myself standing beside the road, looking at the sun setting across the field on the opposite side. The stairway had brought me out at a point where the road curved sharply, but when I followed it round a little the view widened. I could then see up ahead the hill I had recently climbed – the outline of the little hut was visible against the sky – and Hoffman's car waiting down in the lay-by where he had dropped me earlier.

I walked on towards the car, my thoughts filled with the exchange I had just had with Pedersen. I remembered the time I had first met him in the cinema when his esteem for me had been obvious in his every word and gesture. Now, for all his good manners, it was clear he was deeply disappointed with me. I found this thought oddly troubling and, as I continued along the roadside gazing at the sunset, began to feel more and more annoyed that I had not proceeded with greater caution over the matter of the Sattler monument. It was true – as I had pointed out to Pedersen – that my decision had seemed to represent the wisest course open to me at the time. Nevertheless, I could not avoid the niggling feeling that for all the limitations on my time, for all the enormous pressures impinging on me, I should some- how by that point have been better informed. And now, even at this late stage, with the evening's event virtually upon me, there were still certain aspects to these local issues that were far from clear. I saw now what a mistake it had been to miss the Citizens' Mutual Support Group meeting earlier in the day – and all for the sake of a practice session that had proved far from necessary.

By the time I came up to Hoffman's car, I was feeling tired and disheartened. Hoffman was behind the wheel, writing busily in a notebook, and did not notice me until I had opened the passenger door.

'Ah, Mr Ryder,' he exclaimed, quickly putting his notebook away. 'Your practice went well, I trust?'

'Oh yes.'

'And the facilities?' He hurriedly started up the car. 'They were to your satisfaction?'

'Excellent, Mr Hoffman, thank you. But now I must get to the concert hall as quickly as possible. One never knows what sorts of adjustment may be necessary.'

'Of course. In fact, I too have to hurry to the concert hall just now.' He glanced at his watch. 'I must check the catering facilities. When I was there an hour ago, I'm pleased to say everything was going very smoothly. But of course, havoc can set in so rapidly.'

Hoffman steered the car back onto the road and we drove for a few minutes without talking. The road, though somewhat busier than on the outward journey, was still far from crowded and Hoffman quickly built up a good speed. I gazed out at the fields and tried to relax, but found my mind returning to the evening ahead. Then I heard Hoffman say:

'Mr Ryder, I hope you won't mind my bringing this up. Just a small matter. No doubt you've forgotten.' He gave a short laugh and shook his head.

'Which matter is this, Mr Hoffman?'

'I meant simply my wife's albums. You might recall I told you about them when we first met. My wife, she's been such a devoted admirer for so many years . . .'

'Yes, of course, I remember very well. She has prepared some albums of cuttings of my career. Yes, yes, I hadn't forgotten. In fact, throughout all these busy events, it's something I've been looking forward to very much.'

'She's gone about the matter with enormous devotion, sir. Over many years. Sometimes she's taken huge trouble to acquire certain back issues of journals or newspapers containing important articles about you. Indeed, sir, her dedication has been marvellous to witness. It really would mean so much to her . . .'

'Mr Hoffman, I have every intention of inspecting the albums before long. As I say, I'm very much looking forward to doing so. However, just at this moment, I'd much appreciate it if we could take this opportunity to discuss, well, certain aspects concerning this evening.'

'As you wish, sir. But I can assure you, everything is well in hand. You have nothing to be concerned about.'

'Yes, yes, I'm sure. Nevertheless, since the event is now so close, surely it would be sensible to turn our minds to it a little. For instance, Mr Hoffman, there's the matter of my parents. While I have every confidence the people of this city will look after them well, the fact remains they're both in fragile health and so I'd greatly appreciate . . .'

'Ah, of course, I perfectly understand. Indeed, may I say I find it most touching that you should display such concern over your parents. I'm only too happy to assure you that very thorough arrangements have been made to ensure their comfort at all times. A group of very charming and able local ladies has been detailed to look after them throughout their stay. And as for this evening's event, we have planned something a little special for them, a little flourish I trust will appeal to you. As you no doubt know, our local company, Seeler Brothers, was renowned for two centuries for its carriage-making, once supplying many distin-guished customers as far afield as France and England. There are some splendid examples of the Seeler Brothers' craft still in the city and it was my fancy your parents would like to arrive at the concert hall in a particularly distinguished specimen, for which we have prepared a pair of beautifully groomed thorough-breds. Perhaps you can imagine the scene, Mr Ryder. By that time in the evening the clearing in front of the concert hall will be bathed in lights, and all the prominent members of our com-munity will be congregating there, laughing and greeting one another, all of them wonderfully dressed, much excitement in the air. Cars, of course, are unable to reach the clearing, so people will be arriving on foot from out of the trees. And then once a substantial crowd has assembled outside the hall – can you pic-ture this, sir? – there'll come from the darkness of the woods the sound of approaching horses. The ladies and gentlemen, they'll stop talking and turn their heads. The sound of hooves will get louder, coming all the time closer to the pool of light. And then they will burst into view, the splendid horses, the driver in tails and top hat, the gleaming carriage of the Seeler Brothers carrying your most charming parents! Can you imagine the excitement, the anticipation that will go through the crowd at that moment?

379

Of course, your parents will not be required to ride in the carriage for long. Just for that central avenue through the woods. And I assure you, the carriage is a masterpiece of luxury. They will find it as sheltered and comfortable as any limousine. Naturally, there will be a slight rocking motion, but that, in a first-class carriage, becomes a positively soothing feature. I hope you can picture it, sir. I must confess, I had originally conceived this whole arrangement for your own arrival, but then realised you would prefer to be well ensconced backstage by that point in the proceedings. And after all, one wishes nothing to dilute the impact of your appearance on the stage. Then, when we heard the very happy news that your parents would also be honouring this town, I thought immediately: "Ah, the ideal solution!" Yes, sir, your parents' arrival will set the mood very nicely. We do not, of course, expect your parents to stand about thereafter. They'll be led straight into their special seats in the auditorium, and this will signal to everyone else it is time they too were beginning to take their seats. And then, shortly after that, the formal part of the evening will commence. We will begin with a short piano recital by my son, Stephan. Ha ha! I admit this is something of an indulgence on my part. But Stephan was so eager for a platform and at the time I perhaps foolishly believed . . . Well, there's no point in going into that now. Stephan will give a light piano recital, simply to create a certain atmosphere. For this part of the proceedings, the lights will remain up, to give people the chance to find their seats, greet one another, chat in the aisles and so on. Then, once everyone has settled, the lights will dim. There will follow a few formal words of welcome. Then, in time, the orchestra will come out, take their places, tune their instruments. And then, after a certain pause, Mr Brodsky will emerge. He will . . . he will then perform. When he has finished, and there is – let us hope, let us *assume* it – there is thunderous applause, and Mr Brodsky has taken many bows, there will follow a small break. Not an intermission exactly, we will not allow the audience to leave their seats. But a short period of five minutes or so, when the lights will go up again and people will have a chance to collect their thoughts. Then, while people are still busy exchanging their views, Mr von Winterstein will appear on stage in front of the curtain. He will give a simple introduction. No more than a few minutes – what introduction is necessary, after all? Then he'll retreat to the wings. The whole auditorium will be plunged into darkness. And now we come to the moment, sir. The moment of your appearance. Indeed, this is a matter I'd been meaning to discuss with you, since to some degree your co-operation is essential. You see, sir, our concert hall is extremely beautiful but, being very old, it naturally lacks many facilities one would take for granted in a more modern building. The catering facilities, as I believe I've already mentioned, are far from adequate, obliging us to rely heavily on those of the hotel. But my point is this, sir. I have borrowed from our sports centre – which is indeed very modern and well-equipped – the electronic scoreboard that usually hangs over the indoor arena. Just at this moment, the arena is looking very sorry for itself! Ugly black wires dangling down from the space the scoreboard usually occupies. Well, sir, to return to my point. Mr von Winterstein will retreat to the wings after his brief introduction. The whole auditorium, for a single moment, will be plunged into blackness, during which time the curtains will open. And then a single spot will come on, revealing you standing at the centre of the stage at the lectern. At that moment, obviously, the audience will burst into excited applause. Then, once the applause has subsided, before you have uttered a word – of course, this is so long as you are agreeable – a voice will boom out across the auditorium, pronouncing the first question. The voice will be that of Horst Jannings, this city's most senior actor. He will be up in the sound box speaking through the public address system. Horst has a fine rich baritone and he will read out each question slowly. And as he does so – this is my little idea, sir! – the words will be spelt out simultaneously on the electronic scoreboard fixed directly above your head. You see, until this point, owing to the darkness, no one would have been aware of the scoreboard. It will be as though the words are appearing in the air above you. Ha ha! Forgive me, but I thought the effect would serve both the drama of the occasion and at the same time bring added clarity to it. The words on the scoreboard, dare I say, will help some of those present to remember the gravely important nature of the issues you are addressing. After all, it could easily be that in all this excitement certain people will forget to concentrate. Well, you see, sir, with my little idea, there'll be little chance of that. Each question will be there in front of them, spelt out in giant letters. So then, sir, with your approval this is what we shall do. The first question will be announced, spelt out on the scoreboard, you will give your reply from the lectern, and, once you have finished, Horst will read out the next question and so on. The only thing we would ask, Mr Ryder, is that at the end of each reply, you leave the lectern and come to the edge of the stage and bow. The reason for my requesting this is twofold. Firstly, because of the temporary nature of the electronic scoreboard, there are inevitably certain technical difficulties. It will take the electrician several seconds to load each question into the scoreboard, and then there will be an additional lag of fifteen to twenty seconds before the words start to appear on the board. So you see, sir, by moving to the edge of the stage and bowing, thus provoking inevitable applause, we will avoid a series of awkward pauses punctuating the proceedings. Then, just as each round of applause is dying, Horst's voice and the scoreboard will announce the next question, giving you ample time to return to the lectern. There is, sir, a further reason this strategy recommends itself. Your coming to the edge of the stage and bowing will tell the electrician, very unambiguously, that you have completed your answer. After all, we wish to avoid at all costs a situation in which, for instance, the scoreboard starts to print out the next question while you are still speaking. But you see, as I've explained, because of the time-lag problems this could all too easily occur. All it would take, after all, is for you to appear to finish – for you merely to pause – only for some final pertinent point to occur to you. You proceed to make this final point, but meanwhile the electrician has already started . . . Ha! What a disaster! Let us not even contemplate it! So, sir, allow me then to suggest this simple but effective device of your coming to the edge of the stage at the end of each answer. In fact, sir, to give the electrician a few extra seconds to load the next question, it would be enormously helpful if you could in addition give some sort of inconspicuous signal as you approach the end of each reply. Perhaps, let us say, a modest shrug of the shoulder. Of course, Mr Ryder, all these arrangments are subject to your approval. If you're unhappy about any of these ideas, please speak plainly.'

As Hoffman had been talking, an all too vivid picture of the evening ahead had started to form in my mind. I could hear the applause, the buzz of the electronic scoreboard above my head. I saw myself performing the little shrug, then moving into the blinding lights towards the edge of the stage. And a curious, dreamy sense of unreality came over me as I realised just how unprepared I was. I saw Hoffman waiting for my response and murmured wearily:

'It all sounds splendid, Mr Hoffman. You've thought the whole thing out very well.'

'Ah. So you approve. All the details, they are all . . .'

'Yes, yes,' I said, waving my hand impatiently. 'The electronic scoreboard, the walking to the edge of the stage, the shrugs, yes, yes, yes. It's all very well thought out.'

'Ah.' For a second Hoffman continued to look uncertain, but then seemed to conclude I had spoken sincerely. 'Splendid, splendid. Then everything's settled.' He nodded to himself and fell silent for a while. Then I heard him mutter to himself again, not taking his eyes off the road: 'Yes, yes. Everything's settled.'

For the next several minutes, Hoffman said nothing further to me, though he continued to mutter to himself under his breath. There was now a pink hue over much of the sky, and as the road turned this way and that through the farmland the sun would appear in the windscreen before us, filling the car with its glow and obliging us to squint. Then at one point, as I was gazing out of my window, I heard Hoffman gasp suddenly:

'An ox! An ox, an ox, an ox!'

Although this too had been uttered under his breath, I was sufficiently startled to turn and look at him. I saw then that Hoffman was still lost in his own world, staring ahead of him and nodding to himself. I looked around at the fields we were passing but, although I saw sheep in many of the fields, could see no sign of an ox. I had a vague recollection of Hoffman doing something similar once before on a car journey with me, but then soon lost interest in the matter.

Before long we found ourselves back in the city streets and the traffic quickly slowed to a crawl. The pavements were crowded with people making their way home from work and many shop windows had already turned on their lights for the night. Now that I was back in the city, I felt some of my confidence returning. It occurred to me that once I reached the concert hall, once I had had the chance to stand on the stage and survey the surroundings, many things would fall into place.

'Indeed, sir,' Hoffman suddenly said, 'everything is going to order. Nothing at all for you to worry about. This town, you'll see, will do you proud. And as for Mr Brodsky, I continue to have every confidence in him.'

I decided I should at least make a show of being optimistic. 'Yes,' I said cheerfully, 'I'm sure Mr Brodsky will be splendid tonight. He certainly seemed in fine form just now.'

'Oh?' Hoffman gave me a puzzled look. 'You've seen him recently?'

'Up at the cemetery just now. As I say, he seemed very confident . . .'

'Mr Brodsky was at the cemetery? Now I wonder what he was doing up there.'

Hoffman gave me a searching stare, and I thought for a moment about recounting the whole story of the funeral and Brodsky's impressive intervention. But then in the end I could not find the energy and said simply:

'I believe he has an appointment there in a little while. With Miss Collins.'

'With Miss Collins? Good gracious. What on earth can this be about?'

I looked at him, somewhat surprised by his reaction. 'It seems a reconciliation is becoming a genuine possibility,' I said. 'If such a happy conclusion does ensue, then Mr Hoffman, that will be something else you could quite legitimately take much credit for.'

'Yes, yes.' Hoffman was thinking something over, a frown forming on his face. 'Mr Brodsky is at the cemetery now? Waiting for Miss Collins? How curious. Very curious.'

As we went further into the city centre, the traffic became ever more dense, until at one point, in a narrow back street, we came to a standstill. Hoffman, whose manner had continued to grow increasingly troubled, now turned to me again.

'Mr Ryder, there's something I must attend to. That is to say, I'll still be joining you at the concert hall in due course, but just now . . .' He looked at his watch with distinct signs of panic. 'You see, I must attend to . . . to something . . .' Then he gripped the wheel and fixed me in a stare. 'Mr Ryder, the fact is this. Owing to this wretched one-way system and this diabolical evening traffic, it will take us some time yet to reach the concert hall in this vehicle. Whereas on foot . . .' He suddenly pointed past me out of the window. 'There it is. Before your very eyes. No more than a few minutes' walk. Yes, sir, that roof there.'

I could see a large dome-shaped roof looming above the other buildings in the mid-distance. Certainly, it did not appear to be more than three or four blocks away.

'Mr Hoffman,' I said, 'if you have something urgent to attend to, I'm quite happy to make my way on foot.'

'Really? You'd forgive me?'

The traffic moved forward a few more inches then came to a standstill again.

'In fact, I'd welcome the walk,' I said. 'It looks a pleasant evening. And as you say, it's only a short distance on foot.'

'This infernal one-way system! We might sit in this car for another hour! Mr Ryder, I'd be enormously grateful if you'd forgive me. But you see, there's something I must . . . I must see to . . .'

'Yes, yes, of course. I'll get out here. You've been most kind as it is, driving me about like this at such a busy time. I'm most grateful.'

'You'll be approaching the concert hall from the rear. It's a case of just proceeding on towards that roof. You can't miss it if you keep the roof in view.'

'Please don't worry. I'll have no trouble.' Cutting short his apologies, I thanked him again and stepped out onto the pavement.

I soon found myself wandering down a narrow street past a row of specialist bookshops, then past some pleasant-looking tourist hotels. It was not at all difficult to keep the domed roof in view and for a little while I felt thankful for the chance to walk in the fresh air.

By the time I had gone two or three blocks, however, a number of troubling thoughts had entered my head which I found I could not dislodge. For one thing, I could see there was more than a chance the question-and-answer session would fail to go smoothly. Indeed, if the intensity of emotions displayed at the cemetery was anything to go by, the possibility of ugly scenes could not be ruled out. Moreover, if the question-and-answer session went badly enough, it was conceivable that my parents, witnessing the scene with mounting horror and embarrassment, would demand to be taken out of the auditorium. In other words, they would leave before I had had the chance to get to the piano, and then it would be anyone's guess when they would ever again come to hear me perform. Even worse, if things went very badly indeed, it was not impossible one or the other of them would suffer a seizure. I felt as confident as ever that my mother and my father would be united in astonishment within seconds of my starting to play, but meanwhile the question-and-answer session stood massively in my way.

I realised I had become so preoccupied I had allowed the domed roof to disappear behind some buildings. I thought little of this at first, assuming it would come back into view soon enough. But then, as I walked on, the street grew even narrower, while the buildings around me seemed all to be six or seven storeys high, so that I could hardly see any sky, let alone the domed roof. I decided to look for a parallel street, but then, once I had taken the next turning, I found myself wandering from one tiny side-street to the next, quite possibly going in circles, the concert hall not visible anywhere.

After several minutes of this, a sense of panic began to engulf me and I thought about stopping someone to ask directions. But then it occurred to me this would be unwise. All the time I had been walking, people had been turning – sometimes even stopping dead on the pavement – to look at me. I had been vaguely aware of this, though in my concern to find my way I had not given it much thought. But I now saw that, with the evening's event so close, and with so much hanging in the balance, it would not do for me to be seen wandering the streets, obviously lost and uncertain. With an effort, I straightened my posture and adopted the demeanour of someone who, with all his affairs well in hand, was taking a relaxing stroll around the town. I forced myself to slow my pace and smiled pleasantly at anyone who stared my way.

Finally I turned another corner and spotted the concert hall before me, closer than ever. The street I now entered was broader, with brightly lit cafés and shops on either side. The domed roof was no more than a block or two away, just beyond where the street curved out of view.

I felt not only relief, but also suddenly much better about the whole evening ahead. The feeling I had had earlier – that many things would fall into place once I reached the venue and was able to stand on the stage – came back to me and I proceeded down the street with something approaching enthusiasm.

But then, as I came round the bend, an odd sight greeted me. A little way ahead was a brick wall running across my path – in fact, across the entire breadth of the street. My first thought was that a railway line ran behind the wall, but then I noticed how the higher storeys of the buildings on either side of the street continued unbroken above the wall and on into the distance. While the wall aroused my curiosity, I did not immediately see it as a problem, assuming that once I got up to it I would find an arch or subway leading me through to the other side. The domed roof, in any case, was now very near, lit up by spotlights against the darkening sky.

It was only when I was virtually right up to the wall, it dawned on me there was no way to get past. The pavements on both sides of the street simply came to a dead stop at the brickwork. I looked around in bewilderment, then walked the length of the wall to the opposite pavement, unable quite to accept there was not somewhere a doorway, or even a small hole through which to crawl. I found nothing, and eventually, after standing helplessly before the wall for a time, I waved to a passer-by – a middle-aged woman emerging from a nearby gift shop – saying:

'Excuse me, I wish to get to the concert hall. How can I get past this wall?'

The woman seemed surprised by my question. 'Oh no,' she said. 'You can't get past the wall. Of course you can't. It completely seals the street.'

'But this is extremely annoying,' I said. 'I have to get to the concert hall.'

'I suppose it *is* annoying,' the woman said as though she had never before considered the matter. 'When I saw you staring at it just now, sir, I just assumed you were a tourist. The wall's quite a tourist attraction, as you can see.'

She pointed to a spinner of postcards in front of the gift shop. Sure enough, in the light from the doorway, I could see postcard after postcard proudly featuring the wall.

'But what on earth's the point in having a wall in a place like this?' I asked, my voice rising despite myself. 'It really is monstrous. What purpose can it possibly serve?'

'I do sympathise. To an outsider, particularly to one trying to get somewhere in a hurry, it must be an annoyance. I suppose it's what you'd call a folly. It was built by some eccentric person at the end of the last century. Of course it's rather odd, but it's been famous ever since. In the summer, this whole area where we're standing now, it gets completely full of tourists. Americans, Japanese, all taking photographs of it.'

'This is nonsensical,' I said furiously. 'Please tell me the quickest way to reach the concert hall.'

'The concert hall, sir? Well, it's quite a long way if you're thinking of going on foot. Of course, we're very near it just now' – she glanced up at the roof – 'but in practical terms, that doesn't mean very much because of the wall.'

'This is quite ridiculous!' I had lost all patience. 'I'll find my own way. You're obviously quite unable to appreciate that a person might be very busy, working on a tight schedule, and simply can't afford to dawdle about the town for hours. In fact, if I may say so, this wall is quite typical of this town. Utterly preposterous obstacles everywhere. And what do you do? Do you all get annoyed? Do you demand it's pulled down immediately so that people can go about their business? No, you put up with it for the best part of a century. You make postcards of it and believe it's charming. This brick wall charming? What a monstrosity! I may well use this wall as a symbol, I've a good mind to, in my speech tonight! It's just as well for you I've already composed much of what I'm going to say in my head and so am naturally reluctant to change things too much at this late stage. Good evening!'

I left the woman and began rapidly to retrace my steps back up the street, determined not to let such an absurd setback destroy my renewed sense of confidence. But then as I continued to walk, conscious all the time of the concert hall getting further and further away, I could feel my earlier despondency returning to me. The street seemed much longer than I remembered it, and then when I finally reached the end I found myself getting lost again in the network of narrow little alleys.

After several further minutes of useless wandering, I suddenly felt unable to go on and halted. Noticing I had stopped beside a pavement café, I collapsed into a chair at the nearest table and immediately felt what remained of my energy draining away. I was vaguely conscious that around me the darkness was falling, that an electric light was shining somewhere behind my head, that this same light was in all likelihood illuminating me to passers-by and fellow customers, but somehow I still could not find the urge to straighten my posture or even nominally to disguise my dejection. In time, a waiter appeared. I ordered a coffee from him, then went on staring down at the shadow cast by my head over the metallic surface of the table. All the possibilities that had disturbed me earlier concerning the evening ahead now began to crowd all at once into my mind. Above all, the depressing idea kept returning to me that my decision to be photographed before the Sattler monument had irrevocably damaged my authority in this town; that it had left me with a daunting amount of ground to make up and that anything less than an utterly commanding performance during the question-and-answer session would result in catastrophic consequences all round. In fact, for a moment, I felt so overwhelmed by these thoughts I was on the brink of tears. But then I became aware of a hand on my back and someone repeating gently above me: 'Mr Ryder. Mr Ryder.'

I assumed it was the waiter returned with my coffee and gestured for him to place it before me. But the voice continued to call my name, and looking up I found Gustav regarding me with a concerned expression.

'Oh, hello,' I said.

'Good evening, sir. How are you? I thought it was you, but I wasn't sure so I came over. Are you all right, sir? We're all over there, all the boys, won't you come and join us? The boys would be so thrilled.'

I looked around me and saw I was sitting on the edge of a square. Although there was a single street lamp at its centre, the square was largely in darkness, so that the figures of the people moving across it appeared to be little more than shadows. Gustav was indicating to the opposite side where I could see another café, somewhat larger than the one I was now patronising, its open doorway and windows throwing out a warm light. Even at this distance, I could make out a lot of lively activity inside, and strains of fiddle music and laughter came drifting out to us through the evening. Only then did it dawn on me I was in fact sitting in the Old Town by the main square, looking over to the Hungarian Café. As I continued to glance about me, I could hear Gustav saying:

'The boys, sir, they've been making me tell them over and over again. About, you know, sir, what you said, about how you *agreed*. I'd already told them five, six times, but they wanted it all again. They'd barely stopped laughing and slapping each other about from the last time, but there they were again, saying: "Come on, Gustav, we know you haven't told us everything yet. What *exactly* did Mr Ryder say?" "I've told you," I was saying to them. "I've told you. You know perfectly well." But they wanted to hear it all again and I dare say they'll want to hear it all several times more before the evening's out. Of course, sir, although I adopt this weary tone each time they ask, naturally, that's just for effect. In truth, of course, I'm every bit as thrilled as any of them and could happily repeat our conversation from this morning over and over. It's so good to see them wearing such expressions again. Your promise, sir, it's brought new hope, a new *youth* to their faces. Even Igor was smiling, laughing at some of the jokes! I can't remember when I last saw them like this. Oh yes, sir, I'd be very happy to go over it many more times yet. Whenever I get to that moment, when you said: "Very well, I'd be happy to say something on your behalf," whenever I get to that part, you should see them, sir! Cheering and laughing, slapping each other about, it's been so long since I've seen them like this. So there we were, sir, drinking our beers and talking about your great generosity, talking about how after all these years portering would change for ever after tonight, yes, while we were in the midst of saying all this I happened to look out and I saw you, sir. The proprietor, as you can see, he's left the door open. It gives the place a much better atmosphere, to be able to see right across the square as the night's coming in. Well, there I was looking across the square and I was thinking to myself: "I wonder who that poor soul is sitting by himself over there." But my eyes aren't so good, you see, and I wasn't aware it was actually you, sir. Then Karl, he said to me in a sort of whisper, he must have sensed it wouldn't be a good idea to say it out loud, he said to me: "I'm probably wrong, but isn't that Mr Ryder himself? Over there?" And then I looked again and thought, yes, that's possible. What on earth could he be doing out there in the cold and looking so sad? I'll go and see if it really is him. Let me say, sir, Karl was very discreet. None of the others heard what he said, so aside from him, they won't know why I've slipped out, though I dare say some of them might now be looking this way wondering what I'm up to. But really, sir, are you all right? You look like you've something on your mind.'

'Oh . . .' I gave a sigh and wiped my face. 'It's nothing. It's just that all this travelling, all this responsibility. Now and again it just gets . . .' I trailed off with a small laugh.

'But why sit out here like this by yourself, sir? It's a chilly evening, and in only your jacket. And this after my saying to you how welcome you'd be to join us whenever you wished at the Hungarian Café. Did you think you'd be welcomed with anything less than huge enthusiasm if you'd come over to us? Sitting out here on your own! Really, sir! Please come and join us without further delay. Then you can relax and enjoy yourself for a little while. Put all your worries out of your head. The boys will be overjoyed. Please.'

On the other side of the square, the glowing light in the doorway, the music, the laughter all certainly seemed inviting. I rose to my feet and wiped my face once more.

'That's it, sir. You'll feel better in no time.'

'Thank you. Thank you. Really, thank you.' I made an effort to control my emotions. 'I'm very grateful to you. Really. I just hope I won't be intruding.'

Gustav laughed. 'You'll see soon enough if you're intruding or not, sir.'

As we set off across the square, it occurred to me I had better prepare to present myself to the porters, who undoubtedly would be overwhelmed with gratitude and excitement at my appearance. I felt more in control with each step I took and was about to make some pleasant remark to Gustav when he suddenly stopped walking. He had kept his hand gently on my back as we had set off across the square and I felt his fingers, just for a second, clutch at the material of my jacket. I turned and saw in the shadowy light Gustav standing quite still, looking down towards the ground, a hand raised to his brow as though he had suddenly remembered something of importance. Then, before I could say anything, he was shaking his head and smiling self-consciously.

'Excuse me, sir. I just . . . just . . .' He gave a small laugh and began to walk again.

'Is everything all right?'

'Oh yes, yes. You know, sir, the boys are going to be so thrilled when you walk in through that door.'

He moved a step or two ahead of me and led the way determinedly across the remainder of the square.

27

Only when I entered the café and felt the warmth of the log fire at the far end of the room did I realise how chilly the evening had become. The interior of the café had been re-arranged since the previous time I had stepped inside it. Most of the tables had been pushed back against the walls, so as to allow a large circular table to dominate the centre of the floor. Around this were a dozen or so men, drinking beers and carrying on boisterously. They looked somewhat younger than Gustav, though almost all were in late middle-age. A little way away from them, over near the café counter, two thin men in gypsy dress were playing a brisk waltz on their fiddles. There were other customers present, but they all seemed content to sit in the background, often in the shadowy recesses of the room, as though conscious of being present at someone else's event.

As Gustav and I came in, the porters all turned and stared, not certain whether to believe their eyes. Then Gustav said: 'Yes, boys, it really is him. He's come in person to wish us well.'

A complete hush fell over the café while everyone – the porters, the waiters, the musicians, the other customers – stared at me. Then the room broke into warm applause. For some reason this reception took me by surprise and almost brought the tears back to my eyes. I smiled, saying: 'Thank you, thank you,' while the applause continued so intensely I could barely hear myself. The porters had all risen to their feet and even the gypsy musicians had tucked their fiddles under their arms to join in the applause. Gustav ushered me towards the central table and as I sat down the applause finally subsided. The musicians resumed their playing and I found myself surrounded by a ring of excited faces. Gustav, who had seated himself next to me, began to say:

'Boys, Mr Ryder has been good enough to . . .'

Before he could finish, a stout porter with a red nose leaned over to me and raised his beer glass. 'Mr Ryder, you've saved us,' he declared. 'Now our story will be different. My grandchildren, they'll remember me differently. This is a great night for us.'

I was still smiling back at him when I felt a hand grasp my arm and found a gaunt, nervous-looking face staring into mine.

'Please, Mr Ryder,' the man said. 'Please, you'll really do it, won't you? You won't when the time comes, with all the other very important things on your mind, in front of all these people, you won't change your mind and ...'

'Don't be so insolent,' someone else said and the nervous man vanished as though someone had pulled him back. Then I could hear a voice saying behind me: 'Of course he won't change his mind. Who do you think you're talking to?'

I turned in my seat, wishing to reassure the nervous man, but then someone else was shaking my hand saying:

'Thank you, Mr Ryder, thank you.'

'You're all very kind,' I said, smiling at the company in general. 'Though I ... I really ought to warn you ...'

At that moment someone pushed against me, almost knocking me into the person next to me. I heard someone apologising and someone else saying: 'Don't push like that!' Then another voice said, close to me: 'I thought that was you out there just now, sir. I'm the one who pointed you out to Gustav. It's so good of you to come and see us like this. Tonight will be a night we'll remember for ever. A turning point for every porter in the town.'

'Look, I have to warn you,' I said loudly. 'I'll do my very best for you, but I have to warn you, I may not be quite the influence I once was. You see ...'

But my words were drowned out by a number of the porters starting up a chorus of 'hurrahs' for me. By the second one, the entire company of porters joined in, and then the music momentarily stopped as everyone else in the café joined in for the final, deafening hurrah. Then there was more applause.

'Thank you, thank you,' I said, genuinely moved. Then, as the applause began to fade, the red-nosed porter across the table said:

'You're very welcome here, sir. You're a famous and renowned person, but I want you to know we here know a good sort when we see one. That's right, we haven't spent so long in this trade without developing a good nose for decency. You're decent through and through, we can all see that. Decent and kind. You might think we're all welcoming you now simply because you're going to help us. And of course, we're grateful to you. But I know this crowd, they've really taken to you, and they wouldn't have done so if you weren't a decent sort. If you'd been too proud, or insincere in any way, they'd have sniffed you out. Oh yes. Of course, they'd still have felt grateful, they'd have treated you well, but they wouldn't be taking to you like this. What I'm trying to say, sir, is that even if you hadn't been famous, if you were just some stranger who'd stumbled in here by accident, once we'd seen you were all right, once you'd explained you were far from home and were looking for some company, we'd have welcomed you. We wouldn't have received you so differently from the way we did just now, once we'd seen what a good sort you were. Oh yes, we're not nearly so stand-offish here as people say. From now on, sir, you can count each of us as your friend.'

'That's right,' said someone to my right. 'We're your friends now. If you're ever in any difficulty in this town, you'll be able to rely on us.'

'Thank you so much,' I said. 'Thank you. I'll do my best for you all tonight. But really, I have to warn you . . .'

'Sir, please.' It was Gustav talking gently near my ear. 'Please stop worrying. Everything will be fine. Why not enjoy yourself for a few minutes at least?'

'But I just wanted to warn these good friends of yours . . .'

'Really, sir,' Gustav went on quietly. 'Your dedication is admirable. But you worry too much. Please relax and enjoy yourself. Just for a few minutes. Look at us. All of us here have worries. I myself have to be off shortly to the concert hall again, back to all that work. But when we meet like this here, we're glad to be among friends and we forget about things. We unwind and enjoy ourselves.' Then Gustav raised his voice over the hubbub. 'Come on, let's show Mr Ryder how we *really* enjoy ourselves! Let's show him how we do it!'

This pronouncement was met by a cheer and another burst of applause, then the applause turned into rhythmic clapping all around the table. The gypsies began to play faster in time with the clapping, and some of the other customers looking on began also to clap. I noticed too people elsewhere in the room actually breaking off their conversations and turning their seats around as though to witness an eagerly awaited spectacle. Someone I supposed was the proprietor – a dark, lanky man – emerged from a back room and stood leaning on the door frame, evidently just as anxious not to miss what was to follow.

Meanwhile the porters kept up their clapping, becoming ever more mirthful, some of them thumping the floor with their feet to emphasise the beat. Then two waiters appeared and began hurriedly to clear the surface of the table. Beer glasses, coffee cups, sugar pots, ashtrays all vanished in an instant, and then one of the porters, a heavy bearded man, climbed up onto the table top. Behind his bushy beard his face was bright red, whether from embarrassment or from drinking I could not tell. In any case, once up on the table he seemed to have little inhibition and with a grin began to dance.

It was a curious, static dance, the feet hardly leaving the table surface, with the emphasis on the statuesque qualities of the human body rather than its agility or mobile grace. The bearded porter adopted a pose like some Greek god, his arms positioned as though carrying an invisible burden, and as the clapping and the shouts of encouragement continued, he would subtly change the angle of his hip or rotate himself slowly. I wondered for a moment if the whole thing was supposed to be comic, but for all the exuberant laughter around the table, it soon became clear there was no satiric intention in the performance. As I watched the bearded porter, someone nudged me and said:

'This is it, Mr Ryder. Our dance. The Porters' Dance. You've heard about it, I'm sure.'

'Yes,' I said. 'Ah yes. So this is the Porters' Dance.'

'This is it. But you haven't seen anything yet.' The speaker grinned and nudged me again.

I became aware that a large brown cardboard box was being passed around from porter to porter. The box had roughly the dimensions of a suitcase, though to judge from the way it was being tossed through the air, it was light and empty. The box travelled around the table for a few minutes then, at a particular point in the dance, was thrown up to the bearded porter. There was something well-practised about the whole routine. At the precise moment the bearded porter switched pose and raised his arms up again, the cardboard box came through the air, landing smartly in his hands.

The bearded porter reacted as though he had caught a slab of stone – bringing a growl of apprehension from his audience – and for a second or two looked certain to buckle under the weight. But then, with considerable determination, he began to straighten himself, until finally he was standing perfectly upright, the box held against his chest. As cheers greeted this achievement, the bearded porter began slowly to raise the box above his head, until finally he was holding it aloft, both arms absolutely straight. Although in reality, of course, this was no feat at all, there was a dignity and drama to the performance which caused me to join in with the cheering, just as if he really had lifted a huge weight. The bearded porter then proceeded to create with some skill the illusion of his burden getting lighter and lighter. Before long he was holding the box up with one hand, performing little pirouettes as he did so, sometimes tossing the box over his shoulder and catching it behind his back. The lighter the burden became, the more exuberant his colleagues grew. Then, as the bearded porter's feats grew ever more flippant, his colleagues began to look around the table at one another, grinning, egging each other on, until another of their number, a wiry little man with a thin moustache, began to climb onto the table top.

The table wobbled and tilted, but the other porters laughed, as though this were all part of the drama, then held the table firm as the wiry porter clambered up. The bearded man failed at first to notice his colleague and continued to show off his control over the cardboard box, while the wiry porter stood moodily behind him like a man awaiting his turn with a coveted dance partner. Then at last the bearded porter saw the wiry man and threw the box over to him. As he caught the box the wiry porter staggered backwards, and it seemed he might tumble off the table altogether. But he recovered just in time, then, with much effort, straightened himself, the box held on his back. As he did so, the bearded porter, now joining in with the clapping and smiling happily, came down off the table assisted by many hands.

The wiry porter went through much the same procedure as his predecessor, though with many more comic flourishes. He provoked roars of laughter as he pulled funny faces and performed stumbles in the best slapstick fashion. As I watched him, the rhythmic clapping, the gypsy violins, the laughter, the mock hoots of astonishment seemed to fill not just my ears but all my senses. Then, as a third porter replaced the wiry man on the table, I felt the human warmth starting to engulf me. Gustav's sentiments suddenly struck me as profoundly wise. What indeed was the point in worrying so much? It was essential every once in a while to unwind completely and enjoy oneself.

I closed my eyes and let the pleasant atmosphere wash around me, only vaguely conscious that I was still clapping, and that my foot was thumping time on the floorboard. A picture entered my mind of my parents, of the two of them in their horse-drawn carriage approaching the clearing outside the concert hall. I could see the local people – the black-jacketed men, the ladies with their coats and shawls and jewellery – breaking off their conversations and turning towards the sound of horse hooves coming from the darkness of the trees. And then the gleaming carriage would burst into the wash of lights, the handsome horses trotting to a halt, their breaths rising in the night air. And my mother and my father would be peering out of the carriage window, on their faces the first traces of excited anticipation, but also something guarded and reserved, a reluctance to give in completely to the hope that the evening would turn out a glittering triumph. And then, as the liveried coachman hurried to help them down, and a line of dignitaries formed to greet them, they would adopt the wilfully calm smiles I recalled from my childhood, from those rare occasions when my parents invited guests to the house for lunch or dinner.

I opened my eyes and saw there were now two porters up on the table together, performing an amusing routine. Whichever one was holding the box would stagger about on the verge of collapse, threatening to fall off the edge, only to relinquish the box to the other at the last moment. Then I noticed that Boris – who presumably had all this time been sitting somewhere in the café – had come right up to the table and was looking up at the two porters with obvious delight. From the way he clapped and laughed at all the right moments, the little boy was clearly very familiar with all the routines. He was sitting between two large swarthy porters who looked similar enough to be brothers.

As I watched, Boris exchanged a remark with one of them, and the man laughed and tweaked playfully the little boy's cheek.

All the activity seemed to be drawing in more and more people from the square and the café was becoming very crowded. I noticed too that although there had been only two gypsy musicians when I had arrived, three others had now joined them and the music of their fiddles was coming from all directions with greater energy than ever. Then someone at the back – I had the impression it was not one of the porters – shouted out: 'Gustav!' and in no time the call had been taken up at the front of our table. 'Gustav! Gustav!' the porters shouted, turning it into a chant. Soon even the nervous-looking porter who had spoken to me earlier and who was now taking his turn up on the table – a spirited if not particularly skilful performance – joined in, so that even as he manipulated the box down his back and around his hip, he did so chanting: 'Gustav! Gustav!'

I looked around for Gustav – he was no longer by my side – and saw that he had gone over to Boris and was saying some-thing into the little boy's ear. One of the swarthy brothers put a hand on Gustav's shoulder and I could see him imploring the elderly porter to take his turn. Gustav smiled and shook his head modestly, to be met only with an intensification in the chanting. Now virtually every person in the room was chanting his name, and even those standing out in the square seemed to be joining in. Finally, giving Boris a weary smile, Gustav rose to his feet.

Being by some years the eldest of the porters, Gustav appeared to have more difficulty clambering up onto the table, but many hands reached forward to help him up. Once on the table, he straightened and smiled at his audience. The nervous-looking porter handed him the box, then promptly got down.

From the start Gustav's routine departed from that established by the earlier dancers. Rather than pretend the box was extremely heavy on first receiving it, he tossed it effortlessly onto one shoulder and made a shrugging motion. This produced loud laughter all round and I could hear cries of 'Good old Gustav!' and 'Trust him!' And then, as he continued to make light of the box, a waiter broke through to the front and tossed up onto the table an actual suitcase. From the way he swung it and the loud thud it produced, the suitcase was clearly not empty. It had landed close to Gustav's feet and a murmur went around the crowd. Then the chanting picked up again, faster than ever: 'Gustav! Gustav! Gustav!' I could see Boris following carefully every move his grandfather made, immense pride across his face, clapping his hands vigorously and joining in with the chanting. Gustav, noticing Boris, smiled once more to him, then reached down and grasped the handle of the suitcase.

As Gustav – still hunched over – brought the suitcase up to his hip, it seemed clear to me he was not faking its weight. Then as he straightened himself, the box still up on his shoulder, the suitcase in his hand, he closed his eyes and his face appeared to cloud over. But no one seemed to notice anything untoward – quite possibly this was a characteristic mannerism of Gustav's before he performed a feat – and the chanting and clapping continued deafeningly over the squealing violins. Sure enough, the next moment, Gustav had opened his eyes again and was smiling broadly at everyone. Then, lifting the suitcase up further, he managed to grip it under his arm, and in this posture – the suitcase under one arm, the box on the opposite shoulder – he began to dance, making some slow shuffling movements with his feet. There were cheers and whoops, and I could hear someone near the entrance asking: 'What's he doing now? I can't see. What's he doing now?'

Then Gustav raised the suitcase up further and continued the dance with the suitcase up on one shoulder, the box on the other. The fact that the suitcase was much heavier than the box obliged him to lean very much to one side, but otherwise he looked at ease and his steps continued to have a sprightliness about them. Boris, beaming with delight, shouted to his grandfather something I could not hear, to which Gustav responded with a wry twist of the head, provoking further hoots and laughter.

Then, as Gustav continued his dance, I became aware of something going on behind me. For some time, someone had been jabbing an elbow into my back with annoying regularity, but I had assumed this had simply to do with the crowd's eagerness to get a good view of the performance. But I now turned and found that, directly behind me, despite the crowd pushing against them on all sides, two waiters were kneeling on the floor packing a suitcase. They had already filled much of it with what looked to be wooden chopping boards from the kitchen. One waiter was arranging the boards into a more dense formation while the other was gesturing impatiently to the back of the café, pointing angrily at the spaces that remained inside the suitcase. Then I could see more chopping boards arriving, two or three at a time, passed hand to hand through the crowd. The waiters worked quickly, packing the boards in until the case seemed full to bursting. But more chopping boards – sometimes just the broken sections of boards – were still coming down, and the waiters with practised ingenuity found ways to squeeze these in too. Perhaps they would have continued to pack more and more into the case, but the jostling of the bodies around them seemed finally to exhaust their patience and they pushed down the lid, tugged at the straps and, pushing past me, heaved the suitcase onto the table.

Boris gave the new suitcase a stare then looked uncertainly up at Gustav. His grandfather was performing a slow shuffle not unlike that of a matador. For the moment the effort required to hold the box and the suitcase on his shoulders seemed to prevent him from noticing the fresh challenge placed before him. Boris watched his grandfather carefully, waiting for the moment he would see the second suitcase. Clearly everyone else was also waiting, but his grandfather went on and on with the dance, pretending to have noticed nothing. This was surely a trick on his part! Almost certainly, his grandfather was teasing the audience, and any moment now, Boris knew, he would pick up the heavy suitcase, perhaps discarding the empty box to do so. But for some reason, Gustav continued not to see it, and now people were shouting and pointing. Then at last Gustav noticed and his face – sandwiched between the box and the first suitcase – took on an expression of dismay. Everyone around Boris laughed and clapped all the harder. Gustav continued slowly to rotate himself but kept his gaze fixed on the new suitcase, his expression still troubled, and for an instant it occurred to Boris that his grandfather was not entirely faking his concern. But then all around him people were laughing, people who had seen his grandfather perform this same routine many times before, and the next moment Boris too was laughing and urging Gustav on. The little boy's voice caught Gustav's attention and once more grandfather and grandson exchanged smiles.

Then Gustav brought the empty box off his shoulder, and as it slid down his arm, with a contemptuousness that was almost graceful, he flicked the thing into the crowd. There was again a mixture of laughter and cheering, and the box, passed back over the heads of the spectators, vanished into the recesses of the room. Then Gustav glanced down again at the new suitcase and hoisted the first higher on his shoulder. He put on once more an expression of grave concern – this time it was without any doubt entirely mock – and Boris laughed along with everyone else. Then Gustav began to bend at the knees. He did so very slowly, whether because of infirmity or out of showmanship was not clear, until he was crouching, the first suitcase still held on one shoulder, his free arm reaching for the handle of the suitcase at his feet. Then steadily, slowly, as the clapping continued, he raised himself again to a standing position, the heavier suitcase coming up with him.

Gustav was now mimicking enormous effort – much as the bearded porter had done earlier when he had first caught the cardboard box. Boris watched, pride welling inside him, turning occasionally from his grandfather to look at the admiring faces of the spectators pressing in around him. Even the gypsy musicians were now jockeying for a better view, employing the vigorous movement of their bowing elbows as a covert means to jostle. One fiddler had by this method made his way right to the front, so that he was now playing his violin leaning right over the table, his waist pressed against its edge.

Then Gustav again began to shuffle his feet. The weight of the two suitcases, particularly the one filled with the chopping boards which he did not attempt to hoist onto his shoulder – surely a physical impossibility – meant his steps now had only a nominal spring to them, but it was impressive nevertheless and the crowd became ecstatic. 'Good old Gustav!' the cries were going up again, and Boris too, unfamiliar though he was with this way of addressing his grandfather, called out at the top of his voice: 'Good old Gustav! Good old Gustav!'

Again the old porter appeared to hear Boris's voice above the rest and although this time he did not turn and acknowledge the little boy – he was pretending to be much too concerned with his suitcases to do such a thing – a fresh jauntiness entered his movements. He started again to rotate slowly and his back lost the last hint of a slouch. For a moment Gustav looked magnificent, poised like a statue on the table top, one suitcase on his shoulder, the other at his hip, rotating to the clapping and the music. Then he appeared to stumble, but recovered almost immediately, and the crowd gave an 'ooh!' and more laughter at this little variation.

Then Boris became aware of some commotion behind him and saw that the two waiters were back, once more fussing with something on the floor, pushing back people around them to make room for their work. Both men were on their knees and were grappling with what looked like a large golfing bag. Their manner was cross and impatient – perhaps they were annoyed at the way the people pressing around them seemed forever to bump their knees into them. Boris glanced back at his grandfather, and then, when he looked again behind him, saw one of the waiters holding open the mouth of the bag as though something large was about to be slid into it. Sure enough, the other waiter emerged through the crowd, walking backwards, pushing people aside brusquely, dragging some object along the floor. Squeezing a little way back into the crowd, Boris saw that the object was a piece of machinery. It was hard to get a view – people's legs were in the way – but the object was an old engine of some kind, either from a motor bike or perhaps a speedboat. The two waiters were working hard to get it into the golfing bag, pulling at the already taut material, tugging at the zipper. Looking up again, Boris saw that his grandfather was still in full control of the two suitcases, showing no sign of needing to stop. The crowd, in any case, had no intention of letting him do so yet. And then there was a movement around him and the two waiters had heaved the golfing bag up onto the table.

There was for a moment a rise in the hubbub as word of the bag's arrival passed from the front to those further back. Gustav did not notice the golfing bag immediately because his eyes were for the moment tightly shut in concentration, but soon enough the urgings of the crowd made him look around. His gaze fixed on the golfing bag and for a second Gustav looked very serious.

Then he smiled and continued to rotate slowly. Then as before, though with nothing like the ease, he slid the lighter of the suitcases off his shoulder and down his arm. As it fell, Gustav, with a supreme effort, managed to push up his arm so that the suitcase was hoisted up towards the crowd. Being much heavier than the empty box, it could hardly describe a neat arc, and it bounced on the table top before falling into the arms of the porters at the front. The first suitcase, like the box earlier, vanished into the crowd, and all eyes were again fixed on Gustav. The chanting of his name started up again and the old man looked carefully at the golfing bag near his feet. The momentary relief of carrying only the one object – albeit the suitcase filled with chopping boards – seemed to give him new energy. He pulled a long face and shook his head doubtfully at the golfing bag, prompting the crowd to urge him on all the more. 'Come on, Gustav, you show them!' Boris could hear the porter next to him shouting.

Gustav then began to raise the heavy suitcase up to the shoulder on which earlier he had held the lighter one. He did this with deliberation, his eyes closed, crouched down on one knee, then slowly straightening. His legs quivered once or twice, and then he stood steady, the suitcase safely on his shoulder, his free arm outstretched towards the golfing bag. Suddenly a fear went through Boris and he shouted: 'No!' but this was drowned out in the chanting and the laughter, the 'oohs' and sighs of the crowd around him.

'Come on, Gustav!' the porter next to him was shouting. 'Show them what you can do! You show them!'

'No! No! Grandfather! Grandfather!'

'Good old Gustav!' voices were shouting. 'Come on! Show them what you can do!'

'Grandfather! Grandfather!' Boris was now stretching his arms out across the table to catch his grandfather's attention, but Gustav's face remained grim with concentration, staring with enormous intensity at the strap of the golfing bag lying on the table surface. Then the elderly porter began to lower himself again, his whole body trembling under the weight of the suitcase on his shoulder, his hand grasping prematurely for the strap still some distance below him. There was a new tension in the room, a feeling perhaps that Gustav was at last attempting a feat that

404

stretched even his abilities. The atmosphere, for all that, remained festive, the chanting of his name celebratory.

Boris searched appealingly the faces of the adults around him, then tugged at the arm of the porter next to him.

'No! No! That's enough. Grandfather's done enough!'

The bearded porter – for it was he – looked at the little boy with surprise, then said with a laugh: 'Don't worry, don't worry. Your grandfather's magnificent. He can do this and much more. Much more. He's magnificent.'

'No! Grandfather's done enough now!'

But no one, not even the bearded porter – who had placed a reassuring arm around Boris's shoulder – was listening. For Gustav was now crouched virtually down to the table, his hand only an inch or two from the strap of the golfing bag. Then he had grasped it and, with his body still crouched low, positioned the strap around his free shoulder. He tugged the strap closer to himself and then began once more the ascent to a standing position. Boris shouted and banged the table top, then at last Gustav noticed him. His grandfather had already started to straighten his legs, but he stopped and for a second the two of them stared at each other.

'No.' Boris shook his head. 'No. Grandfather's done enough.'

Perhaps Gustav could not hear in all the noise, but he appeared to understand his grandson's sentiments well enough. He nodded quickly, a reassuring smile flashed across his face, and then his eyes closed again in concentration.

'No! No! Grandfather!' Boris tugged again the bearded porter's arm.

'What's the matter?' the bearded porter asked, tears of laughter in his eyes. Then, without waiting for a reply, he turned his attention back to Gustav, joining in more loudly than ever with the chanting.

Gustav continued slowly to straighten himself. Once, twice, his body shook as though it might buckle. His face became strangely flushed. His jaw clenched furiously, his cheeks grew distorted, the muscles on his neck stood out. Even in the heavy din, the elderly porter's breathing seemed audible. Yet no one other than Boris seemed to notice any of this.

405

'Don't worry, your grandfather's magnificent!' the bearded man said. 'This is nothing! He does it every week!'

Gustav continued to straighten more and more, the golfing bag hanging from one shoulder, the suitcase hoisted up on the other. Then at last he was standing completely straight, his face quivering but triumphant, and for the first time in many minutes the rhythmic clapping broke down into wild applause and cheering. The fiddles too broke into a slower, grander melody befitting a finale. Gustav rotated slowly, his eyes barely open, his face a contortion of pain and dignity.

'That's enough! Grandfather! Stop! Stop!'

Gustav went on turning, determined to display his achievement to every eye in the room. Then something inside him seemed suddenly to snap. He paused abruptly, and for a second seemed to rock gently, swaying as though in a breeze. The next instant he had recovered again and was continuing with his rotation. When he had come back to exactly the position in which he had first stood upright, only then did he begin to lower the suitcase from his shoulder. He let it fall to the table with a loud slam – it was too heavy, he had judged, to throw into the crowd without risk of injury to a spectator – then pushed it with his foot until it slid off the edge of the table into the arms of his waiting colleagues.

The crowd was now cheering and applauding, and then a section of it started to sing a song – some swaying ballad with Hungarian lyrics – along with the tune the gypsies were playing. More and more took up the song and very soon the whole room was singing. Up on the table, Gustav was lowering the golfing bag. It fell to the table with a metallic bang. This time he did not attempt to push it into the crowd, but held his arms aloft for a second – even this gesture now seemed to cost him greatly – then hastened to get down from the table. Numerous hands assisted him, and Boris watched his grandfather lower himself safely to the floor.

The room seemed now to have become preoccupied with the singing. The ballad had a sweet nostalgic quality to it, and as they sang people everywhere were starting to link arms so they could sway along together. One of the gypsy fiddlers climbed onto the table, to be quickly joined by a second, and soon the two of them were leading the whole room, moving their bodies in time even as they played their instruments.

Boris pushed through the crowd to where his grandfather was standing recovering his breath. Oddly, although Gustav had only a few seconds before been the focus of every gaze in the room, no one seemed now to pay much attention as grandfather and grandson embraced deeply, their eyes closed, making no attempt to hide from each other their immense relief. After what seemed a long time, Gustav smiled down at Boris, but the little boy went on holding his grandfather tightly, not opening his eyes.

'Boris,' Gustav said. 'Boris. There's something you must promise me.'

The little boy gave no response other than to continue holding his grandfather.

'Boris, listen. You're a good boy. If something ever happens to me, if something ever does, you'll have to take my place. You see, your mother and father, they're fine people. But sometimes they find it hard. They're not strong like you and me. So you see, if something happens to me, and I'm no longer here, you must be the strong one. You must look after your mother and father, keep the family strong, keep it together.' Gustav released Boris from the embrace and gave him a smile. 'You'll promise me that, won't you, Boris?'

Boris appeared to give this consideration, then nodded seriously. Then, the next moment, they seemed to become engulfed by the crowd and I could no longer see them. Someone was pulling at my sleeve, imploring me to link arms and join in the singing.

Looking around me, I saw that the other fiddlers had joined the two up on the table and the entire room appeared to be revolving around them united in song. Many more people had come into the café and the room was now virtually solid with bodies. I saw too that the doors were still open to the square, and that in the darkness outside people were also swaying and singing. I linked arms with a large man – a porter as far as I could guess – and a fat woman who presumably had walked in off the square, and found myself going round the room with them on either side of me. I was not familiar with the song being sung, but then I came to realise that most people present did not know the lyrics either, or have any familiarity with the Hungarian language, and were simply singing vague approximations of what they imagined the words to be. The man and woman on either side of me, for instance, were singing quite different things, both entirely without embarrassment or hesitation. Indeed, a moment's attention revealed they were both singing nonsense words, but this seemed to matter little, and before long I too became caught up in the atmosphere and began to sing, making up words I thought sounded vaguely Hungarian. For some reason, this worked surprisingly well – I found more and more such words pouring out of me with gratifying ease – and before long I was singing with considerable emotion.

Eventually, perhaps twenty minutes later, I saw the crowd was at last starting to thin. I could see too the waiters sweeping up and returning tables to their original positions around the café. There was however a sizeable group of us still circling the room, arms linked together, singing passionately. The gypsies also had remained up on the table, displaying no signs of wishing to stop their playing. As I went around the room, carried along by the gentle tugs and pushes of my companions, I felt someone tapping me and looked over my shoulder to find the man I assumed was the café proprietor smiling at me. He was a lanky man and as I continued to sway along he obligingly kept up with me, adopting a crouched shuffle somewhat reminiscent of Groucho Marx.

'Mr Ryder, you look very tired.' He was shouting virtually in my ear, but I could still only just hear him above the singing. 'And you have such a long and important evening in front of you. Please, why don't you rest for a few minutes? We have a comfortable back room, my wife has prepared the couch with some blankets and cushions, she's turned on the gas fire. You'll find it very comfortable. You could just curl up and sleep for a while. The room's small, that's true, but it's right at the back and very quiet. No one will come in and disturb you, we'll make sure of that. You'll find it very comfortable. Really, sir, I think you should take advantage of the little time you now have before the evening really begins. Please, come this way. You look so tired.'

As much as I was enjoying the singing and the company, I realised I was indeed immensely tired and that there was much sense in his suggestion. In fact the idea of a short rest appealed to me more and more, and as the proprietor continued to shuffle after me with a smile, I began to feel a deep gratitude towards him, not only for this kind offer, but also for having provided the facilities of this wonderful café, and for his generosity towards the porters – an obviously under-appreciated group within the community. I unlinked my arms, smiling my farewells to the people on either side, and then the proprietor had placed a hand on my shoulder and was guiding me towards a door at the back of the café.

He led me through a darkened room – I could make out stacks of merchandise piled up against the walls – and then opened another door through which a low warm light was visible.

'Here,' the proprietor said, ushering me in. 'Just relax here on the couch. Keep this door closed, and if it gets too warm just turn the gas fire down to the lower setting. Don't worry, it's perfectly safe.'

The fire was the only source of light in the room. In the orange glow I discerned the couch, which smelt musty but not unpleasant, and then before I realised it the door had closed, leaving me alone. I climbed onto the couch, which was just long enough for me to lie down on provided I curled my knees, and pulled up the blanket the proprietor's wife had left out for me.

IV

28

I awoke with the panicky sense that I had slept far too long. In fact my first thought was that it was now morning and that I had missed the whole of the evening's proceedings. But when I sat up on the couch I saw that apart from the glow of the gas fire everything around me was still dark.

I went to the window and pulled back the curtain. I found myself looking down on a narrow back yard taken up by several large dustbins. A light left on somewhere was dimly illuminating the yard, but I noticed too that the sky was no longer entirely dark and the fear went through me again that dawn was approaching. Letting go of the curtain, I began to make my way out of the room, bitterly regretting having ever taken up the café proprietor's offer of a place to rest.

I stepped into the small connecting room where earlier I had seen merchandise piled against the walls. The room was now in utter blackness and I twice bumped into hard objects as I groped about for a doorway. Eventually I came out into the main section of the café where not so long ago we had all danced and sung with so much good feeling. A little light was coming in from the windows facing the square and I could make out the jumbled shapes of chairs piled on top of tables. I made my way past them, and reaching the main doors looked out through the glass panels.

Nothing was stirring outside. The solitary street lamp at the centre of the empty square accounted for the light coming into the café, but I noticed again how the sky appeared to carry the first hints of morning. As I went on gazing out at the square, I found myself becoming increasingly angry. I could now see how I had allowed too many things to distract me from my central priorities – to the extent that I had now slept through a substantial part of this most crucial of evenings in my life. Then my anger became mingled with a sense of despair and for a while I felt close to tears.

But then, as I continued to look at the night sky, I began to wonder if I had imagined the signs of dawn breaking. Indeed, now that I studied it more carefully, I saw the sky was still very dark, and the thought struck me that it was still relatively early and that I had begun to panic quite needlessly. For all I knew, it was still possible to arrive at the concert hall in time to witness much of the evening's events, and certainly to make my own contribution.

I had all the while been absent-mindedly rattling the doors. I now noticed the system of bolts and, unlatching each in turn, wandered out into the square.

The air felt wonderfully refreshing after the stuffiness of the café, and had I not been so short of time I would have strolled about the square for a few moments to clear my head. As it was, I set off purposefully in search of the concert hall.

For the next several minutes I hurried through the empty streets, past the closed cafés and shops, without once catching sight of the domed roof. The Old Town under the street lamps had a distinct charm about it, but the longer I went on walking the harder it became to suppress a sense of panic. I had expected, not unreasonably, to encounter a few taxis cruising the night; at the least a few people, perhaps drifting out of some late-night establishment, from whom I could get directions. But apart from some stray cats I appeared to be the only thing awake for miles around.

I crossed a tram line, then found myself walking along the embankment of a canal. There was a chilly wind blowing across the water and, with still no sign of the concert hall, I could not avoid the feeling that I was getting myself thoroughly lost. I had decided to try a turning a little way in front of me – a narrow street going off at a fine angle – when I heard footsteps and saw a woman emerge from out of it.

I had grown so accustomed to the idea of the streets being completely deserted that I stopped in my tracks at the sight of her. My surprise had been compounded, moreover, by the fact that she was dressed in a flowing evening gown. The woman for her part had also stopped, but she seemed then to recognise me and with a smile started towards me again. As she stepped further into the lamplight, I saw she was in her late forties, perhaps even her early fifties. She was slightly plump, but carried herself with considerable grace.

'Good evening, madam,' I said. 'I wonder if you might help me. I was looking for the concert hall. Am I going in the right direction?'

The woman had now come right up to me. Smiling again, she said:

'No, actually it's over that way. I've just come from it. I was walking to take the air, but I'll gladly guide you back there, Mr Ryder. If you don't object, that is.'

'It would be a great pleasure, madam. But I don't want to cut short your walk.'

'No, no. I've already been walking for nearly an hour. It's time I got back. I should really have waited and arrived with all the other guests. But I had this foolish notion I should be there through all the preparations, just in case I was needed. Of course, there's nothing for me to do. Mr Ryder, please excuse me, I've not introduced myself. I'm Christine Hoffman. My husband is the manager of your hotel.'

'I'm delighted to meet you, Mrs Hoffman. Your husband has told me a great deal about you.'

I regretted this remark as soon as it had left my mouth. I glanced quickly at Mrs Hoffman, but could no longer see her face clearly in the light.

'It's this way, Mr Ryder,' she said. 'It's not far.'

The sleeves of her evening dress billowed as we started to walk. I coughed and said:

'May I take it, from what you say, Mrs Hoffman, that proceedings are not yet fully under way at the concert hall? That the guests and so on, they've not yet all arrived?'

'The guests? Oh no. I shouldn't imagine any guests will arrive for at least another hour.'

'Ah. Fine.'

We continued at an easy pace along the canal, both of us turning from time to time to gaze at the reflection of the lamps in the water.

'I was wondering, Mr Ryder,' she said eventually, 'if my husband, when he spoke about me, if he left you with the impression that I was . . . a rather cold person. I wonder if he left you with that impression.'

I gave a short laugh. 'The overwhelming impression he left me with, Mrs Hoffman, was that he's extremely devoted to you.'

She continued to walk in silence and I was not sure she had registered my reply. After a while she said:

'When I was young, Mr Ryder, no one would ever have thought to describe me in such a way. As a cold person. Certainly when I was a child, I was anything but cold. Even now, I can't think of myself like that.'

I mumbled something vaguely diplomatic. Then, as we turned away from the canal into a narrow side-street, I saw at last the domed roof of the concert hall illuminated against the night sky.

'Even these days,' Mrs Hoffman said beside me, 'early in the morning, I have these dreams. Always early in the morning. The dreams are always about . . . about tenderness. Nothing much happens in them, they're usually no more than little fragments. I might be watching my son, Stephan, for instance. Watching him play in the garden. We were very close once, Mr Ryder, when he was small. I'd comfort him, share his little triumphs with him. We were so close when he was small. Or sometimes a dream might be about my husband. The other morning, I dreamt my husband and I were unpacking a suitcase together. We were in some bed-room and we were unpacking it onto the bed. We might have been in an hotel room abroad or perhaps we were at home. In any case, we were unpacking this suitcase together and there was this . . . this comfortable feeling between us. There we were, per-forming this task together. He'd take something out, then I'd take something out. Talking all the time, about nothing special, just exchanging conversation while we unpacked. It was only the morning before last, I had this dream. Then I woke up and I lay there looking at the dawn through the curtains, feeling very happy. I said to myself, it might soon *really* be like that. Later that very day, even, we would make a moment just like that one. We wouldn't necessarily unpack a suitcase, of course. But something, we'd do something later in the day, there'd be *some* chance. I fell asleep again, telling myself this, feeling very happy. Then the morning came. It's an odd thing, Mr Ryder, it happens like this every time. As soon as the day starts, this other thing, this *force*, it comes and takes over. And whatever I do, everything between us just goes another way, not the way I want it. I fight against it, Mr Ryder, but over the years I've steadily lost ground. It's something that's . . . that's happening to me. My husband tries very hard, tries to help me, but it's no use. By the time I go down to breakfast, all the things I felt in the dream, they've long since gone.'

Some parked cars on the pavement obliged us to walk in single file and Mrs Hoffman moved a few steps ahead of me. When I drew up alongside her again, I asked:

'What do you suppose it is? This force you talk of?'

She laughed suddenly. 'I didn't mean it to sound quite so supernatural, Mr Ryder. Of course, the obvious answer would be that it's all to do with Mr Christoff. That's what I believed for some time. Certainly, that's what my husband believes, I know. Like many people in this city I thought it simply a matter of replacing Mr Christoff in our affections with someone more substantial. But lately I'm not at all sure. I'm coming to believe it might be to do with me. A sort of illness I have. It might even be part of the ageing process. After all, we get older and parts of us start to die. Perhaps we start to die emotionally too. Do you think that's possible, Mr Ryder? I do fear it, I do fear that might be the truth of it. That we shall see off Mr Christoff, only to find, in my particular case at least, that nothing has changed.'

We turned another corner. The pavements were very narrow and we moved into the centre of the street. I had the impression she was waiting for my response, and said eventually:

'Mrs Hoffman, in my opinion, whatever the facts about the ageing process, I would say it's essential for you to keep up your spirits. To not give in to this . . . whatever it is.'

Mrs Hoffman looked up at the night sky and walked on for a while without replying. Then she said: 'These lovely dreams in the early morning. When the day starts and none of it happens, I often blame myself bitterly. But I assure you, I haven't given up yet, Mr Ryder. If I gave up, there'd be very little left in my life. I refuse just yet to let go of my dreams. I still want one day a warm and close family. But it's not just that, Mr Ryder. You see, I may be quite silly in believing this, perhaps you can tell me if I am. But one day, you see, I hope to catch it out, this whatever it is. I hope to catch it out and then it won't matter, all these years it's been steadily working on me, they'll all be wiped away. I have this feeling, that all it will take will be one moment, even a *tiny* moment, provided it's the correct one. Like a cord suddenly snapping and a thick curtain dropping to the floor to reveal a whole new world, a world full of sunlight and warmth. Mr Ryder, you look utterly incredulous. Am I completely mad to believe this? That despite all these years, just one moment, the right moment, will change it all?'

What she had taken for incredulity had been nothing of the sort. Rather, while she had been speaking, I had remembered about Stephan's forthcoming recital and no doubt my excitement had made itself obvious. I now said, perhaps a little eagerly:

'Mrs Hoffman, I don't wish to raise any false hopes. But it's possible, just possible, you'll experience something very soon, something that might well be such a moment, exactly of the sort you talk of. It's just possible you'll encounter such a moment in the very near future. Something that will surprise you, force you to re-assess everything and see everything in a better, fresher light. Something that will indeed wipe away all these bad years. I don't wish to raise false hopes, I'm merely saying it's possible. Such a moment might even occur tonight, so it's essential you keep up your spirits.'

I stopped myself, the thought striking me that I was tempting fate. After all, although I had been impressed by the snatch of Stephan's playing I had caught, for all I knew the young man was perfectly capable of crumbling under pressure. In fact, the more I thought about it, the more I regretted having intimated as much as I had. When I looked at Mrs Hoffman, however, I noticed my words had neither surprised nor excited her. After a few moments she said:

'When you found me wandering these streets just now, Mr Ryder, I wasn't simply taking the air as I pretended. I was trying to prepare myself. Because the possibility you mention, it naturally did occur to me. A night like tonight. Yes, many things are possible. So I was preparing myself. And I don't mind confessing to you, I am at this moment a little frightened. Because you see, just occasionally in the past, such moments have come and I've not been strong enough to seize them. Who knows how many more such chances there will be? So you see, Mr Ryder, I was doing my best to prepare myself. Ah, here we are. This is the rear of the building. This entrance will take you into the kitchens. I'll show you to the performers' entrance. I won't come in myself just yet. I think I need to take a little more air.'

'I'm very glad to have met you, Mrs Hoffman. It's kind of you to have shown me here at such a time for you. I do hope every-thing goes well for you tonight.'

'Thank you, Mr Ryder. And you too, you have a lot to think about, I'm sure. It's been delightful to meet you.'

29

As Mrs Hoffman disappeared into the night, I turned and hurried towards the doorway she had indicated. I did so telling myself that I should heed fully the lesson of the false alarm I had just experienced; that it was imperative I did not let anything further deflect me from the crucial tasks in front of me. In fact, at this moment, on the point at last of entering the concert hall building, everything seemed suddenly very simple to me. The fact of the matter was that finally, after all these years, I was about to perform once more before my parents. The priority above all else, then, was to ensure that my performance was the richest, the most overwhelming of which I was capable. By comparison, even the question-and-answer session was a secondary consideration. All the setbacks, all the chaos of the preceding days would prove to have been of no consequence whatsoever provided I could now achieve, on this evening, my one central objective.

The broad white door was dimly illuminated from above by a single night light. I had to lean my weight on it before it would open and I entered the building with a slight stumble.

Although Mrs Hoffman had been confident this was the performers' entrance, my immediate impression was that I had come in through the kitchens after all. I was in a wide bare corridor lit harshly with fluorescent ceiling strips. From all around came the sound of voices calling and shouting, the clanging of heavy metallic objects, the hissing of water and steam. Directly in front of me was a catering trolley beside which two men in uniforms were arguing furiously. One man was holding a long piece of paper which had unrolled almost to his feet, and was repeatedly thrusting his finger at it. I thought about interrupting them to ask where I might find Hoffman – my first concern now being to carry out an inspection of the auditorium, and of the piano itself, before the public began to arrive – but they seemed lost in their argument and I decided to walk on.

The corridor curved gradually. I encountered a good many

people, but they all seemed very busy and somewhat fraught. Most of them, dressed in white uniforms, were hurrying with distracted expressions, carrying heavy sacks or else pushing trolleys. I did not feel inclined to stop any of them and carried on down the corridor assuming I would eventually reach some other section of the building where I would find the dressing rooms – and hopefully Hoffman or someone else who could show me the facilities. But then I realised a voice behind me was calling my name and turned to find a man running after me. He looked familiar, and then I recognised the bearded porter who had opened the dancing at the café earlier in the evening.

'Mr Ryder,' he said panting, 'thank God I've found you at last. This is the third time I've gone round the building. He's holding out well, but we're all anxious to get him to hospital and he's still insisting on not budging until he's spoken to you. Please, it's this way, sir. He's holding out well, though, God bless him.'

'Who's holding out well? What's happened?'

'It's this way, sir. We'd better go quickly, if you don't mind. I'm sorry, Mr Ryder, I'm not explaining anything. It's Gustav, he's been taken ill. I wasn't here myself when it happened, but a couple of the boys, Wilhelm and Hubert, they were working here with him, helping with the preparations, and they sent out the word. Of course as soon as I heard I sped over here and so did all the other boys. Apparently Gustav had been working very well, but then he went to the washroom and didn't come out for a long time. This not being at all like Gustav, Wilhelm went in and had a look. It seems, sir, when he went in, Gustav was standing over a sink, his head bowed over it. He wasn't so ill at that stage, he told Wilhelm he felt a bit giddy, that was all, and not to make a fuss. Wilhelm being Wilhelm, he wasn't sure what to do, especially with Gustav saying not to make a fuss, and so he went and got Hubert. Hubert took one look and decided Gustav had to lie down somewhere. So they got on either side of him to help him, and that's when they realised he'd passed out, still on his feet, gripping the sink. He was gripping the edges, really gripping them, and Wilhelm says they had to prise off his fingers one by one. Then Gustav seemed to come to a bit and they each took an arm and brought him out of there. And Gustav, he was saying again how he didn't want any fuss, how he was all right and could carry on working. But Hubert wouldn't hear of it and they put him in one of the dressing rooms, one of the empty ones.'

He had been leading the way down the corridor at a considerable pace, talking all the time over his shoulder, but now broke off as we dodged past a trolley.

'This is all very disturbing,' I said. 'Exactly when did this all happen?'

'I suppose it must have been a couple of hours ago. He didn't seem so bad at first and insisted all he needed was a few minutes to get his breath back. But Hubert was worried and sent out the word and we were all round here in no time, every one of us. We found a mattress for him to lie on, and a blanket, but then he seemed to get worse and we all talked about it and said he should get proper help. But Gustav wouldn't hear of it, he suddenly got very determined and said he had to speak to you, sir. He was very insistent, he said he'd go along to hospital soon enough if that's what we decided, but not before he'd spoken with you. And there he was getting worse right before our eyes. But there was no reasoning with him, sir, and so we went out searching for you again. Thank God I found you. It's this one here, the one on the end.'

I had imagined the corridor to be a continuous circuit, but I now saw that it came to an end at a cream-coloured wall ahead of us. The last door before the wall was ajar and, stopping at the threshold, the bearded porter peered cautiously into the room. Then he gestured to me and I stepped in after him.

There were a dozen or so people just inside the doorway who all turned to us, then hastily stood aside. I supposed these to be the other porters, but I did not pause to look at them carefully, my gaze being drawn to Gustav's figure on the other side of the small room.

He was lying on a mattress across the tiled floor, a blanket over his body. One of the porters was squatting down beside him saying something softly, but on seeing me stood up. Then within a moment the room had emptied, the door had closed behind me and I was alone with Gustav.

The small dressing room contained no furniture, not even a wooden chair. It was windowless and, though the ventilation grid near the ceiling was emitting a low hum, the air felt stale.

The floor felt cold and hard, and the overhead light had either been extinguished or was not working, leaving the bulbs around the make-up mirror as our only source of light. I could see well enough, though, how Gustav's face had gone an odd grey colour. He was lying on his back, quite still except when every now and then some wave passed over him causing him to press his head back deeper into the mattress. He had smiled at me the moment I had entered, but had said nothing, no doubt saving himself for when we were alone. He now said, in a voice that was weak, but otherwise surprisingly composed:

'I'm very sorry, sir, to have dragged you here like this. It's most galling this should have happened, and tonight of all nights. Just when you're about to do your great favour for us.'

'Yes, yes,' I said quickly, 'but look here. How are you feeling?' I crouched down beside him.

'I don't suppose I'm so well. And in time I think I ought to go along to the hospital and have a few things checked out.'

He paused as another wave swept over him, and for a few seconds a quiet struggle ensued there on the mattress during which time the elderly porter closed his eyes. Then he opened them again and said:

'I had to speak to you, sir. There was something I had to speak to you about.'

'Please, let me assure you at once,' I said, 'that I remain as committed as ever to your cause. In fact, I'm very much looking forward to demonstrating to all the assembled tonight the unfairness of the treatment you and your colleagues have endured over the years. I fully intend to highlight the many mis-understandings . . .'

I stopped, realising he was making an effort to attract my attention.

'I didn't doubt for a minute, sir,' he said after a pause, 'you'd be as good as your word. I'm very grateful to you for standing up for us like this. But it was about something else I wished to speak to you.' He paused again and another silent struggle commenced under the blanket.

'Really,' I said, 'I wonder if it wouldn't be wise to go straight away to the hospital . . .'

'No, no. Please. Once I go to hospital, well, then it might all be too late. You see, it's really time now I spoke to her. To Sophie, I mean. I really must speak to her. I know you're very busy tonight, but you see, no one else knows. About the situation between me and Sophie, about our *understanding*. I know it's a lot to ask, sir, but I wondered if you might go and explain things to her. There's no one else who could do it.'

'I'm sorry,' I said, genuinely puzzled. 'Explain what exactly?'

'Explain to her, sir. Why our understanding . . . why it has to finish now. It won't be easy to persuade her of it, after all these years. But if you could try and make her see why we have to try and end it now. I realise it's a lot to ask of you, but then it's a little while yet until you're expected on the stage. And as I say, you're the only one who knows . . .'

He trailed off as another wave of pain engulfed him. I could sense all his muscles bracing themselves under the blanket, but this time he continued to gaze at me, somehow keeping his eyes open even as his whole frame shook. When his body had slackened again, I said:

'It's true, there's a little time yet until I'm required. Very well, I'll go and see what I can do. I'll try and make her understand. In any case, I'll bring her here as quickly as possible. But let's hope you'll recover very soon and the present situation will prove to have been not as crucial as you feared . . .'

'Sir, please. I'd be very grateful if you'd bring her here quickly. Meanwhile I'll of course do all I can to hold out . . .'

'Yes, yes, I'll set off straight away. Please be patient, I'll be as fast as I can.'

I rose to my feet and started for the door. I had almost reached it when a thought occurred to me and, turning, I made my way back to the figure on the floor.

'Boris,' I said to him, crouching down again. 'What about Boris? Should I bring him here too?'

Gustav looked up at me, then took a deep breath and closed his eyes. When he had not spoken for some moments, I said:

'Perhaps it's best he doesn't see you in this . . . this present condition.'

I thought I saw the faintest of nods, but Gustav remained silent, his eyes still closed.

'After all,' I went on, 'he has a certain picture of you. Perhaps you'll want him to remember you that way.'

This time Gustav nodded more definitely.

'I just thought I should ask you,' I said, rising to my feet again. 'Very well. I'll bring just Sophie here. I won't be long.'

I had reached the door again – I was already turning the handle – when he suddenly shouted behind me:

'Mr Ryder!'

Not only had he called surprisingly loudly, his voice had contained such a peculiar intensity I could hardly believe it had emerged from Gustav. And yet when I looked back at him, his eyes were again closed and he seemed quite still. I hurried to him once more with some apprehension. But then Gustav opened his eyes and looked up at me.

'You must bring Boris too,' he said very quietly. 'He's not so small now. Let him see me like this. He has to learn about life. Face up to it.'

The eyes closed again and as his features tightened I thought he was suffering another fit of pain. But this time there was something different, and as I looked down in concern I realised that the old man was crying. I continued to watch for a moment, not sure what to do. Finally I touched his shoulder gently.

'I'll be as quick as I can,' I whispered.

When I came out of the dressing room, the other porters, who were all crowded near the doorway, turned to me with anxious looks. I pushed my way past them, saying firmly:

'Please keep a careful watch on him, gentlemen. I have to carry out an urgent request and so you'll have to excuse me for the moment.'

Someone started to ask a question, but I hurried on without stopping.

My plan was to find Hoffman and insist on being driven immediately to Sophie's apartment. But then, as I continued briskly along the corridor, I realised I had no idea where to look for the hotel manager. Moreover, the corridor itself had taken on a very different aspect from the time I had come down it with the bearded porter. There were still a few catering trolleys being pushed about, but it had now become overwhelmingly dominated by persons I could only suppose were members of the visiting orchestra. Long rows of dressing rooms had appeared on either side of me, many with their doors open, and the musicians were standing about in twos and threes, chatting and laughing, sometimes calling across the corridor to one another. Occasionally I would pass a closed door from behind which came the sounds of some instrument, but on the whole their mood struck me as surprisingly frivolous. I was about to stop and ask one of them where I might find Hoffman when I suddenly caught sight of the hotel manager himself through the half-open door of a dressing room. I went up to it and pushed it a little further.

Hoffman was standing before a full-length mirror, studying himself carefully. He was in full evening dress and his face, I noticed, had been made up excessively so that some of the powder had fallen onto his shoulders and lapels. He was muttering something under his breath, never taking his gaze off his reflection. Then, as I continued to watch from the door, he performed a curious action. Bending forward suddenly at the waist, he brought his arm up very stiffly so that the elbow was jutting outwards, and thumped himself on the forehead with his fist – once, twice, three times. Throughout it all he did not take his eyes off the mirror or cease his whispering. Then he straightened and looked at himself silently. It occurred to me he was about to repeat the whole action again and so I quickly cleared my throat and said:

'Mr Hoffman.'

He started and stared at me.

'I've disturbed you,' I said. 'I do apologise.'

Hoffman looked around him in a bewildered manner, then seemed to regain his composure.

'Mr Ryder,' he said with a smile. 'How are you feeling? I trust you're finding everything here to your satisfaction.'

'Mr Hoffman, something of great urgency has come up. What I need just now is a car to take me to my destination as quickly as possible. I wonder if this could be arranged without delay.'

'A car, Mr Ryder? Now?'

'It's a matter of the utmost urgency. Of course I intend to return here very promptly, in plenty of time to fulfil my various commitments.'

'Yes, yes, of course.' Hoffman looked vaguely troubled. 'A car

426

should be no problem at all. Of course, Mr Ryder, in normal circumstances I could have provided you also with a driver, or else I would have gladly driven you myself. Unfortunately, just at this moment, my staff have their hands very full. And as for myself, I have so many things to see to, as well as a few modest lines to rehearse. Ha ha! As you know, I will be making a short speech myself tonight. And as trivial as it undoubtedly will seem alongside your own contribution, and indeed, that of our Mr Brodsky, who incidentally is a little late, I feel nevertheless I must prepare myself the best I can. Yes, yes, Mr Brodsky is a little late, it's true, but there's nothing to worry about. In fact, this is his dressing room, I was just checking it over. A perfectly good dressing room. I'm fully confident he'll be here at any moment. As you know, Mr Ryder, I personally have been overseeing Mr Brodsky's, er, recovery, and what a satisfying thing it has been to witness. Such motivation, such dignity! So much so that tonight, on this crucial night, I have utter confidence. Oh yes. Utter confidence! Indeed, a relapse at this stage, that would be unthinkable. A disaster for this whole city! And naturally a personal disaster for me. Of course this is the most trivial of concerns, but nevertheless, you'll forgive me, let me say it, for myself, a relapse on this crucial night, at this point, ah yes, for me it would mark the end. On the very brink of triumph, it would be my finish. A humiliating finish! I could look no one in this town in the face again. I would have to hide. Ha! But what am I doing, talking of such improbable scenarios? I have utter confidence in Mr Brodsky. He will be here.'

'Yes, I'm sure he will be, Mr Hoffman,' I said. 'In fact, I'm sure this whole occasion tonight will be a fine success . . .'

'Yes, yes, I know it!' he shouted impatiently. 'I hardly need reassurance on such a point! I wouldn't have even mentioned it at all, after all there's plenty of time yet until things get started, I wouldn't have mentioned it at all if it wasn't for . . . for the occurrences earlier tonight.'

'Occurrences?'

'Yes, yes. Ah, you haven't heard. How could you have done? There's nothing much to it, sir. A certain sequence of events took place earlier this evening, and as a consequence, when I last left Mr Brodsky a few hours ago, he was sipping a small glass of whisky. No, no, sir! I can see what you're thinking. No, no! He consulted me fully. And after some consideration I relented, coming to the view that in these very special circumstances, a small glass would do no harm. I judged it best, sir. Perhaps I was wrong, we shall see. Personally, I do not think so. Of course, if I did make the wrong decision, then this whole evening – pugh! – a catastrophe from start to finish! I will be forced to hide for the rest of my life. But the fact is, sir, things became very complicated this evening and I was obliged to make a decision. In any case, the upshot of it all is that I left Mr Brodsky at his home with his small glass of whisky. I am confident he will stop at that. My only thought now is that I should perhaps have done something about that cupboard. But then again, I'm sure I'm being over-cautious. After all, Mr Brodsky has made such progress, he can surely be trusted absolutely, absolutely.' He had been fiddling with his bow tie and he now turned to the mirror to adjust it.

'Mr Hoffman,' I said, 'what exactly has happened? If something has happened to Mr Brodsky, or if anything else has occurred that's likely to alter the overall picture in any way, then surely I should be informed of it straight away. Surely you'll agree with me, Mr Hoffman.'

The hotel manager gave a laugh. 'Mr Ryder, you have entirely the wrong idea. There's no need for you to worry in the least. Look here, am I worried? No. My entire reputation rests on this evening, and yet am I not calm and confident? I tell you, sir, there's nothing whatsoever to concern yourself with.'

'Mr Hoffman, what were you referring to just now when you mentioned a cupboard?'

'Cupboard? Oh, merely the cupboard I discovered this evening at Mr Brodsky's home. You may know, he has for many years lived in an old farmhouse a little way off the north highway. I had of course been there many times before, but things being a little untidy – no doubt Mr Brodsky has his own way of ordering things – I had never looked so carefully about his residence. That's to say, it was only this evening I discovered that he did after all have a further supply of drink. He swore to me he had forgotten all about it. It was only when it came up this evening, when I said, well, in the circumstances, in these very special circumstances owing to the upsetting business with Miss Collins

428

and so on, it was only in these circumstances, you see, I agreed with him that on balance, despite the very small risk, yes, it would be best for him to have just one small glass of whisky, just to steady himself. After all, sir, the man was very distressed over this business of Miss Collins. It was only then, when I offered to fetch a hip flask from my car, that Mr Brodsky remembered there was still one cupboard he had not cleared out. And so we went into his, er, kitchen, I suppose you would call it. Mr Brodsky has done very well over the last months repairing the place. He's made steady progress, and now the elements hardly come in at all, though of course there aren't yet any windows as such. In any case, he opened the cupboard, which was actually lying on its side, and inside, well, there were a dozen or so old bottles of spirits. Mostly whisky. Mr Brodsky was as surprised as I was. It did occur to me, I have to admit it, that I should do something. That I should take the bottles away with me, or perhaps pour them out onto the ground. But then, sir, you can see it, that would have been an insult. A great affront to the courage and determination Mr Brodsky has shown. And having already suffered one great blow to his ego this evening on account of Miss Collins . . .'

'Excuse me, Mr Hoffman, but what is this you keep mentioning about Miss Collins?'

'Ah, Miss Collins. Yes, well, that's another matter. That was why I happened to be there, at Mr Brodsky's farmhouse. You see, Mr Ryder, this evening I found myself the bearer of a most sad message. No one would have envied me such a task. The fact was, I had been growing uneasy for some time, even before their meeting at the zoo yesterday. I had been worried, that's to say, on Miss Collins's behalf. Who would have guessed things would move so fast with them, and after all these years? Yes, yes, I was worried. Miss Collins is a dear lady for whom I have the highest regard. I could not bear to see her life torn apart again at this stage. You see, Mr Ryder, Miss Collins is a woman of immense wisdom, this whole town will testify to it, but for all that – and if you lived here, I'm sure you would agree – there has always been something vulnerable about her. We have all come to respect her enormously, and many people have found her counsel invaluable, but then at the same time – how can I put it? – we have always felt *protective* towards her. As Mr Brodsky became . . . more himself over the months, many issues presented themselves that I for one had not properly considered before, and well, as I say, I became concerned. So you can imagine how it was, sir, when as I was driving you back this evening from your practice and you happened to mention so innocently that Miss Collins had agreed to a rendez-vous with Mr Brodsky, when you made it clear that Mr Brodsky was even at that moment waiting for her at St Peter's Cemetery . . . My goodness, such fast moves! Our Mr Brodsky was clearly once something of a Valentino! Mr Ryder, I realised I had to do something. I could not allow Miss Collins's life to be plunged back into misery, particularly as a result of something I had done, however indirectly. So earlier this evening, after you most graciously allowed me to drop you off in the street, I took the opportunity to go and visit Miss Collins in her apartment. She was of course surprised to see me. Surprised I should have come personally on this of all evenings. In other words my presence alone spoke volumes. She showed me in immediately and I asked her to excuse the abruptness of my visit, and the fact that I could not approach the difficult topic I wished to discuss with the care and tact I would normally wish to employ. She of course understood perfectly. "I realise, Mr Hoffman," she said, "what great pressure you must be under this evening." We sat down in her front parlour and I came straight to the point. I told her I had heard about their proposed rendez-vous. Miss Collins lowered her eyes at this, just like a young schoolgirl. Then she said very sheepishly: "Yes, Mr Hoffman. Even as you were coming to my door just now, I was preparing myself. For well over an hour now, I've been trying out different outfits. Different ways to pin my hair. At my age, isn't it amusing? Yes, Mr Hoffman, it's quite true. He was here this morning and he persuaded me. I agreed to meet him." She said some such thing, it was mumbled, not at all the way that elegant lady usually speaks. And so I proceeded. Of course I did so very gently. I tactfully pointed out the possible pitfalls. "It is all very well, Miss Collins." I used such phrases. I trod as carefully as I could given the constraints on my time. Naturally, had it been another evening, had we had time to exchange pleasantries, to make small talk, I dare say I might have made a better job of it. Or perhaps it would have made little difference. The truth of the matter would always have been difficult for her. In any case, for all my going about things in the best way I could, when I eventually confronted her with the truth, when I said to her: "Miss Collins, all those old wounds will be re-opened. They will hurt, they will give you agony. It will break you down, Miss Collins. Within weeks, within days. How can you have forgotten? How can you lay yourself open to it all again? Everything you went through before, the humiliation, the great hurt, it will all come back and more acutely than ever. And after everything you've done over the years to build a new life for yourself!" When I put things to her in such terms – oh, I tell you, sir, it was not easy – I could see her crumbling inside, even as she tried to maintain her outward calm. I could see the memory of it all coming back to her, the old aches starting again. It was not easy, sir, I can tell you, but I felt it my duty to continue. Then finally, she said very quietly: "But Mr Hoffman. I've promised him. I've promised I'd meet him this evening. He'll be depending on me. He always needs me before a big night like this." To which I said: "Miss Collins, of course he'll be disappointed. But I will personally do my utmost to explain it to him. In any case, he'll already know in his heart of hearts, just as you do, that this rendez-vous is ill-advised. That the past is now best left well alone." And she looked out of the window as if in a dream and said: "But he'll be there already. He'll be there waiting." To which I said: "I will go myself, Miss Collins. Yes, I am very busy tonight, but this is something I regard as so important I can only entrust myself with the task. In fact I will go now, immediately, to the cemetery and inform him of the situation. You can rest assured, Miss Collins, that I will do everything I can to comfort him. I will encourage him to think ahead, to the immensely important challenge in front of him this evening." I said some such thing to her, Mr Ryder. And though I must say she looked for the moment completely destroyed, she is a sensible lady and a part of her must have known I was right. Because she touched my arm quite kindly, saying: "Go to him. Straight away. Do what you can." And so I got up to leave, but then realised I still had one last painful duty left to perform. "Oh, and Miss Collins," I said to her. "As far as this evening's event is concerned. Under the circumstances, I would have supposed it best you stayed at home." She nodded and I could see she was close to tears. "After all," I went on, "one has to be sensitive to his feelings. Under the circumstances your presence in the hall might have a certain influence on him at this most crucial juncture." She nodded again and indicated that she understood fully. I excused myself then and showed myself out. And then, although there were so many other pressing things waiting to be done – the bacon, the bread deliveries – I saw that the overwhelming priority was to see Mr Brodsky safely over this last unexpected hurdle. So I drove to the cemetery. It was dark by the time I arrived and it took me a little while walking among the graves before I could locate him, sitting on a tomb, looking despondent. And when he saw me approaching he looked up tiredly and said to me: "You've come to tell me. I knew it. I knew it wasn't to be." This made my task easier, you might think, but I tell you, sir, it wasn't easy at all. To be the bearer of such news. I nodded solemnly and said, yes, he was right, she was not coming. She had thought things through and had changed her mind. Furthermore she had decided not to come to the concert hall tonight. I saw no point in going into it any further than that. And he looked very distraught, so for a moment I looked away and pretended to inspect the tomb next to the one he was sitting on. "Ah, old Mr Kaltz," I said to the trees, because I knew Mr Brodsky was weeping to himself quietly. "Ah, Mr Kaltz. How many years is it now since we buried him? It seems like yesterday, but I see it's already fourteen years. How lonely he was before he died." I was making some such conversation, so as to allow Mr Brodsky to weep. Then I sensed he had brought his tears under control and I turned to him and suggested he come back with me to the concert hall to get himself ready. But he said no, it was too early. He would become too tense hanging around the venue for so long. And I thought he might be right and suggested I drive him home. He agreed to this and so we made our way out of the cemetery and down to the car. And all through the drive, the whole time we were going up the north highway, he was just staring out of the window, saying nothing, the tears occasionally welling in his eyes. I realised then that we were not yet home and dry. That things were not quite so certain as they had seemed a few hours earlier. But I was still very confident, Mr Ryder, just as I am now. Then we arrived at his farmhouse. He has renovated it well, many of the rooms are now perfectly comfortable. We went into the main room and turned on the lamp and I looked about the place making light conversation. I offered to arrange for some people to come and look at the mildew problems on the walls. He didn't seem to hear, but just went on sitting in his chair with a far-away look. Then he said he wanted a drink. A small drink. I told him this was impossible. Then he said, very calmly, that it wasn't like the old way he wanted a drink. It wasn't like that. That sort of drinking was behind him for good. But he had just suffered a terrible disappointment. His heart was breaking. He used those words. His heart was breaking, he said, but he knew how much rested on him this evening. He knew he had to do well. He wasn't asking for a drink in the old way. Surely I could tell that? And I looked at him and I could see he was telling the truth. I saw a saddened, disappointed but responsible man. He had come to know himself better than most men can ever hope to do, and he was fully in control. And he was saying that, in this crisis, a small drink was what he needed. To get him over the shock of this emotional blow. To give him the steadiness he needed for the demands of the evening ahead. Mr Ryder, I heard him ask for drink many times in the early days and this was a different thing altogether. I could see that. I looked deep into his eyes and said: "Mr Brodsky, can I trust you? I have some whisky in a hip flask in the car. If I gave you just a small glass can I trust you that that will be the end of it? One small glass and no more?" To which he said, meeting my gaze full on: "It's not like before. I swear to you." And so I went out to the car, it was very dark and the trees were making a furious noise in the wind, and I got the flask from the car and brought it in, and he was no longer in his chair. That's when I went through and found him in his kitchen. It's really an out-house connected to the main farmhouse that Mr Brodsky has been very skilfully converting. Yes, that's when I found him opening the cupboard, the cupboard that was lying on its side. He'd forgotten all about it, he said when he realised I had come in. And there was the whisky. Bottles and bottles of it. He took out just one of the bottles, opened it and poured a small measure into a tumbler. Then, looking me in the eye, he poured the

433

remainder of the bottle onto the floor. His kitchen floor, I should say, is largely earth, it's not as though it made a terrible mess. Well, he poured it out onto the ground, then we came back through to the main room and he sat down in his chair and began to sip the whisky. I watched him very carefully and I could see he was drinking not in the way he used to. Even the fact that he could just sip like that . . . I knew I had made the right decision. I told him I would have to be returning. That I had already stayed away much too long. The bacon and the bread had to be supervised. I stood up and then we both knew without speaking what was on my mind. That's to say, the cupboard. And Mr Brodsky looked me straight in the eye and said: "It's not like before." That was enough for me. To insist on staying any longer, that would only have undermined him. It would have been an insult. In any case, as I say, when I looked into his face I felt perfectly confident. I left without another thought. And it is only in the last few minutes, sir, that even a flicker of a doubt has crossed my mind. But I know rationally it is simply the tension before a great event. He will be here shortly, I'm certain of it. And the whole evening, I feel very confident, will be a success, a great success . . .'

'Mr Hoffman,' I said, my impatience overtaking me, 'if you feel happy having left Mr Brodsky drinking whisky, well, that's your business. I'm not at all sure it was such a good decision, but then you know the situation much better than I do. In any case, may I remind you that I am myself in need of assistance at this moment? As I explained to you, I need a car as soon as possible. This really is a matter of some urgency, Mr Hoffman.'

'Ah yes, a car.' Hoffman looked about thoughtfully. 'The simplest thing, Mr Ryder, might be if you borrowed *my* car. It is parked outside that fire door just there.' He pointed a little further down the corridor. 'Now, where are the keys? Ah, here you are. The steering is slightly tilted to the left. I've been meaning to get it adjusted but things have been so busy. Please, make whatever use of it you will. I won't be needing it again until morning.'

434

30

I brought Hoffman's large black car out of the parking area and onto a twisting road shrouded on both sides by fir trees. This was clearly not the usual route out of the grounds. The road was pitted, unlit, and too narrow for two vehicles to pass without slowing. I drove cautiously, peering into the dark, expecting at any moment an obstacle or sharp bend. Then the road straightened and the headlights showed me I was driving through a forest. I picked up speed and for a few minutes travelled on through darkness. Then I caught sight of something bright through the trees to my left and, slowing down again, realised I was looking at the front of the concert hall, grandly illuminated against the night.

The building was now some way away and I was viewing it at an angle, but I could make out much of its impressive façade. There were rows of dignified stone columns to either side of the central arch, and tall windows reaching towards the vast domed roof. I wondered if the guests had started to arrive and, stopping the car altogether, lowered my window for a clearer view. But even when I raised myself in my seat, the trees prevented me from seeing anything of the building at ground level.

Then, as I continued to gaze towards the concert hall, the possibility struck me that at that very moment my parents were themselves on the point of arriving. I suddenly remembered with great vividness Hoffman's description of their horse-drawn carriage emerging out of the darkness into the admiring gaze of the crowd. In fact, just at that moment, as I continued to lean out of the window, I had the distinct impression I could hear somewhere not so far away the sound of their carriage going by. I switched off the engine and listened again, leaning my head out further. Then I got out of the car altogether and stood there in the night, listening intently.

The wind was moving in the trees. Then I heard once more the faint noises I had before: the beat of hooves, a rhythmic jingling, the rattle of a wooden vehicle. Then the sounds faded behind the rustling of the trees. I went on listening for a little while longer, but could hear nothing more. Eventually I turned and got back into the car.

I had felt quite calm – almost tranquil – while standing out in the road, but once I started the car again I was seized by a powerful mixture of frustration, panic and anger. My parents were at that moment arriving, and yet here I was, my preparations far from completed, even now driving away from the concert hall in pursuit of some other matter altogether. I could not understand how I had allowed such a thing to come to pass, and I travelled on through the forest, my anger mounting, resolving to get finished whatever I had now to do at the first opportunity and return to the concert hall as quickly as possible. But then the further thought occurred to me that I did not really know how to reach Sophie's apartment or even if this forest road was taking me in the correct direction. A sense of futility began to come over me, but I sped on none the less, staring at the forest unfolding before me in the headlights.

Then suddenly I became aware of two figures standing waving up ahead of me. They were directly in my path and, though they moved aside as I came nearer, they continued to signal with urgency. Slowing down, I saw that a group of five or six people had set up camp on the roadside around a small portable stove. My first notion was that these were vagrants, but then I saw a middle-aged woman in smart clothes and a grey-haired man in a suit leaning down to my window. Behind them, the others – who had been sitting around the stove on what appeared to be upturned crates – were now rising and coming towards the car. They were all, I noticed, holding tin camping mugs.

As I lowered the window, the woman peered in at me, saying:

'Oh, we're so glad you came along. You see, we were just locked in debate and we couldn't come to any sort of agreement. That's always the trouble, isn't it? We can never agree about anything when there's action needed.'

'But certainly,' the grey-haired man in the suit said solemnly, 'we need to come to some conclusion soon.'

But before either of them had said anything else, I saw that the figure who had come up behind them and was now leaning down looking at me was that of Geoffrey Saunders, my old schoolmate. Recognising me, he pushed his way in front and tapped the door of the car.

'Ah, I was wondering when I'd see you again,' he said. 'To be perfectly honest, I'd been getting a bit cross about it. You know, you not coming by for your cup of tea. And when you'd said and all. Still, I suppose now's not the time to go into it. But all the same, it's a bit cheeky of you, old chap. Never mind. You'd better come on out of there.' With that, he opened the car door and stood aside. I was about to protest, but he continued: 'Better come and get a cup of coffee. Then you can join in with the discussion we're having.'

'Quite frankly, Saunders,' I said, 'this isn't the best time for me.'

'Oh, do come on, old chap.' There was a hint of annoyance in his voice. 'You know, I've been thinking quite a lot about you since we met the other night. Remembering about our schooldays and all that. This morning, for instance, I woke up thinking about that time, you probably don't remember it, that time the two of us were marking a cross-country run for some younger boys. Must have been the lower sixth, I suppose. You probably don't remember, but I was thinking about it, this morning, lying in bed. We were standing waiting outside this pub opposite this big field and you were awfully upset about something. Come on out, old chap, I can't speak to you like this.' He was continuing to usher me impatiently. 'That's it, that's better.' He grasped my elbow with his free hand – he was holding his tin cup in the other – as I came reluctantly out of the car. 'Yes, I was thinking about that day. One of those foggy October mornings you always get in England. There we were, standing around, waiting for these third-years to come puffing their way out of the mist, and I remember you kept saying: "It's all right for you, it's all very well for you" and being awfully miserable. So in the end I said to you: "Look, it's not just you, old chap. You're not the only one in the world with worries." And I started telling you about that time when I was seven or eight, when we'd gone on one of our family holidays, my parents, my little brother and I. We'd gone to one of those English seaside resorts, Bournemouth, some place like that. Per-haps it was the Isle of Wight. The weather was fine and all that, but you know, something wasn't right, we just weren't getting

437

on. Common enough on family holidays, of course, but I didn't know that then, I was only seven or eight. Anyway it just wasn't working out and one afternoon Father just stormed off. I mean just out of the blue. We'd been looking at something on the seafront and my mother was in the middle of pointing out something to us and suddenly, off he went. Didn't shout or anything, just walked off. We didn't know what to do, so we just started following him, Mother, little Christopher and I, we followed him. Not close up, always thirty yards or so behind, just enough so we could still see him. And Father kept walking. All along the seafront, up the path with the cliffs, past the beach huts and all the people sunbathing. Then he went towards the town, past the tennis courts and through the shopping areas. We must have followed him for over an hour. And after a while we started to make a sort of game of it. We'd say: "Look, he's not angry any more. He's just playing about!" Or we'd say: "He's got his head like that on purpose. Look at that!" and laugh and laugh. And if you looked carefully, you could believe he was doing a funny walk. Christopher, he was only little, I told him that, I told him Father was doing the walk just to be funny and Christopher laughed and laughed, like it was all a great game. And Mother too, she was laughing, saying: "Oh your father, boys!" and laughing some more. And we kept on walking like that, and I was the only one, you see, even though I was only seven or eight, I was the only one who knew Father wasn't really doing it for a joke. That he hadn't got over it at all and was perhaps getting angrier and angrier because we were following him. Because perhaps he wanted to sit down on a bench or go into a café somewhere, but couldn't because of us. You remember all this? I told it all to you that day. And I looked at Mother at one point because I wanted it all to stop, and that was when I realised. I realised she'd convinced herself, convinced herself utterly that Father was doing it all for fun. And little Christopher, he was all the time wanting to run up. You know, run right up behind Father. And I had to keep making excuses, laughing all the time, saying: "No, that's not allowed. That's not part of the game. We've got to keep a long way back or it won't work." But Mother, you see, she was saying: "Oh yes! Why don't you go and pull his shirt and see if you can get back before he catches you!" And I had to keep saying, because I was the only one, you realise, I was the only one, I had to keep saying: "No, no, let's wait. Stay back, stay back." He looked funny, my father. He had an odd sort of gait when you looked at him like that from a distance. Look, old chap, why don't you sit down? You look completely exhausted and very worried. Just sit down here and help us decide.'

Geoffrey Saunders was indicating an upturned orange crate near the camping stove. I felt indeed very tired and decided that whatever tasks lay before me, I would accomplish them better after a brief pause and a sip of coffee. I seated myself, aware as I did so that my knees were shaking and that I was lowering myself onto the crate in the most unsteady way. People gathered around me sympathetically. Someone was holding out a cup of coffee, while someone else had placed a hand on my back, saying: 'Just relax. Just take it easy.'

'Thank you, thank you,' I said and, taking the coffee, gulped it greedily despite its being very hot.

The grey-haired man in the suit now crouched down in front of me and, looking into my face, said very gently: 'We're going to have to come to a decision. You're going to have to help us.'

'A decision?'

'Yes. About Mr Brodsky.'

'Ah yes.' I drank a little more from the tin cup. 'Yes, I know. I realise it's all down to me now.'

'I wouldn't go so far as to say that,' the grey-haired man said.

I looked at him again. He was a reassuring figure with a kindly, calm manner. But just at this moment, I could see, he was very serious.

'I wouldn't go so far as to say it was *all* down to you. It's just that, given the situation, we each of us have to take some responsibility. My own opinion, as I've made clear, is that it should come off.'

'Come off?'

The grey-haired man nodded gravely. I then saw the stethoscope round his neck and realised he was a doctor of some sort.

'Ah yes,' I said. 'It has to come off. Yes.'

It was then that I looked about me and saw with a start, on the ground not far from the car, a large tangle of metal. The thought vaguely crossed my mind that I had caused this wreck, that I had perhaps been involved in some accident without knowing it. Rising to my feet – immediately several hands reached out to steady me – I moved towards the metal and saw that it was in fact the remains of a bicycle. The metal was hopelessly contorted and, to my horror, I saw Brodsky in the midst of it. He was lying with his back to the earth and his eyes watched calmly as I approached him.

'Mr Brodsky,' I murmured, staring at him.

'Ah. Ryder,' he said, with surprisingly little pain in his voice.

I turned back to the grey-haired man, who had come up behind me, saying to him: 'I'm sure this was nothing to do with me. I have no recollection of any sort of accident. I was merely driving . . .'

The grey-haired man, nodding understandingly, signalled to me to be quiet. Then, leading me away a little, he said in a low voice: 'Almost certainly, he was attempting suicide. He's very drunk. Very very drunk.'

'Ah. Yes.'

'I'm certain he was attempting suicide. But now, all he's achieved is to get his legs entangled. The right leg is virtually unscathed. It's simply stuck. The left leg is also stuck. It's this left leg that troubles me. It isn't in a good condition.'

'No,' I said, and glanced over my shoulder at Brodsky again. He appeared to notice and said up into the darkness:

'Ryder. Hello.'

'We were discussing it for some time before you came by,' the grey-haired man continued. 'My feeling is that it has to come off. That way we might save his life. After some debate, the majority of those present have come to that view. Though the two ladies over there are against it. They are all for waiting longer for an ambulance. But I feel we run a grave risk by doing so. That is my professional opinion.'

'Ah yes. Yes, I can see your point.'

'In my view, the left leg must come off without delay. I am a surgeon, but unfortunately I have no equipment with me. No painkillers, nothing. Not even an aspirin. You see, I was off-duty, just walking out here to get some air. Just like these other good people here. I happened to have this stethoscope in my pocket

440

from earlier, but nothing else. But now you've arrived, this may change things. You have supplies in the car?'

'In the car? Well, actually, I don't know. You see, it's a borrowed car.'

'You mean it's a hired car.'

'Not exactly. It's borrowed. From an acquaintance.'

'I see.' He looked gravely down at the ground, thinking to himself. Over his shoulder I could see the others watching us anxiously. Then the surgeon said:

'Perhaps you wouldn't mind looking in the boot. There might be something there to help us. Some sharp implement with which I could carry out the operation.'

I thought about this, then said: 'I'll be happy to go and look. But perhaps first I should go and have a word with Mr Brodsky. You see, I do know him to some extent and I really should speak to him before . . . before such a drastic step is taken.'

'Very well,' the surgeon said. 'But my feeling – my professional opinion – is that we've wasted a great deal of time already. Please be as quick as you can.'

I went over again to Brodsky and looked down into his face.

'Mr Brodsky . . .' I began, but he interrupted immediately.

'Ryder, help me. I have to get to her.'

'To Miss Collins? I think there are other things just now to be concerned with.'

'No, no. I must speak with her. I see it. I see it very clearly now. My mind's very clear now. Since this happened, I don't know, I was on my bicycle, something hit me, some vehicle, a car, who knows? I must have been drunk, I don't remember that part, but I can remember the rest of it. I can see it now, I can see everything. It's him. All the time, he's wanted it to fail. It's him, he's done all this.'

'Who? Hoffman?'

'He's the lowest. The lowest. I couldn't see it before, but now I see it all. Since the vehicle hit me, whatever it was, a car, a truck, since then I can see it all. He came to me tonight, very sympathetic. I was waiting in the cemetery. Waiting and waiting. My heart pounding. I've been waiting all these years. You don't know, Ryder? I've been waiting a long time. Even when I was drunk, I was waiting. Next week, I used to say. Next week I'll stop drinking and go to her. I'll ask her to meet me at St Peter's Cemetery. Year after year I said this. And now at last there I was, waiting. On Per Gustavsson's tomb where I used to sit sometimes with Bruno. I was waiting. Fifteen minutes, then half an hour, then an hour. Then *he* comes. He touches me, here, on the shoulder. She's changed her mind, he says. She's not coming. Not even coming tonight to the concert hall. He's kind as usual. I listen to him. Drink whisky. It will calm you. This is special. But I can't drink whisky, I say. How can I drink whisky? Are you crazy? No, drink whisky, he says. Just a little. It'll steady you. I thought he was being kind. Now I see it. Right from the start, he never meant it to work. He believed I could never do it. I could never do it because I'm this . . . this *piece of dung*. That's what he thought. I'm sober now. I drank enough to kill a horse, but since that vehicle, I'm sober. I can see it all clearly now. It's him. He's lower than me. I won't let him succeed. I'll do it. Help me, Ryder. I won't let him. I'm going to the concert hall now. I'll show everyone. It's ready, the music, it's all here in my head, all here. I'll show everyone. But she has to come. I've got to speak to her. Help me, Ryder. Get me to her. She has to come, just sit in the concert hall. She'll remember then. He's the lowest, but I can see it clearly now. Help me, Ryder.'

'Mr Brodsky,' I said interrupting. 'There's a surgeon present. He's going to have to perform an operation. It might be a little painful.'

'Help me, Ryder. Just help me get to her. Your car? Your car? Take me. Take me to her. She'll be in that apartment. I hate it. How I hate it, hate it. I used to stand outside. Take me to her, Ryder. Take me now.'

'Mr Brodsky, you don't seem to realise your condition. There's little time to be lost. In fact, I promised the surgeon I'd search the boot. I'll be back in just a moment.'

'She's so afraid. But it's not too late. We could have an animal. But never mind that now, never mind the animal. Just come to the concert hall. That's all I ask. Just come to the hall. That's all I ask.'

I left Brodsky and went to the car. Opening the boot I found that Hoffman had crammed it untidily with assorted items. There was a broken chair, a pair of rubber boots, a collection of plastic cartons. Then I found a torch, and when I shone it around the boot I discovered a small hacksaw lying in a corner. It looked a little oily, but when I ran a finger along the blade the teeth felt sharp enough. I closed the boot and made my way over to where the others were standing talking around the stove. As I approached, I could hear the surgeon saying:

'Obstetrics is a dull field now. Not like when I was studying.'

'Excuse me,' I said. 'I found this.'

'Ah,' the surgeon said, turning to me. 'Thank you. And you've spoken with Mr Brodsky? Good.'

I suddenly felt resentful at having been drawn into this whole affair to the extent that I had, and I said, perhaps a little tetchily, looking around at the ring of faces:

'Aren't there proper resources in this town for eventualities like this? Did you say you'd called an ambulance?'

'We called for one about an hour ago,' Geoffrey Saunders spoke up. 'From that call box over there. Unfortunately, ambulances are in short supply tonight on account of the big event at the concert hall.'

I looked where he was pointing and saw that indeed, standing some way back from the road, almost where the darkness of the forest began, was a public telephone box. The sight of it suddenly brought back to me the urgent business I had been in the midst of, and it occurred to me that by telephoning Sophie now I would not only be able to give her some advance warning, I would be able to get some directions as to how I might reach her apartment.

'If you'd excuse me,' I said, moving off. 'I have an important call to make just now.'

I walked towards the trees and entered the telephone box. As I searched through my pockets for some coins, I could see through the glass panel the figure of the surgeon walking slowly towards the prone Brodsky, the hacksaw held tactfully behind his back. Geoffrey Saunders and the others were circling uneasily, looking down into their tin cups or at their feet. Then the surgeon turned and said something to them, and two of the men, Geoffrey Saunders and a young man in a brown leather jacket, went over reluctantly to join him. For a few seconds the three of them stood looking down grimly at Brodsky.

I turned away and dialled Sophie's number. The phone rang

for some time, then Sophie, sounding sleepy and slightly alarmed, came on the line. I took a deep breath.

'Look,' I said, 'you don't seem to realise just how much pressure is on me now. Do you suppose this is easy for me? I've very little time left now and I've still not had a second to inspect the concert hall. Instead there are all these other things people expect me to do. You think tonight's easy for me? Do you realise what tonight is? My parents, they're coming tonight. That's right! They're coming at last, tonight! They may well be there at this very moment! And look what happens. Do they leave me free to prepare? No, they give me one thing to do after the other. This confounded question-and-answer session for one thing. They've actually brought in an electronic scoreboard. Can you believe it? What am I supposed to do? They take so much for granted, all these people. What do they want me to do, on this night of all nights? But it's the same as everywhere else. They expect everything from me. They'll probably turn on me tonight, it wouldn't surprise me. When they get unhappy about my answers, they'll turn on me, and then where will I be? I might not even get as far as the piano. Or my parents might leave, the moment they start to turn on me . . .'

'Look, calm down,' Sophie said. 'It'll be all right. They never turn on you. You always say they'll turn on you and so far no one, not a single person in all these years, has turned on you . . .'

'But don't you understand what I'm saying? This isn't just any night. My parents are coming. If they turn on me tonight, it will be . . . it will be . . .'

'They're not going to turn on you,' Sophie broke in again. 'You say this every time. From all over the world you phone to say the same thing. Whenever you reach this point. They're going to turn on me, they're going to find me out. And what happens? A few hours later you call again, and you're very calm and self-satisfied. I ask you how it went and you sound mildly surprised I should even bring it up. "Oh, it was fine," you say. Always just something like that and then you move onto other things, like none of it's worth discussing . . .'

'Wait a minute. What are you referring to? What phone calls are these? These phone calls, do you realise how much trouble I go to to make them to you? Sometimes I'm frantically busy, but

I still somehow find a few minutes in my schedule to call, just to make sure you're all right. And more often than not it's you, you pour out all your problems to me. What do you mean implying I talk the way you say . . .'

'There's no point in going into it. The point I'm making is that everything will be fine tonight . . .'

'It's all very well for you to say that. You're just like all these others. You just take it for granted. You think all I have to do is turn up and everything else will just follow . . .' I suddenly remembered Gustav lying on his mattress in the unfurnished dressing room and stopped abruptly.

'What's the matter?' Sophie asked.

For a few moments more I continued to collect myself. Then I said:

'Look. There's something I meant to tell you. It's bad news. I'm sorry.'

Sophie was silent at the other end.

'It's your father,' I said. 'He's been taken ill. He's at the concert hall. You have to come immediately.'

I paused again, but Sophie still did not speak.

'He's holding out well,' I went on after another moment. 'But you have to come straight away. Boris too. In fact, that's why I was calling. I have a car. I'm on my way now to pick you both up.'

For what seemed a long time, the line remained silent. Then Sophie said:

'I'm sorry about yesterday evening. At the Karwinsky Gallery, I mean.' She paused and I thought she was going to go silent again. But then she continued: 'I was pathetic. You don't have to pretend. I know I was pathetic. I don't know what it is, I just can't manage in situations like that. I'm going to have to face it. I'll never be the sort who can travel with you from city to city, accompanying you at all these functions. I just can't do it. I'm sorry.'

'But what does that matter?' I said gently. 'That gallery yesterday, I'd forgotten all about it. Who cares what sort of impression you make on people like that? They were awful people, every one of them. And you were by far the most beautiful woman there.'

445

'I can't believe that,' she said, laughing suddenly. 'I'm an old crow now.'

'But you're ageing beautifully.'

'What a thing to say!' She laughed again. 'How dare you!'

'I'm sorry,' I said, laughing also. 'I meant you hadn't aged at all. Not so anyone would notice.'

'Not so anyone would notice?!'

'I don't know . . .' Confused, I gave another laugh. 'Perhaps you looked haggard and ugly. I can't remember now.'

Sophie laughed once more, then fell silent. When she next spoke, her voice had become earnest again. 'But I was pathetic. I can't ever travel with you while I'm like this.'

'Look, I promise, I won't be travelling much longer now. Tonight, if it goes well, you never know. That might be it.'

'And I'm sorry I haven't found anything yet. I promise I'll find something for us soon. Somewhere really comfortable.'

I could not find an immediate response to this and for a few seconds we were both silent. Then I heard her say:

'Do you really not mind? About the way I was yesterday? The way I always am?'

'I don't mind at all. You can behave in any way you like at functions like that. Do whatever you want. It doesn't make any difference. You're worth more than the whole room of them put together.'

Sophie said nothing. After a while I went on:

'It's partly my fault too. About the house, I mean. It's not fair just leaving it to you to find one. Perhaps from now, provided tonight goes well, we can do it differently. We could look for something together.'

The line remained silent and for a second I wondered if Sophie had gone away. But then she said in a distant, dreamy voice:

'We're bound to find something soon, aren't we?'

'Yes, of course. We'll search together. Boris too. We'll find something.'

'And you're coming by soon, aren't you? To take us to Papa?'

'Yes, yes. I'll be coming as quickly as I can. So try and be ready, both of you.'

'Yes, all right.' Her voice still sounded distant and lacking in urgency. 'I'll wake Boris up now. Yes, all right.'

446

When I stepped out of the phone box, it was my impression there were definite signs of dawn in the sky. I saw the crowd around Brodsky and, as I came closer, spotted the surgeon down on his knees, sawing away. Brodsky appeared to be accepting his ordeal in silence, but then, just as I reached the car, he let out a hideous cry that rang through the trees.

'I have to be going now,' I said to no one in particular, and indeed no one seemed to hear me. But then, as I closed my door and started the engine, their faces all turned to me with horrified expressions. Before I could close my window, Geoffrey Saunders had come running up.

'Look here,' he said angrily. 'Look here. You can't go just yet. Once he's freed, we'll need to take him somewhere. We'll need your car, can't you see that? Surely that's common sense.'

'Look, Saunders,' I said firmly. 'I appreciate you've got problems here. I'd like to help more, but I've done all I can. I've got things of my own to worry about now.'

'That's typical of you, old chap,' he said. 'Just typical.'

'Look, you just haven't the faintest. Really, Saunders, you haven't the faintest. I've got more responsibilities than you could ever imagine. Look, I just don't lead the sort of life you do!'

I had bellowed this last statement, and I noticed that even the surgeon had stopped his work and was looking over at me. For all I knew Brodsky too had for the moment forgotten his pain and was staring at me. I felt self-conscious and said in a more conciliatory tone:

'I'm sorry, but I've got something very urgent to attend to. By the time you're all through, by the time Mr Brodsky's in any condition to be transported anywhere, I'm certain the ambulance will have arrived. In any case, I'm sorry, but I can't wait a minute longer.'

With that I quickly raised the window and set the car moving again through the forest.

31

The road continued through the forest for some time. Eventually the trees began to thin out and I could glimpse the morning glowing dimly in the distance. Then the trees finally disappeared and I came into the deserted city streets.

A red light obliged me to stop at an intersection, and as I sat there waiting in the silence – no other vehicle was in sight – I looked about and found myself slowly beginning to recognise the district I had entered. I was, I realised with relief, already very near Sophie's apartment; indeed, the street directly facing me would, I was sure, lead me directly to it. I recalled too that the apartment was over a barber's shop, and when the lights changed I crossed the intersection and drove down the silent street, studying carefully the buildings I was passing. Then I saw ahead of me in the distance two figures waiting at the edge of the kerb and pushed down on the accelerator.

Sophie and Boris were wearing only light jackets and looked to have grown cold in the early morning air. They came running up to the car, and Sophie, leaning down, shouted angrily:

'You were so long! What took you so long?'

Before I could respond, Boris placed a hand on Sophie's arm, saying:

'It's all right. We'll get there in time. It's all right.'

I looked at the little boy. He was holding a large briefcase resembling a doctor's bag, which gave him a slightly comical air of gravity. But his manner was nevertheless oddly reassuring and he seemed to succeed in calming his mother.

I had expected Sophie to sit next to me, but she and Boris both got in the back.

'I'm sorry,' I said as I turned the car, 'but I don't know my way around here so well yet.'

'Who's with him now?' Sophie demanded, her voice again very taut. 'Is someone looking after him now?'

'He's with his colleagues. They're all with him. Every one of them.'

'You see?' Boris's voice said gently behind me. 'I told you. So don't worry. It'll be all right.'

Sophie gave a heavy sigh, but again Boris seemed to have succeeded in calming her. Then a moment later, I heard him say:

'They're taking good care of him. So don't worry. They're taking good care of him. Aren't they?'

This question was evidently directed at me. I had become somewhat resentful about the role he had assumed for himself – I was not happy either that the two of them should sit together in the back as though I were a taxi driver – and I decided not to reply.

For the next few minutes we travelled in silence. We came to the intersection again, after which I did my best to remember the route back to the forest road. We were still going through the empty city streets when Sophie said softly, her voice barely audible above the engine:

'This is a warning.'

I was not sure if she was addressing me and was about to glance over my shoulder at her when she continued in the same soft voice:

'Boris, are you listening to me? We have to face up to it, this is a warning. Your grandfather, he's getting older. He needs to slow down. There's no point trying to deny it. He needs to slow down.'

Boris said something in reply, but I could not hear him.

'I've been thinking about it for some time now,' Sophie went on. 'I didn't say anything to you before, because I know how much you . . . how much you think of your grandfather. But I've been thinking it over for some time. There were other signs long before this. Now this has happened, we can't hide from it any more. He's getting older and he's got to slow down. I've made plans, I never told you, but I've been making plans for a long time. I'm going to have a talk with Mr Hoffman. A good talk with him about Grandfather's future. I've prepared all the infor-mation. I've spoken to Mr Sedelmayer at the Imperial Hotel and also Mr Weissberg at the Ambassadors. I never said to you before, but I could see Grandfather wasn't as strong as he used to be. So I've been finding out. It's not at all unusual, when someone's

449

worked at an hotel for as long as your grandfather has, it's not at all unusual at a certain stage that he's given a slightly different sort of job. So that he doesn't have to do quite as much as before. At the Imperial Hotel, there's this man, much older than your grandfather, you see him as soon as you go into the lobby. He used to be the chef, but when he was too old to do that any more, that's what they decided. He's got a splendid uniform and he's in the corner of the lobby behind this big mahogany desk with a pen-and-ink stand. Mr Sedelmayer says it works very well, that he's worth every penny. The guests, particularly the regular ones, they'd be outraged if they came into the lobby and the old man wasn't sitting there behind the desk. The whole thing gives the place so much distinction. Well, I thought I'd talk to Mr Hoffman about it. Grandfather could do something like that. Of course, he'd get paid less, but he could keep his little room, he's so fond of it, and get his meals. Perhaps they could set him up with a desk like at the Imperial. But then Grandfather might want to stand. In a special uniform, somewhere in the lobby. I don't mean this should all happen immediately. But before too long. He's not so young now and this is a warning. We can't hide from it. There's nothing to be gained in pretending about it.'

Sophie paused a moment. I had by this time brought the car back to the edge of the forest. The dawn sky had become a purple colour.

'Don't worry,' Boris said. 'Grandfather will be all right.'

I could hear Sophie let out a deep breath. Then she said:

'He'll have more time then, too. He won't be nearly as busy, and you'll be able to spend more afternoons with him in the Old Town. Or wherever else you might want to go with him. But he'll need a good coat. That's why I'm bringing this now. It's time I gave it to him. I've had it long enough.'

There was a rustling sound and, glancing in my mirror, I noticed that Sophie was holding beside her the soft brown package containing her father's overcoat. At this point I was obliged to attract her attention to ask something about our route, and she seemed to become aware of my presence for the first time since setting out. She leaned forward and said close to my ear:

'I've been ready for something like this to happen. I'm going to talk to Mr Hoffman soon.'

I murmured something in assent and turned the headlights up as we entered the darkness of the forest.

'Other people,' Sophie said. 'They just carry on like there's all the time in the world. I've never been able to do that.'

For the next few minutes she remained silent, but I could sense her presence very near me, and for some reason found myself expecting to feel at any moment the touch of her fingers on my face. Then she said quietly:

'I remember. After Mother died. How lonely it got.'

I glanced at her again in the mirror. She was still leaning forward towards me, but her eyes were fixed on the forest going by outside.

'Don't worry,' she said softly, and made another rustling sound with the coat. 'I'll see to it we're all fine. The three of us. I'll see to it.'

I brought the car to a halt in a small parking area somewhere behind the concert hall. A door was facing us over which a night light was still shining and, though it was not the door I had used before, I got out and hurried towards it. When I glanced back, Boris was helping his mother out of the car. He insisted on keeping one hand protectively behind her as the two of them came briskly towards the building and the doctor's bag he was clutching in the other hand banged awkwardly about his legs.

The door brought us into the long circular corridor and almost immediately we were obliged to stand aside for a catering trolley being pushed by two men. The temperature felt a good few degrees warmer than before – it was now positively stuffy – but then I noticed nearby two musicians in evening dress chatting amiably in a doorway and realised with relief that we had entered not far from where I had left Gustav.

As I led the way down the corridor, it became increasingly crowded with orchestra members. Most had by now changed for the performance, but the atmosphere among them seemed still to be a very frivolous one. They were shouting and laughing across the corridor more than ever and at one point we nearly collided with a man emerging from a dressing room posturing with a cello as though it were a guitar. Then someone said:

'Oh, it's Mr Ryder, isn't it? We met before, you remember me?'

A group of four or five men coming the other way along the corridor had paused and was looking towards us. They were in full evening dress and I saw in an instant they were all drunk. The man who had spoken was holding a bouquet of roses and, as he came towards me, waved it about carelessly.

'The cinema the other night,' he said. 'Mr Pedersen introduced us. How are you, sir? My friends tell me I disgraced myself that night and that I owe you many apologies.'

'Oh yes,' I said, recognising the man. 'How are you? I'm very pleased to see you again. Unfortunately, I have something very urgent just now . . .'

'I hope I wasn't rude,' the drunken man said, coming right up to me until his face was almost touching mine. 'My intention is never rude.'

At this his companions all made noises of suppressed mirth.

'No, you weren't rude at all,' I said. 'But just now, you must forgive me . . .'

'We were searching,' the drunken man said, 'for the maestro. No, no, not you, sir. Our *very own* maestro. We've brought him flowers, you see. As a token of our great respect. Do you know where we might find him, sir?'

'Unfortunately I have no idea. I . . . I don't think you'll find Mr Brodsky in this building just yet.'

'No? Not arrived yet?' The drunken man turned to his companions. 'Our maestro isn't here yet. What do you make of it?' Then to me: 'We have flowers for him.' He shook the bouquet again and a few petals drifted to the floor. 'A token of fondness and respect from the city council. And apology. Of course. We misunderstood him for so long.' There were more sounds of suppressed laughter from his companions. 'Not here yet. Our very own beloved maestro. Well, in that case, we'd better while away a little more time with these musicians. Or perhaps we'll go back to the bar. What do we do, my friends?'

I could see Sophie and Boris both watching with mounting impatience.

'Excuse me,' I muttered and started to walk away. Behind us, the men erupted into more muffled laughter, but I decided not to look back.

Eventually our surroundings grew quieter and then we could

see in front of us the end of the corridor and the porters crowded together outside the last dressing room. Sophie increased her pace, but then halted while we were still a little way away. For their part, the porters, noticing our approach, had quickly formed a gangway and one of them – a wiry man with a moustache I recognised from the Hungarian Café – came towards us. He looked uncertain and initially addressed only me.

'He's holding out well, sir. He's holding out well.' Then he turned to Sophie and, lowering his eyes, muttered: 'He's holding out well, Miss Sophie.'

Sophie did not respond at first, simply staring past the porters to where the door of the dressing room was standing slightly ajar. Then she said suddenly, as if to justify her presence:

'I've brought something for him. Here' – she lifted up the package – 'I've brought this for him.'

Someone called into the dressing room and two more porters who had been inside appeared at the threshold. Sophie did not move and for a moment no one appeared to know what to say or do next. Then Boris strode in front of us, his black bag hoisted up in the air before him.

'Please, gentlemen,' he said. 'Stand to one side, please. Over here, please.'

He waved the porters away from the door. The two men at the threshold remained where they were, looking bemused, and Boris gestured impatiently to them. 'Gentlemen! Over here please!'

Having cleared a reasonable space in front of the dressing room, Boris glanced back at his mother. Sophie came forward a few more steps then stopped again. Her eyes fixed on the door – the two porters had left it half open – with a look of some apprehension. Again no one seemed sure what to do next, and again it was Boris who broke the silence.

'Mother, wait here please,' he said, and with that, turned and vanished into the dressing room.

Sophie relaxed visibly. She came a few steps closer and leaned forward almost nonchalantly to see if any of the room's interior was visible. Finding that Boris had pushed the door virtually closed behind him, she straightened and stood waiting as though in a bus queue, her package draped over her folded arms.

Boris emerged again after a few minutes. Still holding his doctor's bag, he carefully closed the door behind him.

'Grandfather says he's very pleased we've come,' he said quietly, looking at his mother. 'He's very pleased.'

He went on looking up into his mother's face and I was at first puzzled by the way he did so. Then I realised he was waiting for Sophie to give him a message to take back to Gustav, and sure enough, Sophie said after some thought:

'Tell him I've brought something for him. A present. That I'm bringing it in for him in just a moment. I'm . . . I'm just getting it ready.'

Once Boris had disappeared back into the dressing room, Sophie placed the overcoat over one arm and began to smooth out the wrinkles on the soft brown packaging. It was perhaps to do with the glaring pointlessness of this activity, but I was at this moment suddenly reminded of the many other calls on my time. I remembered, for instance, that I had still to inspect the conditions in the auditorium and that my chances of doing so to any useful degree were diminishing by the minute.

'I'll be back very soon,' I said to Sophie. 'There's something I have to see to.'

She continued to attend to her package and gave no response. I was about to repeat myself more loudly, but then, thinking better of drawing undue attention to myself, hurried off quietly in search of Hoffman.

32

I had gone a little way down the corridor when I saw a commotion ahead of me. A dozen or so people were pushing against one another shouting and gesticulating and my first thought was that in all the mounting tension a quarrel had broken out among the kitchen staff. But then I noticed the entire crowd was moving slowly towards me and that it comprised a curious mixture of people. Some were in full evening dress, while others – in anoraks, raincoats and jeans – appeared to have come straight in off the streets. A few orchestra members had also attached themselves to this group.

One of the men shouting the loudest looked familiar and I was trying to recall where I had seen him before when I heard him cry:

'Mr Brodsky, I really must insist!'

I then recognised the grey-haired surgeon I had encountered earlier in the forest, and realised that indeed, at the centre of the crowd, moving forward slowly with a look of stubborn determination, was Brodsky. He looked ghastly. The skin on his face and neck had become white and startlingly shrivelled.

'But he says he's all right! Why can't you let him decide?' a middle-aged man in a dinner suit shouted back. A number of voices immediately endorsed this statement, to be met in turn by a chorus of protest.

Meanwhile Brodsky continued his slow progress, ignoring all the commotion around him. It looked at first as though he were being borne aloft by the crowd, but as he came closer I saw he was walking by himself with the aid of a crutch. There was something about this crutch which made me look at it more closely and I saw that it was in fact an ironing board which Brodsky was holding, vertically and folded, under his armpit.

As I stood watching this spectacle, people seemed one by one to notice me and fall respectfully silent, so that the closer the crowd came, the more quiet it grew. The surgeon, however, continued to shout:

'Mr Brodsky! Your body has had a very severe shock. I really must insist you sit down and relax!'

Brodsky was looking downwards, concentrating hard on each step, and did not see me for some time. Then finally, sensing a change in those around him, he glanced up.

'Ah, Ryder,' he said. 'Here you are.'

'Mr Brodsky. How are you feeling now?'

'I'm fine,' he said calmly.

The crowd now stood off a little and he covered the remaining distance towards me with greater ease. When I complimented him on the way he had so quickly mastered the art of walking with a crutch, he looked down at his ironing board as though remembering it for the first time in a while.

'The man who brought me here,' he said, 'he happened to have it, this thing, in the back of his van. It's not so bad. It's strong, I can walk with it fine. The only trouble, Ryder. Sometimes it starts to open up. Like this.'

He shook it, and sure enough the ironing board began to slip open. A catch prevented it from opening more than slightly, but I could see how its repeatedly unfolding even to this extent would prove a serious irritation.

'I need some string for it,' Brodsky said a little sadly. 'Something like that. But there's no time now.'

As I looked down to where he was indicating, I could not help staring aghast at his left trouser leg, tied into a knot just below his thigh.

'Mr Brodsky,' I said, forcing myself to look up again, 'you can't be feeling so well just now. Do you have the energy to conduct the orchestra this evening?'

'Yes, yes. I feel fine. I'll conduct and it will be . . . it will be magnificent. Just the way I've always known it would be. And she'll see then, with her own eyes and ears. All these years, I wasn't being such a fool. All these years I had it in me, waiting. She'll see me tonight, Ryder. It will be magnificent.'

'You're referring to Miss Collins? But is she coming here?'

'She's coming here, she's coming. Oh yes, yes. He did his best to stop her, make her afraid, but she's coming, oh yes. I've seen

456

through his game now. Ryder, I got to her apartment, I walked a long way, it was hard, but in the end this man came by, this good man here' – Brodsky looked around at the crowd and waved vaguely towards someone – 'he came by, he had a van. We went to her apartment, I knocked on the door, I knocked and knocked. Someone, a neighbour, thought it was like before. You know, I used to do that, knock and knock on the door at night, and they'd get the police in the end. But I said, no, you fool, I'm not drunk any more. I had an accident and now I'm sober, I can see everything. I shouted this all up to him, the neighbour, some fat old man. I can see everything now, see everything he's been doing all this time, yes, that's what I shouted up. And then she was coming to the door, her, she was coming, and she could hear me talking to her neighbour and I could see her through the glass, not knowing what to do, and so I forgot the neighbour and started to talk to her. She listened, but she didn't open the door at first, but then I said, look, I've had an accident, and she opened the door then. Where's that tailor? Where's he gone? He was supposed to get my jacket ready.' Brodsky looked around him and a voice from the back of the crowd said:

'He won't be long, Mr Brodsky. In fact, here he is.'

A small man emerged with a tape measure and began to measure up Brodsky.

'What's this? What's this?' Brodsky muttered impatiently. Then he said to me: 'I have no suit. They had one ready, it was delivered to my house, they say. Who knows? I had the accident, I don't know where it is now. They'll just have to get me a new one. A suit and a dress shirt, I want the best tonight. She'll see what I meant, all those years.'

'Mr Brodsky,' I said, 'you were telling me about Miss Collins. Do I understand you've managed to persuade her to come tonight after all?'

'Oh, she'll be coming. She promised. She won't break her promise a second time. She never came to the cemetery. I waited and waited but she never came. But that wasn't her fault. It was him, that hotel manager, he made her afraid. But I told her it's too late for fear now. We've been afraid all our lives and now we have to be brave. At first she wasn't listening. What have you done? she kept asking. She wasn't the way you usually see her, she was

457

almost crying, holding her hands up to her face, almost crying, not even caring the neighbours could hear it all. The dead of night and she was saying, Leo, Leo – yes, she calls me that now – Leo, what have you done to your leg? There's blood. And I said it's nothing, it doesn't matter. An accident, but there was a doctor passing by, never mind that now, I told her, much more important, you have to come tonight. Don't listen to that wretch from the hotel, that . . . that *bell-boy*. There's very little time left. Tonight she'd see what I'd always meant. All those years, I wasn't the fool she thought. And she was saying she couldn't come, she wasn't ready, and besides, she said, all those wounds, they'd open again. And I said don't listen to that bell-boy, that hotel janitor, it's too late for that. And she pointed and said, but what's happened, your leg, it's bleeding, and I said never mind, I shouted at her then. Never mind, I said. Don't you see it, I have to have you come! You have to come! You have to see for yourself, you have to come! Then I could see it, that she knew how serious I was. I could see her eyes, how things changed behind them, how the fear went, how something came alive, and I knew I'd won at last and that cleaner of hotel lavatories had lost. And I said to her, quietly now, I said to her: "So you'll come?" And she nodded calmly and I knew I could trust her. Not a trace of doubt, Ryder. She nodded and I knew I could trust her so I turned and went away then. I came here, this good man – where is he? – he brought me here in his van. But I would have walked, there's nothing so wrong with me now.'

'But Mr Brodsky,' I said, 'are you sure you're well enough to go on stage? After all, you've had a terrible accident . . .'

I had not intended it, but my taking up of this theme had the effect of setting off another round of shouting. The surgeon pushed his way to the front and, raising his voice above the others, punched his fist into his hand for emphasis.

'Mr Brodsky, I insist! Even if it's only for several minutes, you *must* relax!'

'I'm fine, I'm fine, leave me be!' Brodsky shouted and began to walk. Then, turning back to me – I had remained stationary – he called: 'If you see that bell-boy, Ryder, tell him I'm here. Tell him that. He thought I'd never get this far, he thinks I'm dog-shit. Tell him I'm here. See how he likes it.' With that he went off down the corridor, pursued by the arguing crowd.

I continued in the opposite direction, looking for some sign of Hoffman. There were now fewer orchestra members standing about the corridor and many of the dressing-room doors had closed. At one point I was thinking of doubling back and peering in more closely through those doorways that were open, when I caught sight of Hoffman's figure in the corridor up ahead of me.

He had his back to me and was pacing slowly with his head bowed down. Although I was too far away to hear him, it was clear he was rehearsing his lines to himself. Then as I came nearer he suddenly lurched forward. I thought he was about to fall, but then realised he was once more performing the curious movement I had watched him practising in Brodsky's dressing-room mirror. Stooping right over, he brought up his arm, the elbow jutting outward, and began to bang his forehead with his fist. He was still doing so when I came up behind him and coughed. Hoffman straightened with a start and turned to me.

'Ah, Mr Ryder. Please don't worry. I'm sure Mr Brodsky will be here any moment now.'

'Indeed, Mr Hoffman. In fact, if you were just now rehearsing your speech of apology to the audience for Mr Brodsky's non-appearance, I'm pleased to inform you it will not be required. Mr Brodsky is now here.' I gestured down the corridor. 'He's just arrived.'

Hoffman looked astonished and for a second froze completely. Then he collected himself and said:

'Ah. Good. What a relief. But then of course, I was always . . . I was always very confident.' He laughed, looking up and down the corridor as though hoping to catch sight of Brodsky. Then he laughed again and said: 'Well, I'd better go and see to him.'

'Mr Hoffman, before you do that, I'd very much appreciate you giving me the latest news regarding my parents. They are, I trust, safely in this building by now? And your idea of the horse and carriage – I believe I heard it as I was driving past the front of the building earlier on – I trust it created the impact you were hoping for?'

'Your parents?' Hoffman looked confused again. Then he put

his hand on my shoulder and said: 'Ah yes. Your parents. Now let me see.'

'Mr Hoffman, I've been trusting you and your colleagues to take good care of my parents. Neither is in the best of health . . .'

'Of course, of course. There's no need to worry. It's simply that, with so many things to consider, and Mr Brodsky being a little late, though you tell me he has now appeared . . . Ha ha . . .' He trailed off and once more cast his gaze down the corridor. I asked quite coldly:

'Mr Hoffman, where are my parents at this moment? Do you have any idea?'

'Ah. At this precise moment, I have to be honest, I do not myself . . . But I can assure you they are in the most capable hands. Of course, I would dearly wish to oversee personally every aspect of the evening, but you must understand . . . Ha ha. Miss Stratmann. She would know exactly where your parents are. She has been instructed to keep a close eye on the situation regarding your parents. Not that there is any danger of their ever being in want of attention while they're with us. On the contrary I have had to ask Miss Stratmann to watch carefully that they don't become exhausted on account of the hospitality that will inevitably be showered on them from all directions . . .'

'Mr Hoffman, I take it you have no idea where they are at this point in time. And where is Miss Stratmann?'

'Oh, I'm sure she's here somewhere. Mr Ryder, let's walk along and go and see how Mr Brodsky is doing. I've no doubt we'll soon come across Miss Stratmann along the way. She may even be in the office. In any case, sir' – he suddenly adopted a more commanding manner – 'we won't achieve a great deal standing here.'

We set off together down the corridor. As we walked, Hoffman seemed to recover completely his composure and he said with a smile:

'Now we can be certain it will all go well. You, sir, look like a man who knows exactly what he's doing. And with Mr Brodsky here, all is now set. Everything will go just as planned. A splendid evening lies before us all.'

Then his step altered and I noticed he was staring at something in front of us. Following his gaze, I saw Stephan standing in the middle of the corridor with a troubled expression. The young man saw us and came towards us quickly.

'Good evening, Mr Ryder,' he said. Then, lowering his voice, he said to Hoffman: 'Father, perhaps we could have a word.'

'We're very busy, Stephan. Mr Brodsky has just now arrived.'

'Yes, I heard. But you see, Father, it's to do with Mother.'

'Ah. Mother.'

'It's just that she's still in the foyer and I'm due on in fifteen minutes. I saw her just now, she was just wandering about the foyer, and I told her I was going on soon and she said: "Well, dear, I have to see to a few things. I'll try and catch the end of your performance at least, but I'll just have to see to a few things first." That's what she said, but she didn't look that busy. Really, though, it's time you and Mother were both taking your seats. I'm on in less than fifteen minutes.'

'Yes, yes, I'll be along in just a moment. And your mother, I'm sure she'll finish whatever she's doing very soon. Why get so worried? Just go back to your dressing room and get yourself ready.'

'But what is it Mother's got to do in the foyer? She's just standing there, chatting with anyone who happens by. Soon she'll be the only one left there. People are taking their seats now.'

'I expect she's just stretching her legs before settling down for the evening. Now, Stephan, calm yourself. You've got to get the evening off to a good start. We're all counting on you.'

The young man thought about this, then seemed suddenly to remember me.

'You've been so kind, Mr Ryder,' he said with a smile. 'Your encouragement has been invaluable.'

'Your encouragement?' Hoffman looked at me in astonishment.

'Oh yes,' Stephan said. 'Mr Ryder has been extremely generous with both his time and his praise. He's been listening to me practise and he's given me the greatest encouragement I've had in years.'

Hoffman was looking from one to the other of us, a smile of incredulity hovering on his lips. Then he said to me:

'You've been spending time listening to Stephan? To him?'

'I have indeed. I tried to tell you this once before, Mr Hoffman.

461

Your son has considerable gifts and, whatever else occurs tonight, I feel sure his performance will prove a sensation.'

'Why, you really think so? But the fact remains, sir, that Stephan here, he . . . he . . .' Hoffman appeared to become confused, and with a quick laugh slapped his son on the back. 'Well then, Stephan, it seems you might have something for us.'

'I hope so, Father. But Mother's still in the foyer. Perhaps she's waiting for *you*. I mean, it's always awkward, a woman sitting by herself at an occasion like this. Perhaps that's all it is. As soon as you go in and take your seat, she might come and join you. It's just that I have to go on very soon now.'

'Very well, Stephan, I'll see to it. Don't worry. Now you get back to your dressing room and get yourself ready. Mr Ryder and I have just a few things to deal with first.'

Although Stephan still looked unhappy, we left him and continued on our way.

'I should warn you, Mr Hoffman,' I said when we had gone a little further down the corridor. 'You may find Mr Brodsky has adopted a somewhat hostile attitude towards . . . well, towards yourself.'

'Towards me?' Hoffman looked surprised.

'That's to say, when I saw him just now, he was expressing a certain annoyance with you. He seemed to have some sort of grievance. I thought I ought just to let you know.'

Hoffman mumbled something I could not hear. Then, as the corridor continued its gradual curve, what was obviously Brodsky's dressing room – a small crowd was loitering outside it – appeared ahead of us. The hotel manager slowed down, then stopped altogether.

'Mr Ryder, I've been thinking over what Stephan just said. On second thoughts, I think I'd better go and see to my wife. Make sure she's all right. After all, the nerves on a night like this, you understand.'

'Of course.'

'Then you'll forgive me. I wonder, sir, if I could ask you just to check that all is well with Mr Brodsky over there. I myself, yes, really' – he looked at his watch – 'it's time I was taking my seat. Stephan's quite right.'

Hoffman gave a short laugh and hurried off in the direction from which we had come.

I waited until he was out of sight, then walked towards the gathering around Brodsky's doorway. Some people seemed to be standing there out of simple curiosity, while others were conducting heated arguments in subdued tones. The grey-haired surgeon was hovering close to the door, emphasising something to an orchestra member, repeatedly waving his hand in an exasperated manner towards the interior of the dressing room. The door itself, I was surprised to see, was wide open, and as I approached it the little tailor I had seen earlier popped his head out, shouting: 'Mr Brodsky wants a pair of scissors. A large pair of scissors!' Someone went hurrying off and the tailor disappeared again inside. I pushed my way through the crowd and looked into the room.

Brodsky was sitting with his back to the doorway, studying himself in his dressing mirror. He was now wearing a dinner jacket, both shoulders of which the tailor was pinching and tugging. He had on also a dress shirt, but as yet no bow tie.

'Ah, Ryder,' he said, seeing my reflection. 'Come in, come in. You know, it's a long time since I've worn clothes like these.'

He sounded much calmer than when I had last encountered him and I was reminded of the commanding air he had displayed in the cemetery that moment he had appeared in front of the mourners.

'Now, Mr Brodsky,' the tailor said, straightening himself, and for a few moments the two of them considered the jacket in the mirror. Then Brodsky shook his head.

'No, no. A little tighter still,' he said. 'Here and here. Too much material.'

'It won't take a moment, Mr Brodsky.' The tailor hurriedly took off the jacket and, giving me a quick bow as he passed, disappeared out of the door.

Brodsky went on looking at his reflection, fingering thoughtfully his winged collar. Then he picked up a comb and made some adjustments to his hair – which I noticed had been rubbed with a shiny lotion.

'How are you feeling now?' I asked, moving closer to him.

'Good,' he said slowly, continuing to attend to his hair. 'I feel good now.'

'And your leg? You're sure you can perform with such a severe injury?'

'My leg, it's nothing.' He put down his comb and considered the effect. 'It wasn't so bad as it looked. I'm fine now.'

As Brodsky said this, I could see in the mirror the surgeon – who had all the time remained near the doorway – take a step into the room with the look of someone no longer able to contain himself. But before the latter could say anything, Brodsky shouted at the mirror with some ferocity:

'I'm fine now! The wound is nothing!'

The surgeon retreated back to the threshold, but from there continued to stare angrily at Brodsky's back.

'But Mr Brodsky,' I said quietly, 'you've lost a limb. That can never be a trivial matter.'

'I lost a limb, it's true.' Brodsky was attending again to his hair. 'But that was years ago, Ryder. Many years ago. When I was a child perhaps. It was all so long ago, I don't quite remember. That fool of a doctor, he didn't realise. I was all caught in that bicycle, but it was just the artificial leg, the one that was trapped. The fool didn't even realise it. Calls himself a surgeon! All my life, it feels like it, Ryder, I've been without that leg. How long ago was it now? You start to forget, once you get to this sort of age. You don't even mind it any more. It gets to be like an old friend, a wound. Of course, it troubles you from time to time, but I've lived with it so long. It must have happened when I was a child. A railway accident, maybe. In the Ukraine somewhere. In the snow maybe. Who knows? It doesn't matter now. It feels like it's been this way all my life. Just one leg. It's not so bad. You get by. That fool of a doctor. He sawed off the wooden leg. Yes, there was blood, it's bleeding still, I need scissors for it, Ryder. I've sent out for scissors. No, no, not for the wound. The trouser leg, I mean this trouser leg here. How can I conduct with this trouser leg flapping empty like this? But that idiot of a doctor, that hospital intern, he cut off the wooden one, so what can I do now? I have to' – he mimicked with his fingers scissors cutting across the material just above the knee – 'I have to do something. Make it as elegant as possible. That fool, not only does he ruin my wooden leg, he grazes the stump. It's years since the wound's bled like this. What an idiot, with his face so serious. A very important

464

man he thinks himself, and he saws off my wooden leg. Cuts the end of my stump. No wonder it keeps bleeding. Blood everywhere. But I lost it years ago. A long time ago, that's how it feels now. I've had a lifetime to get used to it. But now the idiot with his saw, it's bleeding again.' He looked down and rubbed something into the floor with his shoe. 'I've sent out for scissors. I have to look my best, Ryder. I'm not a vain man. I don't do this because I'm vain. But a man must look decent at a time like this. She'll see me tonight, she'll remember tonight through all the years we've got left. And this orchestra, it's a good orchestra. Here, let me show you.' He reached forward and held a baton up to the light. 'A good baton. There's a particular feel, you can tell. It makes a difference, you know. For me, the point is always important. The point must be just so.' He stared at the baton. 'It's been a long time, but I'm not afraid. I'll show them all tonight. And I won't compromise. I'll take it the whole way. Like you say, Ryder. Max Sattler. But what an idiot, that man! That fool! That hospital janitor!'

These last words Brodsky shouted with some relish into the mirror and I saw the surgeon – who had been looking on from the doorway with an expression of astonishment – retreat sheepishly out of view.

With the surgeon finally gone, Brodsky for the first time displayed signs of strain. He closed his eyes and leaned over to one side in his chair, breathing heavily. But then, the next moment, a man burst into the room proffering a pair of scissors.

'Ah, at last,' Brodsky said, taking them. Then, once the man had left, he placed the scissors on the shelf in front of the mirror and began to stand up. He used the back of his chair to hoist himself up, then stretched a hand towards the ironing board leaning against the wall near the mirror. I moved forward to assist him, but with surprising agility he reached the ironing board unaided and tucked it under his arm.

'You see,' he said, gazing down sadly at the empty trouser leg. 'I have to do something here.'

'Would you like me to call back the tailor?'

'No, no. That man, he won't know what to do. I'll do it myself.'

Brodsky went on looking down at the empty trouser leg. As I watched him, I remembered the various other pressing matters awaiting my attention. In particular, I needed to return to Sophie and Boris, and to find out the latest on Gustav's condition. It was even possible some crucial decision concerning Gustav had been deferred pending my return. I gave a cough and said:

'If you don't mind, Mr Brodsky, I have to be getting along.'

Brodsky was still gazing down at his trouser leg. 'It will be magnificent tonight, Ryder,' he said quietly. 'She'll see. She'll see at last.'

33

The scene outside Gustav's dressing room had not changed greatly in the time I had been away. The porters had perhaps moved further away from the doorway and were now huddled in murmured conference on the other side of the corridor. Sophie, however, was standing much as I had last seen her, the package folded over her arms, gazing at the slightly open door. Noticing my approach, one of the porters came towards me and said in a low voice:

'He's still holding out well, sir. But Josef's gone to fetch the doctor now. We decided we couldn't leave it any longer.'

I nodded, then asked quietly, glancing towards Sophie: 'Hasn't she gone in at all?'

'Not yet, sir. Though I'm sure Miss Sophie will do so very shortly.'

We both regarded her a moment.

'And Boris?' I asked.

'Oh, he's been in a few times, sir.'

'A few times?'

'Oh yes. He's in there just now.'

I nodded again, then went up to Sophie. She had been unaware of my return and gave a start as I touched her gently on the shoulder. Then she laughed and said:

'He's in there. Papa.'

'Yes.'

She adjusted her position a little, leaning to one side as though trying to improve her view through the doorway.

'Aren't you going to give him the coat?' I asked.

Sophie looked down at it, then said: 'Oh yes. Yes, yes. I was just going to . . .' She trailed off and again leaned to one side. Then she called out:

'Boris? Boris! Come out a minute.'

After a few seconds Boris emerged looking very collected and closed the door carefully behind him.

467

'Well?' Sophie asked.

Boris gave me a quick glance. Then, turning to his mother, he said:

'Grandfather says he's sorry. He said to say he's sorry.'

'Is that all? That's all he said?'

For an instant, uncertainty crossed the little boy's face. Then he said reassuringly: 'I'll go back in. He'll say more.'

'But is that all he said to you just now? That he's sorry?'

'Don't worry. I'll go back in.'

'Just a minute.' Sophie began to tear the wrapping off the over-coat. 'Take this in to your grandfather. Give it to him. See if it fits him properly. Tell him I can always adjust a few things.'

She let the torn wrapping fall to the floor and held up a dark brown overcoat. Boris took it without fuss and went back into the dressing room. Perhaps on account of the coat – it sat very bulkily in the little boy's arms – Boris left the door half open behind him and soon a murmur of voices came out into the corridor. Sophie did not move from her spot, but I could see her straining to catch some words. Behind us the porters were still keeping a respectful distance, but I could see they too were now looking anxiously at the door.

Several moments passed, then Boris came out again.

'Grandfather says thank you,' he said to Sophie. 'He's very happy now. He says he's very happy.'

'Is that all he said?'

'He said he's happy. He wasn't comfortable before, but now the coat's come, he says it means a lot to him.' Boris glanced behind him, then back at his mother. 'He says he's very happy with the coat.'

'That's all he said? Nothing about . . . nothing about if it fits him? If he likes the colour?'

Because I was watching Sophie at this point, I did not see precisely what it was Boris did next. My impression was that he did nothing remarkable, simply pausing a little while he thought of a response to his mother's query. But Sophie suddenly shouted:

'Why are you doing that?'

The little boy stared in bewilderment.

'Why are you doing that? You know what I mean. Like this!

468

Like this!' She grabbed Boris by the shoulder and began to shake him violently. 'Just like his grandfather!' she said, turning to me. 'He copies it!' Then to the porters, who were all looking on in alarm: 'His grandfather! That's where he gets it from. You see the way he does that with his shoulder? So smug, so self-satisfied. You see it? Exactly like his grandfather!' She glared at Boris and continued to shake him. 'Oh, so you think you're so grand, do you? Do you?'

Boris pulled himself free and staggered back a few steps.

'Did you see it?' Sophie asked me. 'The way he always does that. It's just like his grandfather.'

Boris took a few more steps away from us. Then, reaching down, he picked off the floor the black doctor's bag he had brought with him and held it up defensively in front of his chest. I thought he was about to burst into tears, but at the last moment he managed to control himself.

'Don't worry . . .' he began, then stopped. He hoisted the black bag higher in front of his chest. 'Don't worry. I'll . . . I'll . . .' He gave up and looked about him. The door to the neighbouring room was only a short way behind him and the little boy turned quickly and disappeared through it, slamming it shut after him.

'Are you mad?' I said to Sophie. 'He's upset enough as it is.'

Sophie remained silent for a moment. Then she gave a sigh and walked over to the door through which Boris had disappeared. She knocked, then went in.

I heard Boris say something, but although Sophie had left the door open, I could not make out his words.

'I'm sorry,' I heard Sophie say in reply. 'I didn't mean to.'

Boris said something else I could not catch.

'No, no, it's all right,' Sophie said gently. 'You've been wonderful.' Then after a pause, she said: 'I've got to go and speak with your grandfather now. I've got to go.'

Boris said something again.

'Yes, all right,' Sophie said. 'I'll ask him to come in and wait with you.'

The little boy now began to say something quite lengthy.

'No, he won't,' Sophie interrupted after a while. 'He'll be nice to you. No, I promise. He will. I'll ask him to come in. But I've got to go and speak to Grandfather now. Before the doctor arrives.'

Sophie came out of the room and closed the door. Then, coming close to me, she said very quietly:

'Please go in and wait with him. He's upset. I've got to go and speak to Papa.' Then, before I could move, she had placed a hand on my arm, saying: 'Please be warm to him again. Like you used to be. He so misses it.'

'I'm sorry, I don't know what you're referring to. If he's upset, it's because you . . .'

'Please,' Sophie said. 'Perhaps it's my fault it's all been happening, but please let it stop now. Please go in and sit with him.'

'Of course I'll sit with him,' I said coldly. 'Why wouldn't I? You'd better go in to your father. He probably heard all of that just now.'

I entered the room in which Boris had ensconced himself and was surprised to find it did not resemble any of the other dressing rooms I had seen in the corridor. In fact, it was much more like a classroom, with its neat rows of small desks and chairs and, at the front, a large blackboard. The place was large and dimly lit with heavy shadows everywhere. Boris was sitting at a desk near the back and glanced up briefly as I came in. I said nothing to him and began looking around.

There was an intense scrawl on the blackboard and I wondered vaguely if Boris had done it. Then, as I continued to move around the empty desks, gazing at the charts and maps pinned up on the walls, the little boy gave a heavy sigh. I glanced at him and saw that he had placed his black bag on his lap and was struggling to remove something from it. Eventually he brought out a large book and put it down on the desk in front of him.

I turned away and continued moving around the room. When I next glanced at him, he was leafing through the pages with an admiring expression, and I realised he was once again looking at the handiwork manual. Feeling not a little irritated, I turned to look at a poster warning against the dangers of solvent abuse. Then Boris said behind me:

'I really like this book. It shows you everything.'

He had tried to say this as though to himself, but I had drifted quite far from where he was sitting and so he had been obliged to raise his voice quite unnaturally. I decided not to respond and continued to wander around the room.

470

After a while Boris sighed heavily once more.

'Mother gets so upset sometimes,' he said.

Again, there was no sense of his having addressed me properly, and so I did not respond. Besides, when I eventually turned to him, he was pretending to be absorbed in his book. I wandered over to the other corner of the room and found pinned on the wall a large sheet marked 'Lost Property'. There was a long list of entries in every kind of handwriting, a column each for the date, the article lost and the owner's name. For some reason, I found this sheet diverting and went on studying it for a little while. The entries near the top appeared to have been written in earnest – a lost pen, a lost chess piece, a lost wallet. Then, from about half-way down, the entries grew facetious. Someone was claiming to have lost 'three million US dollars'. Another entry was that of 'Genghis Khan' who had lost 'the Asian Continent'.

'I really like this book,' Boris said behind me. 'It shows you everything.'

Suddenly my patience snapped and I went quickly over to him and slammed my hand down on the desktop.

'Look, why do you keep reading this thing?' I demanded. 'What did your mother tell you about it? She told you it was a marvellous present, I suppose. Well, it wasn't. Is that what she told you? That it's a splendid present? That I chose it for you with great care? Look at it! Look at it!' – I attempted to tug the book out from under his grasp, but he clung to it, putting his arms down over it – 'it's just a useless old manual someone wanted to throw away. Do you think a book like this, something like this, can teach you about anything?'

I was still trying to pull it out from under him, but Boris, leaning right over the desk, was now protecting the book with his body. All the while he maintained an unnerving silence. I tugged again, determined to take the thing off him once and for all.

'Listen, this is a useless present. Utterly useless. No thought, no affection, nothing went into it. An afterthought, it's got it written over every page. But you think it's something marvellous I gave you! Give it to me, give it to me!'

Perhaps the fear that the manual would be torn apart caused Boris suddenly to raise his arms, and I found myself holding the book up by one cover. He still did not utter a sound, and I felt somewhat foolish about my outburst. I glanced at the book, hanging from my hand, then threw it towards the far corner of the room. It hit a desk and landed somewhere in the shadows. I immediately felt calmer and took a deep breath. When I next looked at him, Boris was sitting up rigidly, staring towards the part of the room where the manual had landed. He then got to his feet and hurried to retrieve it. He had not got half-way, however, when Sophie's voice called urgently from the corridor:

'Boris, come here a moment. Just a moment.'

Boris hesitated, looking once more over to where the manual had landed, then went out of the room.

'Boris,' I could hear Sophie saying outside, 'go and ask Grandfather how he's feeling now. And ask him if he wants any adjustments on the coat. The buttons at the bottom may be wrong. It might flap in the wind, if he stands up on the bridge a lot. Go and ask him, but don't stay and talk for a long time. Just ask him then come straight out.'

By the time I came back into the corridor, the little boy had already disappeared into Gustav's dressing room, and the scene that greeted me was a familiar one: Sophie standing tensely on the spot, her eyes on the door; the porters, a little way behind, looking on with their worried expressions. There was, however, a forlorn look in Sophie's face I had not noticed before and I suddenly felt a rush of tenderness towards her. I went up to her and placed my arm around her shoulders.

'This is a difficult time for us all,' I said gently. 'A very difficult time.'

I began to draw her closer to me, but she suddenly shook me off and went on staring at the doorway. Startled by this rebuttal, I said to her angrily:

'Look, we've all got to support each other at times like this.'

Sophie did not respond, and then Boris came out of the dressing room again.

'Grandfather says the coat's just what he wanted and he likes it even more because Mother gave it to him.'

Sophie made an exasperated noise. 'But does he want me to adjust it? Why doesn't he tell me? The doctor will be here soon.'

'He says . . . he says he loves the coat. He loves it very much.'

'Ask him about the lower buttons. If he's going to keep standing up on the bridge in the wind, it will have to do up properly.'

Boris considered this for a second, then nodded and went back into the dressing room.

'Look,' I said to Sophie, 'you don't seem to realise how much pressure I'm under just now. Do you realise I'm due on stage very shortly? I'll have to answer complex questions about the future of this community. There's going to be an electronic scoreboard. Do you realise what this means? It's all very well you worrying about these buttons and so on. Do you realise the pressure I'm under just now?'

Sophie turned to me with a distressed look and seemed about to say something, but just then Boris appeared again. This time he looked very seriously into his mother's face but said nothing.

'Well, what did he say?' Sophie asked.

'He says he loves the coat very much. He says it reminds him of a coat Mother had when Mother was little. Something about the colour. He says it used to have a picture of a bear on it. The coat Mother used to have.'

'Do I need to adjust it?! Why won't he give me a straight answer? The doctor will be here soon!'

'You don't seem to understand,' I said interrupting. 'There are people out there depending on me. There's going to be an electronic scoreboard, everything. They want me to come to the edge of the stage after each answer. That's a lot of pressure. You don't seem to . . .'

I stopped, becoming aware that Gustav was calling out something. Boris immediately turned and went back into the dressing room, and for what felt a long time Sophie and I stood there together waiting for him to come back. When he finally did so, the little boy looked at neither of us but, striding past, stopped in front of the porters.

'Gentlemen, please.' He made an ushering motion. 'Grandfather would like you all to go in. He wants you all to be with him now.'

Boris began to lead the way and, after a slight hesitation, the porters followed keenly. They filed past us, some of them mumbling an awkward word or two to Sophie.

Once the last of them had gone in, I peered into the room but still could not see Gustav on account of the porters crowded just inside the doorway. There came the sound of three or four voices talking at once, and I was about to move closer when Sophie suddenly brushed past me and entered the room. There was a lot of movement and the voices stopped.

I strode up to the doorway. The porters having formed a gangway to let Sophie through, I now had a clear view of Gustav lying on his mattress. The brown overcoat was draped over the upper part of his body on top of the grey blanket I remembered from earlier. He had no pillow and clearly lacked the strength to raise his head, but he was looking up at his daughter with a gentle smile around his eyes.

Sophie had stopped two or three paces from where Gustav was lying. Her back was turned to me, so I could not see her expression, but she appeared to be staring down at him. Then, after several moments of silence, Sophie said:

'Do you remember that day you came to school? When you came with my swimming kit? I'd left it at home and I was so upset all through the morning, wondering what I was going to do, and then you came with the blue sportsbag, the one with the string strap, came right into the classroom. Do you remember, Papa?'

'This coat will keep me warm now,' Gustav said. 'It's what I've been needing.'

'You only had half an hour off, so you'd run all the way from the hotel. You came into the classroom, holding the blue sportsbag.'

'I was always very proud of you.'

'I'd been so worried all morning. Wondering what I was going to do.'

'This is a very good coat. Look at this collar. And it's real leather all along here.'

'Excuse me,' a voice said close to me and I turned to find a young man with spectacles and a doctor's bag trying to squeeze past. Close behind him was another porter I recognised from the Hungarian Café. The two of them went into the room, and the young doctor, hurrying to Gustav, knelt down beside him and began to look him over.

Sophie silently stared at the doctor. Then, as though acknowledging it was now someone else's turn to receive her father's attention, she took a few steps back. Boris walked over to her and for a moment they were standing almost touching, but Sophie seemed not to notice the little boy and went on staring at the doctor's hunched-over back.

It was just at this point I suddenly remembered again the many things needing to be done before my performance, and it occurred to me that, with the doctor having arrived, this was as good a moment as any for me to slip away. I moved quietly back out into the corridor and was about to set off in search of Hoffman when I heard a movement behind me and felt my arm being grasped roughly.

'Where do you think you're going?' Sophie asked in an angry whisper.

'I'm sorry, but you clearly don't understand. I've got a lot to do now. There's going to be an electronic scoreboard, everything. There's an awful lot depending on me.' I said this, all the time trying to free my arm from her grip.

'But Boris. He needs you here. We both need you here.'

'Look, you obviously have no idea! My parents, don't you see? My parents will be arriving at any moment! There's a thousand things I have to do! You've no idea, you've clearly no idea at all!' I finally wrenched myself free. 'Look, I'll come back,' I called in a conciliatory tone over my shoulder as I hurried away. 'I'll come back as soon as I can.'

34

I was still making my way rapidly along the corridor when I became aware of several figures standing in a line against the wall. Glancing towards them, I saw they were all wearing kitchen overalls and, as far as I could make out, were each waiting their turn to climb into a small black cupboard. Growing curious, I slowed my pace, then eventually turned and walked towards them.

The cupboard, I could now see, was tall and narrow like a broom closet and fixed to the wall a half-metre or so off the ground. A short series of steps led up to it, and from the demeanour of those in the queue I supposed the cupboard contained a urinal or perhaps a drinking fountain. But as I came closer I saw that the man currently at the top of the steps was bent right forward with his rear protruding, to all appearances rummaging busily through the cupboard's contents. Those in the queue, meanwhile, were gesticulating and calling up impatiently for him to finish his turn. Then, as the man came out of the cupboard and was looking cautiously behind him for the top step, someone in the queue let out an exclamation and pointed in my direction. All heads turned to me and the next moment the queue had dissolved as everyone hurried to make way for me. The man who had been in the cupboard came down the steps as quickly as he could, then, bowing to me, made an ushering motion up to the cupboard.

'Thank you,' I said, 'but I believe there were others already waiting.'

There was a storm of protest and several hands virtually pushed me up the short staircase.

The narrow door of the cupboard had fallen shut, and when I opened it – it pulled towards me, obliging me to balance precariously on the top step – I discovered to my surprise that I was looking down onto the auditorium from a vast height. The entire back of the cupboard was missing and, were I reckless enough, I saw that I could, by leaning out and stretching a little, touch the concert hall ceiling. The view certainly was commanding, but the whole arrangement struck me as idiotically hazardous. The cupboard, if anything, actually leaned forward, encouraging a careless spectator to totter towards the edge. Meanwhile only a thin cord tied at waist height had been provided to resist a plunge down into the audience. I could not see any obvious reason for the cupboard – other than perhaps that it was part of some system which allowed flags and such to be suspended across the hall.

I moved my feet carefully until they were both inside the cupboard, then, gripping the door frame tightly, took a look at the scene below me.

Around three-quarters of the seats were now occupied, but the lights were still up and everywhere people were chatting and greeting one another. Some were waving to those in distant rows, others crowding the aisles, talking and laughing. All the while more people were arriving by the two main doors. The array of gleaming music stands in the orchestra pit was catching the light, while on the stage itself – the curtains had been left open – a solitary grand piano was waiting with its lid raised. As I looked down at this instrument on which I was soon to give this most momentous of performances, the thought struck me that this was as close as I was now likely to come to carrying out an inspection of the conditions, and I again felt frustration about the whole way I had organised my time since arriving in the city.

Then, as I watched, Stephan Hoffman came onto the stage from the wings. There had been no announcement and the lights did not dim even slightly. Stephan's manner, moreover, lacked any sense of ceremony. He walked briskly to the piano with a pre-occupied air, not glancing towards the audience. It was hardly surprising then that most people in the hall displayed nothing more than mild curiosity and went on with their talking and greeting. Certainly there was some surprise when he went into the explosive opening of *Glass Passions*, but even then the large majority seemed to conclude, after a few seconds, that the young man was simply testing out the piano or else the amplification system. Then, only several bars in, something seemed to catch Stephan's eye and his playing lost all intensity, as though someone had suddenly pulled out a plug. His gaze followed something moving through the crowd, until eventually he was playing with his head twisted right away from the piano. I then saw he was watching a couple of figures leaving the auditorium and, leaning forward a little further, made out just in time Hoffman and his wife disappearing below me out of my angle of vision.

Stephan stopped playing altogether and, swivelling right round on his stool, sat staring after his parents. This action appeared to remove any remaining doubts in the crowd that Stephan was engaged in a sound check. Indeed, for a moment he looked for all the world like someone awaiting signals from technicians on the other side of the hall, and no one paid any attention when he eventually rose from the stool and strode off the stage.

Only when he had reached the wings did he allow himself to give in to the feeling of outrage now engulfing him. On the other hand, the notion that he had abandoned the stage after only a few bars had for the moment a sense of utter unreality about it, and he hardly gave it thought as he hurried down the wooden steps and through the series of backstage doors.

When he emerged into the corridor it was busy with rushing stage-hands and catering staff. Stephan set off towards the lobby where he hoped to find his parents, but before he had gone far he spotted his father coming towards him, unaccompanied and wearing a preoccupied air. For his part the hotel manager did not notice Stephan until they were virtually about to collide. He then stopped and stared at his son with astonishment.

'What? You're not playing?'

'Father, why did you and Mother leave like that? And where's Mother now? Isn't she feeling well?'

'Your mother.' Hoffman sighed gravely. 'Your mother felt it was correct she should leave at this point. Of course, I escorted her and . . . Well, let me be truthful, Stephan. Let me say it. I tended to concur with her view. I didn't resist the idea. You look at me like that, Stephan. Yes, I realise I've let you down. I promised you you could have this chance, this platform to play in front of the whole town, in front of all our friends and colleagues. Yes, yes, I promised you this. Perhaps it was you yourself who asked me, perhaps you caught me when I was distracted, who knows how it came about? It doesn't matter. The point is I agreed, I promised, I didn't want to go back on it, there, it was my fault. But you have to try and understand, Stephan, how it is for us, your parents. How difficult it is to have to witness . . .'

'I'm going to talk to Mother,' Stephan said and began to walk off. For a brief second Hoffman looked aghast, and then he grasped his son's arm quite roughly, laughing self-consciously as he did so.

'You can't do that, Stephan. What I mean is, you see, your mother has gone to the ladies' room. Ha ha. In any case, I think it best you let her sit things out, so to speak. But Stephan, what have you done? You should be playing. Ah, but perhaps that's for the best in the end. A few embarrassing questions, but no more than that.'

'Father, I'm going back to play. Please take your seat. And please persuade Mother to come back.'

'Stephan, Stephan.' Hoffman shook his head and placed a hand on his son's shoulder. 'I want you to know that we both think very highly of you. We're both immensely proud. But this idea of yours, this idea you've had all your life. I mean about . . . about your music. Your mother and I, we've never had the heart to tell you. Naturally, we wanted you to have your dreams. But this. All this' – he gestured in the direction of the auditorium – 'this has all been a terrible mistake. We should never have let things get this far. You see, Stephan, the fact is this. Your playing is very charming. Extremely accomplished in its way. We've always enjoyed listening to you play at home. But music, serious music, music at the sort of level required tonight . . . that, you see, is another thing. No, no, don't interrupt, I'm trying to tell you something, something I should have said long ago. You see, this is the civic concert hall. Audiences, concert audiences, they are not like friends and relatives who listen sympathetically in the living room. Real concert audiences, they are used to standards, professional standards. Stephan, how can I put this?'

'Father,' Stephan interrupted, 'you don't realise. I've practised hard. And even though the piece I'm about to play is a very late choice, nevertheless, I've practised very hard and if you'd only come now you'd see . . .'

'Stephan, Stephan . . .' Hoffman shook his head again. 'If only it were just a matter of hard work. If only it were just that. But some of us, we're just not born with the gift. We haven't got it in us, and that's something we have to come to terms with. It's terrible I have to tell you this at such a moment, and after having led you on for so long. I hope you can forgive us, your mother and me, we were weak for so long. But we could see how much pleasure it brought you and we didn't have the heart. But it's no excuse, I know that. This is awful, my heart bleeds for you at this moment, it really does. I hope you'll be able to forgive us. It was a terrible mistake, to have let you go this far. To have you go on stage in front of the whole town. Your mother and I, we love you too much to be able to watch it. It would simply be too much to . . . to see our own dear son being made a laughing stock. There, I've said it, I've put my cards on the table. It's cruel, but I've told you at last. I thought I might be able to do it. That I would be able to sit there amidst the smirks and the sniggers. But when the moment came, your mother found she could not, and neither could I. What is it? Why won't you listen to me? Don't you realise this is bringing me great pain? It's not easy to speak so frankly, even to one's own son . . .'

'Father, please, I beg you. Just come and listen, if only for a few minutes, and judge for yourself. And Mother. Please, please, persuade Mother. You'll both see then, I know you will . . .'

'Stephan, it's time for you to go back on stage. Your name is printed on the programme. You have appeared once already. You must now at the very least make a go of it. Let everyone see that you at least did your best. There, that's my advice. Never mind them, never mind their sniggers. Even if they openly laugh as though some hilarious pantomime were being performed on the stage rather than a solemn and profound piece of music, even then, you can remember your mother and father are proud you at least had the courage to see it through. Yes, you must go now and see it through, Stephan. But you must forgive us, we simply love you too much to witness it. In fact, Stephan, I believe it would break your mother's heart to do so. Now you must go, there's little time left. Go, go, go.'

Hoffman spun around, a hand to his forehead, as though reeling from a migraine, and in this manner drifted a few steps away from Stephan. Then he abruptly straightened and looked back at his son.

'Stephan,' he said sternly. 'It's time for you to go back on stage.'

Stephan went on staring at his father for a second, then, seeing finally that his cause was a hopeless one, turned and set off down the corridor.

As he made his way again through the succession of backstage doors, Stephan found himself besieged by a variety of thoughts and emotions. Naturally he was frustrated at this failure to persuade his parents to return to their seats. Moreover, he could feel awakening deep within him a nagging fear he had not experienced for some years – namely that what his father had said was true and that he was indeed the victim of some massive delusion. But then as he approached the wings his confidence rapidly returned and with it came an aggressive urge to find out for himself just what he was capable of.

Stephan came back onto the stage to find the lights had dimmed a little. The auditorium was far from dark, however, and many guests were still on their feet. In various parts of the hall waves of people could be seen rising up as someone else crept along a row to their seat. The hubbub lowered only slightly as the young man sat down at the piano and continued steadily while he waited for his emotions to settle. Then his hands came down in the harsh, precise way they had earlier, evoking a territory somewhere between shock and exhilaration essential for the opening of *Glass Passions*.

By the time he was half-way through the brief prologue, the audience had become significantly quieter. By the time he was completing the first movement, the auditorium had fallen entirely silent. Those who had been standing talking in the aisles were still on their feet, but appeared frozen, their eyes fixed on the stage. All those seated were watching and listening with concentration. A small crowd had formed at one of the entrances where the last of the people drifting in had stopped in their tracks. As Stephan began the second movement, the technicians turned the house lights right down and I could no longer see the audience well. But there was no doubting the general astonishment which continued to envelope the hall. Admittedly a part of

481

this response was down to the audience's surprise at discovering one of their own young men capable of scaling such technical heights as they were now witnessing. But over and beyond his expertise, there was some strangely intense quality to Stephan's playing that virtually refused to be ignored. It was my impression, moreover, that many of those present saw in this unexpected start to the evening a kind of omen. If this was merely the prelude, what did the rest of the proceedings hold in store? Would the evening prove a turning point for the community after all? Such seemed to be the unspoken questions behind many a startled face in the crowd below me.

Stephan rounded off with a wistful, faintly ironic reading of the coda. There was a second or two of silence after he had finished, and then the hall burst into enthusiastic applause, which the young man leapt to his feet to acknowledge. He was clearly delighted, and if he was feeling all the more frustrated that his parents were not present to witness this triumph, he did not allow it to show on his face. He took several bows as the applause continued, and then, perhaps suddenly remembering his contribution was only a modest part of the whole programme, retreated hastily out of view.

The applause continued strongly for some time before subsiding into an excited murmur. Then, before people had had much chance to exchange views, a severe-faced man with silver hair appeared from the wings. As he came slowly and self-importantly towards the lectern at the front, I recognised him as the man who had presided over the banquet in honour of Brodsky on my first night.

The auditorium quickly fell silent, but for a good thirty seconds the severe-faced man said nothing, simply regarding the audience with faint disgust. Then finally he took a weary breath and said:

'Although it is my wish that you all enjoy this evening, I would remind you that we are not gathered here now to witness a cabaret. Gravely important issues lie behind tonight's occasion. Make no mistake. Issues relating to our future, to the very identity of our community.'

The severe-faced man continued to reiterate pedantically this same point for several more minutes, occasionally taking long pauses during which he surveyed the room with a scowl. I began to lose interest and, remembering the queue of people behind me waiting to use the cupboard, decided to allow someone else his turn. But just as I was negotiating my way out of the confined space, I realised the severe-faced man had moved onto a fresh point – that in fact he was in the process of introducing someone onto the stage.

The personage in question, it seemed, was not only 'the corner-stone of the city's entire library system', but was also possessed of the ability to 'capture the curl of the dewdrop on the tip of an autumn leaf'. The severe-faced man stared contemptuously at the audience for one last time, then mumbled a name and stalked off. The auditorium broke into keen applause, directed evidently at the severe-faced man rather than the person he had introduced. Indeed, the latter did not appear for another minute or so, and when he did was greeted somewhat hesitantly.

The man was small and neat with a bald head and a mous-tache. He came on carrying a folder which he put down on the lectern. He then unclipped some sheets of paper and began to shuffle them about, never once looking up to acknowledge the audience. A restlessness began to grow in the hall. I became curious again and, deciding that those in the queue would not mind waiting just a little longer, repositioned myself carefully near the edge of the cupboard.

When the bald-headed man finally spoke, he did so much too close to the microphone and his voice boomed shakily.

'I would like tonight to present a selection of my work from each of my three periods. Many of these poems will be familiar to you from my readings at the Café Adèle, but I trust you will not object to hearing them again in this grand context. And I will tell you now, there will be a small surprise at the end. Something I trust will bring you a modest amount of pleasure.'

He then returned to shuffling his papers and a few murmured conversations started up in the crowd. Then the bald-headed man at last made up his mind and coughed loudly into the micro-phone, restoring the silence.

Many of the poems used rhyme and were relatively short. There were poems about fish in the city park, snow-storms, broken windows remembered from childhood – all delivered in a curiously high-pitched incantatory tone. My attention drifted for a few minutes, and then I became aware that a section of the audience somewhere directly below me had started to talk quite audibly.

For the moment the voices were reasonably discreet, but even as I listened they seemed to grow bolder. Eventually – while the bald-headed man was reciting a long poem about different cats owned by his mother over the years – the noise drifting up to me became that of a sizeable party consorting in more or less normal tones. Overcoming my sense of caution, I moved right to the very edge of the cupboard and, holding on to the wooden frame with both hands, peered down.

The talking was indeed coming from a group seated directly below me, but the number of those involved was smaller than I had supposed. Seven or eight people had apparently decided to pay no further attention to the poet and were now happily conversing with each other, some of them having turned completely in their seats to do so. I was about to study this group more closely, when I caught sight of Miss Collins sitting several rows behind.

She was wearing the elegant black evening dress she had worn at the banquet of the first night, her shawl still around her shoulders. She was watching the bald-headed man sympathetically, her head tilted slightly to one side, a finger raised to her chin. I continued to watch her for a while but there was nothing at all about her appearance to suggest she was anything other than perfectly calm and serene.

My gaze returned to the rowdy group below me and I noticed that playing cards were now being passed around. Only then did I realise that the core of this group comprised the drunken men I had encountered in the cinema on my first night, and then just a little while ago in the corridor.

The game of cards grew ever more boisterous, until the whole lot of them were bursting into cheers or whoops of laughter. Disapproving looks were being cast in their direction, but then gradually more and more people in the hall began also to talk, albeit in more restrained voices.

The bald-headed man showed no sign of noticing and continued to recite earnestly, poem after poem. Then, about twenty

484

minutes after he had first come on stage, he paused and, gathering some sheets together, said:

'And now we enter my second period. As some of you will already know, my second period was ushered in by one key incident. An incident that made it no longer possible for me to create with the tools I had hitherto employed. That is to say, the discovery that my wife had been unfaithful.'

He hung down his head as if this memory still grieved him. It was then that one of the group below me shouted:

'So he obviously *was* using the wrong tools!'

His companions all laughed, then someone else called out:

'A bad workman always blames his tools.'

'His wife did too it seems,' said the first voice.

This exchange, clearly intended to be heard by as many people as possible, provoked a fair amount of tittering. It was not clear how much of it the bald-headed man had heard from the stage, but he paused and, without looking in the direction of his hecklers, shuffled his papers again. If he had intended to say more by way of introducing his second period, he now abandoned the idea and started once more to recite.

The bald-headed man's second period was not obviously different from his first and the restlessness in the audience grew. So much so that when after a few more minutes one of the drunken men shouted something I could not catch, a substantial part of the hall laughed quite openly. For the first time, the bald-headed man seemed to realise he was losing control of the audience and, looking up in mid-sentence, stood blinking into the lights as though in shock. An obvious course open to him was to abandon the stage. A more dignified option would have been to read three or four more poems before departing. The bald-headed man, however, embarked on another solution altogether. He began to read again at a panic-stricken pace with the intention presumably of completing his planned programme as quickly as possible. The effect was not only to render him more or less incoherent, but also to give encouragement to his enemies, who now saw they had him on the run. More and more remarks were shouted out – no longer just by the group below me – to be greeted each time with laughter from all around the hall.

Then at last the bald-headed man made an attempt to regain

control. He put aside his folder and, not saying a word, stared pleadingly from the lectern. The crowd, much of which had been laughing, quietened – perhaps as much out of curiosity as from remorse. When the bald-headed man finally spoke, his voice had gained a degree of authority.

'I promised you a small surprise,' he said. 'Now here it is. A new poem. I finished it only a week ago. I composed it especially for this great occasion tonight. It is called, simply, "Brodsky the Conqueror". If you will allow me.'

The man shuffled his sheets again, but this time the audience remained silent. Then he leaned forward and began to recite. After the first few lines, he glanced up quickly and seemed surprised to find the hall still silent. He continued to read, and as he did so grew increasingly confident, so that before long he was waving his hands about loftily to emphasise key phrases.

I had imagined the poem would be a general portrait of Brodsky, but it soon became clear it was concerned solely with Brodsky's battles with alcohol. The earlier stanzas drew comparisons between Brodsky and a variety of mythical heroes. There were images of Brodsky hurling spears from a hilltop at an invading army, Brodsky grappling with a sea-serpent, Brodsky chained to a rock. The audience continued to listen with a respectful, even solemn attitude. I glanced at Miss Collins, but could see no obvious change in her demeanour. She was, just as before, observing the poet with an interested but detached air, a finger on the side of her chin.

After several minutes the poem shifted ground. It abandoned its mythical backdrops, focusing instead on actual incidents involving Brodsky from the recent past – incidents which as far as I could guess had passed into local legend. Most of these references were of course lost on me, but I could see an attempt was being made to re-appraise and dignify Brodsky's role in each episode. From a literary standpoint, this section of the poem struck me as a great improvement on the earlier, but the introduction of such concrete and familiar contexts had the effect of breaking whatever hold the bald-headed man had established over the audience. A reference to 'the bus-shelter tragedy' set off some tittering again, which grew more widespread at the mention of Brodsky 'outnumbered and battle-worn' being 'forced finally to surrender, behind the telephone booth'. But it was when the bald-headed man spoke of 'a glittering show of valour on the school outing' that the entire hall, as one, erupted into laughter.

From this point on, it was clear to me nothing could save the bald-headed man. The final stanzas, devoted to eulogising Brodsky's new-found sobriety, were greeted virtually line by line with gales of laughter. When I glanced again at Miss Collins, I could see the finger on her chin making quick stroking motions, but otherwise she looked as composed as ever. The bald-headed man, barely audible above the laughing and the heckling, finally came to the end and, gathering up his sheets indignantly, stalked off the stage. A portion of the audience, feeling perhaps that things had gone too far, applauded quite generously.

For the next few minutes the stage remained empty and the audience was soon talking at full volume. Surveying the faces below me I saw with interest that, although many people were exchanging mirthful looks, a significant number appeared to be angry and were gesturing sternly towards others in the hall. And then the spotlight fell onto the stage again and Hoffman appeared.

The hotel manager looked furious and came hurrying to the lectern without ceremony.

'Ladies and gentlemen, please!' he cried, even as the crowd began to quieten. 'Please! I ask you to remember the import of this evening. To quote Mr von Winterstein, we are not here to attend a cabaret!'

The ferocity of this reprimand did not go down well with some of the crowd, and an ironic 'ooh' rose up from the group below me. But Hoffman went on:

'In particular, I am shocked to find so many of you persisting in this idiotically out-of-date view of Mr Brodsky. Setting aside the many other great merits of Mr Ziegler's poem, its central premise, namely that Mr Brodsky has conquered once and for all the demons that once plagued him, cannot be doubted. Those of you who chose just now to laugh at Mr Ziegler's eloquent articulation of this point will, I am sure, very shortly – yes, in the next few moments! – come to feel ashamed. Yes, ashamed! As ashamed as I felt on behalf of this whole city just a minute ago!'

He thumped the lectern as he said this and a surprisingly large proportion of the audience erupted into self-righteous applause. Hoffman, visibly relieved, but evidently unsure how to respond to this reception, bowed awkwardly a few times. Then, before the applause had died down entirely, he collected himself and declared loudly into the microphone:

'Mr Brodsky deserves to be nothing less than a towering figure in our community! The spiritual and cultural fountainhead for our young people. A lantern-bearer for those of us more senior in years, perhaps, but who none the less have become lost and forlorn in these dark chapters of our city's history. Mr Brodsky deserves nothing less! Here, look at me! I stake my reputation, my *credibility* on what I am now telling you! But why need I say this? In a brief moment, you will perceive it with your own eyes and ears. This is hardly the introduction I intended to give and I regret that I was compelled to give it. But let us not delay any more. Let me call onto the stage our highly esteemed guests, the Stuttgart Nagel Foundation Orchestra. Conducted this evening by our very own – Mr Leo Brodsky!'

There was a good round of applause as Hoffman went off into the wings. For the next few minutes nothing happened, and then the orchestra pit became illuminated and the musicians came out. There was another round of applause, followed by a tense hush as the orchestra members shifted around on their seats, tuned their instruments and fiddled with their music stands. Even the rowdy group below me seemed to have accepted the seriousness of what was about to unfold; they had put away their playing cards and were now sitting attentively, their gazes fixed in front of them.

The orchestra finally settled and a spotlight fell on an area of the stage near the wings. For another minute nothing happened, and then there came a thumping sound from off-stage. The noise grew louder until finally Brodsky stepped into the pool of light. He paused there, perhaps to allow the audience time to register his appearance.

Certainly, many of those present would have had difficulty recognising him. With his evening suit, brilliantly white dress shirt and coiffured hair, he was an impressive figure. There was no denying, however, that the shabby ironing board he was still using as his crutch undermined the effect somewhat. Moreover,

as he began to make his way towards the conductor's podium –
the ironing board thumping with each step – I noticed the handiwork he had carried out on the empty trouser leg. His desire not
to have the material flapping about was perfectly understandable. But rather than knotting it at the stump, Brodsky had cut a
wavy hemline an inch or two below the knee. An entirely elegant
solution, I could see, was not possible, but this hem seemed to me
far too ostentatious, likely only to draw extra attention to his
injury.

And yet, as he continued to advance across the stage, it
appeared I was quite mistaken on this point. For although I kept
waiting for the crowd to gasp on discovering Brodsky's condition, the moment never came. Indeed, as far as I could discern,
the audience seemed not to notice the missing leg at all, and
continued simply to wait in hushed anticipation for Brodsky to
reach the podium.

Perhaps it was the exhaustion, or perhaps the tension, but he
did not seem able to reproduce the smooth walk with the ironing
board I had witnessed earlier in the corridor. He was lurching
badly and it occurred to me that, with his injury still unnoticed,
such a gait was bound to arouse suspicions of drunkenness. He
was several yards from the podium when he stopped and looked
down crossly at his ironing board – which I saw had once more
started to come open. He shook it, then began to walk again. He
managed a few more steps, then something on the ironing board
gave way. It began to unfold itself under him just as he was
placing his weight on it, and Brodsky and the board went down
together in a heap.

The reaction to this occurrence was an odd one. Instead of
the cries of alarm one might have expected, the audience, for the
initial second or two, maintained a disapproving silence. Then a
murmur went across the auditorium, a kind of collective 'hmm',
as though conclusions were being reserved in the face of discouraging signs. Similarly, the three stage-hands who approached to
give Brodsky assistance did so with a marked lack of urgency,
and even a hint of distaste. In any case, before they could reach
him, Brodsky, who had been busy wrestling with the ironing
board, shouted angrily from the floor for them to go away. The

three men stopped in their tracks, then went on watching Brodsky with something not unlike morbid fascination.

Brodsky continued grappling on the floor for some moments. At times he appeared to be attempting to stand up, at others he seemed more intent on extricating some part of his clothing trapped in the mechanisms of the ironing board. At one point he broke into a series of oaths, presumably directed at the board, which the amplification system picked up all too clearly. I glanced again at Miss Collins and saw that she had now sat forward in her seat. But then, as Brodsky's struggles continued, she leaned back again slowly and raised her finger back up to her chin.

Then at last Brodsky made a breakthrough. He succeeded in erecting the ironing board in its unfolded position and pulled himself up. He stood there proudly on his one good leg, gripping the board with both hands, elbows pushed out, as if preparing to mount it. He glared at the three stage-hands and, as they began to retreat back into the wings, turned his gaze on the audience.

'I know, I know,' he said and, although he was not speaking loudly, the microphones along the front of the stage seemed to pick him up so that he was quite audible. 'I know what you're all thinking. Well, you're wrong.'

He looked down and became engrossed again with his predicament. Then he straightened himself up a little more, and began to pass his hand along the padded surface of the ironing board as though its original purpose had only now occurred to him. Finally he looked at the audience again and said:

'Dispel all such notions from your mind. That' – he thrust his head towards the floor – 'was simply an unfortunate accident. Nothing more.'

Another murmur went across the auditorium and then there was silence again.

For the next few moments, Brodsky continued to stand crouched over the ironing board, not moving, his gaze fixed on the conductor's podium. I realised he was measuring the distance to the podium, and indeed, the next instant, he began his journey. He proceeded by lifting the entire frame of the ironing board and banging it down again in the manner of a zimmer, dragging his single leg after it. At first the audience seemed taken aback, but as

Brodsky moved steadily forwards, some people, concluding they were witnessing a sort of circus act, began to clap. This cue was quickly taken up all around the hall so that the remainder of Brodsky's journey to the podium was completed against a background of substantial applause.

On reaching his destination, Brodsky let go of the ironing board and, grasping the semi-circular rail around the podium, eased himself into position. He balanced his body carefully against the rail then picked up the baton.

The applause for the ironing board act had by now died down and there was once again an atmosphere of hushed anticipation. The musicians too were looking at Brodsky slightly nervously. But Brodsky seemed to be savouring the feeling of being back at the helm of an orchestra after so many years, and for a time went on smiling and gazing about him. Then at last he raised his baton in the air. The musicians poised themselves, but Brodsky changed his mind again and, lowering the baton, turned to the audience. He smiled genially and said:

'You all think I'm a filthy drunk. We'll see now if that's all I am.'

The nearest microphone was a certain distance away and only a portion of the audience appeared to hear this remark. In any case, the very next instant, he had raised the baton again and the orchestra was plunged into the harsh opening semibreves of Mullery's *Verticality*.

It did not seem to me a particularly outlandish way to open the piece, but clearly it was not what the audience was expecting. Many people started visibly in their seats and, as the elongated discords stretched on into the sixth and seventh bars, I could see on some faces expressions of near-panic. Even some of the musicians were looking anxiously from the conductor to their scores. But Brodsky continued steadily to turn up the intensity, maintaining all the while his exaggeratedly slow tempo. Then he reached the twelfth bar when the notes burst and came fluttering down. A kind of sigh went around the audience, then almost immediately the music began to build again.

Brodsky occasionally steadied himself with his free hand, but he had by this point entered some deeper part of himself, and seemed able to maintain his balance with only nominal support.

491

He swayed his torso. He swung both arms through the air with abandon. During the early passages of the first movement, I noticed some members of the orchestra glancing guiltily at the audience as though to say: 'Yes, really, this is what he's told us to do!' But then steadily the musicians became engrossed in Brodsky's vision. First it was the violins who became quite carried away, and then I could see more and more musicians losing themselves in their performance. By the time Brodsky led them into the melancholy of the second movement, the orchestra appeared to have accepted entirely his authority. The audience too had by this point lost its earlier restlessness and was sitting transfixed.

Brodsky took advantage of the looser form of the second movement to push into ever stranger territories, and I too – accustomed though I was to every sort of angle on Mullery – grew fascinated. He was almost perversely ignoring the outer structure of the music – the composer's nods towards tonality and melody that decorated the surface of the work – to focus instead on the peculiar life-forms hiding just under the shell. There was a slightly sordid quality about it all, something close to exhibitionism, that suggested Brodsky was himself profoundly embarrassed by the nature of what he was uncovering, but could not resist the compulsion to go yet further. The effect was unnerving, but compelling.

I studied again the crowd below me. There was no doubting this provincial audience had become emotionally gripped by Brodsky, and I now saw the possibility that my question-and-answer session would not prove as tricky as I had feared. Obviously, if Brodsky managed to convince the audience with this display, how I answered the questions became far less critical. My task would become one essentially of endorsing something to which the audience had already been won round – in which case, even with my inadequate level of research, there was no reason I should not acquit myself perfectly adequately with a few diplomatic, occasionally humorous remarks. If on the other hand Brodsky were to leave the audience in turmoil and indecision, I would, regardless of my status and experience, have my work very much cut out for me. The atmosphere in the auditorium was still one of unease and, remembering the perturbed anger of the third movement, I wondered what would happen once Brodsky commenced it.

Just at this point it suddenly occurred to me for the first time to search the audience for my parents. Almost simultaneously, the idea flashed through my head that, since I had not noticed them already on the numerous occasions I had studied the crowd, the likelihood of my now discovering their faces below me was not great. I nevertheless leaned forward, almost recklessly, and scanned the auditorium with my gaze. There were certain parts of the hall I could not see no matter how much I craned forward, and I realised I would sooner or later have to go down into the auditorium itself. Then, even if I were still unable to find my parents, I could at least dig out Hoffman or Miss Stratmann and demand to know of my parents' whereabouts. Either way, I saw I could ill afford to spend further time watching proceedings from my present vantage point and, turning carefully, began to make my way out of the cupboard.

When I emerged again at the top of the small staircase, I saw the queue below me had greatly lengthened. There were now at least twenty people waiting, and I felt rather guilty to have taken as long as I had. Everyone in the queue was talking excitedly, but fell silent at the sight of me. I mumbled a vague apology as I came down the steps, then hurried off down the corridor just as the person next in line began eagerly to climb towards the cupboard entrance.

The corridor was much calmer than before, owing largely to a lull in the activities of the catering staff. Every several yards along the corridor I would encounter a stationary trolley, fully laden, sometimes with men in overalls leaning against it, smoking and drinking from styrofoam cups. Eventually, when I stopped and asked one such person the quickest route to the auditorium, he simply pointed to a door behind me. Thanking him, I pulled it open and found myself looking down an ill-lit stairwell.

I descended at least five flights. Then I pushed through a pair of heavy swing doors and found myself wandering through some cavernous backstage area. In the gloomy light, I could make out rectangular slabs of painted backdrop – a castle tenement, a moonlit sky, a forest – propped against the wall. Above my head

493

was a criss-cross of steel cables. The orchestra could now be heard quite clearly and I moved towards the music doing my best not to collide into the many box-like objects in my path. Eventually, after wandering up a set of wooden steps, I realised I was standing in the wings. I was about to turn back – I had hoped to emerge discreetly somewhere near the front stalls – but then something about the music now filling my ears, something problematic that had not been there before, caused me to pause.

I stood there listening for a minute or so, and then took a step forward and peered around the edge of the heavy folded drapes before me. I did this of course with considerable caution – naturally I wished to avoid at all costs the crowd's spotting my face and bursting into applause – only to discover I was looking at Brodsky and the orchestra from a sharp angle and was unlikely to be visible at all to the audience.

I could see much had changed while I had been wandering around the building. Brodsky, I supposed, had taken things too far, for that tentativeness of technique that so often signals a disaffinity between a conductor and his musicians had entered the orchestra's sound. The musicians – I was now able to see them at close quarters – were wearing expressions of incredulity, distress, even disgust. Then, as my eyes grew more accustomed to the glare of the stagelights, I gazed past the orchestra to the audience. Only the first few rows were visible to me, but it was clear people were now exchanging worried looks, coughing uneasily, shaking their heads. Even as I watched, one woman stood up to leave. Brodsky, however, continued to conduct in an impassioned manner, and if anything seemed eager to push things still further. Then I saw two of the cellists exchange looks and shake their heads. It was a clear sign of mutiny and Brodsky undoubtedly noticed it. His conducting now took on a manic quality and the music veered dangerously towards the realms of perversity.

Up to this point I had not been able to see Brodsky's expression very well – I had mainly his back view – but as his twisting and turning grew more pronounced, I began to catch fuller glimpses of his face. Only then did it dawn on me that some other factor altogether was influencing Brodsky's behaviour. I watched him carefully again – the way his body was twisting and clenching to

494

some rhythm of its own dictating – and I realised that Brodsky was in great pain and probably had been for some time. Once I had recognised this, the signs were unmistakable. He was only just managing to keep going at all, and his face was distorted with something more than passion.

I felt an onus to do something, and quickly appraised the situation. Brodsky had still to get through one and a half demanding movements plus the intricate epilogue. The favourable impression he had created earlier was being rapidly eroded. The audience was liable to become unruly again at any moment. The more I thought about it, the more obvious it became that the performance had to be brought to a halt, and I began to wonder if I should not now walk out onto the stage to bring this about. Indeed I was probably the only person in the hall who could do so without the audience sensing a major calamity.

For the next few minutes, however, I made no move, preoccupied with the question of how precisely to execute such an intervention. Would I come on waving about my arms to signal a halt? That might not only appear presumptuous, but suggest a certain disapproval on my part – a disastrous impression. A much better course, perhaps, would be to wait for the andante to commence and then to come on very modestly, smiling courteously to Brodsky and the orchestra, timing my walk to the music as though the whole entrance had been planned long in advance. No doubt the audience would break into applause, at which point I could in turn – all the time smiling – applaud first Brodsky and then the musicians. Hopefully then Brodsky would have the presence of mind to 'fade out' the music and take bows. With my presence on the stage, the chances of the crowd giving Brodsky trouble were remote. In fact with my lead – I would continue to applaud and smile as though for all the world Brodsky had delivered something of indisputable beauty – the memories of the earlier part of his performance might return sufficiently to bring the audience back onto his side. Brodsky could take a respectable number of bows, and then, as he turned to leave, I could be seen genially to assist him from the podium, perhaps folding his ironing board and handing it to him to use again as his crutch. I might then guide him towards the wings, frequently glancing back to the audience to encourage further applause and so on. I could just about see the thing being brought off provided I judged everything absolutely correctly.

But just at that moment something else occurred which perhaps had been on the cards for some time. Brodsky swung his baton in a large arc, almost simultaneously punching the air with his other hand. As he did so, he appeared to become unstuck. He ascended a few inches into the air then crashed down across the front of the stage, taking the podium rail, the ironing board, the score, the music stand, all with him.

I expected people to rush to his aid, but the gasp that greeted his fall faded into an embarrassed silence. And then, as Brodsky continued to lie there face down on the floor, not moving, a low hubbub started up again throughout the auditorium. Finally, one of the violinists put aside his instrument and made towards Brodsky. A number of others – stage-hands, musicans – soon followed his lead, but there remained something hesitant about the way they closed in around the prone figure, as though they expected to disapprove thoroughly of what they discovered.

I came to my senses around this point – I had been hesitating, unsure what impact my revealing myself would have – and hurried onto the stage to join Brodsky's helpers. As I approached, the violinist let out a cry and, dropping down onto his knees, began to examine Brodsky with a new urgency. Then he looked up at us and said in a horrified whisper: 'My God, he's lost a leg! It's a wonder he took this long to pass out!'

There were gasps of surprise and the dozen or so of us who had gathered around exchanged looks. For some reason, there was a distinct feeling that news of the missing leg must not be allowed to get out and we drew closer together to keep out the audience's gaze. Those nearest to Brodsky were conferring in low voices about whether to carry him off the stage. Then someone signalled and the curtain began to close. It quickly became clear that Brodsky was lying directly in the line of the curtain, and several arms reached out and half dragged him away from the front of the stage just as the curtain came across.

The movement had the effect of reviving Brodsky a little, and when the violinist turned him onto his back he opened his eyes and looked searchingly from face to face. Then he said, in a voice that sounded more sleepy than anything else:

'Where is she? Why isn't she holding me?'

There were more looks exchanged. Then someone whispered: 'Miss Collins. He must mean Miss Collins.'

No sooner had these words been uttered than there was a gentle cough behind us and we turned to find Miss Collins standing just inside the curtain. She still seemed very composed and was gazing towards us with a look of polite concern. Only the way her hands were clasped in front of her, slightly higher on her chest than might be expected, indicated any turmoil within.

'Where is she?' Brodsky asked again in his sleepy voice. Then suddenly he began softly to sing to himself.

The violinist looked up at us. 'Is he drunk? He certainly smells of drink.'

Brodsky ceased singing, then said again, his eyes now closing: 'Where is she? Why doesn't she come?'

This time Miss Collins answered, not loudly, but very clearly from the curtain: 'I'm here, Leo.'

She had spoken in a tone approaching tenderness, but when a gangway immediately formed for her she did not move. The sight of the figure on the floor, however, finally brought signs of distress to her face. Brodsky, his eyes still closed, began to hum again.

Then he opened his eyes and looked about himself carefully. His gaze went first to the curtain – perhaps in search of the audience – then, finding it closed, examined again the faces staring down at him. Finally he looked towards Miss Collins.

'Let's embrace,' he said. 'Let's show the world. The curtain . . .' With some effort, he raised himself a little and called out: 'Get ready to open the curtain again!' Then he said softly to Miss Collins: 'Come and hold me. Embrace me. Then let them open the curtain. We'll let the world see.' He slowly lowered himself again until he was lying flat on his back. 'Come on,' he murmured.

Miss Collins seemed on the verge of speaking, but then changed her mind. She glanced towards the curtain, a look of fear coming into her eyes.

'Let them see it,' Brodsky said. 'Let them see we were together at the end. That we loved each other all our lives. Let's show them. When the curtains open, let them see it.'

Miss Collins went on staring at Brodsky, then finally began to walk towards him. People moved away discreetly, some going so far as to turn their gazes in the other direction. She stopped before she had quite reached him and said in a voice that trembled a little:

'We can hold hands if you like.'

'No, no. This is the finish. Let's embrace properly. Let them see.'

Miss Collins hesitated for a second, then went right up to him and knelt down. Her eyes, I could see, had filled with tears.

'My love,' Brodsky said softly. 'Hold me again. My wound's so painful now.'

Suddenly Miss Collins withdrew the hand she had started to extend and rose to her feet. She stared down coldly at Brodsky, then walked back briskly towards the curtain.

Brodsky seemed not to notice her retreat. He was now staring up at the ceiling, his arms spread open as though he expected Miss Collins to come descending from above.

'Where are you?' he said. 'Let them see it. When they open the curtain. Let them see we were together at the end. Where are you?'

'I won't come, Leo. Wherever you're going now, you'll have to go by yourself.'

Brodsky must have registered her new tone, for although he continued to gaze up at the ceiling his arms fell to his sides.

'Your wound,' Miss Collins said quietly. 'Always your wound.' Then her face contorted into ugliness. 'Oh, how I hate you! How I hate you for wasting my life! I shall never, never forgive you! Your wound, your silly little wound! That's your real love, Leo, that wound, the one true love of your life! I know how it will be, even if we tried, even if we managed to build something all over again. The music too, that would be no different. Even if they'd accepted you tonight, even if you became celebrated in this town, you'd destroy it all, you'd destroy everything, pull it all down around you just as you did before. And all because of that wound. Me, the music, we're neither of us anything more to you than mistresses you seek consolation from. You'll always go back to your one real love. To that wound! And you know what makes me so angry? Leo, are you listening to me? Your wound, it's nothing special, nothing special at all. In this town alone, I know there are many people with far worse. And yet they carry on, every one of them, with far greater courage than you ever did. They go on with their lives. They become something worthwhile. But you, Leo, look at you. Always tending your wound. Are you listening? Listen to me, I want you to hear every word of it! That wound's all you have now. I tried to give you everything once, but you weren't interested and you shan't have me a second time. How you wasted my life! How I hate you! Can you hear me, Leo? Look at you! What's to become of you now? Well, I'll tell you. You're going somewhere horrible now. Somewhere dark and lonely, and I won't come with you. Go on your own! Go on your own with that silly little wound!'

Brodsky had been waving a hand slowly in the air. Now, as she paused, he said:

'I might be . . . I might be a conductor again. The music just now, before I fell. It was good. You heard it? I might be a conductor again . . .'

'Leo, are you listening to me? You'll never be a *proper* conductor. You never were, even back then. You'll never be able to serve the people of this city, even if they wanted you to. Because you care nothing for their lives. That's the truth of it. Your music will only ever be about that silly little wound, it will never be anything more than that, it'll never be anything profound, anything of any value to anyone else. At least I, in my small way, I can say I did what I could. That I did my best to help the unhappy people here. But you, look at you. You've only ever cared about that wound. That's why even back then you were never a *real* musician. And you'll never become one now. Leo, are you listening to me? I want you to hear this. You'll never be anything more than a charlatan. A cowardly, irresponsible fraud . . .'

Suddenly a stout man with a red face burst through the curtain.

'Your ironing board, Mr Brodsky!' he announced cheerfully, holding the object up before him. Then, sensing the atmosphere, he shrank back.

Miss Collins stared at the newcomer, then, casting a last glance towards Brodsky, ran out through the gap in the curtain.

Brodsky's face was still turned up to the ceiling but now his eyes had closed again. Pushing myself forward, I knelt down beside him and listened to his heartbeat.

'Our sailors,' he murmured. 'Our sailors. Our drunken sailors. Where are they now? Where are you? Where are you?'

'It's me,' I said. 'Ryder. Mr Brodsky, we must get you some help very quickly.'

'Ryder.' He opened his eyes and gazed up at me. 'Ryder. Maybe it's true. What she says.'

'Don't worry yourself, Mr Brodsky. Your music was magnificent. Particularly the first two movements . . .'

'No, no, Ryder. I didn't mean all that. That hardly matters now. I meant the other thing she said. About me going alone. To some dark, lonely place. Maybe that's true.' Suddenly he raised his head off the floor and stared into my eyes. 'I don't want to go, Ryder,' he said in a whisper. 'I don't want to go.'

'Mr Brodsky, I'll try and bring her back. As I say, the first two movements in particular displayed enormous innovation. I'm sure she can be reasoned with. Please excuse me, I won't be a moment.'

Freeing my arm from his grip, I hurried out through the curtain.

35

I was surprised to find the auditorium quite transformed. The house lights had come back on and to all practical intents there was no longer an audience. As much as two-thirds of the guests had left, and of those remaining most were standing about talking in the aisles. I did not dwell long on this scene, however, having caught sight of Miss Collins making her way up the central aisle towards the exit. Stepping down off the stage, I hurried after her through the crowds and came within calling distance just as she was reaching the exit.

'Miss Collins! Just a moment, please!'

She turned and, spotting me, fixed me with a hard stare. Somewhat taken aback, I stopped in my tracks half-way up the aisle. Suddenly I could feel draining away all my resolve to catch up and speak with her, and for some reason found myself looking down awkwardly at my feet. When eventually I raised my head again, I saw that she had gone.

I went on standing there a little while longer, wondering if I had been foolish to let her go so easily. But then gradually I found my attention being drawn by the various conversations taking place around me. In particular there was a group standing to my right – six or seven quite elderly people – and I could hear one of the men saying:

'According to Mrs Schuster, the fellow hasn't been sober for one day during this whole business. Now how can we be asked to respect a man like that, however talented? What sort of example is he for our children? No, no, it's all been allowed to go too far.'

'At the Countess's dinner,' a woman said, 'almost certainly he was drunk then. It was only by very clever work they managed to hide it.'

'Excuse me,' I said breaking in, 'but you know nothing of this matter. I can assure you you're quite badly informed.'

I fully expected my presence alone to stun them into silence.

But they glanced at me pleasantly – as though I had merely asked if they minded my joining them – then returned to their conversation.

'No one wants to start praising Christoff again,' the first man said. 'But that rendition just now. As you say, it did border on the tasteless.'

'It bordered on the immoral. That's it. It bordered on the immoral.'

'Excuse me,' I said, interrupting this time more forcefully. 'But I happened to listen very carefully to what Mr Brodsky managed to do before his collapse and my own assessment differs from yours. In my view, he achieved something challenging, fresh, indeed something very close to the inner heart of the piece.'

I gave them all a frosty stare. They looked at me pleasantly again, some of them laughing politely as if I had made a joke. Then the first man said:

'No one's defending Christoff. We've all seen through him now. But when you listen to something like that just now, it does put things in perspective for you.'

'Apparently,' another man said, 'Brodsky believes Max Sattler had it right. Yes. He's actually been going round saying it for much of the day. No doubt he was talking in a drunken stupor, but since the man's always drunk that's as close as we'll get to his thoughts. Max Sattler. That explains a lot about what we just heard.'

'Christoff at least had a sense of structure. Some system you could get hold of.'

'Gentlemen,' I shouted at them, 'you disgust me!'

They did not even turn to look at me and I moved away from them angrily.

As I made my way back down the aisle, everyone around me seemed to be discussing what they had just witnessed. I noticed many were talking out of the sheer need to talk out an experience, in the way they might have done after a fire or an accident. As I reached the front of the auditorium, I saw two women crying and a third comforting them, saying: 'It's all right, it's all finished now. All finished now.' An aroma of coffee was pervading this section of the hall and a number of people were clutching cups and saucers, drinking as though to steady themselves.

Just then it occurred to me I should return to the upper level to see how Gustav was getting on, and, pushing my way through the throng, I left the auditorium via an emergency exit.

I found myself in a hushed, empty corridor. Like the one upstairs, it curved gradually, but this corridor was clearly intended to be used by guests. The carpeting was generous, the lights subdued and warm. Along the wall were paintings framed in gold leaf. I had not expected the corridor to be so deserted and for a moment stood hesitating about which way to go. Then, when I started to walk, I heard a voice call behind me:

'Mr Ryder!'

I turned to see Hoffman further down the corridor waving his arm. He called me again, but for some reason remained glued to his spot, so that in the end I was obliged to retrace my steps.

'Mr Hoffman,' I said as I came towards him. 'It's most unfortunate what has happened.'

'A disaster. An unmitigated disaster.'

'It's really most unfortunate. But Mr Hoffman, you mustn't get too down-hearted. You've done all you could to make the evening a success. And if I may point out, I have yet to make my appearance. I assure you I'll do whatever is in my power to bring the evening back under control. In fact, sir, I was wondering if we might not do away with the question-and-answer session in its original format. My suggestion would be that I simply give a speech, something apt, taking into account what has occurred. I might for instance say a few words suggesting we keep in our hearts the meaning of the extraordinary performance Mr Brodsky was in the midst of giving before he was taken ill, and that we should endeavour to be true to the spirit of that performance, something of that sort. Naturally I will keep the whole thing short. I might then perhaps dedicate my own recital to Mr Brodsky or else to his memory, depending on his condition by that point . . .'

'Mr Ryder,' Hoffman said gravely, and it occurred to me he had not been listening. He was very preoccupied and appeared to have been watching me simply for an opportunity to break in. 'Mr Ryder, there's a matter I wanted to bring up with you. A small matter.'

'Oh, what is that, Mr Hoffman?'

'A small matter, at least to you. For me, for my wife, a matter of some importance.' Suddenly his face contorted with fury and he flung back his arm. I thought he was about to strike me, but then realised he was pointing to a spot behind him further down the corridor. In the subdued light I saw the silhouette of a woman, her back to us, leaning into an alcove. The recess was mirrored and her head was virtually touching the glass, so that her reflection slanted away from her. As I gazed towards this figure, Hoffman, perhaps thinking his first gesture had not got through to me, flung his arm back a second time. Then he said:

'I refer, sir, to my wife's albums.'

'Your wife's albums. Ah yes. Yes, she very kindly ... But surely, Mr Hoffman, now is hardly the time ...'

'Mr Ryder, you will recall you promised you would look at them. And we agreed, out of consideration for you, sir, so that you would not be inconvenienced at an unsuitable time, we agreed – do you not recall, sir? – we agreed on a signal. A signal you would give me when you felt ready to inspect the albums. You recall it, sir?'

'Of course, Mr Hoffman. And I had every intention ...'

'I have watched you very keenly, Mr Ryder. Whenever I caught a glimpse of you strolling around the hotel, walking across the foyer, taking your coffee, I would think to myself: "Ah, he appears to have a moment. Perhaps now is the time." And I waited for the signal, I watched you very carefully, but did it ever come? Pugh! And now here we are, your visit here all but over, just a few hours to go to your flight and your next engagement in Helsinki! There were times, sir, when I thought I had perhaps missed it, that I had turned away for a second and, turning back, mistaken the finishing moments of your signal for some other gesture. If of course this is the case, that you have given the signal on a number of occasions and it is I who have been too obtuse to receive it, then naturally I will apologise without reservation, without shame, without dignity, I will grovel to you. But it is my contention, sir, that you have given no such signal. In other words, sir, that you have treated ... treated' – he glanced back towards the figure down the corridor and lowered his voice – 'you have treated my wife with contempt. Look, here they are!'

Only then did I notice the two large volumes he was carrying in his arms. He held them up to me.

'Here you are, sir. The fruits of my wife's devotion to your marvellous career. How she admires you. You can see it. Look at these pages!' He struggled to open one of the albums while holding the other under his arm. 'Look, sir. Even small little cuttings from obscure magazines. Things said about you in passing. You see, sir, how devoted she is to you. Look here, sir! And here and here! And you cannot find the time even to glance over these albums. What am I to say to her now?' He gestured again towards the figure down the corridor.

'I'm sorry,' I began. 'I'm terribly sorry. But you see, my time here just seemed to get very confused. I had every intention . . .' I then saw that, with all the mounting chaos of the evening, I at least had to keep a cool head. I paused, then said with some command: 'Mr Hoffman, perhaps your wife will find it easier to accept my sincere apologies if she hears them from my own lips. I had the great pleasure of meeting her earlier this evening. Perhaps if you would now lead me to her, we shall be able to sort this matter out quickly. Then of course I really should go on stage, say a few words about Mr Brodsky then give my recital. My parents in particular will be getting impatient.'

Hoffman looked slightly bewildered by these words. Then, trying to re-kindle his earlier anger, he said: 'Look at these pages, sir! Look at them!' But the fire had now died, and he looked at me a little sheepishly. 'Then let us go,' he said in a low voice which had a shocking defeat about it. 'Let us go.'

But he did not move for another moment and I had the impression he was turning over in his head some distant memories. Then with resolve he began to walk towards his wife and I followed a few paces behind.

Mrs Hoffman turned as we approached. I stopped a little way away, but she looked straight past her husband and said to me:

'It's very nice to see you again, Mr Ryder. Unfortunately the evening seems not to be unfolding quite as we all had hoped.'

'Regrettably,' I said, 'it would seem not.' Then taking a step forward, I added: 'Furthermore, madam, with one thing and another, I appear to have neglected a number of things I was very much looking forward to doing.'

I expected her to respond to this hint, but she merely gazed at me with interest and waited for me to go on. Then Hoffman cleared his throat and said:

'My dear. I . . . I knew of your wish.'

With a meek smile, he held up the albums, one in each hand.

Mrs Hoffman stared at him in horror. 'Give me those albums,' she said sternly. 'You had no right! Give them to me.'

'My dear . . .' Hoffman gave a little giggle and his gaze dropped to his feet.

Mrs Hoffman continued to hold out her hand, a furious expression on her face. The hotel manager handed her one album and then the other. His wife gave each a quick glance to verify their identities, and then seemed to become overwhelmed with embarrassment.

'My dear,' Hoffman mumbled, 'I merely thought it would do no harm . . .' Again he trailed off and laughed.

Mrs Hoffman stared coldly at him. Then, turning to me, she said: 'I'm very sorry, Mr Ryder, my husband felt the need to trouble you with such trivial things. Good evening to you.'

She tucked the albums under her arm and began to walk away. She had gone no more than a few paces, however, when Hoffman suddenly exclaimed:

'Trivial? No, no! But they are not trivial! And neither is the album on Kosminsky. Nor the album on Stefan Hallier. Not trivial! If only they were. If only I could believe they were!'

His wife stopped but did not turn, and Hoffman and I stared at her back view as she stood there quite still in the low light of the corridor. Then Hoffman took a few steps towards her.

'The evening. It's a shambles. Why pretend it's anything else? Why continue to tolerate me? Year after year, blunder after blunder. After the Youth Festival, your patience with me was surely at its end. But no, you put up with me further. Then Exhibition Week. Still you put up with me. Still you give me another chance. Very well, I begged you, I know. Implored you for one further chance. And you didn't have the heart to refuse me. In a word, you gave me tonight. And what have I to show for it? The evening is a shambles. Our son, our only son, making a laughing stock of himself before the most distinguished citizens of this town. That was my fault, yes, I know it. I encouraged him. Even at the last moment I knew I should have stopped him, but I didn't have the strength. I let him go through with it right to the end. Believe me, my dear, I never intended it. From the beginning I said to myself, I'll tell him tomorrow, we'll have a proper talk about it tomorrow when there'll be more time. Tomorrow, tomorrow, I kept putting it off. Yes, I was weak, I admit it. Even tonight, I was saying, just a few more minutes and I'll tell him, but no, no, I couldn't and he went on. Yes, our Stephan, he went up there in front of the whole world and played the piano! A laughing stock! Ah, but if only that were the half of it! Everyone, the whole city, knows who is responsible for tonight's proceedings. And the whole city knows who took on the responsibility for Mr Brodsky's recovery. Very well, very well, I don't deny it, I failed, I couldn't bring him round. The man's a drunk, I should have seen how useless it was from the start. The evening is collapsing all around us while we speak. Even Mr Ryder here, even he can't save it now. He only adds to our embarrassment. The finest pianist in the world, I bring him here to what? To take part in this disgrace? Why was I ever allowed to put my clumsy hands anywhere near such divine things as music, art, culture? You, from a talented family, you could have married anyone. What a mistake you made. A tragedy. But it's not too late for you. You are still beautiful. Why wait any longer? What further proof do you need? Leave me. Leave me. Find someone worthy of you. A Kosminsky, a Hallier, a Ryder, a Leonhardt. How did you ever come to make such a mistake? Leave me, I beg you, leave me. Do you see how hateful it is to be your prison warden? No, worse, the very ball and chain on your ankle? Leave me, leave me' – suddenly Hoffman stooped forward and bringing his fist up to his forehead, performed the movement I had watched him rehearsing earlier in the evening. 'My love, my love, leave me. My position is now impossible. After tonight, my pretence, at last, it's over. They'll all know it, down to the smallest child in the town. From tonight, whenever they see me scuttling about my business, they'll know I have nothing. No talent, no sensitivity, no finesse. Leave me, leave me. I'm nothing but an *ox, an ox, an ox!*'

He performed his action again, his elbow jutting out oddly as he thumped his forehead. Then he sank down onto his knees and began to sob.

'A shambles,' he was mumbling through his sobs. 'Everything a shambles.'

Mrs Hoffman had by now turned and was watching her husband carefully. She did not seem at all astonished by the outburst, and a look of tenderness, almost of longing, had come into her eyes. She took a hesitant step, then another, towards Hoffman's bent-over form. Then slowly she reached out a hand as though to touch gently the top of his head. The hand hovered over Hoffman for a second without making contact and then she withdrew it. The next moment, she had turned on her heel and disappeared down the corridor.

Hoffman went on sobbing, evidently oblivious of any of his wife's movements. I watched him for a while, not quite sure what to do next. Then suddenly I realised I must now be well due on stage. And I remembered in a flood of emotion how I had so far been unable to find a single sign of my parents' presence anywhere in the building. My feelings towards Hoffman, which until this point had been close to pity, suddenly turned and, advancing on him, I shouted into his ear:

'Mr Hoffman, it may well be that you have made a shambles of your evening. But I will not be dragged down with you. I intend to go out there and perform. I shall do my best to bring back some order to these proceedings. But first of all, Mr Hoffman, I demand to know once and for all. What has become of my parents?'

Hoffman looked up and seemed slightly surprised to find his wife gone. Then, regarding me with some irritation, he got to his feet.

'What is it you are wanting, sir?' he asked wearily.

'My parents, Mr Hoffman. Where are they? You assured me they would be well looked after. And yet earlier, when I looked, they were not in the audience. I am now about to go on the stage and I wish my parents to be comfortably installed. So now, sir, I must ask you to answer me. Where are they?'

'Your parents, sir.' Hoffman took a deep breath and ran his hand tiredly through his hair. 'You must ask Miss Stratmann. She's in direct charge of their welfare. I merely supervised the larger structure of events. And since, as you see, I have been an utter failure in that respect, you can hardly expect me to be able to answer your question . . .'

'Yes, yes, yes,' I said, growing impatient. 'So where is Miss Stratmann?'

Hoffman sighed and pointed over my shoulder. Turning, I saw there was a door behind me.

'She's in there?' I asked sternly.

Hoffman nodded, then, staggering over to the mirrored alcove where his wife had been standing, gazed at his reflection.

I gave the door a sharp knock. When there was no reply, I glanced accusingly over at Hoffman. He was now bowed over the ledge of the alcove. I was about to vent more of my anger on him when I heard a voice from within calling me to come in. I took a last look at Hoffman's hunched-over form, then opened the door.

36

The large modern office I found myself in was quite unlike anything else I had so far encountered within the building. It was a sort of annexe, seemingly constructed entirely out of glass. There were no lights on in the room and I saw that the dawn had finally come. Soft patches of early sunlight were drifting over the tottering piles of paper, the filing cabinets, the directories and folders strewn about on the desks. The office contained three desks in all, but at this moment Miss Stratmann was the only person present.

She appeared to be busy and it struck me as odd she should have switched off the lights, for the pale glow in the room was hardly sufficient to read or write by. I could only suppose she had switched them off just momentarily to enjoy the view of the sun coming up behind the trees in the far distance. Indeed, as I came in, she was sitting at her desk, a telephone receiver in her hand, gazing out emptily through the huge glass panes.

'Good morning, Mr Ryder,' she said, turning to me. 'I'll be with you in just a moment.' Then she said into the receiver: 'Yes, in about five minutes. The sausages too. They should start frying in the next few minutes. And the fruit. That ought to be ready by now.'

'Miss Stratmann,' I said, advancing towards her desk, 'there are matters more pressing than when the sausages should be fried.'

She glanced up at me quickly and said once more: 'I'll be with you in a moment, Mr Ryder.' Then she spoke into the receiver again and began to write something down.

'Miss Stratmann,' I said, hardening my voice, 'I have to ask you to come off that telephone and listen to what I have to say.'

'Hold on,' Miss Stratmann said into the phone. 'I've got someone here I'd better deal with. I won't be a minute.' Then she put down the receiver and glared at me. 'What is it, Mr Ryder?'

'Miss Stratmann,' I said, 'when we first met, you assured me you would keep me fully informed on all aspects of my visit here.

That you would advise me fully about my schedule and the nature of my various commitments. I believed you to be someone I could depend on. I'm sorry to say you've fallen considerably short of expectations.'

'Mr Ryder, I don't know to what I owe this tirade. Is there something in particular you're unhappy with?'

'I am unhappy with everything, Miss Stratmann. I have not had important information when I've needed it. I have not been told of last-minute changes to my schedule. I haven't been supported or assisted at crucial points. As a result, I have not been able to prepare myself for my tasks in the way I would have liked. Nevertheless, for all that, I intend shortly to go on stage where I'll endeavour to salvage something from what is turning out to be a disastrous evening for you all. But before I do so, I have one simple thing to ask you. Where are my parents? They arrived some time ago by horse and carriage. But when I looked for them earlier in the auditorium, I could not see them. They had not been seated in any of the boxes nor in any of the VIP seats at the front. So I ask you again, Miss Stratmann, where are they? Why have they not been looked after in the careful way you promised?'

Miss Stratmann studied me carefully in the dawn light, then gave a sigh.

'Mr Ryder, I've been meaning to speak to you about this for some time. We were all of us very pleased when you informed us some months ago of your parents' intention to visit our city. Everyone was truly delighted. But I must remind you, Mr Ryder, it was from you and you alone that we heard of their plans to visit us. Now for the past three days, and today in particular, I have been doing all I can to ascertain their whereabouts. I have repeatedly telephoned the airport, the railway station, the bus companies, every hotel in this city, and I have found no sign of them. No one has heard from them, no one has seen them. Now, Mr Ryder, *I* have to ask *you*. Are you certain they are coming to this town?'

As she had been talking, a number of doubts had passed through my mind and suddenly I felt something inside me beginning to collapse. To conceal my discomfort, I turned away and looked out at the dawn.

'Well,' I said eventually, 'I was very sure they would come this time.'

'You were very sure.' Miss Stratmann, whose professional pride I had obviously ruffled quite badly, was now fixing me with an accusing stare. 'Do you realise, Mr Ryder, the great trouble everyone here has gone to in anticipation of your parents' arrival? The medical arrangements, the hospitality, the horse and carriage? One group of local ladies has spent many weeks putting together a programme to entertain your parents during their stay. You were very sure they were coming, you say.'

'Naturally,' I said with a laugh, 'I would never have put people to such trouble had I been anything less than convinced. But the fact was' – another laugh escaped me – 'the fact was, I was sure that this time, at last, they would come. Surely, it wasn't unreasonable of me to assume they would come this time? After all, I'm at the height of my powers now. How much longer am I supposed to go on travelling like this? Of course, I'm sorry if I've put anyone to unnecessary inconvenience, but surely it won't come to that. They must be here somewhere. Besides, I heard them. When I stopped the car in the woods, I could hear them coming, their horse and carriage. I heard them, they must be here, surely, it's not unreasonable . . .'

I collapsed into a nearby chair and realised I had started to sob. As I did so, I remembered all at once just how tenuous had been the whole possibility of my parents' coming to the town. I could not understand at all how I had ever been so confident about the matter to the extent of demanding an explanation from Hoffman and then Miss Stratmann in the manner I had just been doing. I continued to sob for several more moments, then became aware that Miss Stratmann was standing over me.

'Mr Ryder, Mr Ryder,' she was repeating gently. Then, as I brought my tears under control, she said in a kindly tone: 'Mr Ryder. Perhaps no one here has mentioned this to you yet. But there was a time once, quite some years ago now, when your parents did come to this city.'

I stopped sobbing and looked up at her. She gave me a smile, then walked away slowly towards the glass and gazed out again at the dawn.

'They must have been taking a holiday together,' she said, her eyes still on the distance. 'They came by train and stayed two or three days looking about the city. As I say, it was some time ago and you weren't quite as eminent as you are today. But all the same, you were hardly unknown and someone, the people at their hotel perhaps, asked if they were related to you. You know, because of the name and their being English. That's how it got out, that this nice, elderly English couple were your parents. There may not have been quite the fuss there'd be today, but they were looked after very well indeed. And then over the years, as your fame spread, people remembered about it, about the time your parents came here. I don't personally have many memories of their visit because I was so small then. Though I can remember people talking about it.'

I looked carefully at her back. 'Miss Stratmann, you're not telling me all this just to comfort me, are you?'

'No, no, it's all true. Anyone will confirm what I'm saying. As I say, I was just a child then, but a lot of people here would be able to tell you all about it. Besides, it's all been pretty well documented.'

'But did they seem happy? Were they laughing together and enjoying their holiday?'

'I'm sure they were, Mr Ryder. By all accounts, they enjoyed themselves very much here. In fact everyone remembers them as a very pleasant couple. Very kind and considerate to one another.'

'But . . . but what I'm asking, Miss Stratmann, is were they well looked after? That's what I'm asking you . . .'

'Of course they were well looked after. And they enjoyed themselves. They were very happy the whole time they were here.'

'How can you remember that? You said yourself you were no more than a child at the time.'

'What I'm reporting is how everyone here remembers it.'

'If any of this you're saying is true, how is it no one has raised the matter with me the whole time I've been here?'

Miss Stratmann hesitated a second and turned again to the trees and the sunrise. 'I don't know,' she said softly, shaking her head. 'I don't know why that should be. But you're right. People don't talk about it as much as you'd think they would. But there's no mistake, I can assure you. I remember it all distinctly from my childhood.'

From outside came the sounds of birds beginning their chorus. Miss Stratmann went on gazing at the trees in the distance, other memories from her childhood perhaps drifting through her mind. I watched her for a while, then said:

'You say they were treated well here.'

'Oh yes,' Miss Stratmann said almost in a whisper, her eyes still far away. 'I'm sure they were very well treated. It would have been the spring, and the spring is so lovely here. And the Old Town, you've seen for yourself how charming it is. People would have pointed things out to them, just ordinary people who happened to be passing. The buildings of special interest, the crafts museum, the bridges. And if they stopped for a coffee and a snack anywhere and weren't quite sure what to order, perhaps because of the language problem, the waiter or waitress would have been very helpful. Oh yes, they would have enjoyed themselves here.'

'But you said they came by rail. Did anyone help them with their luggage?'

'Oh, the railway porters would have immediately gone about helping them. Taken all the luggage out to the taxi, then the taxi driver would have seen to it after that. They'd have been driven to their hotel and that would have been that. I'm sure they didn't have to even think about their luggage.'

'Hotel? Which hotel was this?'

'A very comfortable hotel, Mr Ryder. One of the best there was in those days. They were sure to have loved it there. Loved every minute of it.'

'It wasn't too near the main roads, I hope. My mother always hated traffic noise.'

'In those days, of course, the traffic wasn't nearly the problem it is now. I remember when I was a child, I used to play with my friends in some of the residential streets with a skipping rope or a ball. No question of children doing that today! Oh yes, we used to play like that, sometimes for hours. But to return to your question, Mr Ryder' – Miss Stratmann turned to me with a wistful smile – 'the hotel your parents stayed in was nowhere near traffic. It was an idyllic hotel. It doesn't exist any more, but if you like I can show you a picture of it. Would you like to see it? The hotel you parents stayed in?'

'I would very much, Miss Stratmann.'

She smiled again and came back across the room towards her desk. I thought she was about to open a drawer, but at the last moment she changed course and went to the rear wall of the office. Reaching up a hand, she tugged at a cord and began pulling down something that looked like a wall chart. I then saw it was not a chart as such, but a gigantic colour photograph. She continued to pull it down almost to the floor, where the roller gave a click and held fast. Then, moving back to her desk, she switched on her reading lamp and turned the beam towards the picture.

For the next few moments we both studied the picture before us in silence. The hotel looked like a smaller version of the sort of fairy-tale castle built by mad kings in the last century. It stood right on the edge of a plunging valley covered with ferns and spring flowers. The photograph had been taken on a sunny day from the opposite side of the valley, providing the kind of comfortable composition suitable for a postcard or calendar.

'I believe your parents stayed in this room here,' I heard Miss Stratmann say. She had produced from somewhere a pointer and was indicating a window in one of the hotel's turrets. 'A nice view they would have had, you see?'

'Yes, indeed.'

Miss Stratmann lowered her pointer, but I continued to stare at the window, trying to imagine the view it would have presented. My mother in particular would have much appreciated such a view. Even if she had had one of her bad days, and had had to spend her whole time in bed, she would still have been greatly comforted by it. She would have watched the breeze blowing through the pit of the valley, disturbing the ferns and the foliage on the twisted trees climbing the valley slope on the far side. She would have liked too the wide expanse of sky visible to her. I then noticed in the very foreground of the picture – cutting across the bottom right-hand corner – a section of the hill road from which presumably the photographer had taken the shot. My mother, almost certainly, would have had a view of this road from her room. She would then have been able to watch the local life going by in the distance. The odd car or grocery van would have passed, perhaps even a horse-drawn cart; now and then a farm tractor or some children hiking. Such sights were bound to have cheered her greatly.

Eventually, as I went on looking at the window, I began to weep again. Not as uncontrollably as before, but the tears filled my eyes very steadily and ran down my face. Miss Stratmann noticed my tears, but this time appeared to feel no need to stop them. She smiled gently at me, then turned back to the picture.

Suddenly I was startled by a knock at the door. Miss Stratmann too gave a start. Then she said: 'Excuse me, Mr Ryder,' and walked over to the door.

I turned in my seat as a man in a white uniform came in, pulling after him a catering trolley. He brought the trolley halfway over the threshold so that it was propping open the door and looked out at the dawn.

'It's going to be a fine day,' he said, smiling at us in turn. 'Here's your breakfast, miss. Would you like it on the desk there?'

'Breakfast?' Miss Stratmann looked confused. 'It's not supposed to be served for another half an hour yet.'

'Mr von Winterstein ordered breakfast to commence now, miss. And in my view, he's right. The people are in need of breakfast at this point.'

'Oh.' Miss Stratmann continued to look confused and glanced back at me as though for guidance. Then she asked the man: 'Is everything out there . . . all right?'

'Everything's fine now, miss. Of course, after Mr Brodsky passed out like that, there was a bit of a panic, but now everyone's very happy and enjoying themselves. You see, Mr von Winterstein gave a fine speech in the foyer just now all about the splendid heritage of this city, all the things we've got to be proud of. He mentioned a lot of our achievements down the years, pointed out all the awful problems other cities are blighted with we here never have to worry about. It's what we needed, miss. I'm sorry you weren't there to hear it. It made us all feel good about ourselves and our city and now everyone's enjoying themselves. Look, there's some of them now.' He pointed out through the glass, and sure enough, in the faint light outside, several figures could be made out walking slowly across the grass holding their plates carefully in front of them, looking around for somewhere to sit down.

'Excuse me,' I said, getting to my feet. 'I must go and perform. I'm going to be late. Miss Stratmann, I'm very grateful. For your kindness, for everything. But please excuse me now.'

Without waiting for a reply, I pushed my way past the breakfast trolley out into the corridor.

37

A pale morning light was now permeating the gloom of the corridor. I glanced towards the mirrored alcove where I had left Hoffman, but he had gone. I hurried on in the direction of the auditorium, past the paintings in their golden frames. At one point I encountered another waiter with a breakfast trolley stooping down to knock on a door, but otherwise the corridor was deserted.

I continued to walk quickly, looking about for the emergency door that had originally brought me into this corridor. I had now become seized by a quite overwhelming urge to get my performance under way. Whatever disappointments I had just suffered did not, I realised, reduce at all my responsibility to all those who had waited many weeks for the moment I sat before them in front of a piano. In other words, it was my duty to perform on this evening at least to my usual standards. To do anything less – I suddenly sensed this strongly – would be to open some strange door through which I would hurtle into a dark, unknown space.

After a time the corridor began to grow unfamiliar. The wallpaper became a deep blue, signed photographs replaced the paintings, and I realised I had missed my door. I saw, however, that I was approaching another altogether more substantial door marked 'Stage' and decided to go through.

For a few seconds I groped through darkness, then found myself once more in the wings. I could see the piano in the middle of the empty stage, dimly lit from above by just one or two lights. I saw too that the curtains were still closed and stepped quietly out onto the stage.

I peered down at the spot where Brodsky had earlier been lying, but could not see even a mark. I then glanced back to the piano, unsure how to proceed. If I sat down at the stool and began simply to play, it was possible the technicians would have the sense to draw back the curtains and to turn up the spotlights.

There was always the chance, however – one could not tell what had been going on – that the technicians had all abandoned their posts and the curtains would not even open. Moreover, when I had last seen the audience, people had been standing about talking restlessly. The best course, I decided, would be to step out through the curtains and make an announcement, giving everyone – the audience, the technicians – the chance to prepare themselves. I quickly rehearsed a few lines in my head, then, without further ado, went up to the gap in the drapes and drew back the heavy material.

I had been ready to find the auditorium in some disorder, but the sight that greeted me quite took me aback. Not only was the audience absent in its entirety, all the seating had vanished as well. The idea came to me that the hall perhaps had some sort of device whereby at the tug of a lever all the seats disappeared into the floor – thus enabling the auditorium to double as a dance floor or whatever – but then I remembered the age of the building and decided this was highly unlikely. I could only suppose the seats had been of the stacking kind and had now all been cleared away as a fire precaution. In any case, before me now was a vast, dark, empty space. There were no lights on at all, but instead, here and there, large rectangular sections of the ceiling had been removed, allowing the daylight to come down in pale shafts onto the floor.

Peering into the murky light, I thought I could make out a few figures towards the very back of the hall. They seemed to be standing around in conference – these were perhaps the stage-hands completing their tidying up – and then I heard the echo of footsteps as one of them strode off somewhere.

I stood there on the edge of the stage wondering what to do next. I had, I supposed, spent much longer in Miss Stratmann's office than I had thought – possibly as long as an hour – and clearly the audience had given up hope of my ever appearing. Nevertheless, if an announcement were to be made, the guests could be gathered back into the auditorium in a matter of minutes, and even with the seating gone I could see no reason why a perfectly satisfactory recital could not then take place. It was unclear, though, where the people had all got to and I realised I would first have to find Hoffman, or whoever had now taken charge, to discuss the next step.

I climbed down off the stage and set off across the hall. I had not got half-way across before I began to feel disorientated in the darkness and, changing course a little, made towards the nearest shaft of light. Just as I did so, a figure brushed in front of me.

'Oh, excuse me,' the person said. 'I beg your pardon.'

I recognised Stephan's voice and said: 'Hello. So you at least are still here.'

'Oh, Mr Ryder. I'm sorry, I didn't see you.' He sounded tired and dejected.

'You really ought to be feeling more cheerful,' I said to him. 'You gave a splendid performance. The audience was extremely moved.'

'Yes. Yes, I suppose they did give me a good reception.'

'Well, congratulations. After all that hard work, it must be very satisfying for you.'

'Yes, I suppose so.'

We started to walk side by side through the darkness. If anything, the daylight from the ceiling made it all the more difficult to see where one was going, but Stephan appeared to know his way.

'You know, Mr Ryder,' he said after a moment, 'I'm jolly grateful to you. You've been marvellously encouraging. But the truth is, I didn't come up to scratch tonight. Not by my own standards anyway. Of course, the audience gave me a big hand, but that's because they weren't expecting anything so special. But really, I know myself I've got a long way to go. My parents are right.'

'Your parents? Good gracious, you shouldn't worry about them.'

'No, no, Mr Ryder, you don't understand. My parents, you see, they have the highest standards. These people who are here tonight, they were very kind but really, they don't know so much about these things. They saw a local boy playing at a certain level and got very excited. But I want to be measured by real standards. And I know my parents do too. Mr Ryder, I've come to a decision. I'm going off. I need to go somewhere bigger, study under someone like Lubetkin or Peruzzi. I realise now I can never reach the levels I want to here, not in this city. Look at the way they clapped what was after all a pretty ordinary performance of *Glass Passions*. That just about summed it up. I didn't really see it before, but I suppose you could call me a big fish in a small pond. I ought to go away for a bit. See what I can really do.'

We continued to walk, our footsteps resounding through the auditorium. Then I said:

'That may well be wise. In fact, I'm sure you're right. A move to a bigger city, bigger challenges, I'm sure it will do you good. But you must be careful who you study with. If you like, I'll give the matter some thought and see if I can arrange something.'

'Mr Ryder, if you'd do that, I'd be eternally grateful. Yes, I need to see how far I can go. Then one day I'll come back here and show them. Show them how you *really* play *Glass Passions*.' He gave a laugh, but still sounded far from cheerful.

'You're a talented young man. You've got everything ahead of you. You really ought to be in better spirits.'

'I suppose so. I suppose I'm just a bit daunted. I didn't realise until tonight just what a huge climb I've still got in front of me. You'll think this is very funny, but do you know, I thought I'd have it all wrapped up tonight. It shows what it does to you, living in a place like this. You start thinking small. Yes, I thought I'd do everything there was to do tonight! You see how ridiculous my thinking has been until now. My parents are quite right. I've a great deal left to learn.'

'Your parents? Listen, my advice is to forget about your parents altogether for now. If I may say so, I really don't understand how they can . . .'

'Ah, here we are. It's this way.' We had arrived at some sort of doorway and Stephan was tugging at a curtain hung across it. 'It's through here.'

'Sorry, what's through here?'

'The conservatory. Oh, perhaps you haven't heard of the conservatory. It's very famous. It was built a hundred years after the hall itself, but now it's almost as famous. That's where everyone's gone to eat breakfast.'

We found ourselves in a corridor, all down one side of which was a long row of windows. I could see through the nearer of them the light blue morning sky.

'Incidentally,' I said as we began to walk again, 'I was wondering about Mr Brodsky. About his condition. Is he . . . deceased?'

'Mr Brodsky? Oh no, he's going to be fine, I'm sure. They took him off somewhere. Actually, I heard they took him to the St Nicholas Clinic.'

'The St Nicholas Clinic?'

'It's the place that takes in down-and-outs. In the conservatory just now, people were talking about it, saying, well, that's where he belongs, that's where they know how to deal with problems like his. I was a bit shocked, to tell you the truth. In fact – I'll tell you this, Mr Ryder, in confidence – all of that helped me make up my mind. About going away, I mean. That performance Mr Brodsky gave tonight, in my opinion it was the finest thing that's been heard in this concert hall for many many years. Certainly for as long as I've been able to appreciate music. But you saw what happened. They didn't want it, it startled them. It was much more than they'd ever bargained for. They're very relieved he collapsed like that. They realise now they want something else. Something a little less extreme.'

'Something not so different from Mr Christoff perhaps.'

Stephan thought about this. 'A *little* different. A new name, at least. They realise now Mr Christoff isn't quite the thing. They do want *something* better. But . . . but not *that*.'

Through the windows I could now see the wide expanse of lawn outside and the sun rising over the row of trees in the distance.

'What do you suppose will become of Mr Brodsky now?' I asked.

'Mr Brodsky? Oh, he'll just go back to being what he's always been here. See out his days as the town drunk, I suppose. They certainly won't let him be much else, not after tonight. As I say, they took him to the St Nicholas Clinic. I've grown up here, Mr Ryder, and in many ways I still love this town. But I'm eager to be leaving now.'

'Perhaps I should try and say something. I mean, address the crowd in the conservatory. Say a few words about Mr Brodsky. Put them right about him.'

Stephan considered this for a few steps, then shook his head.

'It's not worth it, Mr Ryder.'

'But I must say, I don't like this any more than you do. You never know. A few words from me . . .'

'I don't think so, Mr Ryder. They won't listen even to you now. Not after that performance from Mr Brodsky. That reminded them of everything they're afraid of. Besides, there's no microphone or anything in the conservatory, not even a platform you can stand up and speak from. You'd never get yourself heard over all the noise. You see, it's pretty big, almost as big as the auditorium itself. From corner to corner, it must be . . . well, even if you kept to a dead straight diagonal, knocking aside any tables and guests seated in your way, you'd still measure out fifty metres at least. It's a jolly big place, as you'll see. If I were you, Mr Ryder, I'd just relax now and enjoy your breakfast. After all, you've got Helsinki to be thinking about.'

The conservatory, right enough, was a vast affair, which at this moment was bathed in morning sunlight. Everywhere people were talking cheerfully, some seated around tables, others standing in little groups. I could see people drinking coffee and fruit juice, others eating from plates or bowls, and as we made our way through the crowd I caught in turn the aromas of fresh rolls, fish cakes, bacon. I could see waiters rushing about with plates and jugs of coffee. All around me voices were greeting one another in delight, and it struck me the whole atmosphere resembled that of a reunion. And yet these were people who saw each other constantly. Clearly the evening's events had made them reassess themselves and their community in some profound way, and the resulting mood, for whatever reason, appeared to be one of mutual celebration.

I could see now that Stephan was right. There was little point in my attempting to address this crowd, let alone in asking them to return to the auditorium for my recital. Feeling suddenly tired and extremely hungry, I decided to sit down and have some breakfast myself. When I looked about, however, I could see no free chairs anywhere. Moreover, I turned to find that Stephan was no longer walking beside me, but had been drawn into conversation by a group at a table we had just passed. I watched him being greeted warmly, half expecting him to introduce me. But he seemed to become engrossed in the conversation, and very soon he too had adopted a cheerful demeanour.

I decided to leave him to it and walked on through the crowd. I thought that sooner or later a waiter would spot me and come rushing up with a plate and a cup of coffee, perhaps show me to a seat. But though on a few occasions a waiter did come hurrying in my direction, each time he pushed past me and I was obliged to watch him serving someone else.

Then after a while I realised I was standing close to the main doors of the conservatory. Someone had thrown them wide open and many guests had spilled out onto the lawn. I stepped out a little way and was surprised by the chill in the air. But here, too, people were standing talking in groups, drinking their coffees or else eating on their feet. Some had turned to face the sunrise, while others were wandering about stretching their legs. One particular group had even sat down on the wet grass, plates and coffee jugs spread around them as for a picnic.

I spotted a catering trolley on the grass not far away with a waiter hunched busily over it. My hunger growing ever greater, I made my way towards it and was just about to tap the waiter on the shoulder when he turned and rushed past me, his arms burdened with three large plates – upon which I glimpsed scrambled eggs, sausages, mushrooms, tomatoes. I watched him go hurrying off, then decided I would not budge from beside the trolley until he returned.

As I waited, I surveyed the scene around me and saw how needless had been my worries concerning my ability to cope with the various demands presented to me in this city. As ever, my experience and my instincts had proved more than sufficient to see me through. Of course I felt a certain disappointment about the evening, but then, as I thought about it further, I could see the inappropriateness of such feelings. After all, if a community could reach some sort of an equilibrium without having to be guided by an outsider, then so much the better.

When after several minutes the waiter had not returned – throughout which time I had been continually teased by the various aromas rising from the hot canisters on the trolley – I decided there was no good reason why I should not serve myself. I had already taken a plate and was bending down searching the lower tiers for some utensils, when I became conscious of a number of figures standing behind me. Turning, I found myself looking at the porters.

As far as I could make out, all of the dozen or so I had last seen gathered together around Gustav's sick-bed were now here before me. As I had turned, some had lowered their eyes, but a few continued to regard me intensely.

'My goodness,' I said, doing my best to hide the fact that I had been about to serve myself breakfast. 'My goodness, what's happened? Naturally, I had meant to come up and see how Gustav was getting on. I was assuming he'd have gone to hospital by now. That's to say, that he was in good hands. I was certainly about to come up as soon as . . .' I paused, seeing the expressions of grief on their faces.

The bearded porter stepped forward and coughed awkwardly. 'He passed away half an hour ago, sir. He'd had trouble on and off over the years, but he'd been very fit, and so it was very unexpected for us. Very unexpected.'

'I'm very sorry.' I found that indeed I felt great sorrow at this news. 'Very sorry indeed. I'm very grateful to you, to all of you, for coming out here like this to tell me. As you know, I had only known him for a few days, but he had been very kind to me, assisting me with my bags and so on.'

I could see the bearded porter's colleagues all looking at him, egging him on to say something. The bearded porter took a deep breath.

'Of course, Mr Ryder,' he said, 'we came to find you because we knew you'd want to hear the news quickly. But also' – he suddenly lowered his gaze – 'but also, you see, sir, before he passed away, Gustav, he kept wanting to know. Wanting to know if you'd made your speech yet. That's to say, the little speech you were going to make on our behalf, sir. Right to the end, he was very keen to hear news of it.'

All the porters had now lowered their eyes and were waiting silently for my response.

'Ah,' I said. 'So you're not aware then of what occurred in the auditorium.'

'We've all been with Gustav until just now, sir,' said the bearded porter. 'He's only just now been taken away. You must excuse us, Mr Ryder. It was very rude of us not to be present while you were giving your address, especially if you were so good as to remember your little promise to us and . . .'

'Look,' I broke in gently, 'many things didn't go as planned. I'm surprised you haven't heard, but then I suppose, as you say, in these circumstances . . .' I paused, then, taking a breath, said in a firmer voice: 'I'm sorry, but the fact is, many things, not just the little speech I had prepared for you, did not go ahead as planned.'

'So you're saying, sir . . .' The bearded porter trailed off, then hung his head in disappointment. The other porters, who had all been staring at me, one by one lowered their eyes again. Then one of them near the back of the group burst out in an almost angry tone:

'Gustav kept asking. Right to the end he kept asking. "Any news of Mr Ryder yet?" He kept asking that.'

A number of his colleagues quickly pacified him, and there then followed a lengthy silence. Finally the bearded porter said, still looking down at the grass:

'It makes no difference. We'll all carry on trying, just the same. In fact we'll now try harder than ever. We won't let Gustav down. He was always our inspiration and nothing will change now he's gone. We've got an uphill struggle, we always have had, we know that, and it's not going to get any easier now. But we won't let standards slip, not one little bit. We'll remember Gustav and we'll keep at it. Of course, your little speech, sir, if it had been possible, it would have been . . . it would have helped us, no doubt about it. But of course, if at the time it seemed to you inappropriate . . .'

'Look,' I said, now beginning to lose patience, 'you'll all find out soon enough what occurred. Really, I'm surprised you haven't made it your business to find out more about the larger concerns of your community. What's more, you seem to have no idea what sort of life I have to lead. Of the vast responsibilities I have to carry. Even now, as I stand here talking to you, I'm having to think about my next engagement in Helsinki. If everything hasn't quite gone as planned for you, I'm sorry. But you really have no right to come bothering me like this . . .'

The words faded in my mouth. In the distance over to my right was a path leading from the concert hall into the surrounding woods. I had for some time been aware of a stream of people emerging from the building and disappearing off behind the trees – on their way home, presumably, for a couple of hours' rest before the start of the day. I now spotted among them Sophie and Boris, walking purposefully along the path. The little boy had once more placed his arm supportively around his mother, but otherwise there was nothing about them to alert the casual onlooker to their distress. I tried to see the expressions on their faces, but they were too far away, and the next moment they too had vanished behind the trees.

'I'm sorry,' I said more gently, turning back to the porters, 'but you must all excuse me now.'

'We won't let standards slip,' the bearded porter said quietly, still looking at the ground. 'We'll do it one day. You'll see.'

'Excuse me.'

Just as I was moving away the waiter came rushing back, pushing the old men aside to reach his trolley. Remembering the plate I was still holding behind my back, I thrust it at him.

'The catering this morning has been appalling,' I said coldly, before hurrying off.

38

The path cut a completely straight line through the woods so that I could see clearly to the tall iron gate at the far end. Sophie and Boris had already covered a surprising amount of ground, and although I walked as fast as I could, after a few minutes I had hardly reduced the distance between us. I was continually impeded, furthermore, by a group of young people walking a little in front of me who, whenever I tried to overtake, increased their pace or else spread themselves right across the path. In the end, when I could see that Sophie and Boris were about to reach the street, I broke into a run and burst through the young people, no longer caring what sort of impression I created.

After this I maintained a steady trot, yet was still not even within hailing distance as Sophie and Boris passed through the gate. By the time I reached the gate myself, my breath was coming in gasps and I was obliged to pause.

I had come out onto one of the boulevards near the heart of the city. The morning sun was lighting up the opposite pavement. The shops were still closed, but there was already a fair number of people walking about, going off to their day's work. I then saw, over to my left, a queue in the process of boarding a tram, and Sophie and Boris bringing up its rear. I broke out again into a trot, but the tram must have been further away than I had thought for, although I kept up a good pace, I did not reach it until after the entire queue had boarded and the vehicle was about to pull away. Only by waving frantically did I manage to stall the driver and struggle aboard myself.

The tram lurched forward as I staggered down the central aisle. I was so out of breath I only vaguely registered that the carriage was half full, and only when I collapsed into a seat near the rear did it occur to me I must have walked past Sophie and Boris. Still panting, I leaned to one side and looked back up the aisle.

The carriage was divided into two distinct sections separated by an exit area in the middle. In the front portion, the seating was arranged as two long rows facing one another, and I could see Sophie and Boris sitting together on the sunny side of the tram not far from the driver's cabin. My view of them was obscured by some passengers standing in the exit area hanging onto straps, and I leaned further over into the aisle. As I did so, the man sitting opposite me – in our half of the carriage, the seats were arranged in pairs facing one another – slapped his thigh and said:

'Another sunny day by the look of things.'

He was dressed neatly, if modestly, in a short zip-up jacket, and I supposed he was some sort of skilled workman – an electrician perhaps. I smiled at him quickly, upon which he began to tell me something about a building he and his colleagues had been working in for the past several days. I listened to him vaguely, occasionally smiling or making an assenting noise. Meanwhile my view of Sophie and Boris became further obscured as more and more people rose to their feet and crowded around the exit doors.

Then the tram stopped, the passengers got out and my view improved. Boris, looking as self-possessed as ever, had one hand on Sophie's shoulder and was regarding the other passengers suspiciously as though they presented a threat to his mother. Sophie's expression was still hidden from me. I could see her though, every few seconds, making an irritated waving motion through the air, perhaps at some insect flying around her.

I was about to adjust my position again when I realised the electrician had somehow got onto the topic of his parents. They were now both in their eighties, he was telling me, and though he did his best to visit them once a day, this was becoming increasingly difficult due to his current job. A thought suddenly came to me and I interrupted him saying:

'Excuse me, but speaking of parents, it seems mine were here in this city some years ago. Just as tourists, you know. It would have been a good few years ago now. It's just that the person who told me was only a child at the time and had no clear memory of them. So I was just wondering, since we were talking about parents, and well, I don't mean to be rude, but I assume you must be well into your fifties, I wondered if you yourself had any memory of their visit.'

'It's quite possible,' the electrician said. 'But you'll have to describe them a little.'

'Well, my mother, she's quite a tall woman. Dark hair, shoulder length. A rather bird-like nose. That would make her look a little stern, even when she wasn't intending to be.'

The electrician thought for a moment, looking out at the city going by outside. 'Yes,' he said, nodding. 'Yes, I think I can remember a lady just like that. It was just for a few days. Looking around at the sights, that sort of thing.'

'That's it. You remember then?'

'Yes, she seemed very pleasant. This would have been, oh, at least thirteen, fourteen years ago. Maybe even longer than that.'

I nodded enthusiastically. 'That would tie in with what Miss Stratmann told me. Yes, that was my mother. Tell me, did she seem to be enjoying herself here?'

The electrician thought hard, then said: 'From what I recall, she appeared to like it here, yes. In fact' – he had spotted my look of concern – 'in fact, I'm *certain* she did.' He reached forward and patted my knee in a kindly manner. 'I'm jolly certain she enjoyed it here. Look, just think about it. She's bound to have done, isn't she?'

'I suppose so,' I said and turned to the window. The sun was now moving across the interior of the tram. 'I suppose so. It's just that . . .' I gave a deep sigh. 'It's just that I wish I'd known at the time. I wish someone had thought to inform me. And what about my father? Did he seem to be enjoying himself?'

'Your father. Hmm.' The electrician folded his arms, a slight frown on his face.

'He would have been quite thin by then,' I said. 'Greying hair. He had a favourite jacket. A tweed one, pale green, with leather elbow patches.'

The electrician continued to think. Then finally he shook his head. 'I'm sorry. I can't say I remember your father.'

'But that's impossible. Miss Stratmann assured me they came here together.'

'I'm sure she's right. It's just that I personally can't remember your father. Your mother, yes. But your father . . .' He shook his head again.

'But that's ridiculous! What would my mother have been doing here alone?'

'I'm not saying he wasn't with her. It's just that I don't remember him. Look, don't upset yourself so much. I wouldn't have been so frank if I'd known it was going to upset you like this. I've got a terrible memory. Everyone says so. Just yesterday I left my tool-box at my brother-in-law's house where I had my lunch. I lost forty minutes going back to get it. My tool box!' He gave a laugh. 'You see, my memory's terrible. I'm the last person to trust about something important like this. I'm sure your father would have been here with your mother. Particularly if that's what other people are saying. Really, I'm the last person to rely on.'

But I had now turned away from him and was once more looking towards the front of the carriage, where Boris had finally given in to his emotions. He was now being embraced by his mother, and I could see his shoulders moving with his sobs. Suddenly there seemed nothing of importance other than to go to him and, muttering a quick apology to the electrician, I rose and began to make my way up the carriage.

I had almost reached them when the tram turned a sharp curve and I was forced to grab a nearby pole to keep my balance. When I looked again, I realised that Sophie and Boris had remained quite unaware of my approach, even though I was now standing very close to them. They were still in a deep embrace, their eyes closed. Patches of sunlight were drifting over their arms and shoulders. There was at that moment something so private about their comforting of each other that it seemed impossible even for me to intrude. And as I went on gazing at them, I began to feel, for all their obvious distress, a strange sense of envy. I moved a little closer until I could almost feel the very texture of their embrace.

Then at last Sophie opened her eyes. She watched me expressionlessly as the little boy continued to sob into her breast.

'I'm sorry,' I said to her eventually. 'I'm very sorry about everything. I only heard about your father just now. Of course, I came after you as soon as I heard . . .'

Something about her expression made me stop. For another moment, Sophie went on regarding me coldly. Then she said tiredly:

531

'Leave us. You were always on the outside of our love. Now look at you. On the outside of our grief too. Leave us. Go away.'

Boris broke away from her and turned to look at me. Then he said to his mother: 'No, no. We've got to keep together.'

Sophie shook her head. 'No, it's useless. Leave him be, Boris. Let him go around the world, giving out his expertise and wisdom. He needs to do it. Let's just leave him to it now.'

Boris stared at me in confusion, then back at his mother. He might have been about to say something, but at that moment Sophie stood up.

'Come on, Boris. We've got to get off here. Boris, come on.'

Indeed the tram was slowing down and other passengers were getting up from their seats. A few people pushed past me, and then Sophie and Boris squeezed by. Still clutching my pole, I watched Boris moving away down the aisle towards the exit. At one point he glanced back at me, and I heard him say:

'But we've got to stay together. We've got to.'

I then saw Sophie's face behind him, gazing at me with an odd detachment, and I heard her voice say:

'He'll never be one of us. You've got to understand that, Boris. He'll never love you like a real father.'

More people pushed past me. I raised my hand in the air.

'Boris!' I called.

The little boy, hanging back in the throng, looked towards me once more.

'Boris! That bus ride, you remember it? That bus ride to the artificial lake. Remember, Boris, how good it was? How kind everyone was to us on the bus? The little presents they gave, the singing. You remember, Boris?'

Passengers had now started to disembark. Boris gave me one last glance and then disappeared from my view. More people pushed past and then the tram began to move again.

After a while I turned and made my way back to my seat. The electrician smiled cheerfully as I sat down again in front of him. Then I became aware of him leaning forward, patting my shoulder, and I realised I was sobbing.

'Listen,' he was saying, 'everything always seems very bad at the time. But it all passes, nothing's ever as bad as it looks. Do cheer up.' For a while he went on uttering such empty phrases while I continued to sob. Then I heard him say: 'Look, why don't you have some breakfast. Just have something to eat, like the rest of us. You're bound to feel a little better then. Come on. Go and get something to eat.'

I glanced up and saw that the electrician was holding a plate on his lap, on which was a half-finished croissant and a small knob of butter. His knees were covered in crumbs.

'Ah,' I said, straightening and recovering my composure. 'Where did you get that?'

The electrician indicated beyond my shoulder. Turning, I saw a crowd of passengers standing at the very rear of the tram where some sort of buffet had been laid out. I noticed too that the whole back half of the carriage had become quite crowded, and that all around us passengers were eating and drinking. The electrician's breakfast was modest in comparison to many being consumed; I could now see people working their way through large plates of eggs, bacon, tomatoes, sausages.

'Come on,' the electrician said again. 'Go and get yourself some breakfast. Then we'll talk about all your troubles. Or if you prefer, we can just forget about it all and talk about whatever you like, whatever's likely to cheer you up. Football, cinema. Anything you like. But the first thing to do is to get some breakfast. You look like you haven't eaten for some time.'

'You're quite right,' I said. 'Now I think of it, I haven't eaten for a very long time. But please tell me. Where is this tram going? I have to get to my hotel to pack my things. You see, I have a flight this morning to Helsinki. I have to get to my hotel pretty soon.'

'Oh, this tram will get you more or less anywhere you like in the city. This is what we call the morning circuit. Then there's the evening circuit. Twice a day a tram goes right the way round the entire circuit. Oh yes, you can go anywhere on this tram. It's the same again in the evening, but the atmosphere's quite different then. Oh yes, this is a marvellous tram.'

'How splendid. Well then, excuse me. I think I'll take up your suggestion and get some breakfast. In fact, you're quite right. Even the idea of it is making me feel better.'

'That's more the spirit,' the electrician said and raised his croissant in a salute.

I got up and went to the back of the carriage. Various aromas came wafting towards me. A number of people were in the act of serving themselves, but peering over their shoulders I saw a large buffet presented in a semi-circular arrangement directly beneath the rear window of the tram. There was on offer virtually everything one could wish for: scrambled eggs, fried eggs, a choice of cold meats and sausages, sautéed potatoes, mushrooms, cooked tomatoes. There was a large platter with rolled herrings and other fish preparations, two huge baskets filled with croissants and different sorts of rolls, a glass bowl of fresh fruit, numerous jugs of coffee and juices. Everyone around the buffet seemed more than eager to get to the food, and yet the atmosphere was extremely cordial, with people passing things to one another and exchanging cheerful remarks.

I took a plate, glancing up as I did so through the rear window with its receding view of the city streets, and could feel my spirits rising yet further. Things had not, after all, gone so badly. Whatever disappointments this city had brought, there was no doubting that my presence had been greatly appreciated – just as it had been everywhere else I had ever gone. And now here I was, my visit almost at its close, a thoroughly impressive buffet before me offering virtually everything I had ever wished to eat for breakfast. The croissants looked particularly promising. Indeed, from the manner in which passengers all around the carriage were devouring theirs, it was obvious they were extremely fresh and of the highest possible quality. Then again, nothing my gaze fell upon looked anything less than enticing.

I started to serve myself a little of everything. As I did so, I began to picture myself, already back in my seat, exchanging pleasant talk with the electrician, glancing out between mouthfuls at the early-morning streets. The electrician was in many ways the ideal person for me to talk to at this moment. He was clearly kind-hearted, but at the same time careful not to be intrusive. I could see him now, still eating his croissant, obviously in no hurry to get off the tram. In fact, he looked set to go on sitting there for a long time to come. And with the tram running a continuous circuit, if the two of us were enjoying our conversation, he was just the sort to delay getting off until the next time his stop came around. The buffet too was clearly here to stay for some time yet, so that we would be able to break off from our

534

conversation every now and then to replenish our plates. I could even see us repeatedly persuading each other to have more. 'Go on! Just one more sausage! Here, give me your plate, I'll get it for you.' We would go on sitting there together, eating, exchanging views on football and whatever else took our fancy, while outside the sun rose higher and higher in the sky, brightening the streets and our side of the carriage. And only when we were thoroughly done, when we had eaten and talked all we could possibly want, the electrician might glance at his watch, give a sigh and point out that the stop for my hotel was coming round again. I too would sigh, and with some reluctance rise to my feet, brushing the crumbs off my lap. We would shake hands, wish each other a good day – he too would be having to get off before long, he would tell me – and I would go off to join the crowd of cheerful passengers gathering around the exit. Then, as the tram came to a halt, I would perhaps give the electrician one last wave and disembark, secure in the knowledge that I could look forward to Helsinki with pride and confidence.

I filled my coffee cup almost to the brim. Then, holding it carefully in one hand, my generously laden plate in the other, I began making my way back to my seat.